The Pretenders

M.L. Bennett

Julia,

Consider this a pass/fail
trial of our friendship.

M L Bennett

For Maggie—you gave me more than just your name.

Prologue
April 2020

Castan heard the crackle and blare of bombs so frequently, he began to imagine a bag of microwavable popcorn was outside Allen Manor. He glanced at the clock above the Major's desk. 08:23:42. Of course, she wouldn't be a minute early, nor a minute late—what a scandal that would cause.

He craned his neck to look at the shelf of books on his right. The unforgivable morning light illuminated the silver and gold lettering on the leather-bound spines. He couldn't read what they said, but he already knew they were the volumes of Taxodium's history. Every tactic, every drill, trial, battle, death was recorded in immaculate print on the inside.

Maybe Rex would be more enjoyable if her library was for pleasure. He couldn't imagine sitting down to read over the minutes of every meeting in 1984. But then again, he couldn't imagine reading anything. Not since—

The doors behind him opened. On cue, he stood up and saluted the Major: right arm with three fingers over his beating heart.

"Cassena," she acknowledged Castan only in the curt nod of her head. Her gaze was elsewhere—her desk. Or maybe the clock to make sure she was exactly on the dot. He knew she was.

"Major Rex." He followed her lead and sat after she tucked herself behind her desk, so large, she was a child in comparison.

The time: 08:25:03.

"This is...?" She picked up the single sheet of paper he had placed on her desk ten minutes ago. She raised a pale eyebrow at him, but Castan couldn't quite find the will to look her in the eye. He stared at the white spikes of her sculpted hair instead.

"That is all the information I could pull from Intelligence, in regard to Corolla Vel's whereabouts," he offered, resisting the urge to cross his arms. The Major wouldn't approve of such body language.

"And?" Again, she raised a brow, and again, he could not look her in the eye.

"And I think this is the best bet we have." He slid forward in his chair, excitement bursting through the formality. "If we can get her to consent, the Gens will think we have their cure. It will distract them long enough so that we can locate their complex and infiltrate."

The Major leaned back in her chair, unimpressed. "I thought I told you to find material on Mena Dentata."

A muscle in his jaw twitched, a dangerous sign of insubordination. His eyes flashed over the Major—she hadn't noticed. She was skimming through the paper, though apparently not reading a word of it. He could smell the crisp new printer paper from where he perched.

"Mena Dentata is a tale." Bitterness replaced his excitement. He sat back in his chair again, though his spine remained rigid. "What we need is a distraction, and Corolla Vel will serve as just that. The Gens will think they have another chance at immunity—and that is a bluff we *must* ensure."

The Major considered his proposal. He could tell by the dense clouds gathering in her irises. She mulled it over, gaze trained on the white paper in her hands. Outside, he was reminded of popcorn in the microwave again. *Boom! Crackle!* An array of explosives on the training field, no doubt. Besides that, the only other noise in the office was the steady *tick, tock* of the clock. He wondered if the Major thought in sync to the thing, like a metallic heartbeat.

"Very well," the Major leaned forward but pushed the paper aside. She caught his gaze, and he could not look away this time. He always thought her eyes were like icebergs, cold and depthless. It made him shudder on the inside, where she couldn't see how she affected him. Her gaze could, after all, paralyze a man like a statue. She was Medusa, ivory spikes instead of snakes.

"Find Corolla Vel and bring her here. I'll speak with Ramsey about promoting her stay. The Gens will more than likely take to her like flies to a flame."

He didn't mention that maybe what the Major meant to say was "moths to a flame." He held her gaze, nodding at her approval. It was just as well, he decided, the Gens were going to be wiped out, regardless of the metaphorical expression.

"Thank you, Major. I know this plan will work."

Major Rex stood, heaving a disgruntled sigh. "For all our sakes, I hope so."

He stood, as was proper to do so, while she stalked out of the room. When the Major was gone, he exhaled into the silence.

It worked.

But his relief subsided almost immediately. His eyes fell on the spines of the books. The volumes only went up to last year, as this year's events had not yet played out. He dreaded the moment that book was published.

2

Your name's not yet in print, Calyx, he thought to the domed ceiling, *but that doesn't make it any less real.* All the weight of the world burrowed inside his chest.

He vowed, again to the ceiling, that he would not fail this time. He would succeed, and all of the Gens would be eliminated because of it.

Book One
Chosen

"Her instinct for self-preservation was stronger than her candour."
-Thomas Hardy, *Tess of the D'Urbervilles*

Corolla
June 2020

The mid-June heat wafts through my open window. I can taste the approaching storm in the air. Metallic and charged. I turn the radio down and strain my ears. Yes, there is thunder, rumbling low and steady in the distance. The rusty windchimes outside my window play a tune from another time, a time when James had a decent job, and I wasn't a pathetic creature searching for cover the same way cockroaches search for shadows in the light.

I throw back my bed sheets because it's too damn hot to sleep. My mind won't quit running a marathon either. Distracting myself with the weather isn't helping. Neither is trying to drown my thoughts in radio waves.

It's almost pitch dark in my room, but I only need to take a half step away from my bed before I'm up against the closet. I find the light switch, ease it up so as not to make any unnecessary noise. I don't want James to hear me, though these walls are so thin, I wouldn't be surprised if he saw the light of my closet through them.

I rub my eyes against the harsh artificial yellow. While my eyes are adjusting, I do a half turn and crank the radio back up again. The commercials are over, and the reporter is back on the air.

"As the number of terrorist attacks increase, Congress is at a standstill. 'Without any organization to blame, we are at a loss for pursuit,' says Speaker of the House, Leo Thackeray…"

I stop listening and look back at my closet. I plunge both arms into the hanging disorder of my clothes—skins of who I used to be—and heave them aside. As if charged by the electricity outside, my fingertips tingle. But I'm not hunting for an outfit. I'm hunting for peace.

On my wall, unbeknownst to James, I've nailed in the outline of a brain. My eyes trace the frontal lobe to the temporal to the occipital. Attached to these makeshift pegs are bunches of yarn, and, where I ran out of the vital string, thin strips of old T-shirts. I run my hand along the coarse texture of my work, through the variation of colors and materials. Some of the yarn is fluffy, some hairy, some fine silk like a spider's.

I sigh and take up the process once more. From the shelf above, I retrieve a loose ball of yellow yarn, bright neon. It's an ugly color. This kind isn't as soft as my last, but its thin enough that I can wrap it around a nail and still have room for ten more rounds. As always, I start with the frontal lobe, where the thoughts always begin. I unravel the ball, hook the string across hundreds of predecessors, to the occipital lobe. That is where the sight began. From there, I move east, then directly west, to the temporal lobe. That is where the deception started, in little whispers, in large waves.

Directly above me, I'm all too aware of the box perched in the rafters. My microscope, like some disapproving god, glaring down at me. I used to want to study the small, the invisible to the naked eye. I believed I could achieve supreme happiness by following that passion for understanding the world on the most basic of levels. And then I met Averil. Everything changed, and I can't touch that microscope—that dream—until I make everything right again. If I don't atone first, I may taint that passion, make it warp under the pressure of all my shame until it's so disfigured, it's unrecognizable.

I may ruin it forever.

I tie off the yarn and stand back to admire my progress. Well, I know this isn't any sort of improvement from what happened, but it is the best that I can do. If James knew about my nighttime endeavors, he'd say yarn is a waste of money. I would say that therapy would only rob his wallet, and words would only sink his heart. So, yarn it is.

I take a piece of masking tape and scribble the date. Then, I fold it around that yellow line. The off-white tag falls limp against the others. It has only been a day since I last did this. We'll see if the remainder of this week will be any better.

As if satiated, the tingling in my fingers cedes until it is only a whisper in the corners of my mind. A whisper like so many other voices tripping, stumbling, and colliding together there already. My arms hang from sagging shoulders as I absorb all the neurotic paths I've woven in the past couple of months.

I have to remember—simply because I cannot afford to forget.

Past
September 2018

"You could still leave," Hadley said from her perch against the concrete wall. Arms crossed, back pressed against the cement, she was all angles and angst. "The guards towards the surface will be drinking—no one would notice you."

Castan grumbled. He finished lacing his boots. They were outside their home bunker, concrete halls stretching like post-mortem arms on either side of them. White lights dotted the wall every few feet, a testament to the darkness underground. The shadows were relentless. The oxygen scrubbers hummed, quiet reminders that the air was being filtered, never fresh.

Living in the Complex was like living in a max-security prison—it was cold, the air was stale, and the food wasn't that great.

Of course, Castan didn't know much about the world above, but from what he'd read, it was better than the layers and layers of concrete he had always called home. No, he decided, living in the Complex was more like the alternate dimension in a sci-fi book he'd picked up once. Maybe that was why he hated fantasy books—because he craved something ordinary, a place to escape to that did not require killing or brutality, or even deranged characters, to survive. He had lived with that far too long, and he would never say it aloud, but Fitzgerald's *The Great Gatsby* was one of his favorite books. Gatsby, despite his love-sickness, possessed honor. That was something Castan saw little of.

He glanced at his sister. Her pale neck seemed to glow in the white light. Or maybe it seemed to glow because her shoulder-length hair was black as pitch. Castan averted his eyes. Sometimes she resembled their mother so much, it physically hurt him to look at her.

"Why don't *you* leave then?" They'd had this conversation more than once, so he already knew her answer. Hadley knew why he didn't just walk out into the world above. For one, he had nowhere to go. For two, the upper levels crawled with guards. For three, he had a sister *here*.

"Women are more noticeable around here," she complained. "I swear, it's almost as if men don't respect us."

"Good thing you're not a woman," Castan teased. All pelari children grew up quickly, but sometimes, Hadley was too severe for a fourteen-year-old.

Hadley tied her flood of dark hair in a knot behind her head, eyes rolling. "And you wonder why I have such strong opinions on the subject."

Castan stood and exhaled. He swore, if anxiety were tangible, it would be a noose around his neck in that moment.

He was sixteen now, as of a month ago, which meant the leader of the Complex, Numen, expected more training out of him. His Essence would soon come and go, like a rare flower at bloom. And like anything extraordinary, Castan had to cherish it while it lasted. At least, that's what Numen pounded into his skull. What he really meant was, *You have to kill as many people as you can, before you lose your gift. Taxodium will pay.*

But his capability also meant Carnage.

Numen created the unique tournament several years ago, as a way to encourage the blooming Essences he ruled over. Numen was impressed with Castan's potential and nominated him after their first training session together. Castan was not particularly religious, but he prayed his nomination was a dream.

It wasn't.

In chalk drawn arenas on the training level below, he would be forced into combat with other pelari his age. And if Castan won, he would be bestowed the honor of the first season's hunting. Human hunting.

Castan blinked, body shuddering as he came out of his own mind. He didn't want this kind of capability, because with it, came cruelty. He remembered all too well the price of such a thing. The *damage* of such a thing.

He still heard his mother's screams in his dreams. And his father, tugging her by a fistful of hair, bellowing in the kind of sadistic voice that says cruelty is merciful. Castan had to shake his head to clear it of the thought.

Hadley pushed herself upright from the wall she was leaning on. She was so small as if she sometimes shrunk.

"But if you really are going to stay," Hadley placed a gentle hand on his shoulder, "then I wish you the best of luck."

Castan offered her a limp grin.

"I would say 'break a leg,'" Hadley quipped, eyes boring into his own, "but that's exactly what I don't want you to do."

Castan, who was no longer in the joking mood, just nodded his head. "I'll see you on the sidelines, then."

"Hey," Hadley caught him by the arm, "life isn't just about survival, okay? It's about being happy, too."

He carefully removed her fingers from his arm. "Happiness is a luxury, Hadley. Maybe one day, we'll have the right currency to afford it."

The Carnage contestants were directed to be half an hour early to the arena before the audience arrived. Castan had to run down several flights of stairs, just to be on time. Each step farther into the Complex squeezed his mind with pressure independent of the actual atmosphere. *What happens if I fail?* He kept wondering, all too aware of the increasing distance between himself and the surface. What would happen to him depended a lot on the people he would have to face in combat. He knew about some but not all. There was a girl from the same floor as him, who could cough up some kind of ravenous bug that gnawed through the skin. But Castan heard she was not very good at controlling these coughs. He also knew that this same pale girl was the one who was always sick as a child. She had little to no experience in fighting and little to no skill in strategy. That's why she was nominated. For a good show.

There was another boy his age who was pretty comfortable with his Essence. It was rumored to be a conjuration of flurries. Cold conjuration was a reasonably common Essence, but the fact that the boy kept it a secret worried Castan more than he was willing to admit. Lying and deception were not uncommon among contestants, but it made him uneasy all the same.

Besides last year's participants, the only other contestant Castan knew of was his brother. People around the Complex called him Mercury because his Essence could drive others mad. Castan would not be permitted to fight him in the preliminary round, as Mercury was a year older than Castan, but that didn't mean he wouldn't have to face him later. Mercury was a problem, an absolute brute. He could alter one's memory with just a well-concentrated look. It wasn't all that interesting to watch, as most of the battle happened between minds, but it *was* dangerous. Because Mercury could only produce horrors. Some people, in their ignorance, speculated that Mercury had driven their own mother to her derangement, even though his Essence wouldn't have come through for another four years.

Last year, Mercury hospitalized two other contestants and was thoroughly vengeful when he lost Carnage. He would be back to win this year. Castan shuddered just thinking about it. It didn't matter that they were of the same blood—Mercury only ever saw Castan as an opponent. And Numen's special attention to his education had not helped this matter.

Castan rounded the last of the winding staircase and entered the level above his father's offices. The arena was laid out plainly before him, broken up into four squares, each one marked by chalk lines done in white. These were situated in the four corners of the floor, to keep matches from spilling into one another, whether it be limbs, Essence, or both. The lone square in the center of the room was reserved for the final pair.

Castan joined the cluster of contestants in the middle of the level. It had been the training floor only hours before, but most of the heavy equipment had been moved to another level. Or up against the walls and out of the way. Castan noted that the display of weapons was still stapled to the concrete walls, up for the taking. Knives, mostly, but also some small axes and even several guns. The goal of Carnage was not to kill your opponent, but, as past participants had acknowledged, the rules said nothing about devastatingly injuring them. There was a reason the hospital wing was above the training level.

Castan hung in the back of the group, peering over heads and between shoulders, when he could, at the man giving the final announcements. Castan recognized the man as Baylor Xander. He was Numen's brother and resembled him much in demeanor but not in physique. Where Numen was on the tall side, muscular and bald, Baylor was squat, barrel-chested and dark-haired. But the brothers had a matched appetite for destruction. It was why they worked so well together.

"You will *potentially* participate in three matches," Baylor explained, semi-uninterested. "You all know that whoever makes it out of the preliminary match the least injured will be the one who moves onto the next round."

Some contestants snickered then. Castan saw Mercury eye another person on the other side of the cluster, though he couldn't make out who. Castan guessed it was Dagger, the guy who won last year. He was turning eighteen this year, though, and would be losing his Essence to the disease within the next few months. Which meant Dagger's vigor in the arena would only be that much stronger—he would cling to his power for the honor of the first season's kill.

For a moment, Castan wondered what it would be like to be neutralized. It was different for everyone, but the end result was the same. Would it be painful? Or would it sap the vitality from his bones and leave him bedridden? In rare cases, the disease killed the host. But that was rare, Castan reminded himself, and it hadn't happened in decades.

But then, shouldn't that worry me even more?

It was because of his contemplating that Castan missed Baylor listing the first-round opponents. It was only when the contestants around him began to move towards their respective corners that Castan snapped to attention.

"I see you weren't listening," Baylor remarked in a dry voice. "Arena One. Make Numen proud. And with that, Baylor took his clipboard and stalked to the far side of the level.

Castan scanned for Arena One and saw that it was close to the back of the area. He wasn't surprised. First-year contestants were usually stuck in the places farthest from the main doors because they weren't typically as entertaining to watch. Trying not to take this as an insult, Castan made his way across the concrete floor and to the arena.

He stepped across the white line.

His opponent was already there, waiting, a figure as thin as a twig and just as frail. Ashley Kerri, he suddenly remembered her name. The girl who lived on the same floor as him. The girl who knew nothing about fighting or strategy. Castan found this a bigger insult to his own skill, but then wondered why he cared if he was insulted. This was not something he desired to participate in. No, it had been forced onto him by Numen. If Castan could have his way, he would be holed up in the library on the fifth level.

"This is one way to keep you from your books all the time," Numen snickered when Castan stepped into his office, flames crackling in his palms and head bowed. "Now you have to focus on your training; otherwise, you'll burn down the library!"

Adrenaline, Castan reassured himself. *It's the adrenaline getting to my head.* He felt it surging through his veins, electricity. This alone was enough to leave him mute: when had fighting someone felt this good? It was dangerous—and he knew this—but some part of him chose to ignore it, decided to ignore the surmounting power in his flesh and the fear it triggered.

Ashley, who was incredibly pale for a living human, regarded Castan with ice-gray eyes. Her white hair was woven into a slick braid, looking so much like a bleached spinal column, that Castan had to do a double take. She was so faded that Castan believed there was still a portion of her that was deathly sick.

"Hello," he said, waving a little. By the disgusted look wrinkling Ashley's profile, he knew he had done something wrong. His mother would have disagreed, but then, most people hadn't liked his mother outside of her research.

"I welcome you all to the 3rd annual Carnage," Baylor's voice came on over a microphone. Castan turned around to see that in the time he was studying Ashley, a large mass of people had flooded the level. Most were stationed near the doors, where the more experienced contestants were posted. Others, like Hadley, were standing around the other two corners of the room. Hadley shot him an encouraging smile, but he saw the apprehension lying just beneath the surface of her skin.

"Alright," Baylor's voice rang out over the speakers. Castan recognized this moment, knew it from the times that his father had escorted him from various corners of the Complex and willed him to watch Carnage. To witness Essences flare, the blood and sweat mug up the air like fog.

"Matches may commence!" There was clapping and whistling from the audience, and other sounds that Castan would not remember hearing in the next couple of seconds.

Everything became a blur of concrete, black and white. He didn't hear Baylor announce Mercury a first round survivor. He didn't hear the amassing footsteps behind his arena, and the buzzing voices that came with them. He heard nothing but the pounding of his own excited heart.

Castan remembered warmth in his palms, heat that was nothing like how his mother's embraces had been. He remembered the putrid stench of flame on human flesh. It was altogether so different from the rats Numen made him practice on, that he gagged. Despite his love for books, he would rather smell burning paper than burning flesh. He remembered the pang in his heart at this realization, but that did not stop him. He remembered Hadley's expression, almost as pale as Ashley and ten times as defeated. That did not stop him either.

But most of all, he remembered the gleam of pride in Numen's black eyes as Baylor announced the Carnage winner: Castan William.

Castan
June 2020

"James won't let her leave."

I suppress a scowl as I toss my aunt a look.

"That's why you're coming along," I remind her, though I know she hasn't forgotten.

"Zoom in, Finis." The man sitting in front of me clicks a combination of buttons. The image goes fuzzy, then adjusts the topography to the new scale. I study the roads, possible entrances, exits, escapes—

"What if it doesn't work?" Aunt Laila pushes back her dark locks, eyes glued to the satellite screen before us. Her voice gives away what her expression does not: she doesn't support my plan.

"It will work." I turn back to the map of Corolla Vel's location. My team and I have spent several months digging through files, social media, government records, and we have finally found her. I would have wanted to snag her a month and a half sooner, but someone has done an excellent job trying to hide her existence. There is next to nothing out there about this girl. I suppose that's a good thing—it means it will take the Gens about twice as long to find her too. *If* they are searching. They didn't look for Calyx, just waited for the right opportunity to strike—

Beside me, Aunt Laila huffs. It is subtle, but it's enough to fix a scowl on Kass's face. I shoot her a warning, but the orange-haired girl just turns so that her back is to my aunt. Talan, who seems to have noticed the exchange, hides a smirk.

"Aunt Laila," I pull her gently by the arm, out of the operations room. "You can't just come in here and criticize the very work we have been managing for months." I love Laila—she's been my ally when no one else was—but sometimes, she is too stubborn to tolerate.

"I'm not criticizing your work," she exhales. "I'm just considering other angles."

"Other angles being the ones where we've failed."

"Well." She shrugs like it's evident she's right and I'm wrong. My temper rises within me like a flame fed on gasoline. I wipe underneath my nose, but the scent of blood crawls into my senses regardless.

"Do you really think I wouldn't have evaluated those outcomes?" I feel the needles of fire surface to my flesh like minnows coming up to

15

feed. I curl my hands into fists to keep it under control. "Do you really think I'd make the same mistake *twice*?"

Her brows unknit, arms droop to her side. She falls apart, while my frustration crests. "No, oh god—Castan, that's not what I meant—"

"Then don't say shit like that, Aunt Laila! We're all trying to restore some sense of normal. I invited you to this team to help, not create a rift."

She drops her eyes to the ground as if my glare is too intense to bear. It may be. I've been told more than once that I look like my father when I'm angry. I force my muscles to relax.

"Castan," Aunt Laila holds my gaze again. "I didn't mean to bring Calyx into this. I just mean that James isn't going to be easy to convince. He was mortified when Adian left and is no doubt the very person who has been keeping Corolla hidden so well for so long. I don't know if my persuasive skills will be enough."

She studies me, dark eyes searching for parts of me that are no longer there. She is so small, so fragile, so like my mother that I have to look away. I don't know what to say to her. She wants me to be a Castan that I wouldn't even recognize in a crowd anymore. She wants me to be whole again.

She sighs, and I smell blood once more.

"It will have to be." I stalk back into the operations room, scowling. Aunt Laila does not follow.

"We'll retrieve her," Talan says from his seat next to Finis when he notices I've returned. By *her* I know he means Corolla Vel. It is all we have been able to think about lately. *When, how, where, if...?* That, and the surmounting Genocide attacks on the pedes population.

An ironic smirk creeps into my lips. "Always the optimistic one."

Kass chuckles, something deep and bitter, from her perch on the counter. She picks at a hangnail. "Someone has to be."

Past
January 2019

Castan dropped to his knees before the great Venefica. He read about her—who hadn't?—and knew all that she had accomplished in her life as a human.

"I am not the Queen of England," Tilia corrected, entertained by the spectacle. She cocked her head and regarded him.

Castan pulled himself upright, but he kept his eyes glued to the earthen floor. The dirt was packed tight, almost as solid as cement. *How many greats have stood where I stand now?*

"You are not like the other students," Tilia concluded. "I knew the moment you bled on the first Hold's entrance."

Castan flushed crimson. He was grateful the Venefica allowed him passage through her Holds. No, he was not like the other students, but he wanted to be something similar.

"An anomaly," the Venefica mused. "And a useful one. You passed all three of your Trials."

"Yes." Castan thought back to the lightning storm, then the arena similar to Carnage, and the final Trial, the one where he had to defend himself from his own doubt. They had all been terrible, crippling situations in which he had to prove his worth to Taxodium, to the Venefica. He had not seen her form, though, only heard her ringing voice explain his objectives.

Obtain this, find that, destroy him, and you will be free to move on.

Castan raised his head then and absorbed the spectral woman before him. In his sight, she was golden. She lounged on a chair, a sort of throne, he thought. Though she had already said she was not royal, the Venefica was regal nonetheless. It was hard not to respect someone of her reputation.

"Why didn't you stop me then, if you knew where I came from?" It was a question that had been dogging on his mind since the moment his *Humanitas* had begun. Tilia knew everyone by their blood before knowing them through their hearts, yet she had not barred his passage through her transportation Holds.

Tilia's solid eyes passed over him. "I took a risk with you, yes, but I also learned something of your heart, young one. You are nothing like your father, or," Tilia added pointedly, "your brother."

17

Castan ducked his head again, ashamed. Even though he had battled those real doubts in Trial three, he still feared his own moral deterioration. And why shouldn't he? Immorality ran throughout his bloodline as much as the disease did. Sometimes he wondered if the two were one in the same.

"You possess information that could help Taxodium, do you not?" Tilia's voice snatched him from his own dark thoughts.

Castan didn't hesitate. "I do."

"So you align yourself with Taxodium now. Why?"

Castan thought about her question. He thought about the day before he broke out of the Complex, and all the suffering he had caused there, fighting for a crowd. It was difficult to put into words why he had abandoned everything he knew for a life far away from Maine.

Finally, he said, "I don't want to be the enemy anymore." It was the simplest he could get his answer, and it sounded right, *felt* right, to say it aloud.

"Whatever was generated for your Trials, I cannot perceive through your mind, only your eyes. I do not read minds either, understand me, I am only part of the circuit through which the Holds generate your Trials. What I mean is, I am not acquainted with your demons. Do you understand?"

"On a basic level, I guess."

Tilia's lips twitched into something of a grin. "With that being said, you fear yourself, yes?"

Castan nodded.

"You have quite the story to tell me. How did you end up at Taxodium?"

So Castan told her about Carnage, how he had almost killed a boy, in his rage. He told her about breaking out, about leaving behind his sister with a promise to return with an army. He told the Venefica about the trains, buses, and taxis he had used to reach the North American Academy. He told her how simple it was to slip inside with the groups of Tax recruits being led past the gates.

"An oversight of Taxodium's guards, no doubt," Tilia said more to herself than to him.

"Well," Castan offered, "it's not a coincidence that Carnage takes place roughly around the same time as the start of a new Tax school year. Rookies are easy prey."

"So I have been told." Tilia was deep in thought now, almost entirely recoiled into her own mind. Even her figure had started to fade as if she were in several places at once. She may have been, as he was not an expert on the mechanics of her dimensions.

Castan ran out of things to tell the Venefica. He folded his hands over his chest and tried not to reel at the very reality of his situation. He had succeeded. He had made it out of the Complex and into Taxodium, with little to stand in his way. Of course, there were a lot of things he still needed to consider, like: What was he going to do now? How was he supposed to help Taxodium *and* keep his identity a secret? He had been at Taxodium a month, and still, he didn't know; he had been avoiding the answers to these tough questions.

Just make it through the day, he would tell himself. So far, the advice had worked, but for how long?

"What did the Major say to you at orientation? Did she notice?"

"No, she said nothing. She gave me papers to sign, just like the rest of the new students. I signed my first name and middle initial—that's how we did things in the Complex. Last names are pretty redundant... I didn't think much of it."

"You lied?"

Castan flinched. "I pretended. I couldn't tell her where I actually came from, could I? *Pride and Prejudice* is more than just a book— people would *murder* me a thousand times over if they knew who I was. Because they don't know who I *am*."

Tilia massaged her temples. "No, I suppose you could not have done anything." And then the Venefica became solid again, no longer transparent. She almost jumped from her seat. "Lucky for you, I have already made arrangements, in regard to your case."

"My case?"

But the Venefica ignored Castan's question.

"There is a woman, her name is Laila Cassena, who will be your ally. She will vouch for your legitimacy. You will call her *Aunt*—no one will question it. The Cassenas are an ancient, reticent family. I have spoken to Laila, and she has agreed to inform the Major that you are her nephew. She is away with business, at the moment, so she has the perfect reason to not have mentioned you before. She will happily comply with this facade."

His knees went weak with relief. "I'm grateful—"

"And I am grateful to you, Castan. If more were like you, I would not have such a headache all the time."

Castan didn't know if this was true, if Tilia could actually have a headache, but he said nothing more on the subject.

"In return," Tilia continued, "I will need to know everything you do. I will then have the vital information passed onto the Majors of the six continents. No one need know my sources. No one need know that the information even came from me. But your contribution to this... struggle... would be crucial."

Castan nodded throughout the whole spiel, eager to volunteer. It meant Hadley had a chance, and it meant people like his father, like his brother, did not. In his hands, he held the balance of an ancient feud. And he was about to tip that scale.

"His name is Jon," Castan offered when Tilia was finished speaking. "The man Taxodium calls Baldwin, and we—they—call Numen. His real name is Jon."

Castan could have sworn Tilia's eyes sparkled. But then he blinked, and that pin of light was gone.

"There is a difference between lying and pretending, Castan. I trust that you are intelligent enough to distinguish between the two. And if I ever find that you are dishonest with me—about this topic or another—you will quickly learn all that I am capable of."

"Yes," he swallowed, "I understand."

Corolla
June 2020

I slam the car into park, but I don't get out right away. I stare at the cracked leather of the steering wheel, tracing the network, though not seeing any of it. The car jolts and hums, the way old machinery does: in agony.

"Is it really so hard to get a job?" I want to scream, but I've done that once before—it hurt my ears more than it relieved my mind. I thought turning sixteen meant more than just getting my driver's license. I thought it meant *instant hire*. I guess I was wrong.

I exhale palpable frustration. James and I have been living off his inheritance money and the little income he makes working at the local grocery store. It's not enough. The inheritance money will dry up before we've had a chance to find our feet again. And then what? We can't lose the house, too. We're already down to one car, so selling this one isn't an option either. Unless we get bikes instead, but something about Michigan winters prohibits this.

All I can think is how badly I owe it to James, about how badly I want to make him proud of me again. My fingers start itching for some yarn, but I can't find the motivation to get up.

My face falls into my hands. The radio crackles.

"The recent shootings in Las Vegas take the nation back several years when a shooting of almost identical initiative struck the area. While people worry about their safety, business owners worry about their profit. Indeed, tourist trends have dropped—"

I shut the car off and climb out. I guess things could be worse. With the recent spikes of global violence, our lives could be a lot more perilous. But I don't think about the shootings, bombings, rising mortality rates in big cities: things happening so far away they can't possibly touch my life. A lost memory surfaces from unknown depths. I don't recall when James told me this sorry tale—I must have been at least six—but his words play through my mind now. Something about a girl he graduated with. Was her name Katie or Kathy...?

"She did everything young—married, had three kids. And then they were in an accident. She was the only one who survived." Here, James turned somber. His vague baby blues pop out at me through a ray of sunshine. *"She's never come out of it."*

I practically scold myself the entire way into the house. *It could be worse. It could be worse. It could be—*

That's when I notice the front door is open.

I freeze, every cell in my body shouting at me to turn around, get back in the car, find a phone, call the police—just don't go inside.

Our little house is surrounded on three sides by cornfields and on the other, thick bundles of trees. If someone broke in, and if something happened to me, no one is around to witness it. My mouth goes dry. I glance around for signs of break and entry, though I don't see any footprints, tire tracks, a car, or shattered glass. Maybe I don't see anything because I don't know what I'm looking for.

I don't know if it's my sense of justice or my sense of stupidity that makes my feet shuffle towards that gaping door. It is a mouth, and it swallows me whole.

The house is drenched in gray light and shadows, spare for a ring of yellow light coming from the kitchen. My psych teacher's voice comes on in my head, *Fight or flight...* I snatch an umbrella from the bench and creep around the corner—

"I wish you'd just put that down."

The sudden voice causes me to jump. I swallow a string of curses as my fear solidifies into a systemic paralysis. I should have run to my car when I had the chance.

There is a man in a black uniform occupying a place at the dining room table. He's thumbing through the library book I keep meaning to return but forgetting to. It hides half his face, so I can't get a good look at his features. Dark hair, intimate posture as if he *belongs* in my house—that's all I absorb.

I can't find words. I only gape, the umbrella clenched so tightly in my fist, I think it's welded into my flesh. I stare at the cover of the library book, read the title over and over again in my fear. It becomes a chant in my mind.

Tess of the D'Urbervilles.

Tess of the D'Urbervilles.

Tess of the D'Urbervilles.

After what feels like ages, he sets the book down. I start—he's not so much a man than a boy my own age, maybe older. "You are one hell of a person to track down," he says in a staccato voice. "It's taken me months."

My own voice cracks. "Excuse me?" I don't know why I don't scream now, why I don't bolt for the door and launch into my car. Something about this boy's eyes, green as emeralds and ominous as criminals, pins me into place.

"I didn't want to frighten you, so I left the front door open, though maybe I should have kept it shut." His nose wrinkles. "Smells like those farmers are laying manure."

I hardly noticed.

He gives me a once over. "I'm sure you're used to it by now."

Despite myself, blood rushes to my face.

The boy leans back in the chair and folds his arms behind his neck. "Take a seat," he gestures with a flick of his gaze, "we have a lot to discuss."

An unknown force grips my muscles, and I am compelled to obey. The chair grates against the cracks in the hardwood floor, cracks I have known all my life and thought little of. I sit. I try not to concentrate on the bulge of his biceps. They are weapons—I can think of no other reason. My practical mind runs through the biological components of muscle, hoping it will help, but I don't make it that far.

"My name is Castan Cassena," the boy introduces, though there is a level of mockery to his tone as if I should already know his name. "I represent the North American division of Taxodium Academy..." He seems to study my reaction to this bit of information. For all intents and purposes, my expression is a muddle of confusion.

"Oh, so you aren't familiar with Taxodium." He sighs, sounding inconvenienced, and folds his hands between us on the table. "Taxodium is an elite school for those who carry the genetic predisposition for..." he struggles to find the right word. I stare at the wrinkle between his eyebrows. "For powers," he settles. The wrinkle disappears.

"Magic?" The word is barely audible, but the boy—Castan—must have gathered meaning from my pale expression. I can feel the blood draining from my face, like one of those Halloween masks that never seems to vanish from the ages.

"Magic is such a crude word for it," he drawls. "It implies that it is something of the fantastical nature, and fantasy is not my type. No," he continues, "not magic, but an extension of science, of the laws of the universe. Those with the gene are referred to as pelari."

My brain concludes simultaneously: *He's insane. What does this have to do with me?*

As if plucking my thoughts from my mind, Castan says, "This concerns you because your mother was one. Pelari, that is."

"My mother?" I cannot hold back my surprise. I have only ever thought of my parents as donors of genetic material, nothing else. My father is alive somewhere, and my mother was murdered young. James never speaks about his sister, and I never ask. I waste no opportunities now.

23

I seem to forget where I am as my mouth shoots one question after the other. It's like when you see a familiar face in a massive crowd, and while I never considered my mother a friend, her mention is something known to cling to in this unknown.

"What about her? How do you know her? *Did* you know her?"

Castan scowls, his dark brows knitting together. The wrinkle in his forehead reappears.

"I'm not here to discuss your family legacy. I'm here because, as I'm sure you're aware of, the world is going to shit." I think about the voices on the radio. My gaze flickers back to his profile. "The trend will only continue unless the Gens are stopped. Permanently." His eyes, which I thought were ominous before, turn a shade darker. His disdain makes me uncomfortable.

I shake my head. "I'm sorry, I don't understand—"

"Naturally," he interrupts, caring little as he does it, "'when a great force of evil arises, nature also creates a great force of good to counteract the effects.' That's science, though I *know* you're not familiar with Rainier. Jacoby Rainier. There are a lot of pelari with the surname." His gaze lands squarely on my own. I wish I could duck my head, but again, some unknown hand holds me steady. My skin starts to prickle. My mouth becomes sandpaper. I wonder if he rehearsed this.

Castan says after a moment, "Rainier would argue that that force is you."

"No." I blink, and my body is freed, breath flooding my lungs all at once. I leap from my seat, clutching the umbrella and aiming to use it. "Get out of my house before I call the police." I have never been more severe in my life, but Castan chuckles—and remains seated. My heart lurches from its cage in my chest to the drums in my ears.

He's not afraid of me.

"Deny it all you want, Corolla, but Taxodium needs bait, and you are the perfect candidate. You carry the Vel name and that… means something to pelari."

I contort my arm behind me for the landline, umbrella pointed at Castan. He spins my library book around the table top.

"I read this once," he twirls it some more, watching it as he goes, "Angel wasn't good enough for her."

I dial 911, put the phone to my ear—and hear nothing. Castan must have cut the lines.

Dammit. That phone was my only chance, save for escaping the house to my car. I don't have a cellphone—James insisted—and I hardly have room to argue with him about it. I wish I'd badgered him a little more about it now, though.

"Corolla," Castan eases out of his chair and steps around the table. I hate that he knows my name. I hate that I have very little power to stop him. I hate that I am cornered.

"Corolla, please put that down." He gestures to the umbrella, all traces of his ill humor gone.

I don't move. This battered old umbrella is the only thing keeping me from succumbing into a fit of wails and curses. I bite my lip, anxious, apprehensive, alone. Alone... I suddenly wish I'd stayed in town longer to find a job. I wish I hadn't left James at the grocer's. I wish I hadn't decided to be courageous and step inside the damn house.

"I'm afraid of how you'll react to what I have to say next," he tries again. Despite the circumstances, I find that he is genuine, almost... caring? No, not caring: guilty. It is written up and down his body as if an amateur artist tattooed it directly to his skin. Ugly. Atrocious. I would know—I see it every time I look in the mirror.

I lower the umbrella end, but only a degree.

"Go on." But I'm not sure I want him to.

"Are you sure you don't want to sit?" He gestures at the chair beside him. I consider the meaning in the fact that he asked it, rather than commanding it. But it's all wrong—his dark crown under the yellow light, the way his eyes follow my every move the same way a predator watches its prey through the tall grass. He is a foreign body in the cell of my house.

"Are you here to kill me?"

"What? God no! I'm here to *recruit* you." He rakes a hand through his hair, thick as syrup and almost as brown. He staggers back a little and pulls out one of the chairs. He lands on it with enough momentum to tousle his hair.

"On my honor," he assures, "I am only here to amend a wrong."

"You broke into my house," I retort. "That says little about your honor."

He sighs and runs a hand down his face. "Yes, well, some things take precedence over others." I notice that his hands are trembling. And his face, which I could not see clearly before, is weighed by black and purple bags under his eyes. He is exhausted.

It's not that I trust him—I don't—but I also don't believe him to be a threat anymore. I know the bulge of his muscles would suggest otherwise, but something about his demeanor... If a person can be broken like glass, the very atoms in his expression display just that. Maybe I just imagine it, but he possesses a quality that cannot be faked.

Tentatively, I cross the floor as if afraid it will fall out from under me. I perch on the chair beside him.

"Thank you. I was getting tired of repeating myself," he admits. "I actually hate repeating myself in general. You're lucky to catch me on one of my gracious days." It is a weary attempt at breaking the tension in the room, and I don't say anything in response. Maybe he is psychologically unstable, or maybe he is telling some form of the truth. I can hardly claim to know his story.

"I have to pick up my uncle soon, so say what you need to say." This is a lie—I don't have to pick James up for another six hours. But I don't want this boy to think I won't be missed. I will be. Dreadfully. An image of James's beet-red face flashes across my vision. He'll have the FBI devour the town if I'm not punctual to picking him up.

For the first time, I'm grateful for James's anxieties.

"No, you don't," Castan lets out a weak laugh. "But don't worry— my aunt, Laila, will be picking up your uncle." He doesn't turn his head, but he must have sensed my rising panic because he adds, "They know each other. My aunt was a friend of your mother's."

There's that word again, *mother*.

Balancing the umbrella across my lap, I fold my arms across my chest. "What do you want?"

"Your cooperation." I startle, but when I look at him, he's staring dejectedly at his hands. Something about the way he twitches his fingers tells me he's seeing anything but what's right before him.

"My cooperation in regard to... what?"

He turns to me then, a wry grin twisting his lips. "You won't believe me." His eyes pin me in place. I wrap my hands around the umbrella's form.

"I'll hear it first." I don't know what else to say. But Castan does.

For the next twenty minutes, the house resounds with Castan's narrative. He tells me remarkable things: there is more than one class of humans. There are pedes, the mundane and ordinary. And there are pelari, the enhanced and extraordinary. He tells me again that my mother was pelari, that she possessed a gene that allowed her to create life forms.

"Nothing like humans or anything," he assures me. "Plants were her talent."

He talks about the Second World War and things that I don't understand like Verum Courts, Tilia Pyrus, Major Rex, and Taxodium.

"It's a school," he elaborates. "Well, it's a lot of things, but it has always been a school. For pelari. A training base." He meets my gaze. "Adian, your mother, went there."

Castan launches into an impassioned speech about the Gens. He says they are responsible for all the chatter I hear on the radio, all the terrorist attacks that have been unclaimed by any organization. He says that Adian's Essence—that's what he calls the pelari gene—was something the Gens craved because it is speculated to be the cure for a genetic disease in the Dentata's blood. He says that's why my mother was murdered, a failed attempt to recover her DNA. *Dentata.* He says that word a lot, and I don't know it's a surname until he mentions a *Rosh Dentata.*

"He's a murderer." Castan comes just shy of actually spitting. "The whole of Taxodium hunts for his head."

I am not stunned, nor disgusted; I am… doubtful.

Castan's expression softens when he sees my skeptical brow.

"Rosh killed your brother."

"I don't have a brother." Castan winces as if the words are economical blows. I didn't mean for them to be.

"No, but you did." He hangs his head. "Calyx was… killed several months ago. He was like your mother, a pelari."

I don't know when I started shaking my head, but I also don't know when the world began to smear into dull colors and nonsense. The blood drains from my face once again. I feel sick. Castan notices nothing of my transformation.

"I'm sorry that you never knew him, Corolla. He was perhaps… the most genuine soul I have ever met."

"I-I don't understand." I grip the edge of the table to stabilize myself. Castan, finally looking up, notices my fading complexion. He places a firm hand on my shoulder. I want to brush him off, but I'm afraid that if I move, the contents of my stomach will end up all over our feet.

"I am so sorry," is all Castan manages to say. I think about what he said earlier, about how he is only here "to amend a wrong." I get this feeling that, in ways I may never fully understand, Castan is related to my brother's death. I swallow more nausea.

Once I've regained some of my composure, Castan's hand drops back to his lap, no longer trembling but shaken just the same. Neither of us says anything for a while. I imagine Castan is seeing things that no words can describe adequately, just as I am feeling things that I don't even know how to process.

A brother? Pelari? I pinch the skin on my hand until it turns white. When that doesn't work, I bite my lip, aiming to draw blood, but Castan decides to open his mouth once more.

"Taxodium is desperate to put an end to the Dentatas. Once the Gens fall, the world will assume some kind of peace." His voice is hoarse and stripped of any pretense. He's gone through so many emotions, it's making my head swim.

"And what," I ask aloud for the first time, "does that have to do with me?"

"As I said before," his voice is calculated, "you are a Vel, and Taxodium needs bait. You would be that bait to draw in the Gens. They'll assume you're another version of your mother and brother. Once you've lured them in, Taxodium's forces will exterminate them like the parasites they are." He ends his lecture with a scowl, directed at my poor cracked floor.

"I don't think—"

"—you believe me? Most wouldn't." He straightens his back several degrees and clasps his hands into loose fists. Then, before I can ask what he's doing, he flips his fists over and opens them. Like blooming flowers, he reveals two identical flames dancing in the center of his palms. They are small and burn a subtle orange. I look closer to examine his hands, thinking, *It has to be a trick.*

But it's not—at least, if it is a trick, I don't understand the mechanisms behind it. The little sparks hover hair-widths above his skin. I think about all the chemistry classes I've taken, and all of the biology ones, too. Out of all the words he just relayed to me, I understand *genes* the most. But this can't be possible. And yet…

I reach out a curious hand, but then remember where I am, who he is—which is no one that I know.

"It's best if you didn't try to touch them anyway," Castan muses. "What I conjure could never hurt me, but I could burn you."

So, he is dangerous.

I don't have time to contemplate the idea further, for he clamps his fingers over his palms once more. When he opens them this time, there are wisps of smoke, but no flames. Blots of red stain my eyes where those twin fires existed. I inhale the smoky scent and am reminded of every birthday I have ever celebrated with James. I feel a little sick all over again.

My gaze is still glued to his open palms. "I can't do anything like that."

He nods his head. "Which is what makes you a perfect candidate."

Part of me hoped that Castan would say otherwise, would say that I am *exactly* like my mother and apparent brother. I chew my bottom lip, thinking. Well, actually, I don't know *what* to think. My thoughts are racing in all directions, clashing and colliding with one another. I feel a headache blossoming behind my eyes.

"Taxodium will pay you."

I nod my head as if I absorbed all this information like a sponge; as if I listened to the careful detail of his explanation. I heard some things, and I lapsed during others. Because what Castan's really telling me is this: I can make James proud of me again.

"So you've been talking about… pelari and pedes," I test the terms out on my tongue, "but what am I?"

"You are volga," he says, "a pretender."

Past
January 2019

Commander Alex Murphy stood in the locker room of the Barracks, shoving his muscular body into the familiar fabric of his uniform. How many times had he adorned the thing in the past two decades?

Enough to make me a Commander, he thought sullenly. He sat on a bench and swapped out the gritty tile for the soft soles of his Caeli boots. He pulled the bootstraps taut. Alex stood, securing the pads of dirt-brown armor to his chest and groin. A jet-black gun hung on his hip, the metal as familiar as the comfortable knit of his soldier's uniform. He fixed his geometer to his utility belt, thinking that the mobile Hold would have been useful fifteen years ago when he and Adian were too lazy to steal liquor from the kitchens. Besides the tattoo on his back, the only other distinguishing object to mark his rank as Commander was the gold band wrapped around his right bicep.

Around him, his men chattered and joked, voices echoing off the locker room walls. Alex imagined the atmosphere was much the same in the women's locker room, too. Gleeful faces, voices lined with adrenaline and impatience. "Surprise the Gens," he kept hearing. "We'll get the bastards now."

I hope. Alex still smelled the smoke from the April Attack in 2004. He still remembered the northern wall, up in flames, and the way the earth groaned and trembled when the Sentries finally started operating again. He still remembered how Adian died. The Dentatas located her, somehow, in her flight to the disgraced Major Alba. And they slaughtered her, blood spattering the pavement and pooling in the potholes of the backroad they found her on. Of course, he hadn't been permitted to see for himself, but Major Rex showed him pictures, not a trace of remorse on her face. That's what being Major was, after all. Emotionless.

Tyto Alba never had that in him.

Alex stuck his earpiece in. His soldiers slipped themselves into their black skins, securing the colors of their ranks to their right biceps. Silver Officials, bronze Sergeants, and maroon Corporals; there would be no Specialists, Privates, or Trainees on this mission—too inexperienced.

Alex took a gulp of water from his silver canister and closed his locker, but the memories of Adian kept coming. Her large, chestnut eyes, and sloppy hair piled atop her head. How she cleaned the house obsessively when she was worried, and how her room was always like stepping through the aftermath of a hurricane. The way her forehead crinkled while she thought, and the way she could never pee on a public toilet without closing her eyes first. She had been his best friend—he knew everything about her.

Well, *almost* everything.

That raw feeling crept into his body as if his heart were being rubbed with sandpaper. The years had compacted his guilt into fine particles, but his regret was just the same. His testimony had not been enough to convict Tyto Alba, but it had been a hit against him. As much as Alex had tried telling himself he testified in Court for the sake of Taxodium, for the sake of justice, that hadn't been the case. He did it because of Adian. Because she ripped his heart out and stomped on it a hundred times over—and she hadn't even known it.

Her son, Calyx, would be sixteen soon. The last time he had seen the boy, Calyx had been crying in his arms as Alex carried him through the underground tunnels connecting Aurum House to an abandoned well outside the Twelfth Wall. It was difficult to imagine that small boy, so afraid and weepy, as grown up. There were rumors that he would be attending the Academy. Alex doubted Calyx would have much of a choice. But maybe, if all the Gens were captured or killed tonight, Calyx *could* have the choice.

"Commander Murphy?" There was a blur of arm, as the soldier striding towards him saluted. *I'll never get used to that.* It was one of his Officials, Cirrus. "The men are ready, and the women are waiting in the field outside. Your orders, sir."

Alex glanced over the Official's shoulder at the rows and rows of expectant, eager faces. How many friends, family members, coworkers had the Gens taken from each of his soldiers? Briefly, Alex recalled Adian, the Alba Atrocities, and the April Attack that had been as much of an ending as a beginning.

Alex cleared his throat, the sound reverberating against the locker room walls. "We take the Hold at Serpent Mound to the coordinates. I want everyone on high alert." He pivoted and led the way out of the Barracks. The rest of his speech, he would save for Serpent Mound, a short drive away from the Academy. There, his soldiers would take that ancient Hold to Maine, to the Gens' headquarters. And they would eliminate every last one.

"This can't be right." It was Cirrus again, the closest thing to being Alex's second in command, though there was no such position. "Where did the Major get her information?"

31

"Ramsey," Alex shrugged, body poised, and ears pricked. "She doesn't tell, and I don't ask. But these are the coordinates, so we'll inspect the premises as if there's a horde of Gens right on the other side of that door." Alex flicked his wrist, and a pack of soldiers moved soundlessly to the east side of the building. Another group moved west, their feet sinking into the deep snowbanks.

There's no way to hide our tracks. He searched the lifeless, black glass of the building and shivered. Alex was suddenly grateful for the thermal tech of the winter skins.

"I don't see any heat signatures, though," Cirrus explained, voice wary. His eyes were peeled, scouting through the snowy darkness.

Alex suppressed a sigh, white flakes like cotton landing on his lashes. The Guard's morale was slipping—and could he blame them? Tax had been searching for the Gens' hideout since World War II. A FedEx shipping and supply was honestly one of the last places anyone thought the Gens would be dwelling. His eyes took in the white brick in the moonlight, the crystal icicles hanging from the roof. Behind him, a train rumbled along its rusting tracks, drowning out the anxious whispers of his Guard.

When the train had gone, Alex turned. The mumbling died, as the uniformed men and women came to attention. Under the light of the moon, and against the silver blanket of the earth, the Guard stood like glaring black shadows in the night. His lips curled with pride. *This is the night. This is the night Tax finally rids the earth of the Gens.*

Adversaries from the two groups he sent out to scout returned. They saluted three fingers over their hearts. *Our brothers, our sisters, our society,* Alex thought, remembering the day he was sworn into the Commander's position.

"The building is clear, alarms disarmed. No signs of life," his scouts reported. Alex nodded and looked back at the array of guards, anxious now for work.

"Falcon," Alex commanded, the strategic code sparking action in his Guard. There wasn't time for speeches of glory, not when pedes were less than a block away.

Cirrus and another Official took up Alex's flanks. Three Corporals took the rear. The remaining Officials gathered units of Corporals and Sergeants, voices soft punches in the winter air. They would follow the Commander's group, at a distance, waiting for Alex's signal. He almost didn't need his earpiece; his Guard was trained so well.

"Look for hatches and openings in the ground," Alex informed, "Intel seems to think they live underground." Leading Falcon, Alex floated across the slight incline of pillowed snow, up to the storefront. He glanced at the rows of snow-heavy hedges that lined the building's perimeter and the white sign above the door that read: *FedEx Center* in purple and orange letters. He wrapped a gloved hand around the handle and pulled it open, his men and women behind him. Alex stalked through the antechamber, opening another door that led into the center. There was a maple-colored desk along one wall and bins of boxes along the other.

"There," Cirrus breathed at his shoulder. Alex followed the Official's glance.

"The scouts didn't say anything about lights being on," Alex replied as he moved towards the glowing doorway. He shot an arm out, signaling for another unit. Soundlessly, they crept towards the unremarkable door, an *Employees Only* label centered on its face.

The unit of Sergeants and Corporals arrived. Official Adriana Dinosco, a girl he remembered being a couple grades below him, headed the front. He spoke to her.

"Scout the premises behind that door," Alex instructed, "and remember to keep an eye out for anything that could look like a way underground. If the Gens are here, that's where they'll be." Dinosco saluted, taking her unit through the doorway. The white light was blinding, and Alex lost the group of the Guard in the radiance.

Alex sent several other units to scout the remaining rooms of the building. He stood, poised and ready with Falcon. Occasionally, the wind would whistle outside, and he saw a flurry of gray and white snow cloud the windows.

Augusta, Maine. Of course, now I see the irony in it. He had been wondering why, of all the places to settle, the Gens had chosen Maine's capital. *Augustus was the first Emperor to rule Rome. Unknowingly, he would have ruled over the first pelari, Phaedra's descendants.*

"Commander Murphy," Official Dinosco came into view, her slim body outlined in the glow of the room behind her. She saluted, but Alex hardly noticed. "The room is clear, but you're going to want to see this." Something about the bitter edge in her otherwise sugary voice made Alex's heart constrict. He followed her into the room, eyes adjusting to the stark white of the bulbs above. He blinked and saw a black rug, the kind that Rainier Hospital had at the front doors for visitors to wipe rain, snow, and salt off their shoes. It was awkwardly overturned, a slab of industrial steel thrown over the top of it. The layers revealed a square jaw. A manhole. Through it, he saw Dinosco's unit, their shadows playing off the concrete walls, expressions pensive.

"Intel was right," Alex breathed, voice raw from shock. "We've found their bunker."

"Yes," Dinosco chimed, "except my unit can't seem to find any Gens. Every room we've checked is scraped clean of... everything. No fingerprints, no possessions, no dust."

Alex's head snapped up, meeting the blue and gold of Dinosco's gaze. "They knew we were coming?" Official Cirrus huffed at his side, confirming what Alex already knew.

"That's what it seems like, sir." The bitterness swept up the remaining softness in Dinosco's voice. She averted her gaze to the scene below their feet.

"How many levels?"

Dinosco planted her hands on her hips. "There's an elevator in the west wing. The buttons on that go all the way down to twenty-three. I haven't sent guards past this first level, though."

"Hmm." Alex kneeled, feet finding the rungs of the iron-wrought ladder plunging into the bunker. "I want to have a look. Cirrus." The Official bent his knees, following Alex's descent into the bunker. When his Caeli boots touched solid concrete, Alex let go of the oxidizing rungs, black gloves stained with metallic powder.

There was a curtain of concrete immediately behind the manhole. Alex glanced around it, seeing Sergeants and Corporals meandering along the two halls shooting out on either side of Alex. He took the western wing, aiming for the elevator Dinosco spoke of. Cirrus was some distance behind him, scrutinizing the rough concrete.

"See anything?"

Cirrus made a noncommittal noise. "My Essence doesn't work through concrete this dense."

"What about the fans?" Alex turned his attention to the contraptions embedded into the walls. The blades hung in remote silence.

"Those are probably oxygen scrubbers," Cirrus commented, "but no, they aren't useful for seeing heat signatures. Based on the fact that they're off, it might be safe to say this bunker has been abandoned for a couple weeks, if not months."

"Months," Alex mumbled to himself. Down the hall, he watched a guard close a steel door, frowning.

"Anything?" Alex called. The guard—a Corporal, by the maroon band on her arm—saluted.

"No, sir. Just concrete." Alex's lips twitched into a frown, as they shuffled past the Corporal. The hall turned several times until a silver elevator came into view. The two stepped inside. The air folded around them like an envelope, causing sweat to prick under Alex's arms.

"Are we checking each level?" Cirrus asked, brushing a thumb across the black stud in his eyebrow. His expression flickered with surprise as the doors slid closed behind them.

"No," Alex said, "I want to see what's at the bottom."

Cirrus grunted as Alex stabbed 23. The quarter-sized button glowed soft orange, and the elevator sank into the depths of the Gens' bunker.

"No annoying elevator music, I guess." Cirrus wiped sweat from his brow.

"I guess," Alex replied, craning his neck to gaze out the bubble of glass in the ceiling. He watched the ropes move, the entryways to each level grew in size and shrunk as they moved deeper underground. The pressure built, and Alex was forced to swallow until his ears popped.

Cirrus stuck a finger in his own ear. "Makes me glad to live on a flat plane *above* ground."

The elevator eased to a halt. Alex glimpsed their hazy black reflections, as the doors glided open. The same square concrete hall stretched before them. The slits of light along the wall flickered, some completely dead.

"See anything?" Alex tried to mask the ominous feeling growing in the pit of his stomach.

"No heat signatures," Cirrus's voice was so low, Alex could hardly decipher his words. Together, they pressed forward, down the ever-dimming hallway.

"There are no doors, either," Alex noted.

"I *do* see that."

Alex strained to catch clues. There was nothing but the winding concrete hall. Not a scrap of garbage, a trace of human existence, only the flickering lights. It was... odd. They moved in silence, each man coiled with apprehension.

"There's a door ahead," Cirrus pointed, but Alex was already leading the way. They paused in front of the double doors long enough for Alex to read the crimson words engraved in the metal: *Numen. Per leges.*

"The bastards shouldn't be allowed to know Latin. It's an insult to Matrona and Phaedra's children."

"That's why they do it, Cirrus." Alex pushed the doors open, noting how fluid they swung on their hinges. *This was definitely the Gens' bunker. Recently.*

Inside, it was much the same as the hallway: concrete walls, flickering lights. Except this room contained black marble floors, the two men's reflection skating along the polished surface at their feet. Cirrus seemed entranced with the ground, tracing the cracks, like shattered glass against an ebony night. But Alex's attention fixed to something else altogether: a mahogany desk. It appeared to be the exact make and model as the Major's desk in Allen Manor. It was empty, scraped clean of possessions, but something glinted in the light. Alex

35

stepped closer, forgetting Cirrus, forgetting the layers and layers of concrete stacked above his head. His heart lurched to his throat as he neared the familiar desktop and the object displayed there. *For me,* a voice in his head whispered. *This is here for me.*

He reached out a tentative hand, fingers gracing the cool metal of the object.

"By Matrona…" Alex scooped the necklace into his other hand. He studied the pendant, the engraving of St. Philomena with her arrows and something Alex had always thought was straw. The girl's face was smothered gray where many thumbs had rubbed it in prayer. He read the inscription: *Prega per noi.*

Alex's head swam, mouth went dry as chalk. There was no mistaking it. He was vaguely aware of Cirrus, coming up behind him.

"This is Adian's."

Cirrus didn't seem to hear. "Commander," he hooked a hand around Alex's elbow. "I said we need to *go*. There's something massive, hot and bursting to *explode* beneath our feet."

Alex came back to himself, seeing Cirrus for the first time. The Official's face was pinched with worry, panic underlying his dilated pupils. Alex glanced down at the ebony-marbled floor. Past the cracks, past his own botched reflection, he glimpsed the shape of something ominous. Red lights pulsing. Bombs.

Cirrus was holding his own geometer, punching numbers and pricking his finger for blood.

"No," Alex shook his head, "we have to warn Dinosco—her people are still in the bunker. There could be more bombs on the other levels."

Cirrus didn't look up as he said, "We can't help them if we're dead, sir. Now stand at my back. The floor is getting hot."

Alex realized, through the soles of his Caeli boots, the black marble was heating up, like beach sand on a ninety-degree day. Alex assumed position, his body brushing up against the Official's back. The geometer beeped, and the lilac seal came over them. Alex closed his eyes, thinking that Adian would have loved geometers, would have loved having a Hold at the tip of her fingers.

And then they were standing outside the shipping and supply building, snow under their feet rather than intense heat. Alex broke away from Cirrus, earpiece ready to call Dinosco out—

The ground shook and shifted beneath them. Alex heard what sounded like a plastic bag popping—the earth tilted beneath them, and suddenly, Cirrus's fingers were gripped around his elbow, yanking him back to the empty road.

"No," Alex protested, legs unsteady. "No, my Guard is still down there—" The FedEx shipping and supply erupted in smoke and flame.

Sparks and flying debris lit up against the pupils in Alex's eyes. He gripped Adian's pendant, knuckles crackling. As the building burned and the Guard retreated, rolling and tumbling into the snow, Alex saw the April Attack. Northern wall aflame, Adian's eyes, pleading him to save her son, to save Calyx. *"Please—I have to go after Tyto. Please, take my son through the tunnels."* The Gens had lost that battle, but they certainly were victorious here.

A Sergeant staggered across the pockmarked plane to meet Alex and Cirrus. Others followed him, wounded dogs returning to their master.

"Somehow, they knew," the Sergeant exhaled, coughing grit into his elbow. "Somehow, they knew."

Clenched between his gloved fingers, Alex felt the pendant like a hot coal.

Prega per noi.

Castan
June 2020

The floorboards creak. Suddenly, a man is standing where Corolla appeared no more than twenty minutes ago, between the kitchen and the couches. If I didn't know better, I'd say he just rolled out of bed: disheveled hair, rumpled polo and khaki pants, sullen eyes.

Behind him, in the white lighting—the front door must still be open—is Aunt Laila. I could pick out her figure anywhere. The long tresses of hair, like shadows, billowing around her shoulders; her nimble but proud frame.

Corolla looks up.

"Is it true?" I'm surprised by how clearly her words ring out—her face has been paling for some time.

The man—James—glances from Corolla to me and back again. As if he doesn't already know. As if Aunt Laila's very presence doesn't confirm it: We are here for *her*.

A hiss of air. An undeniable, "Yes."

Corolla bows her head, biting her lip with enough force to sever the chunk clean off.

James shoots her a wary look, then glares at me. "How did you find her?"

"An overdue library book."

I note the lines of surprise in his profile. *Perhaps he wasn't the one who deleted Corolla's digital footprint.* His own accounts weren't much better. Some overdue bills and a scatter of college debt. A different address on each file. But looking at this shell-shocked man, I'm not sure he could have forged or erased any papers. I'm not even sure he knows how.

James hangs his head. For a moment, I'm not sure if he's crying or praying—his lips are moving, and his shoulders are bobbing. Maybe he's doing both.

Aunt Laila clears her throat. "Maybe you should take a seat, James."

He sways a little, but Corolla is already rushing to his side. She loops an arm around his waist and guides him five steps away to the couch in their cramped living room. It's so outdated—faded plaid pattern, sunken frame—it could have been a poor family's heirloom. They collapse onto it, Corolla a picture of concern.

Shouldn't it be the other way around? It's a small thought, one I don't give much consideration. I follow Aunt Laila to the Vels.

I don't sit. Instead, I tower over both pedes.

Corolla looks so much like Calyx that I blink to erase his face from hers. It's difficult. Her olive skin, like coffee diluted with cream. Her amber eyes, sharp like cognac, dart from my face to Aunt Laila's. She is frightened. If her dilated pupils don't give it away, then the white-knuckled fists at her sides do.

I tear my gaze from her and fix them on James. He isn't like Corolla, with his fair skin, pale hair and blazing blue eyes. But if I thought Corolla was pale from shock, then James is translucent. I'll start seeing his insides at any moment.

"My name is Castan Cassena." I don't reach to shake his hand. I don't care to. "This is Laila. We represent Taxodium."

"I know," he spits through gritted teeth.

Well. I've been trained not to assume.

Aunt Laila takes over. She's better with people, possesses an air of sensitivity that was snuffed out of me before it had an opportunity to grow. She kneels down so that she's eye level with James. "Adian would be proud." As instructed, Aunt Laila already debriefed James on the drive over. He's shaking his head. Maybe he needs to hear it again.

"Adian would be alive had she never gone to that cesspit."

I look around the disarray of his own house, smelling cow manure in the air, and think, *This place isn't much better.*

James says something else as Aunt Laila tries to persuade him. I study Corolla, drawn to her eyes. I thought I'd never see anything like them again. I thought—

I chide myself. I can't allow nostalgia to take root. I can't allow Corolla to unhinge all the doors I've locked and shuttered to keep the ocean at bay.

I look at her as a stranger. I note the intent way she listens but remains silent. She's gnawing on her bottom lip some more, and I force a similar memory of Calyx chewing his cheek from my mind.

She is a stranger, I tell myself, *and she will stay that way.*

"And if she dies?" James almost shouts. He reminds me of a shaken bottle of carbonated pop: on the brink of explosion. "Then what?" He challenges Aunt Laila. His red face illuminates his blonde hair. I can't help but think that he isn't anything like Corolla—pale American features next to dark Florentine ones. At least, Calyx always said his father was of Florentine descent.

39

"The goal of this endeavor," I say tartly, "is only to lure the Gens in. Corolla will be surrounded by Tax guards on campus. The possibility of her death is slim." Corolla shifts a little next to her uncle. For a moment, I feel guilty discussing her mortality as if she isn't in the room.

James doesn't back down. "And what about Calyx? What were his odds?"

I clench my jaw and fists simultaneously. James isn't at all amused by his intentional jab—he's pissed. And now so am I.

Laila cuts in before I can open my mouth. "Calyx's situation was something different entirely."

Through my anger, I hear nothing more that is said. Almost instantly, a wave of exhaustion strikes me. I unfurl my fists, hoping no one will smell the smoke.

I remember how I used to read for hours on end, before Calyx, and before Taxodium. My eyelids would start resembling rusted doors over eroding metal. That's how I feel now, watching Aunt Laila and James work it out—eyes dry and bloodshot.

I wipe the sting from my eyeballs and return to the kitchen. I recall seeing a coffee maker here, while I was waiting for Corolla to come home. I quickly locate the grounds in the cupboard above. No one pays me any attention—Aunt Laila and James are still going back and forth; Corolla is still silent, in psychological shock maybe.

I watch the pot drip with dark amber liquid, allow the scent of it to flood my nose.

James is arguing in circles, and Aunt Laila does her best to break them. It only drains me further. I stay in the kitchen, waiting for the coffee to brew. I wouldn't be much help now—I'd just lose my temper—so I let Aunt Laila do the talking. That's why I brought her with me.

When the coffee is finished, and James is still slandering Taxodium, I pour half of it into a soup mug I found in a different cupboard. No cream, no sugar. Just scorching decaf. I glance to my left and see Corolla watching me with guarded eyes.

I pick up the mug and go outside.

I glance from the rows of flowers around the house to the faded green of the front lawn. Even though I lived with Calyx for half a year, I only recognize one of the species as daisies. I imagine the flowers are attempts to mask the smell of farmland. I wonder if, by some innate calling, Corolla was the one who planted them. I wonder if it stings to know that the Essence gene skipped her. I wonder if she realizes how much good she can do posing as a decoy at Taxodium.

I wonder, I wonder, I wonder.

The sun paints the sky with a soft, warm glow. It sinks farther and farther until it's beneath the cornfields, and my coffee is nearly gone.

Footsteps resound behind me. I don't move from my spot at the end of the stoop. The front door closes with a slight *click*, and Aunt Laila stands by my shoulder.

"He's agreed. I did as Rex suggested—as you proposed."

"Hm." Rex would pay in gold if it meant eradicating the Gens once and for all. And the Vels are conveniently close to bankruptcy.

As if reading my mind, Aunt Laila adds, "It's not about the money, though, Castan. It's about her safety."

"She'll be safer at Taxodium than here. If we could find her, then the Gens can too."

"I know," Laila exhales, "But Taxodium is also the most... obvious place for her. We're putting her on a pedestal and strapping a target to her back."

I blanch. "On my life, Aunt Laila." I don't have to explain further. She already knows that I don't want to repeat my sins twice.

I sip the rest of my coffee, thinking that smelling shit is better than smelling blood.

"One more thing: Corolla wouldn't go unless James could come too."

I groan. "Rex won't like having James the Pedes on the grounds."

"Two," Aunt Laila turns to me, "There will be two pedes at Taxodium. Corolla is not Calyx. Don't forg—"

"I won't." My voice is a whip.

Aunt Laila sighs, facing the sunset once more. "Rex got what she wanted."

"Only half," I remind her. "The Gens are still thriving, and the world is still burning."

Past

April 2019

"Corolla, like the car?"

Corolla craned her neck, pencil scraping across paper. She recognized the dark eyes grinning down at her. *Averil*, her mind filled in. *The sophomore who showed up drunk to Homecoming last year.* Of course, she hadn't gone—she was too young—but people talked. And they loved him for it. She wasn't sure why. It was just one of those things you didn't question.

"No," she suppressed a giggle. "Kore-ah-la. My mother was weird that way." Corolla didn't know why the sentence felt like a betrayal, but it did. She averted her gaze to the wall of glass cabinets behind their row. She was never sure why a chemistry teacher would have fossils, skeletons, and jars of animal parts, but she supposed he was allowed to have hobbies.

Averil flashed white teeth. "I love it."

Corolla nodded and ducked back into her notes. If she weren't careful, Mr. Grubaugh would call her out in the middle of class. He was droning on about covalent bonds, causing some people's eyelids to droop, but Corolla was fascinated. Apparently, she was not the only one.

Averil leaned closer to her, brushing his shoulder against hers. "Diamonds are one of the strongest materials on earth."

"Yeah," Corolla dared to glance at him. Meeting his gaze, she grinned. "Mr. Grubaugh just said that. Network covalent." She was all too aware of his body heat seeping through the fabric of their clothes and burning her shoulder. She propped her chin on her left hand, leaning away from him. She scribbled bits and pieces of Mr. Grubaugh's lecture on her paper, but her mind snagged on Averil. Why was he talking to her? He had been in her chemistry class all year and barely uttered a word, spare for usual niceties here and there.

"Are your cheeks always that red, Cor?" Corolla was suddenly grateful to be in the back row. If they had been in the first two rows, Mr. Grubaugh surely would have written them detentions by now.

Her maple-brown eyes flitted to his chocolate ones. "Cor?"

Averil leaned back in his chair, tossing his mechanical pencil aside. Corolla watched it slide across his blank page of notes. He ran a hand through his dirty blonde hair.

"Well, I can't call you the same thing as my car," he explained, a wry look flickering in his eyes.

"Oh." Corolla followed Mr. Grubaugh's pen on the overhead, drawing a sloppy model of the diamond. "Do all of your lines suck?" Averil spluttered. Mr. Grubaugh paused, flinty eyes peering over the top of his gold-rimmed glasses. Averil ducked his head into his notes, pretending to write something. Corolla bit her lip to keep from laughing. Mr. Grubaugh sighed, continuing his lecture about bonds.

Averil shot her a look, head bent over his notebook. "What makes you think that was a line?"

"Because," Corolla hissed, massaging the cramps from her hand, "you've never talked to me before. And school gets out in two months," she pointed out. "Hell of a timing."

Averil regarded her, mouth slightly agape. "Wow. You're pretty forward, aren't you?"

Corolla shrugged, picked up her pencil again. "I guess."

"Well," Averil spread his hands out on the gray top of their table, "I can be pretty forward too: I like you, Cor, and I want to take you out sometime."

Corolla's heart thrummed in her throat. Liked her? Nobody *liked* her, they only ever pitied her, tolerated her. Everyone knew Corolla's mother was murdered, and her father was absent. Some people thought her father *was* the murderer. It used to bother Corolla, but it was just another piece of her profile.

She studied Averil's crystal eyes, so dark brown, she couldn't glimpse his pupils. Strands of his straw-colored hair tickled his ebony lashes.

Averil probed, "So how about it? Dinner and a movie, or whatever you want. I can pick you up at five."

"Yes," Corolla nodded, lips splitting at the corners, "that sounds perfect."

Corolla
June 2020

It's early the next day when the Cassena's instruct James and me to take a seat at our own dinner table. The sky is gray, the windows cracked open. I taste rain on the wind and watch the faded curtains flap and billow in the bursts of Earth's breath.

I don't look at James, afraid that the very eye contact will unravel the hours of debate and eventual agreement from last night. He'll cave and say I don't know what I'm getting myself into, which may be true, but that doesn't mean I don't want to help. I want to help *him*. A million dollars, we've been offered—*I've* been offered—and I'm giving it all to James. I slept like the convicted last night, and in my sleeplessness, envisioned the things James could do with that kind of money. He could build the house he's always wanted, leave this farmland and manure-air behind. Great oak doors, open concept, kitchen armored in stainless steel, an office on the second level, and a personal library that would make the town's look like an amateur's collection.

Yes, I am doing this for a reason. And I don't need to be reminded. Only assured.

"There are a few things you should know walking into this," Laila Cassena says, severing the flow of my thoughts. She's across from us, Castan on her right, sipping coffee from a mug I got in sixth grade. Forrest Community Schools, it reads in block letters. I don't have to wonder if James minds that Castan has been pawing through his coffee reserve—the subtle exhale from my uncle reveals it all.

I guess I'll add coffee grounds to the list of things James can buy.

"We won't be going straight to Taxodium," Castan says, setting the mug on the table. I think his hands are trembling, but he hides them underneath the table before I can study them further.

"Why not?" James practically growls. I see him from the corner of my eye, wringing his fingers in his lap.

Castan directs his gaze from the contents of the mug to my uncle's face. I don't know how James can withstand a gaze of such... irritation, but he does it effortlessly. Years of experience at the grocer's, I guess.

"She needs to be properly Marked." Again, they are speaking of me as if I am not in the room. And again, I allow them. "The Gens will know she's volga otherwise."

Volga. Pretender.

Laila adds before Castan can spew more venom, "You know each student must complete a *Humanitas*, James. Corolla isn't pelari so she won't be going through the three Trials initiation requires. However, we have to go through the motions as if she were pelari, for the sake of this plan to work. Which means a slight detour to Matrona in Iran. It'll be a day or two journey and stay, and *then* Corolla will be safely deposited to the North American Academy in Ohio."

Deposited. Like a check.

"A day or two?" James shakes his head. "This is idiotic. I—"

"And after that?" I speak up. "What do I do while I'm at Taxodium? Attend class?" I don't say what I meant to ask: *Stand on a platform?* My stomach flops at the idea: being the center of attention, malevolent or otherwise. I've been under the radar for so long, I'm not sure I *can* surface.

Laila's expression softens, but it's Castan who answers.

"You'll be chained to me."

"Excuse me?"

"Not in a literal sense," Laila scrambles. Then, more controlled, "Castan has been assigned your Regent. A bodyguard, if you will."

"Oh." I really *don't* know what I'm getting myself into.

"Anyway," Castan pauses to sip more coffee. I watch his Adam's apple bob in his throat. "Major Rex has been working on leaking the information that you'll be attending Taxodium by the end of this month. It'll reach the Gens' ears and this whole affair should be over with by the end of July."

"And the money?"

"Corolla!" James hisses.

"You can have it now if you'd like," Castan offers. I don't like the look of his wry grin, the way he fails to mask it with the rim of his mug.

"No."

Castan opens his mouth, but the sudden patter of rain on the roof cuts him short. He looks up as if daring the weather to be louder than him. Then he glances down and says nothing. I wonder where the Castan from yesterday is, the one who pleaded me to sit down so he could explain; the one who had the gentle voice and large, vulnerable eyes.

Maybe that was another one of his tricks.

I fold my arms across my chest.

"We have guards patrolling the premises," Laila informs. She mentioned something similar last night. "They will help escort the two of you to the various checkpoints we've planned for your journey."

"Which are...?"

"Look," Castan snaps at James, "it's not your place to know every detail of our pursuit. Corolla will be safe."

James leans back in his chair, the ancient woodwork groaning under his weight. "And what about Calyx? Was he safe?"

Something flickers across Castan's face, something sharp and ominous and sad all at once. The hairs on the back of my neck stand like posts.

Castan glowers. "He was safer at Taxodium than Corolla is now, locked in this house."

James is silent, a calm storm brewing at my side.

Laila intervenes, albeit too late. "We'll leave early tomorrow morning. Any more questions?" She clasps her hands together, the gold bracelets around her wrist jingling like coins.

"James has to be taken to Taxodium," I hold her careful gaze, "otherwise, I'm not going."

"As I said yesterday," Laila says, a kind smile slipping across her profile, "there is already a house waiting."

I nod and chew my lip some more.

The world continues to rain, a drizzle of tears outside, but our conversation reaches a standstill. It seems, no matter how much James opposes Taxodium, we are both already too far into our agreement to back out. I wouldn't want to, but James would do it in a heartbeat. He shut himself up in his room, without breakfast, face brighter than blood.

I return to my room and sit on my bed facing the closet doors. I need to pack some clothes, a toothbrush... But I keep thinking about Averil, about the disappointment and shame—my hands can't make a web of yarn out of these emotions, though. I'm waterlogged.

I look at my fingertips, where the skin is raw from brushing against the nails in my closet. Playing with yarn isn't going to make James proud, but maybe—if he can get over his resentment—helping Taxodium can. Maybe.

"Do you always sell yourself so easy?"

I look up to Castan clotting my doorway. His question catches me off guard, and for a moment I'm mute. Then I notice his expression: a raised eyebrow, half-grin.

My eyes narrow. "You don't always have to be a dick."

"Hey, I'm helping you out, too—"

"Don't," I bite back the worst of my fury, "bring our financials into this." I rise, making my way around my bed for my backpack—

"Corolla, wait." I glance at his fingers wrapped around my forearm. He drops his arm to his side. "I'm sorry. I should have been more considerate..." He seems to think for a moment, for once. I cross my arms, impatient.

Castan brightens up. "How about a session with your mom?"

My defenses falter. "What?"

"I know a girl," Castan gushes, "at Taxodium. She can locate spirits and communicate with them."

I consider his proposition, mind swirling, thoughts tumbling. I don't think about my parents much, but curiosity is something else...

"James is welcome to join you," Castan adds.

"No," I shake my head. "James was pissed when he found out they cremated Adian's body. He wouldn't approve."

"Ah, a traditionalist." As if that explains everything. "But Tax had to cremate her body. If the Gens... you know, stole it, well, nobody wants to find out what they can do with a corpse."

"Burn the witch, huh?" I didn't mean it as a joke, but Castan chuckles.

"Yeah," he scratches the back of his neck, "gives it a whole new meaning, doesn't it?"

I bite my lip, realize what I'm doing, and stop. "Fine," I say if only to make him go away. "I accept."

"Good." He must be out of words, as he gives me a curious look and retreats down the hall.

It's only when he leaves that I realize I'm blushing.

Past
August 2019

For as long as Calyx could remember, the creatures of the night always sang him to sleep. The screeching of owls, the humming of cicadas, even the occasional yipping of coyotes. But this time, the nighttime sang a melody that would not lull him into dreams. Every tune seemed to clash with one another. The effect was atrocious, like an orchestra of the worst musicians.

It's different because I am different. But it's probably for the best I don't sleep. He was afraid too, he realized. Terrified of what his dreams would demand of him. Because they weren't just dreams. No, he recognized the spirit that haunted him.

Calyx tossed and turned in his bed, hearing his father snore down the hall.

Tyto had warned him from a young age that turning sixteen may bring about specific changes in his body chemistry. Yes, he would sweat more, grow hair more, and feel certain emotions more, but that was not what Tyto meant. He meant that Calyx would have an Essence, either like his mother's or completely independent. He meant that Calyx was pelari and would change as such.

So it was no surprise, to either of them, when Calyx woke up one morning in June, *months* after his sixteenth birthday, with vines coiling around his forearms.

"You're like your mother then," Tyto had said. There was no pang of grief in his voice, in the lines of his face, only joy. "My son," Tyto beamed, "pelari."

Calyx was trained as a child to keep his family's secrets locked tightly in his heart. The vines were just an extension of these secrets, and he guarded himself well. Nobody at school suspected. If he suddenly craved an open field of dirt to plant his hands in, he would calmly walk to the bathroom and drown his hands with water. Sometimes, aquatic plants would come out when this happened, and Calyx would have to feign sickness and go home. But Tyto never blamed him, only saw his potential for making something useful of his Essence.

"Your mother almost killed a man when her Essence first came to light," Tyto chuckled one evening when the sun set across the

48

mountains. "Just don't do anything like that, and I won't have any reason to worry."

Besides the occasional, uncontrollable floral outbursts, Calyx was the same. He still pursued his regular schooling, still saw friends on the weekends, and still wanted to get a degree in engineering. He was not, however, destined to continue these endeavors. And he should have known better than to dream.

But it was just that, his *dreams.* Once, they used to be unremarkable, spontaneous and unmemorable things. Lately, they grappled with his mind and presented themselves—always—with a vibrant yellow light. He suspected he knew exactly who this light was, but Calyx was not ready to leave behind the average life he had envisioned for himself. He was not prepared to depart this safe world at Alba Creek Farm.

He knew about Taxodium, about the Gens and what his body would mean to them if they found him. But that would never happen, he assured himself. Alba Creek Farm was buried in the mountains for a reason.

But even distance and a thousand trees could not keep Tilia Pyrus from wedging herself into Calyx's mind.

"Child," she would coo. "Calyx." Her voice was honey, sweet and delectable. He craved the feeling of her light on his skin, but always, always, he found the strength to pull away. He would think of his family here, his life, and he would be appalled that he had ever considered following that light elsewhere.

But he was human, so, despite what his heart wanted, his body was weary. Calyx fell asleep.

He felt her presence before he felt her light. Together, both filled the planes of his mind, expanding into the corners and crevices.

"Calyx." Yes, he was sure now. Tilia Pyrus, the great Venefica, was calling for him. He knew Taxodium's history as well as any child raised in a pelari household. He knew all about Tilia, how she had created ingenious devices with her enchantments, how she had revolutionized the Hold system. How she placed the threads of a ruinous curse in the genes of the Dentatas. Her human body was long dead, yes, but her spirit dwelled in an ancient cypress tree called Matrona. Curious, that she should exist in the center of Iran and his dreams simultaneously. But the Venefica was capable of many things.

Calyx opened his eyes but kept his back to Tilia. "What do you want?" He blinked at the brightness, adapting.

"Would you blame me, child, for asking something of you?"

Calyx turned then, to meet the face of his tormentor.

Yellow as the sun, but not so harmful. The shape of a woman, slim and slender. Calyx blinked again, but finally decided it was better to keep his eyes closed. Through his eyelids, orange and red swirled.

"I don't understand how someone of your... aptitude would need me."

"Then you overestimate me, young one." The light shifted as if Tilia were pacing. She may have been, but there was no other sound, spare for her soothing voice. "You are also afraid of me."

"No," Calyx said, embarrassed. "Not of you, anyway. Of what you want."

"Help, that is all I desire."

Calyx swallowed. "I can't commit to something that vague."

"So it seems," Tilia mused. "I have been trying to communicate with you for several weeks, yes? You run away each time."

Calyx bowed his head, wondering why the Venefica made him feel ashamed.

"You mistake my comment for insult. I only meant that you think through your options before hurling yourself down a path. You mother was not so gifted, in that respect."

"And?"

"And I like how you think, Calyx. You possess your father's perception. I want you on my side."

"Side? You mean Taxodium's side."

"No," the syllable punctuated the air. "I mean *my* side."

Calyx dared to crack open an eyelid. "Are you saying you're not aligned with Taxodium anymore?" Tilia oversaw the *Humanitas*, from what Calyx understood of Tyto's lessons. She Tried and Marked incoming pelari students. Tyto had shared with him stories about his own *Humanitas*.

"I am merely saying that, should advocates of Taxodium come knocking on your door, you let them in. Times are changing in ways I do not fully comprehend yet, but," Calyx felt her gaze on his shuttered face, "when I do understand them, you would be a detrimental ally to my cause."

Calyx chewed the inside of his cheek. His body swayed a little, guided by hearing alone to keep himself upright.

"You're talking about war," he said finally.

Tilia inhaled a sharp breath. "If that is what it must come to, yes."

"Why are you telling me this? Here, in this way?"

"Because I fear that if I do not intervene your life will be lost, and the world's along with it."

"The Genocides?" Calyx guessed at her vexation, eyes still clamped shut.

"For me to relay more to you, young one, I need to know that I can count you as my own."

He didn't *have* to go to the Academy—there was such a thing as pelari parents homeschooling their gifted children. But if he stayed home, stood by and let Matrona knew what happen, then how could he live with himself?

Calyx was acutely aware of his heart pumping in his chest. He was aware of his fingers, twitching to conjure something. He was aware of his head nodding.

"Very well. I advise you to go to Taxodium then. That is the first step."

And so, when a man in a slick black suit showed up on the front porch four days later, Calyx opened the door. Tyto would not, and did not, argue with Calyx, once he expressed that his Essence was becoming too much to handle; he needed training and skill. It was half-truth and half-lie, of course, but no one was the wiser.

That's where his web began.

Calyx hugged his stepmother and shook his cousin's hand. Tyto saluted his son, and they embraced for a brief moment. Calyx said goodbye to his family, and closed the door on one ending, only to open the door to another.

Castan

June 2020

I know this place. I thought I left these corridors behind, the concrete's grooves and stale air. I thought—

"Castan!" The shriek pierces the air, a lightning strike. My legs respond with less urgency than the cry for help demands. It *is* a cry for help, there can be no doubt. So why am I so painfully sluggish?

I find the door the screaming is coming from. I open it.

"Castan!" My mother's shrill voice penetrates my ears, stabbing, bursting in a rush of noise.

Hadley is here, in the corner of the room. She's mouthing words at me, a mask of agony, but the echoes of our mother drown her out. I swear I see waves of the wailing reverberate off the concrete walls of this cell.

"Castan," my mother clutches my hands, her kneeling figure trembling. She gazes at me with those wide-open eyes, the type that makes my heart feel like it has little paper cuts all over. Each beat, I bleed.

"Don't let them take me. Don't let him."

I reach out a hand to smooth back the black wisps from her forehead. Her hair was always short, cropped close to her skull because it made lab work safer. But she disintegrates like ash before my eyes. I stare at the pile of gray and white, so much like the concrete surrounding me, that I lose sight of it.

I hear Hadley now.

"You were supposed to preserve her," she moans, collapsing on the floor. She curls into a tight ball and is hardly recognizable as my little sister. She is a bundle of skin and bones and crippling sadness.

"You were supposed to come back for me."

I take several tentative steps towards her as if the ground will give way under my feet. It may. I don't remember how this dream continues. Part of me knows this is not reality. The dominant piece in me ignores that fact.

"Hadley," I crouch beside her.

"And what did you think?" She whispers into the ground, not meeting my eye. "You knew I'd be long gone when you came back. You killed me, Castan."

"No," I choke on emotion. Tears stain her pale cheeks. "No, I meant to protect you."

Her gaze fixes on mine, but these are not Hadley's eyes. Black. Feral. Inhuman.

"*I* protected her," answers a masculine voice. The room clouds with the wretched scent of old cologne. If smells had expiration dates, this one would have gone bad decades ago.

Hadley's form takes the mold of a new body.

I rise, almost immediately, as the shape unfolds. I stagger backward, running up against the cool concrete. It absorbs all the warmth from my body, from the room. Or maybe that is credited to the man before me.

Behind me, I fumble along the wall, searching with desperate hands for the doorknob. I don't want to speak to this man. I don't want to kill him. Already, I feel flames in my palms, blistering under my skin. I am itching to murder. And that frightens me.

I locate the knob, just as the man turns to face me. I take one look at the familiar angles of his profile and fling the door open.

I'm falling, not out of the room, but down, farther into the Complex. I pass through three levels of concrete, steel beams, and sights I had hoped to never see again. The cafeteria, vacant but harboring a dark presence. The living quarters, where Hadley and I used to throw basketballs down the passageways. The labs. I know the order of these places do not make coherent sense—the living quarters were always above, near the surface of the Complex, and the labs were farther beneath the cafeteria—but the effect is the same. My anger and hatred slip from me like a fish out of water. What replaces it is pure dread, like a hundred arms enveloping me all at once. I cannot move.

I land, not gently, on a floor that I don't recognize because it did not exist in the Complex. A vast plane of gray and concrete, shadows and fear.

I recognize the scene before me, though.

Metallic zings through my nostrils, straight to the pit of my stomach. I suffocate in the perfume of his death.

Splashes of blood, pools of crimson, stains of ruby. And Calyx, wrapped in the middle of it all. I want to look away from his body, so still, so pale, but I cannot. It is a moment I relive more often than I care to admit. Every position of his body memorized, every drop of blood on his brow. Every molecule, I know.

His right knee is cocked at a strange angle, making it look like he's a painting of a man running, a canvas of blood behind him. His arms lay miserably at his side, unable to conjure help, unable to move. His face so weary, and, despite his Mediterranean origin, porcelain white.

I can't, however, look at his eyes.

There is a hand on my shoulder, firm and unfamiliar.

I turn.

"Calyx," I breathe, unable to fathom how he is dead on one side of me and alive on the other. I accept it as truth, though. So eager for him to be alive, for my sins to be forgiven.

I open my arms to embrace him, but somehow, never complete the action.

"I'm sorry."

Calyx regards me, raising an eyebrow. "How far did my ashes fly? Far enough that you will never see them again."

The shadows build around us, construct and contort into walls, furniture, a table and burning incense.

Júlia's place, the place I have been hunting for his soul. To say sorry. To say goodbye.

"You can't find me because I am punishing you," he says in a mellow tone that is not like Calyx at all. It is a dehydrated version of himself, I realize. All of his vitality and charisma, gone.

The paper cuts in my heart burst at the seams.

I falter, choking on blood. It gushes from my mouth, from my abdomen. I am swollen with the stuff, a balloon.

And with each gasp for air, with each panicked glance at Calyx, the corners of his lips climb a degree higher.

My body lurches awake. I forget where I am, but then I see the wooden frames of Corolla on the wall. I relax, heaving a sigh.

You're in an old recliner, not the Complex.

I rub weariness from my eyes, cursing myself for falling asleep. Usually, any sleep is welcome, but not today, not when other people's lives depend on it.

Through the thin walls, I hear murmured voices in what I have established as James's room. Corolla and James, I conclude, which means it must be Aunt Laila in the shower across the hall.

I stand up too quickly, and my vision blots with red and black. I take a deep breath, thinking about my dream. I have different versions of it a lot. My mother, my sister, Calyx... all the blood on my hands.

I go to the back windows, checking for anything unusual. I touch a hand to my throat and inhale the fresh air. There's still a trace of blood in my senses, leftover from my dream, no doubt. I check the front windows next and wonder if Kass has noticed anything strange around the house. She's stationed some miles or so away, along with two other guards. Together, they form a triangle around the house.

I run a hand over the rectangular bulge in my pocket and glance at the clock on the wall. It's almost noon. Kass will be sending a report soon.

Kass. It's difficult to think about her and not remember Calyx. I let my mind wander for a moment, allow it to travel through old memories. But then it gets stuck. I groan. I know I have a temper, and I know I can be rude, but—Well, there is no *but*, is there? I have no excuse for my demeanor towards James and Corolla. Except that whenever I look at either of them, I remember that it's my fault Calyx isn't here. It's my fault they never got to know him, just as it's my fault Kass never got to love him.

Calyx would apologize, a quiet voice mumbles. It sounds like Aunt Laila. I groan again and make my way towards James's room.

I'm not surprised to find that the door is shut. I raise a fist to knock, but then I catch a fragment of conversation on the other side. I pause.

"...don't know where he lives. These came without a return address."

That's James. I can't imagine what he's talking about and I don't want to. It's not my business to know. I make to turn away, but James's low humming voice draws me back in.

"You don't owe me anything," he says in a tone noticeably gentler, more intimate, than before. Curiosity roots me in place. I wipe a finger under my nose, irritated by something but unable to take the time to acknowledge it. I lean closer to James's door.

There is a gap of silence. Then Corolla's faint voice:

"I owe you more than most."

I don't know what she means by that, and I don't have the opportunity to ponder it.

"Castan," Aunt Laila whips the bathroom door open behind me. "I told you, no fires inside." She rubs her damp hair with a towel. I stare at her, confused.

And then I smell it.

Smoke.

"Aunt Laila," my tone is a fist of apprehension, "that's not—"

"Castan!" The front door erupts with an explosion of curses and clouds of smoke. Glass shatters, and my muscles tense at the deformity in the entrance. Kass. No, Kass shouldering the weight of Kat, one of the other guards.

"Phage and Lola," Kass spits, setting Kat against the wall. The woman is dead. That much is evident in the loll of her head, the slump of her spine. The black discoloration, like a noose, around her slender neck.

Macrophages.

"Shit."

Kass looks up at me, not bothering to wipe the sweat, blood, and ash from her brow. It's plastered to her skin like a collage of a mask. We communicate silently: *Carnage*. Phage and Lola must have won it this season, as their faces keep appearing like pesky pop-up ads on the Internet. They aren't as dangerous a threat as Rosh Dentata was the previous year. Where Rosh was ruthless, leaving no survivors, Phage and Lola are somewhat clumsy: Phage can't think on her own, and Lola can't fight on her own. Or so scout intel says.

"They set fire to the field," Kass spews, gesturing out the door. "Ashten stayed behind. Probably dead. We have to go. *Now*."

I'm already moving for James's door, already calculating a list of coordinates to someplace safe. James is in the hall now, sputtering words I don't bother to comprehend.

"James is yours," I instruct Aunt Laila, grabbing Corolla by the wrist. She shrinks away from my touch. I let go, ignoring the way her syrup-colored eyes flinched.

With one hand, I pull a device from my pocket. "How far behind?"

Kass slams the door, but smoke still creeps in through the windows, through the cracks of the house.

"Not very." I hear the scowl in her words, but I don't look up from the geometer. I punch in some numbers and secure our destination with a drop of my own blood. Taxodium. We have to regroup. We have to plan. Because the Gens shouldn't have found us, not this soon.

By Matrona, I swear, *don't let this malfunction*. Geometers are touchy devices. The wrong handling could land you on your neck or drop you from the sky. Potentially both.

"What the hell is going on?" James squawks. Aunt Laila summons the wind, clearing a pocket of breathable air. When disaster strikes, she is always an essence of calm. The worse the situation, the more tranquil she becomes. Right now, her expression is one of relaxed concentration. She swirls her arms in a cyclical motion.

Across the room, I meet Kass's indigo eyes. We share a look. The geometer will only work in open spaces. At least, spaces more open than this cramped living room. We can't risk the Gens jumping our bubble either.

I turn to Corolla, "Is there a back entrance?"

She shakes her head, eyes huge.

"What kind of house doesn't have a back entrance!" I want to scream. Kass's impatience beats me to it.

"Fuck. Ing. Hell," Kass groans. "We can't wait any longer!" She storms to the back wall and raises her hands. I know what she's thinking, and I don't stop her. We have no other options.

Acid spurts from her palms, a milky toxin. It chews away the drywall and part of a window. I expect James to shit a brick, but he must have realized that this is beyond his petty gripes.

"Kass." I don't have to say it. She already knows. I watch her take off through the archway she made in the wall. It's drizzling outside, I realize, but that won't stop the fire from spreading; it won't prevent the Gens from coming.

Laila and I watch Kass, a black and orange blur across the open lawn. When nothing happens to her, it's Laila and James's turn.

"No," James becomes animated once more, "I won't leave Corolla behind—"

Laila places a hand on his back, and her Essence does the rest. They are whisked out into the clearing, feet barely scraping the ground.

Just get close to the trees, I think. *Get close to the trees and use the geometer*. We all possess one, courtesy and convenience of operating outside of Hold domains.

I clutch Corolla tighter. "We run until I tell you otherwise, okay?"

She nods, mute and frightened. Like a calf for slaughter.

I gaze out through the mesh of rain. Aunt Laila and James are just now disappearing into the air. Where they stood by the tree line, James a stooped mess, there is a bubble of pale light. And they are gone. Kass is waiting for me in the trees.

I pull Corolla closer. This is our window.

Past

September 2019

Kass stabbed the prongs of her fork into her bowl without looking. She brought the victim to her mouth, an explosion of salt.

A green one, she thought absently. Beside her, Jura and Dani were talking about Talan.

"Does he prefer gun or knife?"

Jura cocked her head and considered. "Neither."

"What?" Dani balked. "That wasn't an option."

"Well," Jura shrugged, "he's stronger than Hercules and as peaceful as a plant. What do you expect?"

"Okay, okay. Rain or shine?"

"Shine."

"Oh," Dani lamented, massaging the navy and white polka-dotted band wrapped around her hairline. Apparently, it was a fashion from her hometown. "We have nothing in common."

"Well, that's my brother for you," Jura replied, apparently distracted by something else. Kass noted that she hadn't cracked a textbook open like she usually did while they ate. Jura studied incessantly.

Kass brought another olive to her lips.

Black one.

"Hey," Dani leaned towards Kass's shoulder. It took much of Kass's restraint not to stab the girl with her fork. She was not in the mood for Dani's gossip today.

"How much do you want to bet he'll walk in here and think he owns the place?"

The scowl on Kass's face deepened. She knew who Dani meant— the entirety of Taxodium was breathing his name. *Calyx.* The Dining Hall hummed with the syllables, up and down the lines of tables. Kass heard the echoes off the walls. Some of it was speculation. Most of it was resentment.

It was no secret that the disgraced Major Alba and current Major Rex had reached a decision. Calyx was to attend Taxodium, with one condition: he must always have a bodyguard. It did not take Rex long to whip up a position for such a compromise. Regent, that was what it was called, and whoever impressed the Major during training was the

58

one who would be selected. It would be an honor to serve a Vel, even if his very presence provoked outrage.

It was also no secret that Kass had failed this aspiration. The bearer of this honor was some tables away from her, his head bowed over his food.

Castan Cassena.

He was nephew to Communications Master, Laila Cassena. Although Kass knew she should admire Castan for his combative skill, she despised him. He was the same age as her, true, but what did Castan do for Taxodium? Did he volunteer for early scouting shifts? Did he place himself at the Major's mercy? No, he had no ambition here. It was not right. Still, the Major had chosen Castan to be Vel's Regent, and Kass was left to brood.

"Well you're fun to talk to," Dani said, hurt that Kass was ignoring her.

Don't take it personally, Kass wanted to say. She was ignoring everyone. Everyone, except Castan Cassena.

Kass stuck another olive in her mouth and regarded her subject across the room, over the heads and murmuring bodies.

He was an oddity off the training field. Cowardly, almost, but not entirely. He kept to himself, Kass noticed, but that was precisely what made him odd. Everyone at Taxodium integrated into one body, but Castan kept his distance. Kass wasn't even sure he knew this about himself, as he was always absorbed in one novel or another. It was no wonder that Castan was paired with Finis as a roommate. But even the independent Finis contributed to the social circles of Taxodium.

She noted how, while Castan sat between two other guys, he did not partake in the conversation, the frequent glances at the door—any of it. He would probably be sitting alone, had there been space for that in the crowded Dining Hall. He didn't touch his food.

Nerves, Kass considered. Castan was about to be tied to the most essential body on campus. She was sure Finis would be glad that Castan was moving out to live in Aurum House with Vel. If her own roommate, Maggie, were silent all the time, Kass would probably scream.

It was as if all the clashing of his name, all the betting, and nasty remarks had summoned him to the Dining Hall.

The glass doors opened, and there he was, the disgraced Major's son, Calyx Vel.

The Dining Hall plunged into silence.

Finis Fletcher, a student a year older than Kass, grazed the room for the Regent, his now ex-roommate. Kass's eyes flitted back to Castan, in time to see that the person near him nudged his elbow. Castan stood, a flurry of clumsy limbs and messy hair. He practically tripped over the bench. There were snickers in the crowd, as Castan hurried towards the doors, and Kass fought to bite one back herself.

The Major chose him. The whole room was charged with this thought and many others.

Kass turned her attention to Calyx. Since all the pictures and portraits of Alba were taken away, she had nothing to compare him to. She imagined he looked like his father had, all those years ago. He was tall, almost the same height as Castan. Dark hair, caramel skin and, most likely, dark eyes. His eyebrows, she saw, exhibited a graceful posture. But that didn't mean he wouldn't be a bag of arrogance. Son of Alba, son of Vel—the guy was bound to think himself higher than everyone else, Kass was almost certain. She didn't like Calyx, but that didn't mean she wouldn't have appreciated being Regent.

Calyx said something to Castan, who was staring at the floor. His head snapped up then and the two shook hands. They could have been brothers, Kass thought, except that one was incredibly robust and the other, incredibly tan. Finis departed the way he came, and beside Kass, Jura sighed quietly.

Castan glanced over his shoulder at the sea of unfriendly eyes. Kass thought she saw the color fade from his cheeks.

What a sight it must be to a man who doesn't belong here any more than his charge does. Kass felt wicked, and she didn't care.

Castan motioned for Calyx to follow him outside, but Vel stood where he was. Those closest to him ducked their heads and ceased their staring. But those farther still gaped and gawked, each gaze a dagger at Calyx's being.

Instead of following Castan towards the doors, Calyx did something extraordinary.

He waved.

There was no trace of pomp in the gesture, only a friendly beam of light. Kass wasn't the only person who felt it. Little by little, the heavy, disdainful silence melted into something else.

Awe.

And then Calyx was following Castan out the building. Before the doors swung shut, Calyx's voice struck the silence of the Hall.

"I think I'm going to like this place." He had just a shadow of a twangy accent that Kass was sure would fade in time.

And then he was gone.

Kass ducked her head, irritated that one person could have so much influence over hundreds. Dani and Jura began a conversation again, this time about Calyx. The Dining Hall rang with demanding tones about Vel. There were no more bets about his arrogance, no more snide remarks about his father's failure and his mother's murder. There was only admiration.

It was then that Kass knew why she didn't like him.

In a world painted gray and stained red, he smiled too much.

Corolla
June 2020

Castan doesn't tell me what's going on, but I gather from the sharp lines of his expression (and the surmounting smoke in the air) that this is everything he had hoped to avoid. I do not look at the slumped form by the front door.

He tightens his grip around my wrist, and I fix my own grip on the photographs in my hand. James gave them to me only minutes ago. I don't know why I'm still clutching them, but I don't think I could let go if I wanted to. I am terrified.

I duck my head into my sleeve, choking on gray clouds. Castan frowns.

"I can't control this fire. It's not mine. Corolla," he tugs my rigid body, "we have to *go*."

I nod, still wondering why we're here. I would have run with the redhead if Castan wasn't holding my wrist in a death grip, like a parent afraid to lose his child in a crowd. Or his commodity.

Castan tenses, body bracing for our flight to the forest. I note the way his arm flexes, how each cord of muscle becomes one band. I focus on things like to this to distract me from things like James, who has disappeared. Despite myself, I imagine a spider's web, saturated with crystal dew drops. I can't help but tie this image to my nervous system: each neuron weighed down with growing beads of panic.

For a moment—just a hair of a second—the pattering of rain lets up, and the clouds shift. A stray beam of sunlight breaches the storm and smoke. But it is in this space of calm that disaster strikes.

The front door opens.

Castan turns, muttering a string of curses under his breath. I follow his narrowed gaze.

Stepping from the cloud of fumes, with a flaming torch in hand, is a willowy woman. Her hair is white as snow, ash particles sticking to her tresses like miniature doves. She would be elegant, but slapped across her left cheek, is pockmarked skin, warped and wrinkled. *Burns.* From the look in her catlike eyes, I know immediately that I am destined to despise her. Whatever I have gotten myself into, I am no longer a neutral party.

The woman, without a glance in our direction, tosses her torch under the kitchen table. I bite my lip to keep from crying out. My home—James's home—is dying.

"Phage."

The woman regards Castan, regards me. Her pale lips quirk into a grin. She says nothing. I wonder if she *can* talk.

"Hold this," he says without looking away from the white woman, "and don't touch any buttons." He shoves a device in my hand and releases my wrist. I examine the thing. It's something like a glucometer—there's even a strip of blood shoved in the bottom. It's slightly larger and squarer, with buttons and a little screen glowing white, digital numbers printed in neat lines across it.

I glance at the bunch of photos in my sweaty hand. Something clicks in my brain. I carefully place them in my back pocket. I can't let Adian and Calyx burn twice.

Castan takes several tentative steps from where I stand, and I almost wish he hadn't. Even though my wrist will likely be bruised, he was an anchor in this madness.

"Castan," I try to say his name, but the smoke and ash plunge down my throat. I cough, holding the photographs and strange device to my chest. Water, I wish I could have some water. Not for me, but for the flames.

Castan says something to the woman—Phage, he called her? I don't see her open her mouth. Instead, a black shadow peels itself from the ceiling, dropping between Castan and Phage like a sludge of slime.

It is another woman, this time short and squat, square as some of the farmers that live around here. Her hair is curled and tied into two ponytails, one on each side of her head. Childish. Strange. But I am afraid nonetheless.

Castan takes a step back, embers in his palms. I swallow the chalk in my throat as flames erupt from the kitchen table. They lick the round edges of the wood, creep up the back of the plaid couch, a chariot of destruction.

"Don't look so shocked," says a voice like sugar, sweet and overbearing. "You led us right to her."

Her. It takes me a moment to realize she's referencing me. I think the smoke is starting to affect my brain.

"Lola," Castan growls. His embers expand into golden stones.

"Fire with fire," muses Lola, seeing Castan's palms. The irony slips from her expression and is replaced with a coldness that even a blizzard cannot possess. Calculated. Personal. "Phage. Secure the Vel."

Lola's body dissipates and clouds. I lose sight of her, though a newly formed shadow flits along the floor towards the blackening window. Or maybe that's my imagination. Maybe that shadow isn't a person at all but the flicker of spreading fire or lakes of ash clouds. Sweat drips down my back, along my forehead. I swallow again, but my tongue sticks to the roof of my mouth, sandpaper.

Castan becomes a sort of blur, a structure with arms and legs. Light shoots from his being. For an odd moment, I think his body is consumed with it. I hear my heart in my ears, feel lethargy sink my limbs.

A voice in my head is screaming at my legs to move, but I don't. I can't. The world is coming down around me, and all I can do is watch.

The kitchen is lost, obscured by a wall of orange and yellow. The couch, too, is on its way to becoming a pile of ash. I can't say that I will miss it. I think of my room, of the nails and yarn and all the memories that live there. Shoved in the rafters of my closet, the microscope and all the aspirations that went with it. The chipped paint, the blemishes in the floorboards—all stories. All gone.

All gone. James said those were my first words. Said I used them for the most trivial of things: the ending of a storybook, the draining of the bathtub, brushing my teeth. I had no *mother*, no *father*. I had *all gone.*

And then there is a boulder crashing into me. I stumble back into the wall. My shoulder prickles with arrows of pain. A picture frame falls near my feet. Glass sprays like sparks.

I open my eyes and see Phage advancing towards us. Castan pushes himself to his feet, hair glued to his skin with sweat. He's in worse shape than Phage. Deflated, haggard. He's losing.

Castan raises an arm at Phage, but her counterattack is faster. Her expression is a sneer of teeth and pink gums as she grabs him by the collar, eyes like embers, and throws him backward again. This time, his back slams square against my chest. Luckily, my arms are still crossed and most of the force is deterred. I gasp for breath all the same.

Castan pants, hands on his knees.

Phage steps closer. From behind Castan, I see her open her mouth: and a flurry of black vapor exits her body.

The device in my hand starts beeping like a microwave.

Castan's head whips around. "Corolla, no!" A look of terror, a cry of warning.

The device vibrates once, twice: A veil of transparent matter bubbles around us, pale lilac. It expands over me, over Castan, and over Phage. I don't have time to rationalize it. I don't even have time to stare—

We are thrown, the three of us, into blackness. For a moment, I sympathize with clothes, tumbling in a cold, dark washer.

It is only when I hear the crack of bone, a shrill pitched ringing, that I understand.

I have done something horribly wrong.

Past
October 17th, 2019

"Did you hear about the scouts?" Castan pushed aside Calyx's door, ignoring the fact that it had been closed. Calyx had the bigger room between the two that Aurum House had to offer. He claimed he remembered it from when he was younger, but Castan wasn't sure you could remember being alive when you were only two years old.

The room sported a single, neatly made bed, tucked in the farthest corner, a plain desk near the door, and some bookshelves lining one of the walls. Calyx didn't bring many possessions with him, so the shelves were empty, spare for some textbooks and a frame of his family. His closet door hung open, coats and sweatshirts flung over it, masking it as an actual door.

Calyx was cross-legged in the middle of the space now, a heaping bin of Legos at his side. His attention seemed to be on the project before him, but Castan knew better. He watched his roommate dig through the bin, jam some pieces on a platform, only to rip them off again. His fingers were raw-red, and Castan wondered how long Calyx had been sitting there doing just that.

"I'll take that as a yes then."

Calyx sighed and tossed the colorful chunk of Legos in the bin, sending a spray of pieces to the floor. "Yes, I heard." His voice was tight, expression pinched. He raked a hand through his chocolate-colored hair and looked around himself at the mess he made. He chewed the inside of his cheek, something Castan noticed he often did.

Castan's grip loosened on the brass doorknob. "Are you alright?"

Calyx glanced up at him then. He seemed to see Castan for the first time. Recognition flashed over his brown irises, and a quiet grin toyed with his lips. Calyx stood in a single, swift motion.

"It's your birthday today."

Castan was taken aback. "That's hardly the first thing on my mind," he frowned, "when the Gens are out there apparently decimating our scouting units."

Calyx turned his back to Castan and pulled something out from between his textbooks. Castan could see the glaring, overly optimistic *Happy Birthday!* wrapping paper from his place in the doorway.

"Here," Calyx handed him the slim, rectangular package. "Happy seventeenth."

Castan hesitated before grasping the present in his hands. For Calyx's sake, he opened it. Castan cocked his head, staring. It was a magazine, the kind with a half-naked woman on the front.

"Calyx…" Castan began, "what is this? I appreciate you buying me a gift, but I'm not really interested in porn." Calyx's grin widened, eyes glinted as if he had been expecting Castan's lackluster reaction.

"'Don't judge a book by its cover.' Isn't that what you're always saying about your classics? Well, looks can be deceiving, I agree with you there."

Castan exhaled, a smile taking shape in his lips. *Of course. Leave it to Calyx to remember my birthday* and *give a meaningful gift.* Castan flipped the cover over, and there, instead of another nude, was sheet music.

"'Pachelbel's Canon,'" Castan read the title at the top, eyes dipping down into the stanzas of music notes. For a moment, he wasn't in Aurum. He was sitting on a worn piano bench, Hadley on his right, his mother on his left.

"The best musicians move with the music," his mother explained. "Like this." She played the melody from "Für Elise," body swaying ever so slightly along with the movement of her hands across the keys. Castan wasn't really paying attention to her lesson. The music swallowed him whole, took him away from the burdensome concrete of the Complex.

His mother stopped playing the keys, and Castan was deposed in the concrete room once more.

"Again!" Hadley demanded, giggling. Castan knew she felt it too, the way the music transported them far away.

"But now it's your turn," their mother laughed. She swapped "Für Elise" on the music rack to a book, the page open to larger notes and fewer stanzas. Castan's heart sank. He wanted to play "Für Elise," not something from the *Basic Piano Library*.

"So, you like it?" Calyx's voice yanked Castan back to the present. He blinked the black spots from his vision.

"Yes. Thank you, Calyx. I'll enjoy this."

"I will too—I'm tired of listening to that same old sad song you play."

Castan was about to say something smart, but the front door burst open, a plethora of voices filling the house.

"Castan! Calyx!" One of the voices shouted, mild annoyance flaying the tone's edges.

"That would be Kass," Calyx sighed. The pair made their way past the kitchen and into the living room where a crowd of people was waiting. Castan had to do a double take—in only a short month, Calyx had brought all of these people together. It was extraordinary, how talented he was at making people feel like they belonged. Castan felt that glow in his chest, and the sheet music pinched between his fingers only made the *belonging* intensify.

Espirit de corps, I think that's what they call this.

Castan looked about the room. Before Calyx arrived, he had only known these people as faces or names. Talan and Dani were splayed across one of the sofas, fingers intertwined. Finis, his old roommate, was perched on the coffee table, adjusting his silver-rimmed glasses. Maggie and Júlia hovered anxiously behind him. Kass stood near the front door, arms folded across her chest, frustration burning brighter in her eyes than the flame of her orange hair. Jura, Talan's fraternal twin, was trying her best to soothe Kass, muttering silky words at her shoulder.

"It's okay," Jura was saying, "at least it's no one we knew—"

Kass shoved away from her. "But it could have been someone we knew!"

Talan and Dani stopped whispering. Out of the corner of his eye, Castan glimpsed Calyx. They were all here because of him. Because he always knew what to say, always knew how to put their problems into a manageable perspective. They may not have been aware of the fact, but Calyx was a sun in the darkness.

"Kass," Calyx went to her, lightly touching at her shoulder. She was in her black uniform, the material hugging her willowy body. Calyx mumbled something privately to her, and Jura skipped over to Finis.

Castan met Finis's flinty gaze. "Did Major Rex say anything else about the attacks?" It was, after all, Finis who had initially broken the news to Castan: There had been a disturbance in Phoenix, Arizona, a rumor of Gens in the area. A scouting unit had been called in to investigate. Apparently, that rumor had been correct. None of the scouts survived the encounter.

And Calyx was supposed to go on his Humanitas *next week. He won't be able to leave for another month now if the Gens are this active.*

Finis replied, in his reserved and calm way, "The bodies are being brought back tonight. Rex wouldn't say what... state... they were in, but I imagine not a good one."

"Right," Castan nodded, thinking. Carnage was months ago, but that didn't mean there couldn't have been another one, especially considering... But who won this time? Castan tried to remember faces, but all he recalled was smoke, cheering, the scent of scorched flesh—

"Castan, are you looking at a porno?" Júlia shot him a coy look. He felt heat creep into the sides of his face, as eight pairs of eyes latched onto him.

"No," he ducked his head at the booklet. "It's sheet music. Calyx got it for me."

"Ah," Kass said knowingly, sharing a look with Calyx. "Happy birthday, Castan."

"What?" Dani shot to her feet, brushing the honey-colored hair from her eyes. "It's your birthday today? Oh my god—we need to celebrate." She smoothed hands over her face in mock distress. She always seemed to wear a cloth headband, a different pattern for each outfit. Today, she wore a simple red one to complement the roses on her pale pink shirt.

"No," Castan waved his hands, desperate, "we don't need to celebrate." But his pleads were lost in the cacophony of Dani, Júlia, and Jura planning the evening's events. He heard a tangle of words, something about glitter, banners, confetti, cake—

"Oh," Júlia squealed, "and a donkey. I know where we can get a live one." He thought he saw Maggie roll her eyes.

I guess it's better than talking about dead bodies.

Castan's eyes flitted to Calyx and Kass. She suppressed a look of amusement, fingers brushing Calyx's forearm.

"Thanks a lot."

Calyx raised an imaginary glass, eyes glinting, "A party fit for any old Gatsby."

Castan

June 2020

I jackknife awake, coughing ash from my lungs. Fine razors of pain shoot down my spine. Dust, dirt... I am lying in the street. The street where Calyx died. I know I am not dreaming either: Corolla is on the other side of me, sprawled in the evening sun. She's not moving.

"Corolla," I groan and stagger to my feet. I reach for her crumpled form. There's blood drooling from a wound on her skull, and she doesn't move when I touch her. There's black around her mouth and nose from all the smoke she inhaled. She's breathing, a wheezing rise and fall of her chest. I inspect the rest of her being for damage, cursing myself the entire way.

I shouldn't have given her the geometer. I shouldn't have taken so long to get her out of there. I should have been stronger. I scan the premise for Phage, almost positive that she fell in the bubble with us. I don't see her. The geometer is some feet away, though, crushed into fine plastic shards. We're stuck here.

I lightly touch Corolla's left shin, where there's a severe bruise, black and blue. She twitches but doesn't open her eyes. I think her leg may be broken. It's only when I examine it closer that I see it's not a bruise at all. It's macrophages, burrowing into her flesh like miniature power drills.

Shit.

I weigh my options. I can carry Corolla to the Botros's or to Matrona. It doesn't take me long to decide: no way in hell am I transferring her to die in the same room that Calyx did. And no Gens are milling the streets this time, so why wouldn't I go to the Venefica?

I look up at the sun, which is just beginning to set. Another object catches my eye. Phage, body hanging over the side of a building's roof. Pale limbs, silver-white hair and marred profile, neck angled unnaturally. She's dead.

Legs stiff, I walk over to the building. It's low enough that I can yank on Phage's limp hand. Her body crashes to the ground. I glance from her twisted expression to the charcoal handprint on the building's facade and curse myself again for not clearing the history of my geometer. During the struggle, Corolla must have accidentally pressed *scroll* and *jump*.

Rex is going to have my head when she finds out I've been using my geometer to come back here. Or she'll have me sacked for letting Corolla die.

I toss a flame on Phage's hair, not bothering to look at the geography of her face again. *Let someone else worry about the body,* I think, *I'm tired of doing it.*

I return to Corolla and loop a tender arm under her shoulder. She is much lighter than Calyx ever was. Smaller too. I scoop her up in my arms, thinking that it will be a smoother flight for help this time. And if any nightwalkers see us, I don't care. As long as they are not Gens, I don't care.

I only hope Corolla will wake up.

The sun is well below the line of buildings when I reach Matrona. Under the umbrella of branches, I set Corolla against the thick burrows of the cypress tree. Earth and dirt mingle with my senses, almost drowning the soot and sorrow. I feel between one of the grooves for the Mark carved into the trunk. Drawing a little knife from my boot, I run it against my palm. I slap the blood over the Mark, grabbing Corolla at the same time. We are absorbed into the confines of the Venefica's headquarters.

"Castan?" I blink at the shift of atmosphere. The cavern is dull, even with little roots hanging overhead like glow worms. Absently, I feel the flesh in my palm stitch itself back up, a characteristic of my enchanted knife.

"I don't have time for niceties," I say, shouldering Corolla to an upright position. "I need you to save her leg, her life, and get Rex on the line when it's all done."

Tilia's angelic face is grave, something I have never seen before. "Bring her this way."

I follow Tilia to a back room and watch as she swipes an arm in space. The neat stacks of papers from what appears to be her desk are whisked into the air and deposited a yard away. I wonder if Tilia meant to drop them in a pile, scattering them all along the floor.

I set Corolla on the desk, which somehow has become a mattress, complete with pillow and blanket. Corolla twitches. I step away to marvel at my failure.

"This wasn't supposed to happen again." I am struck by how similar this scene resembles another. I am struck by my own stupidity.

Calyx's blood, Corolla's blood… there's no difference. Except that there must be. Where Calyx was defenseless to a fault, Corolla is entirely incapable. She requires more protection than Calyx ever did.

"Out," Tilia commands.

"Can you save her? There are macrophages in her bone."

Tilia brushes past me. "I cannot do anything with you hovering over the room like a monsoon."

I open my mouth to protest but then clamp it shut. I will just have to trust that Tilia knows what she's doing.

"Of course I know what I am doing," Tilia bends over Corolla's shin, inspecting it. "Leave." I don't have to be asked again. I round the corner and sink to the floor.

Soft images of peace replace the apprehension and fatigue in my body. The scent of old books, musty and dry. Coffee brewing, luxurious and relaxed. From the depths of my mind, an old fantasy surfaces: the little log cabin buried in the woods.

"Don't enchant my mind," I call, though I am not confident I'm coherent.

"You need it," I think I hear Tilia reply, but I am asleep before I care to piece it together.

The second time I wake up, my mouth is dry as sand. I ignore it and pull my sore body from the claws of an unnatural sleep.

I'm not on the ground anymore, but in a bed similar to the one Tilia conjured for Corolla. I throw back the sheets and clutch my aching head. I wince—the spot is tender, bruised.

"The adrenaline masked it." Tilia is perched on a throne of intricately tangled roots, some feet away. Despite the fairy tales, Tilia can't read minds. She is only very cultured in the language of facial expressions.

I swing my legs over the bed.

"She is resting," she informs me, "so please do not wake her. There is a pitcher of water by her bedside."

I take this as permission to leave. "Thank you," I say, more grateful than any words can express. I pause by the archway to the second cavern. "Is her leg…?"

"It will heal."

I consider the luck in this. I consider the luck in it all. Corolla or I could have easily landed the same way Phage did. We could both be dead, wasted lives, wasted purpose.

"When you return," Tilia adds, "I expect a detailed explanation of what happened out there. You were not due to arrive here in this state."

I nod.

I remember Tilia's headquarters from my own *Humanitas*—Calyx's too—but I was never allowed in the back room. I didn't notice it before, but the wall near the entrance is a map of the world, constructed in roots twisted to form the continents. Each pulsing dot of light marks the location of a Hold. That is, places where pelari can jump through space to another destination. Some Holds are natural, some are Pyrus-made. All of them are more reliable than geometers because they operate on a larger plane of enchantment.

I stop avoiding Corolla and sit in the chair by her bedside. Tilia left it here for this very reason, I'm sure, as she never needs to sit. Her perception always catches me off guard.

I grab a glass and pour some water. I sip it, restrained, as a wave of blistering anger passes over my body.

Corolla is bruised, like a peach that has been tossed around too many times by careless hands. Besides the bruising, her left shin is wrapped in gauze, and her eyes are closed. I look at the freshness of her face, and wipe a hand down my own, realizing that Tilia cleaned the grit from my skin as well.

The great Venefica, a nursemaid. I suppose that's what happens when one's human form perishes and spirit is left behind in a tree.

I set my glass on a ledge in the earthen wall.

Would this have happened, had I not been napping? Yes, I am certain. My carelessness—it's always my carelessness that creates problems. Of course, my plan all along was to use Corolla to draw the Gens in, but not like this, not taken by surprise, miles away from the Academy's army.

My brow furrows because somewhere, I messed up. The Gens shouldn't have known about Corolla, not yet. Rex's campaign, her leaking of rumors, should not have bled this quickly into the underworld. I backtrack my movements, all the way up until the beginning of this year when I read through the medical records of Corolla's birth. She was born in Rainier Hospital, only a month before her mother ran away. Pelari children come into the world laughing—a reflex I don't understand the science behind. Corolla's records indicate that she didn't laugh but cried until she was blue in the face. That's when I decided using her as bait would serve a more natural way to draw the Gens out of their hole in the ground. They wouldn't know that classified detail.

That information couldn't have slipped, couldn't have found its way into Gen intelligence; otherwise, there would not have been an attack to secure Corolla this afternoon—the Gens wouldn't kill for any pedes. They must still believe Corolla's pelari. So I must have made an error sometime after that. Sometime when I was logging the coordinates of the Vel's home, perhaps? Maybe the Gens stumbled upon the same digital slip about the library book before Intelligence could wipe the record. Maybe.

Rex, Pyrus, Ramsey, Murphy, Aunt Laila, Maggie, Kass, Finis, Talan, Umar, Nasreen. They are the only people who know Corolla is a ruse. And none of them would have betrayed confidence. None of them are traitors, if Tax even has people like that. Somebody always knows someone who died by the Gens' hands. Somebody always wants vengeance.

There must be something else that I'm missing. I'm sure Rex will make that point very clear once Tilia gets ahold of her.

I heave a sigh and pinch the bridge of my nose. I don't know how the Gens found us. I don't know, and my head is beginning to throb. I've made a mistake, and it almost cost Corolla her life.

Just make it through the month, maybe two, and this entire nightmare will be over.

Two months.

And I thought half an hour of terrors was long.

Past
December 30th, 2019

Calyx noticed the glass panes vibrating and opened the doors. A flurry of snow followed him into the Dining Hall, but it wasn't the Dining Hall anymore. The tables had been stowed away. What remained was a floor slick with sweat, flashing lights, throbbing music.

The training uniforms and black boots had been left behind tonight. Women glittered, as did some men. Ties and tuxedos, gemstones and dresses. Even in the dark, Calyx could make out the finery.

Taxodium's New Year's Eve party. The Academy had one every year, apparently, the day *before* New Year's Eve. Calyx thought this tradition strange, at first, until he learned that it was decided this way so that students could return home for the actual New Year to be with family. Tyto hadn't wanted Calyx to come back in the blizzard, though, and he couldn't regardless: he was leaving for his *Humanitas* in two days.

Calyx wove between jolting bodies, an ocean of movement. Arms reached out to trace his shoulders, maybe to brush the snow off. Voices called out greetings; he recognized some, but not all.

"Calyx!" The familiar voice was almost drowned out in the music.

He craned his neck to see Dani bouncing between Finis and Talan. Calyx made his way towards them.

"Coming to the after party?" He asked when he was sure they could interpret most of what he said.

"Yes," Dani purred, dipping down the front of Talan's body. The skirt of her dress was split down the leg, and Calyx flushed when he saw how much it revealed. Dani popped back up again, still dancing circles around Talan and Finis. Talan, at least, was moving with Dani. Finis loosened his tie, gazing out over the sea of heads.

Calyx leaned towards his ear. "Jura's by the punch," he gestured. Finis patted him on the shoulder and disappeared in the crowd.

"Is Castan here?" Dani shouted, straining to be heard. Calyx took a moment to understand what she'd said.

"Oh, yes," he nodded. "Took some convincing, but he's somewhere around here."

Dani grinned. "Good. He's got to stop reading books all the time."

Calyx ducked his head as Talan twirled Dani by her fingertips. He pushed through the people, hoping to find—

Ah, there she was, standing behind the pulsing crowd by the wall. He hardly recognized her without glasses and scrubs.

"Maggie," Calyx's grin faltered as he approached. "Did you...?"

"What?" Maggie cupped a hand to her ear. Then, reading the lines on his face, "Yes. Slipped them between the books on your desk."

"Okay," Calyx nodded, "good." He exhaled, ran a hand through his hair and wiped the sweat from his brow. "It's hot in here."

Maggie nudged his arm, pointing several feet away to another woman. Calyx lost himself in the mold of her body, the vibrant orange of her hair—

"Go," Maggie said, "but don't hurt her, Calyx. Just because it's New Year's, doesn't mean 'no attachments' can be disregarded. We have an assignment to accomplish first."

Calyx only caught a third of what Maggie said. He gravitated towards the other woman without so much as a "see you later" to Maggie.

Calyx wasn't aware of his feet on the floor, the cacophony enveloping the Dining Hall, or anything else. He slipped an arm into the crook of her elbow.

"Kass."

She looked up from her cup of punch, a rare smile breaking the steel of her profile. He drank in her slim form, accented in an elegant black dress. Or at least, he thought it was black.

Calyx bent his head, mouth to her ear, "You look... incredible." The fake diamond of her earrings tickled his lips.

Kass set her drink down and flung her arms around his neck. His hands gravitated to her waist.

"I don't dance," she said, expression changing. *Her eyes,* he thought, *they always look like the ocean's horizon on a stormy night. Such dark blue.*

"You don't have to," Calyx grinned, swaying her back and forth for a moment. "Come with me to the Sun Room? I want to talk to you."

She nodded, and he led her through the crowd to the back room of the Dining Hall. It was called the Sun Room: three of its four walls were made of glass. It was drenched in natural darkness now, save for the sconces on the stone wall. There were some other people here, sitting at tables adorned in white cloths, but Calyx didn't mind. He took Kass to one of the tables in the far corner, snow swirling outside. He felt like he was in a snow globe.

When he sat Kass down, her smile had decomposed into a frown.

"What's wrong?" He reached for her hand on the table, but she snatched it away.

"Kass?"

She wouldn't look at him.

"You're leaving for Matrona soon."

"Yes," Calyx replied slowly, "January first." Kass was crying, he realized. He had never seen her like this before, picking at the skin around her thumbs, eyes dripping tears stained black with makeup. He had never seen her afraid.

"Well," she huffed, tossing the long, fiery tresses of her hair over her shoulder, "be careful." She bit her lip as if suppressing the strength of her tears.

Calyx jumped from his chair and knelt at her side.

"Kassandra," he cooed. "It will be alright." His stomach clenched at the half-lie. He didn't *know* if it would be alright, but he had to have faith. He just prayed she couldn't see his ears flush with guilt. "I will come back. To you."

She sniffled and glanced at him then. "I don't want you to promise me anything. I don't want you to say—"

"—I love you," he interrupted. It was the first time he had said it aloud, and, to his surprise, it was a relief. Like uncorking a bottle of explosive champagne.

"Calyx!" Kass smacked his shoulder, pulling her hand from his grip once more. "You can't say things like that."

For a moment, Calyx thought she was upset because she was afraid someone else might have heard, fearful that Major Rex herself would appear and put them on trial the same way his parents had been fifteen years ago. But it wasn't the Attachment Laws she feared. It was something else. He saw it in the terror of her indigo eyes, the rapid rise and fall of her chest.

"Oh, Kass," he bowed his head, deciphering her like code. "You're afraid to love me back."

"Calyx." She met his gaze, eyes watery and tortured. She swiped at her waterline, a smudge of black eyeliner. "Don't say you love me because there is no reason why you can't come back dead. The scouts... people talk about a war with the Gens. I know I'm not the only one who's heard the rumors, so don't tell me you love me because you can't, Calyx. You can't."

He should have walked away then. What was it Maggie had been saying to him earlier? He couldn't remember, but he was almost positive she would have advised him to leave, too.

He couldn't.

Instead, he crushed her to his chest. She didn't fight it, but she also didn't mold into him the way she used to.

"I won't be your widow, Calyx," she said in his ear.

"Wear that dress at my funeral, and I might just come back to life."

Despite it all, she chuckled against him. He felt warm tears soak through the weave of his shirt.

He drew her away. "Kassandra Ashdown," he held her marine gaze, "I wanted to tell you: if I die in the next week, I will have died a happy man. Because of you."

Was she blushing? He couldn't quite tell.

"Castan must have fed you those lines from his books," she fought back a grin. "But you're not going to die."

Calyx tugged her back into an embrace. "Say the magic words," he murmured against her hair, "and I *will* come back."

Kass sighed, but he felt her lips move against his chest. "I love you, too."

Calyx only wished he had been telling the truth.

Hours later, when the celebrations were over, Calyx located Castan in Aurum House, the place they shared on campus. He was alone, standing by the fireplace tucked in the rear of the house near the back door. The washing machine thrummed quietly behind them.

"Did you enjoy the dance?"

"Hm?" Castan shifted. "Oh, yeah, Júlia's pretty cool."

"You pulled off three different shades of black, and nobody noticed."

"That's what I get for shopping last minute," Castan considered. His brow wrinkled. "But to be fair, I was only wearing one when Júlia was finished with me."

Calyx chuckled. "Everyone is asleep—but I'm not surprised you're still awake."

"Someone has to keep this place warm," Castan mused. "Is Kassandra sleeping in your bed?" He half turned around, smirking.

"Yes," Calyx sighed, a lopsided grin dominating his face. "I gave Kass, Jura, and Dani my room, since it's bigger. Finis and Talan are in yours. I'll probably just crash on the couch."

"Why aren't you asleep then?" Castan crossed his legs and sat in front of the fireplace. Calyx joined him.

"I like watching the snowfall. Also, I knew you wouldn't be sleeping, so I stayed up." He said nothing about the guilt developing in his gut like a tumor, eating all the exhaustion from his pores. Calyx chewed his cheek.

"Oh." Castan blasted some more sparks into the pit of wood and ash. Calyx watched the heat sprout from his friend's palms the same way plants sprouted from his own. Not all Essences manifested this way, via the *manos*, as one of his profs put it. But it seemed to be Nature's favored choice.

"Kass seemed upset tonight. She didn't even touch the hard cider."

Calyx inhaled sharply. "Maybe she's saving the alcohol for tomorrow's celebrations. Tonight is just the Eve Eve of New Year's."

"You don't have to lie to me, Calyx." Castan toyed with the fire. Calyx stiffened, afraid Castan had shuffled through his desk—*why would he?*—and seen the files Maggie stashed there. "Kass thinks I can't protect you."

Calyx relaxed when he heard this, though there was evident hurt in Castan's tone.

"No, that's not it exactly... I told her that I love her."

It was Castan's turn to chuckle, though the noise lacked a degree of amusement. "Usually people find that endearing."

"Well," Calyx shrugged, "you know Kass. If she had her way, I'd be fifty before I went out on my *Humanitas*."

"It's routine," Castan remarked, "the Trials aren't even that difficult. Tilia just has to Mark you, and we'll be on our way back."

"Right." Calyx looked at his hands. "Do you think this blizzard will keep going into the New Year?"

"Maybe," Castan shrugged. "No thing cares about time the way people do. Nature won't stop for anything." Castan glanced at Calyx. He watched Castan fix his eyes to the dog tag around his neck. He was allergic to peanuts, so Tyto made him wear the thing in case something happened. Calyx tucked his knees under his chin, hiding the tag from Castan's view.

Castan said, "The weather won't put a damper on your Trials, though, if that's what you're worried about."

It wasn't what worried him, so Calyx said nothing. They sat there for a moment, the fire popping and crackling in its brick cove.

"You know," Calyx began, "sometimes I wonder if Tax has it wrong."

"What do you mean?" Castan did not look away from the fire. Shadows played across his features, the hollows of his eyes and cheeks.

"I mean, maybe we're going about it the wrong way. With the Gens. Maybe violence isn't the answer. If my DNA could cure the—"

"No, 'exterminate the brutes.'" Castan's tone was jagged. Calyx rolled his eyes.

"If you're going to quote literature, quote an author I like. Conrad is racist."

"I think he's just misunderstood."

"That's beside the point. All I'm saying is that this feud between Tax and the Dentatas is getting old. Why are we even destroying each other in the first place? Imagine who we'd be if we worked together.

Though I guess Tax would be more lost than anything. What are we, without *them* to pursue?"

"It doesn't matter either way. The Dentatas only know how to destroy. And whatever they *do* build is only temporary enough to help them achieve their goal: chaos." Castan shot little arrows of flames into the fire pit. Calyx regarded him, grinning sadly in the dark.

Castan, Castan, Castan, he wanted to say and so much more.

"Hmm." Calyx rose to his feet. "Or maybe they're just misunderstood."

Corolla
June 2020

When my consciousness is finally steered away from the darkness, several realizations strike me at once.

One: I owe the library a new copy of *Tess*.

Two: James and I no longer have a home.

Three: I can't feel my left leg.

I think that perhaps I'm in a hospital, but then my senses return to me. Earthy, damp air. Stiff sheets under my fingertips. And a sort of calm silence. My eyelids flutter open. Lights suspended from the ceiling on strange fixtures... No, not fixtures, roots. Not ceiling either, really, but dirt, solid-looking as stone.

Where am I?

"Underneath Matrona," says a voice like bells. I must have vocalized my thought.

I turn my head, noting how each movement of muscle causes a wave of dull aches to wash over my body. What towers before me is a mold of a woman who looks as if she has been cast in the broth of chicken noodle soup. Even her eyes, which never once blink, are a solid, shimmering yellow.

"Tilia Pyrus," she introduces, tucking her chin a little as she does so.

A part of me knows I should be shocked, but the other part of me is too tired, too drained to put much effort into the endeavor. I slump against my pillows, exhausted.

"Why can't I feel my leg?"

Tilia reaches for a glass of water somewhere behind my line of vision. She brings the cup to my lips and does not answer my question until I've drunk some of the refreshing liquid. She puts the glass back where she found it.

"From what Castan told me, there was a confrontation between Taxodium and two Genocide warriors. You accidentally pressed some buttons on the geometer during the fight."

Geometer? And then I remember the device Castan thrust in my hand. Oh, yes. I recall Castan crashing into me. I must have done something then.

"I don't understand this world," I blurt, head swimming.

Tilia chuckles, the sound a symphony of musical chords. I could almost smile at the beauty of it, but I find that, somehow, my lips are stuck in a straight line.

"You are not the first to be perplexed," Tilia admits. "I confess I was truly daunted by the pelari community when I first came to know it, as well. But that was... many years ago. Times have changed since then." Tilia's lips seem to be stuck in a straight line now, too.

"You didn't tell me what happened to my leg, or anything else, for that matter. Is James okay?" Sudden panic clips my tone. I know James disappeared before I did, but where is he? Did he injure himself?

"Oh, right!" Tilia jolts upright from her chair. She falls back into it almost immediately. "James is well—he is with Laila Cassena. And your house... Well, there was not much to be done about it. And your leg. The woman with the white hair must have unleashed some of her macrophages during the unprecedented jump you three made to Iran." Tilia beams, "I was able to prevent further damage to your insides."

Iran? It hurts my head to file this new information away. James is safe, though—that's all I could ask for.

"You are lucky the macrophages only met your leg—I do not think I could have preserved you, had it been anywhere more vital."

"Thank you. But I can..." I hesitate, "... still walk, right?"

"Oh, of course." I release a breath of relief. "But not for several days, at least."

Several days. I can live with that.

"And Castan?"

"He is in the other room. I had to place his mind in an induced sleep-fullness."

"But he's... alright?"

Tilia considers this, I can tell by the lilt of her tawny eyebrow. The action makes her appear more human than she actually is.

She says slowly, "I do not think he has been alright for some time, but he is not injured beyond repair."

I make a face. "You mean—"

"Tilia!" An exasperated cry erupts from where I imagine the other room is.

Castan.

"I am here."

I note the mischievous grin creeping into Tilia's lips.

"Stop giving me dreams about Calyx being alive," Castan calls, his voice nearer than before. There's something different about the tone, but I can't grapple what.

"I did no such thing. I have as much control over your brain as I do your tongue. I simply provoke your good nature. I cannot help where that leads you." I could take a spatula and scrape the amusement off Tilia's bright face.

"It hurts to wake up to a world where he is dead." Castan rounds the corner. And then I see it: Castan without walls. There is more to him than guilt and honor—there's personality crawling beneath the surface of his pale skin. His eyes land on my own, and his defenses are thrown up without a second thought.

"Oh. You're awake." Muffled relief. At least, I think that's what it is. A pang of longing shoots through my core—I wish James were here in Castan's place. I wish we were home and I was just sick with the flu or something. I wish Tilia were actually just a bowl of chicken noodle soup. I wish I could go back, reject Castan's offer—

No. No, I don't want that last part. Because no matter how much I suffer, it will have been worth it. James. I will do it for James. I won't be able to move on with my life until this... guilt inside of me is reconciled.

"Corolla?" I turn my head. Castan has taken Tilia's place in the chair by my head. I don't know when she left, but she is no longer in the room.

"What?"

"I..." He shoots me a quizzical look. "I asked you if you want me to get James on the line? He probably hasn't slept since he saw you last, if what Aunt Laila says about him is true."

"He's a worrier," I confirm, "but wait." Castan stops, mid-rise. He lowers himself back into the chair. My eyes trace the bruise above his eye. It looks like a smudged version of Australia.

And then I am all too aware of being stuck on a bed, a strange man hovering over me. I tug the sheets a little higher to my chest, even though my whole body suddenly feels hot as the flames that swallowed my house.

Castan senses my discomfort. He shifts in the chair. My embarrassment has embarrassed him.

"I haven't been fair to you," he apologizes, ducking his head. "There's no excuse for my behavior towards you and James. It's just..." And now he hesitates. I wait, focusing maybe too hard on the sound of his voice. I have to tell myself that Castan is not Averil; that he is a soldier, yes, but he will not hurt me.

He won't hurt me.

Castan clears his throat. "Whenever I look at you or James, I think about how I failed Calyx," his eyes dart to mine, "You have to understand, he was my first real friend... I-I'm sorry," he shakes his head. "I don't know how to explain it to you. But you're right. I don't always have to be a dick."

83

I don't know what to say. Instead, I push aside my own distress—it's always getting in the way. I reach out and squeeze Castan's hand. I only know how to take care of James, and this is what he would need.

Castan offers me a sad smile. "What were you going to ask?"

I bite my lip. I don't want to say anything. I don't want to admit my own faults to Castan, who is a product of his environment. Broad shoulders, reliable and able body. If he is a reflection of his environment... Then it terrifies me to become a part of his world.

I admit quietly, "I can't be afraid like that ever again."

"I know," he bows his head, "I'm sorry. I'll protect you better next time." He clenches fists in his lap.

"No," I say, a little taken aback, "I don't mean that you were incompetent, I mean that I was. I need to know how to defend myself." Because if I hadn't been standing around like a dumbstruck fool, maybe none of this would have happened. Maybe I would be at Taxodium with James, showing him all that I can be to this world, no matter how much it terrifies me.

This part, I keep to myself.

"Yes," Castan nods, "alright. We can start when we get back to Taxodium." Something is reassuring about the heavy lines on his face. For a moment, I stutter, baffled. Because he's not patronizing me. He's taking me seriously.

"Thank you."

Castan stands. "I'll get you the phone."

He makes for the archway.

"Castan," something just occurred to me, "You said it took you months to find me, but then, how did the Gens know where I was?"

Castan's entire body seems to droop. The lines in his face grow weary. "I don't know," he replies, "but my superiors are anxious to find out."

"And Castan?" I bite my lip to keep the questions from shooting from my mouth like darts. He must read the conflict in my expression.

"You can ask about anything," he tells me, chuckling softly under his breath. "You're part of this world now, just like anybody else. Granted, your initiation was more precarious than most."

"Well..." I grasp for the right words, "how did you know I wasn't pelari? How did you know I was pedes?" It's important that I ask both these questions. Maybe there are specific Essence-indicators I'm not aware of. Maybe there's something he's missed.

"Because," he shrugs as if it's obvious, "when you were born, you didn't laugh. You cried."

True to his nature, James is livid.

"Two days, Corolla," he bursts through the little mobile phone. "Two days and I have heard nothing about you, except that you haven't woken up. Do you know how much I worried about you?"

"I know," I stare at the lights on the ceiling, like distant suns, "I'm sorry."

James exhales into the phone. I can imagine him with one hand on his hip, smoothing the lines of his face that have already become permanent. I know he hasn't slept since our separation, and that only makes me feel guiltier.

"The architecture here is spectacular, though," he says after a quiet moment. "Cobbled roads, too. The old-fashioned kind."

Well, I want to say, *thank God for that*. Any longer and James would have found a way to climb through the phone.

"I can't wait to see it."

"You'll be coming here soon?" He is so eager, so hopeful.

"I don't know." Because I really don't. I'm sure I can leave as soon as the feeling returns to my leg, but if I told James that, he really would come through the phone. I squint at the ceiling, a weak attempt to ignore the complete and utter disappointment on the other end of the cell.

"I shouldn't be upset with you, Corolla, and I'm not—"

"It's not the Cassena's fault either, James," I say before he can fling accusations. "They couldn't have known this would happen."

"No," James is incredulous now, "but they should have been prepared if something like this *did* happen. Because it did!"

I sigh, giving up. I can't argue with James, and I don't want to.

"Are you alright, though? How are you feeling? How is your leg?" The waves of his worry could sink a large boat.

"I'm fine. Don't worry."

"Okay," he says. "Well, I'll let you sleep. Call me later or I will."

And just before I think he's going to hang up, he asks again, "Are you sure you're okay?"

"Yes. I love you. Goodbye."

"I love you, too."

I snap the phone shut. It's a good thing Castan stumbled upon me— I happen to be incredibly good at telling lies.

Past
January 5th, 2020

Castan's lungs screamed in agony. His legs carried him down the empty streets, dust flaring up behind him. Beads of sweat trickled down his back, under his arms, on his neck. It was so humid there, even in January. Castan turned a frantic corner towards the sound of Calyx.

Death, that's what that sound is.

In the confusion under the moon's watch, Castan and Calyx had been separated. The Gens appeared from nowhere: it had been an ambush. Men and women cloaked in shadows swarmed Castan, encircling him. In a ring of enemies, he was afraid of losing Calyx, but he was terrified of accidentally hurting him. Castan couldn't unleash his fire to clear a path. Instead, he punched and kicked his way out. But by that time, Calyx was gone.

All my fault, all my fault, all my fault, his thoughts whirred along with the erratic bursts of his heart. How did they go from celebrating Calyx's *Humanitas* to *this*?

Because Castan let his guard down.

"*Ahhhhggg!*" There was that blood-curdling scream again. For the second time. Castan's legs pushed forward. They were numb; they were jelly. He couldn't move fast enough.

Where is he? Where is *he?* He scouted the everyday streets, but they were empty. *Iran is a maze of corridors.* He didn't understand why people weren't emerging from their houses—the screaming was undeniable. A lump lodged in his throat. He banished the thought of Calyx, the strong-willed man he had come to know, being subjected to torture, to death.

It can't come to that.

Castan bolted up a set of stone steps, four at a time, and propelled left around another corner—

The stench of blood smacked him in the nose as if he'd ran straight into a wall. He could hardly make out the figure drowning in a pool of blood, but his heart knew it was Calyx.

There was so much blood. Spattered in the dirt street, on the stone walls of the corridor.

Before he could think to do anything else, Castan rushed for Calyx. His arms outstretched, lines of worry on his face, he burst forward like a flood of babbling water ready to swallow Calyx's agony whole.

"I don't think so," hissed a coldly familiar voice. Before Castan could check Calyx for a pulse—his friend's body was curled in pain—a set of hardened muscles flung Castan backward. He crashed into the stone wall, the air compressed from his lungs. His teeth rattled in his mouth. Dust scattered in the air, tickling his esophagus, but the scent of blood was overpowering. Castan gasped. Cologne, diluted under the coppery smell, slammed into his lungs.

Dentata.

"I could kill you, too," Rosh chuckled. "But then *my* life would become considerably boring without *you* to torment."

Castan scrambled to regain his breath. He glared at the Dentata. "Get the fuck out of my way," he choked through gritted teeth.

"Oh?" Rosh raised his eyebrows in mock surprise. "So, I see you *did* get attached to this one. Numen will be thoroughly disappointed that his training has failed you." Rosh clucked his tongue. In the moonlight, the Dentata was a lean figure. His body boasted muscular superiority, a neck thick as a tree trunk.

From the corner of his eye, Castan saw Calyx twitching.

"Get out of my way," Castan growled, stalking ahead for Calyx—

"No, Castan," Rosh said, grabbing him by the collar of his black uniform. "He's going to die." Rosh's black eyes glinted in the starlight. "He will be the cure for us all."

Castan shook free of Rosh, feeling heat rising in his palms.

"You're delusional if you still believe that," he spat. Castan was too conscious of the flames festering in his hands, too aware of that gripping fear in the back of his throat. Carnage had demanded brutality, but this was no longer a game. Castan wasn't going to hold back this time.

"You wouldn't," Rosh said, eyeing his enemy's glow. "You're too much of a pacifist to unleash your hate."

Castan wished Rosh was wrong. But the rage and frustration crept along his spine like a prowling panther. He lunged for the Dentata, grabbing him by the throat. His neck was hot, pulsating. Rosh gagged, but Castan didn't care. He clamped his fist tighter.

And then Rosh was laughing, a low, curdling sound. It only intensified Castan's fury. "What would Hadley say?" He hissed, blood rushing to his cruel face. "And... Mena?"

"You *deserve* this," Castan snarled. His voice didn't sound right. *That's not me, is it?* Castan felt the flames blooming in his palms, but instead of acting upon their impatience, he reached for the silver blade at his hip. He had never killed a man with his Essence—a fault of his, he knew—but *anyone* could kill with a knife. That was all the reassurance Castan needed to wash the blood from his hands.

Rosh's eyes widened at the burning sensation on his neck, then to the knife in Castan's other hand. Castan brought the blade down—hard—on the Dentata's hand clawing for air. Rosh bit back a yelp, the sound catching in his throat. Rosh sucked in his lips, glaring poison at Castan. From his strike, Castan smelled more blood, no different in scent than Calyx's. He witnessed a chunk of flesh fall to the dirt. A finger.

What have I done? Castan saw himself in Rosh's black eyes, hair askew and snarling, but he didn't recognize the visage.

In his lapse, Rosh broke free of his grip. He shoved off Castan, always the stronger one, even if the Dentata had been neutralized for a year now. But Rosh hadn't been stronger in the preceding moment, had he? No, Castan was then, but… was animosity really *that* honorable?

Castan fought back waves of nausea.

"You bastard," Rosh snarled, clutching his oozing hand. "You little *witch*." Rosh inspected the nub of flesh and bone where his left index finger had been.

There was no difference in Rosh's finger or someone else's head, Castan realized. And it scared him. He heard Calyx moan, something soft and barely audible. Whatever Castan was thinking before slipped his mind. It was just him and Rosh and all the pain of the past in one humid bubble of air.

"Do it, Castan. I *dare* you," Rosh taunted. "I have a fireproof suit on. We were *ready* for you. How does it feel to be predictable? To be outwitted?" Rosh flung his arms in the air, gesturing to nothing in particular. Droplets of blood splattered against Castan's cheek.

Fire surged in his veins, in his palms. Rage welled up in his throat like a fist.

"And you left us for *him*?" Rosh sloshed through the pool of blood, spraying the wall some more. A blade, half submerged in blood, winked at Castan from Calyx's deathside. Rosh grabbed a fistful of Calyx's hair, yanking his limp head into the air. Calyx, jaw slack, eyes half-lidded. Whether Calyx was unconscious or dead, Castan couldn't tell. The scene only solidified his urgency to get his friend someplace safe.

Rosh sauntered over to Castan. "You're wasting your time on *them*," he spat. "Numen would take you back. You have more intel on Taxodium than—"

No, no, no! Castan was shaking his head, sweat mingling with blood. "He murdered our mother!" The flames launched from his hands before he could think better of himself. Rosh easily sidestepped the attack. Castan only managed to char the side of a building, the stone instantly blackened like a *smack* of a handprint.

"Pathetic," Rosh scoffed. "I take back my offer." He stuck his oozing finger in his mouth, sucking on the carnage of severed flesh.

Castan no longer heard him. His ears pounded, vision saturated red—he charged forward for the Dentata once again. His fist met Rosh's jaw. Pain shot through Castan's hand, but he hardly felt it through the adrenaline, through the anger and soul-crippling fear that it might already be too late. *Calyx may be dead.* Castan tossed the thought, sinking a fist into Rosh's gut.

What would Mena think, seeing us at war with each other?

Castan didn't have time to contemplate. Suddenly, Rosh was pounding on him. A heavy boot to his legs, and Castan fell down. He felt his chances of success slowly slip from his grasp. He closed his eyes, cursing himself for not paying more attention during those long days of rigorous Gen training.

Thwack! The air was expelled from Castan's lungs. He gagged. He choked. He didn't bother covering his face for protection. *Calyx is dead. I may as well be too. I failed him.* A pang of grief ricocheted throughout his being, a gunshot cutting through his organs.

"You can't be on both sides, Castan," Rosh barked. Thick liquid dribbled down Castan's face, sticky as syrup. He gasped when Rosh struck his cheekbone. It stung, like a boulder to his face.

Despite Castan's failing grip on reality, a thought rang out in his head: *Is this really fair? Calyx, Mena, Hadley... Is it fair of me to be released into peace?*

No.

No, it was only fair that he should live in agony. Live, not die.

Combustion in his palms, flaring like a grill, and a stunned Rosh. He stumbled back, eyes watering with the spray of sparks. Castan clambered to his feet, ready to end this, to end Rosh. Shouting in the distance caused him to pause. He watched as Rosh, noticing the shouting too, shot him one last menacing glare before taking off into the maze of streets. His dripping hand was pinched in the grip of the other.

Wobbling to his feet, Castan approached Calyx's crumpled, bloody form.

The shouting—Farsi shouting—was growing louder. He scooped Calyx up in his arms. Blood, sticky and slick, soaked his arms and all of Calyx's body. Just barely, he felt the shallow rise and fall of Calyx's chest. Castan's shoulders sagged slightly in relief.

Half delirious, he disappeared into the shadows, the opposite direction as Rosh. He didn't look back, nor did he want to—he would have witnessed a crime scene, one that he had let happen.

Castan

July 2020

The Botros arrive early the next morning with a basket of fresh food, clothes, and news.

"Castan," Umar embraces me, while Nasreen gazes on at us with a quiet but pleased look in her dark eyes. Rainey, their six-year-old daughter, hangs back by her mother's skirts. It is only when Umar lets me go, that she comes barreling towards me with a brilliant, beaming expression. I kneel to catch her.

"Castan!" She throws her arms around my neck.

"How are you?" I ask. She squirms out of my arms.

Her English accent isn't as worn as Umar and Nasreen's, so what comes out is slightly rigid and difficult to decipher. "We gotted another fish after you leave," Rainey announces, pride evident in the tone of her voice.

"Another fish?" I know it's in honor of Calyx, but I don't pursue that route. "How many do you have now?"

Rainey shrugs. "One hundred."

I can't contain my amusement any longer. I burst with laughter. The feeling of my chest heaving in such a manner is more foreign to me than I would like to admit.

I look at Rainey, who's now giggling with me, hands covering her mouth. She has the most apparent dimples I have ever seen, dark complexion and dark brown eyes like her mother.

"The table, gentlemen," Tilia calls from somewhere behind me. I sigh, and the laughter subsides.

"Your father, Tilia, and I have some things to talk about," I tell Rainey.

"Okay," Rainey pats my knee and bounces back to her mother.

"Rainey," Nasreen holds her hand out for her daughter. They go to the back room where Corolla is, no doubt, sleeping.

Umar and I move a table from the back room to the main chamber. Why Tilia doesn't just conjure one up is beyond me. When the task is done, the three of us find ourselves sitting. There is so much anxious energy, though, sitting is a punishment.

Umar combs a hand over his beard, gazing at the plain table top. He's vexed, I can tell because I have been too. The issue has been stuck in the back of my mind since the raid on the Vel's home: how did they know where to find Corolla?

"It's unlikely the Gens located Corolla the same way I did," I say before anyone can prompt me. I loathe being prompted in matters like this. I was prompted day and night about Calyx's death when I returned.

Why don't you tell me about what happened in Yazd?

You said the Gens came out of where?

Rosh Dentata, the very same who...?

"Why couldn't they?" Umar asks. "They are not so stupid as we would like to believe."

"Because I found Corolla from an overdue book charge, and that book," I admit, "has been returned. Intelligence has since wiped clean that digital footprint." They don't ask me how the book was returned, and I don't say. My team and I didn't arrive in a vehicle so they could take a guess. I think about the crushed geometer and wince. I also loathe being grounded.

Umar redirects his next question to Tilia. "But we still don't know who's been erasing her existence to begin with?"

"And James's," I add. "He was almost as challenging to find. I suppose the Gens could have traced his bills to all the different addresses they were listed under."

Umar and I look to Tilia for an answer, but she is silent. Her color is fading again, until she is just barely an outline of herself in the chair, a transparent veil. And then she comes rushing back into herself like a stage light turned on too quickly.

"Major Rex seems to suspect the disgraced Major Alba," Tilia ventures, "and I tend to agree."

"Alba?" Umar is incredulous. "No one has heard from him in years. How would he have the means to access files such as these? I have limited knowledge of technology, but surely, he cannot be so capable of something on this scale?"

"He could've had help from his wife," I offer, "Calyx mentioned once that she works for some agency of the state."

"I do not know..." Umar shakes his head. "That seems out of Tyto's element."

"Well," I say sharper than I mean to, "who else could have done it? James was shocked when I explained to him how we found Corolla. He may have been trying to hide her by keeping her off social media, but he was clueless about the missing files."

"Who erased Corolla's files is really of no matter to us," Tilia cuts in. "What does matter is that our current plan to draw the Gens in succeeds. The fact that Corolla was hunted means that they do not know she is volga. We still have the upper hand."

"Upper hand?" My temper rises like a storm. "Corolla could have died—she almost *did*. I know the plan is to use her as bait, but not like that, Tilia. Not stranded in some cornfield with only me and three guards, two of which who are d—"

"Castan!" I have never heard Tilia raise her voice before. I sit back in my chair, not knowing when I chose to stand. Umar lowers his gaze but not before shooting me a sympathetic look. I don't want his pity.

"The fact of the matter is this: there was an attack, and Corolla could have died—she could die at any moment from any number of causes. The attack happened. The past has passed. We must focus on our next moves now." Tilia doesn't wait for me. "Corolla cannot travel in the state that she is in currently. I gauge she will be bedridden for another week or so, maybe more."

"A week? Tilia, that is dangerous." Umar shifts in his chair, disgruntled. "The Gens could stage an attack. They may know she's here already..."

"They could, but they will not attack. The Gens have a certain stigma when it comes to me. They would rather stay away from the witch who cursed them."

Umar goes silent. I have never known Tilia to be so vulgar, but she's not wrong either. The Gens religiously avoid Matrona as if setting foot on the grounds itself will compound their genetic misfortune.

"Alright," I clap my palms on the table top, "then we'll stay here until Corolla is better. Then proceed with the plan as it was designed originally."

Corolla will be well-protected in Tax this time next week, and the Gens will come like moths to a flame.

Corolla is awake when I visit her later. The Botros have gone, and the underground caverns have returned to their quiet demeanor. I almost miss Rainey's incessant chatter. I don't think Corolla does.

"You don't like kids?" I take a seat at her bedside.

"They're too perceptive." Corolla stretches her arms in the air. Somehow, she's managed to change into clean clothes. I'll have to ask Tilia about someplace to shower. I'm beginning to smell like a foot soldier.

"But you like kids, yeah? I'm surprised."

"Surprised?" I'm taken aback. "Why?"

Her cheeks flush. "I didn't mean it like that. It's just... Well, you're so... military."

"Oh." I nod as if I understand her, but I don't. Not really. I guess where I come from, everyone's military. "I'm human, you mean."

Corolla sighs and lays her head back down, clearly exhausted. "Yeah, I guess that's what I meant."

I glance at the neat stacks of papers in the corner of the room. Nasreen must have cleaned them up earlier. I never associated Tilia as the type who kept paperwork, but she probably does. For the initiation Trials. They probably find their way to a printing press and then Major Rex's bookshelf of boredom. I wonder what my papers say.

"I had a younger sister," I say to Corolla, not really sure why. "Rainey is kind of like her."

When Corolla doesn't respond, I glance up and know she is asleep. For some reason beyond my understanding, I feel a pang of nostalgia. Laughter. I miss laughter.

'The first step to traveling lightly is to unburden oneself.' That's what *The Beginner's Guide to Hold Transportation* taught us in class. I always thought that kind of thing self-explanatory. Of course, if you are going to travel through a Hold, you travel lightly. And to do that, don't carry so much. Common sense. Obviously. Obviously...

"Tilia." I'm lying in my bed, but I can't sleep. At night, Tilia sits on her throne—though it's not really a throne—and fades into herself. I know she doesn't sleep, but I'm convinced she needs something close to absent-mindedness. I think she meditates.

Tilia's glow comes to life, subtle, a gentle flame. I feel her gaze on the side of my head.

"Tilia," I say her name slowly this time. "I want there to be complete transparency between us." She is one of the only people that I *can* be entirely honest with. Aunt Laila is one option, but Tilia... Tilia is where Castan Cassena came into existence.

"As do I."

"Corolla's asleep?"

"As far as I can tell."

"Well," I exhale, closing my eyes for a moment to think. *Yes*, I tell myself, *I want to do this. I want Tilia to know what I've done.* "I lied to you at my Marking. And I know I'm at your mercy now because of it, but I didn't run away from the Complex. I won Carnage, and they let me go. Tilia," I gush because now there's no putting a stopper on my words, "I almost killed three people that night. I burnt the flesh of my last opponent beyond recognition and was told that I had won. I won."

"I know, young one. I could see it in your eyes when we first met."

"I didn't think you believed my story. About escaping. But Tilia, the thing is, I could have easily left all of it that night, all of the fighting and bloodshed and betting. I could have slipped the guards alcohol and been gone within the hour. But I didn't. I chose to stay, and I chose to… hurt. Like my brother. So what kind of man does that make me?"

Tilia doesn't say anything right away. It's agonizing, listening to the heavy silence that drenches the main chamber. The guilt—oh, the guilt I feel for everything I've done wrong. Carnage, my mother and sister, Calyx, and now I've dragged Corolla into this mess…

And then,

"A human one, Castan. It makes you human."

I swing out of bed. "But like Rosh? He's human too, I know he is. Tilia," I'm shaking my head now, "I need to be a *good* human." As childish as it sounds, it is the honest truth.

"I never said you were not."

"But—"

"There is a stark difference between you and Rosh Dentata. Do you know what it is? Intention, Castan. Your intentions are well-meant. His are not. And you are conscious of this. You are aware that you are different from the people you left behind. That is why you left them."

I consider this, and all too quickly I am opening my mouth to protest. I can't be good. I can't be different. I am just as terrible, just as horrible as my father's side of the family.

"Hadley," I splutter, "I promised her an army would come to rescue her, and I failed in that, too. I failed my mother and Calyx. Tell me, what's the difference between coincidence, luck, and nature? It's in my nature to lose." The guilt is pressing up on all sides of me, squeezing my lungs like a steamroller.

"You spend all this time wondering why you deserve this pain," Tilia cocks her head, "but have you ever considered why you do not?"

I thought I wanted someone to tell me I'm good. I thought the Venefica could erase my doubts, cast the shadows from my soul with all the goodness of the hearts she's forged from. "I can't," I surrender, head bowing. Calyx's dog tag is ice searing against my sternum, welding into my flesh. "I can't put my pain aside because then who would I be? There would be no force pushing me to try and do better. I—"

Tilia cuts in, voice not unkind. "It is late, Castan. I think sleep would be to your benefit." Before I can voice my thoughts, she is there, tempting my mind with the soft comfort of peace. I wonder if that was my plan all along. Just a little taste, no matter how artificial. It's not laughter I miss, but peace.

Past
January 5th, 2020

"Nasreen!" Castan shouted. His voice caught in his throat. He coughed up a string of curses as he barged into the little house. His arms were numb from carrying Calyx for so long, for so far.

"Nasreen, help me!" His vision speckled with tears. He willed them away.

Nasreen emerged from her bedroom, Umar not far behind. Lights flicked on, gasps and horrified looks passing over their dark complexions. In her hurry, Nasreen had forgotten to put her hijab on. Castan silently noted that this was the first time he'd seen her jet-black hair exposed.

"What happened?" Umar demanded. Castan didn't bother to answer as Nasreen directed him to a back room. She held beaded curtains open so Castan could pass through unscathed by the jingly, glass decorations.

"Put him here," she said sternly, gesturing to a cot against the wall. Castan gently eased Calyx onto the bed, his blood immediately soaking the white sheet dark crimson.

Calyx groaned, a whisper, a whimper.

In the light, Castan finally saw the horrifying extent of Calyx's injuries. Two long gashes gouged into his side, oozing blood like some twisted smile. The dark liquid trickled and waterfalled over Calyx's contour. In the glaring light, the blood shone. A sick, nauseating feeling overwhelmed Castan; the twangy scent of blood snaked its way up his nose, down his windpipe. It was suffocating. It was unforgettable.

Nasreen wasted no time. She gingerly peeled away the layers of Calyx's suit, revealing the mutilated, butchered flesh underneath. There was so much more blood than Castan had initially anticipated. The black uniform had hidden the carnage well. Calyx's skin was porcelain under the thick red mess of crimson. Castan fought the tingling sensation in his face, the lightheadedness slamming against his brain. He dropped to his knees, knowing that if he did not, he would black out. And how would that benefit Calyx?

"We need a Healer," he croaked. Despair wove its way through his flesh. He fought to shake that off, too.

"We don't have one," Nasreen answered, her voice thick with a Middle Eastern accent.

"Dammit! You have to have one!" Castan blinked the tears away. "He's dying!" By the look Nasreen shot him over her shoulder, his outburst was a punch in the face. He did not even think to apologize.

"I'll do what I can," Nasreen said, soft manners. "But he has already lost too much blood. Who did this?" She pressed a wet cloth to Calyx's forehead. He rasped a breath, a struggle for air.

Castan bent down to Calyx's side. He took the cloth from Nasreen and began wetting Calyx's brow. A part of him knew this couldn't possibly help, yet he clung to the action like a lifeline.

Savehimsavehimsavehim.

"It was Rosh. The Gens ambushed us. They knew we were coming. Even had flame retardant suits." Castan's voice was empty, half-hearted.

Nasreen did not say anything. He wished she would. He wished someone would tell him it would be okay, that Calyx was going to live, that his death would not be on his hands. But it was. Even if Castan had broken out of the Gens' circle sooner, the result would still be the same: failure.

"I shouldn't have let my guard down," he brushed the wet cloth against Calyx's forehead, "I should have taken you straight to a Hold and back behind the Twelfth Wall. You would have been safe." He wanted nothing more than to hear Calyx's voice, to see his lips quirk into that easy grin of his. But his visage was pale, deathly as wax.

"Castan," Umar spoke from behind, the same heavy accent thick in his voice as his wife's. "Maybe you should leave the room. Let my wife do what she can..." Umar didn't dare speak the words aloud: *until he dies.* They were both thinking it while Castan religiously denied it.

Umar placed his hands on Castan's shoulders. He shrugged him off.

"No, I can't. I swore to protect Calyx, to stay by his side no matter what..." The words clogged in his throat. His head swam with memories: Calyx laughing, his bright smile. The way his ears turned pink when he tried to lie, and the way Castan used to make fun of him for it. That carefree attitude Calyx always possessed was squashed, in that moment, as if it had never existed to begin with. Blood crusted over his brow, despite the water, which only managed to stream red down Calyx's cheeks.

Like tears of blood. Death stripped away the person and left a body behind. It was the memories of that body, that person in action, that were eternal—but they were the most painful of thoughts.

Behind him, Castan felt Umar's pressure to leave, but he made no move to get up. He heard Nasreen rummaging in cabinets and drawers. For what, Castan didn't know.

"Castan," rasped a voice. Calyx's voice. Castan practically shouted for joy—he thought he'd never hear that voice again.

"Castan," Calyx breathed again. His eyelids fluttered, cracked a degree.

"I'm right here," Castan replied. It sounded pathetic when he should have been apologizing, but it was the first thing that came to mind. Castan grabbed one of Calyx's hands. It, too, was layered in crimson, like a glove of paint. Earlier, before they left the Botros, Calyx was griping about the heat. He said nothing now, though his hand was cold as snow.

Calyx attempted to shift his head in Castan's direction but gave up. Castan noted the dog tag hanging from his friend's neck.

If only this were just an allergic reaction, then I could save him.

"'To die will be...'" The words came out with great difficulty. His voice grated, nails on a chalkboard. "...an awfully big adventure.'" Calyx's lips twitched but didn't make it into the grin Castan thought his friend desired.

"If you're going to quote literature, quote an author I like," Castan recalled from an earlier conversation.

Peter Pan, he wanted to say, *you know I don't like fantasy.* But Castan didn't have an appetite for humor.

"Calyx?" His heart clobbered wildly, spraying blood against his bones. Castan opened his mouth to apologize—

"Say that... at my Ceremony... won't you?" Calyx placed pressure on his protector's hand. Castan imagined he meant to squeeze it, but he was too anemic to complete the action. Calyx's eyelids drooped closed. Through tears, Castan witnessed the shallow rise and fall of his chest gradually come to a halt.

God, no! Not like this! A tremor passed through Castan's body as Calyx's spirit was whisked away into the unknown. He bent his head into his friend's shoulder. He squeezed his hand, willing it to squeeze back, knowing it never would.

At some point unbeknownst to Castan, Umar disconnected him from Calyx's deathbed and guided him to the little living room. Nasreen and Umar made the calls to Taxodium. Castan heard their muffled voices in their bedroom.

"...dead. Yes, ma'am..."

"No, Gen...ambush..."

Castan stood alone in the middle of the space. He couldn't bring himself to go back to Calyx—he desperately wanted him to be alive. His corpse would only solidify the emptiness carving a hole in his chest, a pit in his stomach.

This is my fault.

Death hung in the air like an early morning fog.

Castan clutched Calyx's dog tag in a fist, wringing the chain around his wrists like shackles.

It was strange how he filed away the details of the room. He noted the dinner table, wiped clean from the meal before their visit with Matrona. The corner of the rug by the door was overturned, revealing a pale underside. The faded blue sofa was sunken in the middle from use, an Afghan blanket hanging haphazardly across its back. He swayed on his feet, glancing at how all the room's contents appeared crooked because the floor was ever so slightly uneven.

But he also filed away the details he wished to forget: the crust of blood under his nails, glued to the back of his hands and arms. The sick void taking root in the neurons of his brain. The agony behind his eyes because this—this was *all* his fault. This was Mena and Hadley all over again, except worse. Grenades compared to an atomic bomb.

Castan wiped hair from his eyes. He ignored the agony of his body where Rosh had struck him. It was a poor comparison of pain. Guilt racked his mind, dragging talons across his neurons.

His gaze flickered over the shelf of goldfish—shimmering, orange bodies each flitting in their own orbs of water. Nasreen kept many of the creatures year-round. The fish were oblivious to the hour's past events. Castan silently envied them.

Ironic how goldfish, symbols of life, can exist in this house of death. A dark laugh erupted in his throat but died before it reached his ears.

The goldfish transformed before his eyes. They were drops of crimson blood suspended in hearts of glass.

Taxodium would send for him in the morning—hours from now. He would explain what happened through the lens of someone emotionless, duty-bound. He knew Umar and Nasreen would not say anything about his outbursts, about his attachment to Calyx, even after the last breath escaped past his friend's lips. No, they would tuck those moments away, as Castan would also, and carry on the facade that Calyx's death, though momentous because he was an asset to Taxodium, meant nothing to him at all.

I failed. I am the enemy.

Castan felt pieces of himself chipping away, leaves falling from a tree. Such leaves had always shriveled up and sank from his branches—ever since he was ten—but Calyx's death left him bare. A hollow skeleton.

Corolla
July 2020

As a courtesy, Tilia dims the lights at night—or at least when Castan and I go to bed. I can't say if it's really day or night in the world above. Castan said it's been four days. The yellow splotch on his forehead confirms the length of time we've spent in Iran—his bruise is almost healed. But my leg is still a numb mass dragging from my torso. The skin surrounding my wound is fading from a pitchy black to a steely gray. Tilia says it's a good sign.

"I have never known a pedes to recover so quickly from an Essence flesh wound. Though, I have never known a pedes to be injured in such a manner at all," Tilia said. Castan scowled and informed me that we "can't go anywhere with crippled bait." I don't take it personally, though sometimes I wonder if I should.

The fixtures overhead aren't very bright, but I reach for the notebook and pen I requested a couple days ago. I open the page to the sheet I've been using for my usual habits: remembering Averil. I take one look at the page, all the half sentences, and chains of words, and know it's wrong. I can't relive this tonight.

I sigh and flip to a fresh page. Since my yarn and pegs are ashes now, I have to do this the old-fashioned way. I begin—always—with the frontal lobe, work my way in dashed lines down to the occipital. When my outline of the brain is finished, I draw a line from the frontal lobe to the occipital. I pause. Usually, this is where I insert the moment I met Averil, the things he said about diamonds having the strongest bonds on the planet. But...

I set the pen on my stomach and retrieve the photos from the back of the notebook. They are creased in new places from their stay in my back pocket, but they did not burn. They survived. Adian and Calyx. My mother and brother. And my father? James didn't have his picture.

"I've never even met the man," he confessed. "He was always working when Adian and Calyx visited."

I think about the moments before the house burned, before smoke filled my nostrils with soot, to all the things James told me. I squint down at that line on my memory map. Lies. I always scribble this brain full of Averil's lies and my own. I don't want to do that tonight. I want something different. To escape the discomfort in my body and in my brain.

I wipe a tear from my eye, not sure why it's there at all. I take a deep breath and pick up the pen.

My mother was adopted. She grew up a hellion, James said. She met my father at Taxodium. He was important—important enough that their marriage was kept a secret from Taxodium; important enough that when their secret was found out, they were forced apart and my father was banished.

I pen in my lines, my loops, and arcs. I fit in Calyx and myself, but I omit the day we were separated. There are too many questions, too many unknowns for me to piece together what *became* of my family. Instead, I imagine what could have *become* of us, had we never been ripped apart. A house in the suburbs. A dog perhaps, or a cat. A tremendous dinner table that's always full. I can't imagine James anywhere else, so he's there too, sitting between Adian and me, smiling in a way I haven't seen since I was a little girl. I didn't know the price of living back then. I didn't know sacrifice. And James has paid that fee twice over.

When it's finished, I admire my work. I am so accustomed to the bitter past that it takes me a moment to recognize this for what it is: a sweet present. My mind wanders to all the reports about burning buildings, devastating bombings, and screaming sirens. The world wasn't like this ten years ago. It wasn't perfect, by any means, but it was… safe. I took it for granted. How can *I* help shift it out of chaos? How can a handful of people like Castan? The task is too much, too daunting for one group of people. For the world to change, the people must change. But the Dentatas, the Gens? They don't seem like the type to embrace a peaceful ideology.

It hits me then what kind of change Castan intends to implement. I don't think I believed him before when he spoke about eradication. I don't think I realized he wasn't joking. Rather than using words, he will use force. And I will be the one to catalyze the bloodshed. Is that really justice?

An animal. There is an animal in the cavern. Moaning. Agony. Its sounds echo off the walls. It's only when I blink that I realize my eyes are already open. Blackness. Utter darkness. The lights are out.

The moaning grows louder as my consciousness threads together into coherency.

That's not an animal.

I swing my legs over the side of the bed, slamming my ankle into the chair. My eyes water with the sudden pain, but I lift myself up anyway. My leg is clumsy, disconnected from my brain. I feel for the wall, guiding my path to the main cavern.

"Tilia? Castan?" Yes, I am positive that's where the sound is coming from. But beneath the agonizing cries, is something else. Gasping, breathing so quick and sudden that I almost miss it.

I don't have time to wonder what's going on. All I know is a sick feeling boiling in the pit of my stomach. I round the sharp corner, and there is Tilia, a pale glowing mass. She's hardly visible, like a two-day-old glow stick, so it takes me a moment to piece her together. She's curled into a ball, grumbling deep sounds into her arms.

Despite my handicap, I stagger towards her figure and drop to my knees.

"Tilia," I reach a hand out to shake her, but it goes right through her. My head snaps up to the bed in the corner.

"Castan!" It's too dark to see anything properly, but there is no answer. Again, I catch a snag of labored breathing. The wrongness compounds and builds, becomes something so incredibly overwhelming, that I fear I may empty the contents on my stomach right here and now. My skin prickles with sweat, flashes of heat.

I glance down at Tilia—she's fading fast—and decide to risk it.

I tuck my hair behind my ears and pull myself upright. My good leg trembles. I chew my lip and push forward. Castan's bed isn't that far away, but I cross the length of a football field to get there. I stub my toe on the frame, swearing and wiping sweat from my forehead.

"Castan." I reach for the mattress and no more than touch the sheets—

There is a cry, something sharp and piercing, and suddenly, my head is smacking against the dirt floor. A gasping Castan hangs over me, fire cradled between arched fingers. His other hand is planted into the ground by my ear, his knees on either side of my hips. If I thought I was sweaty, then Castan is drenched. His bare chest sheens white, slick with perspiration. Around his neck, dangles a string of silver with a metal tag looped around it. I catch a glint of letters: CA... VEL. His dark hair clings to his temples. I could trace the cracks in his lips, but I am terrified. Castan's eyes have many personalities, but I have never seen them so... feral.

He blinks as if seeing me for the first time.

"Corolla?"

"T-Tilia," I splutter.

His brow furrows, forehead creases. My brain is shaken, but I swear he even cocks his head. As if the beast I saw in his eyes seconds ago was only an extension of my imagination. As if he is a child, and I, a dog with five heads. Slowly, his eyes peer out into the darkness, past the bubble of his light. I watch the rapid rise and fall of his chest.

He had a bad dream. Those heavy bags under his eyes suddenly make complete sense. He has trouble sleeping, too.

"I don't see her. What are you trying to say?" Those emeralds glare down at me now, not in anger but in worry. In a swift move, he separates his body from mine. Castan combs back his hair with his free hand. "How did you even get here anyway?"

I say before those eyes can transform again, "Tilia was in a ball by the throne. She was making sounds. I don't know what's wrong, but the lights are out. Have they ever been out like this before?" Maybe this is perfectly normal, and *I'm* the one overreacting. I do sleep a lot during the day, strangely enough. Maybe *this* is routine.

Castan scowls, steps over me. "No." The heat in his palms expands, burns so brightly that I have to look away. There, through our shadows and the ones from the roots above, I spot her. She's transparent, a faint outline of herself. Of all things, I think about all those opaque sea creatures lost deep in the ocean.

I open my mouth, but Castan is a blur. He kneels, holding one arm above his head while the other one's fire dies.

"Tilia?" His empty hand skims the air where her figure should be. Or maybe it goes right through her. It's difficult to tell from my place on the floor. I've found that I can't get up, even if I wanted to. Every cell in my body is a weight, pinning me captive to the floor. My eyelids threaten to close.

No, I plead. *I can't sleep now. I can't.*

My brain has one idea, but my body has another one. I can't fight myself. As my eyes are closing, the darkness creeping into the corners of my vision, a tame light outlines Castan's hunched figure.

"Hong Kong," it rasps. "The Gens have destroyed the Asian Academy."

Past
January 9th, 2020

Corolla peered out the blinds. It was sleeting, thick sheets of ice falling from the gray blanket of clouds above. Just barely, she could make out the dark smear of pines in the backyard. Winter loosened its grip on the land, but only just.

A hand crept up under her shirt, planting firmly on her bare hip. Corolla felt his breath on her neck; giddy sensations spiraled through her veins.

"James won't be home for how long...?" She'd already told Averil twice before, but she answered anyway, laughing as his nose tickled the back of her neck.

"Hours." Through her giggling, her eyes caught the cone-shaped pines. A childlike feeling took hold of her. "Let's go outside." Corolla ducked away from his mouth, tugged free of his hands.

He made a face at her. "The weather is terrible."

"So?" She turned back to the window, imagining the drops of ice falling all around them. "It's romantic."

"It's idiotic," Averil grabbed at her waist again. "I have a better idea."

Corolla's heart stung, but her stomach flopped. She knew what he'd say, was afraid of it.

Averil latched onto her hips again. "I want you," he said into her ear. Corolla was all too aware of his hands reaching for her belt. She noted that, somehow, all the lights in the house had been dimmed. Had he done that?

"Averil—" Corolla protested, but he wouldn't let her speak.

"We've been together for eight months. It's time."

No.

"No," she reaffirmed aloud. And then quietly, "I'm afraid."

Averil let go of her, studying her crestfallen expression in the gray light. Above, she listened to the sleet hammering the rooftop. Below, she heard her heart thrashing against her ribs.

"You're afraid of what exactly?" Averil finally asked. Corolla wished he sounded more tender, less... insulting.

"That," she paused, began again, "That you'll leave me."

"Leave you? Why would I do that?" Despite herself, Averil was the one offended. Corolla raised her eyes to see his dirty blonde hair askew, chocolate eyes brazen.

"I don't know," she admitted. "We're just high schoolers—people change."

"God." Averil ran a hand down his face. "So you're saying you want to wait until *marriage?*"

"What?" Corolla crossed her arms. "No, I'm saying I don't want to... give myself to you when it hasn't even been that long—"

"Stop doubting me," Averil groaned. "Stop doubting *us*. I love you, don't I?"

Corolla found herself in an impossible position. And Averil had flung her there—intentionally.

"Yes," she answered, "but—"

"But *nothing*." Averil reached for her again, maneuvering her onto the couch. His hands were on her belt once more. Her heart was in her throat.

"I love you," he assured. Corolla winced as one of his nails caught on her flesh. "And I want you." His eyes were so close to her own that she saw four instead of two. Corolla swallowed. She didn't think about James; she thought about love and how sometimes that meant sacrifice. Was this a sacrifice? She didn't know. Averil's weight on her torso made it hard to think.

Her belt was off. Averil's hand dove father—

Corolla clutched him by the wrist.

"Wait." She was stalling, she knew, but what she didn't know was *why*. She loved Averil—loved him a lot—so why did this feel so... wrong?

He looked down at her, impatient.

"Cor," he only ever used that nickname to get on her good side, "stop biting your lip. You'll draw blood."

"Oh." She hadn't realized she was chewing her lip.

One word, Corolla, that's all it takes.

Yet she could not cough it up.

Averil grew tired of waiting. He tugged at her pants again, and this time, Corolla didn't stop him.

"I love you," he whispered into her ear. Corolla bit her lip to keep from crying out—the pain was so intense. A knife to her insides.

When it was over, she gathered her clothes and excused herself to the bathroom down the hall. She left Averil naked, panting on the old couch that used to belong to her grandparents.

Once the bathroom door was closed, Corolla scrambled to shove herself back in her rumpled clothes. She glanced at herself in the mirror over the sink—tangled hair, flushed cheeks—and her eyes filled with tears.

The movies are wrong, she thought, *every line, every scene.* But what did that matter? She knew better. No, it wasn't the lack of romanticism that gnawed on her. It was something else.

It was like in a dream where she knew she was in her house, but it appeared nothing at all like it. The same phenomenon occurred when she saw her reflection. She knew it was supposed to be her, but it bore no resemblance to the Corolla she thought herself to be.

She wiped the steady streaks from her eyes. *That's not me in the mirror. It's not.*

It was then that she knew the name of all the wrongness pooling inside her stomach.

It was guilt.

Corolla turned on the faucet and splashed chilled water on her face. She looked in the mirror again, and, dissatisfied, splashed another handful of water on herself. But she knew, no matter the amount of water she used, it would not erase what she had done.

Mr. Grubaugh's voice came to her then, a dull monotony of words, *"In lab, we don't scribble out our mistakes. Science does not condone erasing, which is why we use pens. A single line through the error will suffice..."*

Corolla placed a hand on her midsection, felt pain shooting up between her legs. *It wasn't worth it.*

"GET THE HELL OUT OF MY HOUSE!"

Corolla's heart knocked from its valves and splattered on the tile floor.

James was home.

And Averil—

She was out of the bathroom within seconds, but not fast enough to defend Averil—she still loved him, yes. Despite it all, she loved him.

When she got to the living room, Averil was scrambling to get clothed; James was red-faced, close to eruption. He didn't look right either; his skin was taut over his cheekbones and boiling. She had never known him to lose his temper. Not even when she colored on the walls with permanent marker when she was six. Instead, he sat her down at the dinner table with a paper plate and a tube of toothpaste. He squeezed some of the minty goo on the red plate, and said in a voice so calm, she thought he was anyone but her house-enthusiast uncle, "Now try to put the toothpaste back in the tube."

Corolla did as he asked and tried squishing the paste back into the tube. The only thing she managed to do was squeeze more out and get it all over and between her fingers.

"See? Some things you can't undo, Corolla. Now don't you ever draw on anything *but* paper again."

Now, Corolla gawked at the scene before her.

I didn't just color on the walls—I tore them down. The guilt in her stomach flared up, grappling claws in the back of her throat. She thought she tasted blood and realized it was coming from her lip, pinched between her teeth.

James must have been carrying groceries inside because there was a paper bag turned over by the front door. Corolla watched three oranges roll along the uneven floorboards. Fruit Fly, James had called her when she was a kid. She wasn't sure what he would call her now. Liar, Deceiver, Nothing—she was all of that, wasn't she?

Averil said nothing as he passed her. Without noticing, he kicked an orange. Corolla followed its sad path until it disappeared under the very couch that still radiated their body heat.

Corolla couldn't look at James, couldn't look at herself. Her hands were tingling, her ears, ringing. She swayed and wobbled, crashing to the floor.

She hoped she would never wake up.

It only took fifteen days, and in that time, she was prohibited from seeing Averil. But he was at her doorstep now. She hadn't heard from him in the time that they were apart. He didn't say much now either.

"I learned something today," he said, after she invited him inside, out of the cold. They barely made it two feet into the house, but she didn't care. Once, she would have tugged him to the living room for a movie. Once, she would have been elated just to see him. She was numb, a scrape under her chin where she had crashed into the back of the recliner two weeks and a day ago.

"What?" Her voice was strong; it didn't betray her. She had been crying most of the day. She knew their relationship was over the moment James had walked in the front door and dropped his bags. This was just a formality.

"All diamonds eventually become graphite," he replied as if he'd rehearsed it on his way over. He probably had—a sort of half-assed apology. Corolla raised her head.

I've learned something too, she wanted to retort. *All sins begin with a kiss.*

Averil opened his arms, trying to embrace her one last time.

"Don't," Corolla held up a hand. "Just leave."

Averil offered her a sorry look. "You'll always have a special place in my heart." *Did he really just say that?* Yes. Corolla could have laughed.

You're full of shit. How many lies had Averil fed her? And how many lies had Corolla dribbled to James?

I'm going to the library to study—be back in a couple hours.
And:
I'm spending the night at Ali's. I'll be home tomorrow morning.
Or:
I won't invite anyone over while you're gone. No worries.
Corolla held the door open, snowflakes like dandruff falling from the sky. And Averil left. Would she ever see him again? With a jaded heart, she thought it unlikely.

Corolla closed the door and found James in the kitchen. In the window above the kitchen sink, she watched Averil back out of their driveway, watched his silver Corolla disappear down the road.

"You'll need to eat something," James said from behind.

Corolla turned. "I'm not hungry." She couldn't look him in the eye, only felt dazed and exhausted. Whatever reserve she had been sustaining from was dried out. She felt hot and cold all over. She felt alone.

Averil was gone. Eleven days short of nine months, and he was gone. Just as James had predicted two weeks ago. Just as he had warned her—too late.

Instead of saying, "I told you so," James folded her in his arms. She wept quietly into his shirt, not sure if it was worse that he was comforting her or worse that she let him. She didn't deserve it, either way.

If she could, Corolla would have coughed her heart out and placed it in James's hands. But that wouldn't be enough to restore his faith in her. No, she needed his forgiveness. She needed him to be proud.

So she would work harder in school; she would study longer. And above all, she would not forget what she had done—for if she forgot, then there was a chance her mistakes would find a way to repeat themselves.

Castan
July 2020

Black. Brown. Gray. The entire continent of Asia is gone. Like a depleted vein of ore, Tilia's Holds no longer function in that domain. They collapsed overnight, and she collapsed with them. My eyes dart across the map on the wall at all the other Holds in order throughout the world. Golden, glowing discs. Except that the lights flicker now. They never used to do that. Asia contained about as many Holds as Australia and Europe combined. Now, there is nothing there but shadows.

"The Gens obliterated the Academy," Rex said this morning on the phone. "My hands are tied until sufficient relief can be supplied. The Verum Courts are in shambles, as is the standing Army. You and Vel must keep moving around until it's safe to come back."

The only issue is: Corolla fell victim to a ravaging fever.

"*Castan*," Nasreen practically shouts my name. "You're massaging too hard."

I blink, looking down at my hands around Corolla's burning calf. My hands are sticky with a salve Nasreen concocted moments ago.

"Oh, sorry."

Nasreen scowls—I have never seen so much emotion in her placid profile. "If you cannot do this correctly, then don't do it at all."

Nasreen pushes me out of the way and kneads Corolla's calf herself. Corolla doesn't wake up, just mumbles in her sleep. Her cheeks are as bright as a tomato's.

"How do you know the salve will work? I didn't think Essence flesh wounds had antidotes like this." I glance from the green goo between my fingers to Corolla's wound. The skin around her leg is gray, dead-looking, and dry. Tilia assured me it was only the phages beneath Corolla's skin that were dead, but this sudden fever makes me wonder. I don't know how pedes' bodies handle Essence-wounds, but so far, Corolla's is not taking it well.

"I don't know," Nasreen grumbles. "But I do know that Corolla is in a tremendous amount of pain and, though she may not be able to speak, this," Nasreen gestures to her work on Corolla's leg, "makes her feel better."

It's strange how memories can sweep you up, even in the most mundane of moments. While Nasreen bows over Corolla's fevered form, I think about how Calyx could never lie. He was so bad at it, his ears would flush pink. Sometimes I wonder if that's why he was an open book. Not because he enjoyed sharing but because he couldn't hide anything from anyone.

"We need Maggie," I try to keep the bite from my tone, but it's never been my strength.

"She's needed more in Hong Kong right now." Nasreen doesn't say it, but I know she's thinking it: Maggie will be incapacitated for weeks.

"Four hundred fatalities and counting," Rex spat. That doesn't include the injured.

"Damn Gens and their damn bombs." I clench my fists; the flames blooming there die. Where I should detect smoke from the extinguished fire, my nose catches whiffs of blood instead.

Nasreen says nothing. I hear Umar come through to the main cavern. He's been assessing the Venefica's container, the cypress tree, for damage. Tilia is catatonic.

"Where's Rainey?" I ask Nasreen.

"We moved her out of the city. To my brother's."

"Right." I glance up as Umar steps into the second cavern. He touches a hand to his black beard, drops his arms to his side.

"There's nothing," he exhales. "Matrona is perfectly fine, but Tilia..." He peers over his shoulder. "She was bound to many of those who died. Their hearts... When someone completes their *Humanitas*, a piece of one's self remains with Tilia. Think of it as a flame added to Tilia's fire."

"And she just lost four hundred."

"Yes," Umar nods, "but I believe she will recover fully in a day or so. The fact that she managed these lights is a good sign of her progress."

"Right." My gaze flits to the fixtures above. They aren't as bright as they were before, and by no means are they constant. Sometimes, they are snuffed out for seconds, sometimes for minutes. They flicker terribly when they *are* working, but we carry on as if nothing has changed. That's the thing about pelari—we are taught very young to *keep on.*

The Botros do not leave. I'm relieved Nasreen can interpret Corolla's needs—she's an empath—but I also wish I could be alone. I've spent so much time in Tilia's caverns that it's starting to feel permanent. I've memorized the fractures in the dirt walls, the scraggly roots hanging from the ceiling. I know their angles and their lights, and that bothers me. I only planned to come here for Corolla's Mark. It's the beginning of July and Taxodium hasn't made any progress against the Gens.

Nasreen and Umar sleep quietly in the main cavern with Tilia. The Venefica says nothing, just sits on her throne, a statue. I can't imagine losing four hundred hearts in one day. I don't know anyone who lived in the Asian Academy, but I know people who know people who did. Talan's parents are Judges on the Verum Courts. Rex didn't say who survived, and I couldn't find the opening to ask. For Talan's sake, I hope his parents are alright.

Four hundred less to combat the Gens...

I turn my attention back to Corolla. She's splayed across her sheets, the lights above a dim yellow. There's a sizable bump on the side of her head where I threw her to the ground. Guilt shreds through my stomach, a school of razor blade fish.

I cover my face with my hands. The nightmares are getting worse, stronger. I want to ask someone what's happening to me. I want my sister here. I want—

"James?"

Immediately, I am lurching to my feet, kneeling at Corolla's bedside.

"Corolla. Can I get you anything? How do you feel? What's wrong?"

Corolla wipes a hand across her forehead, knocking the wet rag from her brow. I don't think she realizes she's done it until the cloth rests over one of her eyes. Her movements are slow, clunky.

"My head hurts?"

"Yes," I place the rag back on her forehead. "I'm sorry. That was my fault."

"Oh." Her eyes grow two sizes. "Is Tilia alright?" She tries sitting up, but I place a single hand on her shoulder. She falls backward.

"She's recovering. There was an... attack on the Asian Division. The entire Academy is gone. Four hundred people dead, last I knew."

Corolla's voice goes thick as molasses. "That's awful."

"Hey, hey," I panic. Why is she crying? "It'll be alright. James is safe."

Her shoulders tremble, eyes burning with salt water. "Four hundred people died today? I thought we were supposed to stop things like that. I'm sorry I pressed those buttons on that... thing." Her face scrunches together. I think she's still captive to fever. I place a hand on her cheek just to confirm what I already know. She flinches at my touch. I recoil immediately.

"I'm sorry," I don't know what else to say. "It's not your fault this happened. No one could have predicted it."

"Then why do you look so mad?" Two large tears slip from her eyes. "I'm sorry, James. I'm sorry."

"James?" She thinks I'm James? "No, Corolla, it's me, Castan. James is safe at the North American Academy. He *is* worried about you, though." And then, because I don't want her to think about *that*, "Can I get you anything? Food, water?"

"Castan?" Her expression reminds me of the time Mercury wormed his way into one of his opponent's minds, so much so, that he gave the poor kid a concussion. Big eyes, lethargic tongue. The kind of damage you can't see but jumps out at you immediately.

I comb anxious fingers through my hair. *Dear God, did I concuss her?*

"James," Corolla extends an arm, hand reaching. "I didn't mean it. He made me do it. I thought—" Her voice breaks, tears swarm her cheeks.

What's the point in arguing with her? I find myself wishing I were Calyx. He would know what to do, even if Corolla weren't his sister. He possessed that natural inclination for people and their needs, and he wasn't even an empath. I struggle terribly in that domain.

What would Calyx do? I take in Corolla's outstretched hand, the faucets in her eyes. I know she's hallucinating or delusional or both, but this is all real to her. If there's anything I understand, it's nightmares.

Okay. I take a deep breath and clamp my hand around hers. It's as warm as an ember, smooth as a weathered stone. And so small. Like a child's.

"It's okay, Corolla," I say, hoping it's something James would tell her. "You did your best, and that's all I could ever ask of you."

Her body seems to relax then, but her grip on my hand tightens. A part of me remembers how, not too long ago, I was squeezing Calyx's hand, hoping life would squeeze back. I stare at our clasped hands and see another pair entirely. Blood crusted under nails. Dirt and grime. Death. Calyx. Dying.

That coppery tang fills my lungs, like some kind of radioactive hazard. I drop Corolla's hand at once, blinking rapid fire until the white, blood-soaked sheets disappear, and all I see is Corolla. She's fallen back asleep, thank Matrona. I brush under my nose, but the metallic ghost of that night remains floating in the air.

"You look out of place here."

I startle awake—too quickly—and my neck kinks. "Ow," I wince, sitting upright in the rigid chair I fell asleep in. I warm my palm and massage my neck.

"Maggie?"

The Healer stands in the doorway, hair pulled back in her characteristic ponytail. I think the only time I've seen her hair down was at the New Year's Party last year.

She uncrosses her arms and takes to examining Corolla. I blink, confused.

"I thought you were in Hong Kong?"

"I was," her voice is clipped, mechanical. I know better than to ask.

"I'm sorry."

Maggie gently places Corolla's leg back down. "It's not your fault."

"No, but if Corolla weren't hurt, then we would be back in Ohio right now. The Gens would've been drawn to the North American Academy, and fewer people would have died."

Maggie's head shoots up to look at me. Her keen blue eyes narrow. Sometimes, like right now, I wonder at all the things she's seen. It's one thing to watch someone die when no other help can be provided. It's another to *be* the help and still lose people. Maggie *is* the last resort.

"I just meant that the Gens' attention would be on Corolla, not on completely destroying the Asian Academy."

Maggie looks back to Corolla. "I know what you meant. I just don't agree with it. The Gens wanted to destroy Tax's law offices. They would have done so anyway, just to say, 'Hey, we're powerful now, and your Laws can't stop us.'"

I never thought about it that way. I guess it makes sense, though. If the Gens despise any branch of Tax, it's the Verum Courts, the very system that tried and exiled them.

Maggie collapses onto the end of Corolla's bed so that she's sitting next to me. She smells like smoke and debris. Her uniform is torn in places and patched in others. If clothes could talk…

"Are Talan's parents alright?"

Her face could be carved from stone. "Vera's alive. I don't know if 'alright' means anything anymore besides just that: alive."

"I guess that's a relief."

"Of course." Judging by the soft concavity of Maggie's expression, I decide not to pursue the subject further.

"Is Corolla…?"

Sighing, Maggie glances over her shoulder at the sleeping girl. "I can't do anything for a fever. It'll have to be waited out."

"Rex won't like that."

"She doesn't have a choice. Speaking of Rex." From the satchel around her torso, Maggie withdraws an object.

"Here's your new geometer," she tosses it into my lap. "You're going to Florence."

I have to sit up a little. "I'm what?"

"As soon as Corolla is better, you have to go to Florence, Italy. I've already logged the coordinates. There's a TI informant, Issak Park. He's made some headway on the Gens' HQ location. Rex doesn't trust any kind of communication right now, except face-to-face. I imagine Rex'll call a Board meeting if the information is helpful."

"Wouldn't a Board meeting already have been called?"

"Hardly. The Majors are spinning. Soto is dead, and the Academy is buried in too much rubble to even *think* about calling an emergency election. They need something concrete to anchor to first."

"I see." I stare down at the shiny new tech in my hands. At least I won't be grounded anymore.

"Every other able body is either defending Hong Kong or preparing for another explosive attack. Park will find you. Just make sure you don't use this geometer for any errands or day trips. This is important, Castan."

My eyes flit to hers. "Of course it's important! Hell, why don't you stay with Corolla and I'll go to Florence right now?"

Maggie shakes her head. "I have to return to the field hospitals, and your first priority is Vel. Second is Florence. Rex wanted me to make sure you know that. Once things are cleaned up a bit, Corolla will be our best chance to deliver the Gens a blow. We don't know for sure what Park has to offer, so don't botch this." Maggie rises, securing her satchel to her side. I notice how she uses it to mask a dark, rust-colored blotch on her pant leg.

She says, almost under her breath, "This wasn't just an attack on pedes, this was an attack on *us*."

"This is really war then, isn't it?"

She stares down her dirt-smudged nose. "Castan, it's been war since the day Pyrus put that curse in their bodies."

Past
February 2020

James shuffled through his sock drawer, unearthing a mustard-yellow envelope. He slipped it out from under the mess of old socks and thought absently that he should discard the ones with holes in the bottom. But that would mean throwing away most of his socks, and he didn't have the money to replace them.

He unsealed the envelope and sat back on his bed. The old box springs groaned under his weight. He hardly noticed. He was suffering from one of those nostalgic episodes, the kind that grips one's mind in an unbearable clasp. Maybe it had something to do with finding Corolla and... *that boy...* together. But even that thought was a dim flame compared to the longing in his heart.

James dug a hand in the envelope, fumbling with the pictures it contained. The sensible part of him said that he should just dump all the photos out on the bed. The sensitive part of him said that he couldn't tolerate so much loss in the same breadth of time. That was the part that won.

Carefully, one photograph at a time, James set them out side-by-side. Only when he had studied one, would he retrieve another. James thought it childish, this slow process of adaptation, but it was necessary. For maybe the fifth time, he thanked God that Corolla was at school.

When all the photos were laid out, James sucked in a deep breath. Most of the pictures were of his late sister, Adian. Some of them were of the Taxodium gardens she had created and designed. Several others were of various places James did not recognize but supposed they were structures from Taxodium as well.

James examined the last picture in his grid. His sister was at least eighteen and bursting with pregnancy. She was glancing over her shoulder, a daisy tucked behind her ear. She had a gentle hand wrapped under her swollen belly, something mischievous in her eyes, in her smile.

James's shoulders sagged. He had not taken this picture. He assumed Adian's husband had, but then, what did he know? He had been a state away studying architecture.

In the background, was a chapel, white-walled and crumbling. James guessed it was eighteenth century, but vines of some variety webbed and masked the building's features. He wondered—not for the first time—if the chapel had been a place that meant something to his sister. They were raised to be in the Faith, but Adian never took to it. Not entirely. Perhaps she found something in the chapel's deterioration.

"Corolla has her mother's eyes," he found himself mumbling. His gaze skated to another scene, one where Adian was arm wrestling her roommate, Laila. Though the camera snapped a blurry moment, both women possessed an Amazonian quality. It was impossible to tell who was winning, as the place where their arms met was a smear of gray. James always imagined Adian earned a crushing victory. It pained his heart to realize that he would never, in all honesty, know. James would never get the opportunity to ask his sister about the moment, about her life at Taxodium. He would never know, and that thought pierced him with a sharpness no blade could brag.

He ran a hand down his face, weary with emotion. In the months following Adian's death, James had received this envelope in the mail. It had no return address, only his residence scrawled in shaky handwriting. Immediately, James knew it was from Adian's husband, Tyto. He had never met the man, but somehow, he just *knew*. The contents of the envelope only confirmed his suspicions.

James gulped to keep tears from sprouting from his eyes. He reached across the bed for the pile of mail he'd gathered from the mailbox earlier. He pinched the top envelope between his fingers and examined the handwriting again. There was no mistaking it—this letter was from Tyto.

Before he knew what he was doing, James ripped open the top. From it, he extracted a single, faded picture.

James stopped breathing.

It showed a boy, maybe four or five years old. He had a smear of mud across his chubby face, a glob of the oozing stuff cupped in his hands. He was grinning at whoever was snapping the camera—Tyto, no doubt—and two teeth poked out from between his pink lips. He had Adian's eyes too, dark as the mud in his hands and invariably innocent. Like Corolla, the boy had an olive complexion—Tyto's genetic contribution, not Adian's. The background was a blur of green forest and mountains, a red barn in the distance.

James gasped, choking on a sob that had been threatening to overcome him since he collected the mail that afternoon. His body shook with grief, was struck with an ache he had no name for. Because Calyx would never know his mother's voice, would never know his sister's, his uncle's—would never know a full and peaceful life.

Though there was nothing else in the white envelope, James knew, like Adian, the boy was dead.

Corolla
July 2020

Hunger claws the lining of my stomach. I roll over and pull myself into a sitting position. I'm so hungry, I could throw up.

"Corolla?" My name on tentative lips. Castan is at my bedside. Rumpled hair, baggy eyes. If he looks haggard, then what do *I* look like? I'm too starved to care.

"Is," I croak, clear my throat and try again. "Is there anything to eat?"

"Yeah," he almost falls out of his chair, so eager is he to fulfill my request. He reaches for a container on the table behind him. My stomach grumbles, and I cough to try and mask the awkward noise.

"Here," he hands me a plate with a long flat piece of bread. Resting on top of it is what looks like orange or apricot jam. "It's lavash bread and quince jam," Castan says. "Nasreen brought it this morning. She's out shopping for dinner right now. Tea?" His hands slide over a silver kettle. I shake my head and devour the thin bread and sweet topping.

Castan takes the plate from my hand and fills it with whatever is left in the dish. I scarf down that, too. Once my stomach is grateful and full, my head begins to throb. I touch lightly on my skull, feel a lump there. Memories of darkness, stumbling, and Tilia curled up on the ground come back to me. I only have to glance at Castan for him to understand the question in my eyes.

"She's recovering. Umar is here to take care of her and Matrona, though the tree sustained no damage." As if hearing his name, Umar appears in the archway separating the two caverns. My gaze dances between Castan and him.

"What happened to her?"

Castan makes a face, and, rather than answering my question, he tosses a newspaper on my lap. I can't read it—it's printed in Arabic—but the cover photo is enough. Crumbled buildings, piles of rubble against an orange and gray sky. People in all colors of uniforms—black, red, yellow, white—pick their way through the devastation. Every September, I've been forced to watch videos of 9/11, but this picture is something else. This is in *my* lifetime, not a video recording. In the article, I pick out the words Hong Kong and a date, something 4. July 4th.

"The attacks are getting worse."

"No, that *is* the worst," Castan growls. "That's half of Taxodium's forces!"

Umar observes, "That's not completely true. There is still St. Helena Island."

Castan glares hard at the ground. I wait for the earth to crack and split open.

"St. Helena is for the crippled and retired. They aren't soldiers anymore."

"They may have to be now."

Castan says something about "combative inability," and the rest is lost in the low timbre of his voice.

"Well," Umar puts in, "I need to go tend to Matrona up above. Nasreen will be back within the hour, no doubt." And with that, Castan and I are left alone. He does not wait for the inevitable silence to settle over us.

"How are you feeling? Besides the head." He gestures to his own crown while I squint at him. If I stare hard enough, maybe his strange spell of patience will crack and break open. Then I think about his question.

"I can actually feel my leg," I mutter, more to myself than to him. I throw back the sheet and examine my shin. "Did that green stuff come from *me?*"

"Huh? Oh, no. Nasreen rubbed a salve into your skin. Said it made you feel better."

Skeptical, I stare at the dried crust along my healing wound. "It's repulsive."

Castan clutches the back of his chair. "Yeah, well, she's an empath. Your emotions didn't seem to mind it at the time."

"Oh." This new world takes some time to get used to, I guess. I refrain from sticking my fingernail into the dried chunks and peeling it away. My leg starts to itch just thinking about how grimy it is. My hands glide down the shape of my thigh. It's been too long since I've used my leg. Or at least, it's been too long since I could *feel* myself using my leg.

"Can we leave soon?" The question comes rushing out before I can stop it. Once it's out, though, a strange relief passes over me. I know there isn't really a home for me to go back to, but anywhere has to be better than this underground cellar. Is this what a grave feels like? Without meaning to, I find myself looking up, past the lights and at the packed dirt of the ceiling. I'm not claustrophobic, but suddenly, this place is a shoebox, and I'm trapped inside.

Castan says slowly, "If you're sure you feel better, then as soon as Tilia can whip up your Mark."

Right. I forgot that was our original intention of coming here. That conversation with Castan in my kitchen feels like decades ago, some sun-faded photograph like the ones James gave me. James. He, too, is sun-faded.

"But," Castan continues, "there's been a slight change to our plans."

I meet his gaze.

"We have to go to Florence."

"Italy?"

"Yeah, there's a TI—that means Taxodium Intel—who claims to have information on the location of the Gens' headquarters. Since Taxodium's resources are being directed to Hong Kong, I've been assigned the task of meeting up with him."

"I see." James's blonde hair, pale eyebrows, and creased forehead fades a degree more. He'll have to wait.

Castan, the walls breathe. I startle, eyes darting in every direction for the source of the sound.

"That'll be Tilia," Castan sighs, wiping a hand down his face. I follow him into the main cavern, my shoulders hunched in anticipation. Last time I saw Tilia, she was bundled on the floor groaning in agony. Castan heads for the tangled throne. I stop and peer behind his broad shoulders. Tilia's resting atop her mound of roots. The things resemble snakes, curling around her limbs protectively. The Venefica herself is the color of hard-boiled egg yolk; she is not the golden nymph from before.

Castan reaches a hand towards the fallen figure. The lights flicker overhead. I can only watch, wide-eyed. So much of this world is foreign to me, I can't find my footing. If I even breathe the wrong way, I'll be plunged into an abyss. The only way I can make my place in this world is by observing first, doing second.

Tilia's eyes, half-lidded, study Castan. I could scoop the sadness from her being with buckets. She's waterlogged with the emotion. I don't need to be an empath to notice that.

Tilia's jaw slackens; Castan leans in to hear her. I shuffle closer.

"Rosh. Rosh Dentata was there," Tilia hisses. Her jaw clamps shut just as Castan's clenches so hard, I'm afraid it'll break. His spine stiffens. Castan goes pale, then red, then there are flames in his hands, and he's excusing himself for the exit. Wisps of smoke follow him through the Hold.

Rosh Dentata. The name taps a vein of memory. Castan under the yellow light of the chandelier above the dining table.

"Rosh killed your brother," he said. Calyx. Rosh murdered Calyx.

I go to Tilia, searching her as if the answers to all my questions are engraved on her body. Flashes of the newspaper photograph slice through my wondering. How can someone be responsible for that scale of destruction? How can a human be so...? I have to stop or else the lavash bread will splatter all over Tilia's roots.

"I want to understand." And there is so much more meaning in that phrase than the words will ever convey.

Tilia tucks her chin an inch—a nod.

"Let me show you," she deflates.

Before I even know what that means, my sight is swirling, watercolors and rinse water. I slam my eyelids shut, willing this dizzying sensation away. I remember, vaguely, a similar impression: when I accidentally jumped through space with the geometer. The lavash bread threatens to make an appearance again.

"Open your eyes." Tilia. Voice stronger. Normal.

I obey.

And wish I hadn't.

We're standing on a boat, tranquil water lapping the sides, wooden planks solid under my feet. My heart climbs to my ears—I'm *terrified* of vast bodies of water. My eyes shoot upwards, away from the water and to the masts. I focus on the red sails, like dragon's wings, flapping in the wind.

"Look," Tilia commands, and I have no control to do otherwise. My head angles towards the skyline. Skyscrapers, disappearing into blankets of white cloud. Sun, sparkling behind a green mountain. Across the bay, city sounds scratch my eardrums. Cars blaring honks, people chattering, cell phones ringing.

I forget all about the water.

And then:

An object careening through the clouds, cutting through the thick white with the velocity of a jet. My eyes follow its path—and worry hikes up my esophagus. The object is destined to crash in the mountainside. And it does. A spray of orange sparks. A mushroom of smoke. Screaming. The world stops spinning. Cars brake. Phones drop. People pause.

It was a missile.

Tilia and the boat disappear, and I'm amidst layers of ash and flame. I'm trapped in a building, trees crashed through my office window at unpredictable angles. One pins my legs under my mahogany desk. I shift, straining to move. Pain torpedoes up my femur. I bite my lip to keep from crying out.

"Xiaomi!" I shout for my guard, but she doesn't answer. The building vibrates. I feel the structure give way, know that it's plunging for the earth. I'm not the only one. From the staircase, come inhuman echoes, desperate cries for aid. The last thing I hear are the sirens going off, belated and stunned.

My perspective shifts. I'm on the ground, neck craned at the sky. Huaxia Tower is tipping, snapping into pieces. It'll slide down the mountainside, and our people will be lost. My legs do what my brain warns against: they run. I can't move fast enough for the Tower, weaving through a sea of people. I knock some to their knees, to their backs. Why is no one else moving for the Tower? Major Soto is trapped at the top. He'll—

I'm one of the students rushing in a crowd of people, digging elbows and gritting teeth. Towards the gate. *Get down the mountain. Get down.* I wish my Essence were flight, then I could save myself—

A man propels into me, splaying me across the concrete. The rush of bodies behind me threatens to crush me. I'm forced to my feet, panicked eyes glazing over my annoyed ones. I glare back at the guard who hit me and immediately regret it. A second missile strikes several feet from his path. The guard is killed instantly. From the second missile, yellow smoke oozes. The wind carries it through the Courthouse windows. It's only a matter of time before it finds me. I suck in two lungfuls of oxygen and scramble for the gate.

The scene transforms once more. It is slow, hazy and blurred. I should be panicking, should be grabbing my wife and racing for the Courthouse door, but… thoughts are difficult… to connect.

My body sways, but I manage to cross from my office to my wife's.

"Vera," her name is molasses on my tongue. I fan the fog from my eyes, but my brain is still cloudy.

"Vera." I find her at her desk, pen dangling between her fingers. I clasp my hand around hers and reach for her desk drawer. There's a mask buried in the back. Vera has the worst allergies to cut grass that I have ever known. I could laugh. In fact, I think I do.

I strap the mask to her face now and lower her to the carpet with me. The yellow fog multiplies. Blinds. Asphyxiates. I hold Vera to my chest, still tender from getting that pacemaker a couple days ago. I don't think it'll do me much good now.

The Gens could have attacked anywhere in the world, but it was us. Lawmakers and Judges. A hell… of a statement to make. Taxodium should have anticipated something like this. My eyelids seal shut. I see my son. It's Independence Day in America. He'll be watching explosions of a different kind. I see my daughter, and I know my fight is almost through…

I gasp, whimpering. I feel each of those memories squirming and burrowing through my body. Escaping. My vision clears, and my nails are digging into the earth at the foot of Tilia's throne. I grasp my temples, eyes traveling the distance to Tilia's. She stares down a sharp nose, somber.

My tongue is fat and strange in my mouth, but I manage, "You are a vault of memories. Of pain and suffering." Those people are all dead, yet their experiences survived. Through Tilia.

"I lost four hundred," she says, but my ears absorb a different message: *I have to help these people. I have to help the pelari. I have to lure in the Gens.*

I blink away dirt and tears. I find my feet and dare to square my shoulders.

"Mark me."

Tilia blinks acceptance. Maybe she planned this. Maybe she's been waiting for a chance to temper me, make me bolder. She gave me perspective.

"Turn around. Bare your back."

I comply and peel off my tee shirt. Modest Corolla is grateful Castan walked out, but she's a sliver compared to this new Corolla expanding in my bones.

Intense heat scrapes across my flesh. I wince, biting my mouth. It's nothing compared to the deaths I just witnessed. My bottom lip slips between my teeth.

"Repeat," Tilia exhales, clearly exhausted.

I wait, shirt clenched between white-knuckled fists.

"For our brothers" she draws in a breath, "Our sisters. Our society."

I parrot the phrase. "For our brothers, our sisters, our society."

Tilia dabs her heat upon the small of my back, makes a smear above those points. The warmth retracts. My Mark of Tribulation is complete. I carry the burden of Taxodium on my back now.

I turn, flesh stinging, and tug my tee back on.

"We all pretend something, child." Understanding passes between Tilia and me. She retreats into herself just as Nasreen passes through the Hold entrance.

"Is Castan up there?"

"You're awake." She sets several baskets by her feet. I smell cooked meat and something else savory. "How do you feel?"

I meet her by the Hold. "Thank you for taking care of me," I say, "but let me up. I need to speak with Castan. Now. Please."

Nasreen—bless her—doesn't question me further. Maybe she senses the boldness tumbling through my body like a pack of wolves. Maybe she detects my strength. Her palm still bloody, she loops an arm through mine. We step into the Hold—and are spit out under Matrona. I blink at the brightness. My ears clog with the shift in pressure.

"Thank you—" But Nasreen is already gone. I'm alone.

I glance at my surroundings. The sun is setting, ribbons of yellow and red in the distance. Matrona is an umbrella above me, and around the cypress, is a ring of hedges. It's behind one of these that I find Castan.

I don't know why I expect to see him in that strange black uniform, but I do. It occurs to me that, like me, he's changed his clothes, something I didn't even notice earlier. He's wearing khaki shorts and a white tee shirt. The fabric stretches across his broad chest, and I imagine, beneath the thin layer of cotton, there's a Mark between Castan's shoulder blades, too.

I plant myself near him, folding my arms over my knees. He doesn't acknowledge me, just watches the sun wink on the horizon.

I speak first.

"Tilia Marked me."

If this news is surprising, he does a splendid job masking his shock. A muscle in his jaw twitches. My courage hits a wall. I fight the urge to shrink into myself.

I try again, softer. "Can we leave in the morning?"

Castan opens his mouth. Shuts it. He leans back onto his palms, attention glued to the horizon.

"Do you wish you'd said no?" His voice is like silk, nothing at all like the jagged-edged venom from earlier.

"To you? To this offer?" I don't have to wonder. "No." I try to picture what my life would be like, had I chosen otherwise. I would go on for a couple weeks, puzzling over what Castan had to say. I would imagine myself a hero, lugging home bricks of gold for James. Enough time would pass that I would believe it had all been a dream. But a part of me would always wonder what my life could have been had I said yes. Even if the Gens never found me, even if James already possessed all the wealth in the world, I would feel as if some ancient, spellbound door were slammed in my face. I would be ordinary. Average. I don't imagine this being an easy path, but I believe it is a worthy one.

"Well," Castan clears his throat, ducks his head, "I'm sure I don't have to explain how dangerous this life can be, but I don't want you to think I forced you into it." I read the lines in his expression, the low notes of his voice.

"You didn't."

His shoulders sag, relieved. "You just mentioned something the other night, while you were drunk with fever, about some guy forcing you to do something. You thought I was James and kept apologizing."

"Oh." My cheeks flush with shame. "I don't remember that." I don't. Honestly. But I could guess at what my feverish self was referencing.

"Anyway, I'm sick of this Arctic climate, so we can leave in the morning, yes."

And like that, Averil is dismissed from my thoughts. A grin creeps into the corner of my lips.

"I'm no good at jokes, am I?" Castan stands, wiping fine particles of dirt from his hands.

"No," I laugh, despite myself. "You most definitely are not."

Castan smirks. "Let's head back." He thrusts an arm towards me.

There is a lapse in time where I stare at his outstretched hand. I study the veins popping under his flesh, the lines of sweat where his skin creases. If a kiss can destroy a life, what damage can this simple act unravel? I stop myself: I can wonder all I want, but I want to *know*.

Don't I?

I slide my hand into his.

Later, I'm on the phone with James. I don't know what Laila has done to him, but he only asks me *forty-nine* times how I'm feeling, rather than fifty. "I really am fine now. I'm one hundred percent myself again."

Oh, how I lie. The Mark—three dots in a triangular formation, under a black smear like an umbrella—has settled on my skin, but something else is out of place. Not my newfound fearlessness. That awaits, like a great, pulsating orb of potential energy. No, there's something else different.

"Alright, Corolla," James relents. He launches into an incredibly detailed narrative about the Academy's architecture. I imagine he's avoiding the subject of Hong Kong. Or Laila's holding a dosage of narcotics to his vein in case his worry rockets through the phone. Maybe both.

I clutch the phone to my ear, only half listening. Castan's low voice vibrates through the cavern. He's talking to the Botros about something, our plans for tomorrow, I'm sure.

I study my hand, my own veins, and creases. Tilia and Nasreen assured me the phage infection has passed, so then why is my hand tingling?

I know at once why: Castan.

I interrupt the thrilling history of Gothic spires. "I'm sorry, James, but I should get some sleep. We're leaving early tomorrow morning. And with the time shifts and all…"

"You've been sleeping for days," James chuckles, "but okay. Goodnight, Corolla. I love you."

"Love you, too." I clap the phone shut and lie in my bed for a moment. I take a deep breath and reach for the notebook and pen under my mattress. I find a clean page. Dashed lines. Frontal lobe. Temporal, parietal, occipital.

Averil.

I thought I was ready to set him aside, but I just... can't forget. I write, scribble, connect until the tingling in my hand submits and dies.

Past
February 2020

Jura always knew—deep down—that the killings weren't over. But when the opportunity came for her to go out with a routine scouting unit, she said yes. It's what her mother would have done.

"Gain as much experience as you can during *school,"* Vera taught, *"that way you look that much better on paper* after *school when you apply for a job."*

Think ahead. Plan ahead. *Be* ahead. That's what the Taylors did. They took the advanced classes. They left good impressions on their superiors. So how did this one go over *her* head?

Because there wasn't any warning. There wasn't a disturbance or a pedes' murder—we were just taking a tour of the British Columbia/Alberta border. It was routine. And the Gens still found us.

By Matrona, how?

A savage scream resounded behind her, grating against her ears like a razor.

Cirrus. She hadn't known the Official very well, but she knew his face around campus, quietly observing everything. He had an ebony stud buried in his blonde eyebrow and had a rare Essence for detecting thermal heat signatures. He helped out in Defensive Training, sometimes, with Commander Murphy.

And now he was dead. She was acutely aware of his body slumping behind her, the screaming coming to an abrupt end. Her knees ground harder into the grass, damp with morning dew. Ahead of her, a flock of birds sprang from the white hills of the mountains, escaping. Her heart flew with them.

Take it to Talan and Finis, she instructed. *Don't let them think the worst.*

Her thin black vest said STUDENT on the back and flapped in the wind. It was safety protocol to wear it, but Jura wondered now if STUDENT was more a target on her back than anything else. She clasped her chapped hands together and focused on the beauty of the Canadian scenery. There was a lake, nestled in the land below Mount Assiniboine. From this distance, it looked of crystal. Jura imagined dunking her head in the frigid water—

"Lola," a rough voice called from behind, "that one still has a gun."

Shit, Jura blinked. *I was hoping they wouldn't notice it under the vest.* She had been waiting for the right time to use it.

Jura's hair stood on end. Only this morning, Dani had twisted a little braid in one side of her short, wavy hair. "The last thing you want is for it to get in your way," she'd volunteered. Dani enjoyed beautifying others, maybe because she was already so gorgeous herself.

Head ducked, the braid was in her way now. The Gen bent down to retrieve the gun from her waist. Jura tossed her head back, flinging the dark braid from her eyes. She met the eyes of her captor.

The plump girl couldn't be much older than Jura was, which surprised her. *I guess they have to do as much damage as they can before the disease corrodes their Essence gene.* She was square-shaped and had hair similar to Jura's: short and wavy. Except the girl's—Lola's—hair was strawberry blonde, scraped into two ponytails, one on each side of her head. She wore a low-cut red blouse and a fanning, floral skirt. Jura thought she saw blood splatters mixed in with the rose petals.

"Try anything on me, girl," Lola warned in a high-pitched voice, "and I'll kill you last."

Despite Lola's odd appearance, Jura's skin tingled. Her blood ran cold in her veins: there were only five scouts, including herself. Cirrus was dead, which just left three others. Four, if she counted herself. But how could she tally herself among such an ending?

Growing up, she had heard tales about pelari heroes. She knew about Phaedra, the first pelari, all those centuries ago. She knew about how Tilia Pyrus extended her life by entwining her soul with the cypress tree named after Phaedra's mother, Matrona. She knew about Gentry and Dawson Allen's brutal tactics that defeated the Dentata traitors during World War II. And she knew, from her parent's accounts, about the humble farewell of Major Rainier's Ceremony after lung cancer claimed his life.

She knew Calyx. She was sorry when he died—they all were. Castan held him on a pedestal, but she had only ever seen him as a modest spirit. And a detached one: he never went home on the holidays, never cared for material wealth, and even though they had all been his friends, he never spoke about himself. Not really. Maybe, she thought, some part of him knew he wouldn't make it. Perhaps that's how destiny worked, and this was hers—just another thread in the tapestry of time.

At least I'll know somebody in the afterlife.

Her heart, which felt like it had been folded a million times, crumpled up and shoved down her throat, began to unfurl. She inspected the creases, the tears, and she held it in her hands tenderly.

Jura knew she was going to die. And it was a calming thought.

Talan would be upset, but he had Finis and Dani to watch out for him. Maggie never claimed to be capable of repairing broken hearts, but maybe there was something she could do to mend the loss. Jura was sorry to leave so soon, but Talan would understand... Being her twin, he would know she hadn't suffered.

Lola cleared her throat, grinning at something over Jura's head. Jura studied Lola's hazelnut eyes. She didn't want to memorize them. She didn't even want to know they were hazelnut, but the yelp of pain and crunch of bone at her back forced her to stare harder. A smudge of mascara, crinkles at the corners... There was actually something almost familiar about them.

And then they were beaming her, those eyes, like two acorns in the Gen's head. Lola flashed a wicked smile. "You're next."

Jura was captive to an impulse. She shot daggers at Lola, unleashing her own Essence, which weakened others'. It's why she was such an effective tool against Talan when they trained together. He was impossibly strong, but her Essence could strip that away from him. For just a moment, she would erase his strength and have the advantage.

Lola's body flickered before Jura, but her eyes did not change. Jura's heart froze, broke and screamed, shredding into thousands of paper strips all at once. She knew those eyes. But she knew that mind, too. Or at least she thought she had.

"You twisted, traitorous, *witch*!" It didn't sound like her voice but it was. Barking and mangled like a rabid dog's. *Betrayedbetrayedbetrayed,* her thoughts rang out like a car alarm.

"I said no tricks," Lola snarled. The butt of Jura's handgun razed across her forehead, knocking her sideways. Blood oozed down the length of her braid. Vibrant green grass obscured her vision. A beetle crawled, oblivious, on one of the blades.

Head stinging, Jura tried righting herself, but Lola kicked her in the gut. She folded into herself, clutching her aching stomach. Men's cologne swam in her nostrils, but she was sure she imagined it.

"Lola," said that rough voice through Jura's rolling pain. "I won Carnage, so I get the kills. I only said you could tag along because Numen willed it."

"Oh, no," Lola sneered down at Jura, "your Numen wills anything I damn well please." Lola unsheathed an ax from her back. It was decorated, notched along the ebony handle. The blade shone in the morning sun, glinting through rust-colored stains. Jura tried not to think about that. Her eyes flitted upwards.

Under the pale blue of the gaping sky, Jura could almost imagine she was back at the Academy with Finis, watching him create snowflakes in the heat of the afternoon sun.

"Five seconds. That's how long they last today." He shot a spray up into the air, and, seconds later, they splattered cool drops on her face.

"Hmm. Yesterday it was eight." No one came to the Mausoleums, but they did when their schedules permitted it. As odd as pedes may have found it, the Mausoleums were a private place, where the only people watching were the spirits in their resting slots.

Jura felt his chilled breath on her neck, saw the gleam of the ax at the bottom of her blurring vision. Tears, there were tears, like two little rhinestones, stuck to her lashes. Blood coated the side of her face, but she no longer felt the sting of pain from the laceration.

"They'll find out," Jura croaked, gaze still in the vast swell of blue above. "They aren't idiots."

Lola cocked her head, almost sympathetically. "Oh, but even the most perceptive can be the most ignorant."

Jura's attention fluttered back to her memory.

Finis mumbled against her collarbone, "The life of ice is fleeting, but water lasts forever."

She stroked a hand through his silver-blonde hair. He would buzz it soon, as that was what was expected from a Trainee of the Guard. "That's poetic."

"Is it?" He kissed the hollow of her neck. She swallowed as his icy fingertips skated down the side of her cheek.

"Say it again, please."

Jura heard his calm demure voice repeat, "The life of ice is fleeting, but water lasts—"

Castan
July 2020

"Tea?" Nasreen pours me a liberal cup. She hands it to me and decants her own teacup. She sets the transparent pot back on the table, dark liquid sloshing within its container.

"I would love some." I hate tea. I would never tell Nasreen, but it's true. I inhale the herbal scented steam. Nausea swims in the pit of my stomach, but I take a sip of the liquid, so dark, it's black. I force myself to swallow. Tea is nothing like coffee.

I direct my attention to Corolla. Nasreen gave her a backpack for her possessions—a notebook, I guess—and my uniform. Corolla has it slung over her back now. My gaze follows her across the main cavern. I didn't hear Tilia call her name (I was too revolted with my tea to notice), but Corolla steps towards the throne of roots. Tilia, at least, is more herself today than yesterday, a soft straw color.

Tilia touches Corolla's shoulder—Corolla's body goes stiff for a moment, and I wonder if pedes react differently to the Venefica's advancements than pelari do. Except Corolla was Marked yesterday without issue, so I quickly discard the idea.

Corolla relaxes, spine flexible. She mumbles something to Tilia, who quirks the corner of her lips. When Corolla pivots, she's grinning ear to ear, and I understand. Tilia showed her a memory. I duck my head to the cup of dark liquid between my hands. I shove down a wave of hurt more revolting than the tea I just swallowed.

Tilia never showed me Calyx's memories because I told her... it's too painful to see him alive. My stomach twinges. I haven't forgotten the dreams Tilia was supplementing me with. Since Hong Kong, I've been thinking about those utopias more and more. Because I can only ever create nightmares on my own.

Corolla cuts across the earthen floor to me.

"Ready to go?" She eyes the full contents of my cup, eyebrow-raising.

"Yeah," I set my cup on the table. "Issak Park is expecting us."

We say our goodbyes to Nasreen and the Venefica. Umar left earlier this morning to take care of something for Matrona. I expect Tilia to say something to me, but she just nods. A muscle in my jaw twitches.

"C'mon." I stalk over to the exit, slipping my blade down my palm. Only pelari blood opens Holds, I want to explain, but I suspect Corolla already knows this. She's catching on fast.

I loop my arm through Corolla's. She flinches, almost backing into the cavern wall.

"You won't go with me unless we're linked," I tell her, somewhat irritated.

"I know," she bows her head. I think her cheeks flush red, but the lights above cast too heavy of shadows to know for sure.

I slap my palm against the Mark of Tribulation carved in the wall. When I open my eyes next, we're standing under Matrona's broad canopy of branches. Corolla is already out of my grip, standing two feet away.

I pull the geometer out from my shorts. I punch some buttons on the device, and the pre-existing coordinates Maggie supplied me show up on the little screen. Next, I examine the area. The bubble requires a decent amount of open space to operate safely. I gauge the location I'm standing in is about as good as I'm going to get, without being in direct view of any pedes.

"Okay," I face Corolla. "Geometers are a little different than Holds. Unless you want a repeat of what happened last time, or something worse, stand directly back-to-back with me. Jumping is easier if the people traveling are as compact and uniform as possible."

"Okay." Corolla takes off her pack and holds it to her chest. I position myself between Matrona and the hedges where we'll have enough space to jump. As graceful as a shadow, Corolla comes up behind me. She barely brushes my clothes. I realize Matrona isn't a bed and breakfast, so I probably smell like a barn animal, but I can't afford another delay because Corolla got injured *again*. I sigh.

"You'll have to be closer than that." After a second, Corolla pushes herself up against me. She's so short, the back of her head rests between my shoulder blades. Calyx and I used to be the same height— people said we looked alike all the time—but then I hit a growth spurt. Calyx was probably only inches taller than Corolla.

I duck my head at the geometer just as Corolla asks, "What are pelari families like?"

I place a drop of my blood in the end port of the device. "What do you mean? They're like any other family, I guess, just with Essences." I make to punch the JUMP button, but Corolla speaks again. I think she's a nervous talker.

"Well, what's *your* family like?"

My irritation melts into waves of flushed surprise. I quickly mask it, though Corolla can't see my expression anyway. I angle my neck, so she can hear me ask, "What did Tilia show you?"

Corolla bubbles with excitement. Or anxiety. "My mother meeting my father's family. I... I never knew what my father looked like until I saw that memory."

The words stick to the back of my throat. *Calyx looked like your father.*

My thumb presses JUMP. It'll take a moment to process the energy waves. Intelligence is trying to create a better model that's faster at computing, but technology and enchantments are difficult to mix. Especially when Enchanters are few and far between.

"She can only show memories of dead people, right?"

I make a noncommittal noise and nod.

The geometer beeps, and Corolla startles against me.

She practically screams, voice tight. "Did Tilia ever show you... Calyx?"

"No." The geometer vibrates once, twice. "There wouldn't be a point. I was with him all the time." The pale lilac veil begins spreading over us. There's a reason why pelari call it a bubble: it shimmers transparent just like one. Corolla starts squirming. I reach a hand back to still her, but she clamps her own, sweaty one around mine.

For the second time this morning, I mask my surprise.

"Hold still."

Her hand, fingers knotted with my own, relaxes.

Apricot and salmon tickle under my eyelids. No one, not even Júlia, has ever *held* my hand. I'm surprised by the ghost of warmth from where her fingers—so small, they're almost child-sized—locked with mine. Behind me, Corolla sucks in her breath.

I open my eyes.

My gaze meets the sun, a disc rising in the east.

"We're on top of a building." I glance at the pigeon-splattered ground and see that Corolla's not wrong. I step away from her to the ledge. The Arno River is a ribbon, glinting in the morning sun. The people are dots, some on the streets, some on the black-wired balconies attached to the building we're stranded on. *Apartments.*

I watch a riverboat crawl through the water. Staring down, I feel giddy. Maybe it's because I spent most of my life in the Complex, but heights have always made me want to jump. Even standing at the top of the steps of Rainier Hospital, my stomach flops. Fish swim, pedes walk, but me? I want to glide through the open air.

I go back to Corolla, who is gazing at the skyline. She embraces the scenery, all traces of fear evaporated in the plane of infrastructure.

"There's the Dome of Santa Maria," she says under her breath. Corolla turns to me, strands of her caramel hair whipping in the delicate wind. The sun shimmers in her eyes as she says, "I've always wanted to come to Florence."

I squint at the white-speckled rooftop. "Tyto Alba was Florentine."

"Yeah," Corolla chimes, "growing up, it's all I knew about my father." I wonder, not for the first time, why Alba never reached out to his daughter. Surely, he knew she was in Michigan with Adian's brother. Corolla would still be pedes, but at least she would have grown up knowing that the pedes' world isn't the only one that competes for this planet.

"I never knew I had so many uncles. And an aunt." She asks her next question slowly as if it has been swirling around her brain and she doesn't want to mess it up. "They're still alive, right? I mean, they weren't that old in the memory, but still…"

"Corolla, I… I don't know why Tilia showed you that memory," my tone is harsher than I intended. I scan the horizon, eyes locking on the Dome of Santa Maria, like a tent among the flat lines of the rooftops.

Corolla is wary. "Why?"

I wish she hadn't asked.

"You know how your dad was Major? Well, he wasn't supposed to be. He was too young, but he caught a Dentata spy sneaking around Intel. Tax loved him for it."

"Okay, but what does that have to do with the Albas?"

I sigh, fists clenching and unclenching at my sides. I tell her. "That was the first reason. Not too long after your mother was killed, the Gens attacked the Albas. The Dentatas… they didn't like how your dad stuck his neck out to save your mother during the April Attack. That was the second reason why the Gens did what they did."

"But *what* did they do?" Corolla reaches, as if to clutch my arm, but thinks better of it. She hugs herself instead. "Castan, what happened to my father's family?"

I swallow, staring down into those brown eyes squinting up at me. "They were… killed. Valeria Alba and her son, Tate, are the only ones alive besides your father."

Corolla's grip loosens. Her arm falls to her side. "But my father is alright? Did the Gens hurt him?"

I glance back at the Dome. "No. That's the way the Dentatas work. They take away what you love most in the world, and they make you suffer through it alone."

Corolla is silent. She's usually quiet, but it hangs around her now like an eerie cloud. Vacant eyes, chewed lip. I wonder if I've broken her. Nobody talks about the Alba Atrocities because nobody wants to admit how horrific it may have been. Some of their homes were burnt to ash, others were splattered in blood. But the bodies were never found. I was too young to remember when the stories hit the news. I'm not surprised James never knew about it either—Tax likes to keep things hush, hush whenever pelari are involved. Especially rogue ones, like the Dentatas.

"Corolla, I'm sorry. I honestly don't know why Tilia showed you that memory. It's cruel, but now you see why the Gens need to be stopped. Forever. They aren't human. They're—"

"Why do people say that?" She glances up, wind in her hair. "Why do people apologize for things they didn't do? You didn't kill them, so don't say sorry."

I consider her words for a split second before answering, "Because so many of our words are for ourselves, those two were for you." Corolla opens her mouth but then clamps it shut. She folds into herself, those coffee-brown eyes seeing things I never will.

I don't need Tilia to show me his memories—Calyx is on the fringes of my mind. Always. When someone's blood is on your hands, can you ever truly be washed clean of him?

Movement in the corner of my eye captures my attention. I come back to myself, remembering why we're standing on a roof in Florence. *Coordinates.* I couldn't conceivably wear my soldier's gear this deep into pedes territory, but khakis shorts and a tee have never hindered my instincts. The muscles in my body tense, coiling and ready for combat.

"Always anticipate a fight," Commander Murphy taught us in Defensive Training. *"Let your guard down, and your enemy won't hesitate to use that to his advantage."*

The Commander didn't have to tell me that—my father religiously preached something along the same lines. That was *my* childhood.

"Woah, soldier," a friendly voice calls, "at ease." A man, no older than myself steps into the center of my vision. His gait is staggered as if his knees don't bend as well as they should. His black hair is shaved close to his head, almost like a Trainee's cut. He's wearing close-knit cashmere and dark wash jeans. I relax a degree.

"Issak Park," he thrusts an arm in the space between us. His sleeves are bunched above his elbows, and I notice his skin is riddled with scars.

I reach to embrace the TI's gesture and hear Calyx laughing in my head, *"You know you're supposed to look people in the eye when you shake their hand."* We used to have mini-lessons between classes.

Calyx would teach me how to be more... "charismatic" was his word for it. I would teach him how to lie. His ears always flushed shades of pink and red.

I grin to myself, but Issak must think I'm smiling for him. He returns the favor, flashing white teeth in my direction. It's then that I notice the color framed in his almond eyes: pale, milky-white.

He's blind.

"Ms. Vel," Issak tucks his chin. Corolla, who has been standing some inches behind me, steps out from my shadow. "I'm enchanted."

"Hello." Her voice is flat—I know she's still digesting what I said. She's been absorbing so much lately, it's a wonder her small body is still standing.

"You know," Issak remarks, "facial expressions have sounds. Yours is like the creak of an old man's knees. And yours," he faces Corolla, "is like the beat of a butterfly's wings. I'm blind, but I'm definitely not deaf."

"Er..." I run a hand through my hair. "That's... interesting." Corolla crosses her arms, the canvas straps from her pack digging into the fabric of her shirt. She's staring at Isaak like legs just sprouted from his ears. Head cocked, lips slightly parted... I'd laugh if I could.

Issak appears to take us both in one more time. The muscles in his face settle.

"Anyway," he says, "you're, no doubt, anxious to hear what I have to say." I am, but Issak doesn't leave room for me to say that. He takes a scrap of paper from his back pocket and locks it in a tight fist.

"At the Euro Academy, my team and I have been studying and synthesizing earth vibrations, like after earthquakes and etcetera. Since we know the Gens occupy underground bunkers, my team and I have been listening to what noises these vibrations make when they travel through the ground. I won't bore you with the mechanics behind it, but we know a certain scale of hollow cavities distort those vibrations and create a different type of sound, once the vibration passes through it. Well..." Issak holds out his fist, grinning so hard, it's a wonder his lips don't split at the corners. I wonder how often he gets out.

Next to never, I conclude. *And Calyx thought I was socially awkward.*

I take the paper from his hand, read the words scribbled in black ink. My head swims. I don't even try to hide the coordinates as Corolla peers over my elbow.

"Are you sure this is accurate? How do you know your... vibrations didn't just cross into an underground cave?"

Issak is smug. "You may have your flames, and you," he nods his head in Corolla's direction, "your vines, but I have my hearing. And it is never wrong."

"But Belarus? I thought the Gens only had bunkers in the Americas."

"Which is precisely why we turned our attention elsewhere," Issak supplies. He becomes more animated, arms slicing through the wind. "Think about it, we haven't been able to locate the Gens because they've tricked us all into believing they live in the New World. Europe is the perfect place for them to hide. My team is already working on setting up stations worldwide, though, just in case they have multiple bunkers. Who knows how many there are?"

"Right," I stuff the paper in my pocket, "who knows."

"After what happened to the Asian Academy," Issak says with a certain sprinkle of vengeance, "we may have an advantage over the bastards." Redemption sounds out of place on his tongue, like an off-key note.

"Park," the word tumbles out of my mouth with a revelation. "Are you related to Kat Park?"

"Yes." There is no trace of grief in his voice, in the pale skin of his face. "My cousin died fighting, I am told." Images of Kat's slumped body, amidst the Vel's burning house, floods my vision. Corolla is silent beside me.

"She did. *Bellatrix, vale.*"

Issak brushes his hands down the front of his sweater. "Well, I won't keep you. Major Rex will want that piece of paper," Issak points to my pocket, "as soon as your geometer can jump you back to the Academy. Major Crivelli has probably already sent word."

I nod. When Issak doesn't move, I discover he means to see us off. My thoughts scatter like cockroaches. I have a hard time grasping any one. There's no way the Gens have a Complex in Europe. I would have heard about that, surely. If Belarus is a trap, I can't let the remaining Taxodium forces walk into it. But I can't place Corolla in harm's way either.

I make a split decision. I take out the geometer and punch a series of buttons. Corolla is a quick learner—I don't even have to tell her to stand at my back this time. Just as the lilac veil enfolds the space around us, Issak waves, "Give Major Rex my regards."

"I will," I call back, grateful that lies are soundless.

"This is some house in the Academy?" Corolla asks. I run a hand through my hair and pull it out right away.

"No," I scowl at my hand. "It's a cottage in Wales. I thought we should freshen up first." At Corolla's puzzled look, "The shower's down the hall."

I throw myself back on the plush sofa and stare at the empty fireplace. Shadows curl where flames used to. Calyx and I came here months ago for his *Humanitas*. I remember the coordinates because Calyx disappeared to the castle ruins uphill for his Trial with Tilia. He came back, two hours later, red-faced and gasping for breath.

"I think that was my Valor Trial," he said, hands on his knees, huffing.

"No," I replied, "it was to prove how out of shape you are. I told you to lay off the Little Debbie's."

Corolla interrupts my thoughts. "I thought you were supposed to deliver those coordinates before anything else?" She raises an eyebrow, suspicious.

I shake my head. "We can't show up at Allen Manor smelling like *this*."

Corolla flushes. "Issak made it seem pressing, though."

I shrug. "TIs make everything sound pressing." I prop my feet on the coffee table. "It's fine. Rex can't do anything about it right now anyway—too busy with damage control and stuff."

Corolla stands, one foot in the kitchen, one in the hall.

"There are towels in the cabinet by the sink." Corolla doesn't ask how I know, and I don't volunteer the information. She takes one last look at me and heads down the hallway.

I inhale the musty smell of cut wood and admire the rustic decor. Goat horn sconces light the wall. Wooden planks, peppered with brown swirls of knots, make up three of the four walls. The east wall is a puzzle of glass panels. It showcases the fog outside, hovering over the sheet of black pond water. Gray ash spills from the fireplace to the stone hearth. I'm lucky no one else was using the cottage—Corolla would have known I was lying.

I hear the bathroom door shut. The water spikes on, traveling through the plumbing. I fling my body from the couch, knocking a stack of wool blankets to the carpet in the process. I kick them aside and shove all the furniture against one of the walls, that way, Corolla will see it and hopefully know I jumped, not died.

I locate her canvas pack in a pile on the kitchen table. I don't have the patience to put all my gear on, but I kick off sneakers and shove my feet in my Caeli boots. I stuff my knife in the waist of my shorts.

I whip the geometer from my pocket, along with the scrap of paper Issak gave me. Rex will kill me, maybe throw me in a cell for torture, but I have to *know* what's in Belarus.

My heart climbs to my throat.
Hadley.
My thumb stabs JUMP.

Past
February 2020

Kass hated sleeping in, but lately, it was becoming a challenge just getting out of bed. Like hiking up a mountain. Or running a marathon. She didn't have motivation.

Golden rays of sunlight, from the window behind her bed, touched the rumpled sheets of her mattress. She wasn't religious, but she swore, the gods were taunting her. Kass knew she was demanding, knew she was brash and rude and hard to understand—but Calyx had known that. And Calyx had stayed. Until he couldn't anymore.

"Wear that dress at my funeral, and I might just come back to life."

Kass curled into the white mass of her sheets, cursing the Gens, the *Humanitas*, and all of Taxodium. She used to wish Calyx would leave her bed—he wasted too much of the morning sleeping in. But now, she only wished he would come back. *You can sleep in until 20:30 if you would just come back.*

If grief were a language, then she was just beginning to understand it. It was a language with no rules or guidelines, a tongue she didn't sign up to learn. But it wasn't a dead language either—Castan spoke it, too.

Every now and then, Castan disappeared from campus using his stolen geometer. He went back to Yazd, back to the alley where Calyx was—Kass couldn't think it, but Castan said it aloud, sometimes, his voice burning with bitterness. Even if he had claimed a piece of Rosh Dentata, a lost finger was not justice for Calyx's lost life. Major Rex would probably suspend Castan if she knew he hadn't turned his geometer in yet. But that didn't stop him from going back. He told her once it helped, but Kass wasn't stupid. He was tormenting himself.

She glanced at her display case on her dresser. Resting in the red velvet, protected by the glass, was her *cantus* blade. It had been given to her several years ago by her parents, before she left the charming slopes of Colorado for the gentle plains of Ohio. It was ebony, a graceful, subtle *S* shape. Tilia Pyrus made the enchanted blades shortly before she integrated her soul with Matrona. It was for Hold transporting, so a pelari could draw blood and the wound would completely heal, minutes later. Kass rarely used the antique, but Calyx had been intrigued by its properties. He was probably the last person to touch it. Was his DNA still on the hilt, his fingerprints still on the glass of the case? It nauseated her, these little bits of himself that he left laying around. Because he was gone, right? Then why was he still everywhere she looked?

Calyx isn't coming back.

Her empty stomach twisted, and she felt bile rise in the back of her throat. Disgusted with herself, Kass sat up. She flung her legs over the edge of her bed and planted bare feet on the cold wood of the floor. The world was spinning, but wasn't it always? She just never noticed before.

Kass managed to stand, scrape her snarled hair into a loose braid, and tug on some decent clothes. The actions exhausted her. She was grateful it was a Saturday, thankful that she didn't have to wear a mask today and pretend like Calyx's death wasn't a jagged-toothed saw to her heart.

Maggie wasn't home—she could tell by the stale silence of their dorm. *Probably working a shift at the hospital.* Kass didn't know how Maggie could do it, how she could watch people's lives fade from their eyes. How could she bear to lose a life?

Kass reached for her phone for something to do, screen bright in her dim room. There was a missed phone call from her younger brother, Lark. He would be coming to the Academy next year. *I should give him the* cantus *blade,* she thought in a haze. She also had one message from Talan:

Aurum. Now.

Kass shoved the phone in her back pocket, determined to make an effort to call Lark later, and slipped her Caeli boots on. She didn't really own any other shoes, a fact Calyx had found comical.

"What do you wear in the summer then?"

"My boots," she replied, flicking him on the sternum. *"It's not funny."*

"No," Calyx looked at her with something vibrant in his eyes, *"it's endearing. Soldier boots. You're too symbolic for your own good."*

There was snow on the ground, layering everything in a white blanket but the walkways. Kass locked the dorm up behind her, breath coming in gray clouds around her. She fought the instinct to hug herself. She didn't forget a coat, just like she didn't forget to eat breakfast. There was one upside to Calyx's untimely death: he died in the thick of winter, and the cold was numbing. Kass welcomed it.

Aurum House was the unofficial, unspoken meeting place for Kass and her friends. It was a Ward Residence, so it was actually a) large, b) comfortable, c) away from prying ears of other students. Maybe it was a false sense of privacy, as the Major's residence, Allen Manor, was just up the hill. But stepping into the square of Tudor-style houses, Kass felt a strange sense of ease. Strange because this was where Calyx lived.

I haven't tainted Aurum with my sadness yet, though. Back at her dorm, she festered in it quietly. Kass didn't cry, refused to. Even when she raced Talan to the gates to meet Castan, even when she saw him alone, leaf-green eyes vacant, she didn't cry. She nodded her head and went back to her dorm to think.

"Hello?" Kass stepped into the house, and immediately smelled Calyx: sandalwood and cotton. She blinked away the memories the same way one swats at pesky flies. *Not now.*

She seized up the room, vaguely aware of Finis, Talan, Dani, and Júlia in the spread of pastel brown couches. Calyx said they reminded him of the dinner rolls they served in the Dining Hall at Thanksgiving and Christmas. "They look more like folds of skin," she'd replied.

"Where's Jura and Castan?" Grim expressions answered her question. Finis shifted his glasses on his nose, attempting to mask a sniffle. Júlia buried her face in her hands, shoulders shaking. Dani ducked her head, daring to glance at Talan. Kass sucked in her breath.

"Talan—" In two blinks of her eye, she was kneeling before him. "Allen's spotted mare—what the hell happened?" His thin face was white as fresh snow. His eyes were puffy, rimmed red. There was a hefty pile of used tissues occupying the cushion next to him. Dani smoothed a hand down his back, lips set in a frown.

Talan just shook his head and reached for another tissue.

"Jura," Finis's voice cracked, raw from grief. He sighed. "Jura went out with a scouting party this morning. She's not... coming back."

Kass swallowed, hard. "It's just too much," she breathed, picking herself off the floor, whisking herself away. She was outside again, slamming the door on the sandalwood and cotton.

Her Caeli boots carried her past the square, down the red brick road. The rectangular shape of the Barracks loomed before her, archaic and steady. She passed under the familiar stone arch, teeth chattering in her head. The field was clear (of course), shining bright green turf in a world of white. In the far corner, yards away from her, was a flaming mannequin. A figure adorned in black slashed fists at it.

Castan. She bowed her head and inspected the raw look of her chapped hands. Wind toyed with the loose strands of her hair, biting the tips of her ears and nose.

She couldn't bear to hear her thoughts.

Jura. Dead.

Jura, the one they all believed would be a Judge on the Courts one day. *She has big aspirations. She has dreams. She has ambition.*

Had.

"Oh, *fuck* past tense!"

Her legs stopped moving. Kass breathed gray clouds of vapor. She remembered hating Calyx for smiling so much, but what she wouldn't do to see the curl of his lips again. What she wouldn't do to bring either of them back to life. Her heart hurt so much, she wished it would just stop. Her acid was useless against her own flesh, but maybe she could trick one of the freshmen into killing her. Freshmen were always doing stupid things, especially for money.

"Ahhg!" Castan pounded the training mannequin again, the sound echoing in the enclosed field. Castan always moved with the fluidity of a dancer, but today, his body sagged, arms flailed. The language of grief. She wished to go back to English, please.

Her Caeli boots decided she wanted to be near the fire, so that's where Kass went. Years seemed to pass her by, so far was the stretch of field that separated her from Castan. Her legs stopped again, several feet from him. He didn't acknowledge her.

"Hg," she read the black letters scorched into the chest of the mannequin. *Isn't that an elemental symbol?* She despised chemistry and didn't care to ask.

"Your knuckles are bleeding," her voice was muffled as if someone had placed hands over her ears.

"Your lips are blue," Castan retorted, clipping the defenseless mannequin in the jaw. Its mouth was a permanent O shape, eyes blank. The flames licking its profile now made it look menacing, like a PG-13 version of a Disney villain. She watched Castan's bloodied hands slice through the orange blend of flames, unscathed by the heat.

Maybe Castan would kill me?

No, he's too moralistic.

"The Gens who are killing our scouts," Castan delivered a fatal blow of flames, "are doing it because they won Carnage, a sort of game the Dentatas host. Our scouts are the prize."

Kass's head snapped. She focused on the strained muscles in his neck. "How do you know that?"

Castan shrugged. "I heard Commander Murphy talking about it with some of his Officials. I guess they don't want us to worry."

"Or," Kass spat venomously, "they don't want us to know we're goddamn toys for the Gens to play with! Why do they keep sending us out there if they know we'll just get slaughtered?"

Castan paused, wiping sweat from his brow. A smear of blood followed his hand across his forehead. He glanced at her, seeming to take in her haggard, frozen appearance, and he accepted it. That's one thing she liked about Castan: he didn't try to change her. *Maybe because he sees himself in your eyes.* His own were hollow, bruise-black. Where she slept more often, Castan never slept at all. She'd seen his room—Styrofoam coffee cups littered every inch.

"Tax didn't know before. They do now. Students aren't allowed to go anymore. Soldiers only."

"But we are soldiers!" Her Caeli boots were hot coals on the bare soles of her feet.

"No," Castan scowled, "we're not. Let the Army do their job, Kass, and just... take care of yourself."

Kass scoffed. "I should steal a geometer and start hooking up with Júlia now then too, right? Because that'll fix things. That'll bring back the dead. That's me *taking care of myself.*"

Castan looked as if she'd slapped him with a brick. The blood on his forehead ran like crimson paint in his sweat. Silver flashed in the hollow of his throat.

Calyx's dog tag.

"I'm sorry." She bowed her head, eyes stinging with salt. They all pretended—didn't they?—that this sick feeling drilling through their bodies was normal. Maybe it was. Maybe it was just one of those things Taxodium failed to include in their brochures. *Train to harness your Essence*, and in the fine print: *suffer from eternal grief.*

"Kass." She choked at the sound of her name, Castan's voice as raw and shattered as she felt. She met his gaze.

The syllables squeaked past her lips, "Why is everyone dying?"

Castan spread his arms, the mannequin glowing sunshine-yellow behind him. Its entire figure burned now.

Her Caeli boots took her into his arms. She never let people embrace her, so when Castan's arms folded around her, she expected him to be Calyx. Her body shook as the tears spilled down her cheeks. Because he wasn't Calyx. His chest was broader, firmer. He smelled different, felt different—even his body temperature was different. The sensation stripped her bare, a harsh slap in the face.

Kass pulled away, wiping tears with the back of her hand. The salt stung the cracks in her flesh, the same way Castan's presence stung the cracks in her heart. Kass didn't feel hungry or cold or even numb. She felt destruction.

"Thank you," she murmured, "I needed that."

Corolla
July 2020

I all but close the bathroom door and turn the water on, when a sick feeling takes hold of my body. It grips my stomach in a cold, clammy fist. I ignore the patter of rain against the tiled shower, ignore the bright white of the LED lights surrounding the vanity. My head pounds with the wrongness pulsing in my veins.

Castan. His eyes said everything his lips didn't. I quickly shut the water off and race down the hall, almost running into a display case of glassware on my way. The trinkets rattle in the case as if shivering against their near destruction.

At the end of the hall, Castan's body is a statue. If not for the displacement of all the furniture, I would think he's just admiring the painting on the wall ahead of him. I hear the distinct *beep* of the geometer.

"Castan!"

His figure twists, composure cracks like a sculpture coming to life, as he sees me coming up to him.

"Corolla. Don't," he warns. Already, the lavender curtain is forming a shell around him. If I extended an arm, I could touch it.

I don't know I'm shaking my head until my legs are carrying me forward. Castan yells something, but I can't decipher it over the waves crashing in my ears. I don't know if the Mark makes you fearless or foolish, but I *do* know I don't want to be abandoned in Wales.

I launch into the bubble.

My skin tingles as if I'm soaking in a bath of needles. My eyelids flutter—

"Get off me," Castan growls. His eyebrows are knitted into a single, dark line. There's no room for that familiar wrinkle between his brow. His hair sticks up at every angle, sharp blades of grass shooting up through the mangy clumps. He wasn't lying about needing a shower. He smells of sweat and stale onion. I don't know how I didn't notice it earlier.

Castan glowers, the lines in his face forming one word: pissed. My face scrunches together. *Oh,* my brain comprehends. *You're* on top of *Castan.* I clamber to my feet, unsteady. I brush bits of gravel from my knees, hoping the blush in my cheeks isn't apparent. I turn away from him, just in case.

I take in our surroundings—I feel like I just waltzed onto the set of a fantasy movie, and I'm in the center of the Enchanted Forest. Fairies will flit out of the woods any minute now. We're standing in a clearing, vegetation stacked to the gray sky. My gaze travels from the tangled masses of trees, so twisted and gnarled, they barricade us in, to the grassland drowning my legs.

So, this is Belarus, but—

Castan stands in a single fluid motion. His face is one of forced calm now, like when James holds back the floods of his worry. Except Castan reminds me of a volcano anxious to erupt: magma bubbling impatiently just beneath the surface of his skin.

"Do you," his voice is so controlled, I almost wince, "realize what you could have done?" His head snaps up to meet my gaze. I stare into those blazing emeralds, and something snaps inside of me. Because I always put my feelings aside for others: I did it for Averil, I do it for James, and I have been doing it for Castan. I can't keep laying myself down for people to walk over.

"What *I* could have done?" I shout. "If you were going to ditch me, then you should have left me in Florence!"

Castan's fists are at his sides, smoking. My gaze flits from his white knuckles to the tight line of his lips. His shoulders sag.

"You can't get hurt again." There is no fight in his words, only raw honesty. He has that look in his eye, that same one of defeat. Not everyone can acknowledge when they have lost. But Castan does effortlessly.

Still, I am merciless.

"Stop treating me like a china doll." I jab a finger in his sternum. He flinches, and the momentum of my impact forces him to take half a step back. I would grin if my frustration weren't burning up all other emotion. A small part of me celebrates: maybe this is the Adian in me. Perhaps I'm not as motherless as I've grown up believing.

Castan opens his mouth, each muscle defined beneath his pale skin. "I was going to come back. Once I investigated. You don't know what it's like."

"I'm not your redemption case, okay? This," I gesture to the primeval forest, "isn't about you." I don't know what I mean, only that Castan isn't supposed to be here. *We* aren't supposed to be here.

His ears flush red. "Of course it's not about me! It's about the greater good." A scowl shapes his expression. An array of emotions flickers across his face, but I can't identify a single one. My words carved deep.

"Whenever I look at you or James, I think about how I failed Calyx."

Guilt rips through me, shredding sinew and muscle. Maybe this is why I never let myself go—because I will only ever regret it in the end.

A noise interrupts the heavy silence between us. At first, I think it's a gong, but the sound is brash and distinctly metallic, grating against my ears. Something falling. Flocks of birds take flight, cawing and swarming in a black mass above. I feel water on my face and see that it's misting.

Castan and I share a look. All of the anger, the regret evaporates between us. What's left behind is *fight or flight.*

Castan lifts his white tee, revealing the pale skin of his stomach stretched taut with muscle. He snatches a blade from his hip, fist around the hilt. If there were flames in his palms, there aren't anymore. His body is poise as a spring. I envy his instinct as I stand tall and useless in the grass.

Castan doesn't say a word to me, just barrages into the shroud of greenery in the direction of the noise. I wipe the sheen of rainwater from my face and follow him through the thicket of trees. Branches brush my cheeks; shrubs tickle my bare legs. As we plunge deeper into the forest, the sky vanishes. The air is dry here, unscathed by the moisture of the clouds. Shadows weave through the trees, massive, lurking sails.

Castan is catlike, graceful and noiseless, cutting through the forest floor. If the earth silences his movement, it amplifies mine. Every crunch and snap sends shivers cascading down my spine. Castan makes no comment. His elbow is bent, muscles tense beneath his skin. The knife flashes silver in his hand. It's not an unusually large weapon, but something tells me he doesn't require one. His veins are wires burning hot under his skin. They are a dull orange, burnt like the auburn color of fireworks. I'm almost certain he illuminates in the darkness.

The shadows fade from black to gray. The forest thins and we step out onto gravel. Gray and white stones crunch under the soles of my shoes. Fine mist sticks to my lashes, obscuring my vision.

Castan holds out an arm as if to stop me from pressing forward. My eyes absorb the sight before me. Even with this reserve of fearlessness bundled up inside my body, my feet are frozen in place. I'm minutely aware of the clouds of breath squeezing past my parted lips.

A brick building stretches across the earth before us. Plants sprout precariously around its foundations, vines creeping up the grooves of red and brown brick. Glass windows line one, two, three stories, reflecting the gray sky. On the second story, there is a gaping hole where a window used to be, and through it, a tree spills onto the cracked pavement of an old parking lot below. A spiral staircase shoots up from the ground to the third story. Foliage drapes from the metal railings like curtains. Whatever this place used to be, it's clear that it is no longer in use.

"I thought the Gens lived underground."

"They do," Castan looks past me. "The bunkers are usually beneath infrastructure of a sort." Something flashes in his irises, finite and bright as a falling star. He makes for the building. The air shifts, and the James in me begins to dread the worst: We could die here, and no one knows where we are.

"Hold on, Castan," he glances over his shoulder, "haven't you ever seen that show on Netflix? The one—Wait, do you even know what Netflix is?"

"I know what Netflix is," he quips. "Pelari aren't *that* uncultured."

"Well, anyway, there's this show, it's actually kind of terrifying, like this—"

"You talk when you're nervous," he cuts in. His eyes rake over my body, and I know he's replaying our argument in his mind. "You want to be independent? First lesson: don't talk so much." He pivots, movement soundless.

Timely of him to respect my wishes now. I clamp my teeth on my bottom lip and follow him down the overgrown path. Grass and wildflowers grow in the middle, so we walk in the grooves of ancient tire tracks. Weeds lick my ankles. I swipe a spindly-legged spider off my arm and crane my neck towards the building. I trace the towering chimney stacks, three fingers poking the sheet of gray clouds.

"I think it's an old factory."

"What makes you say that?" Castan asks, though by the lazy tone of his voice, he's not really listening to me.

I say more to myself, "It reminds me of the old paper mill back home."

"I've never known the Gens to live under a factory in the middle of the forest." Sarcasm laces his words. "But at this point," he sighs, exasperated, "nothing's impossible."

"But don't you find it odd that there's no sign, no logo, nothing?"

"I find all of it odd."

I study his profile, but we reach a door, and his expression transforms. He's all lines and angles, carved out of marble.

"Something had to of made that noise," he mutters under his breath. With his free hand, he clutches the tag around his throat. I don't think he knows he's doing it—it's a reflex, an instinct, just as much as the coil of his muscle and the dilation of his pupils are.

"A deer?" I suggest, taking in the black, soulless glass of the door. My skin prickles as if the windows are eyes tracking our movements.

Castan shrugs. "Stay behind me," he brandishes his knife, "and stop making your lip bleed."

My tongue skates across my lip—coppery liquid explodes on my taste buds. I wipe the blood away just as Castan eases open the door. The metal groans on rusted hinges. As he enters, Castan's head snaps left and right. The first thing I notice is the smell: smoke and sulfur.

Castan notices the same thing. He inhales, chest expanding. In a hushed voice, "It's not fresh."

That doesn't make me feel any better, but I keep this to myself.

My rods and cones adjust to the room. It's longer than it is wide, stretching about ten yards of flooring between walls. I take in the herd of chairs, some broken-legged, all knocked over on their sides. There's a circle desk resting in the middle of the floor, rising up to Castan's waist. He's already behind it, pawing through drawers and cabinets.

"A receptionist's desk," I say, stepping over chairs to get to him. The counter is smooth, albeit layered in inches of dust. "No one's been here in years." I reach to swipe a finger through the dust but think better of it. Perhaps people *are* living here, and this torn up waiting room is just to scare visitors away.

Castan nods, rising from a crouch by an empty filing cabinet. "Maybe, but there's nothing here." His emerald irises dart left and right, scanning for anything he missed.

A door directly behind the receptionist's desk leads us farther into the strange building. As the entrance diminishes from view, my throat constricts to the size of a pen. I think about all those horror movies Averil took me to see, all of those twisted, gory scenes where more than one character seemed to disappear or die. As we creep down a hallway striped with cracked walls and labeled doors, that's what this feels like. Except I'm not on the other side of a screen this time. I can't escape the dread filling the hollow cavities of my body like glue.

"Library, Break Room, Custodian," Castan has been reading the names of the doors as we pass them. "Bath House, Kitchens..."

"Unless Belarus suddenly became an English providence, these signs should be in Belarusian or Russian, right?"

"Maybe our Tiresias wasn't wrong after all," Castan replies, eyes flickering. He doesn't have to say anymore.

The hall ends with a set of double doors. *Labs*, reads the black and gold-lettered sign above the door frame. Castan grips his knife with a new purpose; a tiny flame pops out of the flesh in his empty hand.

He presses a shoulder to one of the doors—it swings open, and the putrid scent of sulfur and smoke slams my sense of smell.

I pull the collar of my tee shirt over my nose and gag. "That's awful."

And then I look past the threshold.

Castan's flame dies immediately in his hand. "I don't know what other substances are in the room," he explains, "so don't touch anything you don't have to." He steps past me, but all I can do is gape.

The floor is a sea of shattered glass and twisted metal. Stainless steel tables are overturned, upside down, and sideways. Beyond that, something catches my eye: Black as pitch, splattered like spray paint, is a stain.

"An explosion."

My feet are moving toward the far wall, my mind barely registering the ruin around me: chipped microscope slides, shattered lenses, steel cabinets, and test tubes—all in pieces. The ground shifts from glass to gray ash the closer I step to the wall. A lone microscope stands in a pond of ash, out of place in the wreckage.

Castan has a hand on his hip, head cocked. The tip of his knife hovers over the wall, tracing the blotch there. On his tiptoes, he can barely reach the top of it.

"I don't understand. If this place belonged to the Dentatas, then why hasn't Taxodium mentioned it before?"

"Would they?"

Castan turns, arms falling to his sides. His eyes blaze, and I think back to the first day at Tilia's when Castan rounded the corner, and I saw a human boy, not a dark soldier. "Of course. They found a bunker in Maine several months ago. It was abandoned, but every pelari heard about it. No one's likely to forget something like that."

I shuffle my feet in the ash. "How do you know Tax was the one who did this?" I gesture to the ruin around us. "You're assuming a lot here. This may not even be the Genocides'. It could just be a random facility, abandoned due to a 'lab explosion.'"

Castan's brow furrows, his lips press together. I recognize his thinking face, the way his eyes crinkle at the corners.

"If you leave out the pelari and focus on the facts," I continue, "then you'll see that there's nothing here but glass and metal and dust. No paper."

Castan's eyes scatter, and I know he sees what I do. Piles of ashes, here and there, as if someone made deliberate fires *after* the explosion. This was planned.

"Whoever was here last," Castan finishes my thought, "had something to hide."

Castan's eyes flicker and attach to something behind me. I look over my shoulder—and relax. There's nothing there.

"I'll be right back," urgency molds the angles of his body. "Don't move."

"What is it?" I spin, eyes following him to a different set of doors. *Stairs*, the sign reads above it.

"I just want to check the other levels really quick—" The rest of what he says is lost as the double doors swing shut behind him.

My attention falls to the microscope, how perfectly it stands in the ruin of the room. A rectangular patch of sunlight shines through a glass-less window. It disappears almost as soon as it came, and I remember the storm clouds above us.

While I wait for Castan, I go to the microscope. It's an old model, bulky and white. My own was similar, though thinner and compact. James gave it to me for Christmas last year, giddy and impressed with himself when I tore through the paper and saw what it was. I had to stop myself from demanding how he'd managed to pay for such an expensive item. What he wanted to hear was *thank you,* so that's what I told him instead.

An arrow of loss shoots down my spine. I hope James and I can find someplace nice to rebuild after all of this is over. I hope James can finally just relax.

I pick the microscope up by the stem. It's heavier than I anticipated—

"What's this?" I kneel, mind working to place the shape that was concealed under the microscope. Circular, metallic. And utterly rid of debris.

It's a latch. In the ground.

I examine the floor with a new perception and see the flaws in this patch of ground. The pattern is wrong. Where the ash around the explosion spots the level, this ash blankets it as if it were swept over to conceal something underneath.

I shift on the balls of my feet, jaw unhinging. Apprehension zips through my veins like icy water. Castan's name is in my arsenal—

Something wraps around my mouth. Chills flow down my spine; adrenaline spikes my blood. I struggle, but the grip is ruthless.

"Don't," cautions a familiar voice, "shout."

But I don't need to: the microscope crashes to the floor, releasing a barbaric wave of metal clashing metal.

Past
March 2020

The silence never seemed so… *silent*. For as long as Talan could remember, there was always noise. Jura was always bent over her desk, flipping pages of her textbook, tattooing spindly letters to notebook paper. When they were younger, she was always *doing* something. She possessed enough aspiration for both of them. Even in the pedes' world, before they enrolled in the North American Academy, Jura was doing something with herself. She participated in sports, won ribbons and trophies. Though material things had never mattered to his sister, they mattered to their parents—and that, Talan was positive, was all Jura had ever truly wanted. Just a smidge of their approval. Just a mote.

It wasn't the quiet of their dorm bothering him, not at all. For as long as Talan could remember, there was always *Jura*.

Even now, he saw her image, stained black against the morning sun. Her short-cropped hair hung in loose curls, framing her angular face. They were fraternal twins, but he sometimes saw his likeness laced into her being so clearly, it was like staring into a mirror. The same eyes, same straight-edged nose, same eyebrows, like smears of mud above their hazel-green eyes.

In his mind, she was wearing one of her political shirts. *Nevertheless She Persisted* shone out in silver-white letters. Talan never understood why she bothered with feminism—Jura never belonged with pedes. Some pelari went back to that life after the Academy, after their Essences were mastered. But Jura was climbing the ladder to be a Judge. She was going to *be* somebody.

Talan sat up in his bed. He rolled up the sleeves of his cotton shirt to his elbows, taking pleasure in the pain that followed the movement. Bruises, hideous black, blue and purple, overlapped each other all along his arms. The print of his fingers stained his flesh like spilled ink. Some were yellow, healing underneath all the new marks. Talan's eyes shuttered. Dani would find out—she always did—and he would have to sit through another one of her lectures about the difference between self-harm and grief.

Grief.

Jura's Ceremony had taken place only hours before. His parents hadn't come, though they sent their love. Callous, was what Vera and Nikolai Taylor were, but Talan couldn't think about his parents right now. Not when Jura had arrived in two pieces—Rex explained—head and body. His mind couldn't wrap around the idea of Jura, headless. Jura, bodiless. His mind couldn't wrap around anything—not the silence, the grief, the desire for revenge. None of it seemed real, and maybe, just *maybe*, if he ignored it long enough, it wouldn't be. Real.

Pelari did not mourn in public—emotions were saved for behind closed doors—but with each fallen soldier, there was a procession. Off-duty soldiers, instructors, students, and other staff would join the march from Allen Manor all the way through the training field and empty out into the land reserved for the serene Mausoleums. Those who died during active duty were laid to rest there. Honor meant everything. Grief meant nothing.

Talan heard the cries of the crowd's goodbyes, one for each fallen scout. *Bellator, vale! Bellator, vale! Bellator, vale! Bellatrix, vale! Bellatrix, vale!* The phrase was a bell, tolling and vibrating against his skull. He had heard it too many times this year. First with Calyx, his ashes flying in the wind. Then with the other scouts, their bodies wrapped in gray cloth and shoved in a shelf of one of the mausoleums.

But why did it have to be his *sister*? The Scouting Tragedies (as pelari were beginning to call them) were sporadic attacks, sometimes back-to-back, sometimes spread out over weeks and months. But they were always provoked by a murder, disturbance, or rumor about Gens. Jura had only signed up for a routine scouting party, one that didn't involve any anomalies. So why did she have to die?

Talan clenched his fists, realizing that his vision was blurry because there were tears in his eyes. Jura wasn't there to soothe him. Jura wasn't there at all—it was enough to make him want to throw up his heart.

A knock on his door caused Talan to flinch—noise, but not the sound he wished to hear. Jura, amiable Jura. Dependable and responsible, Jura. *That's* what he wanted to hear. *That's* who he wanted to walk through his doorway. It was late, and she would be coming in any minute with the idea of going out for dinner at the Dining Hall.

Instead, he got Finis.

Talan scrambled to tug his sleeves down, wincing at the dull, tender pain. He wasn't fast enough.

"What did you do to your arms?" Finis sat beside him, the bed sagging with the added weight. Without meaning to, Talan leaned against him. He quickly righted himself, flustered.

Talan shook his head, wiping the tears from his eyes. "It's nothing, Finis. Don't worry about it."

The older boy nudged his silver-rimmed glasses up the bridge of his nose. With ginger hands, Finis took one of Talan's arms and revealed the sleeve of bruises decorating his skin. Alone, Talan had always found the mix of black and blue strangely beautiful. But his thin arm propped against the black denim of Finis's thigh, suddenly made the bruises ugly and repulsive. Shameful.

"Why?" Finis, whose face was always a mask of careful calm, was surprised, uncertain. Talan thought he saw cracks in the gentle ice of Finis's expression. Self-harm, it seemed, was something Finis could not compute.

Talan pulled his arm away, shoving his sleeve down over his wrist. In that moment, he felt so alone—so terribly lost in a vast, open world, as if he were falling from the sky. There was nothing to tether to anymore. There was nothing to lose.

"You'll never understand, Finis. No one will. Kass has Lark, and Maggie has Kass. You have all your brothers and sisters, even if they are half a decade older than you. Maybe... maybe Castan would know what I mean, but he's not all there anymore, driven by some guilt no one can even begin to comprehend. But Jura," Talan's voice cracked, "Jura was me. My Essence may be strength, but Jura was always the stronger one. And now, and now..." Talan bowed his head into his hands. He didn't want to cry in front of Finis, but the tears were flowing now, spilling into the creases of his palms.

"I don't have to lose a sibling to understand you, Talan." And for some reason, Finis's admission only made Talan weep harder. *Lose a sibling. Lose a sibling. What a nasty way to think about my sister.*

But Finis wasn't done. "We met in Field Med. She was this close— this *close*—to getting her license."

"And now she never will," Talan commented, voice flat and muffled through his tear-soaked hands.

Finis changed the subject. "Your parents didn't come...?"

"No," Talan shot him a look through his fingers. "They only care about Jura's head if it's getting straight A's, not severed... severed from her body." Talan's face pinched, eyes clouded. He still couldn't quite grasp the idea of his sister in two pieces, rather than one.

Finis's energy sapped as he said, "I loved Jura."

Talan's sobs cut short, hands fell away from his face. A scowl twisted his features. "I *love* Jura, too. I want to see her at graduation, and I want to see her lips crack at the corners from smiling when she finally makes it to the Verum Courts. I want to tell her how proud I am of who she is. I want to rub it in her face when she has more wrinkles than me, and I want her to rub it in my face when she has more degrees than me—"

"Talan—" Finis interjected, expression laced with pain. But Talan wasn't finished.

"—I want her to grow up with me like she always has. I want her to grow old with me like she n-never will now," Talan inhaled, chest heaving. His throat was raw from speaking, from crying. "Some people have tattoos to tell them life will be okay. I have bruises." He was breathing rapidly, but he hardly noticed over the look in Finis's robin egg eyes. It was a lance to Talan's already aching heart, the way Finis's calm demure crumbled away into hundreds of pieces. It was like watching hail fall from the sky and repeatedly strike an unsuspecting child down below. With each chunk that fell, Finis became more and more vulnerable. Talan noted how his friend's chest barely moved beneath the frayed cotton of his shirt.

Talan didn't think about it—an instinct gripped him, and he dove for it.

He reached an arm out, cupping Finis's cheek. And he kissed him, their lips brushing just enough for Talan's brain to register: *He tastes like cinnamon.*

Finis jerked back, not angry, but confused. Talan studied his reaction, glasses sliding down his nose again. Lips slightly parted, Finis was breathing now, chest rising and falling, stretching the fabric of his tee shirt. The pink flush of skin was visible between the knit of cloth.

Finally, Finis met Talan's imploring gaze. "Dani... I thought you and her...?"

Talan choked. He'd never told anyone, not even Jura. He just shook his head. Finis seemed to understand. His shoulders relaxed, and he leaned back against the wall, hands folding in his lap. Talan watched the cogs in Finis's eyes turn, grind, comprehend. His own mind didn't know what to think.

Finis sat up, shuffling to his feet. Talan watched him from the bed, too drained to care about anything anymore. Exhaustion crept into his mind, stealing away all else. He laid his head on his pillow, curled his body like a cat. Finis stepped towards the door. Through the glare of his glasses, he glanced at Talan over his shoulder.

"We bury what we can and learn to live with what's left," he said. "But life *will* be okay. It will."

Castan

July 2020

"Hadley!" My body propels up a set of stairs, eyes scanning everything. The chipped blue paint of the walls, the rust of the railing, the gray clouds through the shattered window. The glimpse of black hair, like a waterfall, disappearing around the corner. I tuck my knife back into the waistband of my shorts.

I take a sharp turn, dash up the steps two at a time. The muscles in my legs ache, the familiar sensation of running up stairs flooding my memory. I never used the elevator—Numen forbade it, said stairs would make us stronger, powerful. Elevators were for the dead, dying, and elderly.

"Hadley!" I call again. "Hadley, it's okay. I won't let them hurt you anymore. I can help—"

I fling open the doors at the top of the stairwell. There are no walls to carve this level into rooms. It is all one, vast space of... cribs? I weave through the rows of thin white mattresses, metal frames, searching. Glass glitters along the brick walls where the windows shattered.

"Hadley!" My attention catches on the tree spilling through the window at the far end of the building. My legs move before my brain thinks. I dash through the neat rows of bed frames, dirty mattresses, and glass.

"Hadley, wait!" I disappear under an umbrella of leaves and branches, hunting for the window. My palms find the window ledge, concrete. I peer out the window, through the tangle of silver-green leaves. Rain beats through the branches, damp against my skin.

"Hadley!" My voice cracks, gravel and vegetation all that I can see. A voice hisses in the back of my head, *She was never here, Castan. Your sister is lost.*

I stagger backward, out of the foliage, clutching my head. Is this what the disease does to you? Hallucinations? My legs feel like water, weak and formidable. I raise my hands to my face, gaping at the lines and creases there. A thought pops into my head—a spurt of fire flares in my palms. I focus. Urge the little orange flecks to grow. *Grow.*

They don't.

"No," I breathe, "it's not supposed to happen so soon, is it? It's not—"

There's a clatter, a clash similar to the one Corolla and I heard in the forest earlier.

"Shit." *Corolla.* I left her alone.

And then I am sprinting, jumping around crib frames, cutting across the columns. Through the first set of doors. Down the steps. Thank God for all Numen's training, or I would have tripped down the flight of stairs and broken my neck. I yank the knife from my hip, burst through the doors—

Through the broken equipment, is Corolla, squirming against a black uniform. A wisp of orange wrestles her back.

"Kassandra?" My weapon drops to my side. Kass turns, smirking, even though Corolla is panicking against her slight frame. "Let her go—What are you doing here? *How* did you get here?"

Kass releases Corolla, and she falls to the ash-layered floor, coughing. "What the hell?" Corolla gasps, glaring at Kass. I extend an arm to her, though I'm staring at Kass. She covers her mouth as if stifling laughter. Knowing Kass, she probably is. Beside me, Corolla brushes her body, sending a spray of ash into the air. I clear my throat.

"Kass."

Her azure eyes flit to mine, hand dropping from her mouth to her hip. She's so pale, each freckle along her nose is visible from where I stand. She cocks an amber eyebrow.

"There's a tracker in your geometer. That's how I found you. When Maggie came back to the NA for instructions to deliver to you, she was incredibly suggestive about your new geometer and incredibly correct." Kass reels on me, "You were supposed to come straight back to Tax!" Even though she's yelling, her voice barely wavers over a harsh whisper.

I shrug, "I didn't." I don't have an excuse. "I acted on instinct."

Kass gives me a disbelieving look. "You went off alone. With precious cargo," she gestures to Corolla. "If that's your instinct, then it's shit."

I fold my arms across my chest. "In my defense, Corolla was supposed to stay in Wales."

Kass shoots me an exasperated look. "I don't even want to know *why* you were in Wales. Castan, geometers aren't for flitting around like some sixteen-year-old with his first car."

"I'm not—"

"Oh my god!" Corolla yells. "Just shut up!"

I pivot, about to say something about earlier, how she is the last person to be telling me to quit arguing, but I stop. Every hair on my body stands on end when I see what she's done. The floor, which was a blanket of gray ash seconds ago, is now a gaping, cylindrical hole in the ground.

The style is so similar…

"Neither of you is very observant." Corolla crouches down by the open latch and swings her legs into the pit.

"Corolla, wait," I come up to her. "You can't go down there first. You're—"

"Precious cargo?" Her whiskey eyes slide over Kass. "Yeah, I know. Damn you both." She drops into the black shadows.

"Corolla!" Panicked, frustrated, and slightly discouraged, I follow her descent. My feet find solid rungs.

"Well," Kass theorizes, "maybe I misjudged her."

As my vision levels with the ashen floor, I shoot Kass a look. "I think we all did." Below me, Corolla drops, feet thudding against solid ground. Seconds later, I touch down on what feels like concrete. I wouldn't be surprised. Darkness envelops us, the light from above cut from view as Kass wriggles her way down.

"Make a flame." Corolla's tone is jagged around the edges. I don't have time to argue with her.

Relief washes over me: I manage two quarter-sized flames. The yellow-orange glow bounces off concrete walls. Ahead of us, there appears to be an opening.

Kass resounds behind us. "If the Gens didn't know we were here before," she grumbles, "they do now."

"I don't think this bunker is currently occupied," I say, eyes scanning the cracked walls, hollow shadows. Corolla is already pressing forward. I follow, cursing myself for not leaving the cottage first before I jumped to Belarus. Cursing myself for being *predictable*, even to Corolla.

Kass falls into rhythm beside me. "Is that all the light you're giving us?"

"We don't need anymore," I reply, hoping I'm right. "How is everything back at the Academy? Since Hong Kong, I mean."

Kass's atmosphere changes immediately. Her voice is plated with sobriety as she says, "I don't know where to begin. Kat and Ashten are dead, bodies in mausoleums. There was an honorary Ceremony for what happened in Hong Kong. Classes have been canceled, and students are now only required to train for combat instead. We lost a lot of the Guard with the fall of the Asian Academy. Even with the Reserve, I don't know if our forces are large enough." Kass pauses to catch her breath. "And then there are the ambassadors. One from almost every Academy is coming to a conference with Major Rex on behalf of the Board. I don't know why the Majors don't just call a

Board meeting. Too scared to leave their Academies, I think. Afraid of which one may be bombarded next."

"The Verum Courts?" Kass knows I mean Talan's parents, so she answers my question as such.

"Nikolai is dead, and Vera was found unconscious in his arms. She had a hepa mask over her face, but... No one's quite sure how Vera managed to survive the chemical toxins the Gens pumped into the Courthouse. She's the only Judge who lived. She's a little... shell-shocked, I guess is the word for it. Talan won't go see her because—"

"—of Jura," I cut in, "Yeah, I know." My eyes watch Corolla. She hovers on the border of my light and the depthless shadows ahead. Her arms hang limply at her sides, swaying with her gait. Not once has she turned to look at me.

Kass ducks her head, "He still blames them for her death. I don't think he even cares that his father is dead, and his mother may as well be, she's so fucked up in the head."

"Maybe he does, maybe he doesn't. Family doesn't necessarily mean allegiance."

The tunnel ends. The light from my palms reveals a more massive pit than the one we crawled down to get here. It's wider around than the silos at the Academy, though just as tall, I imagine. Concrete walls, oxygen scrubbers... the place screams *Genocides*. The air is so dense and humid, sweat trickles down my brow in large droplets. I thought I left this climate behind when Corolla and I jumped from Yazd this morning.

"There's a grate over here," Corolla calls from the ledge, voice flat. "Looks like it could go down." Kass and I meet Corolla where the cement floor shifts to slotted metal. I don't know what she means until my eyes catch sight of the metal grate and the lever by its side.

"I think you're right, Vel," Kass chimes in. I wonder how much it hurt her to say that. To say Calyx's name. We step onto the grate, and Kass slams the lever down. It groans, jolts, and begins its descent. The cogs in the wall *click-clack* as we go farther down. We pass several levels of ledges, wide enough to be called walkways. They seem to round the circumference of the bunker, dull metal doors here and there. Letters and numbers are painted on the door faces. I scan the entries nearest the platform as we descend. A2, B1, C3, D1. The grate stops at D, apparently the ground level.

Kass steps off first, head craning this way and that, hands planted firmly on her hips. I see why Calyx loved her—she's brash and callous and cynical... and he wasn't. He always teetered towards the things he didn't understand, and Kassandra was perhaps the biggest enigma of them all.

"It's a prison."

"Yeah." I lower my gaze to the subtle grooves of the ground, worn from use. The Complex was like that too, grooves flattened smooth from generations of treading. Corolla, some distance from us, coughs into her elbow.

Kass turns, and I meet her steady gaze.

"And Tilia? Every *Humanitas* has been canceled, not even postponed."

I shine a light on the rough concrete walls. "She's recovering. Lost a lot of hearts, Umar said."

"I'm thoroughly assured with the gardener's diagnosis," Kass scoffs. She peers behind one of the gaping steel doors.

"Umar's good for more than just gardening. He keeps Til—"

"What happens if Tilia doesn't recover?" Her voice climbs higher and higher. "We'll lose all of the Pyrus-made Holds and then who will filter hearts? If Tax loses that... Then what's to keep the Gens from slipping through the cracks of Taxodium?"

"It won't come to that." My gaze slides past Kass to Corolla. Her back is to us, but that doesn't mean she isn't listening. "And if it did, we would find the traitors the same way Tyto Alba did." At the mention of her father's name, Corolla's back straightens. I press farther into the darkness, the glow from my hands forcing the shadows back.

"I don't think there's anyone here," Kass opens one of the cell doors. "This is empty." Her voice shifts, "Wait. Castan, come closer." I jog over to Kass, her knuckles white as she clenches the door handle. I poke an arm into the cell. It illuminates orange-yellow like candlelight.

"Is that...?" Kass says, then stops. Wiping sweat from my brow, I take several more tentative steps into the room towards the dark pile on the ground. Kass and Corolla breathe softly at the cell entrance.

If it was humid outside the cell, it's a furnace in here. The air clings to my skin, bathing my body in sweat. I inhale and cough on something putrid in the air. It smells like feces and decay. I cover my nose with an arm and creep closer. I use a foot to poke the pile at my feet.

It groans, barely audible.

"I think it's a person," I call through my drenched arm. Footsteps tap the silence behind me—Corolla's because Kass only ever wears her Caeli boots. They choke on the scent too, Corolla soprano to Kass's alto.

I kneel, killing the pathetic flame in one hand. I touch the crumpled fabric, pulling it back carefully—

"It's a... man?" I picture Kass cocking her head as she says it, unsure. I can't really tell either. A pile of bronze skin, bones poking flesh. Gaunt face, hollowed eye and a stained eyepatch. Scruffy, balding hair. Near his—I'm assuming it's a man—head, are two plastic dishes, like the kind you buy for dogs. One crusted white where water evaporated, and the other edged with what looks like hardened bacon grease.

"It is a man," Corolla observes. She kneels beside me, glued to the specimen before us. The sand-colored eyepatch wraps around his head, beaded with sweat. I note the minute rise and fall of his chest. Sweat shows through the threadbare cotton of his olive-green tee shirt, torn in some places and shredded along the hem in others. His abdomen is layered with signs of torture. Bruises, cuts, scrapes, and scars.

Now I am confident the Gens were here.

Kass kneels now too, jabbing gentle fingers into his neck. "He's got a pulse." Her head lowers a degree. "What's in his hand?" My attention drags from the scars lining his bronze skin to the pad of yellow paper clutched between his cracked and bleeding hands. Three words scrawled in bloodred letters, lurch out at me:

Jon Xabier Dentata

"Is that…?" Kass meets my eyes, wide with realization. Out of the corner of my eye, Corolla extends a hand towards the man's face. I think Corolla strokes his cheek, but then Kass shoots to her feet, incredulous, and I'm just as charged as she is. The flame in my palm burns brighter.

"Numen," I breathe. "*How?*"

Kass scrapes back the loose hairs around her forehead. She paces, says the very thing screaming in my mind right now, "What's going—"

"This is my uncle," Corolla's voice, no more than a whisper, cuts in. "This is Luca Alba."

Past
March 2020

The dorm room reeked of lavender. The wispy clouds of incense were meant to relax Castan's nerves, though it didn't seem to be having that effect. He shifted on his cushion. Júlia imagined his gaze fixed on her. He would see her alpine face submerged in candlelight and shadows. She clamped her eyes tighter in concentration, palms face up on the low coffee table between them. Across her lips, ruby-red lipstick was painted perfectly in the shape of her mouth.

Finally, unable to ignore his attention, she opened her eyes.

"I don't think we're going to find him." She noted the way she said *we*, rather than *I* or *you*. She noted the way his throat bobbed as if he were bracing himself for defeat.

"Why not?" Castan had this terrible habit of not *letting go*.

Júlia cast her eyes to the table. "I think it's because he... died too far away." She could probably locate Calyx's spirit if they ventured to the Iranian street where he was attacked, or the gardener's house, where he died. She didn't say this. She was exhausted from his frequent night sessions. She was exhausted from his disappointment.

And I don't enjoy speaking to the dead that I knew, either. It was a pact she had made with herself a year ago when her Essence came through. Such power required limitations. There was something almost obsessive, almost dangerous about her ability to communicate with the dead. Though she hadn't known very many spirits by name when she created her pact, she definitely knew souls now. *First Calyx, then Jura...* Júlia just wanted to move on.

"Castan." His expression had gone to stone; he had sucked back into himself. Calling his name did not remedy this appearance. He was lost in thought, she knew, and it dogged on her own soul to see him like this.

"Let's take a break." Instead of waiting for his approval, she sprang to her feet.

His body tensed as she walked around the table, sensing her crouching behind his back. Her hand found its way to his shoulder. He placed his own on top of hers.

"I'm not ready." His voice was a croak, dry and stretched thin with emotion. Once, he would have tried to mask his grief. She supposed he couldn't any longer because it had consumed him. Kassandra was almost as bad. Except where Castan *felt*, Kass *suppressed*. Júlia knew which strategy worked better, and it was neither of them. What her friends needed was to communicate and be open, not live in the past or pretend it never happened.

"I know." And she did. She knew he wouldn't be ready to move on for some time. But perhaps she could be his catalyst. Matrona knew she had been trying to make him better for weeks. They all had been, in their own way. Maybe this could be hers.

With little effort, she freed her hand from his grip. She bent down to whisper in his ear, "Let's go to bed." He seemed to sit up straighter at the proposition, and her enticing fingers crept down the front of his shirt. She felt his heart racing and wondered if tonight would be his first time. Plenty of girls certainly asked about him. *Obscure*, they called him, but what they meant was *sexual*.

Júlia pulled away from him, her touch skating across his skin in a taunting manner. She sauntered towards her bedroom, thankful that her roommate, Dani, was out for the evening.

One, two, thr—

Castan stood, his figure black against the harsh glow of candles. Júlia drank in the sight of him—broad shoulders, fabric taut over his back, biceps straining against the sleeves of his shirt.

"What are you staring at?" Júlia knew he'd turned to look at her. Her eyes flitted from his body to the half-grin on his face. It had been so long since he'd smiled, she was beginning to think he never would again.

Wait till I tell Dani and Talan.

"Are you coming?" She inched backward some more just as he took several steps forward. She stopped, bumping up against the door frame. He caught her there, just as she wanted. His hands dug into her thick troves of black hair. His lips devoured her own. He tasted like coffee and the bland chemicals of her lipstick. He rocked into her pelvis, moaning against her mouth. Júlia grinned with satisfaction.

Castan pulled away, stealing her breath. She said nothing, only offered him a wry look and took his hand. His lips were brushed red, cheeks flaming. His eyes shone with something dark, something curious and desirous. It was all the affirmation Júlia required.

Lavender may not work but sex might. It was a selfish thought, but wasn't that look in his eyes the very essence of selfishness? He asked so much of her, to try and locate Calyx's spirit, the very least he could do was... *this*.

Castan caught her body once more, nails digging into the flesh of her hips, nudging her backward. For a moment, Júlia forgot about them all—about Jura and Calyx, about Talan and Dani, Maggie and Finis.

Kass. In a world strung up on pain and misery, any amount of pleasure was a gift.

They disappeared into the shadows of her room and the silky sheets of her bed.

Corolla
July 2020

"He's my uncle." The words echo off the barren walls, slicing through the shadows. Castan's flame flickers as he and Kass fall into stunned silence.

And then my hands are grabbing for that threadbare shirt. Body temperature skin. Fingers dancing along fine cuts and bruises. Luca groans, a faint whisper of a sound. Thoughts, erratic: *Ihavetohelphim.Ihavetohelp.*

All of this happens in a heartbeat.

Castan reaches for me, hooking gentle fingers around my wrist. I stop, a bunch of olive-colored cotton scrunched between my fists. Even though he appears small, I can't lift Luca.

A hiss in the back of my mind, *Dead bodies are heavier than live ones.*

"Corolla," Castan's voice tangles with the looming shadows. It takes effort to sort out the difference between the two.

"My mother loved him." I choke on a strange cocktail of emotion. I haven't forgotten what it was like to be in Adian's skin, to feel what she felt when she met my father's family. The way Adian's nerves fell away and her soul embraced the Albas. I don't know if she felt it, but I did, how she attached a piece of herself to each of them. Maurizio, Giovanni, Luca, Pasquale, Orsino... Even Reino.

Adian was whole again. And if I can preserve any piece of the Albas, then I can preserve her too.

The crumpled pile of olive, bronze, and black blurs before me. My eyes dart to Castan's fingers pinched around my wrist. *Let go of me.* But I can't speak.

In the quiet, Kass huffs, "We need to get out of here. If Numen's name is on that list," my gaze flashes over the yellow notepad, "then who knows what kind of hidden security measures we've triggered just by being here."

My torso twists, teeth flashing, "We can't *leave* him."

Kass softens, "I didn't say that, but we need to *go*."

Castan's grip vanishes. "Kass is right. It's not safe here. It never was." His irises blaze brighter than the candle wick flame in his palm.

"How are we supposed to get Alba out of here?" Kass shifts in the darkness, orange braid gleaming. "Geometers aren't meant for altereds. He's barely conscious."

I relax my muscles, the fabric slipping through my fingers. Luca doesn't react to anything. He just lays there, head propped on a thin arm. The bones in his wrist and elbow jut from his skin, so many angles.

"We have to risk it."

Castan rises, double flames illuminating the concrete cell. "I agree with Corolla. It would be a bigger risk to leave him here and then send for reinforcements. Clearly, he's worth something to the Gens, buried so far in the ground."

Kass finishes his thought, "After all these years, alive." Her head snaps up. "Okay, so you fix him to your back, Castan. Corolla and I will jump together."

Castan nods, running a thumb across his lips. The fire casts strange shadows in the hollows of his face.

"Take the notepad," Castan instructs, though Kass is already plucking it from Luca's weak grip.

"Rex will shit her pants when she sees this," Kass breathes, flipping through the yellow pages. "Jon Xabier Dentata."

I swear, Castan shudders, but it's too dark and humid to tell. I move out of his way as he crouches down beside Luca. In a delicate manner, he wraps one of Luca's arms around his neck. I help Luca find his feet. His body is weak, knees folding like a lawn chair. Castan grunts, beads of sweat streaming down his hairline. Kass is too absorbed in the notepad to notice our struggles. We move out of the cell, clumsy in the sparse light of Castan's single flame.

"This should be enough space to jump," Castan exhales. He flashes a half-grin. "Not exactly a feather, is he?"

"Castan," Kass saunters out of the shadows, brows pinched. "The only name on these pages is Jon Dentata. What do you think it means?"

Castan shrugs with the shoulder Luca isn't slumped against. "I don't know, but could you help with this?"

Kass shoves the notepad in my hands and assists Castan. She flails with Luca's limbs.

"Careful!" I hiss, suddenly conscious that the Gens could be above us right now. They could be descending the ladder this very moment.

"Too bad we don't have rope," Kass mutters. "Then it'd be just like rucking." She aligns Luca's legs directly behind Castan's.

"Hold these," with a flick of his head, Castan motions to the arms around his neck, "so I can keep a flame going."

With one hand, Kass grips Luca's wrists at the base of Castan's throat. With the other, she pulls out her geometer just as Castan is punching buttons on his. The twin lights from their screens glow white in the orange-tinted darkness.

"Training field is the only place with 'comfortable parameters.'"

Castan sighs. "After all the lessons Commander Murphy gave us with geometer tactics, the training field is the only internal Tax coordinate I have memorized."

"East?" Kass glances up from her screen.

"West."

The drone of their conversation fades away as my eyes adjust to the handwriting between my fingers. In the cell, I thought the ink was crimson. Without Castan's light looming directly overhead, it's difficult to tell.

Jon Xabier Dentata

I flip the pages, confirming what Kass has already noted. It's the only name on the paper, along with dates and times. The most recent is July 3rd, 2020, at times 03:42 AM and 10:03 AM.

It's a log.

The orange firelight is snuffed out, drenching the cylindrical space in darkness, spare for the white glow of Kass's geometer. She clamps onto my forearm. "Time to go." Kass tugs me several paces, more towards the center of the area, I assume.

"Hold tight to that notepad." We stand back-to-back, heads touching. I hug the notepad closer to my chest, gaze darting around the bunker. It's so dark now, I can't make out the grate that lowered us down here. Without Castan's fire, the shadows are suffocating. The darkness seems to be gathering. It flows all around us, impenetrable, thickening. Irrational fear strikes my heart, the same way crashing waves paralyze me. I am drowning in darkness, just as I would drown in the vast, open waters of the ocean. Is that really so irrational? To be afraid to die? A tingle cascades from the top of my head to the ends of my toes.

The geometer beeps, the only sound in the eerie silence. My breath catches in my throat. I squint at the curtain of ebony as the lilac veil blooms around us.

"Quit squirming," Kass snaps, annoyed. "You're worse than my little brother."

I freeze, suddenly remembering something.

Lola. Amidst the crackle of flames and devastation as my home came crashing to its knees, I lost sight of Lola in the shadows.

My knees buckle, scraping green turf. For a delusional moment, I think I'm back at Forrest High, standing on the football field. But this field is far more extensive, a green sea in the evening sun. Brownstone snakes around the perimeter, turrets poking the four corners. A breeze picks up my stray hair. I inhale the fresh air—I didn't realize how humid the bunker was until I tasted the cool wind caressing my cheeks.

"Get up," Kass brushes imaginary dirt from her black sleeves. "And welcome to Taxodium!" Her words turn sour. I stand, the notepad still gripped furiously in my hand. I squint at the mass of people trickling onto the field through an archway in the brownstone border. I recognize their black uniforms. There's a clump of people about twenty yards away. The crowd parts and a yellow-skeleton stretcher plunges into the gathering.

Luca.

Kass takes the notepad, but I barely notice. She vanishes from my vision as I stumble towards the black uniforms. Voices, excited and alarmed, snag my awareness.

"…finally got someone back…"

"The Gens spared his life…"

"Valeria and the disgraced Major Alba will want to see their brother…"

"Excuse me." I brush past the chattering bodies, staggering against jutting elbows and precarious body parts. "Excuse me."

I shove past the crowd until I practically trip into the clearing. The first thing I see is Luca, tucked in the stretcher, his consciousness unchanged from the bunker. A small, mousy-haired woman sits at the foot of the cot, a medical kit sprawled across on Luca's lap. The woman clenches and unclenches gloved hands and barks a series of commands. Some of the people in black and brown grip the sides of the stretcher. I watch, entranced, as they cart my uncle away, past the stone archway.

My uncle.

Where's James?

The second thing I notice is Castan. With the back of his hand, he swipes the sweat from his brow. A man, broad chest and thick biceps, crosses his arms. His blonde hair is shaved close to his skull, and without fully knowing, I conclude that he's involved in Taxodium's armed forces. The man, who also fashions the black and brown uniform, nods his head while Castan speaks. I can't make out what he says—not with all the voices buzzing around me—but from the subtle shock on the man's face, I know Castan is telling him about how we found Luca Alba.

And then I am aware of the buzzing ending abruptly and leaving the air humming with silence. My eyes dart from the guarded faces of the crowd to Castan. He's turned, the military man by his side. Everyone seems fixed on something behind me—

"Ms. Vel," a firm voice cracks through the silence. As I pivot, I take in the flashing gazes around me. It occurs to me that these people all know who I am. Have faith in me, even. Though the majority of them aren't aware of the truth.

Volga.

I blink, my attention capturing white-spiked hair, steel-gray eyes, and an expression so cold I briefly wish to be back in that humid bunker. Without exactly knowing how, a name surfaces in the pathways of my mind.

"Major Rex." Her piercing gaze only rests on me a moment longer. She sidesteps around me, slate-gray pantsuit carrying her to Castan and the blonde, muscular man.

"Major Rex," the man does some kind of salute, three of his fingers over his heart.

"Commander." But the Major's gaze slides past the commander and lands on Castan.

"My office," her icy tone is edged with controlled fury, "now."

Castan's expression betrays nothing. Together, the two exit the field, leaving behind a gawking, hissing crowd and one, shuddering pedes.

"Corolla!"

That voice... Relief floods my bones. My hands begin tingling. James struts across the clearing, blonde head bobbing. Before I can think, I close the distance between us, propelling into his familiar arms.

"Oof." I think I've knocked the wind out of him, but then he buries his face in the crook of my neck, murmuring, "You're safe."

I don't care if we have an audience, and I don't care if I'm covered in weeks' worth of grime. James is okay. James is okay, and that's all I could ever want.

Over his shoulder, my eyes crack. I glimpse Castan, disappearing around a bend. And despite it all—despite James's arms around me, despite the wholesomeness quaking throughout my body—my heart fractures a degree.

Laila came for me an hour later, raven hair tucked behind each ear. I knew what she was going to say, and I dreaded it.

"Major Rex would like to speak to you, Corolla." Laila whisked me from Aercus House—James's new residency—up the gentle slope and into Allen Manor.

Now, I follow her through a set of French doors, into an open room. Wood-panels line the walls like an exoskeleton. The guards posted by the main doors surprise me for a moment, then I remember where I am, who these people are, and what we are facing together. Their brown armor is lighter than I remember on the other uniforms, silver and bronze bands around their right biceps.

My eyes dart from the stony expressions of the guards to the vast room. Between each window, is a plant, leaves curled brown with decay. Electric candles shine in each window, too many to count. A golden chandelier drips from the ceiling, drawing my attention to a terrace overseeing the entire room. Alabaster and wood, the balcony does not disrupt the archaic persona of the room. I can just barely make out the tip of a chair. It reminds more of seats in opera houses than a throne.

Laila disappears down a short hallway, and I follow her up a flight of dark wood stairs, so polished, they shine. My palm runs along the smooth, worn banister. *How many times did Tyto or Adian, or even Calyx touch this same banister?*

"Laila?" She hasn't said much during the majority of our plight, but the silence isn't unfriendly either. It's just... there.

"Hmm?" We tread down another stretch of hall. Through a glass door, I glimpse a second set of stairs. These ones are lined in steel and iron. I get the feeling they lead someplace important. I scrape my attention back to Laila.

"James said you were a friend of Adian's," the woman's back goes taut, "but I was wondering... I mean, were you very close with her?"

Laila halts. Over her shoulder, are white walls, drooping plants, and what appears to be another right turn down a hallway.

Laila faces me, tossing her locks over a shoulder. In her crimson jumper, she appears almost childlike. But her expression adds fifty years.

"Adian and I were roommates," Laila says, voice light. "We lived in Aurum House." Laila palms her forehead, eyelids fluttering. For a moment, I fear I've made her cry.

"We were like cousins," she shrugs. "I knew about her secret relationship with Tyto before anyone else because that's just how we were. I... I'm sorry, Corolla," she glances up, laughter hissing through her teeth. "Everyone's adolescence is complicated, but those years with Adian were something of a different variety. I could tell you more about it later if you'd like?"

I nod, maybe over-eager. "Yes, please."

Laila grins, shoulders relaxing. She touches pale fingers to my shoulder before continuing our trek through this maze to the Major.

The next hall manages to take my breath away. I ignore the impending doom twisting in my gut and marvel at the collection of oil paintings garnishing the entire stretch of hall. We pass a portrait bearing a striking resemblance to the Major, reminding me all too soon what's waiting for me behind the French doors at the end of the hall. Even on canvas, Rex is all angles, though her spiked hair is just beginning to streak with white. *Neva Rex*, reads the golden engraved plaque.

Beside her portrait, is a blank space of alabaster wall. As much as my eyes want to skip over it and admire the rows and columns of previous Majors, I am drawn to that empty area.

I'm all too aware of Laila's urging presence, and the two guards posted outside the French doors. I've heard what pelari call Tyto: the disgraced Major Alba. Disgraced. I can't muster the words into life.

This was my father's place.

"Corolla," Laila calls me back to the present. I blink, the afterimage of that empty space glaring against my eyelids. I find myself at the end of the Gallery Hall. Laila beckons to a downy-cushioned bench between two houseplants. I sit, hands folding in my lap, as Laila waves a goodbye.

"The guards will escort you out if you think you'll get lost," she adds over her shoulder. I glue my attention to the plant at my shoulder. The spear-shaped leaf is spotted with holes, crisp brown where the cells have already died. My hands start tingling, itching for something. For yarn or a pen, so I can document things I already know. Like how much I hurt James. Or why Adian was murdered. My nerves clatter like cowbells in the pit of my stomach. Can the guards hear it? Averil flashes through my mind—Where is he right now? What is he doing?

One of the doors yawns wide, and I lurch to my feet.

"Castan." The word is more a question than a statement. He glances at me with half-lidded emeralds. Seeing him in the same grass and dirt-stained clothes reminds me how grateful I am to be grime-free. Laila had fresh garments delivered to Aercus while James and I feasted on his famous lasagna. Besides the strange setting, it all felt somewhat ordinary.

"Hey, Corolla." He ducks his head once more. "Don't forget to salute." Before I can utter another word, he is gone.

What happened to him in there?

One of the guards huffs, "Major Rex is waiting." I tear my gaze from the Gallery Hall to the gaping glass-paneled doors. Dread soaks through my flesh, piercing my heart.

For James, I tell myself. *For James.*

I step through the door, the cream-colored, satin curtain licking my ankles.

The low hum of voices tickles my ears. Major Rex perches behind an enormous mahogany desk, straightening papers. The same man I saw with Castan on the training field murmurs something to her, expression pensive. There is another man, in a strange tailored suit, leaning against the bookshelf along the wall. He has short-cropped hazelnut hair, and a face that reminds me of a snapping turtle.

I stop in the center of the room, two black-cushioned armchairs inches away. But I don't sit.

Rex catches me in the corner of her eye, though something tells me she knew I was here as soon as I walked into Allen Manor. The conversation dies away immediately, but the tension in the air remains the same. The blonde man runs a hand down his mouth, expression pinched. I swallow, meeting the Major's intense gaze.

"Corolla," she welcomes, voice strained, "please sit."

As I occupy one of the armchairs, I think about what Castan said about saluting. My arms are frozen at my side, nerves on edge.

C'mon, Corolla! How many job interviews have you braced yourself for? This is the same.

But it isn't. Not by a long shot. This is my life in Taxodium's desperate hands.

Rex doesn't bat an eye as she says, "Commander Murphy, head of the Guard, and Ramsey, Chief of Intelligence, were just leaving us. Thank you, gentlemen." The two men place three fingers over their hearts and slink out of the room, Commander Murphy maybe a little hesitantly. The doors *click* behind them, glass rattling in their panes.

Major Rex clears her throat, shoving a stack of paper to the corner of her desk. Through the window behind her, the wall of trees surrounding the Academy is a silhouette against the slate sky.

"I would like to express my gratitude, in regard to your agreement to assist Taxodium in this war against the Genocides."

I drop her gaze, unsure of what to say. "Well, thank you for the opportunity, I guess." My skin prickles with heat. It's not about the money, but Rex must think that's the only reason why I'm doing this, why I'm risking my life for a group of strange, extraordinary people.

"But there are some things I would like to ask you." She folds wrinkled hands atop her desk. I dare to gaze at her pursed lips. "I suppose the first round of questions pertains to Luca Alba. How did you know it was him?"

"Well…" I formulate my words quickly, "Tilia showed me one of Adian's memories—it was the first time she met the Albas. I recognized Luca, though he's… thinner now."

170

"He is a lot of things now," the Major practically growls. "But he may recover in Rainier Hospital. Another thing nagging my mind: it's quite convenient that Tilia should share a memory with Luca Alba tangled within it." Rex's voice is one of frightening calm.

"I don't know how that happened," I admit. "The way Umar described Tilia was that she's like a fire, right? So after Hong Kong, maybe all the lost sparks opened up a subliminal channel inside of her?" I refrain from wringing my hands, convinced the Major will take it as a sign that I'm lying. What about, I couldn't say, but she makes me feel like I've done something wrong. And if *I* am more or less innocent, I can't imagine what she said to Castan.

The Major seems to consider what I've said. Her gaze flashes over the stack of papers on her desk, then back to me. *Decision* glints in her ice-blue eyes. The atmosphere shifts.

"Your life at Taxodium, I can assure you, will be less precarious than your journey here. I must apologize, on behalf of my staff and students, for your mistreatment."

"No, I wasn't—"

"With that being said," Rex raises her voice to be heard, "there are only a handful of people who know the truth about your presence on campus. Your Regent will introduce you to them later, but you must— *must*—ensure the secrecy of this task. I can't control your fate if the entire Academy knows you are volga."

I nod, swallowing a dose of anxiety.

Rex continues, "Since the devastation of the Asian Academy, I have canceled classes. My students will only be focusing on combative skills and Essence training. Now, I don't expect you to pretend you have an Essence on the field, and frankly, my students will be too preoccupied with lessons to notice your absence from such classes. However, I do expect you to take part in Defensive Training."

Again, I nod. I want to learn how to fight. After Phage and Lola, I *need* to know how.

"Your uncle, James, may live in Aercus House—for now—but you will live in Argenti with your Regent. I want you to be a visible presence on campus, though not necessarily an active one."

"Okay."

"One last thing, before you may be dismissed." A desk drawer slides and Rex pushes a slip of paper across her desk towards me. I lean forward to read it.

"No," I shake my head, eyes bulging from my skull. "This is too much money—"

"Consider it an extension of my sincerest apologies. In your agreement to help end this blight, you are doing something remarkable, Corolla."

The dread gnawing the lining of my stomach ceases: A drop of humanity sparks her otherwise firm tone.

"Trading your life for money is wrong. Corolla—"

"James." There are so many unspoken words in the response, my uncle ducks his head with the weight of it. Around us, Aercus House flares with yellow lamplight, casting soft shadows around the living room. James holds my steady gaze, soft blues swaying.

"Just let me do this. Please." *For you.*

He exhales, massaging the bridge of his nose. "I don't have much of a choice, do I? I promised your mother that I'd keep you safe, but... What can one man do that an entire organization can't?"

I don't entirely know what James is rambling about, but I sense the acceptance settling in the many lines of his face.

He spreads his arms, and I tuck myself within them, grateful.

James murmurs against my skull, "You're making the world a better place, Corolla."

For you.

Past
March 2020

Maggie tightened her ponytail, feeling the familiar tug of hair and scalp. She crossed her arms, a thin manila folder pinched between her fingers. Above, the white lights flickered, fast enough that most people probably wouldn't notice. *Especially Intelligence,* Maggie smirked. *The way they barrel down these corridors, they wouldn't notice if the ceiling were falling on top of them.*

It was after hours now, all TIs retired to their bunks in the Barracks or their homes off-campus. Maggie glanced over her shoulder, down the empty corridor. The wood paneling and cramped space was suffocating. She would have preferred meeting in Rainier, where the ceiling was tall enough for a giraffe, but even the hospital couldn't beat the seclusion of the underground Intelligence tracks.

And we call the Gens ants.

She turned her attention back to the line of photos pressed behind glass frames. Each year displayed a picture of the men and women serving in Intelligence at the North American Academy. Maggie flicked her eyes a little farther down the wall, where the ID photos were so old, they were black and white. The Barracks boasted a similar photographic set-up, though they honored guards. Maggie hadn't been inside the belly of the Guard in weeks, not since she was called to the scene of a potential myocardial infarction. In the end, though, it had just been an anxiety attack.

Damn Gens have everyone worked up.

While she waited, she made a game out of studying the many, many faces grinning back at her. *Which ones, which ones...?*

"You won't find what you're looking for in photographs," a nasally voice resounded behind her. Maggie pivoted, coming face-to-face with the Chief of Intelligence. His long face caught the shadows in all the wrong places. Glaring nostrils, small eyes set deep into his skull—he wasn't the most attractive man. But Maggie needed him.

"Plain sight is a good idea, though, isn't it? Who would suspect their neighbor?"

Ramsey rolled his eyes. "It would be the Salem Witch Trials all over again. The last thing this Academy needs is more pointless genocide."

Maggie bristled, remembering why they were holding a rendezvous underground so late at night. She thrust the folder into Ramsey's arthritic hands. He didn't bother opening the envelope to read the documents.

"He followed instructions then?"

Maggie nodded, "To the letter."

"Good. The Valence needs this."

"I know," Maggie shuffled her feet, still strapped in her comfy hospital shoes. "Castan is pursuing Vel's younger sister, Corolla."

"I know," Ramsey sighed, exasperated. "Perhaps she will be of true use. If not that, then a distraction." Amusement flickered in his otherwise stern expression.

Maggie nodded, though she wasn't entirely aware she was doing so. "What happens now?"

Ramsey tucked the folder under one arm, making for his office some distance down the hall and buried in the maze of Intelligence.

"We wait."

Castan
July 2020

"There's only so much I could say over the phone while you were in Yazd."

I shift in the leather chair, all too aware of the grit under my nails and the disapproving angle of the Major's eyebrows. They're so pale, she may not even have any, but they exert power in their own right.

"Castan," Rex folds her hands on the glossy surface of her desk. Her ivory hair glows like the moon against the orange and yellow streaks displayed through the glass behind her. "Almost a year ago, the Commander and I chose you to fill the role of Regent because of your combative skills and impeccable insight into Dentata motivations."

I brace myself, though my callous expression does not change. Calyx's dog tag quivers against my bare sternum to the pounding of my heartbeat. If she *knew*, then I would be imprisoned right now. But that doesn't ease the anxiety burning through my body.

"However," the Major grimaces as if smelling something unpleasant, "ever since Calyx Vel's murder—"

"I don't want your sympathy."

Rex bristles. "I'm not giving it to you."

I don't miss a beat. "I appreciate it, ma'am, but I know you didn't escort me to your office to hand out compliments."

"No," Rex purses her lips, "I escorted you here because I'm demoting you."

Despite my self-control, my jaw comes unhinged. Rex can't fire me—Corolla will die without my thorough knowledge of the Gens. I move my tongue to say just that, but Rex cuts in first.

"Perhaps Corolla Vel is a poor influence on you, or perhaps you are slipping. But I can't have insubordination, Castan. I understand the attack on Vel's home was an unprecedented accident, as was the geometer mishap, but you disobeyed my orders in Florence." The Major scowls. "Jumping to Belarus without backup? *Think*, Castan— Had the Gens been there, what could have become of Vel? And besides the two pedes now under my protection, the Euro Academy is demanding jurisdiction over Luca Alba—who, I may add, is nowhere near fit to travel, much less *jump* two continents. Even if he had been well enough, did it ever occur to you the risk in bringing him here? He could have been a vessel of infectious diseases." Major Rex shakes her head, though her hair is so stiff with gel, it does not move with her.

I clench and unclench my fists. "I couldn't just leave Alba there—"

"No!" Rex slaps an unexpected palm on her desk, "But you could have obeyed your instructions and returned immediately after your encounter with Issak Park. *That's* what is expected of you. *That's* what soldiers are meant to do. They are *not* their own Commanders. They are willing pawns for the greater good. Do you understand me, Castan?"

I hold her scorching gaze, feeling fire in my own veins. Through gritted teeth, "Yes, ma'am. I understand."

Rex relaxes a minute degree, expression pinched with anger. "Things are getting worse, Cassena. They may be bigger than your plans now, but I believe Corolla is our last chance. Focus on managing your team. Oh," she adds as an afterthought, "and I will need you to move your things out of Aurum House. The ambassadors require sufficient lodgings during their stay for the conference. You will move back in with Finis Fletcher."

I barely register her string of words. I am numb, the reality of it all sinking far deeper than I care to admit. *Demotion?*

The French doors rustle behind me, and Commander Murphy and Intel Chief Ramsey appear in the edge of my vision. They are here to make it official, to bear witness to such humiliation. I can't meet the Commander's solemn gaze. Ever since I came back from Iran, and word spread that I cut Rosh Dentata's finger off, the Commander has been my biggest supporter. I can't bear to face his disappointment.

The Major rises behind her desk, body stiff as the creaseless gray pantsuit she adorns. Unforgiving as a block of cement.

"Castan W. Cassena," Rex says, voice grating against my eardrums, "I hereby discharge you from your post as Regent."

Book Two
Awoken

"Nothing is so painful to the human mind
than a great and sudden change."
-Mary Shelley, *Frankenstein*

Past
August 1988

The girl waited, perched on her mattress, bony knees tucked up
under her white dress. She glanced at the empty bed beside her where a
boy with pale blonde hair and striking blue eyes usually slept. Though
it was daytime, and the children were allowed to wander the third floor,
the boy was not there. He had been gone almost two hours, by the girl's
watch, and she was beginning to wonder why. The doctors only ever
required a small chunk of the children's playtime, so where was the
blue-eyed boy?

A voice flashed through her curious mind, *Maybe he's sick*. The
boy—B6C8, she thought—had seemed rather weak-limbed, these past
few days.

The girl relaxed her knees, setting her slippered feet upon the solid
wood floor. A nursemaid approached her, red lips beaming. The girl
found herself smiling back.

"Hullo, AD1," the nursemaid said. The girl had learned to answer to
such a name, though this nursemaid had a strange accent and twisted
the sound of *one* into more of an *in* noise. For some reason, the girl
preferred her name this way. AD-*in*, rather than AD-*one*. Her name
used to be A1D1, but the doctors and nursemaids thought it more
efficient to keep track with the current method.

The nursemaid crouched down to the girl's eye level. She
recognized this woman, the black mole on her cheek and the frame of
her plump body in her white smock. She never knew their names—they
never said—and she wasn't confident she was allowed to ask.

"The doctors are very excited to see you today," the nursemaid
grinned, brown eyes glinting. "Give me your hand." The girl slipped
her small fingers into the outstretched hand of the nursemaid she had
come to like so much. Sometimes, one of the other nursemaids
collected her for the doctors, but they weren't as friendly. This one was
friendly.

They passed through the cordial play of the other children, some
white as winter snow, others black as night. The girl herself was brown
as the films of dust that swept through the open windows in the
summertime. The watchful eyes of supervising nursemaids followed
their plight out the double doors. These nursemaids never seemed to
watch any of the other children as closely as they did her, but the girl

hardly thought it odd. The supervising nursemaids tended to blend into the brick walls, despite their bright white uniforms. They became visible when the children became too rowdy, or someone got hurt, but this was rare. The nursemaids truly only became visible if someone was ill. Which was often.

As they slunk down the heavy, metal steps of the stairwell, the girl forgot all about the blonde boy. She was, after all, only six years old. Missing blue-eyed boys was not on her list of worries, if she could claim any worries at all. She enjoyed living on the third floor with the older children and likewise. It was far more appealing than the second floor, where babies screamed throughout the night and the younger children sobbed with every stumble.

The girl and nursemaid passed the second floor, baby cribs showing through the little glass windows on the double doors leading inside. They reached the first floor, and the girl's heart suddenly fluttered. It wasn't that she was afraid of the doctors, but sometimes, she didn't understand what they did. She wasn't sick, wasn't ill—not like the other children, anyway. Maybe that was why the doctors checked in with her so frequently, but then, shouldn't doctors spend more time on the sick than the healthy? The girl wasn't entirely sure.

The nursemaid opened one of the heavy double doors, and they stepped into the shiny world of stainless steel and a vast, open ceiling. The girl knew the doctors intentionally built the brick building so that the second and third levels didn't rest over their offices. She had heard them say as much, something about the noises and disturbances children often caused.

The two waited by the glass shelves of metal objects, the voices of two men carrying like thunder through the air.

"I'm telling you, she is the only one. Out of all the children we have raised, AD1 is the only child with the breadth of potential—"

"So take samples from the hosts again. Create more offspring from A1 and D1." The girl only recognized one of the voices as a doctor's. She wasn't sure who the second man was.

"No, no, no," the doctor said. The girl imagined him shaking his head. "Genes are like—"

"Pulling from an unpredictable deck of cards, I know, Doctor, but if we pulled the right pair once, we may as well try pulling a second time."

"It doesn't matter, not really. If their bodies can't handle the serum… The other children are suffering already, growing weaker. We lost one this morning—"

"Everyone dies. You can't honestly care about *test subjects?* We have enough supplies to keep at this experiment until we find a cure. I'm not funding this project for you to give up."

"Ahem," the nursemaid cleared her throat. The conversation ground to an abrupt halt.

"Come in," the doctor's voice called, tone silky now, rather than strained. The girl clutched the nursemaid's hand tighter as they wove through the doctors' shelves and tables of equipment. Some things she recognized, such as the rope-like thing the doctor listened to her heart with or the white contraption on the counter he put her drops of blood under. Most things, though, she didn't recognize, and she clung tighter to the nursemaid with innate fear. The girl was a curious creature, but the way these objects glinted in the white light struck her as horrifying. She didn't cry, but she suddenly wanted to.

The pair stopped feet away from another couple entirely. The girl knew the one in the white lab coat. *Doctor.* Or at least, one of them. She had met with many. This was the doctor with white plastic glasses, large frames on his sunken face. He looked like the bugs the girl sometimes found crawling around the window panes.

The other man was quite large, thick arms and a chest two times the size of the doctor. He wore a black sweater and dark gray trousers. There was something sinister in his grin, something that burned his face into the girl's memory. Black, beady eyes, shiny bald head. She could have sworn that was blood smeared across his cheek, but, as the nursemaid pushed her forward, the girl realized it was just dirt.

The doctor kneeled to her eye level, a warm grin spreading across his wrinkled face. "Hullo, AD1," *AD-one,* "Are you well today?"

Feeling the crushing gaze of the other man, the girl only managed to nod her head. Hands empty, she grabbed fistfuls of her white dress and stared at the doctor's shiny black shoes.

"Wonderful," he tucked a strand of hair behind her ear. "This is Numen," the doctor gestured to the bald man, "he would like to observe your examination. Is that alright?"

Again, she nodded.

"Alright," the doctor mumbled under his breath, heaving himself to his feet. He went to work at one of the metallic counters while the nursemaid helped the girl onto the examination table. Paper crinkled beneath her, but she paid it no attention. She watched the doctor, hands flitting from one cabinet to another as he prepared his supplies.

Compared to the bald man, there was something almost fragile about the doctor. The girl recalled a time when one of the other children—a girl with thick black hair—had accidentally smashed her head into one of the windows during playtime. While the nursemaids crooned and cared for the bump on the other girl's head, she had sat in her own bed, awed by the jagged cracks in the once flawless window. Could the bald man create such breaks in the doctor?

She didn't have time to wonder. The doctor stood at her side then, a syringe pinched between gloved hands. Behind him, the bald man crept closer, licking his lips.

The doctor angled the needle towards the inside of her elbow. She knew the cold liquid on the inside would make her sleepy—that's how examinations went. "Just a slight pinch, AD1."

There was a stinging sensation, and then the girl was aware of cool liquid traveling throughout her arm. Her body tingled, eyelids drooped.

The doctor's technical voice, somewhere distant, "Once she has completely—"

A loud crack. And something zipping through the air. The girl forced her eyes open, curiosity taking root. Crimson splattered her white dress. She looked up, heart pounding in her neck, at the bloody mess that had become the doctor's face. The nursemaid screamed; the doctor fell backward with the sound of shattering glass.

"Taxodium!" A booming voice rose above the screaming. "Show yourselves, Dentatas!"

And then the nursemaid was whisking the girl's numb body from the examination table. She lost sight of the bald man, but another took his place in her vision: between the cabinets, a man adorned in skin-tight black with mud-brown plating. Even though her eyelids were drooping, something was captivating about this man. She had never seen eyes like that, eyes full of—

The nursemaid took a sharp turn, swallowing cries of her own as she pressed the small girl to her chest. The girl's eyelids fluttered; the world came to her in pieces. The nursemaid flinging a gray cupboard open. White sheets strewn among the floor. A sweet, familiar voice cutting through the gathering shadows, "Stay hidden, AD1." *AD-in.*

The last thing she saw, was the nursemaid's ruby lips disappearing in a crack of white light. The girl was swept up in an icy current of blackness.

When she came to, there was darkness. And muffled voices.

A high-pitched one, apparently a woman's, "By Matrona, are you sure?"

"What do you want me to do, Holiday? If Taxodium discovers how close the Dentatas came to deriving a cure, there will be chaos." A man, the girl decided. A leader like the doctors were.

"But they're innocent people down there—"

"And if the Dentatas get ahold of them again, then what?" The frustration in the man's voice grated against the girl's ears. "We can't have them talking—they're just pedes. God knows what the Dentatas put them through. It's mercy, what we're doing. For our society—"

"Okay, Alistair," the woman relented. "I'll send for gas."

"There may be some around here. One of those Dentatas in the nurse's costume was a suicide bomber. Nearly caved the building in. Couldn't get the kids to stop screaming..."

"Are they going to die, too?"

There was a long pause of silence. The girl shook her head, trying to clear the fog hovering over her mind. She only managed to slam her forehead against the cupboard door.

"What was that?" The man.

Cautiously, the woman, "I don't know."

The girl cowered in the base of the cabinet, hair grazing the shelf above her. When she didn't hear footsteps, she began to relax—

Then the door swung wide, revealing a heavyset woman in black skin and brown plating. The girl whimpered, and immediately coughed on smoke and something putrid that made her facial muscles twist. She sucked her limbs into the folds of her stained dress, wishing her favorite nursemaid would rescue her.

The man, "What is it, Holiday?"

"A girl." The woman cocked her head, warmth in the form of a grin breaking her stern appearance. "Are you hurt, little one?"

The girl pretended the woman wasn't there. She clamped her eyes shut, trying to remember why she was in a cabinet. Red lips, crimson blood—the girl shuddered, choking on the fumes in the air.

Solid hands reached for her, pulling her out of the cubby the nursemaid had been so clever to store her in. The girl dared not squirm, dared not breathe. Through slitted eyes, she glimpsed the ruins of the doctors' room. Tables and cabinets were overturned, glass shards littered the floor, and equipment was thrown about. It was madness. Unable to help herself, the girl sucked in a lungful of the poisoned air.

The woman halted beside the man. At his feet, was a gaping black hole, a section of the floor flung open like a door. The girl had never noticed it before, but the shadows it displayed frightened her. She averted her gaze.

When the man saw her, the black line of his eyebrows softened. He had friendly, hazel eyes and a scruffy black beard. Like her, his skin was a soft, dirt color. For some reason, the girl found his appearance calming.

The man's gaze flitted to the woman carrying her, "I want all evidence of this cruel place destroyed—the papers, the prisoners... But the children," the man frowned, eyes dropping to the girl. "The children will be placed in orphanages. Different ones. And if the trauma hasn't erased their memories, I need Kowalczyk to clear them up. They shouldn't have to grow up with demons. Matrona knows they've been living under the Dentata's roof long enough."

The woman's voice echoed in the girl's ear, "Of course. We can trust Kowalczyk to keep this under wraps. I'll make the necessary preparations."

The man nodded, but his hazel eyes were glossy, unseeing. "The medics say most of these children are sick beyond repair," his low voice cracked. The girl wanted to tell him it was okay, she wasn't sick. Anything to bring back that look in his eyes.

The woman placed a soothing hand on his shoulder. "We can at least give them a drop of normalcy."

The man said nothing for some time. The woman smoothed back the girl's long, caramel hair. The nursemaids had never done something like that, and the effect was... pleasant. She suddenly longed for the comfort of her bed on the third floor.

The man's rigid body snapped to attention. He blinked as if realizing where he was. The girl wondered if he found the air as horrid as she did. He looked like he was going to say something to her, but it was the woman who spoke.

"I'm Joyce Holiday, and this is Theodore Alistair. What's your name, little one?"

The girl scanned the devastation, saw the horrible black splatter on the far wall, and made up her mind.

"AD-in."

"How lovely," the man mused. "Adian."

Corolla
July 2020

"Averil?" I blink, incredulous. "What are you doing here? James will be back soon—"

"Stop talking so much, Corolla." He glowers at me, eyes pitch black. I sink deeper into the ugly plaid couch, the wooden frame digging into my spine through the ancient cushions. Averil towers above me, sneering. He combs a hand through his strawberry blonde hair and reaches for his belt buckle.

"Averil," horror strains my voice. I draw my knees into my chest. "Averil, no—"

The world explodes into fiery wrath. Bright orange and crimson-red flames lick the walls all around me. I squint at the glare of thermal light, shielding half my face with the back of my hand. The paint blisters with the heat. Frames crash to the floor and shatter. Fear spikes my blood, though there's something oddly familiar about the surmounting fire. Smoke clouds my lungs. I cough into my hands.

A hand claps over my mouth, the force of it grinding my spine into the couch's underlying skeleton. I look up, expecting Averil, and see another profile altogether. Ebony shadows stitch into a silhouette. Even a black mass, I recognize the square, brutish outline of Lola.

"Don't shout," she mocks, voice ringing like bells in my ears. I struggle under Lola's grasp until I've managed to free myself. Ash and debris float from the ceiling. The fire spreads to the Bible James keeps on the coffee table.

"How did you know Kass said that?" I scoot farther down the couch, only stopping when my back hits the solid arm.

If the shadow woman could smirk, she would now as she replies, "I was there, Vel, watching. *Always* watching." Her body quivers, like trembling silk, and she vanishes beneath the floor.

Flames crowd my vision. There are so many shades of oranges, reds, and yellows now that I can hardly make out that consuming bundle of energy before me. It's too bright. Too bright...

And then there is a pale woman, standing in a veil of fire, long ivory hair spilling in straight lines from her skull. Phage. She cackles, shoulders rocking, jaw unhinged. But no noise comes from her cherry-red mouth. I don't understand what she's laughing at until my eyes happen upon the olive and bronze shape occupying the coffee table: It's not the Bible burning. It's Luca.

My arms deploy from their places at my sides. I shove them into the pulsing flames, crying out when the thermal radiation kisses the skin of my palms. Through great wells of tears, my fingers grace a charred cheek. Instinctively, I pull away, my own hands sweltering with throbbing, bright red blisters.

Luca moans, blackened jaw crunching with the effort of moving against charred muscle and tendons. "Corolla," Luca croaks.

I inhale sharply and immediately cough the toxic air back up. That wasn't Luca's voice. It couldn't be. Because it's James's.

I peer over the edge of the couch, trying to get a closer look. Sweat coats my face, pools under my arms and at the base of my neck.

"James—"

A force knocks me off my knees, sending me crashing into the ocean of fire. Mouth agape, I cannot scream—the oxygen is squeezed from my lungs, from each individual cell in my body. Agony rips through my core as if James's disappointment has been crafted into a thousand daggers. And each one plunges unforgivably into my flesh. It is worse than burrowing macrophages, worse than my own shame: it is unforgiveness, and it is punishment. I am tumbling through a pit of flames, and the face above me, on the other end of this hellish tunnel, is Castan's.

My eyelids flash open. At once, sleep evades my body, and I sit up in a strange bed in a strange room, no doubt in a strange place. I blink away images of crackling flames, my burning home. I take a deep breath of untainted air, willing the ghostly grasp of my nightmare away.

Memories from last night flood my senses. Major Rex, James and lasagna, Argenti House and the tall, lanky boy who escorted me here. Castan, ducking his head and practically running away from me at Allen Manor.

Better running than burning.

I swallow, and to my relief, there's no ash coating my esophagus. I untangle my legs from white sheets and a plush, pale green comforter. Legs now dangling over the edge of the queen-sized bed, I gaze at the gray shadows of my new room.

Lola. I shake my head, dislodging the thought.

Unclouded light streams through a narrow skylight above my bed. Besides that, there is only one other window bragging a view of distant brick buildings and the medieval architecture of the Barracks.

I skim over the empty white shelves and matching desk, also vacant. I make for the shuttered ivory doors of the closet. Laila left a note on my bedroom door, saying that there was a stockpile of new clothes stashed here. With all the money Rex just wrote away to James and me, I could buy my own boutique.

The closet doors swing open on their own volition. On the right, are dresses of all colors and lengths strung up on black hangers. I ignore those and search through the towering shelf riddled with color-coded stacks of fabric. Fashion has never been my forte, and even with so many options and potential combinations, I gravitate to the familiar: a black V-neck and whitewash jean shorts. I consider slipping socks on when clattering pans interrupt my process.

Castan. Guilt surfaces in the pit of my stomach. *I need to apologize for Belarus.*

I snatch a random pair of socks and zip down the walled-in staircase leading up to my room. I take the steps two at a time, grasping the metal railing to keep my balance. The straight-edge staircase caught me off guard, at first, because each of the five Ward Residencies possesses identical faces: red brick, white stucco, and exposed wooden beams. Classic Tudor exteriors, or so James says. But the insides are different. Aercus boasted varying shades of chestnut paint, alabaster furniture, and sleek, mahogany flooring. Argenti is more... pastel. Pastel paints, pastel couches, lampshades, bathroom towels, kitchen appliances. I'm still deciding how I feel about the color scheme.

The stairs empty out between the kitchen and living room, so it's there that I land on the balls of my feet. A dark crown pokes up from behind the (pastel) yellow countertop.

"Cast—" I catch myself in time as the head rockets into the air, and an unfamiliar figure bends over the counter. Tall and proud as a flagpole, thin arms and a mop of rich brown hair. I don't recall his name—he told me in a rush last night—so I gave him my own nickname: Roman. Because his hair is shoulder length, tucked behind one ear, and screams ancient culture. He mutters something to himself, and my face pinches with a mixture of confusion and curiosity.

Roman transfers the pans—colored pale red, like tomato soup overloaded with too much milk—to the stovetop. When he turns for a cabinet and still doesn't realize I'm gawking at him, I clear my throat. He glances over his shoulder, lips blooming.

"You're awake! I thought I'd have to splash cold water on your face." Roman levels his entire body and pours chunky tomato paste into a measuring cup. I wonder what kind of experiment he's conducting.

"Erm... Where's Castan?"

Roman's hand slips, and the chunky paste runs down the side of the glass cup. He sets the can down, biting his lip. As he stares down at the spillage, a look of consternation occupies his expression.

I step closer. *Maybe he didn't hear me?*

I try again, lighter this time. "Where is Castan?"

Roman is a statue, but from his lips come the nonchalant phrase, "Oh, he got demoted." He screws up his face and cocks his head, muttering something under his breath.

"Demoted?" For some reason, waves crash in my ears.

"Yeah." Roman pivots, yanking a shade of green from a peg by the sink. He wipes the paste from the counter and measuring cup. Gold glints on his hand. I notice a ring, ridged like a mountain range. "Rex stripped him of the Regency," Roman grimaces, adding, "unfortunately. He was good at what he did, and I won't let you down, but... Castan's not very gifted with processing emotions."

"I'm sorry," I grip the back of a barstool, "but what's going on exactly? I thought I was living with Castan. Here. Until the Gens come, and..." I trail off, not quite sure how that sentence ends. Until they what, attack or kill me? Either way, devastation is bound to happen. To someone.

Roman rakes a hand through his thick head of hair. He tears his eyes from his mess and meets my gaze. "I'm your new Regent. I thought I mentioned that last night?" He doesn't wait for my input. "Well, I was incredibly excited last night—Regency, it's something we all had to fight for, back before Calyx came. But we couldn't fight for the honor this year, not with the Gens... But anyway, I was the runner-up last year, after Kassandra, so... here I am!"

I blink, unsure of what to say. *Castan isn't my Regent...?* It's near impossible for me to imagine someone replacing him, even if he is short-fused and bad at jokes. I glance at Roman. *At least Castan wasn't hyperactive.*

"Well," I swallow, "where is Castan now? I need to tell him something."

"He's packing up his stuff in Aurum. The rest of the ambassadors are coming today, and we need Houses for them." Roman frowns. "Where are you going? I was making us lunch."

I pause by the door, somewhat touched and somewhat annoyed. "What I have to say to him is really important," I explain. "And I appreciate you making us lunch, but..." I don't know how that sentence should end, either.

Roman shrugs, apparently uninjured. "It's fine. I forgot Jura's recipe for stovetop pizza, anyway." He taps his temple, "It was all in her head."

"You were making pizza with a measuring cup?"

Roman shrugs again. "Yeah, but I'll just go snag some slices from the Dining Hall." In three long strides, he's ahead of me at the front door. "I'll bring you back a plate," he slips past the threshold, "Oh, and Castan left something this morning for you over there on the counter."

I follow the direction of his pointer finger, locking onto the bright green notebook in this pastel kingdom. The front door clicks shut behind Roman, whose real name I still can't remember.

I set aside the pair of socks still crumpled in my fist. My fingers hover over the notebook. *So, he must have gone back to that cottage in Wales.* There's a Post-it stuck to the journal, along with a pack of Wrigley's spearmint gum.

So you don't chew your mouth off.

—Castan

Despite myself, I grin. I flip open the notebook, thumbing through the pages until I find the photographs of Adian and Calyx. I study the absolute joy in their youthful faces. And then my spirits plummet. Neither of them died here, but they died because of Taxodium... right? Taxodium murdered my family.

You sound like James.

Well. Suddenly, I see the sensibility in his hesitancy. If the roles were reversed... I don't know how I would function without James. He's not a crutch, but he's the only family I have left. Correction, the single, mentally stable and *present* family I have. Until Luca is well again. For as long as I can remember, it's just been the two of us. I don't know if I'd want it any other way. It's difficult to imagine the Albas in my life, most of all, my father.

Carefully, as if the photos will disintegrate at my touch, I return them to the confines of my notebook. I do the same thing with Castan's note, though I'm not really sure why. Laila's Post-it was just as grudgingly heartfelt, but I threw it in the bathroom trash regardless.

I try not to think about it.

I tuck the pack of gum in my back pocket, slip on a pair of sandals, and cross the courtyard to Aurum House.

"Castan?" The door creaks on old hinges. The front door was locked, so I had to walk around back. Thankfully, the courtyard was empty of prying eyes, and the rear door wasn't deadbolted. Behind me, the leaves of the Twelfth Wall flutter like so many sheaves of paper in the wind.

I shut the door behind me, eyes adjusting to the darkness. Underneath the stale, musty air, is a scent like warm vanilla. The house is eerily quiet. The only light comes from ahead, twin windows like two eyes at the end of the narrow hall. There's a brick fireplace on my right, gray ashes swept into the hearth. On my left is a washer and dryer, so many crumpled piles like anthills, around them. A closet door hangs ajar. Various chemicals peer out from the darkness.

Was this how things were when Calyx lived here?

"Castan?" My voice is softer now as if anything above a gentle tone could trigger some sort of alarm system. I tread down the hall, not bothering to leave my sandals by the door. Something about the state of the house tells me to keep my shoes on. I step into the living room. Or at least, what *was* the living room. If Argenti's theme is pastel, and Aercus's is rustic/modern clash, then Aurum's is disarray.

White sheets are draped over the furniture—a pair of sofas and an armchair, I think. Each piece has been crudely shoved against the wall. Beams of sunlight illuminate the layers of dust coating the vibrant white sheets. Particles float through the rays of sunshine, and for a moment, I'm afraid to breathe them in. Each mote, I realize, is how long Calyx has been dead. How long Castan has been here alone.

The only furniture not cloaked in white is a simple coffee table. It, too, is shoved to the side, but sheets of paper draw me to its flank. I recognize Castan's handwriting from the Post-it note. His sloppy hand is scrawled all over mismatched papers, reminding me more or less of barbed wire fences. I manage to decipher a line:

If Shelley can imagine it, then Júlia can help me achieve

it—

***Where** is his spirit?*

I feel the muscles in my face pinch. What is Castan talking about? His frustration and hopelessness seep through even the black ink on the paper. Strangely, it pierces my heart. I set the documents aside. Trespassing property is one thing, but trespassing thoughts is another.

I look about once more—where is Castan? Clearly, he hasn't been packing, as there are no signs of boxes or bags. Junk litters every surface. On the ledge separating the kitchen from the living room is a massive flat screen TV. Games are stacked atop an old PS4 console. On the island behind that, I glimpse precarious towers of dishes, most likely dirty. I think about how much I don't want to be around when they fall.

There's a door some paces behind me. I start there, flitting past a piano only half-covered with sheets. I grasp the brass knob, pushing my shoulder into the ivory door.

"Castan?" I peer through the crack. Sunlight spills through a window I can't see, highlighting the mess around the room. I swing the door wider, enough to see that Castan isn't here. I pause—only for seconds—to take in the room's contents. Styrofoam cups litter the carpet. In the near corner, dark bedsheets flow from an unkempt bed to the floor, and on the far wall, there is a maple bookshelf. Its shelves are packed with various heights of books. Leather-bound spines. Faded, peeling spines. Broken spines.

A memory comes back to me. Castan, twirling my overdue library book around the kitchen table.

"I read this once. Angel wasn't good enough for her."

He was a demented stranger to me then, but what is he now? I shut the door and examine the bundle of emotion that's making my heart behave like a caged bird. But it's not the emotions I see, it's Castan. His weary expression the day he broke into my home. And again, during the fire, the way sweat dripped down his brow and a look of utter concentration commanded him. In Tilia's cavern, when he rounded the corner, groggy and rambling about Calyx and dreams. His tame hand extended towards me.

I exhale a breath I wasn't aware I had been holding. I think about the contents of my back pocket, aware of it as if it were a ticking time bomb, not a pack of gum.

I want to apologize to him, I decide. *And I want to know about Calyx. That's why I'm looking for him.* I have to give myself a motive for this hunt—have to, or else my heart will start drawing its own conclusions.

I moved past the kitchen and find another door. It's open. And Castan is lying, face down, in the center of it.

Before I can rush to his side, one of his arms twitches, the one not crushed underneath his abdomen. He shifts so that he's lying on his back, chest heaving.

"It's impolite to stare."

I flush, grateful that he can't see my color from his angle. "What are you doing?" I ask because I can't bring myself to say the words, not yet.

"I could ask you the same thing, Vel. Though I suppose this is, in a way, the home of your predecessors."

I lean into the doorway, somewhat stunned at the lack of possessions in this bedroom. Compared to the other—Castan's, I'm guessing—this one is twice the size. Only a neatly made bed, a sparsely occupied bookshelf, and a desk are contained within the vast confines.

So, this is my brother's room.

"Roman told me you were here."

"Roman?" Castan's tone shifts, but he remains supine on the carpet.

"The really tall guy living in Argenti now."

"Oh, Talan, you mean. I would have thought Kass would get the Regency. But then, she broke protocol also."

There's a small breath of silence. Castan hooks an arm over his eyes as if shielding himself from the sunlight, though there isn't much in the room. The Wall peeks through the windows; the sun will be glaring on the front of the house.

"I'm sorry about your job." My voice is small, hardly audible in my own ears.

Castan's Adam's apple bobs, but his voice betrays nothing. "I'm sorry I can't be there for you."

I gravitate towards him, placing myself cross-legged near his torso. Except for the rapid rise and fall of his chest, he is a statue. He's at least cleaned up since I last saw him in Allen Manor. He's wearing khaki shorts again and a heather gray tee shirt. A part of me contemplates the reason why his arm is still draped over his eyes. Maybe he's been crying.

"Castan," I inhale, then exhale. "I shouldn't have said what I did in Belarus. I just—"

"It's alright, Corolla." His voice is low, smooth as honey. "You don't have to explain yourself. Matrona knows I couldn't do the same thing for you."

His words reverberate in the large, near-empty room. I think about the strange phrases on those papers in the living room and know he's probably right. Human motivations are a monster of a gray area. If my heart could just stay out of it, I would never have to explain. I would never have known Averil on that couch, in that way. I would never have known James's disappointment.

I bite my lip, eyes fixed on the weave of carpet.

"Didn't you get the gum?"

My attention snaps, and Castan sits up to face me. I take one look at his sunken, black-rimmed eyes and know why his room is littered with Styrofoam cups. He hasn't been crying, he's been awake all night. He's as pale as the moon, leaf-green eyes a ghost of his dark emerald ones.

"Are you sick?" He's not, and I know this. The words fly from my mouth all the same, "You look like death on a cracker."

Breath hisses through his teeth. He ducks his head, a grin breaking across his pale features. "Death on a cracker? Pedes are so... unconventional."

Despite myself, I laugh. "Unconventional? You shoot flames from your hands!" Cackles crack through my chest uncontrollably. Castan meets my watery eyes, head shaking. But the moment only lasts for so long. He frowns, thumbing the tag around his neck.

"What?" I resist the urge to touch his shoulder, to feel the heat of his skin under my fingertips. To know that he's human. He has that look in his eyes that makes me wonder.

He looks around, eyes darting between memories I will never know these walls contain.

"You must think…" He trails off. Frowns.

"I think that Calyx was more your brother than he was mine. And you miss him."

Castan rakes a hand through his unruly chestnut hair. "Like hell."

I don't know how to comfort something as broad and jarring as death, so instead, I say the first thing that jumps into my mind. "Is that Selena Gomez?" I point above our heads at a poster tacked to the ceiling I noticed earlier. I recognize the smooth shoulders and dark hair of the pop star, but someone's taped an oval cutout of a face and placed it where Selena's should be.

Castan doesn't even look up. "Yeah, Kass put it there with her face on it after Calyx was weirdly jealous of the poster of Brendon Urie in her room. He did the same thing. With his face, I mean."

"I hardly recognized her without the red hair." And then it occurs to me. My eyes flicker from the poster to Castan. "You said jealous? Were he and Kass…?"

Castan makes that hissing laughter again, but this time, he's not grinning along with it. "Yes and no, I guess. Calyx only ever loved her, but Kassandra… She's always been acid, but Calyx was her base. I think she loved him back but was afraid the Gens would catch up to him eventually. And they did, so she wasn't wrong." He scowls at his palms. I know that wrinkle between his eyebrows too well. "Hesitating didn't do her much good, though."

I don't know what he means by that, and I don't ask. Despite the parameters of the room, it's suddenly suffocating. I rise to my feet. Castan does the same, though I notice the way his elbows buckle as he pushes himself upright.

"Shouldn't you be packing?"

"No," he scans the room with a distant look in his faded eyes, "I don't want any of this stuff." He seems so inwardly deflated. He's trying so hard to keep it together, I can tell. All I want in this moment is for him to be okay.

Tilia's robust and silvery voice trickles into my consciousness: *"I do not think he has been alright for some time, but he is not injured beyond repair."*

I get lost in my thoughts. It's only when Castan says something that I come back to myself.

"That's how he thought through problems sometimes." I blink, seeing the cardboard box I've been subconsciously staring at for a while now. *Legos*, it reads in bold Sharpie. "He liked building things. Said he wanted to be an engineer before all of this."

All of this. "And what did you want to be?"

He shrugs, and some of his grief falls with the movement. "I know *where* I'd be. Someplace like that cottage in Wales, except dropped in the middle of a coniferous or deciduous forest where no one can interrupt me."

"Friendly."

"Hey, I was antisocial first." Some glimmer returns to his eyes. "What I am today is because of Calyx."

"Really?"

He shrugs again. "Rarely does one walk out the Academy gates the same person who walked in. Funny how people change to adapt to their environment. I could tell you a great Rainier quote, but you haven't read his theories."

"Technically," and I smirk because I can't help it, "I never walked through those gates at all."

"Well," Castan's eyes grow in diameter with mock exasperation, "then you need to cross that threshold right now! You can't skip out on a legit *Humanitas* and fail to walk where the ancients have." He grips my shoulders, and for a small eternity, I am only conscious of his curled fingers, pressing into the curve of my shoulders.

I thought you were broken, I want to say. *When we first met, I thought you were broken.*

And then he draws away, and like an intoxicating fire, steals the oxygen in the air with him.

But you're much more.

I blink, cold realization spreading through my veins. Castan's talking, low voice humming with excitement, but I don't hear his exact words. Faces flash over my vision of the dusty room, but there is only one I latch onto: James, cheeks burning with rage, blonde eyebrows twisted to match the fury clouding his blue eyes. A jolt of regret shreds through my heart, like a great white shark shaking its helpless, dying prey. I could crumple right here, in my dead brother's room, but Castan's voice strikes my ears with astounding clarity.

"...before the ambassadors move in. Will you come back tonight, at like, 8:00?"

I meet his glistening, green eyes, the vibrant color of avocado flesh. Just as soon as the arctic cold came, it melts in the fire of Castan's gaze. I have no idea what he's asking me to do, but he is so inwardly fractured, so crippled with grief, how can I say no?

I must have agreed, nodded maybe, as he beams and says, "Great, I'll see you then." If my own eyes betray the emotions in my heart, Castan doesn't see it.

Or maybe, whispers a voice buried deep in the caverns of my neurons. *Maybe he doesn't see you at all.*

Past
July 1998

"Should you be smoking, sir?" Tyto's skin prickled at the disdain in the old man's wrinkled face. He pursed his lips, blowing a breath of flame to light the Marlboro pinched between his yellowed fingertips. When Tyto came down this hall, he heard the nurses muttering about genetic predisposition. And while they could have been referring to genes Tyto wasn't aware of, he was almost certain they meant the old Major's Essence. It was, after all, a direct line fueling the old man's habit.

That disdain trickled into a form of cynical amusement. "They can't deny me my last wishes." He took a drag, and Tyto stifled a cough against the brash smoke the Major released.

"I just meant," Tyto added quietly, "should you be smoking that in a *hospital?*"

The Major huffed laughter, which quickly turned into heaving, wet coughing. Tyto ducked his head as the Major's face went beet-red, nasal cannula glinting in the glare of brilliant white light. Out of respect, Tyto focused on the slit of the near-blinding reflection of the light bulbs on the linoleum tiles.

Beep, beep, beep.

Major Rainier regained his breath, though his cigarette still bled gray wisps in his gnarled hands.

"Probably not," the Major grimaced and pursed his lips again. This time, his weak breath sucked in the flicker of flame. He frowned at the cold cigarette, that look of disdain once again taking up his features. He yanked the cannula from around his face. "Oxygen is a formality," he snapped. "It won't do anything to stop cancer."

Beep, beep, beep.

"Sir," Tyto couldn't wait any longer, "with all due respect, why did you summon me?"

Major Rainier settled back into his hospital bed, head propped on a stack of crisp pillows.

"You know why you're here," his voice was gravel, a ghost of the booming strength it had been four years ago. Tyto barely recalled how that voice sounded when he had first entered the Academy. He would have forgotten what the Major's profile had looked like too, had the portrait in the Majors Gallery not reminded him every time Rainier summoned him to his office. By Matrona, the man had changed. So many wrinkles. So many cigarettes.

Tyto sighed. *This won't be a quick talk.* He snagged a stiff plastic chair from the far wall and set it beside the Major's bed. The monitors beeped, as much a constant as the clock ticking on the wall.

"Well," Major Rainier cast him one of those knowing looks. "What do you have to say for yourself, boy?"

Beep, beep, beep.

Tyto ducked his head. "It was an accident. I... I never would have seen the man, had you not called me to your office—"

"Is that an apology?" The Major's lips twisted into a grin. "You captured a spy, lad! Matrona only knows how the devil slipped through security, but you saved decades of confidential material from the bastard Dentatas." Rainier gasped for breath, lungs crackling. "Probably even saved Taxodium lives. So why are you apologizing?" His voice was softer now as if seeing Tyto's drooping shoulders for the first time.

Beep, beep, beep.

"People want me to be something I'm not. Or at least, I'm not ready to be what they want. Not yet."

Beep, beep, beep.

Major Rainier inhaled, and Tyto winced at the sound. *How long does he have before...?*

"I've already met with the Board of Majors," Rainier said, voice an even calm. "There are no Laws that prohibit you from running. The tradition has been to nominate and elect Commanders, but it's the people's choice."

"I don't want to run! That's what I'm telling you, Orland. I don't want to be Major, and I don't want anyone else to come up to me and shake my hand. I didn't *do* anything! I noticed a suspicious figure, who just ended up killing himself with a cyanide pill anyway. I didn't get any information, and I didn't save any lives. So why are people treating me like I have? The Dentatas haven't been controlled—they probably haven't even been delayed. All I did was stop a man riddled with scars, okay? I'm not like Gentry and Dawson Allen. I'm not like Tilia Pyrus. I'm not a hero." Tyto's chest rose and fell fast enough to breathe for the both of them. He didn't know he was standing until he met the Major's gaze and realized he was looking down.

Beep, beep, beep.

Major Rainier regarded the young man, who, even now, was so full of that passion the people found so addicting. Tyto scowled, feeling more like his older brother, Orsino, as he did so. The Major only grinned with a wisdom Tyto wasn't sure he would ever understand or possess.

Beep, beep, beep.

"Sit down, Tyto Alba."

He sat.

The Major folded his large-knuckled hands in a pile on his lap. Had they been in his office, Tyto realized, the old man would have folded his hands on his great mahogany desk. But Major Rainier had been hospitalized for weeks now. As unsettling as it was, the act was becoming familiar to Tyto. Even the stack of paperwork on the nightstand seemed normal. A desk for a bed. A Marlboro for lung cancer.

"I remember when I met your older brothers. I wasn't Major when Valeria passed through those gates, but I do—vividly—recall each of your brothers. Giovanni enjoyed his alone time in the library, and Luca... he enjoyed just about the opposite. He told you about the time he organized a pack of students to streak across campus, I'm sure."

"You suspended him for a week."

Rainier continued on as if Tyto had never spoken. "Orsino trained and fought like a panther. And Pasquale was always the quiet, devoted one." Major Rainier drew a slow, haggard breath. It was agonizing to watch, Tyto thought. This man, who he had come to idolize... on his deathbed.

Beep, beep, beep.

"So where are your siblings now?" The Major prodded. Tyto clenched his hands behind his back. *Rainier knows exactly where.*

"Valeria works at the Euro Academy, in Intelligence. Pas is in the Guard for another year. My other brothers returned to the pedes' world. Giovanni's a musician. Luca is... Luca. And Orsino works in management for some mining company out West."

"Yes," the Major nodded approval, "and your last year of instruction is coming to a close. Which do you see yourself in for two years of service, Intel or Guard?" Rainier squinted his eyes, and Tyto clenched his fists tighter, not in anger but in frustration. Because the old man knew the answer to that question, too. Tyto didn't want either. Despite Academy law, Tyto could never put his heart into either denomination. Even a temporary two years in either branch sent claws down his spine. It was a different kind of agony, this not knowing how to spend the rest of his life.

"Look," Tyto leaned forward in his chair, "I don't know why you mentored me. I don't know why, out of the entire Academy of more qualified, more prepared students and faculty, you chose to focus your attention on me, but I can't be Major. I'm too young to make that decision."

The Major made a noise, half laughter, half cough. "Who told you that, Tyto?"

"My parents."

"They talk you down from this great honor?" He huffed. "If you were my son, I'd push you into the Courthouse myself."

"I'm not your son." Tyto deflated in his chair. His eyes darted from the Major's wistful expression to the flashing numbers on the monitor screen. Thanks to Field Med, he knew what those numbers meant. And they were not good. At least, they were not destined to last.

Beep, beep, beep.

"Death is a trivial thing, Alba. I'm not afraid of it, and you shouldn't be afraid for me, either."

Tyto bowed his head, feeling tears prick his eyes.

"I chose you, Tyto, because you have potential. And you *do* have experience, despite what you may think. You've been with me for two years. Don't tell me you didn't pick up anything from my lessons on commanding this ship."

Beep, beep, beep.

Tyto sucked in his breath, taking his emotions with it. Pelari didn't grieve in public, and even if his only witness was the Major, he was not about to break that ancient tradition. Orland Rainier was not dead yet. He fixed his eyes on his mentor.

"But don't you regret it, being Major? I mean, you are that last of the Rainiers..." Coming from such a large family himself, Tyto couldn't fathom being alone for the rest of his life. He knew the price he would have to pay if he pursued the Major's position. The Attachment Laws spelled it out very clearly: *"The Majors of the Pelari's Academies shall not partake in romantic relations of any sort, i.e., partnerships, liaisons, marriages, and any other intrigue the Verum Courts find fair and just to prosecute..."*

"My boy," despite the Major's condition, his eyes twinkled, "heading this Academy has been my greatest joy, and mentoring you has been my greatest pride. Had I become anything else, where would any of this be today?" He gestured to the hospital, the one he founded decades ago as a medical haven for pelari. "But it's not just the Hospital, Tyto, it's every mind I ever influenced, every Law I ever upheld and encouraged others to uphold, too. Majors are beacons of guidance and morality."

"Commander Rex is a better choice. She has *more* experience and respect..." *And nothing to lose.* Tyto's stomach churned with guilt. But it was true. Commander Rex didn't have a family—her husband and sons were butchered in an encounter with the Dentatas nearly a decade ago. She deserved the Major's position. She deserved—

"But she has no charisma. Believe me, Neva is a perfect fit for Commander, but she doesn't have that... link with people. She is cut from the same cloth as the icy rings of Saturn, and the people know that. Acceptable quality for the head of the Guard but not for the head of this Academy."

Beep, beep, beep.

Tyto opened his mouth, but the pale, yet jaundiced Major cut him off.

"You didn't catch a spy, Tyto, you caught this Academy's dignity and Taxodium's respect. These are progressive times. Don't forget what you've done for our people. I can promise you this: they won't."

Castan
July 2020

Boxes packed, and garbage bags tied, I stand in the heart of Aurum, looking out at all the memories this House contains. Every late-night cramming for exams. Every party and every dinner. Calyx and Kassandra. Talan and Finis. Júlia, Dani, Jura, and Maggie. Me. We all came and went. Aurum is a vault, as much as the Venefica is, only I will never know all that these walls have seen. Like the years Aunt Laila lived here with Adian Vel.

I heard somewhere—maybe one of Ms. Hampton's lectures—that nostalgia is supposed to be a good feeling. But when my eyes flit across the furniture, uncloaked and reorganized, there is nothing good in the churning of my stomach.

In my hands are three things: "Pachelbel's Canon," and folded inside that, my brief derangement in the form of scribbled paper; in the other hand, is a hard copy of *Peter Pan*. The ribbon marker is still set to the line, "To die will be an awfully big adventure." Out of the whole book, I have only read that line, over and over. I despise fantasy, just as I'm learning to despise these three remaining objects. I couldn't just pack them away to be donated. It didn't seem right. But keeping them, storing them away in my new/old dorm with Finis, doesn't seem right either.

A vision of me, crossing the few feet separating me from the piano, overcomes my senses. I imagine sitting on that cushioned bench as I did so many times before. I would flick my wrists like I always did, and I would play "Pachelbel's" one last time. Not for Calyx, but for myself. Yet… To strike that first key would be the same as sailing my mind back to a time when the only death on my mind was Jay Gatsby's. And *that* would be the same as torture.

I inhale the scent of blood, which is quickly masked by the overwhelming stench of Pine-Sol and Clorox wipes. Leaving this place behind will be good for me. Moving in with Finis will be good for me. Not being Regent, I think, will be good for me. Better for me. A step in a different direction, though who could say if that direction is good or bad? I guess I'll find out.

But I can't avenge Calyx's death when his allusive ghost strangles me day in and day out. I need some space from this grief.

I look once more at the objects in my hands, and I know what to do with them.

As if on cue, there's a knock on the front door. Through the windows, I catch the caramel skin of Corolla's arm. The sun is just beginning to sink behind the Twelfth Wall, casting long shadows in the yellow light of the courtyard beyond the front stoop.

I realize, maybe a little late, that Corolla is waiting for me to let her in. After all the outbursts from Kass and the others, I find it odd to let my guests inside—usually, they just waltz in. Harmonies to the melody that exists here. Existed.

Shifting the book and roll of paper to one hand, I make for the door.

The glow of the sun glints off Corolla's smooth hair. She grins when she sees me, and I can't help but mirror her expression. Even with her back to the sun, her large, whiskey-brown eyes glow with a light of their own. Calyx's used to shine with something like that, too; as if he knew something none of us did, and that knowledge made him all the more like the sun. But if Calyx was the sun, Corolla is the moon. She is more subtle than her brother, but she illuminates just the same.

How different she is, from that saucer-eyed girl wielding an umbrella. Even if Corolla doesn't recognize it, the Venefica changed her. Maybe it has something to do with the Mark between her shoulder blades or the foreign memory stored inside her brain.

We're inside, though I don't recall when that transition happened. Corolla's head turns every conceivable direction, taking in the restored Aurum House. For some reason, the inspection causes my skin to prickle with heat. I almost laugh at the reaction—I haven't felt this self-conscious since the day I met Calyx.

"The place looks… better. I see you've moved the furniture back."

"Yeah, well." I don't have a geometer to jump with anymore, not that I would risk offending Major Rex again by doing so. "I've nothing else to do on a Saturday."

Hands on her hips, she exhales, resting those eyes on me once more. "So why did you want to meet here again? I didn't know what excuse to give Talan."

I wave her off, "I already texted him permission or whatever it is he calls it."

Corolla makes a face. "He's almost as anxious as James."

Rather than respond to that, I pad across the floor to the pantry door. I swing it open, revealing empty shelves and white walls.

"I thought you'd want to see this before one of the ambassadors moves in."

I imagine Corolla stifling a laugh as she asks, "See what, exactly?"

I grin, careful that she doesn't notice it, and push aside a panel in the wall space not decked out with storage shelves. That familiar, musty draft licks my ankles. I stare at the human-sized gouge where the wall should be. Rimming the edges of the uneven rectangle are the rough ends of wooden planks that Calyx sawed through almost the same day he arrived on campus.

"My dad told me about these tunnels," his eyes gleamed. "One from Aurum, one from the Major's bedchambers... They lead just outside the Wall, to an old chapel."

Corolla groans, though it doesn't entirely mask the excitement in her tone. "I've had enough of tunnels."

I glance at her over my shoulder. "Calyx said these tunnels are how your parents used to meet up. They're also part of the reason why they were forced apart."

"Well," Corolla's tone practically shoves me into the dark mouth, "by all means, give me the grand tour."

My feet land on uneven ground. Darkness cloaks us, making these narrow tunnels slightly more claustrophobic. The air is metallic, though not because I smell blood. Behind me, Corolla slips from the last of the ladder's iron rungs. I tuck *Peter Pan* under one arm and pour my focus into coaxing a flame to light. It takes longer than usual, that natural pathway like a sticky key on a piano now. I try not to think about how weak I was earlier, about how awkward things could have been, had Corolla shown up moments before she did. I didn't faint, I keep telling myself, but I definitely didn't have the strength to stand either.

It wasn't supposed to happen so soon.

My palm glows, and I place the bundle of energy on the tips of the scroll of music sheets and my delirious *Frankenstein* notes. I don't know if I could possess a flame bright enough for these tunnels. Calyx was cremated, so it only fits that these mementos of him should burn, too. It's not the objects that bound me to him anyway: it was always the memories. And even though I sometimes wish I could fish those out and discard them, I will always possess them. Pieces of him, I guess the poets would say.

"So," Corolla's voice wavers in the harsh orange light. "What exactly happened between my parents? James told me what he could, but he admitted the topic was beyond him." The tunnels aren't wide enough for two people to walk side-by-side, so Corolla scuffs behind me. I put a hand out to the wall, fingertips brushing the old planks that shape it. It always reminded Calyx of a crypt, but I thought it looked more like a mineshaft. Of course, he frequently got splinters, while all I had to do was light up my hands and watch the wooden fragments disintegrate to ash.

"Well, I'm not an expert, but every pelari knows about *Taxodium v. Alba and Vel.*" Fine dirt gets stuck under my nail. I pull my hand away from the walls.

"That sounds... daunting."

"They got married. In secret. Majors aren't allowed to be involved in any sort of relationship, especially with your mother." I laugh, incredulous at the prospect of marrying a Vel. "She was the Dentata's target, and if they knew about her relationship with the Major of the Academy—you can only imagine the hostage crisis the Dentatas could have pulled off. During World War II, taking hostages was part of the Dentata's tactics. Leverage over their fighters. That's why the Attachment Laws were ratified. But anyway, your parents, the two most important pelari on the continent, and they were involved."

Corolla doesn't say anything, and I wonder if I've crossed some sort of line. Calyx never really invested in the details of the trial—claimed he remembered it from when he was two years old!—but Corolla isn't Calyx. She didn't grow up with any pelari, only the ghost of what her parents *weren't*. Maybe it's too much to take in all at once.

"I'm sure you have a lot of questions," I add, pinching a stray strand of flame dripping down the paper and placing it back on top of the roll. "You should ask Talan to take you to the library. There are a lot of volumes about your parents' case. It's not usually busy on Sunday mornings."

"Can't." If Corolla's upset, her exasperated voice doesn't betray her. "Talan's determined to be my friend, so he's taking me to the Training Field in the morning, then breakfast."

My stomach twinges as I recall my own promise to teach Corolla Defensive Training. I shake my head and pluck some more traveling flame from the spine of paper.

"These tunnels are so far underground, they're beneath Intelligence."

Corolla stumbles. The sound of her shoes scraping packed dirt is noticeable. It reminds me of all the nights Hadley and I ran to get home before curfew, our heels scraping concrete, breath coming in quick bursts.

"Is that... a building?"

"No." I blink back the memory. But the noise of her tripping echoes down the tunnel, down pathways in my mind. "Intelligence is where the second branch of Taxodium operates. Its facilities are underground because they're easier to defend."

"What's the first branch?"

"The Guard—"

"Sorry!" Her hands fly from where they landed on my back as if she might burn on contact.

"Talan has his work cut out for him, I guess." I shake my head and rearrange my bouquet of flames. The paper is almost burned down to my fist. I frown. "You may actually want to hold onto my shirt or something. We're almost to the fork, and the torch is almost out."

"Can't you just use your Essence?"

"No," I grin, "it's more appealing to follow the sound of the river." Or at least, that's what Calyx always claimed. And besides, I don't have the flames in me, at the moment.

Tentative fingers pinch the fabric of my shirt. The thought of her fingers, so close to my skin, causes the hairs on the back of my neck to stand on end. I don't know why.

We make our way past the fork. "That one," I gesture with an elbow, "leads up into the Major's bedchambers, though it was sealed off before your parents' trial." My fire dies soon after, and the only thing guiding us in the ancient arteries is the coarse babble of rushing water. This tunnel is less of a distance than the first. We reach the cavern in minutes, golden light spilling from the old well above.

I go to the underground river, *Peter Pan* in my fist.

"We call this river Phaedra's Blood, after the first pelari," I say without looking at Corolla. The water appears black, glinting yellow where the sun's fingers can reach. It runs through a chasm, no wider than ten feet or so. It then cuts through rock on one end and disappears through a channel of rock on another. It is just a glimpse of the river flowing beneath the whole of the Academy and its fields, but it's enough.

I hear my father's harsh cackle, "If I can't keep you away from those damn books, then your Essence surely will." In those days, I wouldn't touch any paper, convinced I'd lose control and it would burst into flames. The river's steady current streams past. I feel none of that old taboo in my bones.

I toss *Peter* in. It slaps the surface of the inky water. I watch in reverent silence as gravity pulls that turquoise book under and the current carries it away.

"To die will be an awfully big adventure."

The book vanishes in the black water, no doubt already downriver where no pedes or pelari has ever been.

A pocket of pressure in my chest absolves.

All this time, Corolla has been speechless, observant, a few feet from my shoulder. Her eyes followed the book's path just as well as mine did, though she couldn't have felt that jolt of peace in her chest.

Rather than ask why I just tossed a perfectly good copy of *Peter Pan* in Phaedra's Blood, she wonders aloud, "Who is Phaedra exactly?" I step away from the chasm and move towards the exit ladder. "Phaedra was the first pelari, daughter of Matrona. She grew up to be a Healer, under the reign of Emperor Augustus. The first pelari began in Rome, you know. That's why the oldest pelari families have Latin surnames." I wrap my hands around the oxidized rungs and climb towards the brilliant evening light. A stairway to heaven.

"Fascinating."

"Look, I don't want to sound like a know-it-all, but you need some serious catching up."

Corolla scoffs. "I'm only volga."

"That has origins, too. About thirty years ago, the first pretender was a man with the last name of Volga. And I say first because the Dark Ages were strange times. Any charlatan probably could have gotten in with the pelari. We were only clusters back then. The Rome Accords brought those clusters together, thus Taxodium." Below, Phaedra's Blood echoes off the cavern walls, reaching my ears in waves. I pull myself up more rungs, feeling the ladder tremble with the movement.

"Anyway, Volga tried getting into the Euro Academy, but the guards found him out. A woman named Kowalczyk—I think that's how you pronounce it?—had to remove Volga's memory of pelari and the Academy."

"That seems wrong."

"Maybe." The calluses on my palms begin to ache. I suspect Corolla will have blisters by the end of the day. "But part of the Rome Accords binds every member of Taxodium to look out for 'our brothers, our sisters, our society.' Pelari don't completely discredit pedes—Tax was involved with fighting in the World Wars—but Tax usually operates in its own interest, as any organization would. The pedes around Ohio just think this Academy is a school for agriculture." I steady myself on the last few rungs, stretching my arms over my head to slide the metal grate from the well's mouth. It scrapes against the stone lip, maybe too loudly, and I pray to Matrona there isn't a scouting unit out tonight. I take my chances and climb into the open air.

The sun sets due west, its golden tendrils flowing over the foliage of the old chapel. I hop over the stone lip, feet digging into the overgrown grass. My back to the Twelfth Wall and all the little lights of Taxodium, I help Corolla out of the well. Her head breaks the russet glow, hand clasped in my own. She's lighter than I remember, though I suppose that's because she's conscious this time.

"Why does this feel like a prison break?" She takes in our natural surroundings. "This is the place from the photo," she mutters.

I glance at the scenery with her eyes. The staggered wall of pines branching out from either side of the old chapel, so layered in vines and wildflowers, that one cannot tell a building is there at all. Even the steeple, maybe a little sunken since last I saw it, has vines twined and twisted about it. I look over my shoulder at the spires enclosed in the Twelfth Wall. From the border, stray trees speckle the grassy plain. Through the pines, I just barely glimpse the orchards on my right. On my left, the rust-stained silos loom above the far corner of the Wall. This is a different kind of bubble.

"I suppose it is a prison break," I shrug. "But Taxodium isn't that stifling, is it?" I make my way across the land. Corolla follows some paces behind me.

"I guess not. I just… It's difficult to imagine myself in this world, is all. I don't know how to describe it."

Finding a decent place, I pause. The grass isn't as overgrown here, and the break in the pines allows for an unobstructed view of the sunset. I sit, turf digging into my palms.

"If you can survive macrophages almost devouring your leg, you can survive the Academy." It's supposed to be uplifting advice, but out of the corner of my eye, Corolla frowns. I glance at her leg where the flesh around her old gash is pink with new skin. My eyes dart back to her face. Her rosy lips are puckered in thought, eyebrows soft angles. Do I want to know what's brewing behind her intense eyes? I don't have to ask.

"*Jon Xabier Dentata.*" The name sends chills down my spine, though July heat spikes the air. I turn back to the mosaic of color in the sky. Pinks, burnt orange, yellows as gold as the Venefica herself.

When I say nothing, Corolla dares to continue, "What do you think it means?" Her words are cautious as if she can read the lines hardening my worn features. Maybe she can.

Because I know Corolla will just ask again, I huff, "Well, Dentatas usually go by their first two names, as Dentata gets redundant after a while living underground. Xabier isn't much to go off of, though. It only means that Numen's siblings—if he has any—would also possess an X initial." I exhale, the sound heavy. "I don't know. I honestly don't."

Corolla gives me a look, though I keep my gaze fixed on the transforming sky ahead. "Is there a Dentata 101 class? How do you know all of that, about the names?"

I crane my head to look at her inquiring eyes. Shrug. "I've made it a personal study." That severe pucker mutates into a smile.

I find myself saying without really meaning to, "Sorry about earlier. Sometimes the grief is just so... isolating. It's all I see, and I get lost." A corner of my mind flinches at the emotion my voice carries, but I can't tell her the real reason I was on the ground. A more significant chunk of me recognizes Corolla's intent listening. Calyx was the same way.

She raises a loose fist, as if she's going to brush her knuckles against my shoulder, but then she digs her hand into the lush grass instead. Disappointment prickles my skin. I rub a hand down the back of my neck, oddly flustered.

A half-hearted laugh brings me back. "You don't have to apologize." She draws her attention back to the sunset, and I see that the yellow orb has almost disappeared behind the horizon.

I bolt upright. "You need to meet Júlia!" I turn on Corolla, wide-eyed. "She can coax your mother's spirit from wherever it is people go when they die—"

"Thanks, Castan," her profile is one of distress, "but I don't know if that's such a good idea. I never knew how many murdered relatives I actually have."

"Oh," *the Alba Atrocities*, "right." Gray and blue shadows fill the voids where the sun abdicated. In the tall grass, crickets and cicadas chirp, harmonizing with the screeching bats and twittering birds. I watch a pair of mourning doves flit from one of the pines across the falling night sky. I lie back on the grass, arms cushioning my head.

Her back to me, Corolla's voice is muffled. But I hear each syllable like an alarm. "Do you think they suffered?"

I consider her question. She doesn't know about the bloodstained walls, or the homes, some burnt to the ground. Maybe the Albas survived. Luca, after all, is supposed to be sixteen years dead.

"I don't know," I finally answer. "I've always imagined dying as closing your eyes really tight until all you're conscious of is blackness." I sigh, knowing my answer isn't what she wanted to hear. "I don't know."

Corolla shifts. I blink, and she's lying beside me, arms crossed over her stomach. I can almost feel the heat of her body against my arm. I think of her radiation spilling into mine, and my heart does something painful in my chest.

"James said dying is peaceful, no matter what. Kind of like watching a sunset, I guess."

An image of Calyx, blood-soaked and pale as porcelain, flashes across my vision. I don't believe that for a minute, but... I banish the thoughts and images away. I don't want to think about that, or *him*, or anything else beyond the tree line, beyond this moment. The first of the stars wink down at us, paving the way for the moon. We lie in content silence for a while. Bats dart across the darkening sky above. Somewhere, an owl coos like the chime of the Bell Tower. Maybe it is the Bell Tower, marking the new hour.

"Can I ask you something? You might get mad, which is fine—I certainly can't claim to have an even temper."

Wary, Corolla's irises swivel in my direction. "What?"

"Who's Averil?"

She clenches fistfuls of her shirt in her hands. "You read my notebook."

"Not intentionally. It may have fallen open once or twice on my jump back." I think back to that page. Broken sentences, scribbled thoughts. Swirls and dashed configurations taking the blurred form of a brain. And woven in almost every line: Averil.

She says nothing for some time; only the cicadas and night creatures stir. Night cloaks the earth now. If I cared to look back, I would see the bubble of the Academy, illuminated in white light.

Corolla breathes so faintly, I almost don't hear her, "It's not an easy story. Or a quick one." Sleeplessness makes some people menaces; it makes me relentless.

"We have all night."

Corolla readjusts so that she's on her side, arm pillowing her head. Turning my head, I watch her twirl a blade of grass between her fingers. Her pulse jumps in her throat. The grass quivers at her quickening breath.

"You don't actually have to answer that question," I amend.

She makes a noncommittal noise. "No, it's okay. It's just that I don't know where to begin..." She inspects the blade between her tiny fingers, though I know she does not see it.

"He's your ex?"

She nods.

"Broke your heart?"

She shakes her head as best she can with one ear to the earth. "I did that myself."

I shift on my side, a reflection of Corolla. She meets my imploring gaze. Heavy eyes, half-grin. She sighs, her sweet breath hooking my senses. Spearmint gum.

"Have you ever been in love?" Her question catches me off guard. I blink, and the ghost of Júlia's body wraps around mine. I blink again, and it's gone.

"No."

Corolla's mouth twists. "I thought I was. I thought a lot of things." Her tone is clipped. By observing other students, I consider myself

209

adept at reading into relationship conflict. I know what heartbreak looks like, and I know what it sounds like. Corolla isn't like any other person I've ever noticed before. The edge in her voice isn't knifelike with anger—it's piercing as an arrow dipped in remorse. Most people brandish arms against the person who hurt them. Corolla draws the knife on herself.

Now it's my turn to be wary. "What did he do to you?"

If words could be bruised, her next ones are. "Whatever he wanted," she breathes, plucking the blade from the earth. It's too dark now to tell, but I swear her eyes glisten with tears.

"Corolla—"

"And then James found out, and I couldn't bear his disappointment." She scoffs, "I actually fainted. Cut my chin on the way down. I woke up seconds later, and I wanted to die."

"Corol—"

"I know how selfish that is now. I mean," she hurries, voice thick with unshed tears, "I could never die and leave James behind. Especially when I have so much debt. He sacrificed his entire future to raise me, and that look in his eyes said it all: I let him down. Severely. Absolutely. Completely."

I want to hold her, to tell her that I will string up Averil's corpse— even if it is a Genocides' tactic, innocent people have been murdered in worse ways. And Averil is anything but innocent.

Corolla's curled into a little, shivering ball. I think about stretching an arm around her and pulling her close, but given everything she just said, and everything she *didn't* say, that's probably the last thing she wants.

We lie there for several long moments. The only sound is the nightlife around us. Crickets, cicadas, bats, owls. It seems impossible, but somehow, there are even more stars in the sky than I have ever seen before. I really don't know how much time has passed. We've been gone so long, I'm not sure society will exist when we return. It is just the two of us and the planet we inherited.

"I just thought," her voice is hoarse, lips loose, "that if I did well in school, secured a prosperous future, James could finally have a reason to be proud of me. And I know how sappy that sounds, but he's all I've got. If I don't have his respect, then what do I have besides a bunch of meaningless things? Things don't forgive you. They don't love you." Her voice is soft and strained with exhaustion, I believe. I can only imagine her mental fatigue—she's brave enough to admit her sins aloud. I can hardly manage to think mine.

For something to do, I tug the blades of grass separating us. "Did you ever tell James that?"

"How could I have?" She's appalled, but she doesn't shift from her cocoon. "I didn't want to reopen that wound. Not until I have something credible to show for, anyway."

"So..." each syllable is a question, "you agreed to help me... for James?"

"Yes," she folds tighter into herself, "For James."

I may never understand her sketch, or the trauma residing so fresh in her mind, but at least I know now why she's so skittish sometimes, why she talks so much when nervous: because she never did before with Averil.

Corolla yawns, long and deep. I retreat into myself, absorbing everything she's said. A piece of me wants to laugh, *This must be what Corolla felt like when I broke the news to her about Taxodium.* But that voice is drowned in the somber, sober chunk of my consciousness.

Corolla's not like me, and yet... she is. She doesn't deny her past: she keeps it close enough to remember—to *remind* her—to atone. Everyone has a story, especially here, but I had no idea the poison of hers. I remember something Aunt Laila told me during those hazy days after Calyx's death, *"The past can never be buried. It can only be endured."*

"You're a Tess."

"What? No, my name is Corolla." She's disoriented, half-asleep. Through another deep yawn, she enunciates, "Kore-ah-luh."

"Corolla of the Vels."

"My life was mundane." I don't think she knows what she's saying anymore. Exhaustion slurs her words.

"Was? What's changed?" I expect her to say everything. I expect her to say Taxodium, Calyx, Adian—

"I met you."

I glance at her, but I see someone else entirely. It's not Calyx, but it's not Corolla either. It's as if I've just finished a 10,000 piece puzzle without a guide, and this is how it looks: A small, caramel-haired woman lying in the grass, her head nestled in the crook of her arm. Eyes closed, her chest rises and falls gently. She is a doe.

But she is the most unshakable person I know.

It's well past the 10:00 curfew when I unlock the russet door to my new/old dorm. My head is reeling with Corolla—from her spearmint breath to the smooth curve of her fingernails—and everything she told me tonight.

I close the door behind me as softly as I can manage while not paying attention. I must have been loud enough, as a light in the kitchenette flicks on. I slip my shoes off and turn to face Finis.

The smaller dimensions of the dorm wash over me. The kitchenette, the single sofa and chair in the living room, a bathroom and two bedrooms shooting off from the main space. Definitely not as spacious as Aurum House. The ceiling is low enough to touch with my fingertips.

At my look, Finis raises a pale eyebrow. Talan, I'm sure, texted him. He wasn't too pleased that I kept Corolla past curfew.

"We have plans early in the morning!" Talan scolded. I prayed James couldn't hear him from Aercus. He tugged Corolla inside Argenti, barely allowing her the breath to say, "Good night." Talan whisked her away, practically slamming the door in my face.

But Finis doesn't ask about why I was out so late. He folds his arms over his chest. "No books?"

"No books."

A quiet smirk tugs one corner of his mouth. "Welcome back, then."

"Surprisingly," I say, each word an admission, "it's good to be back."

Past
July 1998

Major Orland Rainier, the last of the great Rainiers, passed away on a Wednesday night. Not a soul was around to bid him farewell, but the pelari thought this best—he was the type of man who preferred dying alone. His lifeless body was carted to the Hospital's basement. He was prepared in a morgue designed by his own hand, not ten years before his death day.

His Ceremony was held Friday morning, under a rising, golden sun and pink clouds. Four Major's guards held the platform carrying his pampered, yet cloaked, body from the Hospital. Behind the pallbearers, the procession was headed by Commander Neva Rex and the remaining Major's Guard. Their heads did not dip to the cobbled roads. Their eyes did not glisten with tears. No, the only emotion roaring in their chests was pride—and a curious sense of peace. How long had they watched their Major suffer from lung cancer?

Mingled within this first clump were two Judges, Vera and Nikolai Taylor. It was not often that Judges left the halls of the Verum Courts for Ceremonies—pelari died all the time—but these two, stiff-neck Judges wanted to make a statement. Major Rainier had upheld their every Law, and the Taylors would stay at the Academy to ensure the election of the next Major resulted in a leader with similar morals.

Some heads behind the Judges, a young man marched with a weary heart. Tyto felt the peaceful atmosphere of the procession, but beneath that, he also felt the tug of expectation. It was this expectation, in the form of sideways glances and knowing smiles, that grappled his mind.

Facilitating the election fell to Intelligence, and there was already talk of nominations by Sunday. The people would nominate him and then what would he do? They would get what they wanted, regardless of what Tyto needed. But what he did need, he couldn't say, only that being Major was *not* it. He was only twenty years old, for Phaedra's sake! Why did the people want a child leading them anyway?

"You didn't catch a spy, Tyto, you caught this Academy's dignity and Taxodium's respect."

Tyto thought back to that moment, the start of all this unwanted attention, often. Major Rainier had called him to his office, so that was where Tyto was headed when he just happened to glance through the Intel doors. He saw a man, riddled with scars, at the top of the steps.

Tyto had watched him for a split-second before alarms chimed in his brain. Flinging the door aside, Tyto tackled the man. He didn't put up much of a fight, just stared at Tyto with wide, steel-gray eyes. And then he had killed himself. His mouth foamed, effects of the cyanide pill embedded into his gums, no doubt. Eyes locked onto Tyto's, he watched the stranger die. Major's guards, hearing the struggle, came. But the Dentata spy was dead, quivering against polished tile at the mouth of Intelligence.

"These are progressive times."

As the procession continued down the cobbled streets, students, instructors, TIs, and off-duty guards joined the tail until the swarm of people resembled a snake. The procession slithered through campus, past the Dining Hall, past the dormitories, and towards the Mausoleums.

One arch: the people flooded the Barrack's field. Another arch: the people of the Academy spilled onto the flat, green plane of the Mausoleums. The stone structures stretched far into the distance, each row and column dizzyingly aligned.

The pallbearers ascended the Ceremonial stage where Commander Rex would recognize the Major's life. Tyto knew he should be the one leading the late Major's Ceremony, but the Commander was determined to show the people just how attractive a candidate she was.

The pallbearers set the Major's cloaked body on the dais. For a moment, a breeze caught at that gray cloth, lifting it just enough to create the illusion of breaths. But those breaths were too fluid to have been the Major's, rose and fell too easily for a man with lung cancer. Still, Tyto stared at the gray sheet longer than he should have.

Tyto redirected his attention to the pallbearing guards. They stood erect behind Orland's body. Their elbows were bent in tandem, ebony bodies frozen in the three-finger salute. Mouth a firm line, Rex overlooked the people of the Academy. She was only three feet above them, but the Commander had the type of aura that made her tower over the procession. Tyto found himself scoffing. He wasn't the only one. As was protocol, Judges always seemed unimpressed, but there was something even more lackluster about their expressions now.

Commander Rex raised her arms, subduing the crowd for the moment. The students around Tyto shifted on their feet, exchanging glances. They didn't want the Commander up there any more than Tyto did. But their reasons were different from his own.

"People of the Academy," Rex's flat voice seemed to make the once beautiful morning ugly. "We have lost our Major, but it is important to remember all that he represented." Tyto raised an eyebrow. The Commander appeared to be grasping for words. "Orland—"

"Stop!" Tyto didn't know he cried out until hundreds of heads, like so many fluttering wings, shifted in his direction. He cleared his throat and stalked towards the stage. Commander Rex shot him icy daggers. He was almost certain she would have literally paralyzed him with one of her infamous looks, had the whole of the Academy and two Judges not been gathered before her.

He knew the stage wasn't that high off the ground, but gazing out at the sea of people, his head swam. Were there really so many people in the Academy? He recognized some students from his graduating class, the gray and black of the TIs, the brown and ebony of the Guard.

He cleared his throat again, and, not meaning to, stood center stage. He was quite aware of Rex glaring at his backside, aware of the dead Major laying under a sheet behind them both.

"People of the Academy," Tyto felt a natural grin shape his lips, despite the anxiety in his chest. "One of my last visits to the Major consisted of this conversation: 'Should you be smoking in a hospital, sir?'" Tyto's voice dropped an octave, matching the late Major's gravelly tone, "'They can't deny me my last wishes!'" Tyto chuckled and was surprised when hundreds of others echoed his own. He thought he heard the Commander hiss, but he knew she wouldn't dare.

All eyes were on him. A strange thing happened then. Later, he would recall the odd moment as something like when he started a new wood carving project. He would look at the raw lump of wood, and its desired shape would pop out at him. With no guide but his own eyes, he would take his blade to the grain and know precisely what marks to make where. That's how it happened, up on that stage. His anxieties evaporated, and he just *knew*.

Tyto continued, "Our Major was not a vain man—the artist who did his portrait can attest to that, I'm sure!" More amused noises followed; he waited patiently to speak again. "But he is the last of his breed, and that hospital," Tyto gestured to the spires in the distance, "he once told me it was his greatest pride. We all know he wouldn't have asked himself, but what greater honor for our late Major and the Academy both, if the hospital he helped design and loved so dearly bore his own name. 'Rainier Hospital' has a certain ring to it, doesn't it?" People nodded, many clapped and cheered. "The Rainier name will not die with Orland but will exist in the form of that beautiful building." Tyto sucked in a breath that the whooping crowd could not hear.

"Helping people, after all, was his greatest joy," he said more to himself than the crowd. He stopped himself from retreating into his thoughts. There was one thing left to say:

"Bellator, vale!"

The crowd parroted his words, the pelari's final goodbye swallowing the serenity of the Mausoleums. Tyto stood, the edge of the stage digging into the soles of his shoes, clapping and cheering along with the procession. The pallbearers set out for the Major's final resting place.

He came down the worn cement steps, pausing to watch the Major's guards tread between two rows of mausoleums. Some people joined him, clasping firm hands on his shoulders. Tyto caught Vera Taylor's sharp glance. She tucked her chin and vanished as more people swelled at the foot of the stage.

Tyto swallowed, knowing fully well that he had just sealed his fate. If the excited rush of people around him didn't confirm it, then the Judge's support certainly did.

Maybe being Major wouldn't be so bad. Orland had believed in him, and maybe that would be enough.

Tyto's blood hummed in his veins.

And the first thing I'll do, he vowed, *is amend that damn loophole so the next accidental hero will have a choice.*

Corolla
July 2020

I slept like the dead and dreamt like the drunk. So when Talan came up to wake me at 6 AM, I lashed out like the diseased.

"Ow!" Through my slitted eyes, he clutched a smarting cheek. He scowled. "It's not my fault you were out until midnight. Now get dressed. Something athletic." He ducked his head under the doorway and stormed down the stairs.

And that's how my day started.

From there, Talan dragged me across the campus, chatting all the way about the infrastructure we passed. "There's the Courthouse," he would point. "That cluster of brick buildings is the classrooms. And over there, is the library." My ears pricked at the sound of that, mind wondering if I could somehow find refuge from Talan there. Castan did say Sunday mornings weren't very busy.

Several times, I asked if we could stop and look inside the places we passed, but Talan refused, leading the way to the Barracks in the most roundabout ways possible. Even *I* gathered that. We pass under the brownstone archway now.

"You're already familiar with the Training Field," Talan comments. I squint at the sun spilling over the Barrack's wall. A breeze toys with my hair.

I catch Talan frowning. Again. "What is it this time? You said my outfit was fine." I look down at the black athletic shorts and Nike shirt. Apparently, I now own ten Dri Fit tee shirts, each a different color. Being fashionably inclined as I am, this one is slate gray. I managed to scrounge up a sports bra, though its hot pink. Whenever I breathe, I feel it constricting my chest.

"No," Talan pinches his bottom lip between two fingers. He's wearing his black uniform with brown armor but no belt. "Your outfit is fine, but I forgot about hair ties."

"Does it matter?"

"Yes—I'll be right back," he's already trotting across the turf, "I have some in my locker!" He vanishes behind a copper-colored door, and I enjoy the lapse of silence in his absence. I know I'm grumpy—I don't *mind* Talan—but I wish he would've let me sleep in at least until seven. I glance at the massive clock topping the Dining Hall. It *is* only seven. I grimace. If this is what Talan has planned for our morning, I dread what he has scheduled for the rest of the day. And every day after that.

I wonder what Castan's doing.

Talan is back too soon. His own hair is pulled into a stub at the base of his neck.

"Here," he hands me a black hair tie. I scrape more snarls than hair into a ponytail.

"Thanks."

"We need to get you a locker and some proper gear," he says more to himself. "But I guess that's my job."

I shrug, suppressing a yawn. "I guess."

"Alright," Talan does a couple jumping jacks. "Have you ever done anything like this before?" Up, down, up down, my eyes follow his.

"Nope." *How does he have this much energy so early?*

He pauses briefly. "Well, jump with me, Corolla!" He starts up again, faster than before. "We've got to loosen those muscles."

"Alright," I relent, trying to match his pace. Some of the sleep abandons my eyes, and my pulse pounds in my ears. I gasp after a minute or so, "I think I'm really out of shape."

"Don't be self-conscious," Talan is undeterred. "I'll whip you into shape in no time!" I'm not self-conscious—it's hard to be when Talan is so… bubbly… and the nearest soul is yards away from us beating a poor mannequin.

I clutch my cramping side and huff, "I believe it."

"Okay," Talan grins, "you can stop jumping now." I do. Immediately. My calves burn. "I think we should just focus on some basics today, then maybe end with a combat routine."

"Sure," I brush a stray hair from my eyes and add, "Thank you, by the way. I *do* want to know how to defend myself. It's just so early."

Talan looks wistful, sweat gleaming on his brow, when he says, "You'll adapt. Especially with such a dedicated personal trainer."

I laugh, and Talan rewards me with a set of thirty squats. Drill after drill eats an hour away. I hunch over, hands on my knees. Sweat pours down my back, between my breasts, and under my arms. I probably smell similar to the Corolla who jumped here two days ago.

"Can we stop for a water break?" I rasp. Talan's eyes grow to the size of baseballs. He smacks his slightly flushed forehead.

"I always forget water!" Before I can say anything, he takes off for the locker room again. I suck in another lungful of air, suddenly aware of the other people on the field. I don't recognize any of them, though some have to be students—they're too young to be guards. I know from Talan that the Academy's Guard dwells in the Barracks, which exist under the expanse of the Training Field. Some of the Guard congregates on the turf now, their colorful bands marking them as official soldiers. While Talan stepped on my toes so I could do sit-ups, he mentioned that the bands represent different ranks.

"Shimmering yellow for Major, gold for Commander, silver for Officials, bronze for Sergeants..." I would have to ask him about the rest of the ranks. At that point in the conversation, the pain in my abs was deafening.

I don't hear Talan approach, but he taps my shoulder with a dripping bottle of glorious water.

"Thank you!" I snatch it from his hands and down half the bottle in a single breath. Talan sips his quietly, looking more like a beanpole than ever before. I realize why: this is the first time today that he's been *still*. The questions flicker across my mind: Should he be taking medication? Is he already?

When he opens his mouth again, his voice is not as springy as before. "There are a couple places I haven't shown you yet." Without another word, he cuts across the field at an even pace. I don't have the heart to remind him that he promised a combat routine; my muscles are liquid fire, body weak with growing hunger and want of sleep.

I manage to keep up with his long, elegant strides. We pass a cluster of students, and I fight the urge to duck my head. If my face was flushed before, it's neon red now.

Talan passes under the second arch and cuts right.

"Slow down," I dare to jog to keep up. The grass here is cut short to the earth. The land is just as level as the Training Field, yet when I look back, I notice there's a slight dip to the ground beneath the arch.

"What is this place?" I take in the precise rows of stone prisms like so many teeth poking from the earth. I could have guessed first.

"The Mausoleums." I'm not sure how to reply to the wound in his words, so I say nothing.

He turns at what could be a random row, but the unwavering set of his boots tells me that he's been this way before. A fist of apprehension clutches my stomach, and I forget all about my scorching muscles and aching body.

Talan stops at the fourth mausoleum on the left. He orients himself with the far side, coming face-to-face with silver plaques and square doors sealed in concrete. A quick calculation reveals that there are twelve shining plaques on each side, three rows of four. Talan stands feet away, and like a guiding rope, my eyes follow the middle row of engraved names.

Ashten E. Sienko, Kat S. Park. I shudder. I know these names. They died in the place where I grew up.

My eyes stutter on the name masked in Talan's shadow: *Jura L. Taylor*. And the smaller print below that: *05/08/02-02/21/20*.

"Talan." I can't tear my gaze from the stone, afraid of what I will glimpse on Talan's face. But I know exactly what I'd see: grief. I hear Castan's voice in my head, *"Those two were for you."*

"Talan, I'm so sorry." The sun warms my back; a drop of sweat trickles down my neck. Gold catches in my eye. I notice Talan's ring, not for the first time. I thought the ridged metal was just another fashion statement. But looking at it through this new lens, I see it for what it is: Jura, like the mountain range. His sister, bound to his heart the same way married couples bind their love to their fingers.

"Jura wouldn't want it to ruin me, but she's not the one who has to *live* without her twin." I flinch at the venom in his tone.

My voice is small, "You're angry with her for dying?"

He whirls on me, fists at his sides. "No! I'm angry with the world for taking her, angry with my parents for not coming to her Ceremony, *furious* with the Gens for—for... decapitating her." His rage peters out; his gangly body droops.

A scene flashes before me: wrinkled arms reaching for his unresponsive wife. Vera... Vera Taylor.

Talan's mother.

"Why don't you speak to your mom now?" I can't seem to tear my gaze from his ring.

Talan sneers, this venom so unlike the character from ten minutes ago. "She wasn't there for me when Jura died, and I won't be there for her now. Her mind is broken: I call that karma."

"But, Talan..." *Your father is dead.* Does he know? Of course he does—He must. Kass mentioned an honorary Ceremony for the Hong Kong victims. Talan must have seen or heard his father's name somewhere.

But he doesn't know his father's final thoughts were of his children.

And then I catch sight of the fourth plaque. All other thoughts are forfeited.

Calyx M. Vel, 12/18/02-01/05/20.

I've been trying not to think about Castan, but he floods my senses now. Pale skin, faded irises. I know my brother's body was cremated, ashes were thrown in the wind to litter the very earth he once walked upon. I know this stone slot is as hollow as the hole in Castan's heart. How many times did he make this same, lonely pilgrimage through the stone mausoleums? How many times did he stand where I stand and torment himself with my brother's death?

My empty hand curls into a fist. How many people will the Gens take? I can't keep up anymore.

I feel sick.

"Can we go back now?" I nudge Talan's shoulder, though it's almost a head above me. "We still have a combat routine."

Talan's expression transforms completely.

"If you dare," he taunts. "But if you beat me back to the Training Field, then we can call it a day." His dark eyebrows raise on their own volition.

"That's tempt—" Talan becomes a sudden blur of limbs, me following hopelessly behind. The nausea in my stomach is replaced with another cramp. I shouldn't have drunk so much water at once.

Talan wins, coming to a dead stop at the locker room doors. Thirty seconds later, I am beside him, once again, struggling for air.

When Talan laughs, I swear it is the essence of joy. He laughs now, infecting me with a derivative of elation.

"We should work on endurance tomorrow," he clutches his stomach. "But I can tell you're spent. Let's get cleaned up, and I'll show you the best breakfast combo the kitchens have to offer."

"Alright, sounds good."

The men's locker room door swings open, and a man with sky-blue eyes appears. He has silver-rimmed glasses and a calm demure. His blonde hair is buzzed so close to his head, I can see the flesh of his scalp.

"Talan," he comes up behind my Regent. I notice the soft blush creeping into Talan's cheeks, the way their fingers just barely touch. Apparently, they know each other. Talan frowns.

"Finis, what's wrong?" I study Finis's expression. It doesn't appear to display a trace of... anything. I think back to my childhood dreams about robots disguised as humans. Finis makes me wonder if such nightmares have become a reality.

Finis's voice is low, but I make out the words, "Group chat." And then he is leaving. Still frowning, Talan whips out a phone from a concealed pocket in the thigh of his uniform.

"He's not much for words, is he?" But Talan can't seem to hear me over the worry settling like snow on his face.

"What is it?" I almost read over his elbow but catch myself. Talan glances up, looking after Finis's trek across the field.

"Castan's called a team meeting."

A familiar voice growls, "You're half an hour late, Talan. Where have you been?" Though I saw Castan when Talan first opened that oak door leading to this office, I search his face now. A scowl dominates his features, chestnut eyebrows drawn into a subtle, yet distinct, V.

There's no trace of the Castan from last night. He doesn't even look at me.

So. He's military man again.

"There was a line," Talan shrugs and slides a couple yogurt cups across a frosted glass table along with plastic spoons. "In case you guys didn't get breakfast." He faces Castan, "Sorry I didn't have enough arms to swipe you a coffee." Was that...? No, Talan isn't like that.

Talan pulls out an egg-shaped chair across from Finis and gestures for me to sit. I do, propping my forearms on the cool glass of the table, grateful that Talan allowed me the time to shower before we came. He barely managed five minutes to wash before he was yanking me out the door.

Talan plops down at my left, and Laila occupies the place at my right. Kass shoots Talan an indecipherable look, her hair a stream of orange. She could have just crawled out of bed—I spy several tangles in her long, unbraided locks.

Castan doesn't sit. He crosses his arms and leans against a marble counter.

"Before I delve into our discussion," he says, voice unpleasant, "Finis, this is Corolla. Corolla, Finis." Castan doesn't allow a space for cordial words. "Besides, Rex, Ramsey, and Commander Murphy, these are the faces you can trust at the Academy." Why won't he look at me? "Oh," he adds, staring so hard at the clock, I'm surprised the hands don't cease moving, "and Maggie. She's busy with patients, though."

The tension in the air is palpable, most of it emanating from the dark figure against the counter.

Laila pushes out of her seat. "Well, I don't need to be here for this, as you and I have already had this conversation." Her gaze falls to my own. "C'mon, Corolla. I promised you answers." Without waiting for Castan's permission, Laila thrusts through the glass door separating the office in half. I don't hesitate to tag along.

Laila didn't go far, though this office isn't big enough to get lost in. She's perched in a maroon armchair, one knee folded over the other. Her own sleek gray slacks and rose-pink silk blouse emphasizes my fashion handicap. For a moment, guilt stabs my insides. Should I be showcasing something more than tee shirts and shorts? I make a note to myself to wear something more elegant tomorrow.

"Thank you for the wardrobe," I gush, setting up in the other armchair. "I love it." I intentionally put my back to Castan, knowing he can see me through the transparent walls. It probably doesn't matter, but in case he *happens* to look my way, I want him to feel as ignored as I do. Was it something I said last night? I try not to think about it.

I can't hear past the glass. Is it bulletproof? After all, Intel is underground because it's easier to defend—Talan made sure to drive that point home on our way down. We took so many rights and lefts, if there were a fire, I wouldn't know which way to go to get back to the staircase in Allen Manor.

Considering how foul Castan's mood is right now, this is a legitimate concern.

"I'm glad," Laila's eyes glint. I've never seen her raven hair pulled back before, but she has it in a tight bun at the base of her neck today. I count three studs in her ears. She knits her fingers together, dozens of gold rings accenting her slim hands. "What would you like to ask me?"

"Um…" Put on the spot like this, I draw a blank. I curse myself—because I have always wondered about Adian. Even if I tell myself otherwise. "I guess just whatever you feel like sharing."

"Well," a sly grin creeps into her pink lips, eyes fixed somewhere ahead. "Where to begin with Adian… She didn't really have a filter. I mean, she had self-control, but she definitely wasn't afraid to speak her mind."

"She was forward?" I can imagine that.

Laila meets my gaze and nods twice. "Very."

Questions come to me, slowly. "How did you guys become roommates?"

"Adian said Tyto twirled his finger in the air like this," she demonstrates, making a helicopter motion with her right index, "and whatever name it landed on the roster was who Adian would dorm with. That was probably the first encounter your parents had."

I consider this. "Calyx and I were born here, in Rainier, right?"

"Yes."

"Then how did Adian keep two *children* a secret?"

Laila shifts her legs so the one is now draped over the other. "She didn't. Since she was a ward of the Academy, she wasn't required an additional two years of service in the Guard or Intel. After the normal four years taking classes, right. Which means she wasn't technically bound by the Attachment Laws—those Laws prohibit graduated Tax members from getting involved romantically before those two years of service are up."

Laila inhales, organizing her next words. "So she secretly married Tyto but told everyone else she married a pedes man in the Marines. Marcus the Marine, we called him. If people asked after him, she would just say he was deployed somewhere confidential or whatever. People resented the fact that he was pedes, so they rarely did ask. It was a flawless lie."

"Wow. Deception is in my blood." Laila chuckles, but she couldn't know the double meaning behind my choice of words.

I don't ask about the trial, and I don't ask about the murder. I ask about her habits, her favorite colors, hobbies, and places to go. Gradually, my concept of Adian expands from a single memory to a continent of information. Warmth fills my core, like drinking hot soup on a cold evening.

Laila says, "Tyto—maybe a little biased—permitted her to start a garden in what *was* an empty lot behind the West Dormitories. It absolutely flourished, even still today. After she was killed, Major Rex commissioned a statue of Adian and placed it in the Garden."

"Oh," I screw my face up and turn to shoot Talan a look through the glass, though his own back is to me. "Talan failed to show that to me during this morning's tour."

When I can't think of any more questions, and the meeting behind us doesn't show any signs of ending soon, I surmise, "You were best friends."

Laila makes a face. "Adian and I were more like really close cousins. I'm sure she considered me one of her best friends, but Alex Murphy was, hands down, her best, best friend."

I'm on the edge of my seat. I know that name. "Murphy, as in the Commander?"

Somber, Laila tucks her chin. "The same."

I lick my lips. "Could I speak with him, too?"

"I don't know if he'd want that. Adian and Alex fell out before she... left."

"Why?"

Laila flashes one of those smiles nurses do when they're trying to understand your symptoms but failing miserably. "Because he testified against her and Tyto in front of the Verum Courts."

I fall out of my chair, catching myself with sore arms. From the floor, "What do you mean, *testified?*" I put myself back in the armchair.

Laila exhales. It's a dense, weary noise. "You're aware the Dentatas attacked the Academy in April before you were born?"

I nod, not wanting to waste time answering with words. I'm on the chair's edge again, threatening to crash a second time.

"To protect Adian and Calyx, Tyto ordered three of his Major's guards and a Trainee to go to Aurum and take the Vels through those secret tunnels. Well, after the smoke cleared, the people needed someone to blame for the damage the Dentatas caused. And where was Tyto throughout the attack? Saving Adian. Mind you, there weren't many casualties, but pedes were poking around for weeks, asking questions and whatnot."

"So they blamed my father."

"Almost as soon as he was well enough to leave the Hospital, too." I don't dare interrupt to inquire about *that*. "But people saw the way Adian doted and wept for him. They questioned Calyx's and your parentage. The Verum Courts flew in like vultures, and that was that."

"Wait," I shake my head, not quite comprehending. "But you said Alex testified?"

"He did," Laila's smooth skin stretches taut over her facial bones. "He was the Trainee in the group of Major's guards Tyto asked to escort Adian and Calyx through the tunnels. That was another drop of evidence in the case against your parents. Tyto was exiled, and Calyx—another hostage risk in Tax's eyes—was to go with him. Adian gave birth to you the *very* next day—stress-induced, the doctors said—but Tyto and Calyx were already gone. She was... heartbroken."

"She was betrayed."

"Yes," Laila tucks imaginary hair behind her ear, "but the other evidence against your parents—the marriage license, the paternity tests—was so substantial, Alex's testimony was just another narrative. Adian never forgave him for it, though."

My mother was betrayed by someone she loved.

I know all about that variety of pain.

Past
August 1998

Adian stood so closely to the raging bonfire, she was almost certain her red lipstick would melt. Raucous voices swelled with slurred song around her so that she couldn't recognize the tune they were trying to belt even if she wanted to. She glanced at her wristwatch, but rather than seeing the time, she saw something else.

Dammit! I scratched my timepiece. Adian froze, eyes half-lidded in the vibrancy of the fire. The words in her head were her father's, and if that wasn't confirmation enough that this party ate dirt, she didn't know what was.

Adian stepped away then, the afterimage of the great blaze blinding her. She wove through a scatter of lawn chairs and into the darkness. No one stopped her; she didn't expect them to. Alcohol stung the air, and Adian was grateful for the long walk back to her car. If her mother smelled booze on her clothes, Adian would be sentenced to sing in the church's choir until the day she died. At that thought, Adian shuddered.

"This was not worth James's silence," she muttered, feet squelching in the mud.

Muddy shoes. Another thing I'll have to hide. It usually didn't go like this—Adian and her friends would hear about a raging party, go, get drunk on good times; and James would stay up to let her in the back door. As if she were a cat. And promising her brother the Oldsmobile for the week would be worth it.

But this party, despite the secluded venue in a cornfield, was definitely not worth it. For one, her friends appeared to have ditched. For two, she didn't really know anyone else here. She should have listened to her gut when she parked the Oldsmobile on the side of a long stretch of dirt road. She hadn't recognized any of the other cars, nor had she heard from her girlfriends in the hours leading up to the party.

Half miserable for wasting her time, half relieved to be leaving, Adian marched through the winding cornfield paths. Her hands itched, and she uncrossed her arms to swat at mosquitoes humming around her ears. The din from the bonfire faded as she put distance between herself and the congregation of tone-deaf drunks. Soon, the only noises following her were the gentle wave of cornstalks in the wind, cicadas buzzing in hidden places. The waning moon shone ahead, outlining the farmhouse in black.

Tomorrow was Saturday, which meant Sunday was in less than forty-eight hours. Adian's already low spirits plummeted. She didn't mind church or the congregation, or even God. But she did mind the way her mother became some kind of manic woman, possessed with the Holy Spirit itself. Everything in church, Adian learned young, was an unspoken competition. And her mother's reputation was the unspoken champion.

Even the day Adian was adopted by the Vels, her new mother had exclaimed, rosy-cheeked, "Oh, the congregation will just adore her! I can just picture you in a white, lacy dress. Can't you, Adian?"

She had shaken her head then. "No, I hate white dresses," and Mrs. Vel appeared somewhat shocked and pleased at the same time. James, who had been cowering behind Mr. Vel's short legs, had edged some inches into the open.

"Why, my dear?"

"I don't know." She hadn't and still didn't. Childhood whims. Maybe she had a bad dream about white dresses before. James couldn't eat rice for a month because of a nightmare, though he refused to disclose precisely what horrors his brain had scrambled up.

Rustling cornstalks brought Adian back to the present. She paused, ears pricked. The rustling, maybe imagined, was no longer.

A raccoon, probably.

She continued along the path, feeling solid ground beneath her feet now, rather than mud. The farmhouse was twenty yards away, at least. She ducked her head to recheck the time and realized she never actually had before.

Holy hell! It's already past midnight. Adian's pace quickened. *James will be having an aneurysm by now.*

So caught up in her own anxieties was she, that Adian failed to notice the scent of alcohol in the wind. So loud was she, pushing through bent and buckled cornstalks, that she didn't hear the heavyset body encroaching upon her.

"Adian," a harsh voice said. A hand clasped her bicep, grip painfully firm. Irritation boiling in the back of her throat, Adian turned.

And knew, without really knowing, that she *really* should have stayed home.

A guy, two-times her size, towered over her, with round shoulders and a round body. A hoodie masked his face, but Adian thought she recognized the plaid pattern of the fabric.

Caleb. She didn't know his last name, wasn't really sure how she knew his first name. He was from her school, like the rest of the people

227

here, and she could vaguely place that red plaid hoodie somewhere among the clusters of band kids at lunch.

"Let go of me," her voice was even, though her heart threatened to burst from her chest like a fleeing bird.

"I wanted to talk to you, but you left." His words were so choppy, it took him about a minute to manage the sentence. In that time, Adian glanced around, looking for something to grab with her free hand. There were only cornstalks, and she knew they were the most stubborn plants to uproot in all of Forrest, Michigan.

Caleb shoved her, his weight and sheer power causing her to fall on her backside. She landed on her forearms, splayed across the corn. Stalks dug into her side, elbows sinking in moist dirt. Adian bit her lip and glanced up in time to see what her captor was doing.

Her voice wavered. "Stop, Caleb." Her eyes darted from his hands on his belt buckle to the hollow where the hoodie masked his face. "You don't want to do that."

"I do, though." He crouched on his knees, grubby hands grabbing for her waist. Adian screamed—and a sweaty, bitter hand clapped over her mouth. Adian slapped and tugged at his hands, but he was merciless. Caleb struggled with her impossible belt, and Adian, though terrified, was a hundred times thankful that she had worn a belt at all.

But then the clasp came undone, and the buckle was cast aside. Adian forgot about the time, forgot about church, and even James. As Caleb yanked the buttons and pulled the zipper, some primitive instinct took hold of her body. But what escaped her being was not wholly primitive at all.

Creatures sprang near her hands, and in the dark, Adian thought snakes were crawling around her body as well. She watched the beings curl around Caleb's hands and tighten. He made a noise, slurred yet terrified. The snakes slithered up, past his shoulders, and into the darkness of his hood. In the moonlight, Adian saw the creatures were not snakes at all.

They were vines.

Caleb choked, gagged. Adian realized as he fell backward, bound hands desperately clawing for his throat, that she was somehow responsible for his fate.

She was horrified. She wasn't aware of the tears streaming down her cheeks, just as she wasn't aware of the diminishing pressure in her palms. Adian scrambled out of the corn and found her feet, weak-kneed. Caleb sprawled like a mountain, limp. His barrel chest rose and fell, and that was enough for Adian.

The vines were gone. And Adian wasn't about to stay back to investigate.

She ran.

Adian was grounded, but she didn't care. Mrs. Vel made her join the church choir, and Adian didn't put up a fight. Mr. Vel revoked her driving privileges, and Adian let him. James, voice hovering between concern and curiosity, asked why she was complying so easily, and she couldn't bring herself to speak the words aloud.

Because somehow, in that dark cornfield with only the moon as a witness, vines had shot from her hands. And almost killed a kid, no matter how despicable he had been.

The shock of that night should have smoothed itself out and faded like every inconceivable occurrence eventually did, but every time Adian looked at her hands, she remembered. How was it possible? *Had it been a dream?* But no, the nasty, yet terrified glances from Caleb confirmed it enough. Nobody else noticed it, but he flinched every time she walked in the cafeteria. He wore high collars for days, hiding what, Adian didn't want to think about.

It had been real.

And then, three weeks later, came a knock on the front door. Adian was sitting at the kitchen table, doing her homework under her mother's watchful eye. She heard James answer the door, and, with Mrs. Vel's back turned, went to see who knocked when there was a perfectly accessible doorbell to ring.

Peering around the corner, Adian glimpsed a man in a tailored black suit. His ebony hair was slicked back, a grin set on his somewhat youthful face. He shook James's hand. "Mr. Dailey, from the North American Recruiting Office. And you are, young man?"

Adian saw James's knuckles whiten as he gripped the doorknob tighter. "I'm sorry, sir. We don't want any brochures—we're Calvinists."

Mr. Dailey didn't miss a beat. "You misunderstand me. I represent Taxodium. We heard about the incident." Mr. Dailey stifled a laugh. "That poor boy didn't know what he was telling the police. But our very own Tilia Pyrus confirmed Ms. Vel's case: she is pelari, and an extraordinary one at that."

James fumbled with words, trying to close the door in the significant presence of the oil-haired man. Adian should have been afraid, but fear was something she didn't typically acquaint herself with. She bit her lip. This man knew something. He had answers.

Still, she hesitated.

Yes no yes no yes no—

"James," Adian stepped out from behind the corner, "let him in."

Castan
July 2020

My eyes skip right over Aunt Laila and follow Corolla out the glass door. Her hair falls in wet ropes down her back. Her cheeks are flushed, possibly sunburnt. I'm guessing she had something to do with why Talan was late. I tear my eyes from her frame and clear my throat. Talan looks up from peeling the foil lid off a yogurt cup.

"We need to talk about the attack on the Vel's home." Kass swivels in her chair, scowling. Her expression mirrors mine. "The Gens shouldn't have known where Corolla was located."

Finis pushes his glasses up the bridge of his nose but says nothing. I look to Talan, who shovels Greek yogurt into his mouth.

"Does anyone have any thoughts?" I hate prompting as much as I hate being prompted, but no one is talking. I take a seat next to Talan, hoping that will spark some conversation.

"I don't know," Kass picks at the skin around her thumbnails. "I thought Vel was impossible to find to begin with. Whoever deleted her from the records did a pretty splendid job." Those words, in anyone else's mouth, would have conveyed the compliment that it is. But in Kass's mouth, they are scornful, critiquing, though I know she was just as impressed as the rest of us.

"What about you, Talan?" *You're the genius.* Now I sound like Kass.

Talan shakes his head, choking down a generous portion of yogurt. "You're the Genocide expert here." Words thick with more yogurt, "Wow, that was poorly phrased."

I'm not in the mood for jests today. I can't think.

"We're missing something," I pinch the bridge of my nose, "unless one of you is a spy."

Kass bursts out laughing. "That's rich of you!"

"Well, what else am I supposed to think?" My eyes pinball from Kass to Finis to Talan. "You guys aren't saying anything to Dani or Júlia, right? I know you didn't want to exclude them, but this stuff is confidential—the Major, Commander, and Ramsey handpicked us for this assignment."

"Maybe they're the traitors," Kass mumbles, ripping a chunk of skin off. "Shouldn't we be preparing for a massive infiltration instead?"

"Sure, but how can we prepare for that if our information is compromised? If the Gens knew where to find Corolla, then what else do they know?"

"Not that she's volga." This is the first thing Finis has said.

"Right, but—"

Finis, apparently, isn't done talking.

"Castan, I think you're paranoid. If our team were compromised, then wouldn't the Gens have left Corolla alone in the first place? The fact that they pursued her means that they still think she's valuable. If one of us were a traitor, the Gens would know Corolla's volga—and not worth their time."

"The Gens aren't just a bunch of sporadic bullies anymore," I scoff. "They're more organized."

Talan licks his spoon. "Good point, Fin." He nudges my elbow. "Maybe Ramsey leaked the right *false* information down the right underground alleyway. Who knows what kind of places he sprinkled Corolla's name. The words could have found the intended ears immediately." Talan shudders and reaches for another yogurt cup. I want to slap his extended arm.

"Kass," I turn to her for some support. Her expression is a mask of concentration. She rips more skin from her thumb. By the end of this meeting, she won't have any left. "You've been quiet."

"Have I?" There's blood pooling around her thumbnail. She sticks the oozing thumb in her mouth, scowl deepening. I knew she was upset when Rex gave Talan the Regency, but I didn't think she would be petty about it.

"What's wrong?" Finis's cool tone never changes, and it doesn't now. It tends to do the trick for Kass, as she's mentioned once or twice before that she finds our care and concern *demeaning*. I think she just hates admitting that we love her.

Kass takes her thumb out of her mouth but doesn't look up from her savage work. "Rex is allowing teams of students to manage the scouting demands now."

Finis goes stiff, and Talan exclaims, "She can't do that—they'll be slaughtered!"

"She doesn't have a choice," Kass blazes, "Hong Kong was more than just a statement about Tax Law."

Finis breaks in, "Then the South American Academy should send some of their Guard. Everyone knows the Gens harbor more grudges against this Academy than any other." I'm surprised Finis suggested such a hopeless solution. Kass is unimpressed.

"The SA Academy won't. They've unofficially adopted some sort of isolationist policy. They wouldn't send an ambassador, and they won't send soldiers."

There's no yogurt in Talan's mouth when he demands, "Then someone else should send guards! The Reserve—"

"Kass," I recognize that determination on her face. I know why she won't look at us. "Did *you* volunteer to lead a unit?"

She looks up then, indigo fire jumping from her eyes. "Yes," she slaps a hand on the table, "I did. And don't any of you *dare* tell me I can't." Her gaze is a challenge, eyes flickering over each of us.

Talan simpers. "What did Maggie say? She wouldn't—"

Kass shoots to her feet. Her chair crashes to the floor, just missing the computer monitors behind her. Though the table separates her from him, Talan flinches.

Jaw set, each word is a strategic blow. "Maggie is doing her part in the hospital, and I will be doing my part in the field." Kass grinds her teeth. "If you'll excuse me, I have another meeting to attend. Consider this my formal resignation." She weaves past the table, the air radiating her anger. She pauses at the door and glances over her shoulder. "But don't worry, Castan. My lips are fucking sealed." Her hair is a cape of flames behind her. Through the glass, I feel Aunt Laila and Corolla's curious stares burning the side of my face.

When Kass slams the oak door behind her, Talan faces me. "Talk to her, Castan." His eyes are the size of saucers. "She can't get involved with the scouting units. You said it yourself: the Gens are more organized. And even if there hasn't been an attack on the scouts in months, things are escalating. Things can change."

I open my mouth, but it's Finis's words that ring through the air.

"Talan, no one can talk her out of it. She threw herself over a cliff when Calyx died, and a soldier's death is all she can count on anymore."

It's late in the evening when I find myself wandering the cobbled streets from the Dining Hall. I caught myself making that turn towards the Ward Residencies.

You live in the East Dorms now, Castan.

My conversation with Aunt Laila replays in my head over and over again.

"Should it be happening so soon? I don't turn eighteen for another three months."

Aunt Laila's expression softened. "It happens differently for everyone, Castan." Across the table, she gripped my hand. "But I am here for you. We'll get through this. Together."

I comb fingers through my messy hair.

"She threw herself over a cliff when Calyx died, and a soldier's death is all she can count on anymore."

I want to be angry with Kass, but I can't. It's my fault, isn't it? Even when my Essence burned its brightest, I couldn't save him. And Corolla is worse off.

Nothing is going how I thought it would. I should have run for the woods when I escaped the Complex. I should have barricaded myself against the world and melted in isolation. I should have brought Hadley with me.

I exhale and receive weird looks from a pair of girls passing by. I trudge on until the Dorms stretch on either side of me. The red clay buildings aren't as architecturally appealing as the Ward Houses with their Tudor-style exteriors. They tower, four stories high, patios and ground level porches to make up for their apartment dimensions.

As I pass down the road, all the identical Dorm complexes blur red in my vision. I stop at a brown door. Knock. Know I shouldn't. Swore I wouldn't do this again. But the thoughts are in a loop, and I need to break it.

Of course, when the door opens, I don't tell Júlia this.

"Castan!" She pulls me inside before I can explain myself. Lips painted a pale shade of pink, she studies me now. Her alpine features and thin, black eyebrows stir something in my being. Or maybe it's the way she's looking at me. Like I am a plate of the Dining Hall's brownie special: steamy and savory.

"I was beginning to think you weren't going to come back. At least to say hello."

"Hi, Júlia." I rub the back of my neck, not sure what else to say. The dorm is almost exactly how it was when I saw it last. Living room cluttered with incense, tarot cards, and more decorative pillows than one sofa requires. Júlia is the same, too. Her long, brown-black hair frames her face, falling somewhere at her waist. I realize, with a start, that what I thought was a black dress is actually an oversized tee shirt.

She notices my gaze traveling her slim legs.

"I was out back setting up my telescope," she skips towards the kitchenette, and I glimpse the lacy lingerie under that tee shirt. "Want something to drink? I still have some hard cider, I think." She opens the little fridge, shuffling through its contents.

My throat is dry, but I manage, "No, I came here to see you."

"Did you?" Júlia whirls around, cider in hand. "I hope you don't expect another séance." She quirks a thin eyebrow and takes a swig of her drink.

"No," I slip off my shoes, "nothing like that."

"Oh," her voice is low, knowing. "Dani isn't home tonight." But I knew that, didn't I? She works kitchens Sunday evenings.

And then her hands are around my neck, fingers cold from the cider. I grasp her waist, pulling her against me. I crush her lips with mine, and my desire grows. She tastes sweet, and my head swims. Júlia's icy hands are traveling up my shirt, fingertips gracing my bare sides. I shudder, and she pulls away.

"I knew you'd come back to me," she purrs, leading me to her bed. I let her.

I don't want this—I know I don't—but I'm so *tired* of trying, so *tired* of taking care of people and worrying that it's not enough. So even as I discard my clothes, even as Júlia climbs on top of me, even as our noises clash with each other, I tell myself it's okay. The world will still be the same when I leave here. Calyx will still be dead, Kass will still be suicidal, and I will still be me. But right now, with Júlia, I am nobody. Least of all myself.

When it's finished, I lie, gasping, with Júlia draped across me. Our sweat mingles, and we stick to each other like melted candy.

"I heard about your late night with Vel," Júlia says, voice subdued. I can't tell if it's her throbbing or me. I close my eyes, not wanting to think.

"Yeah?" Absently, I toy with her hair and manage to create a tangle. Júlia props on her elbows, and I meet her half-lidded gaze.

"If I didn't know any better, Castan Cassena, I'd say you're replacing Calyx with Corolla. Maybe even pushing for a little more." There's no jealousy in her voice, no trace of bad blood. Only coy observation.

Júlia sighs and rolls off me. But I can't move. While Júlia tugs her clothes back on, my stomach lurches. That temporary veil vanishes, and reality comes crashing down on me.

"Here," she tosses my clothes at me. "Dani will be back soon, so you should probably go."

I don't have to be told twice.

Past
September 1998

The Courthouse loomed above Adian, a domed ceiling formed in panels of painted masterpieces. Though none of the depicted scenes meant anything to her, the awed chatter surrounding her confirmed what she already knew: these were famous pelari moments.

"Look," a girl at her shoulder shouted above the din. For a moment, Adian thought the girl was talking to her, but then the girl tugged a boy by the elbow. "That's Matrona and Phaedra… and there! That's Gentry and Dawson Allen on the battlefield." The girl's excitement was so extreme, Adian felt the need to introduce herself. Then a hush fell over the room, and her opportunity was lost.

She watched as a man, maybe only a few years older than James (it was difficult to tell from the back of the room), stepped across the dark wood floor. Against a cold backdrop of the courtroom, his easy smile and welcoming body language were out of place. Adian wasn't sure how pelari law operated, but she was confident the massive desk behind that man was a source of feared power. Or at least, she wondered about it. What kind of people filled those seats?

All of this, she found herself thinking in a heartbeat. Adian adjusted her stance so that she could see between the many heads. There were seats towards the front of the Courthouse, but they were filled. Had her father been here, he surely would have complained about the lack of accommodation. After all, this was orientation.

"Welcome all!" The man raised his arms, and the last of the whispers died away. Adian's scattered thoughts scattered some more. This man had a lovely voice, didn't he? If her girlfriends were here, they would probably say something about his broad shoulders, lean frame. Even from the back, Adian could see his skin was bronze, and his eyes glinted a powerful, yet charismatic, aura.

He spoke again, lips grinning. "I'm Major Tyto Alba. I oversee this Academy, which means I now oversee you." He gestured to a stiff woman beside him, and introduced, "Commander Neva Rex, though I'm sure many of you have already heard of our head of the Guard." The man paused—briefly—and she thought he was looking directly at her. Adian grinned, not at the Major, but at the foolish idea that he could possibly see her through the thick of the crowd and the distance separating them.

Major Alba spoke once more, long paragraphs about where to go to schedule classes, where to pick up dorm keys, and even about the best foods to try in the Dining Hall. But Adian heard little of this. She was terrible at listening, even if the speaker's voice carried a note of... allurement.

Instead, Adian was distracted by the many faces and backs of heads against the alabaster marble of the Courthouse. *Pelari... And I am just like them.* Her body tingled with raw excitement. Not even Mr. Dailey's ominous words could deter her.

"The Dentatas have been searching for a cure since the day Tilia Pyrus diseased them. Because of your Essence's ability, you are that cure, Adian. Taxodium will do everything in its power to protect you." He mentioned something about Sentries—a sort of gun—being installed atop the buildings for protection. She couldn't imagine that, so yes, amidst these jittering teenage bodies, Adian only knew that she belonged.

She half expected to see Mr. Dailey here, but scanning the room now, she couldn't find that slick ebony hair. She was impressed with Mr. Dailey's skills of persuasion and had a mind to ask him some of his tricks. Mr. and Mrs. Vel hadn't been easy to convince, yet somehow—to Adian's delight—Mr. Dailey had managed it. The last she had seen of him, he was escorting her down the incline from Serpent Mound to one of the black vans waiting in the parking lot to take her here. Other recruits were there, tossing duffle bags and exchanging numbers. She lost Mr. Dailey in the chaos and, even in the promising crowd outside the Courthouse where everyone's possessions had been dropped in the front lawn like some kind of summer camp, there had been no trace of the man who liberated her from Forrest, Michigan.

Major Alba's words reached her ears. "...and of course, I will see each of you again when we sit down together and schedule your *Humanitas*." The man exited the stage, which really wasn't a stage at all, but rather, a raised floor where the guilty party would plead his case before the judge's massive desk. A roar of clapping followed the Major from the stage.

Adian screwed up her face, silently cursing herself for not paying more attention. *What's a* Humanitas*?*

As if he read her mind, the boy at her shoulder said, "You must be from a pedes family, too. I arrived a couple days early and read up on as much pelari culture as I could in the library." He had beach-blonde hair and kind eyes. Adian liked him immediately. *"Humanitas* is like a form of initiation," he explained, looking more at the crowd than at her. "Three Trials must be completed before Tilia Pyrus, to prove that you have what it takes to be… here," he gestured to the Courthouse, stifling a laugh, "and also to make sure you're not volga."

Adian turned her body, and even though Commander Rex was speaking now, she asked the boy, "Volga?"

His hazel eyes slid over hers. He crossed his arms and licked his lips, the corner of his mouth curling as he spoke, "Volga are pretenders. Pedes. From what I read, pedes sometimes catch wind of the operations happening right under their noses. Others are… What's the name for it? Conspiracy theorists? It varies."

Adian was sure she was missing some vital orientation information, but she was more amused by this boy than the rigid Commander. "What happens to them?"

"Each Academy has a guy who molds minds like clay. The text said, 'Very honorable and gentle,' but…" the boy shrugged one shoulder. "Whips up new memories and sends them on their way."

"Isn't that… kind of wrong?"

"Humane, I think is how the book put it. You and me, we grew up with pedes, so I think our definitions of *wrong* are slightly different than Tax's."

Adian puckered her lips, considering this. From the corner of her eye, she glanced at the boy. *So he's from a pedes family too.* Mr. Dailey mentioned the Essence gene was nondiscriminatory, but she didn't think she would meet someone with so similar a background as hers so soon.

The boy caught her staring. He thrust an arm out, and Adian clasped her hand in his.

"Force fields."

"Plant conjuration."

The boy's eyes expanded. "By Matrona—you're Adian Vel!"

Adian chuckled, ignoring the glances and succinct *shh*s from the students around them. "And you are…?"

"Alex," his grin widened, "Alex Murphy."

"Come in, Ms. Vel." Tyto straightened a stack of papers, in an attempt to organize, but it was hopeless. The number of documents a new school year demanded was beyond him. Rainier's desk was littered with pamphlets, rosters, and various other forms he had to review.

My desk, Tyto corrected himself. Before his mind could wander to the impossibility of his position, Adian Vel glided through the French doors.

"Please," Tyto gestured, "take a seat, and we'll discuss your housing arrangements."

Adian tucked a stray hair behind her ear and planted herself in one of the leather chairs opposite his desk. Besides the change of proximity, she was exactly how he'd seen her in the Courthouse. Large, chestnut eyes, and glowing, tanned skin. Her hazel hair was swept into a bun on top of her head, resembling a donut more than anything.

Her gaze fell to his desktop. She raised an eyebrow. "Busy day?"

Tyto cleared his head. Glanced at the array of papers scattered before him. He frowned. "Busier." He opened a drawer and extracted a crisp white contract. "But this paper is for you." He handed it to her, noticing a spark of interest in her eyes.

"Do I have to sign it? Because I think I've signed about fifty papers today." Again, her gaze gravitated towards the mess of his desk. "Though I probably shouldn't complain."

Tyto's frown twitched into a grin. "I do need your signature on the back. That paper just explains your rights as a Ward of the Academy," he knitted his fingers together. "Basically, once you've completed your four years at the Academy, you'll be expected to remain at Taxodium until the Dentata threat is no longer imminent. You won't be required to join the Guard or Intel for an additional two years, as your safety is more pressing than your service." Tyto noticed Adian's frown. "Of course, you can join Intel, if you wish, but the Guard is out of the question."

Adian glanced up, brow furrowed. "I can never leave?"

"Well, you can visit your family and whatnot, but we'll have to be careful about that. If the Dentatas discover you're leaving—"

"They'll kill me," Adian's voice was frigid, "I know."

Gently, Tyto added, "But that isn't likely to happen. Intelligence has already secured certain... precautions around campus. And besides," Tyto shrugged, "you weren't attacked on your way here, which leads me to believe the Dentatas aren't aware of your Essence yet. Maybe they never will be."

Adian didn't say anything. She scowled at the paper, flipped it over, and the scowl deepened.

"I hope your day has been enjoyable so far?"

"When will the Dentata threat *not* be imminent?" Adian looked up, her chocolate gaze piercing Tyto's.

"That's not for me to say."

"Hmm." She skimmed the paper again. "It says I'll be staying in a Ward House. The tour guide boasted five, so which one is my prison?"

"It's not your—"

"I know," her eyes glinted with mischief. "I'm joking with you. I love it here. Do you have a pen?"

Tyto opened another drawer and withdrew one. Adian snatched it from his fingers, bun bobbing.

"But I do want to know which House. Before I sign, that is." Adian uncapped the pen, waiting. "And also, no one's told me who my roommate is, so that would be good to know as well."

Tyto masked his nerves with a chuckle. "You don't give signatures easily, do you?" He thumbed through his papers until he found the roster for the class of '02. He drew imaginary circles in the air and pointed. His index finger landed on:

"Laila Cassena will be your roommate and your lodgings..." It was a split-second decision. Tyto remembered Major Rainier telling him about the old tunnels connecting the Major's bedchambers to Aurum House and outside the Wall. They were rumored to have been used in the Underground Railroad but were now long forgotten. "...will be Aurum House."

Adian grinned. Using the surface of his desk, she scribbled her name and handed him the contract.

"Thank you. If there's anything else you need, don't hesitate to ask, Ms. Vel."

Adian turned to go, then stopped. "Actually, there is one thing," a wry grin dominated one corner of her mouth. "Aren't you a little young to be at the helm of this Academy?"

Corolla
July 2020

"Oh, you're already awake." Talan pauses just inside the doorway. I look up from my shameful scribbles and set the notebook aside. I had that nightmare again, the one where I'm falling down a tunnel of flames, suffocating, and Castan's face peers over the distant opening. I thought writing it down would help, but traces of smoke still linger in my nostrils.

I suck in a sharp breath.

I would rather live that nightmare again than meet Talan's gaze. Because I remember what I was going to tell him yesterday. I didn't know what I was asking of Tilia then. I didn't know I would cross paths with one of the deceased's children. I don't know if I would take that memory back, but it's too late now.

"I got you a locker and a uniform." He tosses an orange-tagged key at me. "Let's go before the sun rises and the Monday meeting commences." He claps his hands together. I fiddle with the key ring and take another deep breath.

"Can we visit the hospital soon?" I dare to look at him. A muscle in his jaw twitches. I bow my head to the key once more.

"Between training and Monday meeting, there won't be any time." His cheerful, rational voice does not betray the irritation I saw in his eyes seconds ago.

"Talan, there's something I really need to tell you." In the edge of my vision, I watch him plop down on my bed.

"Look, Corolla," he combs long fingers through his thick hair, "if it's about what you were *actually* doing out so late the other night, you don't have to tell me. I *am* your Regent, but it's none of my business how you spend your free time."

"What?" Blood floods my cheeks, skin burning. "No, it has nothing to do with that, Talan!" I slap him across the shoulder with my notebook. He recovers quickly.

"Oh. Well then, what is it?" His eyes flicker to mine, and I can't look away. So I tell him what Tilia made me relive, and I tell him about his parents, about his father's death. How he sacrificed himself for his wife, how his last thoughts were about his children.

"I would never wish for you to see what I saw, but..." I suppress a shudder, "I wish you could feel what I felt from your father. He—" I stop myself, voice choked.

Talan's no longer sitting. His fists are clenched at his sides, long hair spilling into his eyes.

"By the Pyrus disease itself," he breathes. He begins pacing, and with each succinct turn, his exasperated curses escalate. Had there been any glass trinkets in my room, he surely would have pitched them all against a wall. "Allen's spotted mare. Rainier's left lung. Phaedra's mother!" He's reaching for an empty bookshelf, and before I can quiet him, he's raising it over his head as if it's only a piece of cardboard.

And here I thought his Essence was speed.

Though my muscles scream in protest, I'm on all fours, crawling through the nest of bedding to reach him. "Tal—"

"That bastard witch actually loved me." And with that, he sets the shelf back against the wall and heads for the door. "Change of plan," he calls over his shoulder, steps creaking under his slight weight, "we're going to that damn hospital."

This Academy has gone 27 days without a death.

I read this, and other posters tacked on a corkboard in Rainier Hospital. This place doesn't smell like a hospital, though. It smells like something more... earthy. I don't really know what I mean by that, except that the scent reminds me of fall when wet leaves litter the ground and the sky is golden hues. Maybe all pelari hospitals smell like this.

The off-white halls are bustling with so many people, I don't know where they're all coming from. Some are employees, some are patients. Black uniforms pepper blue scrubs.

Visitors sit in the half-rectangle arrangement of chairs in the waiting room, magazines or tissues folded in their hands. Talan said Rainier was built for all pelari, not just Taxodium. Maybe that's why some of these people look out of place. Or perhaps I'm the one out of place.

But I was born here.

"What's an... EsAp?"

"Huh? Oh." Talan glances over his shoulder, eyes flickering to the posters. "Essence Aptitude. It's for pelari parents to test their offspring's potential Essence." He faces the visitor's desk again, arms twitching with impatience. I read the poster with the bright-eyed baby again.

Want to be prepared?

241

I glance around, see that Talan's moved up in line, and I move up beside him.

"Are you nervous?" My gaze darts from his hand, wringing his wrist, to the wince in his expression. He's knotted his hair behind his head, but too-short locks fall around his ears, framing his thin face.

"No," a muscle in his jaw twitches, "I'm confused."

I startle. "Why? I'm sure it will do your mother good to see you."

Talan scoffs, a vein bulging in his exposed neck. "My mother..." The smart comment falls dead in his mouth. His expression changes, and we move up to the front of the line. A woman with dark highlights streaked with suicide-blonde hair sits behind a slate-gray desk in front of a computer.

"How can I help you?" Her unremarkable eyes glance from Talan to me and back again.

"I'm here to visit Vera Taylor," Talan says. The receptionist narrows her attention to him. The woman prattles off some information, makes Talan sign something and hook a Visitor badge to his shirt, then she takes him away. I watch him disappear in the artificial light of the hallway.

People press up behind me, anxious to be helped, but I don't leave the line. Asking Talan to come to Rainier was for more than just his reunion with Vera.

"Excuse me," I catch the eye of the returning receptionist. "I'm here to visit Luca Alba."

The receptionist frowns, clacking on her keyboard. "Luca Alba doesn't have visitation hours. Major Rex made that quite clear." She sucks on the straw of her fountain drink.

"But can I at least know how he's doing? I'm his family—"

The receptionist's eyes turn cold, cutting off any pleading words springing to leap from my tongue.

"I'm sorry, Miss, but Major Rex was explicit. Luca Alba is off limits to the public. Even family."

"Oh," I recoil from the desk, "thank you anyway." I slip away from the line, feeling like a kicked puppy. Without thinking, I take a seat on one of the waiting room chairs, the kind that could be green or blue but is ugly no matter what.

Not even family? Do Tyto and Valeria know Luca is alive? Elbows on my knees, I raise my head to the corkboard advertisements.

This Academy has gone_27_days without a death.

Hopefully Talan has better luck.

A figure storms through the visitor doors. I watch as Castan stalks past the corkboard. He stops abruptly, ripping a white paper from its tack. People turn their heads, following Castan's furious pace to the front desk.

"I need to speak with Maggie Delphi." The words come out a low growl and would not have been heard moments before, but the room has gone silent.

The receptionist takes one startled look at Castan. I can only guess at what she sees. Fire leaping from his dark green eyes, smoke curling from the corners of his mouth.

A wounded soul.

His eyes have so many personalities, it's difficult to keep up.

"Room 312," she says, voice even but eyes quite large. Despite myself, I grin.

Serves her right.

Castan storms down the hall, papers clenched between dangerous fists. In his wake, he leaves opportunity. I don't waste it.

Rising from my seat, I eye the frazzled receptionist. She primps her hair, recovering from her encounter. The visitors speculate in hushed tones, "...Cassena. He took a chunk out of Rosh Dentata in Yazd."

My legs stop in their tracks. I almost swivel around to ask the man who whispered Castan's name what he's talking about. Almost. My eyes dart back to the receptionist. She sucks on her straw again, back slightly to me. Without another thought, I tail Castan's exit through those winding halls.

In my hesitation, I've lost him. Only the mixed expressions of awe and irritation in passing nurses and doctors supplies clues as to where he went. It's just as well that I lost him—he hasn't spoken to me since the tunnels. I try not to think about what that means. Not because I don't understand why he's ignoring me, but because I don't understand why his disdain makes my stomach ache.

Heart thrashing in my ears, I scan the signs above.

E.R., Intensive Care Unit, Recovery, Restricted Cases.

I stop, and in that moment, all thoughts of Castan are gone. I step down that hallway, the lights humming like robotic mosquitoes above.

I read somewhere that reliving memories too often can distort them, but I don't think my mother's memory ever could be. It's pure and impenetrable. It's contentment and wholesomeness and love. My father, so dark and charismatic, loved my mother. So why hasn't he tried finding me? This is an old thought, worn and frayed around the edges like a page from a book thumbed over too many times.

But I still want an answer.

Luca Alba.

I reach a turn in the hall, tiles so polished they reflect the glaring lights above. I don't know why I peer around the corner—maybe it's the still, eerie atmosphere or maybe it's the clatter of my own heart—but I'm instantly grateful that I did. Two guards, adorned in black, flank a double set of doors. I can't see anything past that sturdy entryway, but behind one of the guard's elbows, I make out a gray keypad.

My heart sinks with a mixture of relief and disappointment.

That's when the alarms start screaming, like so many wailing sirens, and I know the Gens have come for me.

Past

October 1998

Tyto tried his best not to furrow his brow, but the task was proving more challenging than he initially thought. From his dark leather armchair, he watched the portraitist. He made brush stroke motions, elbows jutting from behind the large canvas. Tyto was all too aware of his face being transferred in oil onto that canvas. And he felt the cold bite of betrayal.

How can you think about her while this man paints you for generations of pelari to look at? Convinced the portrait would depict his conflicting thoughts as legible as a newspaper headline, Tyto relaxed his facial muscles once more.

TYTO ALBA LIKES ADIAN VEL. A childish thought. A traitorous thought. Tyto refrained from shaking his head just to prove to his mind how incompatible its ideations were. His position prohibited such relations—he may as well be a castrated monk—and he knew it. So why was Adian Vel tormenting him? It wasn't sex that drove him to her. No, it was something else, some other distinct quality in her deer-brown eyes.

The painter—Mr. Nepeta, if Tyto remembered correctly—glanced over the side of his canvas. Frowned. Disappeared again, elbows stabbing the air.

Tyto's genial smile slipped into a frown. He quickly amended it, though, willing himself to think about anything else.

The South American Academy, he goaded himself. *Contemplate their isolationism in recent months. Or even better, think about ways to solve it!*

But no matter the policies and paperwork he bribed his mind with, thoughts of Adian swirled across his own mental canvas, stronger than before. He had been—shamefully enough—keeping tabs on her progress. Though, it wasn't difficult to look up her grades, nor was it difficult to hear the chatter around campus. Adian Vel was otherworldly. She was fearless. And if the Dentatas didn't know about her before, they surely did now.

There was a knock on the bedroom door. Tyto dared to glance behind him—

"Luca! Orsino!" Forgetting his role as an immovable statue, Tyto sprang from his armchair to greet his brothers. His stiff muscles welcomed the interruption just as much as his mind did.

"Speak of the Pyrus curse," Luca grinned, clapping Tyto on the back.

"What are you doing here?" Tyto glanced from Luca to Orsino. Both were just as dark in complexion as himself: dark eyes, dark skin, dark hair. Such was their Florentine heritage. Luca, however, was taller and wore an eyepatch, the scar on his cheek gleaming. Orsino, ever the better groomed, wore a tailored gray suit, his hair combed back in style. Tyto, fashioned in his own trim-fitting suit, could never hope to boast the debonair Orsino did. The two visitors exchanged looks, and it took Tyto several seconds to piece together their hesitancy.

Tyto pivoted then and saw the rather displeased Mr. Nepeta.

"If you could just give us a moment," Tyto said, tone gentle. Mr. Nepeta set aside his palette, an expression of irritated submission marking his face as clearly as the paint strokes staining his apron.

When the portraitist had gone, Luca clasped Tyto's shoulder, a familiar gesture.

"Pas came out to Mom and Dad."

"He *what?*" Tyto shared a look with his brothers. They had all known for some years now, but Pas was adamant their parents not know at the time. "Well, good for him then."

Orsino sighed and collapsed onto Tyto's four-poster bed. He loosened his tie. "I suppose, but you know how the Guard is with..." Orsino struggled to find the right word, "...homosexuals." He smirked. "That just doesn't roll off the tongue nicely, does it?"

Tyto folded his arms across his chest. "So what? The Guard doesn't have to know."

"Actually," Luca cut in, leaning over Tyto's portrait with a mischievous eye, "our dear Pasquale has caused quite the scandal. Got himself suspended for two weeks."

The blood drained from Tyto's face. He felt his body sinking onto the cushioned armchair, but he didn't remember his feet carrying him there.

"What do you mean, scandal?"

Orsino raised his head. "I thought you would have heard about it? You are Major."

"Of this Academy," Tyto said, voice stripped, "I don't know everything that happens in the rest of them. Least of all, the South American. That's probably why Pas chose to be stationed there."

"Hmm," Luca mused, still bowed over the canvas. "He got your nose all wrong."

"Well, *Tito*, let us just say that our brother is a very *passionate* lover, and that attracted some," Orsino coughed, "attention."

Tyto spun about to face Orsino. "From?"

It was Luca who answered, "Major Tieko. She's quite... displeased." He stepped away from the portrait, not a trace of mockery left in his being. It was rare that Luca was severe, which only made the situation that much worse.

Tyto scowled, feeling like a child amid his older brothers.

But I'm not a child. I'm Major of this Academy.

"What are you proposing I do?" Tyto's eyes darted from Orsino sprawled supine on his bed to Luca, who prowled the mahogany flooring with less grace than a blind cat. It wasn't Luca's lack of depth perception that made him such a clumsy being: it was simply who he was. "I am assuming," Tyto continued, "that's why you came?"

Orsino bolted upright, a snarl in his voice. "Pas will be a dishonorable discharge if you don't intervene."

"He's stationed at another Academy—it's hardly my place to tell Major Tieko how to do her job!"

"No," Luca said, voice soft, "but you can endorse a better fate. Here, at this Academy. This is the most progressive of all six Academies—one word from you could change how the whole of Taxodium looks at gay pelari, whether they're in the Guard or on the streets." Luca added when Tyto opened his mouth, "You know it's true. You have the Taylors wrapped around your little finger. It's no secret how much you've impressed the Judges these first few months."

Tyto bowed his head, not with shame but with the weight Luca's demand carried. But he was right—Tyto seemed to have all Taxodium's attention. He inherited so much more than the Major's position. He inherited expectation. Some, like Commander Rex, expected him to fail. Others—a vast majority of others—expected him to triumph right up until his death. His predecessor had been much the same, and Tyto's bond with the late Rainier was no secret either. Taxodium thought him Rainier's incarnate, his contemporary, perhaps with a little less nicotine addiction. And Tyto could not let them down.

When he looked up, Luca and Orsino were gazing at him, a different kind of expectation. "You realize I can't bring down the Attachment Laws. If Pas broke those..." *There would be a trial, and he would be disgraced for the remainder of his life.* It was not a simple matter. To break the Attachment Laws—precautions set into place to avoid hostage crises with the Dentatas—was to break a very fundamental rule within the Taxodium Doctrine.

Tyto didn't say this. Instead, he asked, "So I'm to proclaim some sort of 'Don't Ask, Don't Tell' like the Americans?"

"No," Orsino scoffed. "Pedes are always solving problems with silence, rather than truth. Just make a speech or something. And throw in there that bit about the Spartan's Sacred Band of homosexuals. They fought twice as hard for their partners because they were all bound in the same, bloody fate!"

"I think," Luca's solemn eye slid from Orsino to Tyto, "what Orsino means to say is that Taxodium's stigma needs to change. There's really no difference between two men, two women, or a man and a woman. So long as it doesn't interfere with the job and no hindering attachments are made, it shouldn't matter."

Tyto mulled it over for several minutes. He could draw up a Mandate for the Board of Majors. Or, at the very least, speak to the Board about the absurdity this social stigma created. *We are better than pedes,* he could rally. *We are better than—*

He glanced up suddenly. "How are Mom and Dad taking it?"

Orsino shrugged. "They just want him to be happy." Something flashed in his dark eyes but was gone before Tyto could name it. "This Academy harbors Adian Vel, the great antidote. When the Dentatas strike, will it matter so much your guards' sexual preferences, or will it matter that Vel is protected?" Orsino raised a dark brow. "Just saying. Perspective means everything."

"Right," Tyto pressed his palms together, thinking. "Of course. I'll come up with some way to present this to the Board. Thank you for bringing it to my attention." He looked around at his brothers, realizing that this was the first time they had visited him in his new position. They seemed to read his thoughts.

"Well, brother," Luca's eye gleamed. It was a normal eye, despite its abnormal capabilities. Luca could see anyone's truest intention if he bothered to look for it. Intel had offered him quite a price for his abilities, but Luca, never one to be tethered, declined the position. Tyto almost ducked his head, praying that his brother didn't see his heart then and there, splayed before him. "No matter how convoluted that portrait is, your head hangs in the Gallery before hanging in either the Barracks or Intel. That's a first. I'm proud of you."

Orsino saluted him. "Just because you're the big cat now, doesn't mean we can't still drag you from your bed in the middle of the night."

Tyto shuddered, remembering his childhood horrors. "I guess that's what big brothers do. Speaking of—What's Giovanni up to? I haven't had so much as a phone call from him."

Luca rolled his one eye at the mention of his twin. "Oh, you know, lost in his violin or something of the sort. I can't keep track of *what* he plays anymore. I swear it's everything short of an actual human being."

"Are you available later?" Orsino asked, readjusting his tie. "Luca and I can stick around for dinner, if you are."

Tyto felt the presence of the unfinished canvas behind him, the stack of papers on the desk on the floor above him. "I'll need more than a last-minute notice if you guys want to get me out of the Manor." Tyto ran a hand down the back of his neck. "I'm sorry, there's just so much to do."

"Ah, well," Orsino sighed. "At least we know you're actually doing something these days." He pulled his younger brother into a hug. "You are the symbol of progress, *Tito*. Don't forget it."

"And don't forget your family either," Luca clasped his shoulder. "It was just yesterday we were all rolling like maniacs down the vineyard hills in the light of the setting sun."

Tyto pulled out of his brother's grips. "Don't go soft on me, Luca. But I'll talk to you both later. Mr. Nepeta will have my head if I don't start behaving like a proper model."

"Alright, *Tito*," Orsino hissed with laughter. "Talk to you later." He slipped out the door, leaving Luca hovering not too far behind.

"And Tyto," Luca glanced over his shoulder. "Your next endeavor should be to amend your life sentence to die alone." With a knowing look, Luca disappeared in the same manner Orsino had.

Tyto stood, grinding his teeth, and silently cursed his brother for reading his heart.

Adian. Was it his imagination or did the tunnel entrance in his closet call out to him?

He was only a man. A progressive, powerful man, but a man nonetheless. He could never hope to slay the Attachment Laws, which had been a foundation for Taxodium during those strange times when the Dentatas turned on other pelari. The Verum Courts established such laws to protect Taxodium from infiltration through the weakened hearts of its people. Perhaps the Laws were brutal, but they were necessary.

They were necessary.

Mr. Nepeta, quiet as a mouse, entered the room once more. He saluted, three fingers over his heart, though the gesture was perhaps less enthusiastic than ever before. The man was old, Tyto thought, old enough that he painted the late Major Rainier when he began his career twenty-five years ago.

"Shall we continue, sir?"

"Yes, of course." Tyto sank into the armchair, resuming the stiff-necked position his muscles were all too keen to forget. His lips twitched into a slight grin, and he found himself even more tormented by thoughts than before.

Of course, he would do his best to assist Pas (it would benefit more than just his brother). But that was not what gnawed his neurons. No, he was choking on something Orsino had said.

"They just want him to be happy."

Happy. Tyto wasn't sure if he could claim such an emotion, though shouldn't he? He had Taxodium in the palm of his hand, yet... He was afraid to admit how lonely he was. He remembered something Major Rainier told him once. They were discussing the history of the Guard, no doubt one of the man's subliminal tactics to encourage Tyto to choose a branch.

"It's evolved," Rainier said, a cigarette clamped between his teeth. His habit wasn't as dire back then, though of course, Tyto suspected it would only become worse. "Taxodium never needed an army until the world did. And then the Dentatas happened, and we couldn't take it back."

"It's difficult to imagine Taxodium as just... a school," Tyto commented. How young he had been, only just beginning his junior year at the Academy. But Rainier laughed a sad sort of noise, one filled with nostalgia or perhaps regret.

"Yes, Taxodium was just a school, a place where pelari could learn to control their Essences. A place where they wouldn't be alone." Something flickered in the Major's eyes then. He didn't look at Tyto as he said, "It is incredibly isolating to be pelari, you know. Taxodium was a chance to abate some of that loneliness."

"It still is, though." That's not what Tyto wanted to say. He wanted to say, "Sir, you sound like your great-grandfather, Jacoby Rainier." But he didn't know Orland well enough to speak like that yet. He was just trying to make it through junior year. Shadowing the Major seemed like an easy way to do that, especially since the Major enjoyed his company.

"Yes, my boy," Rainier's eyes flitted to Tyto's then, "but our generations never knew the purity in that old order. The Dentatas ruined everything with their greed and destruction, killing those pelari who masked their talents to help the pedes in their Second World War. The great Venefica herself could not pass over into peace because of the bastards, but... I suppose that's a conversation for another time."

Young Tyto opened his mouth to speak, but he had no words for the Major.

The memory was so fresh in Tyto's mind, only the scent of oil paints reminded him that it was just that. A memory. But late Major Rainier had been correct on two matters: 1) To be pelari was to be lonely, and 2) The Dentatas did ruin everything.

That's why, Tyto decided, neither factors would hinder his chances with Adian Vel.

Castan
July 2020

I fling back the door to Room 312, which, by the looks of the vending machines, mini fridge, and assorted couches and chairs, is a break room. The air reeks of lukewarm pizza. Maggie, a granola bar in hand, jumps at the sight of me.

"Oh," she relaxes. "You scared me, Castan."

I hold up one of the two crumpled papers in my hand. "Did you see this?" In my mind, I still do. The Mark of Tribulation, like an umbrella at the top of the page. Below that, the Major's Mark, eight black circles gradually becoming larger as they travel down the paper. The words scattered stylistically about the page: *For our brothers, our sisters, our society. Join the scouts today!* I don't have to ask—I already know this is Kass's doing.

I lower the paper and ball them both up into tight wads. I toss them in a nearby trash can with more force than is necessary. With the palm of my hand, I rub sleeplessness from my face. "She can't get involved with the scouts, Maggie."

The Healer glances at me above the rims of her glasses. "It looks like she already has." There's sleeplessness, and there's exhaustion. Maggie is the latter, great bruise-blue circles under her eyes. Her expression is pinched, eyes half-lidded. On the couch, her entire body sags into the cushions. Sometimes I forget the Healer is just as old as me.

"Castan," Maggie takes a bite of her granola bar, "I know your job conditioned you to believe that you were responsible for someone else's fate, but you can't save everyone. Not because you're incompetent, but because that's not how the universe works."

"Are you really lecturing me on destiny? You think it's Kass's destiny to die? You think it was Calyx's?"

"I think you take too much responsibility for things out of your control. Kass needs to figure things out for herself."

"And leading a scouting unit is going to help her do that?"

"I think it's a start. At least she's not lying in bed all day anymore; at least she's trying to live her life."

"It's a death sentence—she's suicidal, Maggie, and we have to help her."

"She's not suicidal, Castan," Maggie gives me a hard look. "She was born into a family of soldiers. This is what she's always wanted." She looks so tired, it's almost painful to witness. Of course she believes in destiny—hers was sealed the moment Tax found out she's a Healer.

"I bet Phaedra took days off."

Maggie sinks farther into the couch, eyes closing. "Phaedra was a humble slave. She didn't get days off."

"So then why don't you?" I pull up a chair from the small circle table, prop my elbows on my knees. There's coffee on my breath, but I wish I had another cup in my hand.

"What with Hong Kong and Corolla Vel's presence on campus, there hasn't actually been as many outside pelari coming here. They all know to stay away. Even the registration for next year's freshmen is suffering. Some people aren't even coming back for next semester." I already know this, heard echoes of the same thoughts in the locker room this morning.

"How do you know that?"

"I have friends in Intel."

"This will be the summer we finally destroy the Gens."

Maggie, who could have been asleep seconds ago, jolts upright. "See, that's what's wrong with Taxodium these days. We're all so vengeful or afraid, and it's because of the Gens. It didn't used to be like this."

"You're an idealist, Maggie. Things have been different ever since the end of World War II."

"I just wish pelari weren't always out for blood—it would save me money on new scrubs." She finishes off her granola bar and retrieves water from the mini fridge.

"When's the last time you actually went home?"

She sighs, stretching her arms behind her back. "If you didn't keep bringing me special case patients, I would get to leave more often." Only by the slight quirk of her lips, do I register her comment as a joke. She's so drained, she doesn't even have the energy to properly do that.

"Why, what's up with Alba?"

"He's under lock and key. I legally cannot tell you anything about my patients. You know that."

"Yeah, I was just wondering. Corolla is anxious to know."

"Then you can tell her he's stable, but I really can't say much more."

"Right—"

Just then, Maggie's pager goes off with three high-pitched squeals. She snatches it from her hip, frowns, and that exhaustion is set aside. It has to be.

"What is it?" But Maggie's already tucked her water bottle in her satchel, dashing for the door.

"Cardiac arrest," she calls over her shoulder. Maggie plunges into the hallway, and I take after her. I watch her go, down that snow-white hall, it's almost blinding. She jogs up until the corner, dead stops with a look of superior calm that even Finis couldn't possess. She pushes her glasses up the bridge of her nose and disappears around the bend. *Recovery*, I read the sign above her departure. Several other darting nurses disappear after Maggie, in the same rushing and then tranquil manner. Maybe they slow themselves down so as not to put themselves into cardiac arrest, too.

A flicker of movement in the corner of my vision catches my attention. A girl crouches, shoulder pressing against the wall. I know who it is, even before she turns her head, caramel hair whirling about her face.

"Corolla?" And then I am before her, staring at her parted lips, eyes so full, I'm afraid they'll explode from her head.

"I have to get James," her voice is a strained whisper.

"No, Corolla, no." I press her face between two hands. Because of course she knows about the Academy's alarms, but not what they sound like. "The Gens aren't here, okay? Those were just pagers going off for one of the patients." Beneath my pinkies, her pulse clobbers in her throat. Her saucer-round eyes dart from the hands framing her face to my own eyes. I quickly step back, hands dropping as if the surface of her skin is a hot pan.

"They're just pagers," I repeat, just as breathless as she. Her chest flutters rapidly. I nod to the segue behind her and rake a nonchalant hand through my hair. "Those guards have them too."

"I thought…" Color returns to her cheeks.

"I know. At least you were on your feet," I say, meaning it as a compliment. "C'mon, let's get out of here." She doesn't protest, just follows deflated at my side. I glance at her.

At least she's chewing her gum not her lip.

We break into the wing's main artery. There's no trace of the rushing staff. It's as if the pagers never went off. I wonder which patient went into cardiac arrest.

I ask gently, "What were you doing in that hall?"

Corolla flushes scarlet. "I wanted to see Luca." The telling note in her wavering voice makes me believe there's more to her visit than just that. I don't press for more.

"Oh." I've done enough hospital shifts to know that Restricted Cases are as unobtainable as the gold in Fort Knox. I grin. "Did you think you could get past the guards and locks?"

"No," Corolla ducks her head, "I just wanted to know if he was alright."

I think about the scant information Maggie supplied. "He's stable."

Corolla doesn't say anything. We walk the remaining distance in silence. The waiting room looks just about the same as when I stalked past earlier, though I wasn't really focused on visitors. This time, I really do see Rainier as Maggie described it. There aren't as many people flooding the visitor's wing as usual. The chairs are peppered with bodies, and most of the people passing through are adorned in the garb of the Guard. The fall of the Asian Academy affected more than just Taxodium's morale. It affected pelari morale.

I duck my head, thinking about everything I overheard in the locker room this morning. *"Tilia's relapsing,"* the Commander said. *"Pelari are losing faith in Taxodium."* I didn't want to believe it, but Rainier is evidence enough. Still, I felt no guilt for ripping down as many of Kass's propaganda posters as I could find.

I glare at the corkboard across the way. A fresh wave of mingled frustration and apprehension sweeps over me. I didn't make any promise to Calyx to watch over Kass once he was gone, but I know he would want me to. Just as he would want me to watch over his sister. I think of my own sister, buried somewhere underground. Where did Numen move his people?

Another question arises, filling the chambers of my heart with a strange mix of terror: Will my plan work?

For the first time, I doubt my preparations.

Maybe I would have been better off hunting for Mena Dentata like Rex initially wanted. I glance at Corolla. *At least then, she would be out of harm's way.*

"Talan," Corolla cuts across the waiting room floor, nearly severing a woman from her small child's grasp. Corolla mutters an apology, but her attention is fixated on Talan. He's standing on the far side of the room, near the drinking fountain and kid's corner of toys and coloring books. I almost missed him back there, wringing his wrists, skin stretched taut over his face.

"What's wrong?" Corolla beats me to it. Talan glances in our direction. I narrow my own eyes at the fist locked around his thin forearm.

I know what you're doing.

"I was visiting my mother," his voice is soft as snowfall, though it carries the weight of rocks, "and she's still a little out of it, you know? Well, she started muttering something—Alba, I think—and then her heart monitor was screeching."

"Oh my god," Corolla's mouth is an O, "Is she alright now?"

Talan catches my gaze, and his arms drop limply at his sides. "I don't know… Maggie was there. So were other nurses." He fixates on something behind us. "Corolla, we should go. Morning meeting starts soon."

Talan," I read his expression, "I'll take care of it. You should stay here for when Vera recovers."

Talan shoots me a grateful look, and Corolla squeezes his hand. Does she know what he hides under those long sleeves?

"Keep me updated." Talan nods, sinking into a chair. Corolla and I make for the glass doors. I feel the visitors' stares on my back like laser beams, hot and aggravated. Word travels quickly among pelari as if we are all tethered to one another with electric wire. *Castan Cassena cut Rosh Dentata's finger off,* the silence whispers. I ignore them, just as I did the first time I shot through the room. If I cared to check, I would probably see condemnation side-by-side with their awe. The April Attack, Alba Atrocities, Scouting Tragedies, the fall of the Asian Academy: The people are losing faith in Taxodium.

Outside, the wind caresses gentle fingers across my cheeks. Gray clouds no longer lurk in the horizon but hover above campus. A faint mist travels on the wind, but I'm so tired, I hardly take much notice.

"Why would Vera say 'Alba'?" Corolla grips the iron handrail and descends the layers of stone steps. I note the suspicion in her tone, but only one Alba makes sense in this scenario. I don't answer her until we reach the bottom.

"Maybe she didn't say Alba at all, but if she did," I guide Corolla right, "then maybe it's because she feels guilty for banishing your father." Our shoes clap against the red brick road. The earth begins to slant. I see the Garages ahead, black vans stationed in the parking lot. There's another lot near Rainier, but this one is reserved for visitors' vehicles.

Corolla is mechanical when she says, "The Taylors put my parents on trial."

I comb fingers through damp hair. "Yeah."

A heavy silence falls over us like a stage curtain. Corolla lags several paces behind me, no doubt mulling over the unspoken.

Then, under her breath, "I hope she's alright." I stumble but not because of the uneven bricks. Her heart is an ocean brimming with selflessness, passion, love. And if I could just catch one drop of that goodness, then maybe I would be a better person because of it.

I shake my head of such sappy thoughts, but the wonder doesn't go away. Her reaction shouldn't be such a surprise, but it is. Maybe pelari *are* always out for blood, like Maggie said. But Corolla isn't pelari. She's volga.

When we make it to the bottom of the slope, the light mist has transposed into a sprinkle. Cool water droplets soak into my scalp, slide down my arms like tears.

Corolla slows. "I thought we were going to a meeting. This is—"

"I said you had to walk through the gates, so here we are!" I sidestep so she can view the magnificent gate. It's iron-wrought, though the weave of flora through its bars masks that characteristic. The gate reaches almost as high as the coniferous trees of the Twelfth Wall, which branch out on either side of it so that one cannot tell where the gate stops and the Wall begins. The Wall groans as a stronger current sweeps through it, rustling the leaves and hedges like the flapping wings of a flock of birds.

Corolla is only feet away from the gate now, head craned to read the block letters capping the gate's arch: Taxodium Academy, North American Division.

I come up beside her, crossing my arms. "Guess who did those flowers in the bars?"

"Adian." She touches tentative fingertips to the bell-shaped blossoms drooping from delicate vines.

"They come back a different color every year." I watch her trace one's rose-red outline. Last year, they were white as snow.

"What type of flower are they, do you know?"

"No one really knows," I poke one of the bells myself, "people call them *Adian's Doorbell.*"

She shoots me a sidelong glance. "That's not very elegant."

"No," I chuckle, smelling coffee on my breath, "I suppose it's not."

"I expected something symbolic and Latin."

"I was never very good at that class, but maybe..." I cock my head, thinking. "Maybe *Adian's Animus* does her work better justice."

"Animus?" Spheres of rain collect in her black lashes. She blinks them away, though never seeming to break her hold on my gaze.

"Heart, spirit," I translate. When she bows her head, I add, "I think."

Her eyes, like the sun shining through whiskey, makes some of the fog of sleeplessness scatter. Something indecipherable stirs in my breast. I think about Júlia. It never mattered before, never meant *anything* before. But in Corolla's presence, it means shame.

"Anyway," I say louder than necessary, pivoting on my heel, "let's get this gate open." I make for the white box, to scan my student ID, when suddenly, the gate groans with the voice of the ancients. Adian's Doorbells jolt, some plummeting like parachutes to the asphalt. Drops of blood on pavement.

Corolla startles back into the grass as the doors swing on their own volition. Three black vans appear from the shadows in the tunnel of overhanging branches. I always liked the entrance better than the exit. Something about feeling encased in a tunnel of trees is appealing to me. *The ambassadors.* Behind us, I hear the welcoming entourage barreling down the hill in a golf cart. Commander Murphy steers with all the elegance of pedes just learning to drive. Ramsey is green with sickness. I pick out Major Rex's ivory spiked hair among the group. Suddenly, the atmosphere becomes severe, frigid as a winter blizzard.

I glance back at the black vans, which have swung round to the private lot across the cobbled street. Their passengers clamber out just as the Major's party reaches them (maybe with a harder stop than Rex was prepared for). I recognize the sashes of the Australian, European, and African Divisions.

"Are those the ambassadors?" Corolla asks, voice strained at the sight of so many strangers. Except they aren't all strangers.

A figure breaks away from the cluster of chattering dignitaries.

Issak Park.

It's beyond my understanding of Essences as to how he knew Corolla and I were standing, gawking, across from the lot. I suppose he heard Corolla's unanswered question. He saunters up to us, his gait as mechanical as a puppet on unpracticed strings.

"Miss Vel," he grasps her hand and plants a kiss upon her knuckles. "Cassena," He turns that milky white gaze upon me, "you stole my patient."

I launch a counter, "No—"

"He's my uncle." I'm so used to Corolla's soft wonder that it takes me seconds to process that such acid could come from her mouth. Park startles as if his enhanced hearing is unaccustomed to such a response. And I know, no matter how subtle Corolla's bite was, Issak heard every syllable with painful clarity.

"If you'll excuse us," I nod to Corolla, "we have someplace to be. I hope you enjoy your stay." *Not in Aurum,* I pray. *Any House but there.*

With the tangled noise of many welcomes, salutes, and small talk at our backs, Corolla and I tramp down the road. Pellets of rain prickle our skin and wet our clothes. Corolla doesn't seem to mind.

She says, "I think we missed morning meeting."

I shoot Corolla a sidelong glance. "How about breakfast instead?"

My insides constrict with shame again. Because when she looks at me like that, like I am one of the Allen brothers reincarnate, I want to tell her everything. I want to tell her why I can't sleep at night, why I can't be pleasant, why I can't get attached to her. Because in a month or so, Taxodium will be liberated, I will be stripped of my Essence, and she will be starting her life over with James once more.

She looks at me like I am a hero. And I am not.

Or maybe I am just tired.

Past
September 2000

"'Tilia Pyrus, the Mother of Enchantments, achieved which of the following a) cantus blades, b) Holds, c) the Dentata disease, or d) all of the above.'" Adian gnawed the end of a No. 2 pencil, puzzled.

Alex lifted his head from the stack of textbooks he was pouring over. He propped his elbows on the library desk. "That's a stupid question."

They were in the campus library, dark shelves of books aligned around them in neat rows. The first time Adian had been here, she was sure she would need a map to find the front door again. Luckily, Alex had a sense of direction. It was unspoken between them that this lone desk was theirs. It was tucked in the farthest corner of the first floor, near the Biographies and Memoirs section. Adian was still surprised pelari libraries even contained pedes books.

"That's why I read it aloud." Adian circled D. "Why is this quiz so easy?"

Alex sighed and flipped the page. "I wish Field Medicine weren't such a mess. I read it, and everything jumbles together like a ball of Ramen noodles."

"I have that next semester. Just take one thing at a time, Alex. You tend to get ahead of yourself." Adian turned back to her quiz and answered several more questions. Pelari History 101A was perhaps the most straightforward class she had taken yet. When she would ever apply it to real life, she didn't know. James used to wonder the same thing about trigonometry. That was before he found architecture so alluring. Adian felt a little pang jolt her heart. She patted the packet of seeds in her pocket: James sent her something new every month, it seemed, and she was eager to plant them. Pumpkins, this time, for Halloween.

Adian's concentration broke. She felt Alex's eyes on her face as tangibly as if he were touching her himself.

"What?" Adian kicked his shin under the table. "Why are you looking at me like that?"

"Nothing," Alex ducked his head, grinning into his textbook. "I just remember when you didn't know what volga meant. You've come so far."

"Don't patronize me," Adian crossed her arms and leaned back in her chair, smirking. "I'd never met a volga."

"We're all one, in a way. Don't tell me you've never pretended to be something you're not."

Adian's blood ran cold. Did Alex know? Had he somehow found out? But then Alex slammed his textbook shut and stood, the demure brushed clean off his face.

"I've got to get going, or I'll be late for Fight Club." He shoved three textbooks in his backpack. The buttons fixed to the canvas of his bag rattled.

Adian relaxed, counting the number of heavy metal bands and political references on his bag. It was 2:1.

"Am I supposed to know that?"

"Har, har," Alex jibed. "It's not *that* kind of Fight Club. With the Commander as the instructor, it's more of an early year boot camp." He flung his pack over his shoulder, blonde hair glowing in the artificial light above.

"Rex probably just enjoys seeing a bunch of sweaty, bare-chested boys running around the field every Friday night. Or girls," Adian made a face of mild confusion and wonder. "I guess I don't know which way she swings." It was, after all, about a year ago that Major Alba established new precedents for Taxodium's branches. A good chunk of pelari adored him for it; a smaller chunk despised the changes. Older generations always had troubles with progress, it seemed.

Alex only shook his head, lips curling. "She doesn't swing *any* way, Adian. She's absolutely, irrevocably heartless."

"That was probably her campaign slogan, too. You should get a pin for it."

"God," Alex exhaled, tossing his head back in mock frustration. "I'll see you later."

Adian waved goodbye and watched Alex's blonde head disappear between the shelves of books. She happened to glance at her wristwatch.

"Holy hell!" She scrambled to shove her things in her bag and ran out of the library with a trail of *shhh*s chasing her through the door.

"You have a bad habit," Tyto revealed, as the white face of the chapel came into view, "of always being late."

Adian was suddenly grateful the tunnels were under her house—after today's Defensive Training, she didn't have the strength to carry her backpack full of books out of the well, too. She pulled herself up and over the lip of the old stone well. "Full disclosure," her breath came in short bursts, "I sprinted here all the way from the library, so don't say I didn't warn you about the sweat."

Tyto chuckled under his breath. Her eyes cut through the foliage and shadows of the sinking sun, locating him. He was sprawled in a clearing, surrounded by unruly pasture. He twirled a blade of grass between two fingers, but he wasn't watching his hand. He was watching her.

Adian had to stop, half sitting on the lip of the well, half standing in the overgrown clumps of grass. She caught her breath, but it had nothing to do with the amount of running she just performed.

How did I get here? Her eyes traveled down the lean body of the Major—*the Major*—and her knees felt weak. Stolen glances, stolen moments. This was not the first time they'd taken the tunnels to rendezvous at the chapel, but her head was still swimming with the impossibility of it all. She knew what her family would think if they found out: *whore.* Hell, it didn't matter she hadn't done anything with the Major, they would all think it—Alex (probably), Laila (maybe), all her classmates and all of her instructors (most definitely).

But that didn't stop her from going to him.

Tyto's complexion was dark—hair, eyebrows, eyes—but a certain brightness shot his brown irises with flecks of gold. Like a moth, she was sucked into the light.

Tyto propped on his elbows, eyes reflecting the want in Adian's. He pulled her down into his lap, her knees on either side of his hips. She felt his breath on her neck, his hands on her waist. He smelled of mahogany and cedar, and she knew he had been carving before he left the Manor.

And then he kissed her.

It was slow, at first, lips brushing. Then Tyto's hands were in her hair, pulling it free from the loose bun she'd tied it in. Her hair spilled over them, and she pushed into him, hungry. His teeth tugged at her lip, tongue pressing gently. He tasted like iced tea.

Her hands were suddenly yanking at his tee shirt. Her fingers skated across his bare stomach, feeling the warmth and sprinkle of dark hair. He reached for the hem of her blouse, and Adian shrugged off her windbreaker.

Can you go to Hell for having premarital sex on a chapel's lawn? She never really paid attention when her parents dragged her to church, but she thought maybe yes, God would be offended if they stripped to their skin in front of the Cross.

Tyto pulled away, fingers gliding down her bare hip. She felt his chest rise and fall against her own. It pleased a raunchy part of her to know that she made him breathless.

"I want you to meet my parents," he whispered against her cheek.

Adian fell back on his lap. He pulled down his tee, covering the bronze skin of his abdomen. *I guess it is kind of chilly outside.* Adian shivered and stood. She snatched her jacket from the grass and shoved her arms through the sleeves.

She didn't notice the fleece blanket they had been lying on, but it didn't surprise her that Tyto brought it. He was the type to recognize the subtle percussion in the background of loud music. He paid attention to detail. It's why he was such a talented wood carver, such a meticulous Major.

Adian climbed back into his arms, resting her head on his shoulder. They had their backs to the Academy, but Adian was aware of it lurking in the background, just as one is aware of a shark fin poking through the waves.

"What are you thinking?"

Adian shifted against him so that her head rested on his chest. His heart thrashed beneath her ear, loud and steady.

"I was thinking about babies, actually." Tyto's heart stuttered, and she grinned into the black cotton of his tee.

"Pelari babies are born laughing," she continued, "and I think laughter is the best part about a person."

"Yes," Tyto played with her long tresses, "it's a shame pedes are born squawking."

Sometimes she wondered who had been there when she was born. Her birth mom, yes, but had her birth father also been present? Why couldn't they keep her? The only thing they had given her was her first name: Adian. She held that word close to her heart as if it were all the words her birth parents could never say to her. *Adian.*

Adian was adopted by Mr. and Mrs. Vel when she was just six, and, strangely enough, she could only truly remember her adopted parents. Her skin was pale enough to resemble the Vel's, but there were parts of her that would never belong. The strange twist of her words whenever she was exhausted and weary. The feeling, buried deep inside her being, that there was something about her early life lost. She thought she recalled her real parents, in fading memories of red lips and glasses like goggles. But the faces always blurred into one of a menacing-looking man with a shiny bald head and black eyes.

Adian shivered and Tyto, thinking she was cold, hugged her closer. She never voiced these thoughts because she knew it wouldn't lead anywhere but to fatigue.

They watched the sun plunge behind the tree line. Yellow and gold bands faded from the fields bursting with corn and beans. Adian listened to Tyto breathe, in and out. She closed her eyes, memorizing the sound of his heart in her ear.

After a while, Tyto said, "You don't have to say yes. It's just that it's my sister's birthday, and we're having a small celebration." He didn't say what was really on his mind: *We've been together for almost two years now. It's time.*

"Can you afford to leave the Academy? Won't that look bad to your political opponents? You know, since you're new to being Major." *New* was an understatement—Tyto was decades too young to be the leader of the Academy, but his valor and charm had broken convention and landed him at the top of the election last year. He was modest, though, and hated talking politics with Adian.

"Dee," Adian's own heart skipped a beat, her name on his tongue, "you're not usually like this. What's wrong? I've told you before, my parents couldn't care less about Tax's Attachment Laws. They just want me to be happy." Tyto sat up, positioning her so she could see his face. "And I *am* happy, Adian, more than I ever have been."

Adian's gaze fell on their hands, bronze fingers intertwined with her tan ones. She remembered when her palms were delicate, untempered. Now, they were callused, proof of hours spent training. Tyto's were much the same, though there was an edge of softness to him. A feeling of déjà vu swept over her, making her head swim.

This was always how it was meant to be. But that didn't address the unspoken between them.

"If you're so happy, then why do we have to go to Cali?"

"Adian," Tyto blew air between his teeth. She glanced up, strands of hair tangling in her lashes. Tyto was incredulous, massaging his stubbled chin with a hand. He looked at her and tucked the hair behind her ear. His hand brushed her cheek, and she fought the need to hold it there.

"You're afraid things will change if my family finds out. What happened to 'full disclosure'?" Adian didn't say anything because it was true. Part of her was grateful she didn't have to say it aloud, the other part of her cursed his perception.

"Can you blame me?" Her flinty gaze connected with his. "My whole life transformed in a day, and I ended up in a strange place with strange people, with a strange ability. I can barely manage to leave Taxodium to visit my family without the Board throwing a hissy fit. My life will always be in danger because the Dentatas will *always* want my DNA—you know how apprehensive people acted when I left for my *Humanitas*. There's a new anxiety every day, but the fear is always the same." Adian sucked in a breath of frigid September air. "So, can you blame me for not wanting this, what's between us, to change?"

Adian was breathing hard now, not quite sure if she was making coherent sense. But in her heart, she knew exactly what she meant: This Tyto belonged to her, and no one could hold him over her head.

"Change isn't always the bad kind," he mumbled. "You know you're safe here, at Taxodium. And you know I would lessen the Board's restrictions if I could, but it's too much of a risk. But Adian," Tyto cupped her cheek, "you can't live your life in fear. We don't run and hide, okay? That's what the Dentatas do."

Despite the ache splintering her heart, Adian grinned. She leaned into Tyto's hand and kissed his knuckles.

"Pelari don't give anything freely, except for our lives. It's always been that way, whether the pedes need wartime allies or the Dentatas need to be put down. We work for the greater good. Always." Adian met Tyto's eyes, suddenly pinched with worry. *What's he getting at?* "But my heart is yours. The moment I saw you across the Courthouse, I placed it in your capable hands."

I love you.

He didn't say it, and he didn't need to: it was written up and down his face, in the soft curve of his lips, the gentle lines in the corners of his eyes. Her expression mirrored his, and she was content. Adian leaned into him, locking her arms around his waist.

"Fine, but I'm not going to the Board to request a leave of absence. You better figure something out."

Tyto stroked the back of her head. "I was thinking you just ditch. I'll reprimand you when you get back."

Adian laughed, giddy with the idea. It could work—what could the Board do to her anyway, if Tyto intervened first?

"We can take a plane, so Pyrus can't accuse us of using her Holds for personal reasons."

Adian mocked shock, "She would never!"

"But I would," Tyto chuckled. "In the meantime," he lifted an arm, displaying a packet of pumpkin seeds. *Must've fallen out of my pocket.* "You better plant these before the ground freezes over. By the time we get back, they may even be ripe."

Corolla
July 2020

The Dining Hall rings with its usual cacophony, but the chatter is more excited than usual. Castan and I take several steps inside, smearing rain from our cheeks, when two girls wave Castan over to their bench. One of the girls has tawny hair and fair skin. The other is dark-haired and alpine. We weave our way through other students and staff, my ears filling with a jumble of noise. My stomach grumbles, and I realize it's a little late for breakfast: the kitchen appears to be serving cold cuts for lunch already.

"Castan," the alpine girl calls. She scoots down the bench, making room for the two of us. "You missed Monday meeting."

Castan ignores the half-whine. "Corolla this is Júlia and Dani." He gestures to the dark-haired girl, then the honey-colored one.

"Hey," I manage a wave, though I am suddenly weak with hunger. Dani locks her pale brown eyes on my dark ones. She extends her hand across the table.

"It's a pleasure to finally meet you." I clasp her hand in my own, taken aback. I try not to stare, but it's incredibly difficult not to: Dani is the most beautiful girl I have ever seen. Sharp jawline, beige eyebrows thin, symmetrical smears above her intense eyes. She's wearing a stretch of apple blossoms around her forehead, honey hair curling around her in so many billows.

Dani is so captivating, I hardly know what Júlia is saying to Castan until he exclaims, "Banquet! What the hell?" Castan bristles. "I'm not going to that."

"What do you mean?" Júlia puckers pink lips. "You have to go. It's for the ambassadors."

"Yeah," Dani cuts in, leaning an elbow across the table, "it's not exactly optional either. Rex made that pretty clear during morning meeting." But Castan doesn't seem to hear her. His eyes fixate on something over Dani's head. He clambers to his feet.

"I'll be right back. Corolla, you want anything?"

"Sure—" But he's vanishing in the thick of people before I finish my sentence. I follow the angle of his desperate gaze and spy a crown of flame-orange hair. Kass.

"So," Dani pats the table between us. I notice the remains of a bowl of salad before her. "Do you have plans for the banquet?"

"Erm, no. This is the first I've heard of it, too."

"Right," Dani smacks her forehead. Her gaze flits to Júlia then back to me. "We can help you get ready for it if you want? I mean, Talan is good at many things, believe me, but the only hairstyle he knows how to do is the Pull Back."

"Yeah," Júlia nudges my elbow. "I have so many dresses—you could definitely borrow one." I don't know why, but I feel like a battered mouse trapped between the paws of two cats. I glance over Dani's head, heart sinking when I see that Castan is deep in conversation with Kass.

I manage a smile, voice small in the swell of the Dining Hall. "Sure, I would really appreciate that. Thank you."

"Great," Dani beams, flashing perfect white teeth. "It's Friday. You can meet up with us around..." she makes a face, glancing at Júlia, "...two? Yeah, that should be enough time if it starts at six."

"Oh!" Júlia grips my wrist. "I bet you don't know when your DT is either." I meet her gaze, head shaking.

"What's D—"

"Defensive Training," Dani gushes. "You can come with us to the afternoon session. It really doesn't matter what session you go to. But Commander Murphy teaches the afternoon one, and he's hella attractive."

"Oh, alright." I hardly know what I'm agreeing to anymore, head spinning with hunger and the anxiety of being prodded by strangers.

Dani's lips twist into a frown. "Where is Talan, by the way? He wasn't at morning meeting either."

"Oh." For a moment, that's all I can manage. I inhale and relay the events of the morning to two captivated pairs of ears. I leave out the part where I thought the guards' pagers were the Academy alarms, though.

"That's awful!" Júlia breathes, mirroring Dani's expression of utter horror.

"I hope Talan's okay," Dani ducks her head. "He hasn't even texted me."

"I'm sure he's alright," I find myself saying. "He said Maggie was there, so that's good, right?"

"Oh!" Júlia exclaims, clutching my wrist again. "Yes, that's good. Maggie's a Healer—the only one on the continent, actually."

Dani looks like she's about to say something, but then Castan returns, squeezing himself between Júlia and me. He sets down a Styrofoam cup of steaming black coffee and a plate of sandwiches. From under his arm, he hands me a Dasani.

"I didn't know what kind you wanted, so I got ham, turkey, and Matrona knows what that one is."

"Thank you." I pluck a ham sandwich from the stack, grateful for food in a way I never have been before. Castan eats from the same plate, and though Júlia and Dani scold him for it, some small sliver of me relishes in this allowance.

I only have enough time to scarf down one and a half sandwiches, and a third of my water, before Júlia and Dani are dragging me, elbows linked in my own, out the Dining Hall doors. I glance over my shoulder, half wishing Castan will come after me, but he's already gone.

A prisoner between two girls, I am on my own.

Staggering with the pace of Dani and Júlia, the two quickly learn that I know nothing about makeup. Their conversation about the best brands for eye palettes and foundation travels through my ears like whispers in a hollow tunnel. Despite the rainfall, their industrial masks of glimmering eyeshadow and rose-colored cheeks remain untouched.

The Barracks loom before us, those brownstone turrets familiar faces. Dani and Júlia untwine their elbows from mine, and I think about two guards releasing their captive. I swipe away the stray hair that's been poking my eye since we stepped outside the Hall. We pass under the stone archway, trickling into the pool of bodies.

The only thing keeping me from bolting in the other direction is the ghost of the Major's words, an icy wind across the landscape of my mind: *"I do expect you to take part in Defensive Training."*

Dani whirls so that she's walking backward. "You have a locker, right?"

I grasp my back pocket, feeling the key there. "Yeah."

She flashes me one of her grins, eyes crinkling at the corners. "Great!" Dani pivots then, Júlia and her treading the familiar, unmarked path to the women's locker room.

I shadow their pace, some length behind. The Training Field is alive with students of so many shapes, sizes, personalities, the only thing my brain comprehends is: black uniform, mud-brown armor. And if sparks crackle from one guy's fingertips, if one girl's feet hover inches above the ground, I ignore it.

What a volga you are. Blood rushes to my cheeks, skin prickles like so many insects crawling under my clothes.

Once inside the locker room, I avoid as much human interaction as possible. Mostly because the humans in here are slightly naked, half-naked, or completely bare-assed naked. My modesty doesn't know how to process this, so I locate my locker in the back, withdraw my fresh uniform, and dash to a bathroom stall to change.

I peel my damp clothes off and sling them over the door. I slip into the smooth, ebony glove. On my side of the door, is a mirror, peppered with smudges and lipstick-kisses. Through those obstructions, I come face-to-face with my plainness. The uniform's fabric hugs me in all the right places, bestowing liberal curves to my otherwise straight-edged figure. It compresses my chest, even without the plate of armor, but strangely enough, I breathe better in this material than any sports bra.

My judging comes to a halt, however, as loud complaints reach my ears.

"Toilets are for pissing, shitting, and bleeding. *Not* changing your fucking clothes."

Embarrassment overwhelms every cell in my body, so much so, that the word *apoptosis* flits across my mind. I scramble with my possessions, throw my wasted clothes in my locker, and bolt from the locker room with enough speed to break the sound barrier.

Outside, I force my hands to stop trembling, will the blood in my cheeks to recede. Girls can be vicious, flesh-eating creatures. I learned that in elementary school when Mackenzie Clark started those rumors that my dad murdered my mom. And rumors die hard. I'll make sure not to forget it again.

I take in the growing crowd once more, the somber and the excited. I don't see Dani and Júlia, but I'm not looking for them either. An ache rattles through my being—I miss Talan. No matter how much he chatters and twitches, I would do anything to see him waltz through that archway right now.

I move through the clusters of people, doing my best to keep from hugging myself. The breastplate makes that action somewhat tricky anyway. I almost bite my lip, but then I remember the pack of gum in my thigh pocket. For reasons I don't wish to acknowledge, I've been conservative with my gum supply. I unsheathe a stick and shove it in my mouth.

Emerging from under the stone canopy above, I allow the rain to wet my body. Every time it used to storm back home, I'd call Averil, if he wasn't already with me. *"I love the rain."* And if James wasn't around, he would kiss me until my lips were swollen with passion unspoken between us. He wasn't all bad, but he wasn't as good as he led me to believe, either.

At the edge of the crowd, I close my eyes. I forget the bodies at my back, cool rain drops following the frame of my face.

Corolla, you can do this. For James.

For James.

My eyelids flutter, water droplets speckling my vision. Across the turf, in the folds of gray and veils of rain, is a man. His back is to me, hands propped on his hips. He's too far away to discern further, but he's close enough to make out the color of the band around his bicep.

Gold for Commander.

"Alex Murphy," I mutter.

"He's sexy, isn't he?" Dani comes up beside me. Inferiority sweeps over me as I take in her body. Like mine, her uniform is a glove. The only difference is that Dani has more to offer than curves: She has confidence. And boys take to that like ants to sugar. I glance away, chewing against my left cheek.

The Commander confronts his class now, though he remains a steady distance. His eyes are gray hollows, but I swear, even with Dani at my shoulder, he's glaring right at me.

"Alex's testimony was just another narrative. Adian never forgave him for it, though."

And then that dreary specter moves, voice carrying across the field in a masculine timbre, "We'll take the first thirty minutes to run through our circuits."

There is a roar of "Yes, sir" and the smacking of hands over plated hearts. The Commander's eyes rake across the crowd, but when his gaze reaches me, it glazes right over my figure. The act says what words cannot: I have her eyes, her skin, fragments of her face.

DT begins.

Dani sticks by my side, expression pinched with concentration. Sometimes, I see Júlia, a flash of long black hair, but she never rejoins us. I'm in debt to Talan a hundred times over, as many of his morning drills were stolen routines from DT. Muscles sore from my previous training session, I grit my teeth and learn to welcome that burn in my limbs. Now and then, Dani speaks, but I couldn't repeat a single word she says. I make the right noises, the right movements.

While we work through the circuit, the field crawling with waterlogged students, I retreat into a private nook of my mind. I imagine a new house for James and me. We'll have two Greek columns on the front stoop, and leading inside, two oaks doors, so heavy a child couldn't pull the handle without help. The kitchen will sparkle with stainless steel, and the dining room will shine with the glossy finish of a mahogany table large enough to seat ten. The floors will be dark (tile or wood?), and the walls will be pale—not pastel—but shades of brown, gray, and off-white.

In the center of our open-concept living room, is a glass dome above, and the room will be consumed in a waterfall of natural light by day, a lake of stars by night. A spiral staircase will carry us upstairs, where James will have the study of an Oxford professor. Bookshelves to the ceiling, crammed with so many leather-bound volumes, we'll need a ladder just to reach half of them.

Castan is there, sitting in one of the armchairs by the fireside. The hearth is empty, as the windows on the far wall allow the yellow sun to pool at our feet. I go to him, questions on my lips but none of them asking him why he's here.

"It's not a cabin in the woods, is it?" I comb my fingers through his crown of hair. He tosses his head back, chuckling. He's unrecognizable, cheeks full, skin glowing. Because in my mind, he sleeps. In my mind, he's not haunted by his failures.

"No, it's not." Castan plucks my hand from his hair, curling my fingers into a loose fist. I find myself in his lap, head against his broad chest. He presses my knuckles to his lips, emerald eyes scorching my own. I clasp my other hand on the back of his neck. The heat of his skin burns under my fingertips. But Castan doesn't burn with vengeful fire, he burns with—

"Alright," Commander Murphy's stern voice crashes my train of thought. I'm on the ground, doing extra sit-ups I didn't realize I was doing. Clambering to my feet, I exhale a breath I didn't know I was holding either. I blink at the world before me. The rain's let up, sun spilling across the horizon. The clockwise circuit of groups has ground to a halt. I guess that means the first half hour is over.

Commander Murphy says something about moving on from the circuits to individual skills, but I still feel the heat of Castan's lips on my left hand. I pinch the bridge of my nose, bowing my head so Dani can't hear me mutter, "What the fuck?"

I swear to God—if someone has an Essence to compel daydreaming... I glance from the slick turf to the flowing tide of students breaking for water. *No, Corolla, you came up with that on your own.* And thank God my cheeks are flaming with exercise, masking any blushes my imagination could have conjured.

I brush the back of my hand against my thigh as if washing away the imagined kiss in the damp fabric of my uniform. I follow Dani with the crowd.

"What are we doing now?" I come up to her shoulder. She shoots me a half-grin, chest heaving.

"We're working on personal skills so the Commander can monitor our progress. Most of these people," she gestures to the ebony wave surrounding us, "will practice with their Essences. I, however, can't exactly use astral projection in combat, so I work on hand-to-hand stuff."

"Astral projection? You mean like, out of body experiences?"

"Sure," Dani shrugs, taking a swig of water. "Want to be my partner?"

"I don't know what else to do, so sure." Dani offers me a drink from her bottle, and I'm so flustered, I don't think twice about it. I normally wouldn't share drinks, but I gulp down the icy fluid now. "Thanks."

"This half of the field is designated for non-Essence training." Dani beckons me to follow her, and we walk some yards away from the thick of the crowd. She cracks her neck. "Sorry, I can never really fight unless my whole body feels... loose?" Her face screws up. "I don't like how that sounded, so never mind. I'm just not a warrior, is what I mean."

"Well," I flick my hand because that imaginary kiss survived, "I'm not much better, but maybe that's a good thing. I've only ever worked with Talan, and his skill far exceeds my own. Obviously." I watch a pair of girls practice archery, and another pair, near the arch to the Mausoleums, fight with silver daggers and brute strength. I wonder what their Essences are.

Dani cracks her knuckles. "Alright," she exhales. "I think I'm ready. You good?"

"Yeah," I face her. "I'll follow your lead if that's alright?"

"Of course! Talan helped train me before Jura died," Dani flinches, "so my instruction *should* be as good as his. No prom—"

"Hey!" A dark-skinned guy strides across the field. Judging by the beard wrapped around his chin, he's older than Dani and me. "Hey," he calls again, raising an arm, "You're Corolla Vel, right?"

"I—"

"You should come practice with us," he nods over his shoulder at a group of students. As if summoned, they prowl closer until Dani and I are walled in. The faces blur together, so many colors, so many glowering eyes.

"Corolla's practicing with me, Kale." Dani's voice doesn't betray her usual candy, but her eyes flash with... annoyance? I don't have time to study further.

"C'mon, Dani," the guy—Kale—tips his head, smirking beneath that burly beard, "if Corolla is anything like her brother, she'll need to practice her Essence." His predatorial eyes flicker over me. He licks his lips. His entourage follows my every breath. Lightning crackles at one guy's fingertips.

"Well, no," I find my voice, "I'm with Dani today. Sorry." My voice is not so feeble as I imagined in my head. My hands curl into fists to hide the trembling. Kale steps closer still, eyes glinting with something that makes my hearts lurch to my throat. Averil had eyes like that, and yet... I thought pelari would be different, safer.

"Back off, Kale," Dani snaps, slapping her forearm across his broad chest. Kale stares down a brown nose, seizing Dani up. The other students inch closer, like so many loyal wolves. And their pack leader has just been challenged. The air is charged, but it has little to do with the lightning zapping in the tense silence.

Dani meets Kale's glare, each a statue in their own right. Dani, one arm still barring Kale, is even more beautiful when furious. I don't dare breathe, eyes darting to each of the thugs.

"What's going on here?" The deep timbre of the Commander's voice slices through the tension like a whip. The circle of students breaks away, cockroaches fleeing light. Still, Dani doesn't move. Kale turns first, meeting the solemn gaze of Commander Murphy. He salutes.

"Nothing, sir."

"Good answer." The Commander flicks his wrist, and Kale scurries back the way he came. Dani exhales and salutes the head of the Guard. Words, questions bubble in my throat, threatening to explode in the sunny afternoon air.

"Commander—"

"You are dismissed, Corolla." He meets my imploring gaze then. Those hazel eyes, shot with green, haloed in blue, penetrate my soul. But just as he sees my soul, I see his. I read a story I wasn't meant to know: Unrequited love.

And then he pivots, eyebrows furrowed, and he's stalking down the length of the Training Field. Dani says something, a hand on my shoulder, but I don't hear her.

I watch the Commander's broad back, until black speckles my vision and I'm forced to blink. He proposed a valid question, one I cannot quite fathom.

Had Adian chosen Alex, would she still be alive today?

Past

September 2000

"**M**y family is very... passionate," Tyto warned, a gleam in his eye as he climbed out of the rental car. "So I apologize in advance for anything they say or do."

"I'm sure they're lovely." Adian wove between the haphazard line of cars. Tyto was the youngest of six. The number of siblings he had was evident in the tally of vehicles blockading the driveway.

Adian straightened her blouse, hoping she looked presentable. She glanced up the incline at the Alba's home. It seemed to come out of the hill, straight edges and a hint of Tuscany in the brown-gold of its exterior. They walked up the steps to the front door, overhanging butterfly bushes, purple, and magenta, gracing their ankles.

Adian imagined a young Tyto, galloping in the hills and planes of the Alba vineyards. The lands *were* vast, she saw, as they rose higher on the mountain. From up here, the vineyards were dizzying rows, and Adian felt as if she were a figure in one of her terrariums. *Like a small kingdom,* she thought.

"But if you're ever not sure what to say to them, just mention drinks. Some families like hunting, some like grilling, but the Albas like their drinks." Tyto shifted the box of gifts to his other arm and tucked a stray strand of hair behind her ear. He planted a kiss on her forehead.

He's such a gentleman, she thought, *it comes so naturally to him, he makes me want to be polite.*

"Drinks," Adian nodded her head, watching her sandaled feet on the steps. "Lemonade, cranberry juice, coffee, and alcoholic beverages."

"You're always leaving little worlds behind." Tyto tightened his grip on the cardboard box of terrariums. The contents shifted against thick wads of newspaper cushions.

"It's not too much, is it? For your sister and mother, I mean."

"They'll adore them." But now, looking around the extravagance of Maurizio and Marilena's home, Adian wondered if it wasn't *enough*.

"Yes, well." They stopped on the concrete stoop. She absorbed the patio furniture, the pink drops of bleeding hearts spilling out of expensive-looking pots by the threshold. It wasn't like Adian didn't know Tyto came from money—she came from money too—but she was all too aware of the pair they made: Major Alba and Adian Vel,

Taxodium's commodity, plucked out of Pedes, Michigan less than two years ago. Next to him, she was a child.

She heard Alex's voice in her ear, *"Don't tell me you've never pretended to be something you're not."*

Maybe I am volga, pretending I'm good enough, mature enough for Tyto Alba.

Before Adian could brace herself, the front door swung open. Sunlight scratched the glass panes, reflecting in her eyes like pools of rippling water.

"Ah!" Exclaimed a short woman. She was wrapped in a black cardigan and too many necklaces for Adian to count. Her raven hair was cropped close to her skull, tousled with hair product. *"Tito, my little son."*

Tyto bent down to embrace his mother, though the box in his arm made it difficult. She pecked her son on the cheek.

Marilena turned on Adian. "And you must be Adian." Her bright smile touched something in Adian's heart. She couldn't remember why she had been so nervous before. Marilena, despite her short stature, crushed Adian to her voluptuous chest.

"Come in, come in," Marilena spread the door open wider, practically dragging Adian by the sleeve of her shirt. "Valeria and I are just finishing up dinner."

"Would you like some help?" Adian offered, thinking, *My own mother would drop dead if she could hear me now.*

"No, darling. It's almost finished. Besides, the boys are eager to meet you." Marilena turned to Tyto. "Orsino will be here soon—I told him to leave his secretaries and yoga instructors at home, though." Marilena padded down a hall, through which Adian glimpsed the kitchen. Italian scents tickled her nose, sparked the claws of hunger in the pit of her stomach.

"What was she talking about?" Tyto slipped off his shoes on the doormat, and Adian did the same. He set the box of terrariums by the stairwell shooting upward to the second floor.

"About Orsino?" Tyto scratched the back of his neck. "He's just really into the bachelor scene. He goes through women the way someone with a cold goes through tissues."

"Oh." Adian wasn't sure if she should laugh or be horrified.

The stairwell behind them creaked. Adian turned, recognizing one of Tyto's older brothers from the dark Alba complexion of his face. He was slighter than Tyto, though his biceps bulged in his simple, maroon tee. Adian recalled Tyto saying that his family was enrolled in Tax's Reserve, even though they'd all graduated the Academy years ago.

"Pasquale," Tyto greeted, shaking his brother's hand in a firm grip. *Pasquale. So, this is Ty's* younger *older brother.* "This is Adian," Tyto introduced.

Adian extended her hand, grinning. "Nice to meet you," Pasquale's voice was an octave lower than Tyto's. His dark eyes, almost black, skated over Adian. He followed his mother's earlier footsteps into the kitchen without another word. Adian felt snubbed.

"Don't take it personally," Tyto leaned into her shoulder. "Pas is always a shade. And his boyfriend—well, *ex*-boyfriend—just ripped his heart out."

"Oh." Adian's watched Pasquale float through the bright lights of the kitchen, a scowl plastered on his face. It was hard to view him as *vulnerable.* It suddenly struck her, though, that *he* was the brother who caused such an uproar at the South American Academy years ago.

They made their way left, opposite from the kitchen, into the living room. Hardwood floor transitioned to soft carpet, and Adian absorbed her surroundings like a sponge. Black frames lined the rich, dark gold paint of the walls. Some of the photos were singular, displaying the Alba siblings through various stages of their childhood. Some of the frames were collages, neat print arched overhead *The Alba's 1989* and other odd years. Adian barely recognized Tyto with chipmunk cheeks and coffee-brown hair to his shoulders.

"Don't look at those," Tyto chuckled. Adian glanced at the impish grin transforming his face. His hands dug into the pockets of his jeans. She fought the urge to touch him, but the clash of voices and sudden flare of "Happy Together" broke her trance.

"I can guess who that would be," Tyto groaned, but Adian saw the glint in his eye. *He's home,* she thought. *And he's missed it.*

Tyto and Adian followed the trail of noise, leading them off into a segue from the living room. The walls were the same warm gold color, but shelves of books and knick-knacks stood erect against them. There was a desk in the corner, a computer monitor glowing with the Windows screen. A brick fireplace took up the farthest wall, sprays of gray ash highlighting the metal wrought grate. Beside that, were two men hovering over a sleek black stereo. As far as Adian could tell, they were identical in every way except their clothes, one in slacks, the other in denim.

And their taste in music, apparently.

"You said you wanted to listen to classics, so that's what we're doing!" The one in denim shot, voice laced with mischief. He swayed with the beat of the song. The music blared from the stereo, sinking deep into Adian's bones.

The brother in slacks smacked a hand on top of the stereo—the music cut off immediately. "I meant Beethoven, Bach, Mozart, not *The Turtles*."

The brother in denim puffed his chest, about to spew slander, Adian was positive, but Tyto interjected, "Giovanni, Luca!"

The twins turned sharply, apparently unaware that they were being watched.

"Tyto!" They exclaimed in unison, all disputes forgotten.

Tyto clasped an arm around each of his brothers' necks. It endeared her, the way only large and chaotic families could, to see Tyto like this. Her own family was so... stripped and sterile compared to the Albas. Even when Adian had been at her most reckless, her parents never raised their voices; James never provoked her back. There was no... passion.

Adian's head snapped up at the sound of her name on his tongue. Tyto was introducing her again. She grinned, shaking hands, placing faces with names. In this case, though, the twins were so alike, that she could only tell them apart from their pants. *Denim for Luca. Slacks for Giovanni.*

She noticed things about them the way one does when encountering something new. The long curl of Giovanni's eyelashes, the pale scar tattooing Luca's cheek. The way the corners of their eyes crinkled with mischief and discord.

"Time to eat!"

"That would be Mama," Luca ducked his head, a half-grin tugging at his lips. The twins made for the kitchen, and, though they were grown men, Adian could almost see their child-selves walking in their places. What was it like to grow up in the Alba house? She was beginning to find out.

"What's this?" Adian padded to the mantle above the fireplace. She touched a finger to a wood carving of an angel holding a pale pink conch shell to her ear. The angel kneeled beside a small, ornate wooden box. Around the box, a silver chain gleamed. She turned to Tyto. "You made these, didn't you?"

"Yeah." The spark in his eyes dulled into something pained and careful. He came up beside her, hand gracing the small of her back. "For Reino. He passed away when he was a baby. He would be about your age now."

"Oh, I'm sorry."

"Sometimes these things happen." He shrugged, but she sensed the weight stooping his shoulders. Pelari hearts were guarded—they didn't mourn openly, but they did have two words for loss:

"*Bellator, vale,*" she squeezed Tyto's hand. *Goodbye warrior.*

277

Tyto brushed back her hair, tenderness taking the place of his pain. His voice was husky, tickling her ears, "You're so beautiful, Adian." She was all too aware of his breath against her lips, his hand pressing against her back.

Words stuck to her throat. What did he see in her? Tyto Alba, risking everything he was. For her. Adian knew love did strange things to pedes, but nobody ever told her what love did to pelari.

For all that they believe themselves to be, pelari are just as vulnerable. They're just as easy to break.

Tyto leaned in to kiss her—

"It's not *your* birthday," a rough voice called out, "but I do enjoy this spectacle all the same." Adian jolted backward and would have slammed her head on the mantle, had Tyto's other hand not been there to hold her. They looked at the figure standing under the arch. He was fashioned in a trim black suit, shirtsleeves rolled to his elbows.

"Orsino," there was a smile in Tyto's flustered voice, "how was your drive home?" He stepped towards his brother, and Orsino folded him into a quick hug.

"You think I drove? I took a Hold." Orsino inspected his fingernails, eyebrow quirked.

Tyto dug his hands into his pockets. "You know Holds are really only for current Taxodium personnel, right?"

Orsino blew air on his nails. He glanced up, offering the two of them a rather charming grin. "I'm in the Reserve—that counts for something. I don't know why Tax is always playing within the lines the pedes drew up. Think of what this planet could be if pelari dominated."

"You can't be that dense, Orsino, because you're not a Dentata." The hair on the back of Adian's neck stood on end as Tyto spoke. "If pelari were dominant, where would we stop? Pedes would be enslaved, casualties and everything in between. Especially if pelari shared your same twisted *beliefs*."

"You're always so quick to talk politics." Orsino shot Tyto a forgiving look, nostrils flaring. "I'm sorry, *Tito*. Mama barred my guests again. Don't pay me any attention. Anyway, it's time for dinner." And with that, Orsino stalked away.

"Well," Tyto clapped a hand on the small of her back. "You've met all my brothers now."

"The twins are something else," Adian admitted. "But I'm not sure what to make of Pas and Orsino." She thought about the scar on Luca's cheek, the way Orsino kept studying his fingertips. Essences could manifest into almost anything, but she had never known someone to be gifted with *nails*.

"Full disclosure: I've never really been a cat person."

Tyto chuckled under his breath, guiding her along. "Drinks, Dee, just ask about drinks."

"Adian Vel, Maurizio Alba." Adian folded her hand in Maurizio's steady one. She liked him immediately. His eyes crinkled around the corners, much like her own father's. Except where Mr. Vel's yelled exhaustion, Maurizio's screamed vitality. The pale blue of his irises surprised her, as all his children possessed dark shades of brown. But, she concluded, his children all had similar versions of his bridged nose.

Essence and eye color from mother, nose from father.

Tyto sat her next to his father and occupied the seat on her left. Orsino was prowling around the room for a place himself. Pasquale hung by his older brother's side, a rare smile breaking the surface of his brooding expression. Adian could only guess at what they were talking about.

"Do you drink, Adian? I have a nice selection of merlots in the cellar."

"Well," Adian began, startled. "I'm only eighteen."

"No matter," Maurizio winked, "as long as you aren't driving to the airport. I'll be right back." He ran a hand through the graying hair of his beard and disappeared in the kitchen doorway.

Tyto put a glass of water in her hands. "What did I say?"

Adian sipped the iced liquid, eyes darting every which way. The dining room overlooked the vineyards. Adian almost lost herself in the scenery—gentle sloping hills, stakes of grape vines twisting up and down like railroad tracks.

Her gaze landed on the dinner table. It was cut glass and large enough to sit ten people. Marilena and Valeria kept dashing between the kitchen to the dining room with platters of steaming noodles and sauces. They filled the space down the middle of the table now. Hunger sounded like thunder in her stomach again. But the room was ringing with noise, and her small addition was swept up and lost in the cacophony.

Giovanni and Luca took up seats across from her and Tyto. They seemed to have resolved their dispute about the stereo. If Adian listened close enough, though, she thought she heard "Happy Together" weaving through the din of the house.

Giovanni took a swig of ruby-red liquid. He met Adian's eyes. "How was your flight?"

It was crowded and uncomfortable, and they almost missed it. She would have preferred to use a Hold, but Tyto insisted it was wrong to do so.

"Enjoyable." She had spent every minute worrying about her terrariums, praying they wouldn't tip over or spontaneously die.

Luca put in, "How did you manage to get away from classes?"

"Well," Adian shared a look with Tyto, "I just left. I mean, my roommate thinks I went up to Michigan to visit my own family, so no one should worry too much…" Adian and Tyto already had it planned: she would fly back tomorrow morning, and he would return later the next day. They had to stagger their vacations, lest someone notice their absences were linked.

"A girl after my own heart," Luca slung an arm over the back of his chair. "I remember cutting class every Friday when I was at the Academy."

Tyto was amused. "I'm sure Major Rainier appreciated that."

Luca shrugged. "I gave him a run for his money." Giovanni choked on his wine, laughing, and the two engaged in a conversation Adian couldn't follow. Something about setting uniforms on fire and broken windows.

Adian was acutely aware of Orsino at Giovanni's shoulder. She dared to glance at him. Thin nose, prominent cheekbones—he could have been cut from stone. She saw how women could fall for him, despite the deficits in his morals. Adian averted her gaze before he noticed her staring.

There was a bouquet of red and white roses on the table. One of the buds was browning in the middle, sick or diseased, she couldn't tell. Without thinking, she stuck an arm out, fingertips brushing the dying bud. It swelled white and whole once more.

"Wonderful! Splendid!" Maurizio exclaimed from the doorway, and she realized she had an audience. Seven pairs of eyes were glued to her. Even Pasquale appeared intrigued.

"Sorry," she ducked her head, suddenly bashful and not knowing why. She rarely felt shy.

"I wouldn't apologize for a gift, my dear," Marilena beamed, taking her seat at the opposite end of the table as Maurizio.

"Here, pour this girl a drink!" Maurizio handed Tyto a bottle merlot. Within moments, Adian's glass of water was replaced with a glass of dark, blood-red liquid.

"Now," Marilena exhaled, "we eat."

Adian glanced around at the steaming plates of noodles, sauces, and bread. She reached for a dinner roll but stopped herself. "Where's Valeria?"

"I'm here." The birthday girl appeared in the kitchen doorway. From where Adian sat, Valeria's bronze skin was pale, eyes half-lidded. She was an everyday woman, gentle curves, gentle beauty, but something altogether different marred her features.

Marilena stood, her short stature somehow filling the room. "Valeria, darling, what's wrong?" She went to her eldest child then, placing the back of her hand against Valeria's forehead.

Valeria ducked her head, brushing Marilena away. "I'm fine, Mama," Valeria sucked in her breath and shot an evil glance at the table of food. "I'm pregnant."

The chatter of the room plummeted into silence. Adian's eyes darted from Valeria's ill expression to Marilena and Maurizio's shocked ones. Drifting in the background, the upbeat lyrics of "Happy Together" could be heard. Then everyone was talking, the rumble of so many men competing to be heard. Marilena dashed from the room.

Adian whispered to Tyto. "Is your mother alright?"

"Just wait," a grin toyed with his lips, "My mother is very superstitious when it comes to pregnancies." Marilena came rushing back in. She flung a chain around Valeria's neck.

"Wear Philomena, Val, my baby." Mother and daughter were so alike in that moment, they could have been looking through a mirror of twenty years. Adian recognized that silver chain from Reino's shrine.

"*Grazie*, Mama." Valeria looked anything but thankful. She looked… overwhelmed, pale and nauseous. Adian felt sorry for her.

"So," Orsino wore a devilish grin, "who's the father?"

Valeria scowled, adjusting the chain around her neck so that the pendant fell atop her heart. "No one you know."

"Is it someone *you* know?"

"Orsino!" Maurizio snapped. "Watch your mouth in my house."

Orsino shrugged. "Sorry, Papa, I just wanted to know—pedes or pelari?" He turned coy eyes back to Valeria. "Volga?"

"I think," Valeria said, "that I'm going to bed early tonight." She clutched her stomach and vanished from the doorway. Marilena watched her go, tisking under her breath. For a moment, Adian thought she was condemning her daughter. Marilena returned to the head of the table.

"Poor Valeria." And as if it were a toast, each Alba tossed back his or her glass. Adian marveled. She didn't know how her own parents would take such a declaration, but she was positive it wouldn't be like this. They would be ashamed, not supportive.

Pasquale drained his glass, smacking it on the tablecloth with more force than necessary. "I'll kill that deadbeat."

"Amen," Orsino raised his glass, and Giovanni and Luca touched theirs to it. Their *clinks* reverberated in Adian's head. She thumbed her own glass, not sure if she dared to move. How could she drink to that, sitting there at Tyto's elbow, the outsider? God knew what these people actually thought of her, beneath those Florentine masks.

"Excuse me," she shuffled out of her seat.

"Adian…" Tyto reached a hand out to touch her elbow. She managed a tight-lipped grin.

"I just need some," she glanced at the crimson liquid at her place, "water." Adian found herself in the kitchen then, the chatter in the dining room chasing her up against a polished cabinet. She clutched her temples, staring down the stainless-steel sink and yet not seeing it at all.

She knew Tyto was true—he didn't know jealousy, control, or anything but love, devotion, and care. But what about his family? Was it wrong to confess to them, to come here? Was it a choice she would later regret? Tyto and she already put too much planning into hiding their secret, and now a whole household knew. What would that mean in the future?

There was a hand on her shoulder then, a deep voice saying, "If you want water, you'll have to do more than stare at the tap."

Adian whirled about, seeing Luca, not Tyto. Still, his lips were drawn into a gentle grin.

"I'm sorry," Adian admitted, "I just needed a minute."

"About Valeria? Don't worry about it—Albas never forsake their family."

"No," Adian shook her head. "I mean, I know that. I know you all are very… close-knit. I just…" She trailed off, not sure why she was saying anything to Luca. It should be Tyto, shouldn't it?

As if reading her mind, Luca said, "Tyto was out of his chair the moment you walked into the kitchen. Papa made him sit down, so I came instead."

Adian nodded, not sure what to say to this. Why would Maurizio deny Tyto to come after her?

"Come here," Luca beckoned, "there's something I want to show you." He made towards a sliding glass door. It revealed a back patio, raised on tall steel beams, that wrapped around the rear end of the house. If Adian took several steps to her left, she would come face-to-face with a view of the dining room and all its inhabitants. However, she didn't. Adian took in the rich russet of the sky, the shadows playing across the expanse of the vineyard. It was a breathtaking view of all the land the Albas commanded.

Luca, someplace behind her, said, "The Venefica once told me that reading hearts is a dangerous Essence, almost as dangerous as harnessing one of the elements."

Adian craned her neck and watched him over her shoulder. His long body was draped across a cushioned chair, expression pensive.

"Giovanni is pretentious, Orsino is shallow, and Pas is just... pitiable." As he spoke, an array of expressions crossed his face. A smirk, a frown, but here, Luca was somber.

"And what does Tyto's heart read?"

Luca's eyes flitted to hers. A knowing grin swept his forlorn expression away. "I think you know."

Adian crossed her arms, not in defense, but to mask the shivers cascading down her spine. "Is that what you wanted to tell me?"

Luca rose, coming up beside her. Adian dared to meet his peculiar gaze, and it was then that she noticed his right eye. How did she not see the light there before? The place where his iris *should be* glowed, like so many starbursts on the Fourth of July. Luca ducked his head.

"I usually wear an eyepatch. Unpredictable thing." He touched tentative fingers to his eyelid. "What's it doing now?"

"Sparklers."

Luca huffed with hands on his hips. "Interesting." He gazed out at the sinking sun, and Adian caught sight of his standard, brown iris. She followed Luca's stare, hoping she hadn't embarrassed him. Essences were strange, to be sure. Her own was unique enough to make her a target for a rogue pelari family.

Luca gripped the iron rail. "But anyway, I wanted to show you something," he faced her, "something inside yourself you may not even be aware of."

Adian found herself shivering again. "What?"

"I read your heart too, Ms. Vel, and what do you think I found?"

Breath escaped past her lips in foggy clouds. She shook her head. "I don't know."

"All your life, you've wondered about the family that never was, wondered about the family that is, yet neither meet your demands."

Adian shrank away from him, bumping into a piece of outdoor furniture as she went. "My demands?"

Luca chuckled, the sound a derivative of Tyto's own laughter. "I don't mean to frighten you, Adian. I just thought you should know."

"Know what?"

"Your greatest desire: you want to be whole."

Adian hugged herself, teeth clattering in her head. "What," she spoke through gritted teeth, "does that have to do with anything?"

"Well," Luca let go of the rail and faced her, "you think my family will condemn you the first chance they get. We aren't like that. Believe it or not, Tyto told us about you long ago, and we accepted it then as we do now."

"*What?*" Adian's chills were replaced with the scalding heat of horror. "Why did he do that? I—"

"Because he loves you. He always has. So don't be so quick to discredit us. We're a loyal lot, and Tyto's a powerful fellow. Who knows," Luca shrugged, "maybe he's even powerful enough to put an end to the oppressive Attachment Laws?"

Adian clutched her temples, head swimming. "I still don't understand. Why—"

"He completes you, Adian. If your doubts weren't so occlusive, you'd know that by now."

"But why are *you* telling me that? Why say anything at all?" Her hair was spilling into her eyes, bun lopsided.

Luca shrugged once more. "Because without the right shoves, you two may never take those leaps you deserve."

Castan
July 2020

The Academy's library, despite its common name of "library," is actually dedicated to someone by the name of Sanne Dare. She labored extensively over the contents of these shelves, putting down her foot when the Board refused pedes literature to be cataloged among pelari. "Literature is literature," or something like that. As I take a seat in the corner of the fourth floor, I recall this bit of information. It's not important—at least, not essential in regard to my other thoughts—but maybe that's why I think it now. Not every pelari is destined for bloodshed and loss. Just most of us.

With this grim thought, I take a swig of coffee and tuck into the breakfast burrito I smuggled inside. I couldn't begin to count how many "No food or drinks" signs bedeck the library's walls, but I *can* say they are wholly ineffective. The librarian, Ms. Lindsey, didn't even look up from her desk when I pushed through the front doors.

On a Tuesday morning, the library is usually bustling with students doing some research project or another. But since summer classes have been canceled, even the first floor is vacant. It's really a testament to the number of book-lovers residing in this Academy.

I choke down a massive bite of scrambled egg and maple sausage, avoiding my thoughts, avoiding my emotions. The list of things I allow myself to examine is becoming shorter than I ever anticipated. That's why I left behind the noise and clutter of the Dining Hall and came to the Sanne Dare Library. Books are a small comfort, even if I refuse to read them anymore.

I occupy a table in the corner farthest from the stairwell. It's an unspoken rule that the fourth floor must be the quietest. It is perhaps the only place utter silence exists on campus. Even the preceding three stories are not as soundless as they are meant to be—that is, when people bother to come here. Dark shelves of books tower in neat rows before me, blocking my view of the stairwell. Behind me, the original brick walls of the first three floors have been replaced with one-way glass. On the inside, I can see everything of this campus, though the library does not reach so far into the clouds as the spires atop Rainier and the Dining Hall. On the outside, the windows are mirrors, reflecting all that this Academy has to offer.

But what does it have to offer?

I sidestep the question and think about the only other library I have known. The one in the Complex was much smaller, much more outdated, than Sanne Dare's. My own mother enjoyed spending time there, between the cramped, concrete walls that were gouged out to create makeshift shelves. The Complex's library was almost an afterthought, and, gazing out at the immaculate detail of this one, I am almost certain that it was. It had no desks, no devotees, and no named dedication. It was just *there*, collecting dust, a crypt of information about the outside world. My father hated it. It's a wonder it thrived as long as it did.

I glance down at the polished table top, notice my burrito is gone, and groan. I wash the taste of egg from my mouth with scorching black coffee. It's bitter, almost as bitter as I have become, and I smile at this connection.

What would Calyx say, seeing you so jaded?

I couldn't fathom to guess.

I'm draining my coffee cup when a noise tickles my hearing. It's faint, so spectral, that I think I might be imagining it. Then my eyes catch sight of a tight ponytail, pale blue scrubs.

Maggie.

Something about the way she's running her finger along the book spines tells me not to speak, to move, to breathe. I become a statue, eyes slits and brow furrowed.

What's she doing? I can't see which section she's hunting through, but the fourth floor only contains History and an Archives that's three times as small as the confidential one down in Intelligence. So what would Maggie be doing in History? I'd expect her on the third floor where all the biology and human systems and diseases are located. But even more than that, I'd expect her in the hospital, especially since she's wearing her scrubs.

Maggie glances down another aisle. While her back is turned, I creep out of my chair and conceal myself behind a shelf's end. I peer over the side, my view of Maggie slightly obstructed by a row of bronze busts. But I see enough. Maggie's wearing Caeli boots.

And then she is gone, vanished as quickly as she came. I leave my hiding place, letting out a breath I hadn't noticed I was holding. Around me, the air tingles with suspicion and a strange sort of silence. The shelves, which were once a comfort, now wear an eerie facade. The hair on the back of my neck stands pin-straight.

Once I check that Maggie is indeed gone, I go to the shelf she was first searching through. Dust can tell as great of a story as any book if one looks hard enough. I thought I saw her slide a volume out, and I was right. There's a dustless slit where a book has been removed and pushed back in place. *In His Own Words: Dawson Allen's Account of the Battle of Brothers.* I remove the old volume from the shelf. Judging by its title, it's about how the Allens fought the Dentatas during World War II. But when I open its cover, not a single sentence remains intact. It's been hollowed out. And there, resting in the carved compartment, is a thin slip of paper. The letters are printed, though I suspect Maggie is the one who typed them up.

TGMBKHMX G OL UENW

GQM FOX—

I had to take a class last year on decryption and ciphers—as every freshman did—so I'm not astonished that Maggie knows code. I'm surprised that she's using code at all. Questions ricochet through my mind: Who is this intended for? What does it say? Why is Maggie planting secret messages in the library?

My stomach splatters to the floor, blood draining from my face.

Is Maggie a traitor? And if so, then *who is she communicating with*?

I slump to the ground, the coppery tang of blood flooding my nostrils. The book falls in my lap, but the note is still clutched in my hand. Is that possible? Can Maggie—the Academy's own Good Samaritan—be a traitor?

I stare at those block letters once more. Maybe I have it wrong. Maybe this is just a romantic tryst and has nothing to do with how the Gens found Corolla so quickly. But even if this note does contain sensitive information, it means there's at least one other person on campus who shares Maggie's discretion.

My mind whirs with possibilities. I could put the note back, see who comes to read it, but who knows how long that will take. I could deliver this straight to the Major, but what if it is only just a note, a game Maggie plays with someone else? Major Rex would think even less of me, *and* I will have embarrassed Maggie.

I could confront Maggie myself.

I push through the fatigue, the weakness in my limbs, and consider this route. She'll be at the hospital by now. I could just ask her what the note is—she would understand my concern, be grateful I didn't take it to the Major at once. And she'll explain herself. There's a reasonable explanation, I'm sure.

My pulse jumps in my throat, and I breathe like a cow about to give birth. I sit down before my malaise knocks me to my feet.

Damn disease.

I lie there, between the towering shelves of books, and wait for my body to return to a sort of homeostasis. The white lights are blinding, but my eyes don't see them. Instead, there is Calyx, sprawled across those white bedsheets. Like watercolor paint, his blood soaks through the cloth.

"We need a Healer," I croak. Despair slams my body with the force of a freight train. I want him to live—I want him to live so badly—but a part of me recognizes death in his whiskey-brown eyes. I ignore it.

"We don't have one," Nasreen answers. Her voice is thick with her Middle Eastern accent, but I understand her perfectly: there is little hope for Calyx's survival.

"Dammit! You have to have one!" I blink tears away. "He's dying!" Nasreen shoots me a reproachful look, and I know I've crossed a line. But my best friend is dying. What are unkind words in the face of death?

"I'll do what I can," Nasreen says, "But he has already lost too much blood. Who did this?" She presses a wet cloth to Calyx's forehead. He rasps, chest rising with the ease of a rusted door.

I bite my tongue until I taste blood. Tears well in the corners of my vision, smearing everything together in white and brown mixtures. My breathing slows until there is only a trace of blood in the air. This disease makes my mind feeble, makes my heart *more* broken.

What would Calyx say now, seeing you so pitiable?

He'd extend an arm, help me to my feet.

But I can't move. Guilt, grief, and all the misery in the world are bricks upon my chest, pinning me in place. Maggie's note gripped in one hand, the hollowed book splayed across the floor near the other, and my back, pressed upon the carpet as cold as the concrete of the Complex. I came here to forget everything—if only for a moment—and now it's all come crashing down upon me.

And yet...

This is what I deserve.

It is near afternoon when I find myself in the hospital's break room again. I've swept all my misery back under the rug and steeled myself with a scowl. Maggie gazes at me with exhausted eyes, though I know she recognizes the slip of paper in my hand. The air is just as thick as before, scented with leftover spaghetti now, rather than room temperature pizza.

"You're interrupting my routine because of *that?*" Her eyes flit to the paper.

"What is it, Maggie? You know I can't just forget about it, not with the Gens prowling outside Taxodium's gates like so many starved lions."

"I'm not a traitor," Maggie adjusts her glasses, "I've been consulting another doctor about Vera's condition." Before I can move, she snatches the paper from my hand.

"Maggie—"

"I will show you, Suspicious One, what I mean." She takes a pen from her breast pocket and leans over the little circle table to write. "There," she steps back and crosses her arms.

I come closer, bow over that little scrap of paper and read:

ANTIDOTE N V's BLUD

TGMBKHMX G OL UENW

GQM FOX—

NXT MVE?

"I'm not a traitor," Maggie repeats.

"Then why go through all the trouble of encryption and a... a hollowed-out book?"

"Well," Maggie smooths back her hair, "it's not exactly legal to share patient information with outside sources, and now, thanks to you, I've just broken that law ten times over."

"Why do you need to consult another doctor...? Warners is capable enough."

Maggie glances over the rims of her glasses. "Yeah, he's capable, but second opinions are always nice."

I reread her scrawled letters. "What antidote?"

"For the gas that took out the Verum Courts. Vera's bloodwork came back with a heavy concentration of a counteragent. Which means someone gave it to her before the attack because I doubt—highly doubt—Vera Taylor knew that attack was going to happen. She lost her husband."

"The Gens needed a messenger," I mumble to myself. "What about her rambling 'Alba'?"

Maggie shakes her head, collapsing back onto the sofa. "I don't know. Guilt, maybe, for banishing Tyto Alba. She couldn't have known Luca Alba lived."

"Well, what about Valeria Alba?"

Again, Maggie shakes her head. "Valeria has been holed up in Euro Intel for years. Major Crivelli has already confirmed that she's been working night and day." Maggie huffs, "I don't know about Vera. Everything is wrong with her case, and it doesn't help that Talan's asked her to be moved to St. Helena."

"He has? Why? *When?*"

"Says it's too dangerous for his 'mental mother' to be stuck in a targeted Academy. She's being shipped off tomorrow."

I lean back against the table. It's not so much of a shock, but it makes things even more *real*. The Gens could be on their way here right now. I pray to Matrona the alarms will resound loud enough, the Academy with be prepared enough. Defensive Training might not be adequate precaution, not if the Gens are using chemical agents now.

Maggie checks her wrist, frowns. "I have a surgery in ten. Kidney transplant."

I want to ask if she's awake enough for that, but she's out the door and gone by the time I blink. And then I want to kick myself—I never asked who this coded message was for. I glance out my shoulder. *Next move?* I shrug. I suppose it doesn't matter. At least she was honest with me. At least she's not a traitor.

I exit the break room, frowning. Why would Vera have an antidote in her blood? Why would the Gens need a messenger?

I don't ponder those questions any further, as a sobbing shape takes form down the hall. Issak Park makes cooing noises, smoothing a hand down the figure's back. I know right away who's weeping outside of Luca Alba's containment.

And all the emotions I'd been avoiding strike me like arrows in the chest. They won't be as easy to stash under a rug now.

Past
March 2002

A specter came through the closet, vaguely thinking, *This isn't how it goes.* But she hadn't seen Tyto in weeks. Of course, his presence was always hovering over campus, occupying vacant spaces like oxygen. Or pollution. Adian wasn't sure anymore. That's why she was creeping into his room, rather than waiting for him to come to hers.

Adian didn't bother to shut the closet behind her. Tyto was always so neat, always so manicured, she took one look at his swept pile of wood shavings in the corner and tore her bare feet straight through it. How much she had grown up for him, no instrument could measure. She only knew that last year, she and Alex would steal cider from the kitchens and stay up late drinking it all. And now, she found no thrill, no satisfaction in that pastime. But perhaps that had nothing to do with Tyto. Perhaps that was just a facet of the aging process.

Adian clutched her stomach.

You're not done growing yet.

She turned from the mess she'd created and made towards the sound of Tyto singing. Once, she would have grinned at the noise. Once, she would have come crashing through the bathroom door. Now, she squeezed through the crack of the Major's master bath. Steam clouded her lungs, and Adian wanted to throw up. She wanted to scream, to rip the mirror from the wall and watch it shatter all over the white-tiled floor—

Instead, she clamped her jaw shut and stripped her clothes off. She was emotional this week, for reasons now clear to her. But she didn't want to cry in front of him; she didn't want him to see what he'd done to her. So the water would mask her tears and muffle her voice to anyone listening outside the Major's bedchambers. All the while, Tyto sang in his warbling tenor:

"'I've seen your flag the marble arch and love is not a victory march…'"

Adian slipped between the shower curtain. His back was to her, bubbly suds sliding down the smooth skin of his torso, curling in pools by his feet. She watched those suds circle the drain, disappear forever.

"'But remember when I moved in you and the holy dove was moving too?'"

Adian bit her lip, hugged her arms across her bare chest. The spray from the shower was just close enough to speckle her calves. She dared not draw any closer.

Instead, she fixated on the Major's Mark running down his spine. She studied the Mark of Tribulation between his shoulder blades, and the eight points beneath it. Each one represented a rank in Taxodium's Guard, though Tyto had bypassed them all, spare for one. Her eyes traveled the ebony dots, each one growing larger as her gaze plunged downward.

And then Tyto turned.

Adian could have slapped that breathtaking grin from his face. Because it spelled out everything she wasn't sure she wanted to read. His love in a single, potent expression. It was enough to make her cry, but Adian bit her lip, clenched her fists to keep flora from bursting free.

Tyto brushed the hair and water from his eyes, reaching long, muscular arms for her. Adian did not move, but Tyto didn't seem to notice this. The most perceptive man she knew, and he didn't notice the heartbreak in her eyes. He swept her to him, their bodies bound in burning water.

"I was just thinking about you," he mumbled into her ear. He swayed, and she couldn't find the motivation to yank herself free of him. She closed her eyes and let him hold her. The weeds in her fists vanished along with the tears.

Even underwater, he smells like cedar.

The shower was large enough that Adian could spread her arms out and twirl without touching the walls. And when she opened her eyes, saw Tyto holding her out before him, she felt the expanse of that space the same way one perceives the unfathomable depths of the ocean beneath fearful feet. It was terrifying.

Tyto's eyebrows knitted together. "What's wrong? Is school becoming too much for you again?" It was, after all, her senior year at the Academy. And while everyone in her graduating class would be dedicating two years of service to the Guard or Intel, Adian would remain on campus. In Aurum House.

Adian slipped from his hands and sank to the floor. She crossed her legs because this wouldn't be a quick conversation, nor would it likely be an enjoyable one. Behind the veil of water, Tyto crouched on his knees. Like the many drops of water trailing down him now, Adian followed the contours of his sculpted body. His throat, his chest, his torso and that black ribbon of hair, like an arrow, directing her eyes. Her gaze stopped at the bulk between his legs.

The source of all evil.

"Adian, love," Tyto's finger was under her chin, reaching through that curtain of water, "my eyes are up here." But she didn't want to look him in the eye. She swallowed the water that had pooled in her mouth from the rivers cascading down her forehead.

Tentative, wondering, "Did something happen?"

She felt her shoulders stoop; her stomach dropped to her feet. It was enough to make her weep. But she didn't want to do that either.

"I'm pregnant, Ty."

Water pounded the floor, steam swirling between them. Adian looked at him now, but he was staring someplace behind her, someplace far away. He was thinking. How she wished he would sing again, hold her again! If he could just tell her it would be alright... But no, he wasn't saying anything, and the water was loud enough to burst her eardrums.

Adian stood, lilies dripping from her palms. They tangled at her feet, clustered in the water and were swept towards Tyto. Why did she think she needed his help? Why did she think he *would* help? A baby put his job on the line, put his entire legacy on the line, and while Tyto wasn't an ambitious man, he was a proud one. He wouldn't want her to ruin everything he was acclaimed for.

Palms free of foliage, she reached for the shower curtain. But a hand on her wrist stopped her flight.

"Come here," Tyto whispered, voice barely audible over the roaring water. Rather than wait for her, he swept her up in his arms once more. His hands were on her waist, gripping her so close, her lungs couldn't expand to breathe.

"I love you, Adian," Tyto's arms loosened, "and we'll figure something out. I don't want you to worry, okay? I will take care of you."

Something Luca once told her came ringing through her mind now, *"He completes you, Adian. If your doubts weren't so occlusive, you'd know that by now."* Why *had* she doubted him?

Adian couldn't speak. She was numb, but with what—relief, anxiety—she couldn't say. She felt the heat of his skin against hers, heard the thrashing of his heart in his chest. Would their baby laugh or squawk?

Their baby.

"I missed you, Ty." *Full disclosure* was a game from the past. It had been four years. Four years of what, though? Of hiding, of sneaking around like criminals. And... And Adian loved it. She loved him. She knew his body as well as her own; she knew his mind better than her own; she knew his heart.

Tyto chuckled under his breath, "I was actually going to propose to you tomorrow."

Adian drew back, saw he was serious and said, "You better have a ring to prove that." *Are these the leaps Luca meant, all those years ago?*

"I have more than a ring to prove my devotion to you, Adian Vel." And then her back was to the wall. He kissed her, lip-biting, and she had to clamp her own hands on his hips to keep from falling. He was always so gentle, even when they were first learning each other. All Adian wanted to do was crash and burn with him, but Tyto made her patient, made her wait.

"I should warn you," she sucked in a breath as Tyto moved to kiss her neck, "pregnant pelari have stronger Essences. Self-defense."

Tyto's lips were in her ear, "I know. Our ancestors used to host games. Who needs gladiators, right?"

Adian chuckled, and Tyto cradled her in his arms, laying her down upon the shower floor. Her lilies were caught in the drain at their feet, but Adian paid them no attention.

He was above her now, the shower a gentle hum raining down upon them. Adian hooked her legs around his torso, tracing his lips with her thumb. Water spilled down his forehead, and she cupped her hands at his hairline to shield his eyes.

Tyto stopped, despite the burning ache between her legs. She felt him there—so eager—how could he just quit?

"Will you marry me?"

Adian slapped a hand on his breast. "Is now the time to ask that?"

Tyto looked from Adian's naked chest to his own nether regions between their hungry bodies. He traced her belly button, and she could have sworn he blushed.

"Is that a...?" He raised a dark brow.

Despite her place against the shower floor, she cocked her head. "You're doing this on purpose."

Tyto traced her collarbone now, making her skin tingle with electricity. But she wasn't watching his movements. She was watching his eyes. Focused. Amused. Wanting.

Adian clasped her hands around his neck, drawing him closer. "Of course I'll marry you," she whispered. "Now f—"

But Tyto caught her mouth with his, wiping the vulgarity from her lips. Adian gasped against his him, and their bodies were moving together. And it was like their first time, butterflies flitting in her stomach, passion charging their limbs. Adian tossed her head back, mist collecting on her eyelids. Pleasure consumed her until the only thing she was aware of was Tyto's body against hers.

Tyto mumbled against her neck, "I suppose we should invent a more PG engagement story to tell our children."

"Children?" But Adian let it go. Without opening her eyes, she wove her fingers in his wet hair. "That would be wise, yes."

Corolla
July 2020

The Twelfth Wall hums with birdsong and so many leaves flowing in the occasional breeze. It's colder this morning than usual, and I hug myself to capture body heat. I am alone, sore legs trudging the red brick roads through campus. Silently, I applaud myself for thinking to bring my Caeli boots (and the rest of my uniform) back to Argenti—I am as soundless as a ghost. And I was this morning too, creeping down the stairs and sneaking past Talan's door.

He came home late last night, Finis glued to his side.

"Vera?" I asked, forgetting all about James's task to brainstorm a list of new house features.

"She's alright," Talan said. "Recovering." I would have hugged him, had Finis not been there beside him, their hands knotted together. Unbreakable. Finis stayed the night, and I found myself wondering, up in my own bed, if Castan appreciated having the dorm all to himself. I wondered if he would finally get some rest.

Yesterday, on my trek home after Defensive Training, I glimpsed a voluptuous garden behind the West Dorms. I couldn't escape from Dani and Júlia long enough to check it out, and I was already late for dinner with James and Laila. But nothing is keeping me now. Not a soul wanders campus this early.

After some wrong turns and troubleshooting, I land myself at the edge of the garden. Butterfly bushes line the perimeter. Their fragrance catches in the breeze, easing my senses. Black and blue butterflies flit here and there, and I imagine Adian among their numbers. I walk the narrow mulch paths, suddenly feeling warmer, brighter. What did Calyx think about our mother's garden? I pass colorful perennials—pinks, reds, yellows, peaches—and I have no name for any plant. My heart soars with an almost childish exhilaration. Troubles cannot follow me through the garden paths. This place is as pure and compassionate as Adian's memory of the Albas.

My hands tingle for something to weave these new memories together with. Though I don't recall Laila saying Adian liked Victorian history, this garden is a clipping from another time. My mother's time.

But where is the statue?

Something glints in the morning sun. My question is answered. I loop around a circle of what looks like miniature weeping willows, and the mulch transitions to gray slate. Under the shade of the weeping willows, are stone benches. Birds scatter as I make my presence known. I hardly notice them, my eyes reflecting gold.

Adian overlooks her horticulture creation. Standing in her shadow, it's difficult to imagine Major Rex commissioning this lavish piece. And it is extravagant, towering at least eight feet tall. Her golden-bronze arms are cupped before her, and resting within her welded fingers, is a sproutling of some variety. Her lips are full, grinning. Her eyes are as solid as the Venefica's, glinting in the sunlight. She has a slim face, high cheekbones, and her hair is piled atop her head in a bun. The artist molded her body in a flaring gown of lilies, tangling and spilling over the concrete base. Adian is more a faerie queen than my mother.

I step up onto the concrete slab, grasping Adian's wrists for support. Not knowing why, I trace her jawline. Is this really how she was? An Amazonian beauty? I bow my head at her cupped hands. A green-backed tree frog is resting in her fingers, along with a crumpled piece of paper.

I purse my lips and snatch the paper from Adian's hands. The tree frog blinks slow, yellow eyes my way. I jump down from the statue, unfolding the article as I go.

Adian, should I go to the banquet with this girl I like or no?

My brow knits together. What is this?

"Your mother's tribute seems to have become Taxodium's own Juliet of Verona."

I whirl about, wild eyes landing on a figure clad in cream-colored cashmere and dark wash jeans. A silver pin adorns his breast, but I can't make out what it says. Maybe something about being an ambassador.

"I didn't know you were standing there," I laugh. It's a nervous laugh, the kind you wish you could take back as soon as it escapes.

Issak shoves his hands in his pockets. "Caeli boots," he grins, "they're a wonder."

I glance at my own feet, feeling a smile blooming across my lips. "Yeah..." I crumple the paper in my fist and set it back in Adian's hands. Part of me wonders if Issak put that scrap of paper there. "Um... How did you—"

"Hearts also have distinct beats." Issak clears his throat. "I actually wanted to speak with you."

Though he can't see me, I meet his milky gaze. "Why?"

"I wanted to apologize for the other day. I didn't... I mean, I didn't know Luca was..." Blood creeps into his neck. I bet he wishes he wore a higher collar.

I scuff my heels against the slate, though, of course the action is soundless. "It's alright."

Issak exhales. "Good because I felt so incredibly guilty. I—"

"Actually," an idea strikes me, "could you get me into his room?"

Issak clasps his hands together, face screwing up with thought. I am close enough now that my brain deciphers the silver pin on his breast: an intricate tree branch. My gaze slides from the pin to the fingers fondling it. I forgot how scarred his hands are as if he's received a million paper cuts. I want to ask about it, but I scrape enough decency together not to.

After a short forever, Issak says, "Okay. Let's go." He puts out an arm, and I twine my elbow in his. I know he's perfectly capable of walking on his own, but the skeptic inside of me believes he needs my guiding arm. The grateful heart inside of me doesn't know how to turn him down.

Adian at our backs, we make our way through those winding garden paths. Every shrub, every blossom, I imagine my mother the day she put her plants in soil. Was my father a witness? Did he choose some of these plants to showcase?

I frown. Adian's garden outlived her.

But then, so did I.

"Heavy thoughts?" Issak tugs me from my reverie. I blink, glancing up at him. His unseeing eyes stare straight ahead, but a grin toys with his pale lips. His skin is porcelain, but Issak is anything but fragile. I see that in the set of his jaw, the determination in his gait, even if it's odd.

"No," I duck my head, "I mean, I guess. I don't know anymore."

Issak slides a hand over the top of my own. "You don't *know* anymore?" Amusement laces his question. I study the pale white lines marking his flesh.

"What happened to your hands?" Blood rushes to my face, and my eyes come close to exploding. "I didn't mean to ask that."

"I know I've told you this before, but you talk when you're nervous."

Issak chuckles, and that too is odd. Breathy but not forced. In fact, it's such a natural sound on Issak's lips, I find myself grinning. "It's a fair question to ask. I'm just too much of a pacifist to be a guard. We all learned that the hard way, back when I learned combat."

"Defensive Training?"

Issak nods, and I see that we're out on the cobbled road now. "It has nothing to do with my blindness," he shrugs, "I'm just not deft enough to be a fighter. Nor do I have the heart for it. I prefer science to it all."

Not knowing what else to say, I blurt, "Your hearing is impeccable, though."

He turns pearl-white eyes on me. "More than you know."

My breath catches in my throat. I bite my lip to keep from embarrassing myself further. We tread soundlessly down the cobbled road, passing only a few other students as we go. It's then that I realize Issak is the one leading *me*, tugging in his gentle manner. I match his pace.

"Does it overwhelm you, hearing everyone all the time?"

"No—it's liberating. Before I turned sixteen, I had a guide dog. Before that, a cane. My parents were thrilled when my Essence came through, and so was I."

"Oh, that's... It sounds like the first happy story I've heard since I got here. Everyone else's seems forged in blood and grief."

Issak pats my hand. "Well, the Gens have taken much."

"Oh," I remember his cousin, "I'm sorry. I didn't mean to bring your cousin into this."

"It's okay," he grins. "I gave you the wrong impression when we first met. Vengeance isn't my path. Kat died, but she wouldn't want me to take it personally. I think people forget that sometimes."

Castan flashes over my vision of the looming hospital. *Don't take it personally.*

"That seems callous."

Issak shrugs, lifting my arm with his. "I don't think it's callous. I just think people lose themselves to grief sometimes, and pelari are no exception. Especially since we don't typically feel in public. We're a stubborn lot."

"A suffering lot," I mumble, as we climb the stone steps to Rainier. We pass a father and daughter, the little girl jumping down the steep steps one at a time. I tear my gaze from the pair, but when they pass out of my line of vision, I glance over my shoulder. The father sweeps his daughter into his arms, and they descend the remaining steps that much quicker. The little blonde girl wriggles with laughter. Gold winks in the horizon.

Maybe our suffering today will save that little girl suffering tomorrow.

Issak flashes an ID before the two hefty guards. They don't ask questions, just scan his badge and punch in a password on the keypad. The doors *click*, and the guards push them open.

For the first time, Rainier smells like a hospital: sterile, hand sanitizer, and other cleaning products. Issak let go of my arm long ago, but he shows me around a corner now, to a room divided into glass cells. Hospital rooms. Occupying the nearest hospital bed, buried under white sheets, is Luca Alba. The remaining rows of beds are empty, and the silence strikes me like an arrow. A room has never been so quiet, so desolate.

Issak slides his ID through another keypad. "I should warn you," his voice is stern enough that I tear my gaze from Luca and stare into those gray eyes, "he's been comatose since they brought him in. His brain activity is astounding, though." The thick glass door slides open. Beeping monitors meet my eardrums, disrupting that grim silence.

"Okay," I manage. "Thank you."

Issak offers a small smile. "Of course. I'll wait outside the wing if that's okay."

"Yeah," I nod, two steps into Luca's box. "Thank you." The door slides shut behind me, and I don't care that I thanked Issak twice. All I see is Luca, his frail body cocooned in stiff hospital sheets, electrodes pasted to his forehead and scalp. They shaved his head, but the electrode wires resemble so many sprouting gray hairs.

There's no chair in the room to sit, so I settle on the edge of his bed, careful not to jostle his arms too much—there are IVs taped to each antecubital. Underneath all the wires, I notice they took his eyepatch off. His ragged clothes have been replaced with a clean gown, and his cheeks appear fuller. I only ever saw him in the dark, so maybe he's just as gaunt as before. But this isn't the Luca Adian knew. The Luca she knew was mischievous and genuine, caring and careless all at the same time. He wasn't so feeble, so fragile.

He was so much more than a pile of skin and bones.

I glaze over the many monitors, the color-coded numbers. *Jon Xabier Dentata... What did he do to you?*

My hand sweeps over the sheets, fingers knitting between Luca's.

"I'm Corolla Vel," I whisper, "your niece." Tears choke my next words, "My mother loved you. Adian loved you."

I imagine his atrophic fingers twitching in mine. I imagine my words reviving his consciousness. His eyelids fluttering, meeting my longing gaze. And then I will tell him who I am again and again until we're both weeping tears of joy. "You're my uncle," I'll say, clutching his hand for fear of losing that spark in his eyes.

But none of this happens. The monitors beep, monotonous, and Luca remains unchanged. I watch his chest rise and fall. Tears blur my vision like watercolors.

"What did he do to you?" My gut twinges, as all the possibilities flood my mind. I haven't forgotten those bruises and scars on his torso. "He broke your spirit, collapsed it like a lawn chair and tossed it in the dumpster." I chew my lip and brush tears from lashes. "Why won't they come to visit you? Why won't Valeria and Tyto come to see you? Even if Rex won't let them, why don't they try?" Maybe they have tried, but my emotions stifle logical explanations. Powerful waves crash over my body, chilling the marrow in my bones and taking me under.

It's too much, all this devastation.

I give Luca's fingers one last gentle squeeze and climb to my feet. The doors slide open. My arms wrap around my torso. And then I'm out in the main hall, Issak fluttering about me like a concerned matron. Maybe he would stop if the tears did, but they don't. They are two streams down my cheeks, unrelenting.

"Corolla," he smooths a hand down my back, "it's alright. He'll be okay. We'll probably reach the decision to send him to St. Helena. He'll get better there, be safer there—"

"What's going on?" My head snaps up, fingertips tingling with so much energy, I have to make fists.

In Castan's presence, Issak fumbles.

"She um… Corolla—"

"My synapses are firing." I fling tears away with knuckles.

Castan laughs, the sound rumbling through my head like a summer breeze. "That's one way to explain it." My insides thaw, and I wipe glossy eyes. Issak is appalled, pale and insecure. I hardly notice him.

Castan loops an arm around my waist—*why do people always link themselves to me?*—and turns to Issak, a familiar grin on his lips. "I'll take her home. I'm sure she appreciates seeing Luca," his emerald eyes flit from Issak to me, "but it's been a long… month."

I nod—it's the best I can do—and Castan is taking me away. We're staggering down the halls, through the waiting room, and, through watery eyes, I perceive awed and irritated looks from staff and visitors. But they aren't staring at me.

We burst through the main entrance. Castan's fingertips dig into my hip, helping me down the steps. It's not an unpleasant feeling.

My voice wavers, "Why do people look at you like that?"

Castan pushes a strained breath through his teeth. His gaze angles towards the sky. "I cut Rosh Dentata's finger off, and they all wish they were the ones who'd done it."

"What the *fuck?*"

Castan turns on me, shushes exploding past his lips. Amusement crinkles in the corner of his eyes. "Tess—there are children around!" I don't care to correct or confirm his statement.

Numb. I am numb. How could Luca's family abandon him? Where would he be if we hadn't stolen him back to the Academy? How many others have been lost in the same manner? How many have been forgotten? There were a lot of cells down there... I pull away from Castan's grip, all too aware of his eyes on the side of my salt-stained face.

"I'm not usually like this." My shoulders tremble. As if to convince him, I force laughter through stinging tears. I swipe them away, will them away, but these faucets are uncontrollable.

"I know, Corolla." He swallows and pins his gaze on the horizon. "You have so much love to give."

"I don't know about that."

"But you do—that's why it hurts you to keep it to yourself."

Bitter wind cuts through the thread of my tee shirt. I rub hands down my arms. My breath hitches, as I think about what James would say if he stumbled across me now. The last of my tears dry up behind my eyes. My heart steels, bracing itself for an encounter unlikely to happen—James spends most of his time with Laila these days. All this time, Castan has been studying me, caution masked behind that wall of amusement.

I don't look at him as I say, "I know I shouldn't be so sad, but sometimes you have to cry about the things that never will be, just so you can keep living in the now."

"Can I get that on a mug?"

My eyes slide over him. "You really are bad at jokes."

He digs hands into his pockets. "I already gave you that disclaimer."

The cobbled road gradually becomes steeper, and I know we are close to the Ward Residencies. Panic kneads my stomach—I want it to stay like this, the ease of talking with Castan, for a moment longer. I know I shouldn't care. I shouldn't. But, more and more often, my heart is insubordinate to my mind.

"The ambassadors are voting to send Luca to St. Helena." I heard the rumors yesterday. Somehow, Dani knew all about the Board meeting and let it spill on our way back from Defensive Training.

I glance at Castan. He's thoughtful, with a knuckle to his lips. I look away—because, for some reason, that act stirs emotions I don't want to explore.

He answers, oblivious to my internal parrying, "That's a popular choice these days. Probably the best place for him, though. St. Helena has better equipment to deal with... special cases." The Twelfth Wall roars with thunder as a sharp gust shreds through its branches and shrubbery. If I look close enough, into those ebony shadows, I can see the crumpled stone remains of the Wall's predecessors.

"Why haven't Valeria and Tyto come to see their brother? Why have they abandoned him?"

Castan sighs, combing pale fingers through his dark hair. I don't want to explore how *that* makes me feel either. I focus on the Twelfth Wall again.

"I don't know, Corolla. I will never understand people."

"What about your family? You never talk about them." Immediately, I know I've said the wrong thing. Castan sets his jaw, ducks his head. He's that jaded soldier I met at my kitchen table all those weeks ago. I wish my feet would scuff across the red brick. I wish I could think of rescuing words. I wish there weren't silence between us.

Then, in a tone so quiet and calculated, I have to check and make sure it's coming from Castan's mouth, "The Dentatas."

I know not to ask for more. I can guess what the strain in his voice means.

"I'm sorry." *Those two were for you.*

The Residencies peek over the hill, five welcoming Tudor faces.

I squeeze my abdomen. "Did you really cut his finger off?"

A bitter whisper, "I would have done more."

"Have you ever...?"

"No," his tone is clipped, "I could never murder someone."

I look at him then. He's staring at his feet, but I glimpse the distance in his dark irises. I'm accustomed to the shadows hanging under his eyes, yet they catch me off guard now. He's so pale, worry prickles my flesh.

"Are you alright?"

He laughs, but it's nothing like that glowing laughter from the hospital. It's cynical, frigid. It's the laughter of someone who knows the world offers nothing to be joyful about.

"I'm alive, Corolla." He stops, and I realize we're on Argenti's front stoop. Castan fixes those haunting eyes on me. I know he sees my lashes, still wet with tears, and my eyes, rimmed red from sobbing.

I duck my head. "I shouldn't have asked." My hand is on the doorknob, and my mouth is saying, "I have to get my things together for DT." But my mind is saying, *Ask him to stay. You despise DT—ask him to stay.*

Castan's taken aback. "You're still going to that?"

I shrug. "Well, yeah. I like the mindlessness of exercise." Images from yesterday flicker through my head, from the brutal locker room to the piercing gaze of the Commander. It's so tempting to stay home, to stay with Castan. But I have so much to prove, so much to—

"I guess I'll talk to you later then," Castan runs a hand down the back of his neck. He does this often enough that I know the hem of his shirt will rise, offering a view of his smooth abdomen. I glue my eyes somewhere beyond his head. I wonder if he expected me to ask him to stay, if he *wanted* to stay. I shove the thoughts away.

"Alright," I crack Argenti's door, "thanks for," Castan raises a demure brow, "everything." The door is closing behind me, and I'm collapsing against it, burying my face in my hands.

How mindless is exercise when Castan appears in your thoughts wanting to undress you?

God, I'm hormonal today.

A door creaks to my left. Talan emerges from his room, bedecked in full gear. "I don't want to wake Finis," he whispers. "Are you ready for training?" Something about his lopsided grin summons violent tears to my eyes. Talan is at my side immediately, drawing me to my feet and crushing my heaving body in his lanky arms.

"You're an emotional little creature this morning, aren't you?" He smooths my hair back, and I nod against him. "Is Aunty Flow paying a visit?"

I stumble backward, my face draining and flushing all at once. Talan forces me back to his chest, patting my head.

He exhales a knowing sigh, "Every woman has her days."

Past
November 2002

Adian flipped a weary page of *Battle of Brothers: World War II and the Dentatas*. She kept reading the same paragraph over and over again, though her mind was like a broken vacuum: she only picked up the bare minimum, and even then, she was likely to forget it. Nerves had that effect on her.

She had brought the book as a distraction, but it wasn't accomplishing its job. She didn't even like reading—*that's* how eager she was to forget their destination.

Adian shook her head and turned back to the fine print on the page. She summarized, once again, hoping it would stick this time.

It was controversial for Tax to enter the war, as they stayed out of the first one. The Dentatas wanted pedes to destroy themselves, so pelari could finally rise to power. They attacked pelari who covertly helped the Allies...

"I should be able to remember this," Adian sighed, giving up. "But it's just so awful and contradicting to what I learned in grade school, that I can't." She folded a scrap of paper to hold her place and set the book on the dash. She knew why her mind was elsewhere—she had a son squirming in her abdomen and severe parents awaiting her for dinner.

"My great-grandfather fought in the battle under Commander Allen's lead."

"Really?" Adian was distracted, but at least she knew Laila was referring to the Battle of Brothers. It had been the defining attack of pelari history: the Allen brothers vs. Dentata generals. Bloody and gruesome, it had ended the civil war between Taxodium and the Dentatas.

Or started it, Adian rolled her eyes. Following Taxodium's victory, was the Dentata's trial and sentencing. Tilia Pyrus laced each member's DNA with that dreaded disease, the very reason why Adian could hardly manage to leave the Academy to visit her family for holidays, such as this.

I guess I recall more than I give myself credit for.

In the corner of her vision, Laila shrugged. "I mean, a lot of people's greats did. It was the war of the century." She said this with the air of one who grew up with such history swirling behind her eyes.

It may have fascinated Laila, but it gave Adian a headache. She cracked her window, allowing the frigid air to refresh her. In the cradle of her arms, Calyx pounced. Adian jolted, ever surprised by her child's spontaneous movements. She smiled fondly at her unborn baby.

Life was unpredictable. If Adian knew anything, it was that. In grade school, she remembered being quizzed about what profession she wanted to go into when she was older. The answer always changed. Vet to nurse to biologist. But this… Never could she have planned, post-graduation from the pelari Academy, to be newly married and with child.

She repositioned ginger hands around the swell of her abdomen. Nine months in, and she still wasn't used to the feeling. She was so accustomed to creating plants that it endeared her to create a human. The pendant of St. Philomena hung around her neck. She heard Marilena's, voice in her head, *"Philomena protected my mother's babies, her mother's babies, and my own. She'll protect yours too."* The practice was superstitious, even if Adian wasn't, but she adored being a part of an Alba tradition. She was, after all, an Alba.

Adian wriggled her toes, feeling the soft aloe socks all over again, in the confines of her tennis shoes. Marilena sent them in the mail, cartoon aloe print *and* aloe infused. Strange that she should be armored in Marilena's affection to survive the confrontation with her own mother.

At least I can curse in front of my parents now, and they won't scold me. She'd picked up quite a few phrases, phrases any pedes would raise a brow in response to, as they wouldn't know which venerable beings Adian swore upon.

Adian glanced past her book laying precariously on Laila's dash. The throbbing in her temples intensified. Or maybe that was her imagination.

"Take a right up here," she instructed. They whizzed past familiar markings: Otto's Grocers at the corner, and Pierce Barn in the cornfield where many, many parties had been hosted. The structure was now sagging, heavy with age and rain rot. All around them, Forrest, Michigan swelled with reds, ambers, golds, and memories.

Adian saw herself and James skipping down the uneven sidewalk after long days of school. She could almost feel her younger self, trapped in this body of hers, yearning to fly down to Harmon Park and put her hands around the metallic rungs of the old swings. James used to push her, always warning her to, "Hold tight, Dee." She would let go just to watch his face flood white with fear.

Adian touched the smile shaping her lips, biting back laughter. *I was cruel to him, wasn't I?*

"Are you going to tell your parents about Marcus the Marine or about Tyto?" The click-click of the blinker resounded, as Laila maneuvered the vehicle downtown.

Adian thought about Marcus, the name she had given to her and Tyto's lie. To Taxodium, Marcus was her husband. Only Tyto and Laila knew the truth: that Major Tyto Alba married Aurum Ward Adian Vel. The truth had to remain a secret, had to, or else Tyto would lose his position and Adian would be... Well, between the both of them, Adian wasn't *technically* breaking any rules. As a Ward of the Academy, she was not permitted to participate in the mandatory military service. She was, therefore, not disobeying the Law that stated: *Students and graduates must complete two years of service before attaching themselves to another.* Tyto, on the other hand... Adian couldn't even begin to count all the Laws and oaths his marriage to her severed completely.

If anyone asked after her husband, Adian explained that Marcus was currently deployed out of the country. But since Marcus was pedes, most people didn't ask. Pelari had an awful habit of assuming pedes led terribly dull lifestyles. Which is what made Marcus the Marine the perfect cover. As much as Adian and Tyto had fun with their secret, it pained them both. They lied to everyone. Tyto lied to his advisors, to the Board of Majors, and whoever else supervised Taxodium government. And Adian lied to Alex.

He was preoccupied lately with his new post as a Trainee to the Guard, just as Adian was preoccupied with the life blooming in the confines of her body. But that didn't make the deception any more comfortable. Adian still felt the shockwaves of his surprise when she told him the news.

"I'm pregnant. And married." She held up a hand as if the drop of diamond there was evidence of both. Alex could only stare, at first, his eyes darting from the gemstone to her stomach.

Then, with a wry grin and hazel eyes tethering her own, "A shotgun wedding?" Adian exhaled relief. For a moment, she feared he was angry with her.

"Nothing so scandalous," she assured him. Something gritty and barbed settled in the pit of her stomach. Adian recognized the feel of deception, knew it from all those nights she snuck out of the house to party at Pierce Barn.

"I'm tired of things being complicated," she told Tyto the same day. Yet even now, the words still made her stomach twinge. Adian breathed through her teeth.

"You seem tense."

"I should have just told my parents about Ty when we got married in March."

"But you didn't."

"No, my parents are traditionalists. They fit in better with the Amish than the suburbs."

"Well," Laila's voice stretched thin, grasping for something comforting to say. "They can't be upset with you forever. Especially on Thanksgiving."

Adian's eyes traveled the yellow lines on the road. "Watch them. James once put a scratch on the Oldsmobile, and they still make him park in the street because of it."

"Hmm. Maybe you should wait to tell them *after* we eat dinner then. I'm famished."

Adian looked down at the balloon of flesh in her lap. "I don't think that's going to happen."

Laila didn't have an answer for that.

Adian studied Laila's profile, seeing everything her parents would: too many holes in her ears, too wild of hair, too low-cut of a blouse. She squinted. *Nope*, she decided, *even then, Laila is too liberal.*

"Why are you staring at me?" Laila asked, not self-conscious but apprehensive. "You look like a displeased cat when you make that face."

"Maybe…" Adian trailed off. "Maybe only wear one pair of earrings?"

Laila shot her a look. "You're joking."

"And take off all your finger-things. Except that topaz one. If anyone asks, it's your promise ring."

Mr. and Mrs. Vel lived in a neighborhood that could have been a page from a *Better Homes and Gardens* magazine. Neat rows of two-story houses, black shingled roofs, lawns striped with lines to indicate where the hired professionals had cut the grass. Even the trees, sprinkled here and there, appeared identical, not a single leaf out of place.

"That one," Adian pointed, feeling nauseous. "I always have to look for the flagpole."

"I think your brother's Honda gave it away," Laila smirked, as she passed the silver car parked in the street. She pulled into the driveway of the home with the American flag flapping like a ribbon in the autumn wind.

Adian checked the windows for faces but saw only white curtains of her mother's decorum staring back at her.

"For a pregnant woman of color," Laila began, "you're very pale."

Adian slapped her roommate's thigh, laughter bubbling through her anxiety. "Would you stop starting your sentences like that? It's unnecessary."

Laila shrugged. "I just want to be correct. Ready to go?"

Adian slid her hand around the handle and unlatched her door. She took a deep breath and spilled onto the sand-colored driveway. Laila opened the trunk, duffle bag strap looped around her wrist.

Adian stopped her. "Better wait until after the smoke clears to get the overnight bags out." *If we get past the front doors.*

Grim and anxious, Adian walked to the front door with all the grace of a woman heavy with child. Her feet ached—and her back! The damn thing seemed to be in a constant state of discomfort, no matter which way she positioned herself. As much as Adian relished in the idea of motherhood, she was ready for Calyx to become his own entity. Calyx, yes, that's what she and Tyto decided on before she left for Michigan. Adian had had the name in mind for years, ever since she opened an old biology textbook in the library downtown. She and James had been picking up material for their summer reading list (their parents insisted), but Adian lost herself in the basement of old books.

Adian could still feel the spine, brown and frayed with age, crumple open in her hands, almost submitting to her delicate touch. The book displayed a diagram of a plant. It was such an old volume that the ink was smudged, the pages, thin as the Bible her mother gave her for her eighth birthday. Thirteen-year-old Adian studied the diagram on the left page. Noted how *calyx* and *corolla* sounded on her tongue. They were counterparts, she saw, just like how she and James were. The names stuck with her ever since.

Adian blinked away the musty smell of old paper and nostalgia. She rang her parents' doorbell. On the other side of the door, she heard it chime *bing, bong.* And then there were feet, tramping along the long, shaggy carpet that always stuck between her toes. Even after all this time—it had been a little over a year—Adian recognized the person by the sound of his gait.

The door swung open, the faux wreath tacked to its face swinging.

"James!" Adian exclaimed before her brother could make a face at the size of her midsection. She squeezed his lanky body to hers, glancing over his shoulder for her parents. She didn't see them, but scents from the kitchen wafted out the door. Adian could pick out each dish on the menu: turkey roasting in the oven, stuffing baking in a pot, cranberry sauce, pumpkin pie cooling on the stovetop. Oh, and cheese and basil-seasoned crackers for appetizers.

Being pregnant had its perks. Her Essence was stronger than ever; she didn't have to squeeze her body in that ugly guard's uniform to practice. And she could mostly pick out any ingredient in any dish present.

Adian pulled away, holding James by the shoulders. She inspected him, as he was very obviously examining her. Wide-eyed, flushed cheeks—

"You look great, James!" Adian knew she was too cheerful, exclaiming too much, but she couldn't help it. "And this," Adian moved to allow Laila space, "is my roommate, Laila Cassena."

"Nice to meet you, James." Laila offered him a mock salute—not the pedes salute, of course, but the pelari one: right hand with three fingers over the heart. Adian could have kicked her—how many times had she reminded Laila that she didn't come from a pelari family? At this point, Laila forgot on purpose.

James could only wave, shell-shocked.

"Can we come in, James?" Adian scanned behind him for their parents once more. *Where are they?*

"W-well, yeah," James stuttered. He moved past the threshold to allow them passage. "Mom and Dad are in the kitchen getting something ready for you…" Adian was already shuffling past him.

"Dee…" James turned, the door closing behind him. He scratched the back of his neck, uncertain.

Adian's hands climbed to her hips. "If you think I'm out of wedlock," she hissed, "then get your head out of Mom and Dad's asses. I'm married." She wiggled her fingers, and the diamond caught sunlight.

James paled. He ran a hand through his straw-colored hair. It stuck up like pikes. "Shit," he breathed, fixing his hair absent-mindedly. "Mom and Dad are going to kill you."

Adian flashed a smile that didn't match her uneasy eyes. "You're going to make sure that doesn't happen."

"No," James gushed, "I don't think you understand—"

But he never finished the sentence.

From the corner, came Mr. and Mrs. Vel. Adian's back was to them, but she heard the distinct tread of their feet against the carpet. The hairs on the back of her neck stood on end.

"Congratulations!" Adian felt the spray of confetti on her back.

Oh, Phaedra's Mother.

She turned around to bright grins, white teeth flashing, and her parents, more or less the same way as she saw them last, ecstatic to greet her. Her father's dark hair was obviously gray now, but her mother's remained the same golden blonde. Adian recalled her mother saying something about dyeing it, during one of their rare conversations on the phone.

In slow motion, their eyes traveled to the lump in Adian's stomach. The corners of their lips sank, plummeted as if anchors were now tethered there. In their arms, each held a confetti cannon and an edge of a big poster board sign that read: *Congrats, Dee! (We know it's late, but here's a gift from Mom and Dad).* A neon orange arrow pointed to a box at their feet. No, not a box. A suitcase. And pinned to the gray canvas of that, was a map of Europe. It was marked in red Sharpie, directing Adian's eye all around the continent.

Adian's shoulders sagged. *They bought me a tour to travel Europe.* Tears stained her vision. *It was something we always talked about.* Since no one knew for sure where Adian originated from, her parents used to tell people mixed stories. It was a family joke and maybe the only lies her parents condoned.

"She's a distant cousin to the Queen's cousin."

"Yeah, Dee is actually from Hamburg. Gypsy mom, German dad."

"Italy. She came to us with a Medici stamp on her right ankle."

Adian couldn't face their iron wall of disapproval, so she looked at James instead. He had somehow moved to stand between her and their parents. James the mediator. His eyes were glued to the ground, tracing imaginary designs in the carpet, no doubt.

It was then that Adian noticed how much her brother had changed. She had a bad habit of only remembering him as the child he was growing up, but he wasn't a child anymore. In place of his chipmunk cheeks, were ones sculpted to his bones. His eyes had always been blue, but there was something different about them. They were intelligent, thoughtful, hidden behind pale lashes when they had only ever been eyes to Adian before. And his blonde hair was a shade darker, reminding her more of wet sand now, rather than straw under sunlight.

Adian wondered what Laila saw when she looked at her brother. Was he attractive? Though he was lanky, his arms had some shape to them, as did his chest. Broad, pointed shoulders. He had graduated college two years ago and was interning at an office of architectural design. He's an adult, Adian had to tell herself, not an awkward child with adult-ish tendencies. *Hell, he may even have a girlfriend!*

Her mother, gasping, "What have you *done?*"

Adian came back into her body. Behind her, she felt Laila shifting in the tense atmosphere. Beside her, James was silent and still. She saw the cogs turning behind his eyes, working out ways to fix this. James was always trying to fix her mistakes. Or at least, he was always trying to fix what their parents *viewed* as her mistakes. Adian wasn't sorry for Tyto or Calyx. She loved them both with a fierceness that consumed her aching body, gave her strength.

"Mom, Dad," Adian implored them. "I meant to tell you—"

"Tell us?" Her mother shrieked, voice rising higher and higher. "Adian Marie, you're pregnant!"

Adian winced at the sound of her middle name. *Marie* always made her quake with shame. And defiance. Philomena blazed against her skin, a zap of lightning on her sternum.

"No, look," Adian showed them her left hand. "I'm married to a very nice man. Tyto Alba—"

Her father, one of the most mild-mannered men she knew, smashed his confetti gun in the ground. Adian flinched, the air raining with scraps of shimmering ammunition. Mr. Vel repositioned his glasses, which had slipped in his outburst.

"Dad..." Adian reached for him, but he took a sharp turn and stalked into the living room. He kicked the ottoman, sending it crashing into the coffee table. The poster hung limply in her mother's small hand. Somewhere, past the living room and down the hall, the oven timer beeped.

Mrs. Vel's crumpled expression steeled over. "That'll be my turkey. You may see yourself to the door, young lady."

And that was the last time Adian saw her mother alive— disappearing around the corner, gold hair glinting in the sunlight that poked through the curtains.

Adian didn't remember moving, but suddenly her arms were around her brother. She was saying goodbye.

"I'll write to you," James whispered in her ear. Adian thought she nodded; she was too numb to notice. Her shoes sloshed through a pile of confetti. Laila's hand on her back, guiding her out the door and down the walkway. The car door opening, Adian, plopping back in her seat. It was still body-temperature warm.

Laila started the car. Adian snapped her seatbelt on, motions robotic.

"Thank you for coming with me," a voice whispered, so quiet, it took Adian several seconds to realize it was her own.

"Of course."

"I don't know what else I expected. They were never going to accept me. I guess..." Adian chewed her lip as she said it, "I guess I just hoped they would be more like Ty's parents. That, after all this time away from them, they would be more like the imaginary parents I always give myself." They were leaving the suburbs, leaving the platform of her childhood.

Laila grinned sardonically. "To hell with them both! In fact, let's drive to my parents' place. Right now."

"No," Adian said and not because the Cassenas lived in Montana. "Let's just go home." The words were broken glass in her lungs. Because, despite all their disagreements, Adian always considered her family *home*. But that door had just been slammed in her face forever.

Adian must have said this aloud, as Laila—voice quite full of vengeance—commented, "Then I guess you'll just have to make your own family without them."

Calyx Maurizio Vel was born December 18th, early enough in the morning that Tyto Alba could be there to congratulate his wife. Her brow was beaded with sweat, their pink and red-tinged son suckling at her breast.

"One of the only things your Essence is good for," Adian mumbled. Her tongue slipped with exhaustion, making her vowels sharper than usual. Tyto was invisible, but she sensed the air shift where he moved. The doctor and nurses had all gone, giving her a moment alone with her firstborn. Tyto managed to slip between one of these exits, patiently waiting for the room to clear.

The sun pooled through the slitted blinds, casting their pattern on the white sheets of Adian's hospital bed. Tyto padded to his quaint little family, and his shadow took the place of the sunlight on the end of her bed. He revealed himself to the naked eye.

"I heard the news from my bedchambers," Tyto whispered, awed with the delicate nature of his son's puny fingers. Something shifted in his breast, something fierce and affectionate. He came to recognize this emotion as *fatherhood*. And Tyto knew he would do anything for his son.

"Yes," Adian breathed, stroking Calyx's peach fuzz hair. "He laughed. A beautiful, glorious laugh."

Castan

July 2020

"Are you *drunk?*" Corolla's eyelids smoosh together. I think she's squinting. I almost regret responding to the knock on my door—it's so *bright* outside. Corolla stands in a rectangle of light, stray hair plastered to her forehead with sweat. She's wearing her uniform, skin tight, and I have to do a double take. She's unstrapped her armor; it's slung over one of her forearms like an animal pelt. But her body... If Calyx were here, reading my thoughts, he'd have me strung up from the Bell Tower.

"I am not," I say, rolling my eyes, "but if you're going to be so loud, then step inside before the whole East and West hear you." I pivot, making for the kitchenette where I left my mug and a wadded-up tee shirt. I swipe a hand down my sticky abdomen. Frown. Wonder how I spilled so much Yuengling down my shirt anyway. I use the wasted tee to mop up an amber puddle on the counter.

"It's only 15:00." The door shuts behind her, cutting off the afternoon glow. "What is that *smell?*" I imagine Corolla making that disgusted face of hers, muscles bunched together into an expression that anyone would find horrendous. When I turn around though, her profile is entirely different. My heart sinks as if this calculating Corolla is a stranger where I expected disgusted Corolla to be.

She ditched her armor by the door, and I can almost hear Finis chiding her for such carelessness. Her eyes dart around the dorm, likely counting the collection of empty vodka bottles Finis has aligned atop the kitchenette cabinets. "They're not mine," I want to assure her, but these are not the words flying off my tongue.

"I see Talan has you on his schedule," I smirk at my own joke, though it's been years since Corolla said *15:00*. With my back, I try to mask the number of empty bottles on the counter, like soldiers arranged for battle.

Finis is going to kill me. Thankfully, he won't be back from the Guard until tonight. Maybe I'll ask Talan to jump to Pennsylvania and replace what I drank before he gets back.

Corolla offers me a slight smile. She shifts in place, and clasps her hands in front of her body, not quite reaching my gaze.

"What?" I step towards her, half tripping, "it doesn't smell *that* bad in here. I opened the window."

To the floor, "You have a window?"

I ignore that valid question. "Oh," I wag a finger in her direction, though she's not watching, "I know what your problem is. I'll be right back." I stumble through the living room. My surroundings smudge in the corners of my vision. While I acknowledge this is a problem, I do not care to address it. My tongue feels thick, and I think back to the time Calyx once tried to explain his peanut allergy to me. I'm about to snatch a fresh shirt from a stack of clothes when I catch myself in the mirror hanging on the inside of my closet door.

I glance at myself, the shadows outlining my muscle, the scars and fading bruises of too many unanticipated encounters. *Like Corolla using you as a landing pad after that jump in Belarus.* I almost laugh, but a different memory strikes the bells in my mind.

I'm only twelve or thirteen—a couple years after my mother was taken—sitting at a newly cleaned desk in the Complex's library. *The only bloodshed in this room*, I remember thinking, *is contained between ink and pages.* And until I turned sixteen, those carved shelves in concrete walls, and all the clots of dust in the world, were my sanctuary. For a long time, my only role models came from books. Then I met Calyx.

"I didn't want to be like this," I mutter to my reflection. "I didn't want to be raised a killer." I tug a shirt on—one of the ten plain white tees I own—and rejoin Corolla in the living room. Since there's only a single sofa (Finis wanted extra fridge space for all those beers I just inhaled), I throw myself down beside Corolla. The cotton of my shirt sticks to my skin where I spilled beer. I try not to draw attention to myself by picking at it.

"You're a terrible liar." My blood runs cold with the accusation. I always knew someone would find out, someone would put the pieces together, but how did Corolla know? I didn't just say anything to her, did I? Alert, I glance around—Is there a banner streaming from the doorway somewhere?

"How—"

"You're drunk," her eyes slide over mine. Her hair's askew. I want to fix it. "You reek of alcohol when you normally reek of coffee."

Relief replaces my anxiety. I slump back into the sofa cushions. I point to the coffee table at the Styrofoam cup on its side. "I drank that, too."

"Laila said you were sick, but I didn't think she meant *this*." Corolla raises a caramel brow, and I want so desperately to brush the hair away from her forehead, that I have to sit on my hands to keep the urge at bay. Then I register what she said. Cross my arms.

"Laila doesn't know sickness." No one here does. The fire ripping through my veins, destroying, decomposing. Alcohol was the only way I could water down that fever, though my skin still burns.

"But she knows you," Corolla slides cold fingertips on my wrist. Does she feel that agony under my skin? I don't anymore. "She's your aunt. And she's worried about you."

"*Is* she?"

Corolla angles her body, a complete blur of ebony to me. "Of course she is! I meant to come earlier, but like you said, Talan has me on his schedule." I'm not drunk enough to miss that smirk creeping into her lips, the kind that makes you feel like the third party in a two-party system: excluded. Corolla smells of salt and sweat and spearmint gum, her cheeks flushed pink. I stuff my hands under my thighs again.

I sigh, not bothering to correct her assumption of my question: Laila is as much my aunt as nuns are sisters. But Corolla can't know that, can she? Tilia was explicit...

"Should you go to the hospital?"

I startle at her suggestion. "Like this?" I gesture to myself, a grin breaking my chapped lips. A foul taste swirls in my mouth. I'm half tempted to ask Corolla for a stick of gum.

Corolla tosses her head back. I watch her throat bob as she laughs, "Like this, as in completely shit-faced?"

"Do you even know what shit-faced looks like?"

"Well," she shrugs, "you can't be too far off." Her eyes dip to my chest. "Your shirt's on backwards, too. That's a pretty common side-effect, I think."

I check for myself, eyes straining to see my collar. "Oh, you're right," I say. "Want me to take it off?"

"What?" Heat radiates in waves from her flushed cheeks. Chills shudder down my spine, and I lean closer.

"I'm joking, Tess. I only take my clothes off if I decide to bathe in Yuengling."

"So *that's* what I smelled." Corolla's grin slips into a frown. She runs her thumb over the smooth leather of the sofa. "They voted to move Luca to the island. Dani knew before me."

Something twists in my chest. Sobriety maybe. I sit up straighter. "Oh. Corolla. Shit..." I run a hand through my hair, "St. Helena is a good move, though. They have better facilities, equipment, and staff." I sound like a pamphlet. I almost wince because of it.

"I know," Corolla heaves, "it's just that I feel responsible for him. I mean, he *is* family, and... And I thought he would recover, and we could, you know, *be* a family."

I remember what she told me about James, how she just wants to make him proud. How driven she is to take care of her family. For a moment, my mind spins with this: Corolla embraces her family, and I (with some exceptions) reject everything to do with my kin.

"He'll get better at St. Helena," I say, voice not unkind but a little dazed, "and then you can properly meet him." I don't say anything about Laila's blurb on his character—"He was mischief," she told me, "but I only ever knew him from stories."—because how can I guarantee that Luca will be that person once he's recovered? Phaedra knows what that man has been through.

Jon Xabier Dentata...

"That's what Issak says, too," Corolla bites her lip, and I want to remind her why there's gum in her cheek. Addled, my brain hits *Issak* like a crater in the middle of the road.

"Issak, as in Ambassador Olejar's co-partner, Issak?" I crane my neck, but Corolla's profile is a mask.

"The same."

"You talk to him a lot?"

"He gets me past hospital security. So I can visit Luca."

I scoff, thinking back to yesterday. "He's great at handling situations."

Corolla raises a hand as if she's going to smack my shoulder. She thinks better of it. "Issak's really not that bad. You just got the wrong impression of him."

Instead of arguing with her on the matter, I snag another Yuengling from the mini fridge crowding the living room. The ocean whooshes in my ears, but I toss back the amber bottle until I can't hear it anymore.

"Castan!" This time, she really does smack me. I cough through the beer traveling down my windpipe. Tears sting my eyes.

"What?"

"You shouldn't be drinking any more of that stuff," she scowls. "I think you have a fever."

"Finis is already going to be pissed, so what's another bottle?" I extend my hand, "Want some?" Her facial muscles scrunch together.

"Ah," I say into the lip of my bottle before taking a swig, "disgusted Corolla makes an appearance at last."

"What's that supposed to mean?"

"That I missed you." I down half the bottle, esophagus numb. My limbs tingle with faint distress. This would be *so* much easier if I were a lightweight.

"Whatever." Corolla averts her eyes. I think watching me drink is physically painful for her. My gaze travels up the black fabric hugging her shapely legs, torso, chest... Thoughts from earlier return. I have to balance them out with ideas of less attractive things. Like Major Rex.

"Can I ask you something?" I set my almost empty beer aside, "and don't say that I just did. Asking permission doesn't count."

"If you say so."

"Well, um," I clear my throat and adjust in my seat, "the other week, when you were talking about your ex—"

"Castan."

I disregard the warning in her voice. "Just let me ask? You don't have to answer, but the question has been giving me a headache ever since."

"Just wait until tomorrow's hangover." But Corolla folds her limbs into herself, knees tucked under her chin and arms crossed.

"Did he hurt you? I mean, it's one thing to break up, and I'm sure that sucks, but did he, you know..." I rack my foggy brain for a better way to phrase it. Corolla beats me to it.

"Rape me?" Her voice is a ghost, a breeze through the night. When I look down at her, those doe eyes are as glassy as a doll's. Unseeing. "I don't know," she exhales, swallowing hard, "manipulation is a tricky thing to... to define." She props her chin on her knees. Sighs. Never once blinks.

"I will jump out of here right now and teach that kid a lesson," I growl. "Don't think I won't, Corolla." My hand is on my pant pocket, feeling for a geometer I turned in weeks ago.

"You're intoxicated. Inebriated. Drunk." Rattling off synonyms doesn't appear to make that look in her eyes disappear. I try again.

"You know, not every guy is like that—not every guy wants to use and discard you."

"Yes," her eyes flicker over mine, "I know that."

I lean back, hooking an arm over the back of the sofa. "You just always seemed a little skittish, and I wish you'd told me why."

"Tell you why...?" She blinks then, grounded in this dorm once more. "How was I supposed to? When we first met, you were about as friendly and accepting as a cactus with five-inch thorns. Not to mention James," her voice cracks, "James would die of embarrassment if my shame made it past our home's walls. I'm surprised *I* haven't died of embarrassment yet."

"That's wrong, you know. The way he holds it over you."

Corolla reels on me, nose pink and eyes brimming with tears. "He *doesn't* hold it over me. *I* hold it over me. I can't do something like that to him again, okay? He's all I've got and—" She stops, voice thick with emotion. A muscle in her jaw twitches and she turns away, wiping under her eyes with the back of her sleeve. I wonder if she imagines Luca as a clean slate, a fresh canvas to quietly paint herself across.

When she doesn't continue, I say, "Corolla, I don't know the situation as well as you do, but even from the outside, I can tell that you blame yourself for what happened. Chances are, there's no logical reason for you to torment yourself. But that's how you are, right? If you don't have a logical explanation, you make one up to fill in the blank. It was your boyfriend, so you assumed responsibility for his actions. But that's... not right."

"And what about you, Castan?" Her face is a sneer. It's not bitterness twisting her features, but rather, her attempt to bite back a flood of tears. "You think you deserve all the blame for Calyx's death, but have you ever stopped to wonder why you *don't?*"

I've heard something like that before. The Venefica's words cut through my mind like arrows, *"You spend all this time wondering why you deserve this pain, but have you ever considered why you do not?"*

"That's different."

"It's not!" Tears trickle down her flushed cheeks. I swallow a hard lump in my throat. "I know the story—you were ambushed. Taken by surprise and separated from each other. So how is that your fault?"

"You sound like Aunt Laila."

"I don't have to have dinner with Laila to know you're buried in a grave of your own guilt."

"You talk about me at dinner?" I know James, Laila, and Corolla take dinner at Aercus, but I never imagined my name would come up. Especially tied to Calyx's death, though I shouldn't be surprised. I clench my fists to hide the flames blooming there. Burning. So low. But there.

"Laila isn't the only one worried about you." I don't know when we stood up from the sofa, but I tower over Corolla now. She meets my gaze with eyes almost as icy as my palms are hot. Her chest heaves, eyes dried of tears.

"No one should be worried about me, okay? I've been taking care of myself since the day..." *Since the day the Dentatas took my mother.* "... since forever. Your job isn't to worry about me or anyone else. Your job is to survive."

"Look at you!" Corolla flings an arm my way, fingertips scraping my chest. "You can't even stand straight, and your skin is burning with fever."

"I'm fine." But even I hear the hollow ring in my words. My head spins, thoughts swirling around in a whirlpool of all the beer I've been drinking. Corolla stares at me with wide, concerned eyes. I lose my train of thought. She's so close—only a foot separating our bodies—but the look in her eyes puts years of distance between our hearts.

"Corolla." And I am moving, erasing that physical distance to try and erase that emotional distance too. "Corolla," I say again. Her breath hitches in her chest. I can't tell anymore if the heat in my palms is from the sickness or the embers, so I keep my hands balled in tight fists. It's a leech, that worry sucking the vitality from her visage. I want to touch her, to tug her against me and feel the warmth of her body through the fire of my own. I want to kiss her until that worry vanishes.

So I wrap arms around her head, careful not to let my hands singe her disheveled hair. It doesn't matter if my vision is blurry, that I stink of alcohol and my breath is foul. Corolla is here, and her eyes are her own. I lean forward.

A hand on my chest brings my intentions to a halt.

"Stop," Corolla is breathing so hard, I have half a mind to get her a paper bag.

I move back, but only inches, giving her enough room to breathe.

"You need to drink water. And take an Advil. Or a couple." She ducks out of my half-embrace and snatches her armor plating from the floor.

"Corolla—"

But the door's already slamming behind her.

In its proper cage, my heart squirms and writhes like a bag of worms. It feels things I'm not even sure hearts are meant to feel. I stare after Corolla, the place she disappeared, and then all those Yuengling's are traveling up my esophagus with volcanic power.

I hurtle for the bathroom so Finis can't blame me for ruining the couch, too.

Past
April 16th, 2004

Burnt orange. Fire in the distance.

The northern wall, Tyto wanted to shout. *Put out the flames!* But he couldn't make his tongue work, couldn't make his *body* work.

There was an explosion—he felt the vibrations crawl through the sidewalk and through his back. Ash rained down like cotton. Was it yesterday that he had taken Calyx outside to catch fireflies? Where was his son, his wife? Tyto couldn't remember. They had been—

Oh, there she is.

Adian. Crouching over him. Supple lips frowning, pregnant stomach bulging. *Corolla,* they would name their daughter. Tyto had wanted Marilena, but they agreed that would be Corolla's middle name. He smiled at that long-ago compromise.

Adian was saying something, saying his name. Though Tyto's ears strained to hear her voice, not a sound resonated with him. Only ringing, a sharp soprano.

Ash landed in her pile of hair, a crown. Or a halo. It was difficult to tell at this angle. A chain dangled from her neck, silver catching light from the lamp overhead. *Philomena,* he recognized the pendant and could have laughed at his mother's stupid superstition. But it had worked, hadn't it? Calyx was safe. Corolla was safe. And so was Adian.

Adian. His arm was reaching for her, wiping at the tears dripping down her cheek. What happened to make her cry? He was acutely aware of burning, something searing through his chest. It was annoying.

Moon behind her, full and glowing. A disc of light. Adian grasping, pulling, clutching at his body. Her hands coming away red, dripping with blood.

You're bleeding. Adian... His eyelids shuttered. He thought of the moments before the confusion. Bed. He had been in bed with his wife. Calyx was sleeping in his crib and the night had been serene.

***

Tyto cracked the pantry door, and, out of habit, peered left and right: Aurum House, saturated in shadows and pale moonlight. Adian's terrariums lined the center of the kitchen counter, some oblong, some spherical. The shadows played with the succulents that nuzzled within.

He knew which jagged edges the aloe plants were, which soft, round outlines were the cacti. And amid the dirt, he knew which terrariums Adian had designed with mini figurines. A hunter, his dog, and a bear in one. Fairies and elves. Sunbathers and beach-goers. Adian couldn't help herself from creating tiny worlds. Especially with Preiser miniatures. That's why he gave her a plot of land behind the West Dorms as an anniversary present. To expand her imagination in the form of a life-sized garden.

Through the exposed beams, Tyto heard silence—it had been raining all day, maddeningly beating against his office windows. Maybe it was the paperwork extinguishing his patience. Or perhaps he was just anxious to see Adian, to see his family.

Laila isn't even home. Internship, he told himself, dropping his defensive crouch. *She's in Rome.* Not that Laila would care—she knew about his relationship with Adian. Had known almost since the beginning.

"Dee?"

"Here," his wife called. Tyto followed her soft voice through the kitchen, past the terrariums, around the corner, and into her room. It was the bigger bedroom in Aurum House. Laila hadn't even batted an eye—thought it best for Adian and Calyx to have room to move. Or room for Adian to make a mess.

Tyto was grateful, in a loving way, that he didn't share a room with Adian. The floor was littered with clothes, baby and otherwise. Tyto winced as something sharp and plastic dug into the underside of his foot. He stepped around a pile of laundry that was destined to reach the ceiling at this rate: it had been dozing there for weeks now. And yet... the shelves that adorned the wall were flawless, filled with neat rows of various plants, each contained in its own glass planet. Tyto knew these terrariums too, knew which shelf was designated for the sick and which was designated for the favorites. Clear jugs of water occupied the bottom shelves, where sunlight had a difficult time reaching.

Tyto passed Adian's desk, noted that she was still working on her Mardi Gras universe, which would feature a crown of purple succulents, slick as leather. Mixed between piles of dirt and tubes of glue, were jars of baby food. Calyx refused to eat anything else. Tyto meant to speak to his son about that.

He found Adian tucked in the corner of the room, leaning over their son. He came up beside her at the crib he had built over two years ago. Calyx would be moving out of it soon, making room for his little sister to reside within. Tyto was still working on building Calyx a bigger bed.

"He was hellish today," Adian said from the corner. She didn't look up as he approached.

"Was he? Gets it from you."

Adian chuckled under her breath, sneaking an arm around Tyto's neck. He leaned into her, breathing in the scent of her recently shampooed hair. Bamboo, she had told him once, though Tyto wasn't sure a grass could smell so intoxicatingly sweet.

I thought we would be impossible back then, so much so, that it made me sick to my stomach. But look at us now... It was not being with Adian that had made him sick, he realized. It was the thought of being *without* her. Because once he saw her, he knew what he wanted, knew just as Orland Rainier had known being Major was *his* path to take. But it had never been Tyto's path, not really. Had he only waited a couple months for Adian to arrive, then maybe he wouldn't be sneaking around at night to be by her side. He tried not to think about that.

"I know this is strange, but I feel like this is something my mother did to me when I was a baby. I can't explain it." Tyto studied her face, the gentle curves of her cheekbones, the straight slope of her nose. Her accent—muted and doused in her childhood—tended to slip and surface when she was tired. Her words became crisper, almost sharp, something mixed between Italian and French. No one knew for certain her exact origins, least of all Adian.

"You should sleep, love. I'm here now." Tyto gripped her gently by the waist and led her to the bed behind them, against the wall. It was only big enough for one body, but they somehow made it fit for two. Three, if Corolla, curled within Adian's abdomen, counted.

"I'm not tired." The yawn she mumbled through suggested otherwise. Adian tumbled backward, the bed sinking with her weight. She was heavy with child, after all.

Tyto lied back with her. She folded into his arms, a gesture that had become so routine between them, he couldn't recall a time without her head against his chest, her breath against his collarbone. Even the nights when he couldn't sneak out of the Manor fell away and were forgotten. How could such emptiness be remembered in the company of such fullness?

"Are you feeling alright today? I didn't see you." Tyto closed his eyes, soaking in her body heat, the strange twist of her words.

Adian cradled an arm around her stomach, "I was busy. You were busy." He thought she shrugged, but their bodies were so snug together, it would have been difficult for her to make that motion.

Tyto thought back to the drum of rain against his windows, the ache behind his eyes as he sorted through all the paperwork of the day.

"Just thinking about it gives me a headache."

"Yeah? Lots of proposals or what?" Adian nuzzled her face into him.

"Changes in Administration and such. Boring stuff. If it wasn't for the incessant patter of rain on my window, I would have fallen asleep after the first page. Nobody ever really says how much paperwork being Major requires."

"That was a lovely storm, though." Adian laughed against his chest. They listened to Calyx shift in his crib.

"But you never answered my question, Dee: how are you feeling?"

Adian didn't say anything for a while. Had it not been for the racing of her heart against his body, he would have thought she was asleep.

And then, "Just Braxton-Hicks. Nothing serious."

"Dee!" Tyto struggled to keep his voice down.

"Shh, Ty," Adian chided. "Calyx has been a little monster today, all locked up inside the house. I'm not getting up to put him back to sleep again."

"Alright, but you should tell me next time you have contractions. It might be the real thing." Tyto settled into his skin once more. The silence occupied the space around them. "I may not be able to be in the room when Corolla is born, but I can at least be in the hospital."

Tyto knew she was falling asleep, but he wasn't ready to lose the sound of her voice for the night. "What makes you think your mother stood over your bed when you were little?"

He felt Adian attempt to shrug again. "Sometimes I get these strong senses of déjà vu. I don't know how to explain it."

"Oh. Do you ever see a face clearly?" His own heart rate sped up, thinking about the identity of her true parents forming and swirling just behind Adian's eyes. What would it mean if she had locked up their names and faces in her brain all this time, unknowingly? Were her parents still alive?

"Yes, there is one man..." she shuddered. "He always makes me sick."

Tyto opened his mouth to ask more, but a piercing wail interrupted him. He shot upright, taking Adian with him. Calyx began screaming, his sobs sharp enough to shatter the little worlds surrounding him.

The alarms.

"We're under attack," Tyto said before his brain could comprehend what that meant. *Attack. The Academy is under* attack. My *Academy is under attack.*

"What?" Adian's voice was no longer laced with her strange accent. She was awake. And afraid. She dashed to the corner just as the earth began to shake. The terrariums rattled on the shelves, items rolled off the desk. Things shattered.

Tyto flung out of bed, reaching to steady his wife. "Bombs. You and Calyx need to take the tunnels out of here. I have to ready the Guard—" Tyto turned to go, but Adian gripped him with a strength he didn't know she could possess.

"Don't leave me." Had the phrase been a loving creature, it would have crawled in his lap and died. He remembered a conversation from years ago, Adian curled like a cat beside him. *"Taxodium is safe,"* he'd said to soothe her anxieties. *"We don't run and hide, okay? That's what the Dentatas do."* But what were they doing now?

"I have to, Dee. The Dentatas will come looking for you so get to the tunnels *now*." The ground shook again, and he questioned whether he should send his pregnant wife and toddler son underground.

The tunnels have held up for centuries—they'll hold up now.

"Ty—"

"Don't argue, Adian. My guards will be looking for me, and if I'm not in the Manor, you and I are in serious trouble. Please," his eyes pleaded with hers.

"Take the tunnels back, back with me."

"No, Dee, it'll be faster for me to take the sidewalk. Go."

After some hesitation, Adian nodded.

"Good." Tyto planted a kiss on her forehead and Calyx's. He wiped tears from his son's eyes.

"Remember when we took the tunnels to catch fireflies?" He asked him. Calyx nodded, two fingers in his mouth. Tears flushed his eyes, dark like opals.

"Well, that's what you're going to do with Mamma now. I'll be with you in five minutes."

Calyx nodded, but Tyto was looking at Adian. *Liar,* her brown eyes said. *Come with us now.*

Tyto shifted—Adian grabbed him by the shoulder and smacked her lips on his, desperate, hungry. Time seemed to stop when Adian kissed him. Through her lips, he remembered the first time they formally met. Adian on the other side of his mahogany desk, asking about housing and roommates. He hadn't really been listening to her—he'd been listening to the blood in his veins singing as if some part of her were a piece of him, returned. He knew he could love her then, and, despite all the obstacles, he did. Love her.

His arms folded around her and Calyx as he pulled her body closer: Calyx's head on his shoulder, Adian's stomach under his palm. Her warmth seeped through the cotton of his pajamas. Even heavy with child, Adian fit into him. Some part of Tyto wondered about the symbolism behind this. That no matter her size Adian should fit him like a matching puzzle piece.

But the screeching alarms dragged him back to the present. He knew every inch of her, each mole on her back, freckle along her nose. Strange how her geography felt like his own; in his mind, he didn't know where she stopped and he began.

A voice in the back of his mind, *Well, that's what matrimony does to you.*

Tyto memorized Adian's face one last time, the way her eyebrows angled in disapproval, the dilation of her pupils. Something tangible passed between them: Why did this feel like an ending?

He pried himself from her slipping hold and ran for the door. He tried not to think about the hurt in his wife's eyes. He tried not to think about the tears drooling down his son's cheeks. He tried not to think about what would happen if Adian were captured by the Dentatas. Agonizing, endless experimentation and a painful death.

Outside, he slipped into his invisibility. Tyto doubted anyone would be paying attention to where he was coming from, but he had to get back to the Manor. Commander Rex would look for him there. Tyto's stomach clenched, thinking about what would happen, should someone peer into his room, see his bed was empty. It was essential his marriage remained a secret. People would blame him for this attack, especially if they knew he was not where he was supposed to be when it happened.

I'd have to have some good lie to explain how I escaped my room without once opening my door. His room was naturally secured by two soldiers from the Major's Guard. And despite the chaos around him, students screaming in the streets, ash falling from the sky, he clung to the familiar, to the secret of his relationship with Adian.

But we're being attacked now! His mind screamed. As he passed behind the bushes lining the Manor's walkway, he came into visibility. He would have preferred to enter through the back doors, but there was no time to run the distance. He slipped through the Manor doors, hoping no one would notice. Inside, there was such a flurry of people, Tyto would have been impressed if anyone *had* seen him come in. Commander Neva Rex barked instructions from the center of the room.

"You bunch, reinforce the gate. And you four—go down to Intelligence and figure out why the Sentries aren't firing. You, I need a squad to evac."

"Commander," Tyto greeted, voice tight. "I believe the main breach is at the gate and the surrounding northern wall. We'll need more than just one squadron for defense."

"Of course." She saluted him, but Tyto found himself studying the flinty streaks showing through her fading black hair. She would be completely gray by the end of the night.

"I need you at the Barracks, Rex, rallying the remaining soldiers. Something tells me this isn't just a display of power." Before his time, things like this happened occasionally. The Dentatas would crawl out from their hole in the ground and torment pelari outside the Twelfth Wall. But there was a distinct line between taunting and attacking: the sound of battle at the gate.

"Yes, sir," Commander Rex saluted him once more. There was no disdain in her attitude, no contempt. And it was this lack thereof that sunk reality into Tyto's bones like hooks: The Academy was under attack.

Tyto stared after his Commander as she took off through the main doors. Guards, destined for other tasks, followed her leave. The violence of explosions, gunfire, and desperate screams echoed with each opening of the door. Tyto swallowed the sounds, stored them away to be dealt with later. He glanced around the room, at the forsaken faces. They all gawked at him for courage, for wisdom.

Major Rainier was better under pressure than I was, a piece of him said.

These people elected you for a reason, Alba. Show them you aren't a mistake.

Tyto raised his arms for order. The people—some TIs, Major's guards, and students—quieted their chatter and stared at him some more. He hoped he didn't appear as young and inexperienced as he felt. Even with years of labor under his belt, he wasn't sure he would ever feel old enough for this position.

Calm, Alba, your people will respect you more if you can remain calm. He took a deep breath.

"We have practiced drills for occasions such as this. You are not without the ability to defend our beloved Taxodium. The Dentatas came here for a reason, but they will not leave without suffering for their intentions." There was no time for grandeur. But his words seemed to have an effect. Faces steeled over, tears dried up in eyes. His people went to work.

Tyto turned to three of his guards and a Trainee. He pulled them aside where the crowd would not hear him say, "I need you to go to Aurum. There's an underground tunnel that leads out of Taxodium where the northern wall meets the eastern. Make sure Adian Vel and her son successfully escape by that way. They are in more danger than the lot of us. There's an old chapel where they can hide. If you can, get them off the premises entirely."

"Sir!" The guards and Trainee saluted, three fingers across their beating hearts.

"And," Tyto recognized the Trainee as Adian's friend, Alexander, but he spoke his next words to all four of them. "Nobody can know about these tunnels. They are secret for the very reason that they may need to be used like this another day. I can't have hundreds of people flooding through them to escape. They're for the Vels only. That's who the Dentatas will be hunting. Understand?"

"Yes, sir," they replied in unison.

Tyto bowed his head. "Then go." He watched as his men disappeared past the front doors. The wailing siren drove nails into his ears once again. In the distance, he saw the flaring of fire, wisps of thick gray smoke.

Why aren't *the Sentries firing?*

"Sir," one of his guards came down the hall, "you should leave with us. If the Dentatas breach the gate, they'll pillage the Manor first." Tyto studied the man's face. He couldn't place the stubbled jaw, the dark, probing eyes.

Do I have a bald Official? The sirens flooded his senses, drowned his concentration, and the thought slipped through his mental grasp. Tyto looked around the room. Somehow, it was empty, spare for the cluster of Major's guards clotting the hallway. Had the squadron been standing there the entire time? In the panic, he couldn't remember.

"Okay. Let's go."

The guard nodded and led the way through the front doors. Four other guards formed a wall around Tyto. Something tickled at his brain, but then they stepped outside. The steady trickle of panic collecting in the pit of his stomach escalated, became a hurricane. Every muscle in his body coiled, charged with adrenaline. But where he should have been yearning to defend the Academy, he was only thinking, *AdianCalyxCorolla AdianCalyxCorolla. Should I have seen her off personally? What do the rules matter now? I should be with my family.*

They were close to the Ward Residencies now. Tyto found himself facing Aurum House. The windows were black, reflecting shades of auburn from the northern wall.

"I change my mind," Tyto blurted, "I want you five to facilitate the students. I don't recall if Rex sent a squad there. They are bound to be afraid and disorganized. I need to go check the wards—"

"Oh, no, sir," the bald Official whipped around to block Tyto. "That wouldn't be a good idea." Tyto cocked his head, misunderstanding.

"Soldier, that was an order."

"No, *sir*, you're not as influential as you think."

It was then that Tyto identified the tickle in the back of his brain: This guard never once saluted.

Before he could get the accusation out, one of the imposters slammed into his back. Tyto grated against the cobbled road, cheek smarting. His instinct was to shift to invisibility, but the inclination to use his Essence was gone, severed. He had no connection to that biological piece of him, like a muscle that no longer obeyed commands.

Tyto scrambled to his feet, glaring at the five men. The bald one, set apart from the other four, seemed to be their leader.

He jeered, "Can't use your Essence? My nephew's acts as an off switch on people of his choosing. No tricks from you, I'm afraid."

Tyto swiped at his face, wiping grit and gravel from his flesh.

"Who are you?" He searched the faces of all five men, memorizing them. Square jaws, dark eyes. They all resembled one another. Men, too, no women. For some reason, Tyto thought that strange. And then it struck him.

"Dentata," he breathed. "How did you get into the Academy?" Behind them, the sparks flew from the spires of Rainier Hospital and the Dining Hall. Absently, Tyto congratulated whoever got the Sentries operating again.

If the Dentatas are already inside, we'll need all the gun-power we can get.

"People will learn not to call us that anymore," the bald man said, "*Genocides* has a nice ring to it. Gens."

"Jon," coughed one of the men, "Vel is in one of these houses."

"Right, Baylor," the bald one—Jon—replied. "We'll get Alba to tell us which one."

"No—"

Baylor stepped forward, and a fist found its home in Tyto's kidney. He collapsed to his knees, gasping.

Jon crouched to Tyto's level, a black gun suddenly in his hand. "I don't take hesitation lightly. Which house?" The Dentata jammed the barrel of the weapon against Tyto's cheekbone, angling his head in the direction of the Ward Residencies. Aurum winked at him, called out to him in Adian's voice.

"Ty!" A figure appeared, arms waving in the grayish black of the night. The crackling flames ripping through the northern wall colored her black.

"My, my. Could it really be that easy?" Tyto heard Jon say. His heart sank.

Dammit, Dee.

He watched his pregnant wife come over the hill. Tyto sucked in a breath—

"Warn her, and I will shoot her where she stands," Jon cautioned in a low voice.

329

"She'll see the gun to my head and run anyway," Tyto spat, hoping it was true. Adian was... persistent.

Rather than anger, his remark provoked laughter. Jon practically doubled over chuckling. The gun's barrel pointed dangerously past Tyto's head, towards Adian. Tyto shoved himself in front of it as Jon jolted and wriggled with uncontrollable laughter.

"Ty!" Adian bellowed his name once more. Calyx was not at her side. Tyto had to assume his guards—his *real* guards—had at *least* secured his son. But Adian... It wasn't beneath her to haggle and threaten her way out of his guard's instructions.

Adian, turn around. He was certain she saw him under the amber light of the street lamps. She was close enough that she must see the gun, too. *Turn around. Run.*

Jon's laughter gradually came to an end. "Tell me, Alba, who else is permitted to call you *Ty?*"

Tyto gave away nothing, but Adian wasn't stopping. *Shit, why doesn't she turn around?*

Because she loves you, you idiot.

Tyto straightened his spine a degree. If Adian wasn't going to stop, then he had to do something. *I can't lose Corolla and her both.*

He was aware of the sweat pooling on his brow, of the pebbles crunching beneath the soles of his shoes. Like a spring, the tension in his body was becoming unbearable; he was ready to move. Tyto braced himself—

Adian gasped, the sound of her sucking breath catching Tyto off guard. He glanced at her ghostly face, framed in the amber lamplight. He remembered another night, another time. It was Christmas, and Adian flicked all the house lights off, so the lights winding around their artificial tree glowed like hundreds of miniature suns. "One last time," she said, smiling with pleasure. "One last time before we have to take it down tomorrow." Amber light framed her then, but Tyto blinked, and that memory was swiped away. Adian wasn't looking at him. Or the gun.

"I'm not my father," Jon chuckled, jamming the handgun into Tyto's flesh. He was speaking to Adian. "But I must look like him. I'm surprised you remember."

"Remember?" Tyto's eyes flitted from Adian's slack jaw to the cluster of Dentatas closing in on her.

"You..." Adian began but stopped. She was speechless, motionless, a snapshot of the woman he called his wife. *Never* had she stood so still. *Never* had she appeared so frightened. Yet it wasn't fear etched in her face. It was terror.

Jon spoke, his voice rumbling deep within his chest, "Out of all the children, you were the one with the most promise. My father commissioned the experiment that led to your creation. He escaped Taxodium's raid on those labs, and no matter how many of those children he tracked down later, they all died of their own weaknesses. He's dead now too, and *this* is my coronation. I am the new Numen, and I have come to collect what's mine. I'm a father too, you should know, and this disease is not something I want my children living with."

Adian did not move. Tyto struggled to grapple his mind around Jon's words.

"What are you saying? My wife was a test subject?"

"Wife? Oh, I see now," Jon taunted, "the two of you. How the Courts will reel when they find out. The deaths I'll give you will be mercy compared to what the Courts would decide."

Tyto clenched his jaw, fists forming at his sides. He attempted to catch Adian's gaze. She was someplace else, far away from the scene unfolding before her. If she was pale before, Tyto swore he saw through her now.

"I suppose I can give you the satisfaction of knowing before I hand you over for my nephews to enjoy," Jon divulged. "Nature always creates opposites. But my kin and I weren't made from Nature, now were we? I was diseased by a witch, and your *wife* was grown in a lab."

No, Tyto wanted to say. *That can't be true. Adian...*

Jon flung Tyto into another man's grip. "You two can have your fill now. I don't care what our... allies say. I want the Major dead."

Tyto struggled against the Dentata, all his training slipping between panic. Jon moved for Adian. Willow branches were seeping from her palms.

Willows! Dee, willows won't save you.

His view was cut off by yet another Dentata. This one was much younger—at least sixteen—bony elbows and thick eyebrows. Tyto's gaze landed on the energy festering between the kid's hands. Lightning.

The hair on his arms stood on end.

The Dentata grinned. "You won't remember a thing." He took a step closer, fingers spreading, lightning crackling from one palm to the other. Instinctively, Tyto pulled backward, only to remember that he was pinned in place.

The next four seconds were a blur. He heard Adian cry out, but he couldn't maneuver for his wife. Lightning stretched for him, implanted into his temples. A willow switch wrapped around his wrist, and around it, lightning tangled. There was a sting, a flash of white light—a force knocked him free of the Dentatas. Something whizzed overhead, exploded into the earth. The ground trembled.

The Sentries…

When he opened his eyes, he was laying on his back, ash hailing down from the sky. Dirt and grit on his face. Crumbs of cobblestone. He blinked, and Adian was there, shaking, lips moving. Crying. *Why is she crying?* Blood, oozing down her hand. He reached for her, wiped her tears as best he could manage.

His head lolled, gaze aligning with the earth. There were bodies— one, two, three—laying around a crater.

My guards… But the thought didn't seem right. There was something about those guards, wasn't there? Tyto searched the mangled body parts, an arm, a leg, for clues. Some yards away, several fingers, blackened and bloodied. He looked away, sickened. Sometimes Sentries misfired—they were new installments. It was unfortunate that his guards died because of it.

More guards, towering over him. Adian, being shuffled behind a wall of men and women. He remembered! The Academy was under attack. That's why the Twelfth Wall was highlighted in orange and gray, in fire and smoke. Was that why Adian was crying?

Arms lifting him onto a stretcher. Firm hands gripping the sides. An arm pressing down on his chest. Pain slammed into him; his ears rang. Words flooded him all at once.

"… get Major Alba to Rainier immediately."

"…gunshot wound… misfire… profuse bleeding…"

Oh, that's *why she's crying. Because I'm dying.*

Tyto wanted to reach for his wife, for unborn Corolla, but the darkness cried out for him. He slipped into the folds of a cold blackness.

Corolla
July 2020

"I'm thinking Michigan."

"Michigan?" My voice cracks. This is the first time I've spoken in hours. I set aside the booklet of flooring samples and clear my throat. "You want to go back?"

James peers over a fan of paint swatches. "Of course I want to go back. We can rebuild right over the old house."

"Rebuild...?" I finger-comb my hair, pushing it back over my head. "I thought you'd want to stick around here. Maybe someplace in Dayton?"

James disappears behind teals and pale blues. "I don't want to live in Ohio."

My heart sinks, shoulders sag. "But..." I can't come up with the right words. "I like the people here. I have real friends here." But do I really? I have Talan. And Castan... I can't think about him without my cheeks flushing. James already asked me if I caught a fever from Castan, already felt my forehead as the blood rushed to meet the back of James's hand. *Traitors*, I scorned my red blood cells. But I feigned a laugh, shrugged James off my forehead. "No, you can't catch a fever," I said. "It's not like a cold."

But that was ages ago, before James dumped carpet and flooring booklets into my lap and before my fingertips were raw from feeling all our different options. My RBCs should be tame enough now. Except they're not. I pick up my discarded booklet, open it, and hide my burning face between two squares of what could very well be the same sample of carpet. One is four dollars more expensive, though.

"I thought you'd want to go back," James says, though he doesn't glance up from his search in the paint swatches. "I thought you'd want to go back to being normal, go back to your *real* school."

I know he didn't mean it as an insult, but his emotionless words sting my heart regardless. Little arrows, like the ones Talan says he can't trust me to practice shooting with.

"Why can't we use real swords?" My palms are sticky, clamping down on the hilt of a wooden practice sword.

"Because we're just working on reflexes. And besides, you'd probably be clumsy enough to slice your femoral artery and bleed to death," Talan huffs, licking his lips. He sways on his knees, and I mock

the athletic movement. In uniform, I'm like every other guard on campus. Except for my obvious deficit in experience.

"You're worse than my uncle." *But I'm just glad he's back to normal—Vera and Luca were shipped off to St. Helena early this morning. It's not that Talan was upset to see his mother leave, but I know he felt* something, *seeing her in that packaged hospital bed.*

"You mean," *Talan brushes damp hair from his eyes,* "I'm better."

"No," *I chuckle, moving left,* "I mean whatever Laila did to James, she needs to do to you."

"I think she charmed him." *Talan looks ready to pounce, but he keeps talking,* "I've seen them at the Dining Hall together, eating in the secluded Sun Room."

My body tenses for different reasons entirely. "You mean they like each other—" *Talan propels forward, and our swords connect with a clatter. But Talan is much stronger than me—even without his Essence—and the force of the attack compromises my balance. I groan, scraping myself off the turf. Talan offers me a hand. I give him a dirty look but accept it.*

"I think they more than* like *each other," he shoots me a knowing look, swinging his practice sword like a propeller.*

"Hmm." *I don't know if James ever really had a girlfriend. Growing up, he was so focused on keeping his job and raising me, he didn't really have time for a relationship. But Castan's aunt? I touch my face, finding a wide grin there.* "Well, good for him. It's about damn time."

"Did something happen between you and Laila?"

"What?" The fan of swatches falls between his fingers. "What are you talking about?"

"I just…" I bite my lip. "Never mind. You know Luca Alba was taken to the island this morning?"

James retrieves his booklet of colors. Grunts. "I don't know any Albas." This has been James response to Luca since I mentioned him the day I landed here. I took a psychology course my freshman year, and I know all about self-preservation. But even with baseline knowledge of the human reaction, I don't understand James. I know he desires pieces of Adian—maybe more than I do. He did, after all, keep that packet of photos before they were burned in the fire. Luca is another piece of his sister, my mother. So why does James pretend otherwise?

"Anyway," I rise, stretching my arms behind my back, "I'll see you tonight at the banquet."

James's profile flickers with his usual worry. "You're not coming back after training?"

"No." My eyes dart around the dark wood and paint of Aercus. I can't face him. "I told you already. Some girls from my Defensive Training class want to get ready together beforehand."

"Oh," James sinks into the ebony couch, "okay." The black fabric makes his blonde hair stand out like a lamplight. I recognize his expression and can't ignore it.

"But I'll stop by here after I'm all done," I offer, "and we can walk together." I look at James expectantly. He massages the bridge of his nose, makes a solemn face, and nods.

Since I changed into my uniform earlier, all I have to do now is slip my Caeli boots on and grab my armor from the counter.

"That's wrong, you know. The way he holds it over you."

I mumble to the sun, "He doesn't hold it over my head."

"Hey, Corolla!" Talan waves from Argenti's front door. "You ready for DT?" With Talan, Defensive Training has never been so unbearable as that first day. I just didn't realize it until the second day: he stood by my side and Training became just like another morning session.

I begin buckling my breastplate. "We're using the shooting range today, right?"

Talan grabs the buckle under my arm from my fumbling hands. Straps it in place. He has that type of infectious personality, the kind that makes you love his friendship. Or maybe I love him because the first time we met, he was trying to make pizza with measuring cups. I surprise myself with a pang of sadness: all of this will be over sooner than I would like.

This.

Castan's bloodshot eyes and fermented breath flashes across my memory. I haven't seen him since Wednesday, and I suspect he's avoiding me just as thoroughly as I am avoiding him. Or he's still sick. Laila didn't say, and I couldn't find the reserve to ask.

Talan gives me a look. Unlike Castan, I know exactly what his expression portrays: lifted eyebrows for mockery, wry grin for effect. "Yeah, but stand ten yards away from me, okay? I'm not convinced Murphy knows how much of a hazard you are yet."

I hit him across the shoulder because that's what he expects; that's how we are together. He starts talking about something he and Finis did the other night, but his story doesn't register. I think about James's sad eyes. Whenever he wears them, he gets what he wants. But...

He doesn't hold it over you, Corolla. And even if he did, you told Castan yourself that you hold it over your own head.

Talan's talking a hundred words a minute and doesn't hear me mutter, "I do."

Then why do you have to convince yourself to believe it?

Damn Castan for putting doubt in my head. Damn Castan for—

"Are you alright, Corolla?" Talan nudges my shoulder. "You haven't laughed at anything I've said. That's concerning."

"Yeah," I reach for my pocket to snag a stick of gum but stop myself. "Yeah, I'm fine."

Then why do you have to convince yourself to believe it?

A little after DT ended, Talan escorted me to Dani and Júlia's dorm, while he disappeared into Finis and Castan's down the street. Not only are the dorms ugly on the outside—glaring reddish/orange that reminds me of regurgitated salmon—they are considerably smaller than the Ward Residencies. Of course, I noticed this the other day, when I stopped by Castan's, but I thought maybe my perception was biased. Everything seems smaller when your heart thrashes like a caged animal.

Dani swept me up into a chair across her own vanity, and I don't dare complain. Luckily, I barely have to talk at all—Dani chatters enough for both of us. I saw Júlia walking around the kitchen in her bra and underwear (frilly things that barely cover what they're supposed to), and after that, I vowed never to look for Júlia again.

Dani clips my hair on top of my head and pulls supplies from a drawer so overcrowded and disorganized, I don't know how she manages to locate any of the little bottles and palettes of makeup. Hanging on clothespins along the mirror, are all her patterned and plain headbands. She wears a simple black one now, her curly hair scraped into a messy bun. She makes a face at herself in the mirror.

"What?" I flush, suddenly afraid that my hair smells gross or that Dani thinks one of my moles may be cancerous.

"I'm just thinking," she says, multicolored tubes clamped between her fingers like claws. She cocks her head, eyes sliding to my face. "Hair or face? Hair or face…"

I open my mouth to make a suggestion, but then clamp it shut. This is out of my element, and unlike DT, I don't think I can be taught.

Dani perks up, her rich brown eyes sparkling. "I'll do your makeup first if you don't mind."

"By all means." I slap my hands on my thighs, smooth my sweaty palms on the fabric of my uniform. Luckily, we only practiced shooting guns, crossbows, and bows today, so I'm not drenched in sweat like I usually am. Dare I give Commander Murphy credit for thinking ahead.

Dani displays all sorts of creams, powders, eyeshadows, and tubes on the vanity before me. I'm instructed to close my eyes and to shut my mouth, while she concentrates on filling in my flaws. I think of a failed tattoo, and Dani's skill goes over it to make it at least somewhat better.

Acceptable. That's what she's doing: making me into someone *presentable*. When she does my eyelids, I have to bite my lip to keep the tears shuttered from the outside world. She pokes me so much, though, that this task becomes my main focus for a whole ten minutes at least.

And then the poking stops. Dani's shadow recedes.

"You can open your eyes now." It's only when her bubbly voice reaches my ears that I realize she was silent throughout that whole process.

My reflection greets me, but it's not... me. My hair is still pinned in odd places, but my face... Dani's successfully crafted me an industrial mask to match her own.

"Wow." I reach to touch my skin, remember all the layers Dani plastered on my face, and drop my hand back in my lap.

"I know right," Dani grins, hands clutching my shoulders. "I have the perfect hairstyle for you too."

Dani scrapes all her tools back in the open drawer and kicks it shut with her bare foot. She yanks another drawer of hair supplies right out of the vanity's structure and sets it across the cleared counter space. She spills a handful of bobby-pins across the alabaster surface and slips on a sleeve of hair ties.

"I used to be his proxy, you know, before he came out as gay."

"Who, Talan?" Her outburst should surprise me, but after a whole week of comings and goings to DT, this is just how Dani is. A gossip. I watch as she scrapes my hair into a sloppy bun. I have no idea what she's doing, I just hope it looks more sophisticated when she's done.

"Yeah. I was really into him. Then he told me he doesn't swing that way. But we love each other, you know, the way only best friends can. So I promised to help him because that's what friends do. They help."

"Why did he need a proxy to begin with? I mean, it's 2020..." Dani yanks on my hair with a comb. I suppress a wince. I'm pretty sure she's combing my hair in the wrong direction, but I'm afraid to correct her. Or ask why.

"His parents' approval meant the world to him. Talan didn't want his parents to suspect his sexuality. Graduates aren't allowed to be fully committed to another person until after their two years in the Guard or Intel is served, so Talan was just going to tell his family then." Dani pauses. Frowns at the back of my head. When she speaks again, her voice is subdued, "But then Jura was killed, and neither of his parents made much of an effort to be there for Talan. After that, he said, 'To hell with it!' and came out to the entire Academy by making his relationship with Finis incredibly obvious. I mean, if the Attachment Laws pertained to students, his parents surely would have put Talan and Finis on trial, just out of spite. You know, before the Courts were utterly demolished." Dani makes another face. "I guess it is a little weird, though."

When she doesn't continue, I feel like I have to ask. "What is?"

"That Talan is dating his sister's ex. I mean, Finis and Jura were still together when she was killed, but I guess that's how grief works. It brings people together just as much as it can tear people apart." I bow my head into my hands, as a gallon of guilt sloshes in my stomach. Because I miss Castan. But I can't dwell on that now, so I pluck a paper from the hair-things drawer to distract myself instead.

I skim over patterned squares and the words typed underneath them. It looks like another language, but Dani rips the paper from my hands before I can decipher it.

"That's just so I can keep track of all the headbands I have," she explains, tucking it into a different drawer. "I lose them in the locker room sometimes." I recognized some of the patterns on the paper—the star of life, red roses, purple and yellow dragonflies. I glance at the headbands hanging like pelts around the mirror.

"You do have a lot of those."

"Yeah," Dani beams, "it's kind of a local fashion back home." She pounds a fist over her heart. "Keeps me close."

"Oh, where are you fr—"

"Hold on," Dani sets down a fistful of pins, glancing at the clock above the vanity. "I have to go change my tampon."

I almost balk—I can't imagine saying something so forward in front of anyone. I've lived with James so long, I forget I'm not the only one with monthly troubles. I still cringe at Talan's "Aunty Flow." The only way I even found out about periods was from a presentation in fifth grade, given by the school counselor and a handful of other female teachers. If not for their tips, I wouldn't have survived. James acts like the feminine products under the bathroom sink don't exist. For a guy who grew up with only a sister, he can be an incredibly clueless individual.

Dani saunters into the room some minutes later, her face disturbingly pale. I twist in my chair.

"Are you alright?"

"Yeah," she grins, "I just hate the sight of so much blood."

"Oh." Not knowing what else to say to that—*I'm sorry* or *Me too?*—I face forward once more and let her finish my hair.

When it's done, I can't help but admire her work. Two braids frame my face, disappearing somewhere around my ears and snaking back into the pinned bun at the base of my neck. It's just sloppy enough, just shapely enough, to be considered "stylish." Immediately, I want to show Laila.

"I love this."

Dani shoots me a wry grin. "Wait until you see your dress." She disappears across the hall—to Júlia's room—and comes back with a black body bag. She drapes it over her bed. Silent, I watch her unzip the garment bag. She holds back the flaps, revealing a floor length dress with black skirts. My gaze stumbles over the bust—it's adorned with garnet or ruby gems, sparkling under the light like so many beads of blood.

"Dani... I can't wear this! It's like a prom dress—I thought we were just going to a banquet?"

"Prom? Oh yeah, that's the dance in like every pedes movie ever, right?" She shakes her head. "Trust me, you'll want to wear this. I can't send you out there underdressed!"

Dani slips out of the room so I can change, leaving me no more space to argue. I peel off my uniform, gently lay it aside, and stand over the gown. I chew my lip and taste chemicals. Exhaling, I unsheathe the dress and tug it on. Once I'm positive all the zippers (there's only one in the back) are done, I go to the mirror.

There's an oval cut out, right where my cleavage is, that I didn't notice from the gown's dormant stay in the bag. I smooth my hands down the flaring ebony skirts. My shoulders are bare, except for the thin straps supporting the weight of the dress. I suppose it's alright, but I've never felt more naked clothed.

Dani knocks on the door. "Can I come in?"

I shuffle away from the mirror, four layers of skirts *swooshing* with me. "Yeah."

Dani flings the door open, her arms cradling something metal. She sets the objects on her bed, next to my uniform. They're bracelets, thick metal-wrought bracelets. Dani pairs them up, silvers, golds, bronzes. She makes another one of her thinking faces and plucks a silver pair from her bed.

"Wrists."

I hold my arms out to her.

"It's tradition and fashion, all wrapped in one."

"Tradition?" Dani clamps the bracelets on my wrists. I flinch at the cold metal on my skin.

"*Armatus*. Their engravings tell stories, hence the name. Pelari women wear them to formal occasions. Some people wear them to Fourth of July fireworks or the end of the year celebration Tax has for New Year's, but *armatus* aren't meant for things like that. Things that recognize *pedes* holidays. They're for pelari celebrations, like weddings, Ceremonies, recognitions, and banquets."

I study the intricate design in the silver wrapped around my wrists. Amidst the Greek-like patterns, there's a woman—No, two women. One bows before the other. "What's mine tell the story of?" Dani doesn't even have to look.

"Matrona and Phaedra. There are a lot of *armatus* for that story. Pelari origins." Dani shrugs, goes to the vanity, and touches up her makeup. I don't ask the question charging my tongue: Are Adian and Tyto a story?

"What other stories are there?" I drop my arms to my sides, surprised at how light the metal cuffs are. The other pairs glint on her bed, but even if I were to examine them, I doubt I'd recognize their tales.

Dani lines her lips with a shade of mauve before answering, "Pelari cherish the good and the bad. So as long as a lesson was learned, anything could become *armatus*. But not every story is a happy one."

I guess that answers my question. I change the subject.

"Should Tax be hosting a celebration while we're at war?" There have been new attacks around the world. National monuments desecrated and such, but no organization has taken responsibility for it. The fear is growing, festering like a sour wound. It's not just the pedes who are infected either. At DT, someone asked if it was safe to have a banquet—*"Wouldn't that make it easy for the Gens to wipe us out? If we're all in the same place?"*—and Commander Murphy assured us that special precautions are "going to be put in place to ensure that doesn't happen." I know his Essence involves shields, but can one man stop hundreds?

Dani starts with her hair, and I know I have to get going soon. James is expecting me. "We have to keep up morale somehow," she says. "And the dead must be recognized."

"Talan said pelari don't grieve."

"No, we don't wear mourning clothes or have elaborate funerals," Dani grins wickedly, "we wear dazzling dresses and have extravagant parties."

"But... everyone has to grieve. We're all human."

"Right," Dani primps her crown of honey-colored curls, "but for pelari, it's incredibly disrespectful to be so public about one's pain. It's just how we are."

James, Laila, and I arrive five minutes past six—and the Dining Hall is already bloated with people. The long tables have been stored away. When I wonder how they got past the Dining Hall's doors, I hear someone remarking on "another Pyrus enchantment." Apparently, the tables can shrink.

James and Laila walk arm-in-arm. I don't know where James got a gray suit, but I suspect Laila has something to do with it. She's cloaked in a pale sapphire slip that matches James's eyes. I have suspicions about that too. Her *armatus* are silver, like mine, and when I asked her what story they told, she supplied names I don't recognize. Before they disappeared into the crowd, I caught a glimpse of a bird and a man on her cuffs, though.

Now that I'm alone, the banquet swells around me. I sequester myself to the wall, hopefully out of the way of arriving parties. Without the long tables, the Dining Hall feels as spacious as the Training Field. On the far wall, before the fireplace big enough for giants, a band plays classical tunes. Violinists, a pianist, and a harpist fill the Hall with lyrical notes. The chatter and clinking of silverware drown the music so that I couldn't recognize the pieces, even if I wanted to.

Along the wall leading into the Sun Room, platters and punches bedeck a white table-clothed table. There's a line for food, and I spot James and Laila among the waiting. In the crowd of conversationalists, Major Rex's spiked hair gives her away. I recognize her entourage: Euro Ambassador Olejar, his stomach threatening to pop buttons, the shredded Ambassador Emeko, and Ambassador Collingwood from the Australian Academy. Next to the African ambassador, she's so small, the lacy pink of her dress may be a child's size. Her biceps are sculpted with enough muscle, though, that I know she's not so defenseless.

I hear Talan's informational voice in my head: *"The African Academy specializes in Guard, Australian in prison, Euro in Intel. NA and SA are produce and other natural resources. The Asian Academy used to specialize in Law."*

Among the Major and ambassadors, is Issak. His unseeing eyes stare over the tops of his party's heads.

His name tumbles past my lips before I can think. "Issak." I don't have to shout. Straightaway, a grin transforms his serious composure. I watch him excuse himself, weave through the crowd towards the sound of his name.

"Hey." I take in the trim cut of his maroon suit. "I've never seen a suit that color before."

Issak pats his chest. "I hope it's acceptable. Olejar promised me it was alright."

I'm about to say, "It's maroon. It's fine," but color means nothing to Issak. I clear my throat. "You look great, Issak. Very sophisticated."

"Well, thank you." He ducks his head and tugs his collar. A couple pushes behind him, and he shuffles closer to keep from being plowed over. His breath catches the stray hair framing my face.

"I'm sure you look astounding. If you wouldn't mind me asking, what are you wearing?" He gestures to his eyes, though he doesn't have to.

"Well," I look down at my train of skirts, the glittering red gemstones. "My dress is... I could be one of Henry VIII's mistresses."

Issak claps a hand over his mouth to stifle laughter. He ducks, casting a shadow over his face. But even that can't mask the blush flooding his cheeks. "You say it like it's a bad thing."

I shrug, eyes darting through the crowd for familiar faces. For *a* familiar face. "The way James looked at me makes it a bad thing."

Issak offers me an arm. "Well, Ms. Vel, mistresses aside, would you care to join me for a dance?"

I twine my elbow in his. "I should warn you: I've only been to one dance in my life, so my coordination isn't the best." At least, that's what Averil told me afterward.

"You could really use some athleticism, Cor," he said. *"I think you broke my pinkie toes."*

"Don't worry," Issak turns his head so I can hear him better, "it's the blind leading the blind."

Laughter bubbles in my throat as we make our way through the clusters of people. I recognize Talan and Finis talking with some guys I've never met before. I saw Dani and Júlia some minutes ago, and Kass seems to be recruiting for scouts outside the Hall's doors. I fix my attention on Issak, avoiding the very head I have been searching for since entering the Dining Hall. But even in the corner of my vision, my attention follows Castan's dark crown.

"Pelari dances are pretty simple," Issak says. I blink. Couples spin and sway around us. The music is clearer here, so close to its source. "Hand here," Issak grasps my forearm, fixing it to his shoulder. Automatically, I move my other hand to match my first. He places tentative fingers around my waist. Despite myself, I grin at the color flushing his cheeks.

"So..." I sway a little, mimicking the couples speckling the dance floor, "like this?"

"Yeah," Issak clears his throat. "That's perfect." His grip on my waist tightens as we learn the rhythm of the music. For a moment, I ignore the cacophony and relish in the sound of the violins. I glue my eyes to Issak's almond-shaped ones, and I tell myself I'm not allowed to look past him. Because if I do that, then I'll be searching for Castan again.

I don't want to see him. I don't want to see him. It's the fact that I have to remind myself that makes the longing worse.

"Are you leaving soon then?"

"No," his gentle timbre tickles my eardrums, "the fill-ins still have some things to discuss with Major Rex. Matrona knows how long that will take. Politicians only seem to know how to argue."

"I see." And then, wondering if that was an insensitive response, I shoot, "For someone who lives in Europe, you don't have an accent to show for it."

Issak grins. "I *do* have an accent, but I tend to mask it when I travel." He spins me under his arm, and the Dining Hall becomes a blur of warm colors. Using his shoulders, I right myself.

"I'll need a little forewarning next time."

"Alright," Issak chuckles, flashing white teeth.

"But why do you mask your accent?"

Beneath my draped arms, he shrugs. "I like languages—am good at them, too. I don't know. I just like blending in."

"You mean, you like fitting in."

"When your eyes look like mine, it helps." Where bitterness should ring, amusement does. I think I love his good humor.

"But then, what do you actually sound like?"

"Depends. Korean is my first language, but I was raised to speak six others. At the Academy, my default is British English." His voice shifts, hard T's and succinct S's, "Most of my mates are British."

"That was pretty good."

"I'm spinning you again." He gives me just enough warning to close my eyes. My body twirls, butterflies flutter in my stomach. When I open them again, Issak is grinning at me, eyes crinkled in the corners. But his face is not the one I imagined in my lapse. My lips dip into a frown before I can salvage my emotions.

"Is something… bothering you tonight?"

"I'd like to study your genes." I know he noticed the change in subject, but he doesn't acknowledge the obvious shift.

"There are drawbacks to hearing. For example," he pricks his ears, "there's a couple next door in the Phone Booths most likely having sex."

It's my turn to blush. "I guess that is a drawback, though most guys wouldn't think so."

"I'm not most."

"I know." I squeeze his shoulder. "Thank you for everything you did for Luca, by the way."

"Well, I wouldn't have done anything, had Castan not broken protocol and brought Luca Alba back here. He knows how to make an entrance, I'll give him that."

"Meaning, he's made memorable entrances before?"

Issak nods once. "When he came back from Yazd. At the time, I was here meeting with a colleague, but I heard everything the crowds were saying."

"That Calyx was dead."

"That, yes, but also that Castan Cassena was the only one to leave a mark on Rosh Dentata and live."

I shudder, and my foot lands on Issak's. Thank God I'm only wearing sandals, another tradition Dani explained to me. Something about Roman peasants and Phaedra's slavery.

"I'm sorry. I didn't mean to bring up unpleasant conversation."

"You didn't—I did. But it's fine." I stop in my tracks. Other couples twirl about us, blurs of blacks, silky blues, lacy pastels, and glittering *armatus*. "I'm going to go get a drink. Thirsty?"

Issak shakes his head. "No. I better go stand with the rest of the stiff-necked ambassadors, though. Thank you for dancing with me." He offers me a smile that doesn't match his expression. I open my mouth to ask if I've offended him but stop myself. Issak doesn't wait either. He slips away, leaving me all alone on the dance floor.

Suddenly self-conscious, I cross my arms to hide the window displaying my cleavage and push through the crowd towards the Sun Room. I thought I saw James's blonde head disappearing behind the wall some time ago, Laila's dark crown at his shoulder.

When I emerge in the archway, the sun is just beginning to set in the horizon, bathing the room in golden yellow. Roundtables speckle the Sun Room, though most of them are abandoned. Crew from the kitchen, recognizable in their white aprons, buss the tables, clearing the white tablecloth and resetting the places with neatly folded bundles of silverware.

"Júlia—" My veins freeze. I turn my head towards the sound of that voice.

And my heart shrivels in my chest.

Flush against the stone wall, is Júlia. But my eyes stutter over the figure pinning her there, kissing her there. Castan.

Their bodies are pressed so tightly together, the only way I decipher two figures is the contrast of Castan's black suit against Júlia's mocha ball gown. Her leg sneaks through a slit in the tulle, grappling Castan's ankle. My stomach knots.

I look about, the question *Does anyone else see this?* spurting from my watering eyes. But if the sparse couples and busboys notice, they ignore the dalliance.

I don't hang around to witness more. Turning on my heel, I grab handfuls of my black skirts and dash through the crowd until I find James. He hovers over the dessert table, indecisive as always.

"I'm heading back to Argenti," I say. Laila's eyebrows furrow. "I'm tired," I add, forcing a yawn when a scream threatens to overtake me.

James tongs two pastries onto his plate. "Alright. I'll see you later then."

And for some reason, this gesture hurts more than any stolen kiss could. I recoil, though his words were not unkind. They were dismissive, unlike any James has ever uttered to me before. Even Laila notices. But I pivot, vanishing in the flurry of formal dresses and animated conversation before she reaches an arm out to stop me.

Outside, the evening air cools my skin. Sweat prickles under my arms, across my brow. I stalk past Kass's recruiting table, now empty. She must have gone into the banquet after all.

Fistfuls of dress, I walk the cobbled road not really knowing where I'm going. I don't feel like crying, and this frustrates me even more. Crying is easy. Crying is purging your emotional mind. But it's not my mind that's emotional. It's my heart. I feel sick to my stomach in a way I have only ever experienced once in my life.

I blink, and Averil's car disappears down my driveway. I blink again, and I want James to hold me, to tell me that I need to eat. Because that's never what he meant. He meant, *I love you, Corolla. You're stronger than this.* But James isn't here—he's down the hill with Laila. He doesn't need me to take care of him anymore. He hasn't needed me since the night I first called him from Matrona.

My stomach roils, and I bite my lip to suppress whatever is surging up my throat.

Because it's not Castan. It's not James. It's me. Where I could be one of the victims of the Genocides' attacks, I am not. Yet I'm hurting all the same.

I glance up from the red brick road. I'm in the square outside the Ward Residencies. I go to the fountain splashing in the center of the Tudor homes. Vacant windows follow my movements as I approach the bronze tree blooming from the middle of the stone fountain. I know enough pelari history to recognize this tree as the cypress, Matrona. Streams of water shoot from the tree's teardrop bulk. The sculpture is so detailed, crawling with miniature figures clad in long cloaks. They hold lanterns in their outstretched hands as one of their party is forever placing a hand on the tree's trunk. Though the figure is hunched over with age, I know it's Tilia Pyrus. The fountain depicts her ascension, the coronation of Matrona.

I forget the weight in my heart, the fist in my stomach. But in the noise of trickling water, it rushes back to me. I glance at the pennies, nickels, and dimes littering the fountain's mosaic bed. My vision blurs, and the sky—golden, wispy clouds—reflects in the rippling water like a mirror.

My palms begin itching for yarn, a pencil and paper, *something*. I need to capture these unsettling thoughts. And then, "Fuck paper, and fuck pencils! That's not going to erase what I've done!"

What would Adian do? I don't know why I latch onto this thought, but, through the chaos in my mind, it rings clear.

A bitter voice follows, *Why do you care what Adian would or wouldn't do?*

"Because she was strong, and she was fearless," the words slip easily past my lips as if they have been waiting there my whole life. "And you are not." My own reflection gapes back at me in the pool.

I steel over, scowling at that Corolla.

I clamber over the lip of the fountain, trampling over other people's wishes as I wade through the pool. My skirts drag like tentacles trying to anchor me in place. I don't care. I have enough money to buy a hundred of this dress. I trudge forward to the nearest spout. Cupping my hands, I catch the water and splash it on my face. Scrub. Catch more water. Scrub again. The water dripping down my chin, down my garnet bust, is a shade lighter than my skin tone. My mask is melting, pooling around my legs like gasoline in water.

I move around the fountain, away from the murky water. I focus on my steps, face dripping with lukewarm water. Through the sky's reflection, I think I see a silver chain and pendant lying among the wishes. But then I trip over the burdensome tangle of my skirts and reach out to catch myself on a chute's lip.

Only when I right myself, do I notice the sting in my palm. I pull my hand from the copper ledge and inspect the clean slice down my palm. Like a fish's gill. Blood oozes from the fleshy slit. I make a fist and watch the crimson beads drip into the water.

Past
April 2004

Beep, beep, beep.

Tyto felt his eyebrows knitting together. *I'm not supposed to be visiting Major Rainier tonight.* His arms twitched, and pain shot through his pectorals with the movement.

"Tyto." A cold hand on his wrist. His eyelids fluttered, and there was Adian, sitting at his bedside. Her eyes were swollen and red, hair falling around her shoulders, tangled. She was pale and thin. Tyto sat up—or at least, he tried. He groaned and fell back, gasping at the agony ripping through his body.

"You shouldn't try to move," her voice was raw, hurting. His eyes rolled across the hospital ceiling. His thoughts struggled to come back together, but this, at least, he knew: Major Rainier was years dead, and Adian was raw from crying.

"What happened? Are you resting enough? How's Corolla? Calyx?" Adian laughed, but the shaking of her shoulders only triggered more tears. Tyto stretched an arm out to hold her hand.

Beep, beep, beep.

"I don't have a lot of time," Adian glanced over her shoulder at the room's door. "But I want you to know that Calyx is safe—we all are—and... and I love you, Ty."

Tyto shifted, ignoring the strain it put on his aching body. He yanked the IV out of his antecubital and flung sloppy arms around his wife. She smelled like she always did, of bamboo and sweat. But there was something different about the way she clasped her arms around his neck. Something like an ending.

Beep, beep, beep.

"There was an attack," he said slowly, remembering the smoke and fire in the northern wall. He pulled away. "But you wouldn't be here, unless..."

"They know, Ty. I'm sorry, but when you were shot... I couldn't just stand by—I thought you were going to die. I thought..." Silver tears streamed down her cheeks, falling on the swell of her stomach. Tyto brushed them away with his thumbs. He no longer felt the pain in his own body; Adian's pain was stronger than that, overpowering his everything. He remembered the day they married, how, even in a stuffy courthouse, he said his vows and the world hung on that precious

347

moment. And that look on her face... Where people only ever saw him as the young Major, Adian looked at him and saw him. She saw his weaknesses, his strengths just as he saw hers.

In his mind, he reconstructed her face. Took away her chapped cheeks and red-rimmed eyes. He replaced them with that young, eager face from their wedding day. He scraped her hair into the bun she always tied atop her head. He gave her happiness, gave her joy.

He wanted to give that to her now.

Tyto kissed her knuckles, lips brushing the ring on her finger. "It'll be okay."

And even though his words rang with conviction, even though Adian nodded acceptance, they both knew the futility in such a promise.

Tyto's stomach filled with sickness. *Taxodium's turned their back on us.*

They would be anything but okay.

From Aurum's front window, Adian watched the Verum Courts move into Allen Manor. The black vehicles, she decided, drove through the courtyard on purpose. Taunting. Though she couldn't see through the tinted windows, she sensed Vera Taylor among the vans. Tyto's ally, now his enemy.

Calyx tugged on the hem of her shirt, making noises for lunch. Adian moved away from the window, clutching her stomach. Corolla kicked, but she barely noticed the odd sensation. She plucked Calyx from the floor and held him close.

"Lunch!" The little boy cheered against her shoulder. He squirmed in her arms, pulling his head from under her grip.

"I know," she cooed. "I know." She wished Laila would return from Rome. Wished she had someone to help her carry the burden bowing her back. But she was alone. Alex stayed away. Tyto was locked away. And she couldn't call Maurizio and Marilena anymore—her phone privileges were revoked. She couldn't call her own father, not that she would. The last time she had seen him was her mother's funeral, last year. The grudge he bore against her was as plain as the glasses he wore.

Calyx squirmed again, and Adian set him down before his knobby knees found a home in her stout stomach. He raced to the kitchen and hung from the refrigerator handles. Tyto would have scolded him for that, but Adian let him play. She allowed him to do anything to keep him from asking about his father. Calyx knew Tyto worked away, was used to his comings and goings. But her son wasn't clueless, either. He curled in her arms last night, sensing her distress the same way she sensed when he was hungry, sad, or in need of the bathroom.

"Calyx, love," Adian eased him from the refrigerator handles, and he giggled. Everything was a game to him. She opened the fridge. It would need to be restocked soon, but Adian wasn't sure when she would be able to get out to do that. "Applesauce and crackers?"

Calyx clapped his hands. "Yes! Yes!"

Adian prepared a liberal bowl of applesauce, withdrew half a sleeve of crackers from the cabinet. She steered clear of the pantry ever since some men barged into the house and sealed the tunnel shut. Adian wasn't sure how they knew, and she wasn't given the opportunity to ask. Maybe Tyto said something, but she found this hard to believe.

"Come here, Calyx." Adian patted the seat next to her own. Calyx didn't even question why they were eating in the living room—another thing Tyto scolded him for. The little boy just raced over to his plate and shoveled a spoonful of applesauce into his mouth. He probed her with giant eyes.

Adian offered him a small smile and fetched his water bottle from the fridge. She placed it in his wanting hands and sat back beside him. She sank into the couch cushions and watched Calyx bite into a saltine cracker.

It was sad, wasn't it? The house was gray, while the world was glowing through the twin windows. But Adian couldn't bear to leave Aurum, couldn't bear to leave Calyx. She wasn't afraid of what people would say. She was worried she would make it worse by reacting to what they said. Because they talked. Constantly. It's why she kept the windows shut now. Weeks into this ordeal, it still surprised her how quickly the Academy turned on them. Women who threw her a baby shower when Calyx was due, men who swore to guard her and her children... They would walk past Aurum and fix scornful glares upon her residence. If people were so cruel to her up here, she could only wonder how awful they were to Tyto underground. She didn't want to think about it.

"You lunch?" Calyx passed her a cracker before she could refuse it.

"Thank you." She nibbled on it but tasted nothing. She knew she should eat, but everything was sand in her mouth. She'd lost her appetite anyway. But it wasn't surprising. When your fate was up in the air, how were you supposed to eat? She never thought she took her life for granted, but sitting there with Calyx, Adian knew that's all she had ever done. She would make it through the legal battle, but where the rest of her family landed, she could only begin to guess.

"So this is how this is going to work," Chief of Intelligence Ramsey slapped his palms across the metal table top, "You don't get a lawyer, but you get me. Tell me the whole truth, and I'll make sure you don't hang for of it."

Tyto stared at the Chief's long nostrils. Though Ramsey had never been Chief while Tyto was Major (Chief Bailey stepped down upon hearing of Tyto's incarceration), he thought he had seen a nose like Ramsey's before. As the man paced the interrogation room, Tyto dismissed the peculiar thought. He pinned the resemblance to a tortoise's nose instead.

Tyto clasped his hands on top of the table, the cold metal biting his bare forearms. He wished he had a blanket, but he didn't dare ask for one. He didn't dare permit these people satisfaction at his suffering. So when the healing wound in his breast ached, pinched, or pained him, Tyto would bite his tongue and will it away. He knew now that he had been close to death. But the staff at Rainier saved him, preserved him to be dragged through trial. He was one week released from Rainier Hospital and was transferred from one kind of room to another.

At least the hospital had cable. The holding cells at Intel were large enough for a cot and a bucket. Though he got three meals a day, it was never enough food to ease the claws in his stomach. Tyto passed his time by sleeping, but even his dreams weren't a complete escape. He saw Adian and Calyx sometimes, crying in a crowd of angry spectators. It was only when he heard what the spectators were saying, did he know that he was dying.

"Burn the witch!" They would chant. And Adian's face would go red from crying. "Burn the witch!"

But not all his dreams were like that. Sometimes he would stumble upon pleasant ones, ones where he and Adian were lying under the stars, that crumbling chapel at their backs. Calyx was never in that dream, and neither was the bloated bump of Corolla in Adian's stomach. But whenever Tyto reflected upon this thought, a sense of peace flooded him. He knew his children were someplace safe, chasing each other through the orchards perhaps.

"Alba!" Ramsey barked across the table. Tyto blinked, saw the man had taken the seat opposite him. "I'm here to help you, but no more lies."

Tyto lifted his head. "This society is built on a foundation of lies."

Castan
July 2020

"Kassandra." The redhead raises her eyes to meet mine. She's in full uniform, and I wonder if Rex is giving her points for commitment.

"I would have thought you'd be inside," I nod towards the Dining Hall behind her. Among the suits and gowns trickling inside, her recruiting table is a glaring reminder of the war.

She ignores my comment and hands me a flyer. "Sign up for the scouts today. For our brothers, our sisters, our society." She salutes, but not for me. The *greater good* rings in her practiced words. Talan and Finis have gone on ahead of me, passing Kass with simple "hellos."

I run my tongue along my upper lip. Hand the flyer back.

"Put my name on your list then," I say. Her eyes flicker for a brief moment, but her expression betrays nothing.

"You have to be healthy to join the scouts."

"I don't think you can afford to be so picky." Her hand tightens around a pen. "Besides, I'm not sick." I am better today, after yesterday's long haul of sleep, water, and canned soups. Finis let me borrow a suit (all the same shades of black this time), following my reimbursement for all the Yuengling's I emptied.

Kass pulls a clipboard from under a stack of flyers. Her spreadsheet is maybe only a quarter filled out. Just then, I pity her enthusiasm and sparse returns. She really *can't* afford to be picky. Grudgingly, she puts my name in the next blank space.

"I know what you're doing," she hisses through gritted teeth. "I don't want your protection. You're not my Regent."

"I'm not anyone's Regent. But I am your friend." I adjust my cream-colored tie and continue on my way down the cobbled road.

The Dining Hall thrums with people. I weave through warm bodies and try not to remember the last time I was here to celebrate. December was so long ago, but those memories are fresh in my mind, offering themselves willingly.

"Aunt Laila!" Down the hall, the sight of her dark crown saves me from my thoughts. I move through the crowd towards the Sun Room, where I plant myself in a chair beside Aunt Laila. James takes my interruption as his cue to leave. He wipes a ring around his mouth with his cloth napkin, offers me a curt smile, and mumbles something about dessert before excusing himself.

"Castan," Aunt Laila squeezes my arm. "You're feeling better then?"

I shrug. "I'm out of the dorm at least."

"Go eat something. You look pale. James and I just finished dinner—they have barbecue up there next to the dinner rolls." She rises, figure framed in silky robin's egg blue, the picture of elegance. Her long tresses have been pulled back, but they hang around her shoulders like a Greek goddess's. "I feel weird abandoning James in a crowd like this," she gushes, but I see that glint in her eyes. "Come with me?"

I shake my head. "I think I need a minute. But I'll come find you in a second."

Aunt Laila supplies a sympathetic look, squeezes my arms once more and follows James's earlier path down the hall. The sun glares through the wall of windows. Sweat prickles at my hairline. I run my thumb along the table's edge, absently feeling the coarse thread of the tablecloth.

Calyx—

"Castan!" Arms wrap around my neck, fingers snaking beneath my suit coat. "Black again, you creature of habit."

I pluck her hands off my chest. "Hi, Júlia." She finds an invitation where there isn't one and tugs a chair out to sit beside me. I take in the mocha of her dress, the way she spreads her legs enough to reveal that slit in the side of her skirt.

I look her in the eyes. "I have a lot on my mind."

She scoots closer, leans forward so that the hem of her dress is compromised. "I'm sure you do. But I think I can help with that."

"Not here," I mutter, meaning, *No more*. But somehow, those direct words don't flow from my tongue.

Júlia grabs my wrist, leading me towards the more vacant end of the Sun Room. I focus on her golden *armatus*. My brow furrows.

"Where did you get these?" I clutch her wrist, drawing the cuff closer to my face.

"I had them custom made," she coos. "Do you like them? I had to get a little inventive, but it's all there. You. The finger. That Gen." With her free hand, she twirls fingers around my tie. The perfume she's wearing suffocates my senses, too sweet and too sour all at once. Like rotting food.

"What the hell, Juh?" I shake my head, too astonished to scowl. "I don't want that on *armatus*." Only then do I realize she's backed herself up against the stone wall. And I am the one holding her there. I drop her wrist, pulling away, but she tightens her grip on my tie.

"Júlia—" Her lips crush mine, biting and gnawing. Wanting. Her leg hooks me by the ankle, body pressing into mine. But my body doesn't react to her, not the way it used to.

I yank free of her ferocious grip, chest heaving. "Júlia," heat rises to my palms, but I will the flames away. "You can't do that anymore. You can't be that anymore. I don't..." I run a hand through my hair, successfully undoing all of Talan's earlier work to style it. "I don't want us to be like that for each other anymore."

Júlia's hair spills freely down her shoulders. Her exposed leg bends at the knee, propping her against the wall. She crosses her arms, red lips grinning.

"I knew you had feelings for her. But, Castan," she pushes herself off the wall, "it was fun while it lasted." She moves past me, but I catch her by the arm.

"Juh, the *armatus*..." I can't shake the golden image. Me, brandishing a knife. Rosh, a malicious grin twisting his features. And then my knife chopping through his hand. The finger, a halo surrounding it, fallen on the ground.

She shrugs my grip away, not unkindly. "You are the only one to take a chunk out of that bastard, Castan. I will never forgive him for butchering Calyx and Jura and all the other scouts who died at his hand."

"Right." I blink, stunned by those glinting images. "Thank you."

"Don't thank me," Júlia's voice goes soft. She steps on her tiptoes and plants a kiss on my cheek. "Thank you for serving some justice."

"Justice," but my voice echoes in the silence. Júlia's words come back to me, *"I knew you had feelings for her."* My spine straightens. I don't need her to explain those to me.

Corolla.

Where is she? I rack my brain for any sighting of her, for that caramel skin and caramel hair. Aunt Laila's laughter reaches my ears. She and James enter the Sun Room, carrying little plates of pastries. I force myself not to run to them, not to alarm them.

"Have you seen Corolla?" My eyes dart from James to Aunt Laila.

"Why?" James tenses. "Is something wrong?"

"No, no," I wave him away. "I just... there's something I want to tell her."

Brow furrowed, James opens his mouth to say something else, but Aunt Laila clamps a hand on his forearm. She gives James a look. My skin prickles at the private moment. They make eyes at each other. The eyes of people who have survived much and known little companionship. The eyes of people who understand one another. Aunt Laila tears her gaze from James.

"She went back to Argenti about ten minutes ago. Said she was tired." Aunt Laila grins and shoots me a knowing look. *Am I that obvious?*

I don't hang around to ask. If I had, I would have heard James's bitter last words. I call over my shoulder, "Thanks."

Once I'm out of the Sun Room, all I want to do is tear through the crowd and out the doors. But this is wartime, and I don't want to draw any more attention to myself. I stalk past the dance floor and shoulder my way through the clumps of people. I'm so caught in my thoughts— *what exactly am I going to say to Corolla?*—that I knock right into a woman in pink lace.

"Oh, I am so sorry!" I step back, grasping small shoulders to right my wrong.

And then the woman turns.

"Ambassador Collingwood." I salute the diplomat. My humiliation doubles, but so does my urgency to leave. What if Corolla is already asleep? What if she's in the shower and won't hear me knocking? What if—

"It's alright," Ambassador Collingwood says in that Australian twang of hers. "No drinks spilled yet." She grins, and I think I'm supposed to laugh. Major Rex, who has been watching this whole encounter, raises her thin eyebrows.

"Is something wrong, soldier?" My eyes dart from her blinding white pantsuit to the ambassador's amused eyes. Ambassador Olejar and Issak Park, drawn to the disturbance, turn towards the Major and me. Their stares bore into the side of my face like drills. I hear Ambassador Emeko's low rumbling laugh. Issak's unseeing eyes seem to fix on me then, brow furrowed. And I know he senses my urgency, maybe even knows who I'm searching for.

"I'm just feeling under the weather, ma'am." I salute Major Rex, ducking my head. "Excuse me." I depart the Major's vicious stare, the ambassadors' entertained gawks.

Behind me, Collingwood chuckles, "I've never seen a face so *scarlet*."

I tug my collar, pushing through the remaining crowd. I burst into the evening air, sucking in a deep breath. The sun is setting, the sky, golden. I put the scene behind me, and run, past Kass's vacant table, past the gate, past the hospital, up the hill—

And there she is, swaying in the fountain's pool. Her dress catches sunlight, rubies winking like bloody stars across the square.

My race becomes a canter, the soles of my borrowed shoes clacking on the brick courtyard. I stop at the lip of the fountain to catch my breath. My pulse throbs in my temples. I shake sparks from my palms. They hiss when they strike the water.

"You shouldn't be out here by yourself." Her back is to me, but she makes no move to face me. She is still, wrought in her own kind of bronze. Pins dangle from her drooping hair. Water gushes from the sharp lips in Matrona, spilling into the pool. I used to wonder if Phaedra's Blood supplies this fountain with water, but I never found out.

"Corolla." I give her five seconds to answer before I'm tugging off my shoes and socks. I wade in the pool, the lukewarm water soaking my pants up to my shins. She's less than a foot away from me, but I don't touch her. Her arms hang limply at her side, and it's then that I see her right palm. My heart aches at the sight of her blood, a steady trickle.

"Corolla."

"Fuck you."

I flinch. "I deserve that."

A cynical laugh erupts from her mouth. I don't recognize it as Corolla's. "Out of everything you *think* you deserve... Yes, you do."

"I'm sorry about the other day—"

"Why, because you were drunk? Because it was a mistake? I'm not another Júlia for you to play with."

Without having to ask, I know she saw something of my encounter with Júlia in the Sun Room. I gather from the hurt in her voice, the way her shoulders tense and muscles take shape beneath her skin. "I never said you were."

"Don't you *dare* lie to me, Castan." Her words cut to the bone. I want to confess everything to her, tell her that I didn't have a choice, that I did what I could to survive... But I wouldn't be talking about Júlia anymore. Out of all the things I have done, fooling around with her is the most insignificant. Droplets of water speckle my brow. I wipe them away.

"Júlia was a distraction. After Calyx died, we would stay up through the night trying to find his spirit. But I let things get out of hand. She's just a friend." Dribbling water fills the silence. "And she knows that," I add. "She knows we're just friends. That's why I was talking to her in the Sun Room."

"Oh," Corolla tosses a bitter look over her shoulder. "You sure were *talking*." She raises her arm as if to march away, but I grasp her wrist.

"Corolla, I... I wanted to talk to you. I ran all the way from the Hall. I..." I look up from her oozing palm to her whiskey-brown eyes. Black mascara runs down her cheeks, dripping paint. Any other person would bow under her fierce stare, but I hold her gaze. I read the unspoken words in her eyes. Let go of her wrist.

"I am sorry. Corolla—"

Her arms lock around my neck, chest pressing into my body. Before I can speak, her lips crash into mine. Our noses knock, and I stagger backward half a step. But she's kissing me, cupping her hands on the back of my neck for a better grip. I shove aside my shock and pull her closer, hungry. In my arms, she is nothing like Júlia, who is always taking, always pushing for more. Corolla is eager, biting at my bottom lip. But she's so careful, so efficient, that when we break apart, I'm the one gasping for breath.

She braces herself for my reaction, eyes steeling over with locks and bolts. Her puckered lips pulse bright red. She crosses her arms, shivering despite her defensive expression.

I open my mouth to say something, but no words come. Instead, I cup her face in two hands and kiss her the way I've intended to since she first walked through that door brandishing an umbrella. With a gentle tongue, I ease past her lips. She moans against my mouth, pushing her body against mine until I feel the pulse in her abdomen.

It should feel wrong. Because Corolla is a lure dangling from a short line. Because as soon as she fulfills her purpose, she'll be sent away. Because I am deteriorating and will have to go away too. Because of all the lies I've spoon-fed her.

It should feel wrong.

But it doesn't.

We come apart, Corolla clutching my wrist and wading through the pool. I help her over the fountain's lip, and she snatches my shoes and socks from the ground. I don't have to ask where we're going. Argenti beckons ahead while the whole of the Academy parties below.

Once inside, gray light cloaks our surroundings. I rely on Corolla for guidance. She dumps my shoes at the door before locking it. We tramp up a set of stairs, and I nearly lose my footing several times. Corolla stifles laughter but doesn't say a word.

Then we're in her bedroom, and I'm tossing my tie on the floor. I take Corolla's arms in my own, unclasp her *armatus*, and throw them aside too. She works at the buttons on my shirt, face pinched in concentration. I shrug my jacket off, and next, my shirt. Corolla splays her hand over my bare stomach, and I know she's studying me.

Careful not to disturb her, I weave hands around her back, feeling for her dress zipper.

"Wait." I freeze. Her bust glints red and burnt orange in the filtered sunlight creeping through her curtains. "I don't want you to think I'm easy."

I pull back, but only enough so that I can see her face. I cup her face, smooth a thumb along her cheekbone.

"Who said *this* was easy?" A hand graces the side of my torso. Corolla grins, reaching for my belt buckle. I plant a kiss on top of her head and return to my task of locating her zipper. My hands tremble so badly, that once I do find it, the damn thing keeps slipping from my grasp.

"Here," Corolla snakes her arms around her back, "let me help you." She takes the zipper from my hand, and I hear the thing come undone. Holding her front, she shrugs out of her dress. It falls in a puddle at her knees. I tug off my pants and sweep her into my arms. We fall back on her bed, naked chests pressed together. Her heartbeat matches my own: erratic.

Corolla brushes my hair aside. "You always smell like brewed coffee."

I raise a hand to my mouth and blow air. "I hope that's a compliment."

"Not your breath!" She draws circles on my shoulder. "Your skin. It's... you."

"Dark roast or light?"

"I don't know the difference."

"Corolla, Corolla. And you thought pelari were uncultured."

She raises her dark eyes. "Why are you shaking?" I bow my head into her neck and pepper the curve of her throat with kisses. Her fingertips toy with the waistband of my underwear.

She manages through pleased noises, "You have to answer me."

I raise my head and tuck hair behind her ear. "Because it never mattered before. I—I just never really cared, but I want this to be right for you. I want—" She smooths back the hair spilling into my eyes.

"Now who's the nervous talker?"

I trace her collarbone with a finger. "I don't have a... you know. I'm wasn't prepared for this."

"I didn't expect you to be," she says. And then, "I'm nervous too. But I want this. Do you?"

I bite back laughter. "Can't you feel me? God, Corolla, you've been taunting me since the day we met!"

Her wandering fingers find their way around my waistband. I get the message. I ease off of her and slip off my last article of clothing just as she does the same. She moves farther up the bed. I follow her. My eyes dip to the swell of her chest, the plane of her abdomen.

I catch her against a pile of pillows, and our bodies pulsate together. She wraps a leg around my backside, our hips locking. She inhales sharply, almost painfully. I stop, her body cradled beneath my own.

"Are you alright?"

Her heavy-lidded eyes meet my own, locks of hair fanning around her head. Her irises flicker, all the unspoken settling between us. My lungs swell, and my heart threatens to hammer straight through my chest. She grasps the back of my neck and crushes my lips to hers.

We move together until the sun vanishes and moonlight patches our bare bodies.

Past

May 25th, 2004

Adian swept her hair into a bun. She coated her lips in Chapstick. Maternity shorts and a baggy tee shirt. Socks. Going through the motions was easy. Living with the consequences was... impossible. Had it not been for the baby packed in her flesh, she surely would have died two days ago during the hearing.

Adian sighed, wiping the tears from her eyes. She bit her lip, frustrated. Why was it that she had to lose Tyto and Calyx? Why was it up to the Courts to decide their fates?

At least he survived. Yes, she reminded herself, *at least he didn't die during the misfire.*

Adian stalked over to the window, Calyx's crib in the corner. He was still sleeping in it now, though he was much too old to be in a baby crib. She listened to the sound of him breathing, thankful that he would be slumbering through the sentencing. Not that he was permitted to attend. But it was a small comfort to her heart that her son should be in a dreamscape while his parents were in a living nightmare.

She turned back to the window. It was raining, gray clouds a pressing mass above the earth. She scanned the Twelfth Wall, noting the jagged places among the trees where the fires had damaged the northern section. Trees burn so easily, but the Twelfth Wall was enchanted to withstand a vast amount of the heat. Adian recalled the night of the attack but only in still life's; as if her mind had taken pictures of the events, rather than recording the entire thing. Tyto, lying still, bleeding through his shirt. The crater from the Sentry's misfire. The bodies surrounding that pit. And yet... whenever Adian attempted to remember how she had come to be under the lamplight, her head began to throb, and she was forced to give up.

She glanced up at the sheet of gray clouds once more.

Of course, she thought. *Of course it should be gloomy on the worst day of my life.* It sounded childish, even to her, but she was beyond caring. Corolla squirmed in Adian's midsection, reminding her mother that she was still there. A slight grin crept into Adian's expression. It comforted her heart that Corolla should be safe from the outside world too.

There was a knock on her bedroom door. Adian turned to see Laila peering through the door crack.

Laila's back. Part of her knew this reunion should be joyful. The other knew it was never meant to be. Time declared this moment to be sober and forlorn from the moment Adian was born. Was *this* destiny? To lose her family again and again? She already lost her birth parents, her adopted parents, and now, to lose Tyto and Calyx... But no, she mustn't cry anymore. She mustn't allow her misery to show through the careful mask of her expression.

"Come in."

"Adian," Laila slipped between the frame and the door. "I just wanted to say... I just—" Laila hugged herself, body curling into itself. Adian could only watch as the shoulders of her dearest friend began trembling, shaking and heaving with a sort of grief Adian knew would be her own fate soon enough. She escaped the worst of pain when Tyto escaped death, but now they were to be torn apart. She would rather have a baby than face that agony. No amount of cleaning Aurum could distract her from the impending trauma she was soon to know.

"It's alright, Laila." Her voice sounded strange in her ears. Flat. It occurred to Adian that she never even asked Laila how her internship was. She would probably never know.

Laila glanced up, tears two streams gushing down her flushed cheeks. She tucked her long raven hair behind her ears. Some tresses caught in the row of metal piercings in the arc of Laila's ear. Some snagged on the many rings wrapped around her fingers.

Adian closed her own eyes, hung her head. Why did everything have to be so hard? She swallowed, opened her eyes.

"The guards are on their way," Laila hiccupped. "I just wanted to say I'm sorry. I wish it could have been different for you and Tyto. I wish—" Laila broke off, perhaps realizing the fruitlessness of her own words.

Adian folded Laila in an embrace, pressed her trembling body against the stout bulge of her stomach. St. Philomena battered against Adian's sternum. What were the rest of the Albas doing? If they had tried to contact her, no one was going to inform her.

"It's alright," Adian repeated, smoothing back Laila's tangle of hair. "It's alright." But it wasn't. Tyto and Calyx would be tossed someplace thousands of miles away from her. Adian would never see her family again. This baby in her stomach might never know her father, her brother... What would become of Corolla? The Courts wouldn't allow a "potential hostage" to stay under Adian's wing, but surely, they couldn't take Corolla from her too?

Could things have been different? Had Tyto not risked his life for her, had Adian followed his instructions, would their secret still be intact? Adian wondered. But then again, her children were bound to grow into Tyto's mold eventually. One could not mask genes. Maybe their secret would have lasted until Calyx reached puberty. Or maybe their secret would have faltered once their daughter was born. Maybe Corolla would have Tyto's nose or his eyes or—

"They're here." Laila's choked voice brought Adian back. She blinked at her roommate, but she could not move.

No, I can't do this—

But she had to. Time would keep dragging her along, no matter how rebellious her heart was; no matter how terribly she longed to go *back* in time. Before the hearing, before the trial, before the Dentatas attacked...

"Okay," Adian whispered. "You have to let go of me, Laila." But when she looked down, Adian saw her own hands gripping Laila's waist.

"Oh."

Laila covered her mouth, stifling another cry.

"I am so sorry, Adian. I am so sorry..."

"Just... take care of Calyx while I'm gone." Adian's arms fell limp at her sides. She took one last look at Laila, a watery, raven-haired mess, and walked out the door. Laila's cries followed her like a swarm of bees.

Past the kitchen, five guards waited for her in the foyer. She recognized some, though they would not meet her eyes. Adian gripped the blonde man by the shoulder and shoved her swollen feet in tennis shoes. If the guard was surprised, he did a wonderful job remaining passive. Adian could have spit in his face, a face she had come to know as *friend*. Ever since he testified against Tyto, his face no longer expressed that warmth. So shutdown was he to her, that, rather than pain, anger plated her expression.

You've been promoted for your treachery, she wanted to spit. *You've been rewarded for throwing my family under the bus.* Somehow, the venom wouldn't pass her lips. All she could utter was his name.

"Alex."

He cleared his throat but would not look at her. "You may no longer call me that." He nodded his head to the other four guards. Without a word, they stepped outside.

"What the hell?" Adian gasped when they were alone. He may have saved her son during the attack, but he was no saint. "How can you be here after testif—"

His lips crushed hers. Startled, Adian pulled away and raised a trembling hand. Alex's eyes unclouded. He saw her arm but did not flinch. He stood ready for her blow, eyes swirling gray.

"How dare you," Adian gasped, chest heaving. She lowered her arm, weak. "How dare you come here—"

"I'm sorry. I just—Had it been me, had you loved me, even a single kiss would have been worth the punishment."

Adian, disgusted, confused, and suddenly exhausted, pulled on her raincoat.

"Take me to my husband." Never had words made her shiver so much. Alex flinched, and if he noticed her shaking, he kept the observation to himself. Alex Murphy, her first true friend, was gone.

Since the Courthouse had been partially destroyed in the attack, the Verum Courts moved into the main floor of Allen Manor. People packed around the paneled walls, leaving only a small bubble before the Judges. Upon her entrance, the crowd parted generously around her, condensing farther than she thought possible. Alex led her through the paths, though Adian could have walked herself.

This was the third day of *Taxodium v. Alba and Vel*. Since then, Adian learned to never bow her head. Being proud meant her neck would be stiff at the end of the day, meant people would spin more lies about her. But it also meant Tyto's last memories of her would not be ones of a cowering, bloated, tearful woman.

Adian met her husband's gaze across the room. Hair askew, eyes sunken into his skull, she hardly recognized him. He looked worse every time she saw him. Unlike her, he was forced to stay in the cells underground. But even then, she would take this Tyto over the one with a bullet in his chest. The minute twitch of his lips was meant to reassure her, but her heart bled all the same.

What did he see when he looked at her? Tyto was so perceptive, Adian was positive he saw Alex's kiss, unabsorbed, on her lips. His eyes made no inquiry, though, because he wasn't a fool. He knew her heart beat in his chest.

On instinct, Adian clutched her stomach. Pregnant women were never alone, but in that moment, it was just Tyto and her. He watched her from his seat before the Judges.

It'll be alright, love, he said.

Maybe. But our children?

Blood is thicker than banishment. Adian could have laughed, but the cacophony of the room came slamming back into her. The walls said awful things.

"She's more trouble than she's worth."

"Bastards, the lot of them."

"Why should we save a woman and child whose very genes are a danger to us all?"

362

But above it all, the archetype word from all those witch trials blackening pelari history. The worst insult a pelari could utter:

witch

Witch

Witch.

"The people have spoken," Tyto explained when he was elected Major. "It wasn't in my power to refuse their demands, no matter how many loops the election jumped through."

The people have spoken. And they are saying terrible things. Adian took her seat before the Court. Seven stony sets of eyes glared down at her from the kidney-shaped desk. Adian calmly stared back. Vera Taylor—the hypocrite—shifted in her cushioned seat.

Adian's expression betrayed nothing, but her mind reeled. *You have two babies, just like me! How can you sit there and rip* my *family apart?* But this was "different." Different because Tyto broke his Major's vows, and Adian put the Academy at risk for loving anyone so fiercely.

Vera averted her gaze. Adian followed the angle of the Judge's head. She was staring at her own husband: Judge Nikolai Taylor. Without warning, Adian's heart broke. All the cracks it had endured over the years finally met, became one complete fracture. This was real. Tyto and she would be sentenced, and that would be it. She would have this baby and be forced to find her feet again. The world would continue spinning. She felt it in her core, and she couldn't bear it.

I can't live without you.

The hollow ring of the gavel brought most of the mumbling to an end. Rain beat against the windows, no longer a gentle *patter* but a violent *swish*. Adian blinked back silent tears, grateful Tyto couldn't see her eyes at this angle. She didn't want him to know how wounded she was.

The seven Judges stood, and with them, the seated population. Except for Adian. She couldn't move, and no one asked why. She clutched her stomach. They assumed her weakness. The Judges returned to their seats.

"We will begin now," Vera announced. Behind her, the new Major was perched in the balcony. How many times had Adian sat there with Tyto late at night? Major Rex didn't give Adian a second look. No, she trained her icy beam at Tyto. He was a disgrace—his portrait had already been taken down. Burned, most likely. He was the youngest Major in history and now the most despised one.

"How dare he put his life at risk for a woman, no matter her genes!"

"Our own leader—he disgraces the duties of Major."

"Not sure if that one has got his mind in the right place."

It wasn't that the people hated them. Actually, they had adored them—as individuals, not husband and wife. For two people of such ranks in Taxodium to be involved romantically... Well, Tax would have another hostage situation on their hands if the Dentatas found out the Major's weakness was the very thing they desperately wanted.

None of this would matter if my genes were different. Ty and I could be another Vera and Nikolai Taylor, though not as heartless. Ty could step down from office, and we could be a proper family, pelari or not.

Adian sucked in oxygen, lungs ballooning. There was a knife in her midsection, but she couldn't move a muscle to tell someone.

No! Not now!

Vera's dry voice above it all, "...unfortunate circumstances. However, the insubordination is inexcusable. A crisis has been avoided, a crisis that would have been more damaging than the attack this Academy endured a month ago."

Adian thought she had gotten rid of Alex a while ago, but he was suddenly at her side. Discretely, he asked, "Are you feeling okay?"

Adian clenched her teeth, body rigid with pain. "Get away from me," she hissed. It shouldn't be Alex asking her. It should be Tyto, and they should be somewhere alone together, Calyx bouncing in Tyto's lap.

Then Nikolai, "A Major makes many vows when he or she is sworn into office. One of those vows, as the public knows, is 'no attachments.' This means no romantic relationships and especially no marriages. Tyto Alba broke this vow, and by doing so, placed his own life at risk. Among many witness testimonies, it is pertinent to relay a particular statement, in which Alba urged his personal Guard to escort Adian Vel and her son through tunnels under the Academy. Alba reportedly wanted these tunnels to remain a secret from the public. During times of attack, such tunnels would have been detrimental for evacuation..."

Adian found the courage to move her head several degrees. *Ty...* He was staring at her, had been for some time. Those sharp eyes, alert, expectant.

Baby, Adian mouthed. It was too hot, too loud. Every sound echoed and stretched in her mind like taffy. She heard Nikolai, but how could she be understanding him correctly?

"In accordance with Taxodium laws, this Court hereby finds Tyto Alba guilty of Breach of Duty. He is sentenced to banishment. For the integrity of this venerable institution, his son, Calyx Vel, will be escorted with him off the premises. The unborn child, Corolla Vel, will also be transferred into Tyto Alba's care at the earliest convenience."

It wasn't just her heart that broke—it was her will. Never had she felt so much pain, so much agony—not even when her own parents disowned her, not even when Calyx was born, or now, with the knife-like pain shredding through her torso. No, none of that could compare to the utter hopelessness she felt then, hearing her family's fate reverberate against the wood-paneled walls.

Vera's voice like chalk, "Adian Vel will remain a Ward of the Academy."

Tyto blinked once. Twice. Adian didn't realize the room was smudged because of the tears in her eyes. Tyto leapt to his feet, but the surrounding guards grappled arms around him.

The tears slid down her cheeks as Tyto was shoved through the jeering crowd. Away from her. Away from their daughter.

"She's having a baby!" Her husband's lips screamed. The noise of the people was too great, and his panic was lost in the waves. The things they said...

Adian bowed her head at the puddle in her lap.

The people have spoken.

Corolla Marilena Vel was born ten hours later at 12:01 AM, May 26th, 2004. She was premature, almost two sizes smaller than Calyx had been. While Adian waited for the nurses and doctors to return with equipment, she held her baby girl close.

Tyto was not there to wipe the beads of sweat from Adian's brow. He wasn't there to hear her account of their daughter's birth, and deep down, Adian knew he never would. But she stored the story away in her mind anyway. Maybe she could write it down later and send it in a letter? Maybe she could find out where he was banished to?

This thought alone gave her courage to keep breathing. Adian felt a twinge of guilt and bowed her head at Corolla's pink face. It wasn't her daughter's fault—she had never known her father and brother. No, it wasn't Corolla's fault that Adian lived, not for her daughter's little, fluttering heart, but for the idea of her family, brought together once again. Because if Adian had fixed her world upon that little pulse cradled in her arms, then she may learn to come to terms with her sentencing. However, she had never been very good at accepting her punishments.

Corolla wriggled in her arms, and that was real. Adian felt Tyto and Calyx's absence, and that was real too.

Corolla
August 2020

The tunnel of flames consumes me, a gaping, endless mouth. I choke on sulfur and smoke as fire crackles and scorches my flesh. Though my arms are charring, I don't look at the blackened flesh. I glance above, where Castan's face obscures the tunnel's fiery entrance. He grins, amber and golden light flickering across his features. I want to scream, to call out to him, but the tunnel is a vacuum. And I am suffocating.

My eyelids fly open. As the smoke leaves my senses, my brain perceives the carpet of my room, the pastel green of the walls. I brush hair from the drool trickling down the corner of my mouth. I took out the accessories stabbing my skull before I fell asleep, all the pins and clips scattered along the floor are proof. With a stiff neck, I'm grateful I didn't sleep with a head full of little knives. I shift, massaging my neck, and find that my body is tangled in silky white sheets. I turn over on my side.

And freeze.

I'm not alone.

I thought I dreamt up last night, the sweat and heat of our bodies united. But the nude figure draped across the other half of my bed is evidence that I did not. My eyes travel his bare body, from the hook of his arms over his head to the spread of his legs. He takes up so much of the bed, it's a wonder I didn't fall off in the night. From the skylight, a rectangle of sunlight separates us. In the brilliance, he is so much more than a dream. My imagination could never have conjured the shine of the hair trailing under his belly button; it never could have drawn his expression in such torment, either.

I reach out an arm from the cocoon of sheets to touch him but pause. Raise a brow. Where I cut myself on the fountain chute, my hand has been wrapped in gauze. Something twinges in my stomach, thinking of Castan wandering Argenti at night, naked and hunting through the cabinets and closets for bandages. Color rises to my cheeks; fingers touch my swollen lips. Like a cherished treasure, I tuck this thought away.

I free my other arm and cross through the sunlight to him. I scoot up closer to Castan's head. His dark eyebrows are sloped downwards, facial muscles pinched. With my good hand, I brush the chestnut hair from his eyes and trace the slope of his nose, the curve of his lips, and shape of his chin.

Without warning, he catches my hand and presses my knuckles to his dry lips. He cracks his eyes. A minute grin transforms his face.

"I like that better than an alarm clock," he croaks. His eyes dip to my chest where the sheet has fallen. His grin widens. "I like that better too."

I frown, though my cheeks blaze. "You're feverish again. Do you feel okay?"

His eyes roll back in his skull only to squint at the luminescence of the skylight above. "I feel fine." And then his arms are around me, tugging me across his body so that my head rests on the bulge of his right bicep. Flush against his chest, my cheek cooks on his skin.

"I think you should go see a doctor. Or at least Maggie."

His voice rumbles throughout his chest, vibrating in my ear. "Maggie's not a god," he sounds as if he's falling asleep, "and I'm fine."

With my index finger and thumb, I write slurred messages on his torso that he will never know. "You're shivering."

"And you're drawing letters on my stomach." I pause my work, wondering if I've been found out. He pats my head, and I watch the muscles in his abdomen contract and relax with the movement. He smooths back my tangled hair. I can't help but feel like a cat being stroked. When his movement peters out, I gently push myself out of his grip. He's asleep again, chest rising and falling with ease. I let out a breath I didn't realize I was holding.

I untangle myself from the sheets, careful not to disturb Castan. He's got a peaceful expression—almost a *smug* expression—and I don't dare wake him. I snatch his suit jacket from the floor, admiring the flurry of articles along the carpet. My dress is probably ruined, but I don't let that bother me now. I shove my arms through the sleeves of Castan's jacket and pad downstairs.

The main floor rings with silence. I glance at Talan's door, but it's wide open.

He must not have come back last night.

I move to the kitchen to fetch a glass from the pastel yellow cupboards. I push back the too-long sleeves of the jacket and fill the glass with tap water. Before I climb the stairs again, I lean against the counter. If Talan didn't come home, then he's at Finis's. And if he's at Finis's, where do they think Castan is? My eyes shoot up the walled-in staircase.

"How am I supposed to explain *that?*" I bow my head at the rippling surface of the water. *Do I have to explain that?* My heart squirms. I gasp at the sudden dysrhythmia. What if last night meant nothing to Castan? What if—?

Outside, the world buzzes. I recognize the outburst as the speakers. I've only ever heard them used once—when Rex announced the arrival of the ambassadors and their diplomatic agenda. I go to the front door now and crack it open just enough so that I can distinguish the buzzing for coherent words.

"... at once. Repeat: The Australian Academy is under Genocide attack. All off-duty guards and Trainees report to the Barracks at once."

The glass of water almost slips from my hands. I shut the door, spin, fly up the stairs, spilling water all along the walls. I step around last night's carnage to set the glass on the nightstand by Castan. He shifts in his sleep.

I fling my closet doors wide, shrugging off Castan's jacket. As I hunt for my uniform, my head swims with a mixture of emotion and adrenaline.

Another Academy under attack. Another mass casualty incident—

"What's going on?" Behind me, Castan shuffles out of bed. "Why are you—"

"Just go back to sleep," I say in the most reassuring voice I can muster. "Don't worry about it."

Dammit! I think I left my uniform at James's.

I pull out a different variety of clothes and scurry to shove them on. Castan's opened a window, the message from the lamppost speakers reaching my ears once more.

"The Australian Academy is under Genocide attack. All off-duty guards and Trainees report to the Barracks at once."

"I have to go." Castan's voice is even. Calm. But one look at his expression indicates the level of his sickness. His skin is stretched taut over his facial bones, skin flushed.

I'm beside him before I remember crossing the distance between us. He's managed to slip his briefs on, but the rest of him remains bare. His body trembles with shivers.

"You're sick," I say, apprehension spiking my tone. "And you're not a guard or a Trainee." I ease him back to the bed. When the backs of his calves strike the frame, his knees give out. He collapses on the mattress.

"Just stay here." I move for the doorway, but he grabs my wrist, cautious of the gauze.

"You're not a guard either. Where are you going?"

"James. I have to find James." He nods as if understanding the dire need in my chest to protect the man who raised me. Maybe he does. Maybe he would do the same for Laila.

"But stay here, please? You look awful."

He raises his head, and our eyes meet. For a moment, I forget the noise outside the window, the panic surging through my veins. In that bubble of time, all I know is the glisten of his emerald irises and the way his body felt against mine last night. The feel of his lips and my spine arching just as his head bowed into the crook of my neck, a gust of hot breath on my sweat-soaked skin. In that bubble of time, all I know is that I never wanted to be so close to someone before; I never wanted someone to touch me like that before. I remember when I thought he was too jaded, too military to have a heart. But he does. And it is a gentle one.

"Of course," he says, nodding. "I'll stay."

My heart convulses, and the spell is broken. From below, shouts of command sail through the window along with the monotone call for arms.

Castan brushes his lips across my knuckles. How someone burning with fire can cause such shudders to cascade throughout my being, I don't know. But if I stay any longer, I may never leave.

So I go.

At the doorway, I glance over my shoulder at his figure seated on the edge of my bed. I memorize his solemn expression, the way his hair tickles his eyelashes. His pale skin in the morning light. He offers me a reassuring grin, but the emotion doesn't reach his eyes.

"I'll stay."

I pivot, feet flying down the steps. *James*, I tell myself. *I need to focus on James.* But my heart is fixed on Castan.

I am almost positive he is lying.

Past
June 29th, 2004

Adian cracked open an eye. Laila's footsteps echoed down the hall. She heard the front door open, close. Laila was gone.

Adian flung back the covers of her bed, promises of sleep forgotten. Of course, she hadn't meant it when she told Laila she was going to rest.

"Repairing the northern wall exhausted me, Laila," Adian had practically whined. "I'll be dead asleep as soon as my head hits my pillow."

Adian lied. Repairing the northern wall made her realize something: it was time for her family to be whole again. It was tormenting to stitch together the damage in the line of trees when her own family was in shambles. Tyto and Calyx were almost two months gone from her, and premature Corolla was barely 30 days old, living in the hospital, pink and quiet-mannered as an aloe plant. Adian smirked to herself. If Corolla was aloe, then Calyx was a proliferous forget-me-not, spreading himself over everything like a beautiful contagion.

She missed her son.

Adian slipped on her Caeli boots and took off down the stunted hallway. Anxious, she knew what she had to do: Find Tyto and Calyx.

She opened the pantry door in case she had hallucinated the day those workers stormed her house to seal the tunnel. She hadn't. Where the panel of the sidewall used to slide open and reveal the dank underneath, wooden planks were bolted over the entrance. Adian would have merely grabbed a hatchet to amend this, but she didn't know where to find one. And once she was down there, then what? Surely the other end was blockaded too, maybe with something more than a warning in the form of wooden planks. Getting trapped in the tunnels would only waste time, and time was something she had little of. Before Laila left, she informed Adian that she would be back in an hour to bring her dinner.

Adian backed out of the pantry, blinking away memories of Tyto emerging from those very doors. She went to the back door, with the plan to snake around the perimeter of the Twelfth Wall. She would have to risk being sighted by someone, but what choice did she have? She couldn't just walk into Allen Manor and demand her family's coordinates. If Tyto were here, he could just slip into his Essence of invisibility. But he wasn't here, and Adian had given up on him coming back for her. Something was keeping him from returning to her, she was sure. *She* would not be contained any longer, though.

Adian wrapped cautious hands around the doorknob. She eased the back door open—

"Going somewhere?"

Adian almost jumped out of her skin. She regained her composure, a look of disgust plastering her face.

"Alexander." Perched on the patio, his guard's uniform a second skin, was the traitor. Black sleeves, thick brown armor strapped to his chest, he was exactly as she remembered him. What was different in the hazel set of his eyes? The knowledge of his transgressions, of his betrayals. His testimony. Adian would never un-hear Alex's accusations against Tyto.

She crossed her arms, hoping he wouldn't look at her feet. Seeing as how Caeli boots were only good for battle, training, and sneaking, she—postpartum—could not possibly be doing the former two, which left only the latter.

"What are you doing here?" Adian demanded, maybe a little too defensively. The diamond of her wedding band dug into her arm. Just like St. Philomena, Adian refused to take off her ring. Even if Taxodium expelled her marriage, Adian didn't.

"I could ask you the same thing." Alex, always so irritating. Even when they had been friends, he found little ways to get under her skin. "I like playing with fire," he once laughed when she smacked him for something he'd said.

Adian retorted, "I live here."

"Right, but according to Laila, you're supposed to be sleeping."

Adian was aware of the trap he was carefully setting for her. Her face betrayed nothing. Before, she would have said something smart, like, "Don't you have a Private's ass to wipe?" But that was before. Now, she replied, "Excuse me." Adian moved around his figure and stepped off the patio.

The evening sun was bright, draped over the earth like a napping cat. Wind rustled the trees of the Twelfth Wall. Without meaning to, Adian thought of Laila. Her own Essence was spent after repairing the northern sector; otherwise, she would have spun around and wrapped Alex in a sushi roll of suffocating vines. Had she still been with child, her Essence would have had that spurt of extra energy.

She barely made it out of Aurum's backyard when Alex called, "Adian."

The thought of Tyto, baggy-eyed and deflated, kept her from turning around. She crossed into Aercus's backyard.

"Adian," Alex tried again. She didn't hear him move the distance—he was also wearing Caeli boots—but she felt his presence behind her, a wall. "I came here to apologize."

Adian couldn't tolerate it any longer. James always said she was too much of a spitfire, but her anger was the only thing holding her together anymore. She was losing her mind, and she knew it. Adian spun around, a finger jabbing Alex square in the chest.

"Apologize? You testified *against* my family in front of the Verum Courts!" Adian didn't need to say more. Alex knew what she was accusing him of: *You were my best friend...*

"I bitterly regret what I did—"

"Then why did you do it?" Adian was aware of the tears blurring her vision, of Alex's eyebrows knitting together in thought.

"Because I wanted it to be me. Even when we all believed you were married to a pedes man, I wanted it to be me." The words flowed so smoothly past his lips, it was hardly an admission; it was a fact. Adian sniffled, wiping the tears from her waterline. She knew he loved her—she loved him once herself—but that love was only the kind that two friends possessed. She could never love Alex the way she loved Tyto, just like she could never love Tyto the way she loved her children. There were differences, and Alex knew that.

"Alexander," Adian breathed, "do you realize what you did? Do you—" Her voice cracked, choking on the words in her throat. *You've ruined my life.*

"I know," Alex ducked his blonde head. "I wish I could take it back, Adian. I wish I could take every last drop of it back. I hurt you, and I don't want that." He raised his arms, maybe to embrace her, then dropped them limp at his sides. Adian absorbed his guilt like a sponge. Her anger disappeared beneath the surface. It was still there, but, as she examined it, Adian saw it was not intended for Alex. Neva Rex, Vera and Nikolai Taylor, perhaps, but not Alex. Not *her* Alex. She heard his testimony in her ears. She thought about his promotion, the tattoo on his spine Marking him as a Private. She recalled the way he kissed her once, how she pulled away and wished to slap him. With everyone disappearing from her reservoir, Adian realized she couldn't lose Alex too.

She forgave him.

"Is this you apologizing?" Alex, hearing the shift in her tone, looked up.

"Yes," the word flew from his mouth, eager. "Yes, Adian. I'm so incredibly sorry—"

She threw herself into his arms, knocking the rest of his apology from his tongue. His arms, around her, brought Adian back to her senses. She pulled away.

"I need your help."

Alex glanced at her feet. "Does it have anything to do with your choice of footwear?"

"I need you to distract the Major."

"Oh, God," Alex groaned. A grin toyed with his lips. Despite it all—the hollow pit gnawing Adian's soul, the anchors of guilt in the corners of Alex's eyes—it was almost like normal. Almost.

Alex made good on his word: Neva Rex was outside now, inspecting Adian's repairs to the northern wall. It seemed (and didn't surprise her) that Rex was more than willing to critique Adian's work, hunt for flaws in her designs. Alex and the Major passed by Adian's hiding place in the curtains, and with them, went the guards that stood outside the office doors. In such unstable times, guards were necessary wherever the Major went. When the group disappeared around the corner, Adian slipped into the Major's office.

So much of it was the same, that Adian stood, paralyzed, for a moment. The shelves against the far wall, once dusty but now clean, stuffed full of books. Adian's eyes traveled across the glittering spines. Her gaze landed on the mahogany desk. She possessed so many memories of Tyto sitting on the other side, that they all overlapped and consumed her vision. Adian blinked them away and crossed the floor soundlessly.

She noted the windowsill was bare and wondered if Tyto was permitted to take the terrarium with him. She had tried making the glass orb resemble as much of California as she could. A man with an easel, painting amidst sand and a pointed, pale green dudleya. *Erasmus,* she named the plant, *meaning, the one who loves*. She wanted Tyto to look at it and see his hometown in Napa Valley.

"You're always leaving little worlds behind," Tyto once said after Adian gave his mother a terrarium resembling the beach with a beautiful agave in the middle. Her heart writhed—she still hadn't heard from the Albas. She was almost positive her mail was being watched, and since she wasn't allowed in the Phone Booths, she couldn't call Maurizio and Marilena either.

Adian shook her head and went back to work.

It felt wrong to be on this side of the desk, on Tyto's side. Even after they were properly married, she and Tyto were always careful around Taxodium. One guard overhearing one out-of-place giggle could create an uproar.

Adian, ears straining for noise outside the door, pulled a drawer open. It felt wrong to do this too, not because she was sneaking around, but because Tyto never let her open his drawers.

"It's unprofessional," he explained when she offered to just grab a pen herself. "I can't have you accidentally reading sensitive material."

Adian wasn't sure what she was looking for exactly, but the Major's files seemed like the right place to start. She thumbed through the tabs on the manila folders. Bills, Budgets, Class Rosters, ID Numbers... Registered Essences, Uniforms, Yazd.

Adian closed the drawer and opened another. This one, though promising on the outside because it was big and bulky, was a disappointment. Pens, pencils, tape dispenser, staples, Post-its, and... Adian snatched a glossy square from the back of the supply drawer. She brought it into the light from the window behind her.

It was a family photo. That much was evident in the uncomfortable, forced smiles of the two young men in the front. Clean shaven, clean cut, dirty blonde hair. Twins, Adian knew at once. They had even dressed the same, red knit sweaters and black dress pants. Adian guessed they were nineteen or twenty, maybe just graduated from the Academy. Her eyes skated over Neva Rex and rested on her husband. Her first thought: *How could anyone love Rex?* Then she studied the man herself. His face was wrinkled like a piece of paper folded too many times. Lines across his forehead, lines in the corners of his eyes. Lines at the edges of his lips.

He must have smiled a lot. This observation surprised Adian. Without meaning to, she examined the younger Rex. Adian guessed this family photo was taken before Rex climbed the ranks in Tax's army. There were no streaks of gray in her hair. The skin on her long face was taut, stretched over bone and muscle. But she looked... happy, and that puzzled Adian.

Adian set the photo back in the drawer, slid it shut. Neva Rex lost her family in an encounter with the Dentatas years ago. Rex was a barren widow, Tyto mentioned as much after one of his meetings with the former Commander.

Despite herself, Adian found pity seeping into the hatred within her veins. This woman lost it all. Even though Tyto and Calyx were gone from her, death would be a more devastating loss. For Tyto's soul to be snuffed out forever, forgotten through the passage of time... How many people expired that way, forgotten and all their loved ones with them? How many people lived that no one would ever know about?

These thoughts hurt Adian's head, so she stuffed them away and resumed her search. She pawed through the rest of the drawers and one cabinet but found nothing. Above her head, she felt the pressure of the clock ticking on the wall. The sun was setting, and Alex couldn't distract the Major all night. Adian scanned the office.

"What did I miss?" She mumbled to herself, nerves a set of bells in her stomach. She was surprised the guards on the level below didn't come running at the noise.

If not in her desk, then where would she keep it? Tyto's location had to be documented somewhere. The Board of Majors decided upon Tyto's exile, and every Board meeting had notes.

Notes.

Adian whirled around, scanning the bookshelves. The gold and silver engraved words whipped past her hurried hunt. She didn't find it in the volumes of past Board meetings. She spied it sticking up between *Holds—And Other Pyrus-Made Designs,* and *J. Rainier's Contemporaries: The Evolution Behind the Essence.* With steady, desperate hands, Adian ripped the sheet of paper off the shelf.

She unfolded the thick white leaf, hungry for the coordinates. They wouldn't send him to Cali because that's where he was born and raised; it was too obvious. Maybe someplace out of the States? Adian pictured Calyx running down the slopes of Tuscany, an orange sun pulsing at his back. Alex seemed to think Tyto was banished somewhere South, but Italy would be nice. Italy could be home.

And then Adian read the printed words. Her shoulders sagged.

The Board hadn't only decided Tyto's banishment. They also decided to kill her.

Adian fumbled in disbelief. She reread the Mandate five times. The words were still the same. And Tyto and Calyx's location wasn't there.

Adian thought about shoving the paper back where she found it, but no… No, she folded in half and in half again and jammed it in her back pocket. Rex wasn't allowed to hold her fate her hands anymore. Tyto would know what to do. Yes, when she found Tyto, she would show it to him. He could explain why the very organization she had come to love was plotting—had *approved*—to assassinate her.

How quick people were to change, to betray.

Adian's thoughts tripped over themselves, darting in all different directions. Her heart beat against her ribs, spattering blood. The office, once a familiar atmosphere, expanded and shrank before her. All this time protecting herself against the Dentatas, and Taxodium was the enemy. How could that be correct? Through the panic, her motherly instinct took root.

One thing was for certain: She may never find Tyto and Calyx, but at least she could save Corolla.

Laila flew across the Manor halls, boots scuffing against the polished tiles. Tyto had barely left the office before Neva Rex was voted in to replace him as Major. Rex wouldn't be pleased when she heard what Laila had to say. Laila passed the empty block of wall where Tyto's portrait had been removed. The space usually glared at her—as if *she* had been the one to take down the picture—but she didn't have time to feel its stare today.

"Major Rex!" Laila exploded through the French doors to the Major's office, so quickly, she didn't bother to salute her leader. The office was the exact same in appearance, the exact mahogany desk, bookshelves, and leather-bound volumes. But Tyto Alba's calm eyes were no longer behind that desk. A pair of cool blues were. The atmosphere had shifted. Where Alba had been someone warm and approachable, Rex was an arctic wind. Laila shivered without realizing.

"She's gone!" Laila gasped. "Adian Vel is gone. Stole a car, jumped onto the highway. No idea where she went."

If Laila was a frenzy, Rex was a statue. Her thin hands folded atop her desk, eyebrows a straight line across her forehead, a mop of dark hair salted with gray streaks. A sigh squeezed between her teeth, highlighted the creases around her lips.

"Yes, I know. After Alba, I'm sure."

Despite herself, Laila cocked her head. Breathless, she asked, "You knew she would escape?"

The Major nodded, and Laila found herself wondering why, of all the candidates, Rex had been the one elected by the people. She was too cold, too calculated, nothing at all like Alba.

But that's probably precisely why the people chose her.

"Respectfully, ma'am—I know Adian isn't privy to Alba's location, but that doesn't mean she can't guess. Are you sending people after her and her child?"

"Of course," her voice was pinched, if not entirely calloused. She stood, and Laila noticed for the first time a gold glint on the woman's left hand. A wedding band. But the Major's husband? Laila could only assume he was no longer alive, as Majors weren't permitted to be attached.

The Major must have seen Laila's gaze, for she then said, "He was killed in an altercation a decade ago, along with both of my sons."

"Oh." Laila bowed her head, ashamed to have been caught staring.

"You all think me very harsh, don't you? It's not that I don't understand Vel's situation. To be torn from a husband and a son in a single day... But still, duty before family. Always. What's done is done."

Laila snapped her attention to the Major. "Ma'am, I'm not sure I follow."

"Perhaps not. Regardless, I have sent people after Vel to save her from further harm."

"And Corolla?" Laila balanced on the balls of her feet. She had been fond of Calyx and was looking forward to taking care of Corolla until she was ready to join her brother and father. But more than that, Laila was worried about Adian. She hadn't been in her right mind since… since Corolla's birth, perhaps even earlier.

"Maybe it's best she lives with Tyto now. At any rate, Adian is not in a functional state of mind to care for another's life."

So. I'm not the only one who's noticed.

"'What's done is done,' ma'am?"

The Major seemed to be far away, even as she answered, "Forget I said anything, Cassena. I'm fatigued with paperwork, phone calls, and meetings." Laila twisted the rings around her fingers. Of course the new Major was waterlogged. The Dentatas almost breached the Academy and guards were killed. To make matters worse, pedes were poking around the farmland, asking about the fire and reported "disturbances."

"If you'll please excuse me," Rex continued, "I have an appointment with Chief Ramsey."

The Major left with years of distance spreading across her face. Laila was sure there was something she was missing. What, she could not say, only that the look in the Major's eyes filled her own heart with dread.

Where did Adian go?

Castan

August 2020

I down the half-empty glass of water Corolla brought up for me. Swipe a hand across my brow. My temples throb and I long for a cup of coffee, for the routine of it.

"You always smell like brewed coffee." My blood slows—I wish we had a day, a morning. I wish we had more than a night to be together, to be ourselves without the weight of the world pressing in on all sides. But I can't indulge right now, not with the chaos mounting across campus like rolling waves of a storm.

I brush the thoughts away and scan the carpet. I need better clothes than a suit.

Down in Talan's room, I fling his closet doors wide. Everything is color coded, labeled with white stickers. I locate the one I was hoping for. *Fin's* in neat black print. I can't hope to fit into Talan's clothes, just like I can't hope to go to battle in a dress suit.

I tug on the ebony skin, one of Finis's numerous spare uniforms. The fabric chafes around my thighs, is loose around my shoulders. With deft hands—hands familiar with this motion—I strap the plated armor to my chest and groin. I slip on the Caeli boots and plunge outside.

In the courtyard, my sickness surrenders to adrenaline. Not a soul travels the cobbled streets. All gathered at the Barracks, I imagine. Over the hill on my right, the spires atop the Dining Hall protrude towards a bundle of wispy clouds. These Sentries lay dormant while others will be firing at an Academy elsewhere. I skim over the bronze fountain, water trickling with memories of last night. Ambassador Collingwood's door has been thrown open, a gaping mouth across from Argenti. Aercus's lights are on, but my senses focus on the message relaying over the lamppost speakers.

"The Australian Academy is under Genocide attack. All off-duty guards and Trainees report to the Barracks at once. Repeat: The Australian Academy is under Genocide attack. All off-duty guards and Trainees report to the Barracks at once."

How long has it been playing? How long has the Australian Academy been under attack? Of all the times I don't have a geometer...

All of this takes but seconds for me to absorb. Then I am moving, heart pounding in my temples. In my head, a map of the Academy lays before me. It'll be faster to get to the Barracks if I cut through the gardens. My feet are already pounding in that direction, soundless against the red brick road.

I think about all the times I took this road to class with Calyx, all the times we met up with Kass and Maggie on our way. I meet no one now, the only sound my own ragged breathing and the monotone voice of the speakers. Kass will be flinging herself into battle if she hasn't already. I have to go with her. There is no hesitancy in my decision.

I push on, jumping with the grace of a gazelle over the hedges enclosing the gardens. The stone turrets poke over the vegetation and small decorative trees. Though I run as fast as I can, those turrets don't seem to get any closer. I cough at the aromatic perfume of some of the flowers, each one a gray blur, no matter their brilliant colors. Mulch shifts under my soles.

I duck under a low hanging branch and burst into the garden clearing. The ground solidifies into gray slate, Adian Vel's monument glinting ahead of me. Though my lungs are exhausted, I don't pause for breath. I zoom past the memorial, imagining the truckloads of soldiers leaving without me, the devastation the Gens are creating while my lungs burn and muscles groan—

"Castan."

My whir of thoughts and tensed muscles halt. Amidst the fragrance of the butterfly bushes flanking this trail, a new scent tickles my nostrils.

Old men's cologne.

Without thinking, my hands fly for my waist, but my knife isn't there. A cackle resounds through the air. The hairs on the back of my neck stand on end. Maybe I imagine it, the same way I imagined Hadley in Belarus. Maybe. I turn.

And see the face from my nightmares.

He stands, hands shoved in the pockets of his jeans, among the drooping branches of the two willow trees framing the path's entrance. Behind him, Adian Vel's glimmering backside reflects the morning sun.

"Rosh."

He swipes a thumb across his bottom lip as if to mask the grin taking shape there. "You're defenseless, little brother. What would our father say?"

I take a single step closer, mulch under my boots. "Is he here too?"

Rather than answer, Rosh nods over his shoulder. "Come closer. It's been too long." He pivots, his broad back and dark crown an oddity among such light and beauty of the gardens. Though I am all too aware of the crimes Rosh has committed, my feet follow his loping gait. Like a moth drawn to a flame.

In the clearing, he's seated himself on one of the stone benches. He pats the place beside him. I don't sit.

"How did you get here?" The question tumbles past my lips, but my sense of urgency remains pinned to my heart. If Rosh is here, then who else is? Who is at the Australian Academy? And Corolla?

Flames tickle my palms, the stench of sulfur fumigating the air. Rosh raises an eyebrow.

"It won't be long now, will it? Before you are extinguished for good." He shifts in place so that his elbows rest on his knees. He grins. "When I was being neutralized, killing helped ease that pain. It can help you too."

"No."

He shrugs, and when he meets my gaze again, there is a frown on his face. It doesn't make his expression any less cruel. "Something's wrong, Castan. And I need your help."

"You never needed it before."

"No, but our father was never so weak before. He's a bootlicker, Castan." Black irises, dark hair—I know how much we resemble one another. And if anyone lays eyes on him, they will know what I have strived to conceal since the day I walked past those Academy gates.

When I don't respond, Rosh says, "He disgraces the Dentata name by taking orders from this Renatus fellow." He raises his head, black eyes emanating frustration.

"Renatus?"

Rosh bows his head into his lap, chuckling. "Your Latin has never been fluent, has it? Even when you abandoned your Carnage victory for this venerable institution? It means *reborn*, you idiot! Our father seems to be under this man's spell."

I shrug, palms burning. "I don't care about Jon."

Rosh stands. "Dentatas don't follow outsiders—we make them suffer. I'm going to challenge our father for the title of Numen. I want you by my side when I do."

I have been listening with a stone expression, but now it cracks with surprise. I amend my composure, anger and grief plating my profile. I spit through gritted teeth, "I would kill you first."

"Yes," Rosh chuckles. He holds up the hand he's been concealing in his pocket. "I believe you earned a legacy for this." He wriggles his fingers and the nub of what used to be his left index. I feel nothing, no shame, no sympathy. I want to hurt him more.

Rosh continues, "But you're deteriorating, Castan. How does it feel to suffer from the very disease these people—" he raises his arms, gesturing to the Academy, "—have placed within you? How can you defend them after the pain in your own body because of their actions?"

"Because *this* pain is bearable. What isn't bearable, is the number of people you have butchered just for the sport of it!"

His eyes flicker across my expression. "After you left, we did a rematch. I won Carnage. I earned my right to the season's first kill."

"You have no conscience, Rosh. You're as deranged as your old victims!" Flames jump to my palms. Rosh eyes my fire, the orange and yellow swirls reflecting in his black irises. He grins, and I remember the streets of Iran, the pool of blood and hopelessness laying there in the dirt. I remember crimson-soaked sheets and the raw emotion of loss shredding my being afterward. So I don't care if I'm playing into Rosh's hands. I don't care that he's here or that I'm missing the call to arms. In this moment, I only care that he never hurts another person again.

"Your blood boils with hatred, little brother. Your heart sings with self-destruction. I can help you channel that elsewhere. I can—"

"You are the reason!" I bellow, spit flaring with the momentum of my words. "You are the reason so many lives have been lost, so many families have been broken. How can you expect me to join you after you've taken so much?" My voice snaps with emotion, but the crackling torrents of flames drown the noise. Rosh rolls to the ground, just escaping my fire. The willows combust in spheres of amber, sulfur, and smoke, paying the price for my miss.

On his knees, Rosh pushes himself to his feet. His hands hide behind his back, but I know—after years of growing up with him—I know. He's got a gun in his waistband.

"Our father isn't as powerful as he pretends to be," Rosh wipes sweat from his forehead with the back of his impaired hand, "You and I could overthrow him, lead the Dentatas together—"

"You bastard." Arms arching at my sides, I release a spray of scorching flames towards Rosh. He manages to avoid the heart of the blow, but the bench he was sitting on earlier does not. Sparks ignite the vegetation around it, meeting with flames from my first attack. Rosh bows under the heat, smacking the fire snaking up the side of one arm. All behind him, orange and gray destroy the beautiful gardens Adian Vel created.

"Castan," Rosh pants, "I don't understand you. Why do you stay? Why do you turn your back on your family?" His black gaze meets my cold one.

"You have never been my family." To my surprise, Rosh flinches. But the reaction is quickly swept under a mask of rage. Rosh sneers, rolling the long sleeves of his flannel up to his elbows. He prowls like a lion. I follow the movement, palms ready.

"I won Carnage. I killed scouts all up and down North America. But you know what? Our father still ignored me! What he ever saw in you, Castan, is a mystery. You, pathetic, emotional creature." He withdraws the black handgun from behind his back. I don't even blink. "And after you left, he turned his attention to Hadley. It didn't matter that she was only fourteen and as stubborn as our mother. What mattered was that she wasn't me." Rejection rips through his tone, but my eyes are on the gun clenched in his white-knuckled fist.

"It's because you remind him of himself." Rosh disappears behind Adian Vel, but I saunter to match his pace. We come out the other side of the statue together, opposite one another. Under the statue's cupped hands, Rosh shoots me a wicked grin.

"No," he shakes his head, "it's because I'm stronger than him. He's afraid. You know when our father became the new Numen, he attacked this Academy? Well, he had Adian Vel right there, in his hands—and he got himself blown up. The Gens could never touch her again. But I, I killed Calyx, years later. I came closer to glory than our father ever will. He's a puppet—"

Overhead, something rips through the cloudy sky, air shrieking with its momentum. I crane my head to watch the high-velocity object sink closer and closer to the Academy. My heart stops: it's headed for the Barracks. Before my muscles work, the missile strikes the earth. I feel its vibrations through the soles of my boots. Screams swell in the distance. Black masses of smoke sprout from the direction of the Barracks. The alarms slice through the Academy, the high-pitched squealing cutting my eardrums.

I turn back to Rosh, unable to mask the shock in my voice when I shout, "What did you do?" It doesn't matter that the gardens are ablaze—*this* Academy is under attack.

Laughter bubbles in my brother's throat, but his chest heaves with coughs. Smoke—*my* smoke—fills his lungs. He regains his composure and grins, flashing white teeth. "The thing about Taxodium is that they are too trusting, too gullible. I didn't need Renatus's guidance to know that."

"The Australian Academy…"

"A ruse," Rosh is smug, pleased with himself. "And all the Guard has already left to defend an Academy that is perfectly safe. Defenseless, this place is a sinking ship."

Corolla. I need to find Corolla.

Fury spirals throughout my veins. The flames in my hands burn brighter—too bright for Rosh to gaze upon. He blinks—I lunge past the monument, taking advantage of his blindness. My body rockets into him. We crash to the ground, Rosh groaning at the impact, me grabbing his collar.

"You murdered my best friend!" I clutch his shirtfront, the fabric melting in my hands. Rosh grimaces, bites his lip to keep from crying out as fire licks his flesh. I ignore the smell of his skin charring, his cologne burning up in the heat of my anger.

"I was jealous," Rosh squeals. His profile twists in agony. He raises his gun towards my gut, but I knock the weapon from his hand. My knees dig into the stone floor, and I force Rosh harder into the ground.

Through gritted teeth, I hiss, "Liar. You have always been cruel, just like our father. You take and take and take, Rosh. You felt nothing when our mother was dragged by her hair from our home. You felt nothing when you slashed a knife through Calyx's abdomen. You don't know what love and loss are. You're incapable of such emotions, you fucking monster." Fire laces his neck like a noose. Beneath me, Rosh writhes and squirms. I don't loosen my hold. Not this time.

Tears flood from the cracks of his eyes. I glimpse his black, animal eyes. "How could I not be jealous?" He rasps through the pain. "I saw you two together! You replaced me, Castan, before I even had a chance to be your brother."

Pity crawls into my heart, but I shove it aside. Images of Calyx, drowning in a puddle of his own blood rush back to me. Despite the smoke and sulfur, that metallic stench worms its way into my senses. I clamp my hands down around his neck harder. This time, Rosh does cry out. The sound cuts to my bones. His tears evaporate before they fall from the corners of his eyes as I will the fire to climb his outline. It won't go anywhere I don't want it to, but I want—yes, I *want*—Rosh to feel pain. To feel agony and suffering.

"How many people will you take away from me, Rosh, before you realize that I will *never* love you?"

"It was my job," he struggles, and I know his airway is closing, "to make you tough." A noise escapes past his lips, unlike any laugh I have ever heard. Brittle. It sounds brittle. "I guess I succeeded. Look at you, brother. Look at yourself."

I blink, seeing my hands around Rosh's throat, flames a glove around my fingers. But they aren't just blanketing my hands. I stand, Rosh's blazing body below me. I raise my arms, incredulous: My entire body is coated in an aura of fire. Head to toe, I am burning. But where Rosh blisters with the light, I am unscathed.

I pick up the handgun from the ground. Cock it. I glance at my brother, meeting his scalding eyes. The fire ate away his eyelashes, face black with burns. I cover my nose to escape the wretched smell of igniting hair. He should be dead. He should have died long ago. But Rosh has always been strong.

I aim the gun at his head.

His voice is so stripped of its tone, I barely make out his words. I imagine him grinning, but, strangely enough, not one of his wicked ones. "The gardens... are infamous for... their perfection," each word is a struggle, "but thank you... for destroying them... for me."

The flames protecting my being suddenly vanish. I blink tears from my eyes, throat thick with smoke and something else I try to ignore. Rosh doesn't deserve to live, doesn't deserve my mercy, but staring down at him now, I can't bring myself to walk away and let him burn. I can't bring myself to let him die alone.

"Bellator, vale."

I pull the trigger. The shot is almost lost to the cacophony of screams and wailing sirens. Ahead of me, one of the Sentries fires at the gate. I focus on the missile's path, unable to look at the charred figure below me any longer.

I sniffle, tuck the gun in the belt around my waist.

Every fire has a heart. I find mine easily, grasping it in one fist. The flames gradually disperse, but the damage has already been done. The Adian Vel Gardens sprawl across shaded land, her monument standing tall in the center of blackened earth.

Above the horrors of the battle, a scream pierces my ears. Hands shaking, heart bleeding, I bolt towards that sound—I've heard it before.

Past
June 2004

"Dee? What are you doing here?" James rounded the strange black vehicle in his driveway, recognizing the shape of his sister at once. He hadn't seen her in almost a year, not since their mother's funeral. For a brief moment, he was elated with her arrival. Then he saw her blank, red-eyed expression. She had been crying.

Adian jolted in the driver's seat. James imagined a sort of painful reality flooding into the cracks of her mind. The agonizing look on her face all but spelled it out for him: Adian *was* in pain. But why?

"Has something happened? Where's Calyx? Tyto?" Was it his imagination, or did Adian flinch? It was too dark outside to tell.

"I'm sorry," his sister apologized, though he was not quite sure why. "I... I need to ask a favor."

As if on cue, the lump in the passenger's seat squirmed in her wool blankets.

"Oh my gosh—Adian! I didn't know you had her already," James exclaimed. "Why are you all alone with her? Where is Tyto?" He was serious now, and his tone expressed it.

Adian ducked her head, palmed her eyes. "I woke up one day, and I was grown up, James." She glanced at him then. "Remember when we tried camping in the backyard, and it got so cold, we hallucinated a bonfire in the middle of our tent?"

"Yes," James was certainly confused, "but Dee, what the hell is going on? I'm glad to see you, but *what* are you doing here?"

"You have to take Corolla, James. I have to go on a trip... I have to see Tyto and Calyx again... before... please, take her? Love her?" Helpless. So blatantly helpless, she gazed up at him with those sugar-brown eyes rimmed red and purple with exhaustion. She looked horrible.

James opened the driver's door. "Come inside," he suggested. "Let's talk about this." He had no idea what *this* was, but it clearly gnawed on Adian like a dog on a bone.

Adian was shaking, undoing her seatbelt. "Corolla. Get Corolla please and stay out of the shadows. That's the worst place for her. She must stay in the light. Warmth..." Adian broke off. James hooked an arm under her shoulder.

"Let's go inside, Dee. C'mon." James maneuvered his sister from the seat and half carried her to the house. He came back and unstrapped his niece, so small and so precious, from her car seat. It was then that he really noticed the big black van his sister had arrived in.

Inside, he asked her, "That's not your vehicle. Where did it come from?"

"Taxodium," she answered without pause. She had landed on the couch, a gift from their parents years ago. "I stole it."

"*Stole* it?" James hugged Corolla a little tighter to his chest. He had never been fond of children, as he had never possessed the skills to care for one. In that moment, though, he knew she was his; Adian... Adian was unreachable, and a small part of him accepted this. A larger part of him brimmed with worry.

He took a seat next to her. "Tell me what happened."

Adian was mechanical, almost robotic in her answer. "There was an attack two months ago. Dentatas outside the Twelfth Wall. I..." she struggled to grasp the words, "I don't know exactly how things came to be. Before the Sentry misfired, things are... fuzzy."

"Adian," James felt as if he were sitting on needles. "*What* are you talking about?"

Her crazed eyes jumped to his. "Ty almost died trying to save me. The people... they found out I was his wife. There was a trial, the Verum Courts came, prosecuted us, banished him and Calyx somewhere. South, I think. Alex thinks maybe South. I don't know exactly where. Wasn't allowed to know. I tried finding the papers about his whereabouts, but I-I found something else. I have to say goodbye."

Adian shot to her feet like a rocket. She turned to James, a stream of tears trailing down her cheeks.

"Please take care of my daughter. You are the safest place for her."

"Of course, but—"

"And make sure she knows," Adian was sobbing now, "that I love her. That I didn't turn her out the way Mom did to me."

James wrapped an arm around his sister, clumsy with a child cradled in his other. His eyes, deep blue wells of questions, implored hers.

"No, James," Adian wiped away all her tears with the back of her hands. "I can't explain the universe to you. This is just how it has to be. Protect her from the Dentatas. Protect her from them all. She's... special."

"Stay, Dee. We can figure something out. Something better than you beating yourself up."

Adian ignored him, was already dashing for the door. "I have to go."

"At least stay the night," James pleaded. "You look exhausted."

"Can't," she shook her head. "I have to… James." She looked at him one last time. James felt tears slipping from the corners of his eyes. "James, you were the best brother an orphan could ask for."

"Versailles," he spat around the lump in his throat. "If you were a building, I always saw you as Versailles."

"Oh, James." A hand on his cheek. "I love you. I love you both so very much." A kiss on his forehead and the one sleeping in his arms. Headlights in the driveway, a monster van chugging down the road. Warmth streaming down his face.

James bowed his head at the life in his arms. His tears rested upon her forehead, slid down her flesh. Pink skin, soft skull. *Corolla*, Adian had named her after the petals of flowers. But she was so small, so fragile. How could he transform this little bundle into a capable individual? How could he raise her at all?

"The calyx holds the corolla," Adian told him once in their youth during one of their expeditions at the library. *"That's what I'll name my children one day."*

"You are your sister's keeper, James," his mother often told him when they were young. *"You two are like halves of an orange. Without each other, your flesh is vulnerable and exposed."*

"I'm not your keeper—you're mine," he wanted to tell Adian. But his sister was gone. Gone.

Adian pulled the bulky black van over to the side of the road. After resting through the night in a vacant lot somewhere in Ohio, she had left early that morning. She didn't think about Corolla or James. She thought about Tyto and Calyx, the impossibility stretching between them. She tried calling Maurizio and Marilena, but the number she dialed wouldn't connect. She couldn't remember Luca or Orsino's numbers, and her panicked thoughts were no help. And so, she drove onwards, searching and searching, refueling only when the dash flashed a threatening *Empty*.

She was somewhere in Tennessee now, the roads lined with trees blooming purple. Night was falling, and not a soul could be seen down this backroad. Not a soul, except one.

Adian hopped out of the driver's seat and slammed her door shut. She was aware of the tatters of her mind, but she wasn't imagining the figure standing in the road before her. She couldn't be. *Couldn't* be. He was real.

"Adian," that voice greeted, and she felt tears spring to her eyes. Cicadas hummed in the descending darkness.

"What took you so long?" She wrapped her arms around him, and he did the same. *Ty...* She inhaled mahogany and cedar. She almost asked where Calyx was, but she knew he couldn't be far.

"It's been a war on all fronts," he chuckled into her ear. "But I'm here now."

Adian stepped back, grinning in a way she hadn't in months. "I've been searching for days, waiting for months. Corolla," Adian struggled to speak coherently, "she's just beautiful. Just like Calyx."

"I know. I know. Come here." He opened his arms, and she fell back into him. Relief flooded her body.

"I've finally found—" Something pierced her back just below her shoulder blade. Pain seared her flesh, and she staggered backward.

"What…" Adian looked up at Tyto's face, but it wasn't Tyto. It never had been. She blinked, tripping and crumbling to the pavement. Hot liquid oozed down her backside, but she couldn't tear her gaze from the man towering over her. He adjusted his cufflinks, brushing his lapels, though they were spotless.

"Did you really think the Dentatas would send a man, so obviously out of place?" Adian shook her head and blinked hard at the pain rippling through her body. "No, Tyto didn't catch a spy. He caught a prisoner with nothing left to lose. And in doing so, he catalyzed a change larger than your comprehension."

Bits of asphalt dug into her knees. Shots of clarity struck her thoughts. She sneered at that cordial grin. "What the hell is your game?"

"Freedom." He withdrew a second knife from the inside of his jacket. Adian wondered if the first was still stuck in her back. It had to be, but she couldn't tell.

The man kneeled, and through her pain-clouded thoughts, his awful voice reached her. "Pelari shouldn't be sinking under the pedes' yoke of ignorance. We should be commanding this planet, ruling it and expanding our own people's potential. Because we all have it, but until we can go public, pelari are limited. We've been limited since the days of Emperor Augustus." He drove his second knife under her other shoulder blade. Adian screamed out in agony. Her pain pierced the night, silencing the melody and harmony of creatures. The night became silent as if the world were watching vigil. As if the world had already accepted her death.

"Phaedra curse you," she spat through gritted teeth.

"*Phaedra* set a terrible precedent. I aim to break it," the man tisked. "But don't worry, Adian. Your body will find its way back to Taxodium intact. I still need the Dentatas for my own purposes. And besides," he shot her a wry grin, "I have a feeling your offspring will serve the greater purpose you never could."

"Stay away from my children!" Adian meant to convey the anger spiking her blood, but she was losing so much of her vitality, the words dribbled past her lips in a whisper.

"Didn't you wonder about the Sentries? 'Why oh why oh why aren't they working?' Because of the Genocides. Because I told them to. Did I mean for Tyto to get shot?" He shrugged. "Not really, no. But that bastard Jon paid in blood for that error when the Sentry's missile ravaged his own people. But of course, you don't remember that, do you? Strange what lightning can do to you, the very pelari potential I am fascinated with." He yanked the knives from her back, and Adian bit back vocal cord ripping screams. Her vision speckled black and gray. Her lips mouthed his name.

"No." He placed a foot on her chest and pushed her back with little effort. She fell on her back, writhing in pain. "I don't answer to that name anymore." He kneeled over her once more. "Taxodium will crumble. I need the break to be complete. I need the fall to be bloody. With two worlds wrapped around my fingers, the task will be easy. My life isn't the length of Pyrus's, but it will be a long one. And I intend to take my time with this and enjoy it." A laugh rumbled through his chest, but the noise tangled in Adian's ears. She reached out a hand, willing her Essence to cooperate.

The man regarded her movement. "The Board called for your death, but you should know that I had no hand in that Mandate. I haven't reached that level of infiltration yet, but that's what the rest of my life is for." He inspected the crimson pool surrounding her. "Yes," he mused in a tone she had heard on so many doctor's lips, "you will bleed to death. Not as slowly as I wanted, but it will do."

In her mind, Adian cursed him to Hell. Death was upon her, but she wasn't prepared to face her mother yet; she wasn't ready to relinquish *being* a mother yet. Her eyes fixed on the diamond budding her scraped knuckle. Her heart broke long ago. But still, it throbbed with the knowledge that her last image of Tyto had been flailing arms, a guard escort out of Allen Manor. What was he doing now? Was Calyx behaving himself?

The man pulled a handkerchief from his breast pocket and wiped the edge of his twin blades. Her blood soaked the cloth just as it soaked her clothes and hair. St. Philomena gazed silver eyes from her resting place in the dirt. Adian closed her own eyes and thought the only words she could:

Prega per noi.

"They call me Renatus, Adian. This is a new era, sweet antidote, but you will not live to resist it."

Corolla
August 2020

"James!" I leave the cobbled street, parting from the crowd of people pushing towards the Barracks. I make my way towards that familiar blonde head. "James!" My frantic cry is almost lost to the noise of many voices, the static of the speaker's announcement. I couldn't find him at Aercus, but I managed to slip into my uniform. Just in case.

"Corolla, what's going on?" He grunts as I throw myself into his arms. His arms fall on my back, head resting on top of my own. I pull away.

"I've looked everywhere for you. What are you doing in the library? The Australian Academy is under attack." I suck in oxygen, cheeks stinging red from running so hard so fast.

His blue eyes expand. "It is?" He rubs the back of his neck. "I didn't even hear anything in the library," he gestures over his shoulder at the brick building, "it's so quiet in there. Maybe we should go back. Wait for this excitement to die down."

"James—" I break off. The announcement didn't call for pedes, did it? It called for guards and Trainees. But I can't just sit still while the Australian Academy is under attack. It may be one of the smallest Academies, but people still live there. Lives are still in danger.

"What did you do to your hand?" James catches my bandaged hand between two palms. He meets my gaze, demanding an answer.

"Just a cut," I explain. I shrug, but blood rushes to my face. I think about Castan lying naked beside me, his hot breath on my neck. How would James react if he found out? But I can't think about that now.

"James," I tug my hand from his grasp, "where's Laila? There's got to be something we can do to help."

"Corolla," he sighs, eyes following the scatter of people around us, "I don't think—"

Something whizzes through the sky above. James and I crane our heads, searching for the source of the noise—the earth shakes as the object crashes into the Barracks. Plumes of ebony smoke shoot through the air. Screams rip through the golden beauty of the morning. And then a high-pitched wailing crashes over the top of every other noise.

The alarms.

I clutch James's wrist, his eyes clouded with confusion. Maybe he knows what the alarms mean. Maybe he's too dumbstruck to piece it together.

"The Academy is under attack!" I yell over the discord of injured bodies begging for help, vengeful bodies bellowing for an ordered line of defense. But even I know—I passed so many black vans barreling through the streets for the gates—that the Guard has abandoned us for the Australian Academy. In this battle, we are alone.

"We have to find cover," James shouts into my ear. He tugs me towards the library, but I pull him back.

"No." My neurons fire with so many thoughts, so many possibilities, that I can't pin down any one idea. *The Barracks are in flames: no weapons. The Academy is under attack: no Guard. And what can I do?*

I yank James back again, and yell, "Aurum. We have to get to Aurum House. There's a way out." Despite all those morning sessions with Talan, all those Defensive Training classes, I am useless in a real fight. It's better for me to admit this than plunge headlong into a battle I can't win. But I can get James out of here. I can keep him safe until we figure out what to do.

James doesn't argue. He nods, squeezes my hand in his, and we take off through the crowd of people fleeing the Barracks. As we push through the thick stream of pelari, I don't see any familiar faces. For once, my heart and mind operate in unison, scouring the crowd for two: *Talan. Castan.* Students and staff alike are flurries of voices, eyes wide with fear. They don't understand what's happening. No, they don't know how this *could* have happened.

Dragging James behind me, I ignore the mass confusion. I think about telling these people about Aurum's tunnels, but the opportunity never presents itself. A scream ripples through the crowd of bobbing heads. I hear a fleshy noise, and a body slumps to the ground. The crowd parts and Kale towers over the figure of a small-framed boy with red hair. He's dead. That much is evident in the angle of his neck. Kale beams, blood spattering his chocolate breastplate.

"Let it be known," he raises his head at the bewildered crowd, "that pelari will rise under Renatus. He reigns!"

The speakers on the lampposts screech, and I refrain from covering my ears at the hideous noise. A deep, crackling voice crows over and over, "Renatus reigns! Renatus reigns!"

Kale brandishes his knife, stepping towards the crowd. Behind him, I recognize the same group that always surrounded him during DT. Malicious grins overcome their profiles. From their uniform belts, they each withdraw a weapon—knife, gun, crossbow.

"Traitors!" Someone shouts. The accusation hangs in the air for less than a second. Then all hell breaks loose. Pelari dive towards Kale and his people, who plunge forward with vicious cries shredding through the noise of battle. Knives meet flesh. Shouts meet screams. Blood meets blood.

James is shoving me away from the slaughter. *The tunnels*, I want to say, *go to the tunnels*. But as pelari turn on pelari all around us, I don't know who's a traitor and who's not. And elbow jabs into my side and a limp body flies over our heads. James flinches with each sound, but we manage to break free from the mass uninjured. I hold onto James's damp hand like a lifeline, almost positive my grip has broken his bones.

"This way," I say, though my words are lost in the sounds of battle. We snake around the West Dorms and meet another sight just as terrible as the last.

The gardens are blazing, each supple bud burning with the heat of growing flames. And, as if a beacon amidst the destruction, Adian Vel towers in the glow of orange and red. But the statue isn't the only thing in the clearing. Two figures pace. They could be identical, except that one is of larger proportions. The smaller man turns, and through the tunnel of flames, I glimpse his face.

"Castan."

I'm hardly aware of James pulling me alongside the ugly backside of the dorms. I'm barely aware of the patios we cross, the lawn chairs we kick aside. The larger man turns, and, even at this distance, I know his face too. It is Castan's.

I tear my gaze from the scene across the burning plane, my heart breaking under more than the pressure of fear and adrenaline.

James and I come out onto the cobbled street. I don't have to tell him which way to go—if we just follow this road, it will empty out into the courtyard of the Ward Residencies. My feet are soundless, but James's *clack, clack* on the rust-red bricks. His breath is ragged, matching my own. Not once have we let go of one another.

"Renatus reigns! Renatus reigns!" The speakers parrot. I don't think I will ever be able to forget that ominous tone. The voice imprints into my brain like a stamp.

There's movement to my left—a missile from the tip of the Dining Hall zips towards the direction of the gates. The explosion rattles my teeth. I picture *Adian's Animus* melting in the heat of the blast.

"The Sentries are firing at us, too," I pass the information along to James. He grunts, a grim noise. Once we reach the courtyard, we pause to catch our breath. Hands on his thighs, James sucks in lungful after lungful of air. It's tainted with sulfur.

"Wait," I silence him. "Do you hear that?" James freezes, every muscle in his body tensing. His sky-blue irises scan the square, the houses. Those eyes, which so regularly see the beauty in buildings, now see nothing but potential danger.

"There's nothing to hear," he says finally. "Not even the speakers are on."

"Exactly." I inspect the eerie quiet of the courtyard. Everything is how I left it fifteen minutes ago. Aurum's door flung open from Ambassador Collingwood's flight for the Barracks. Argenti shut up, and Aercus aglow with the lights I left on. The other two houses are dormant, occupants nowhere to be found. I wonder where Issak ended up, if Emeko and Olejar are with the Guard jumping from Serpent Mound to Adelaide, Australia.

The speakers crackle to life. My eyes dart to the nearest lamppost where the system resides.

"Corolla Vel," that gravelly voice says. "I have waited sixteen years to finally speak to you."

I shoot James a look. He pulls me to his chest. Together, we scan the area for the person responsible. We come up empty.

"Let's go," he whispers, head nodding towards Aurum. He places one foot forward, and the speakers flare to life again.

"Make one more move, Vel, and I will shoot you dead. I neither require nor need you alive for my purposes."

Fear drowns any logic I possess until that cold, clenched emotion is all I know. Beside me, James tugs me closer. He doesn't make a move again.

"Who are you?" His charged question radiates through the still air. I imagine his eyebrows furrowed, his cheeks red with the rage in his voice. Down the hill, screams and gunfire pierce the atmosphere.

That gravelly voice answers. "I am Renatus, the reborn."

"What do you want?" I wish so badly to take the responsibility from James, but I am mute.

"To speak to your niece, of course. Though," Renatus drawls, "she's not just your niece now, is she?"

James bristles. His entire body flushes with anger—I feel the heat through the cotton of his clothes. He disengages from my grasp and stalks towards the nearest lamppost. There are fists at his sides.

"James!" I scramble after him, "don't—"

I hear the missile before I see it. It comes from Rainier, its sleek, cylindrical body slicing through the pale wisps of clouds. James understands it too.

He whips around, "Corolla," his eyes meet mine, "Aurum!" We are running, James only five feet ahead of me, towards the mouth of

Aurum. If we can just get inside… If we can just dive down the tunnels…

But we are too late. Even I can't pretend otherwise.

The missile strikes the square. The impact sends me flailing backward. Through the clouds of concrete and ash, I see a spray of crimson, glittering rubies.

James.

I must be screaming. Because the next thing I know, my head cracks against something substantial. Pain sears my left arm. My voice breaks, particulate matter coating my open mouth. Tears blur my vision, as an ache of profound loss pierces my heart. I don't feel the pain in my arm, in my head. I feel only the weight on my soul announcing the meaning behind that cloud of scarlet in the explosion.

I don't know how long I lay there, writhing, unable to get up. Long enough for most of the dust to settle. Long enough for me to distinguish the bronze lump of the fountainhead holding me captive to the ground.

I struggle. Groan. Blackness swarms the edge of my vision. Threatens to consume me…

…I want it to.

James, my mind cries because my mouth can't bear to open. Maybe I imagined the blood in the air. Maybe James is pinned to the ground, like me, and that's why he hasn't gotten up yet.

My body goes slack. Through the fog of dust, I see the same wispy clouds overhead from this morning. I want to go home.

My vision of the sky is cut off, as emerald eyes peer down at me. My thoughts fly back to this morning, back to the words I sketched on his pale stomach:

Saved by a soldier, loved by a man.

What I want to write now:

Murdered by a traitor.

Castan Dentata has come to kill me.

Past
June 2004

"Giovanni will be here any minute now," Marilena called from the kitchen. She turned the burner down on her alfredo sauce and stirred it once more.

Maurizio emerged from the cellar, his cheeks red from jogging up the steps. "I've got the good wine." He held up his prize and Marilena paused to hear his predictable, "But it's *all* good wine." Though she rolled her eyes, it eased the weight in her heart to hear him say something so ordinary. Normalcy was a gift these days.

Marilena kissed his cheek and carried her sauce to the table. Through the windows, the moon was visible, but sunset would not come for another hour. She set the pot down and returned to the kitchen for the noodles. Maurizio had set the table before vanishing in the cellar, and now all they waited on was their son.

They sat at each end of the table. The silence was deafening.

Maurizio eyed the wine's ebony label, something he'd paid a pedes woman to design for the vineyard. *Alba e Vite*, the curling golden letters read on the other side of the bottle. And framing that, seven winding vines, one for each of their children, even Reino.

Marilena hung her head. Her reflection caught in the white ceramic of her plate. Tears clouded her vision yet never fell.

"We need some good news," she said, voice hoarse from disuse. "Giovanni said he had good news."

Maurizio harrumphed, a noise she had never heard him make before. She wished he would say more but knew he wouldn't. Couldn't. How could either of them find words for the grief piercing their hearts? Tyto and Calyx were in exile, Corolla was Matrona knew where, and Adian... Marilena swallowed a solid lump in her throat.

There was a knock on the door.

In his effort to get up, Maurizio knocked his knee on the underside of the table. The bottle of wine toppled. Shattered. Scarlet liquid pooled on the glass table, staining the table runner rust-red.

Maurizio muttered curses under his breath, but Marilena moved past him, careful not to step on any glass. She knew better than to interfere with her husband's anger. Especially when he spilled his wine. It was something he preferred—and needed—to process on his own. It wasn't just a spilled drink to him. No, it was spilled devotion and love.

396

Like Adian's blood...

She heard kitchen cabinets slam, the victims of Maurizio's hunt for paper towels. Marilena wiped under her eyes and yanked the front door open. She frowned. Cocked her head.

"You're—"

But she would never finish her sentence, as a blade the length of her forearm spiked her breast and pierced her heart.

Castan

August 2020

Fear flashes across Corolla's eyes as she slips into unconsciousness. I place a hand on her neck and feel her carotid pulse. Strong and regular.

I gaze out at the aftermath of the explosion. I don't see any other victims among the rubble. The houses appear unscathed, but the courtyard is a minefield of ruin. The stone is upturned, the fountain dismantled. I inspect the bronze bulb now. It's pinning Corolla in place like a cleaver. Her left forearm is crushed underneath the massive metalwork sculpture. Blood pools from beneath the weight.

I situate myself so that I have a safe path to roll the tree off Corolla. Placing hands on the bulk of the sculpture, I brace my feet against a block of stone and push. Sweat beads my forehead, but the tree comes off her arm with enough effort. Corolla whimpers the entire time but does not wake up.

I crouch down by her arm—and bite back emotion. It is ruined. From where the fountain chute landed, I see that the structure completely severed her arm below the elbow. Blood spurts from the free wound, no longer contained by the metal chute. I whip off my belt, gun clattering to the rough stones. I tie the tourniquet above her elbow, tighten it. The bleeding stops, but the horror remains. I look from one bone end to the other. Even Maggie can't put limbs back together.

I take Corolla's good arm, the one I bandaged in the middle of the night, and sling it over my shoulder. Grabbing the gun from the ground, I scoop Corolla into my arms so her feet won't drag through the ruins. She makes a sad noise, enough to prove to me that she's still alive.

I glance at the half of her arm laying on the stones. Blood dribbles from one end. I can't bear to look at her fingers, inanimate. There's nothing that can be done. I manage a flame and turn my back on her burning flesh. The Gens won't have her.

I don't know if she ever found James—she'll hate me when she finds out we left him behind—but we have to move. The Gens have infiltrated the Academy, and I don't have the strength to beat them down. I'll just have to trust that Aunt Laila is looking out for the other pedes.

On Aurum's threshold, a voice cries out, "Corolla!"

I turn my head, shoulders relaxing when I see that orange braid across the square. Dani appears over the hill beside her, casting anxious glances over her shoulder below. I wonder how bad it is down there. I wonder who has died.

"Kassandra! Dani!" I wave them over. "I have Corolla here." The two cut through the crumbled ground with the ease of trained soldiers.

"I thought you would have gone with the Guard," I say when Kass is close enough that I don't have to shout. She scowls.

"We don't have time for this." Her eyes grow three sizes. "What the hell happened to Corolla?" Dani comes up at her shoulder, clasping a hand over her mouth at the sight of Corolla's amputation.

"The Sentries are firing against us," I say. "Is there anyone else coming?" My attention darts between the two women. Grime and dried blood flakes their skin. "Talan? Finis?"

"For all I know, Finis went with the Guard," Dani says. "I don't know about the rest. But the Gens are making their way up the hill. Tell me you have a plan."

I nod. "There are tunnels under Aurum that lead out of here. Let's go." Careful with Corolla, I maneuver past the doorway. Aurum is how I left it: clean. I don't waste time admiring it now, though. I lead the party to the pantry, and Kass opens the door without me having to ask.

"Hold Corolla for a second," I instruct, handing her off to Kass. I position myself in the tunnel's entrance, feet secure on the ladder rungs. "Alright, I can take her."

Corolla's limp form slips into the cage of my arms. Her wounded arm scrapes against the tunnel wall, causing her to whimper. I descend into the darkness of the dank tunnel, Kass and Dani not too far behind.

Once my feet strike solid ground, I shrug Corolla onto my back. One arm supports under her butt, the other grips her by her good wrist. Her only wrist. I swallow a lump lodging in my throat.

Kass and Dani thump behind me, and I strike up a candle-sized flame. I blink away the visions it procures, the scent of boiling human flesh.

"Just follow me," I tell them, though that much is obvious. We travel through the tunnels, an occasional explosion above causing dirt to snow down below.

After the second explosion, Dani quakes, "How can the Sentries be firing at our own people? They're meant to shoot at things outside the Wall."

"They're computer controlled," Kass answers, voice bitter. "Computers can be hacked."

Dani shudders. "That's a big flaw to overlook."

We continue in silence until we reach the fork. Phaedra's Blood echoes down the passageway. I cut my flame, grateful to be rid of the destructive light. Since we are all wearing Caeli boots, our plight is soundless, spare for the babbling of the river. Corolla is quiet, but the irregular rasping of her breath informs me that she's still alive. For now.

We reach the cavern. Sunlight spills through the grate at the top of the long ladder sprouting from the cavern ground.

"I need a break for a minute." I set Corolla down and kneel to inspect the tourniquet. It holds tight, despite all the shuffling movement through the tunnels. Even in the inadequate lighting, Corolla is pale. Sweat drips down her forehead, the point of her nose. I frown.

"She's getting worse—" A thick-toed boot crushes my side, throwing me sideways. I scrape against the ground. The river bank is near enough I could touch the black water with one hand.

"You traitor," Kass spits, acid bubbling at her sides. "You think I didn't see you? You think you could play me *twice*?"

I try righting myself, but Kass lashes me in the gut with her boot. I land on my back, gasping for breath. Kass towers over me. Her acid spills from clenched fists and drops onto my legs. It takes seconds for the substance to eat through my uniform's fabric. The little drops kiss my bare flesh. I bite my tongue to keep from screaming. Behind her, Dani holds Corolla's supine form to her chest, fighting back tears.

"Kass," I raise my arms in submission, "I can explain. I'm not—"

"I don't want to listen to your shit, Castan *Dentata*. You killed Calyx, and you're killing Corolla. You tried pinning traitor on all of us when it was you the entire time." She swings an arm, fist pounding against the side of my head. Acid burns my flesh as the blow smarts. Burning. I just want the burning to stop.

I crawl towards the river, dipping cupped hands into that black water. I splash my face with the replenishing liquid, but the burning sensation isn't satiated for long. Is this how Rosh felt? My stomach churns, but it has nothing to do with Kass's decisive blows.

"Kass, Dani," I try again, "you have to believe me. I'm not a traitor."

I wish Kass would laugh, Dani would smile. "It's all a misunderstanding," I want them to say. But neither do. Dani pulls Corolla closer to her chest. Kass crosses her arms.

"I'll fucking kill you, Dentata." There's a blur of boot, then my head threatens to split with pain. I crumple, eyes rolling. My gaze fixes on the river, and I swear, the water is no longer ebony, but rushing crimson. The blood of a fallen Academy.

Past
June 2004

"Tyto," Valeria said her youngest brother's name for what felt like the hundredth time. They could be children again, she, scolding him for something idiotic he'd done. Just as he had done when he was little, and unwanting of reprimands, he ignored her. He finished stuffing an envelope with pictures and sealed it. Despite her irritation with his behavior, she was just grateful she and Tyto had survived what the Board was dubbing "The Alba Atrocities."

The motel lights flickered, strangely illuminating the cracks running down the mustard-yellow walls. Valeria averted her gaze from the TV stand where a glass containing a drooping plant rested. She knew where that flora had come from. Tate squealed, and Calyx cried, reminding Valeria all too quickly that she and Tyto were not children at all. She snatched Tate from his younger cousin, said something about sharing, and set him down on the other side of the room. Tears dripped down Calyx's cheeks. Tyto made no move to comfort his son, though he clutched his father's pant leg.

"Quit acting like this," Valeria snapped, losing her patience. "You don't get to mope about anymore. You have two children, Tyto, and they need their father."

He wheeled on her then, stepping around Calyx. "I'm not moping, Val. I'm grieving for my wife, for our parents, and for our brothers."

Valeria crossed her arms. "You're running away, is what you're doing."

Tyto flinched as if she had struck him over the head with a lead pipe. She wanted to, but then Tate might think such abuse was permissible.

"You know where Corolla is, yet you hide here. *Why* don't you go after her? *Why* don't you salvage your family like you're *supposed* to do?"

"Like I'm supposed to?" His face twisted, and she thought he may cry. But he pulled himself together when Calyx reached for his hand. Behind her, Tate emptied his backpack of Match Box cars, filling the room with the sound of metallic rain.

Tyto was frozen, staring down at Calyx. His clothes rumpled and dark hair disheveled, Valeria had never seen a man so broken. He hadn't shaved in months, and his clothes were loose on his body. She doubted he ate regularly. Her heart bled for Calyx, who was caught in this emotional crossfire.

Valeria changed her tactics.

"Look, I've been eyeing this house outside of Marble Hill. I thought I would settle down and raise Tate, but that's not going to happen now." *Now that Mama and Papa and everyone we love has been murdered.* Valeria swallowed and continued, "So why don't you buy the house, stay there with Calyx, Corolla, and Tate? I'll still be working at the Euro Academy, but there's a Hold not too far away—"

"Corolla's in Michigan with James."

Valeria waited for him to say more. "Okay," she nodded, "that's doable. Let's get packed and we can drive up there now." She turned to instruct Tate to clean up, but Tyto's deep timbre interrupted her.

"No, Val, I can't... do that."

She crossed her arms again. "Why not? She's your daughter. Do you think Mama and Papa would—"

"Enough about what they would or wouldn't do!" Calyx jolted, dislodging his small hand from Tyto's. Tate screamed, and it took Valeria several moments to calm him down. He was almost seven, but he was more temperamental than most. She smoothed his dark hair back, and held his thin wrists in one hand, lest he tried hitting her again. Once he was settled down, she turned wicked eyes on her brother.

"Corolla needs your protection, Tyto. She can't," Valeria bit back the word *survive*, "grow up without your guidance. She'll be an outsider."

"She already is one."

"That doesn't mean you abandon her," Valeria said gently. She dared to utter the truth, "Adian would want the three of you together." Adian died searching for him—all the reports suspected so. Why else had she run away with Corolla only to be found dead on some backroad in southern Tennessee? Valeria couldn't comprehend why Tyto let her sacrifice be in vain.

A muscle in his jaw twitched. He said nothing.

"Fine," Valeria stood, leaving Tate to ram his cars. "I can't put you back together on my own, Tyto. You've got to help me out here. But if you won't accept your daughter—if you won't protect her—then I will."

Tyto bristled. "Stay out of her life. Let her grow up oblivious to all the suffering our world has to offer."

And there it was, the reason why he denied her attempts to reunite him with his daughter. He thought he was doing Corolla a favor.

Valeria licker her lips, incredulous and trying not to show it. "She won't thank you for this, you know. One day, she may even find you herself, and then what will you tell her? 'I thought you'd appreciate the distance'? 'I thought you'd want to live your life never knowing your brother or me?' She'll hate you."

Tyto lifted his head, not quite meeting her eyes. "You said her paperwork reported she cried?"

Valeria nodded. For hours, she had scrounged the system to find that document. One of her job's benefits, maybe, but she had to keep checking over her shoulder to make sure no one noticed.

"Then it doesn't matter if she hates me. It's for the best."

Valeria crouched, shoving lacquered nails into the pile of diecast model cars. She deposited fistfuls into Tate's corduroy backpack with more force than necessary.

"You're making a terrible mistake, *Tito*," she said over the ruckus, "but at least consider the house—don't make yourself a coward and an idiot all in one day."

Corolla
August 2020

Light penetrates the darkness. I shift, hoping to drown that cheerful glow, but it pursues. My body throbs in places I didn't know could throb. My elbow. My occipital bone. My heart. But I knew that could throb. Knew it could break, but I've loved anyway.

Unable to escape it any longer, I crack my eyelids. That wretched brightness pierces my vision with white spears of vibrancy. I blink until I can see normally.

I'm lying in a four-poster bed. Red velvet curtains are pinned back, displaying the room. Tall stone walls surround the downy bed. Tapestries adorn the walls in no particular order. I can't make out the images, but one vaguely resembles the scene from the fountain in the courtyard: a crescent of cloaked figures around a lone person with a lantern. To my left, an archway of thin drapes dances in the breeze. I imagine a marvelous balcony jutting from the side of the castle. I taste salt in the air. My eyes dart from the wooden door bound in metal braces ahead of me to the stone and mortar of the spacious room again.

James would love this.

Pain rockets through my body. I gasp at the sensation, head spinning.

"Oh, you're awake." A figure moves between the fluttering drapes. Her yellow sundress camouflages with the wispy curtains. Honey-gold curls. A strikingly beautiful face.

"How are you feeling?" She pads across the floor, cutting the distance between us in half. I don't want to talk, but I know she won't go away unless I do.

"Fine," I croak.

Dani is at my bedside now, thin eyebrows furrowed. "I'll get you some food and water. You must be hungry." There's something different about Dani. It takes me a moment to puzzle it out: she's not wearing a headband. Where a patterned fabric should wrap around her hairline, there is nothing but a sprinkle of acne.

I dread asking. I swallow, mouth as dry as chalk. "How long?"

"A couple days." She frowns, eyes brimming with tears. "We cauterized your wound—"

"Don't." I take a deep breath. "I don't want to know what happened." I don't want to think about it too hard because then I'll feel sick to my stomach. Like when you know you've done something wrong and there's no possible way to go back and fix it.

"Taxodium has fallen," Dani mutters, bowing her head. "Kass and I used our geometers to jump to this old pelari fortress. We'll be okay for now. No one will look for us on Cyprus." This information rolls over me, unabsorbed.

"Mostly," Dani makes herself comfortable on the edge of the bed, "Kass chose this place because of the dungeon. We have a traitor down there."

Despite my decree, my brain pieces together several things: *Cauterized wound. Traitor. Emerald eyes obstructing my view of the sky.*

I shift under the covers, sweat pricking my hairline. Chest heaving, I force myself upright with Dani's help.

"You shouldn't be—"

"Well dammit, Dani! I told you I didn't want to know, and you kept talking." The other girl flinches at the venom in my tone. I drag my tongue over an infinite number of cracks in my lips. Ignore my thirst. "So take me to Castan. I want to speak with him."

Dani takes a step back, hazelnut eyes waterlogged with concern. "Kass won't like that. She doesn't even let *me* go down there."

Panting, I swing my legs over the side of the bed. My gravity feels wrong—so wrong—but I tell myself not to dwell on it.

"Then I'll take myself there." I touch toes to the cold stone. My black uniform has been replaced with a white nightgown. Lace scratches my neck. I hold my head high and rise. My legs wobble. I clutch the post at the end of the bed for support. Dani tries to be my crutch, but I shrug her off. When my balance stabilizes, I stagger towards the door, shove it open, and step into a narrow hallway. On one side is a dead end. On the other, is a winding staircase. I trudge past the windows, ignoring the view, ignoring Dani's anxious breath at my back.

"Corolla, please. You lost a lot of blood. You shouldn't be moving about so much."

I make it to the top of the staircase, hand gripping the iron railing to steady myself. *One, two, three...* I breathe. *This will be easy. They're just stairs.* I focus on the things in front of me, the things I can see, rather than the things inside of me, the things I can't see. I don't wonder why my left arm aches, why my pulse pounds in the back of my head. I push on, one step at a time.

"Where are the dungeons?" I huff, smearing sweat across my brow. Dani's indecisive silence rings through my ragged breath and feet scuffing stone stairs. Sconces line the wall between narrow slits of windows. I catch glimpses of pale rock terrain and turquoise water. The Mediterranean Sea.

Then, "The west wing, straight down," she sighs, "I guess I can take you there, but you have to eat something first."

"No," I descend the last two steps, "but you can get me water please." I gaze out at the vast room, the massive table and its hundreds of chairs gathered around it. An empty fireplace occupies a third of the farthest wall. A huge oil painting, framed in gold, hangs above the mantle. Two towering doors shoot from the floor to the loft ceiling on another wall. In my head, I mark them as *front entrance*. I cast a look over my shoulder where Dani hangs back on the staircase. "West wing?"

"Straight," she relents, "then down."

While Dani hopefully scurries towards the kitchen, I embark on my long journey to the other half of the fortress.

For James, I remind myself, *I'm doing this all for James.*

And maybe—just *maybe*—there's a possibility he's waiting for me in another room of this fortress.

The first thing I notice about the dungeons is that they are hot. I expected a cellar of biting air. The second thing I notice is the lack of cells. There are only four, two on each side of the hall. Each is comprised of three walls of sturdy gray stone, one wall of iron gate. A couple have wooden buckets. Some have bundles of musty straw.

The fourth thing I notice is Castan. His cell is easy to find because the third thing I noticed was Kassandra. She's cross-legged on an elegant wooden chair like the ones I saw in the great hall. In her hands, she twirls a gun. She's still in her uniform, an ebony blade tucked in one of the loops of her utility belt. Clasped beside that, is a ring of antique keys. Her pale freckled face is fixed in a scowl, even when she looks up and sees me.

"I want to talk to Castan."

She doesn't stop twirling the gun. "You can't. I'm having a conversation with him."

"Have it later."

At this, she rises. She doesn't aim the gun at me—she doesn't have to. Her indigo eyes are piercing enough. "He's a traitor, Corolla. I don't think you've quite wrapped your head around that yet." Though her body is willowy and slim, our heights mark almost the same. I hold her gaze, unrelenting.

"Then sit at the top of the steps and wait for me to call you." Over her shoulder, Castan raises his head. The hollows of his eyes are black and blue, cheeks scraped red with abrasions.

Kass glances down my body, fixes her eyes on… something. She meets my gaze again. Concern peppers her otherwise callous tone. "I can't just leave you down here alone."

It takes all my self-control when I utter, "I am not a cripple." And that is about as close as my mind will allow me to discuss the subject.

Kass's brows dip. I read the lines in her expression before she can argue further.

"You are not the only one who's lost something." The dangerous calm of my tone strikes a nerve in my opponent. She blinks. Nods.

"Okay, I'll give you ten minutes with him. But that's it." She pivots and saunters over to Castan's cell. "If you do anything out of turn, I'll melt your dick off. Understand?"

Castan drops her gaze. "Yes."

Kass stalks past me. As she ascends the winding staircase, her feet are soundless, but the keys at her hip jangle.

I go to the chair propped in front of his cell, but I don't sit. His uniform is torn in one thigh, feet stripped bare. Sweat causes his hair to clump around his forehead. His cell reeks of human waste.

"You have five minutes to explain."

"Then you may want to sit down." There is no humor in his raw voice, only the tune of confession. I remain standing. He raises his head. I look past his eyes.

"Please, Corolla. You look about ready to collapse." His voice cracks with emotion.

"You're wasting time."

"Okay," he sighs, "I'm not a traitor. Not to Taxodium anyway. My family… my family is the Dentatas. That's my real name: Castan Dentata. And Laila isn't my real aunt. Tilia Pyrus set Laila up as my relative, though."

"Why would Tilia do that?"

"Because I escaped the Complex. I gave her information, the Complex's location, and vowed loyalty to Taxodium's cause. I wanted the Dentata threat dealt with as much as anyone else at that Academy. I wanted—I want—to be the good guy."

"And Calyx? Maybe you did kill him after all."

Castan propels forward, hands gripping the bars of the cell gate. "No, Corolla! I didn't kill him. I tried saving him. He was my best friend—"

"And your own brother killed him, then? Likely story."

"I'm telling the truth. Rosh…" Castan winces, drops his gaze, "Rosh was my brother, but I am nothing like him. I left the Complex to escape that kind of lifestyle. My mother raised my sister and me differently. By that time, Rosh's head was already full of our father's twisted truths."

"You have three minutes to start making sense, Castan, or I'll leave you to get back to your *conversation* with Kass."

"My mother was Mena Scott Dentata," he explains. "She was a brilliant scientist, even before her hand was forced into my father's. Arranged marriages are how they do things, though many are never happy marriages. My parents' wasn't." He clears his throat. "My father is Jon Xabier Dentata. He took my mother away when I was ten. I don't know where to. He probably killed her. She was working on a cure, but then something must have happened. My father never would have taken her if things were going as planned. I'm guessing she acted out against him in some way. Undermined him. But Mena raised Hadley and me with that kind of reserve: to resist our father's—our underground society's—ethics. Rosh never clued into that morality. He was always seeking our father's favor.

"For a long time, I was never sure which parent to obey. When I was ten, I witnessed my father rip my mother from our home, and I knew who I was loyal to. From that day on, I dreamed about leaving the Complex. I didn't want to be like my father or the other men in the Complex. I didn't want to be a Dentata."

I want to cross my arms, but a warning bell in my head says not to.

Do not attempt, it chimes.

Castan continues, "I had to be careful about showing my resistance, though. I read books, mostly. Stayed away from brawls. But things changed when I turned sixteen, and my Essence came through. Jon nominated me for Carnage, and I didn't have a clue about how to drop out. He trained me, groomed me to win the right of the season's first kill. And... and I did. I almost killed my last opponent with my Essence. Hadley was horrified. So when I was finally free to 'wreak havoc' in the world above, I promised Hadley I would return with Taxodium's army instead. But the Complex was vacated by then. Hadley was gone."

I file this information away but remain silent. My heart thrashes in my chest, though my expression remains stone.

I guess this explains his 'insight' into Genocide lifestyles and motivations.

"When I left the Complex, I started over at Taxodium. I put everything behind me and became the person I've always wanted to be. I wasn't a soldier or a student. Not really. I was just... me. I did what was asked of me, yes, but I also did what I wanted. I read books, played the piano—without the fear of my father's shadow creeping up behind me. I left behind the so-called *honor* of winning Carnage and won the Regency instead. Calyx became my best friend."

"And your recent sickness, that's the Pyrus-made disease."

He nods. "I'll be neutralized by October. Maybe sooner. I'm sorry, Corolla." I meet his bruised gaze. "I've wanted to tell you for so long, but I knew you would despise me." My skin flushes with the thought of his hips grinding against mine. Should I despise him?

"I saw Rosh at the Academy."

Castan clenches and unclenches his fists. "I-I killed him. I was the only one who could. He... he loved me too much, in his own, demented way."

I blink rapid fire. "You... you killed your own brother?"

"Burnt him alive. A shot in the head to end his suffering."

I can't find words for that.

"He killed so many people, Corolla. The scouts, Calyx... Matrona knows who else. I'm sure he was at the Asian Academy, picking off the wounded before help could arrive. He was malicious, merciless—"

"Castan, you don't have to convince me," I crouch to his level, staring through the iron bars. Kass marked him up good. Through the holes of his uniform, I catch sight of raw flesh glistening with puss. "I'm sorry it had to be you."

His eyes dip, but he catches himself. I blink. Hard. I can guess what he's trying not to stare at.

"I'm not the traitor, Corolla."

"I know."

"But someone is."

"I know." I think of Kale, the pelari backing his cause. The people they killed. But someone had to have facilitated that. Kale is too thick-headed to be that clever.

"Rosh mentioned a name, someone who even my father takes orders from."

And somehow, without Castan saying it, I know.

"Renatus."

Castan's brow furrows. "How did you—"

"I don't," breath puffs past my lips in hot clouds, "want to explain."

Castan's eyes glow with a certain amount of self-restraint. He wants to ask, but he won't. He changes the subject.

"Someone initiated the attack from the inside of the Academy."

I nod, following his train of thought. "So if you're not the traitor, then who is?"

"Well," Castan and I direct our attention to the flickering figure in the stairwell, "I am, of course."

Past
June 2004

"Stop that racket!" Jon Dentata growled over his shoulder. He paced by the room's main exit, a shark awaiting its prey. He wondered what was taking Baylor so long. Between his thumb and index finger, he pinched his lip. He lost good men in the attack on the NA Academy.

This Renatus fellow better honor his word. The obscure man had come from the cracks, and though Jon knew him as pelari, he struggled to understand him as *ally*. True, they had a common desire for pelari dominance, but one could only trust a ghost so much. They couldn't die twice. They had nothing to lose. Tonight would be the building block of trust. *If* Renatus followed through.

When the string of piano notes didn't falter, Jon whirled about to confront his wife. "Mena, for Rome's sake, you're giving me a headache."

Through the music rack, she met his cold gaze. Smiled. "If you keep shouting, you'll wake Hadley. Then you'll have a *real* headache." She flipped the page of her music. "And Castan enjoys it."

Jon cursed the woman. If she weren't still fragile from childbirth, he would have dragged her by the hair to the back room. She could cut it as short as she wanted to, but he would always dominate her. Their three children were proof of this. His newly appointed position as Numen was proof of this. Had Mena not been working on a cure, he would have bashed her skull in years ago, but—But he needed her brain intact. He had been neutralized for close to a decade now, but he would see that his children were cured. He would see that they had a better life than his own. At this thought, Jon's anger flared. His own father would have smacked him over the head at such tenderness.

"You're only my son so that you can live up to my name. Nothing more." How many times had Bartholomew reminded him of that?

Jon's gaze fell on Castan, his dark head bobbing as he followed his mother's hands along the keys. That anger in the pit of his stomach escalated.

Jon stalked past the kitchen table, made a sharp turn, and stood over his wife and son on the piano bench. Mena's hands flew across the keys, unflinching. In her lap, Castan craned his head to meet his father's gaze. He grinned, drool oozing down the corners of his lips.

"He's got to stop sucking his fingers."

Mena played on. "He's only a baby."

Jon plucked Castan from the cage of his mother's arms. He ripped the two fingers from Castan's mouth. The boy's face turned red, eyes crinkling with the threat of tears.

"He cries too much." Just then, Rosh stumbled down the concrete corridor carrying a pocket knife. "Ah," Jon exclaimed. He set Castan in front of Rosh, the older boy sheathing and unsheathing the old knife. "Play with your brother, Rosh. Make him tough."

The older boy cocked his head, his dark curls spilling into his eyes. Jon regarded his sons, the one brandishing a switch blade, the other stuffing fingers into his mouth. *They may yet fight for the right to take my place as Numen,* he gleamed. His own brother, Baylor, hadn't put up much of a fight, more drawn to drink than responsibility.

Maybe he was the wrong man to send above.

Mena had stopped playing the piano. Jon felt her gaze boring into his back, but he ignored her. The scene below him pleased his eyes. Rosh jammed his fingers into the tool's casing and withdrew the blade. He had been doing this—ever since Jon gave him the knife a couple days ago—unaware of the button that would accomplish the same thing, but with less brute force.

With a *snap*, Rosh flipped the blade back in place and handed the object to Castan. The younger boy clenched the pocket knife in his fist and shook the thing up and down. Irritated, Rosh went to snatch it from Castan's grasp, but as he grabbed it, Castan's grip triggered the button. The blade flicked out from its sheath and sliced the inside of Rosh's wrist. Blood oozed from his soft flesh.

Rosh's lip trembled as he examined his own, dripping blood. At four, he knew better than to cry. But Mena was continually searching for small ways to undermine Jon. She flew from the piano bench and wrapped Rosh in her arms.

"They shouldn't be playing with weapons," she snarled. She yanked the blade from Castan, ever so careful and economical in her movements. Unremarkably, Castan began wailing in Rosh's place.

Jon turned his back, temples throbbing with more than his usual frustration. His eyes flitted to the clock mounted on the wall.

Where the hell is Baylor?

Anxiety prickled his skin. But of course, nothing terrible could have happened—the Complex was built to withstand any attack from the outside, and the FedEx depot sitting above it, was guarded with more than enough surveillance. No, Jon decided, nothing was amiss. His brother was just a fool.

411

He left behind his wailing children—baby Hadley had been awakened by Castan's screams—and made his way to Level 23, his office.

Jon stalked past the office doors, once his father's, now his. And there, standing in the center of the obsidian floor, was the irregular shape of Baylor. It was only the lean form beside his brother that kept Jon from clouting Baylor.

He was supposed to fetch me from my room before bringing the visitor down. Irritation radiated from Jon in rivulets but ceased to exist when his eyes landed on the large cardboard box between his brother and guest. The lean man wrapped a hand around the cart's handle and, in doing so, pulled the box closer to himself.

"Gentlemen." Jon adopted the air of a diplomat, clasped his hands behind his back, and entered the room as if all were as he intended. "I trust there was no trouble with my men?"

"None whatsoever." Renatus tucked his chin, a humble gesture for one so bloodthirsty. The NA attack, after all, had been his idea.

"Announce your birthright as Numen. Make them fear *you."*

"And our package?" Jon's gaze dove to the box on the cart. "Is she still intact?"

Renatus tossed his head in Baylor's direction. "You may open the package, but you should know," the man said over the noise of ripping tape, "I was unable to secure Adian Vel. Her body was lost to me. Taxodium has since burned her corpse."

Jon clenched his jaw. The cruel smile faded from his lips, but Renatus did not flinch. Through gritted teeth, he asked, "Then *who* have you brought for my purposes?"

Baylor stepped back. Cocked his head. "It's a man, brother."

"Yes," Renatus bent his neck and gazed down at the slumped form in the box. "I could not deliver Adian Vel, but I give you a valuable member of the Reserve. To secure our pact of loyalty to one another. This is Luca Alba."

Jon waved him away and approached the cart where the unconscious man lay cramped in the cardboard container. This Alba couldn't be much younger than himself. An eyepatch hung haphazardly around his neck, fallen in the struggle or transport, Jon didn't care. Even in sleep, Alba's expression was lined with the mask of grief.

"I don't care about his name," Jon scoffed. "But what am I supposed to do with this? I fail to see how he is more valuable than the very creature my father created to be our antidote." He met his guest's piercing gaze. Despite the ragged, bloody form separating them, neither man indulged in the creature's misery. Jon searched this man, this

Renatus, for any sign of weakness. He knew his guest was assessing him for the same thing. But in each other's eyes, not a single fracture was detected in the steel-faced expression dominating the two leaders. Neither dared look away first.

Renatus glared out of hooded eyes. "You don't know what he can do yet."

Jon flicked his wrist in dismissal. "My reports mention something about 'seeing true intentions' or the like. He can't replace Adian Vel— he can't cure my family!" Blood rushed to his face, along with the venom slurring past his tongue. "Our agreement was for you to deliver the woman, not one of your—"

"That is just one eye." Renatus ignored the outburst and withdrew a blank pad of yellow line paper from the box's confines. He handed this and a pen to Jon. "Did your reports mention what the other can do?"

Castan

August 2020

"Here's your water." Through the iron bars, Dani chucks the glass at Corolla, who turns away. It strikes the wall beside her. Shatters. Water sprays the skirt of her nightdress. Glass litters the stone floor.

"People get so caught up in beauty, they don't even think to wonder what lies beneath." Dani jumps down the last step. As she falls, her body flickers shadows, like a TV flipping channels too quickly. When she lands, a different figure stands before us. I stagger to my feet, hands clenched around the iron padlock.

"Astral projection?" Lola squeals, scraping her hair into two pigtails. "C'mon, what a joke! And anyone can get a tattoo. Especially one so simple as the Mark." She drops her hands, a sneer twisting her profile.

Corolla is motionless. The only thing between Lola and her is the wooden chair Kass dragged down here two days ago. She obstructs Lola's view of my hands, of the metal liquefying in my heat. I could have escaped this cell anytime, but I wanted Kass to trust me. I wanted her to believe me. One look at the empty, knotted sleeve of Corolla's nightgown summons my defense systems.

Lola clasps her hands behind her back, just as I feel the remainder of the lock melt. She paces in front of Corolla. "It took Jura up until her death to figure it out, but," Lola shrugs her square shoulders, "I can't give you two much credit for putting it all together either."

The padlock oozes between my fingers. Over Corolla's shoulder, I meet Lola's gaze. Those eyes—Dani's eyes—set in a different visage altogether. "*You* murdered Jura?"

"Oh, Castan," Lola smirks, "someone always kills someone. You would know."

Before the jab can sink in, Corolla growls, "That paper of your patterns. That wasn't a catalog, that was a code. You were sending messages with your accessories!"

I shoot a puzzled look at Corolla's back. Why is she shouting? Why is she even talking? And then I see the boot toe at the top of the winding staircase. Kass is prowling.

Keep Lola talking. Keep her from shifting.

"And Talan?" I don't dare open the cell door, though I want so badly to be free of the stench of my own urine. "Did he betray Taxodium too?"

"Talan? No, no," she shakes her head, ponytails wriggling, "I only got close to him because of his parents. I wanted the drop on the Judges, but by the time I realized Talan didn't get along with his parents, it was too late. BFF's. The ironic part is that I can only ever be a woman, no matter the shape or size. Talan, however, was immune to my body. Jura thought he would figure it out, but God, that girl was ignorant. Poetic, the way she died."

Nausea creeps into the pit of my stomach. Past Lola, I glimpse Kassandra's leg crouching down each step with the precise movement of a cat. I fix my gaze on Lola's ugly face. She is nowhere near as chiseled as Dani was, but I suspect that was the point. Disarm people with beauty. I always knew there was something unnatural about her.

"You're not a Dentata." I was never sure, but now I know.

"No, I'm a Noel. Don't you know the Genocides are more than just your convoluted family? We are all pelari who want change, who want the world."

Corolla scoffs, "And how do you think you'll manage that?"

Lola turns vicious eyes on Corolla. "With Renatus, of course." Corolla goes rigid—more rigid than before—and Lola grins with the reaction. She cocks her head like a bird of prey.

"He spoke to you, didn't he?" Kass is on the last step now. "He said he would. Said he—"

"You witch!" Kass's fist comes down on the back of Lola's head, sending Lola sprawling. It's only when she drops that I realize Kass smacked the girl with the butt of her gun. The gun I snatched from Rosh. Lola twitches, a cackle escaping past her lips. Corolla fixes a foot on the edge of the chair and shoves it with all her might at Lola. It smashes into her crumpled form, interrupting the twisted laughter. Lola's body flickers, the figure of so many swarming shadows.

"You cannot win this." The shadowy woman flattens into a patch. It skitters along the wall as I burst from the cell. Lola's high-pitched voice echoes, "They are already coming."

"We have to go!" I usher Corolla towards the stairs, and Kass leads the way.

"Where is she?" Corolla's head whips left and right, scanning the stairwell. I wrap an arm around her waist, help her up the stairs.

"It doesn't matter," I tell her, "We have to get out of here." Banging reverberates along the solid stone walls. Shouts of battle reach our ears.

Kass groans, "That'll be the front entrance." We fly up the staircase, a blur. "I leave to pee for one minute, and shit hits the fan."

We leave behind the sweltering heat of the dungeons and come up upon the main floor. The sounds of pillaging are undeniable now. Our fortress has been compromised.

Kass wheels around, shoving something in my hand. "I took it from Da—Lola. Take Corolla. Get out of here. She's in no shape..." Kass glances over her shoulder as a loud ringing vibrates through the air. She glances back at me, body springing for battle, "Just get out. I'm sorry I doubted you."

"Kass," I reach for her shoulder, but my hands are full. "Kass, you can't go out alone—"

"Go, Castan! I don't want to hear it." She spins, braid a flare of orange, and sprints down the hall. I glance at the geometer she pushed into my hand.

"Let's go." My arm still secured around Corolla's waist, we plunge back into the staircase. It will lead to a room, hopefully. A clear, open space at least. We climb the stairs, my body aching from all the beatings Kass felt inclined to deliver. I blink swollen eyelids, searching for that puddle of ebony on the walls. Corolla rasps at my shoulder, but we can't stop.

The stairwell empties out into a narrow hallway. At the end of the passage, is a wooden door braced in black hinges. I take us there, shoving the door open with my other shoulder. The room is a spacious one, heavy carpets spreading across the unforgivable stone floor. I set Corolla on the mattress of the bed and prepare the geometer for our jump. A drop of blood. The punch of coordinates. Matrona. We will go to Matrona. The Gens wouldn't dare.

"Castan, look out!" Corolla shouts. I turn in time to avoid the heavy blow of an ax. Lola yanks her blade from the floor, grinning.

"Is it justifiable, Castan? That's why you killed Rosh. But you killed Phage, so now it's my turn to take a life in exchange for the one I lost. It doesn't matter that I hated that mute, brainless little creature. It only matters that I get my vengeance." She raises her ax, the fabric of her yellow dress stretched taut over her pure form. I stagger back, willing flames to my palms. They won't come.

A savage cry rips through the air—Corolla lunges between Lola and me, flailing a fire poker in her single hand. The metal rod slashes the soft flesh of Lola's neck. Bright red blood spurts from her wound, splattering Corolla's white gown. I clutch the fabric of her dress, yanking Corolla back before Lola's arms drop, her ax dropping with them. The girl falls to her knees, shock lining her pudgy face.

The fire poker clatters to the carpet with a *thud*. In the protective cage of my arms, Corolla heaves, breath breaking.

I want to comfort her, tell her it will be alright, but there is no time. Another Gen bursts through wooden door. I don't recognize the man. He brandishes a longsword from one of the suits of armor that decorated the great hall. Geometer in my fist, I sweep Corolla backward. Salt air stings my lungs as we stumble onto a balcony. I'm hardly conscious of the decision—I register the Gen pursuing us, the odds of us getting past him, weaponless—and I punch JUMP.

"Over the ledge," I shout into Corolla's ear. We run, bare feet slapping against the smooth plateau of the half oval balcony. The ledge looms closer, low enough for us to scale it. I clasp an arm around Corolla, and we leap—

Wind whips our bodies, cutting through the fabric of my uniform. Corolla's gown flaps in the fall, her hair in my mouth. I don't hear the geometer beep, but it must have. The lilac veil blooms around us, a bubble of faith. Around Corolla's wild hair, I don't see much. The pale cliff face blurring, the turquoise water of the Mediterranean Sea drawing closer. Closer. And above, the Gen, peering over the ledge at our suicide drop.

"Castan," Corolla hides her face in my chest. I squeeze her to my body, my back to the ocean now. I shut my eyes and pray that when I open them next, we'll be on land.

And to think, I always wanted to fly.

I strike a solid surface, the air squashed from my lungs. I gasp, struggling to catch my breath. Corolla rolls off my body, and the burning Iranian sun shines down upon us. I could laugh, could shout with relief, but I can't breathe. There is a crowd of pedestrians surrounding us, foreign faces and foreign words.

I force my chest to rise and fall, force my lungs to cooperate. I stagger to my feet, brushing off helping hands. I don't bother with the dust and dirt, the ache in my backside. Corolla is curled into a ball, crimson blotches staining the knot of her left sleeve. *Her* blood, not Lola's.

"Get away from her," I shove men and women aside. From the differences in their clothes, some are tourists, some locals. I pluck Corolla from the ground. She doesn't resist me, but she whimpers at my touch. I scan over the heads of the crowd. Set my destination. Push through the barricade of bodies.

"Out of my way. Out of my way." By their confused, worried expressions, I know I'm slurring my words. I don't care. I break through the crowd, feet dragging in the dirt. Enter the ring of hedges, the shade of Matrona's branches. Find the Mark carved in the tree's trunk. My palm is already bloody, from Lola or my previous cut, I don't know. I slap my hand over the engraving.

My knees buckle, but when I drop, we are inside the main cavern.

"Tilia," I rasp, setting Corolla to the hard-packed ground. "We need your help." But the cavern is black as pitch. I snap my fingers, willing something to spark. Finally, a flame dances in the cup of my hand. A halo of golden light crowns Corolla and me.

I try again, "Tilia?"

"I know you despise fantasy," a startling voice calls from the shadows. My mouth goes dry as it continues, "But if you'd read the book, you'd know that Peter never dies."

Book Three
Broken

"But the beginning of things, of a world especially,
is necessarily vague, tangled, chaotic,
and exceedingly disturbing."
-Kate Chopin, *The Awakening*

Calyx
August 2020

"Castan," I crush his rigid body in my arms. "God, it's good to see you." I pull away from limp arms. In fact, he didn't embrace me back. I note this and the bundle of white fabric on the floor beside him. I kneel, hand outstretched to touch my sister, but a sudden grasp on my shoulder cuts the action short.

"Don't," Castan growls, "touch her." With economic movements, he clutches the fabric of my shirt and flings me back into the shadows. I catch myself on the edge of a table Tilia left in the main cavern.

"I've had enough of shapeshifters." Flames flare in my friend's palms, casting dark shadows across his scowling face. He's stronger than when I saw him last. Stronger, but also... weaker. I see it in his eyes, how they blaze to conceal agony. Agony from what?

I raise my hands, palms flat. My brain whirls with defensive tactics, but I ease the adrenaline back. "Castan, it's me. It's Calyx."

"No," he shakes his head, adamant, "you're supposed to be dead. You *are* dead. I saw you... saw you..."

Tilia never said this would be easy. Drifting in and out of a distinct shape, she never said a word. If her hand had been solid, I would have held it as she died. Two days ago, she flickered into nonexistence, golden eyes projecting a message in my brain.

It's time.

Castan and Corolla's unexpected appearance only hinders my plans in a sense that I'll have to call the Valence together later. Right now, I focus on the radiation of flames, the fallout of confusion and shock.

"I had to fake my death, Castan. It was the only way to truly escape the Gens."

"No." He shakes his head again, the flames dying in his hands to a low glow. I should feel guilty. I should feel like an ass. But I don't.

"It was necessary, and I'm sorry to have put you through such an... uncanny situation. But I'm not dead," I take a humble step towards him, "I am quite alive."

"How?" His guarded expression collapses. What remains is pure surprise, the kind I imagined when this reunion played through my mind. So many times, I wished to tell him, to pop out of the Twelfth Wall or a locker room stall and say, "Castan, I'm alive!"

"Tilia crafted an enchanted blade, the one you found with me at my bloodbath. It's like the *cantus* blades she created for Hold transportation. My idea too." Here, I can't help but beam at my own cleverness. "I lost a lot of blood, but that was expected. Nasreen and Umar really had to work to get you out of my room; otherwise, you would have witnessed my wound stitch itself back together. Once I was strong enough, I came back to Tilia and we got to work."

"Rosh killed you. There was so much blood." His eyes cloud. Frowns.

I take another step. A foot of space separates us, amber light from Castan's fire dancing across the walls. "Rosh was set up. I had the blade with me, goaded him, and he thought it poetic to cut me down with my own weapon. *He* fell right into my design."

Castan shudders. He turns his head away from me but not soon enough to mask the emotion flickering in his eyes. When he faces me again, that guarded mask adorns his profile once more. I'm not too discouraged. I touch a hand to his shoulder.

He jerks out from under my loose grip and demands, "Where's Tilia? I need her help with something."

I bow my head to that something curled in fetal position on the ground. "Tilia is dead. When the Academies fell, she lost too many hearts. I suspect that was the Gens' plan all along. To get rid of the Venefica, one of our most powerful allies, before she pieced together the number of hearts turning against her."

Castan doesn't say anything. I sense him pondering new possibilities, new solutions to whatever problems my sister faces. Tilia mentioned Castan's protectiveness for Corolla, but I didn't know how much dedication he actually exhibited. I guess a job will do that to a person. Knowing Castan, he blamed himself for my death and funneled more effort into Corolla's case because of it.

He crouches. Brushes back the hair masking Corolla's face. One hand clutching a faint light, he runs a thumb across her cheekbone. Her eyes are open, unseeing the dirt floor before her. I want to hold her, to unburden her mind from whatever is haunting her, but I know Castan may actually kill me if I do. He's not the same person I knew eight months ago. The old Castan would have clapped hands on my shoulders, asked me in his quiet way where I've been, what I've been up to. As he mumbles reassuring words to Corolla, I know that Castan died in the streets of Iran the night I made my escape into the underworld.

That was never part of the plan.

I chew old wounds on the inside of my cheek, comb my hair with fingers. "Now that you're here, Castan, I would like to explain something to you."

The question slips past his lips, a whisper. "The Australian Academy wasn't a ruse then, was it?"

"If you're referring to the—" I stop, seeing that reproachful look in his eyes. "No," I tuck my chin, "it was not a ruse. After the North American Academy fell, the others were soon compromised as well. The loyalists are fleeing to St. Helena for medical attention and refuge."

"Loyalists?" His brow furrows, but his thumb doesn't cease caressing Corolla's cheek.

"Yes," I exhale, propping hands on my hips, "that's what I want to talk to you about. Follow me," I beckon, "there's something you need to see."

Reluctantly, Castan obeys. He scoops Corolla into his arms, and she molds into the support of his body. What incapacitates her so, I can't say. But I know she hears me, as she flinched when I mentioned Tilia's death, the destruction of the other Academies.

Castan's glow follows me into the second cavern. I gesture to the immediate wall. "The Holds relied on her functional being. That is, they weren't dry enchantments that could survive without their maker, like *cantus* blades. The Holds are gone now that Tilia is, too. All except the natural ones." Twenty-six Holds remain, scattered worldwide in arbitrary locations of no strategic importance.

"Our transportation is crippled," is all he says, hugging Corolla closer to his body. She gasps, as if in pain, and he loosens his hold.

He ducks his head, whispers, "Are you alright?"

"Put me down." This is the first time I've heard my sister speak. Her voice is like silk, underneath the haggard, ragged tone of disused vocal cords.

Castan puts her down, her bare feet touching the hard-packed floor.

"Corolla," I reach out to steady her, and see, in the faint glow of Castan's fire, the cause of her pain. Her left sleeve is knotted below her elbow. Crimson soaks the alabaster fabric, like an external blood clot.

My little sister has lost half her arm.

Corolla recoils from my supporting embrace, backing up into Castan's chest. He slings an arm around her shoulders and guides her to the hand-crafted table behind our gathering where he pulls out a chair for her. She sits, sighing as if relieved from an unimaginable weight.

My eyes dart from Corolla's slumped form to Castan's tense one. Something noncommutative passes between the two, though I doubt even they notice the subtle things. Like how Castan's chair is closer to

Corolla's than it was before he sat, how Corolla's body leans several degrees towards his. It seems Castan has replaced me with more than just another job.

I sit across Corolla and capture her foggy gaze. "I am sorry. I didn't know."

Castan clears his throat. "You were saying something about the Holds?"

Again, my eyes flit between them, from Corolla's catatonic state to Castan's protective one. I rest my attention on Castan, an orange bundle of energy flickering in his hand. What I thought were shadows in the hollows of his eyes are actually bruises.

"Yes, well our transportation is crippled, but so are the Gens' now too. They may have snagged some geometers from the Academies, but my sources relay the majority of those clever devices reside in our hands."

"The Gens can't use the Holds. Dentata blood doesn't compute unless Tilia gives—gave—permission. That's how I got through." I duck my head at the blush creeping into his cheeks.

"I know, Castan. I've known you were Dentata since we moved in together. You were too... *correct*. As if you owed the world something. But you don't, you know that?" I don't mention the fact that Tilia confirmed my suspicions about Castan's origins long before that.

"And I thought you couldn't lie."

It's my turn to blush, memories of our mini-lessons between classes flooding my consciousness. My ears always gave me away. They still do, if I don't believe wholeheartedly in my cause. Castan must think I'm selfish, self-centered. But it's not that—not at all. It's that I've given up so much for Tilia's cause, I can't pause to consider how many people I've hurt along the way. I *know* faking your death is wrong. I *know* lying to everyone you love is wrong. But it's less wrong than Taxodium's corruption, the Gens' destruction, and all the pedes who've died in the crossfire.

I tap my fingertips on the table top. "I guess those lessons weren't just a way to kill time after all."

"How..." he shakes his head, unbelieving. "How did you even plot such a thing? I was at your side most of your time at the Academy. I don't understand."

"When she was strong, Tilia could spread her consciousness to any willing heart. She found me in my dreams, months before I came to the Academy. We made most of our plans that way from then on. Nasreen and Umar assisted, of course."

"She recruited you then." Did he put emphasis on the word *you*?

"Yes."

"You have been lying to us all."

"I've been volga."

Corolla makes a noise, and Castan leans back in his chair, exhaling. He drags a hand across his face, wincing as his fingers graze the bruises there. The tension escalates. Suffocates. Castan used to devour my every word. Now, he rebukes me.

Castan mutters, more to himself than to me, "So Taxodium has finally fallen to the Gens."

"But the Gens aren't just Dentatas. Never were. They're all the pelari who want change: domination over pedes."

Castan narrows his eyes. "What are you talking about?"

"Dani," Corolla interrupts. "He's talking about people like Dani."

"So Maggie was right about her. Hmph." I chew the inside of my cheek and taste blood. My gaze slides across the table to Castan's. "Maggie is one of the people Tilia reached out to. Your sister is another."

Castan jolts forward, hand slapping the table top. "Hadley? What about her?"

"She came here, to Tilia. She won those Dentata games... Carnage, I think she called it. Anyway, winning gave her a reprieve. In that time, though Tilia said it was completely unnecessary, she went through her *Humanitas*, passed her three Trials, and earned her Mark of Tribulation. I think she wanted proof of her good-heartedness. Not for Tilia or me, but for herself."

"So where is she then? Here?" He looks about the room as if he'll locate her among the heavy shadows. Corolla perks up but otherwise remains a statue, her spine rigid.

"No, she's been acting a Genocide these past few months. Besides that lapse in Belarus when we followed your tracker, she's been residing in a nice little place in the Cordillera Huayhuash mountain range."

Castan's voice drops. "The South American Academy."

I nod.

"That would explain why we haven't been able to find their Complex." He pinches his bottom lip between his thumb and index finger, contemplating.

"She's been working on locating your mother. Mena Dentata contained a secret, didn't she? Something that may dismantle the Dentata clan for good."

Castan's eyes flicker; he apparently doesn't want to follow that route of conversation. "If the Gens have been staked out in the SA all this time, then why haven't you said something to the Majors? Why haven't you attacked?"

"Because we didn't have adequate forces. We had no idea who we could trust. All Tilia knew was that Taxodium was slipping, and she wanted to find out why. She paid the price for her investigation."

"You think someone caught onto her?"

I shrug. "It's possible. Either way, it's convenient for her to be out of the picture." I swipe a thumb across one eyebrow. "Now that all the Academies have toppled, and the survivors have fled to St. Helena, we know who we can trust."

"Who, exactly, is 'we'?"

"The Valence. Other recruits. There's only a handful of us. We've been operating under Tilia's command for a year now. It was her goal to find the source of all the fatigue she felt."

"Fatigue?"

"The turning hearts, I'm guessing. I don't know. She rarely spoke about her affliction with me."

Castan considers all that I've said, retreating into himself for a moment. I keep my mouth shut, not wanting to ruin the only normal-feeling conversation we've had since he slipped through the cavern wall. When he returns, he asks, "Are you familiar with Renatus?" At his elbow, Corolla flinches, eyes unseeing again. I drag my attention back to Castan.

"No idea who he is. Hadley reports that he never makes appearances, but his name is on every Genocide's lips."

"Wait," Corolla blinks, and her irises become crystal, "why did Tilia think Taxodium was corrupt? Fatigue couldn't have been all that she based her accusation on."

"No," I meet those forlorn eyes, thinking how similar they are to the ones I see each time when I gaze into a mirror, "there were three events in 2004 that didn't quite add up to her." On my fingers, I list them. "The April Attack on the NA, the Alba Atrocities, and our mother's death."

My sister's eyes narrow, but Castan beats Corolla to it. "Why?"

"Because a) the Dentatas should never have broken through the Academy's defenses, b) Adian's body was abandoned, bloody, but untouched, c) Aunt Val and Tate were never attacked by whatever party murdered the rest of the Alba clan."

"Luca is alive, too." Corolla's whispered response sends goosebumps up my arms. Castan tucks unruly strands of hair behind her ears, but that doesn't improve her haunted gaze.

"I know. It's a good thing the proxy Board voted to move him to St. Helena. He'll be safe there with the rest of our people."

"So what, you plan to use the forces on St. Helena to overthrow the Gens?" Castan tosses the ball of fire from one palm to another. To anyone watching, he's playing with his Essence. I know him better. He's trying to remain calm.

"More or less," I nod. "It's what the Valence's plan was all along. It was just a matter of time."

"Your little scheme is going well, I suppose."

I choose to ignore the cynicism in his tone. "For the most part. Corolla," I bite back laughter, "was actually never part of Tilia's plan. That was a spontaneous occurrence on its own."

"It wasn't spontaneous," Castan's voice is even, but his flame fumes, "it was *my* plan to lure the Gens in and destroy them." And just like that, he throws his guards back up. I'm locked out.

Castan pushes out of his chair, running a hand down his face. If his goal is to smooth the scowl from his visage, he fails. He grasps something around his neck, yanks, and tosses the object on the table. The metal glints silver in the light. My dog tag. As Castan turns his back to leave, the furious lines deepen.

"Castan—" I rise, hoping to catch his arm, but he's already past the archway. He takes the light with him, the main cavern glowing a mixture of orange and yellow along dirt-brown walls.

I pull the flashlight from my belt soon enough to see Corolla, body swaying without Castan to catch her. I scramble around the table and press a hand to her shoulder. She glances at me, eyes brazen. In that moment, I wonder if that's the look my father always described when he spoke about Adian. How fierce she was. My heart is overcome with the idea of a family that could never be.

"Even for a moment, I wish I could've grown up with you."

The white glow of my flashlight catches in her pupils. I blink, and that look of surprise is replaced with something bitter. Her face pinches, and she jerks away from me. Before I can react, a hand flies across my face.

I clutch my smarting cheek, incredulous.

Corolla squares her shoulders, chest heaving. "If I had two hands, I would have strangled you."

Corolla
August 2020

"You know, last time we were here, I told Tilia that I wanted transparency between the two of us. She agreed, yet she contained so many secrets... I know she had her reasons, but then why does this feel like a betrayal? She was on our side. They both are." Castan and I sit close enough that our shoulders almost touch. I maintain that centimeter of distance and gaze out between a break in the hedges surrounding Matrona. The sun sets, a fiery half circle in the horizon.

"Because it is. A betrayal."

Castan chuckles, but the sound rings cynically in my ears. Perhaps those are broken too. "No one understands human emotion—Except maybe Nasreen."

I scrape my big toe across the dirt and decide not to answer. He's referring to Calyx. To my brother being alive.

Jesus.

Castan shifts, his deep voice in my ear. "Can I check your arm?"

Rather than respond, I clutch his nearest hand. My eyes trace the veins bulging there, blue and healthy. A sense of déjà vu overtakes me, and my head spins for a short eternity. I've done this before, admired his hands. But then, even though they are the same anatomical structures as before, they are different.

"Burnt him alive."

If he could hear my thoughts, they would break his heart.

I place his hand in his lap and relinquish myself to his purposes. While he unties the knot, I wonder about my brother. Calyx doesn't know how much Castan has suffered since his supposed death. How much he tormented himself for something that was out of his hands in more ways than I could ever imagine. Calyx doesn't know Castan has killed for him. I don't think I slapped him hard enough to realize this, however.

Out of the corner of my eye, Castan's hands roll up the frilly lace sleeve. I avert my eyes while he inspects what the light of the setting sun reveals.

"Part of the wound reopened, and some of the blisters burst."

"Blisters?" I hear myself say. "From the cauterization?"

"You don't remember? I guess you wouldn't. You passed out with the pain." He makes a face as he ties the sleeve together again. I aim my gaze higher into the overhanging branches of Matrona. I follow the limbs, count the rustling leaves, and ignore the strange, painful sensation gnawing on my left arm.

"I want you to see Maggie as soon as possible. You're more susceptible to infections now. Do you feel feverish?" Without waiting for an answer, he places the back of his hand against my forehead.

At the pressure of his hand, I clamp my eyes shut. "That's ironic, coming from you."

"I just want—"

"Corolla, Castan!" A voice calls behind us. Castan turns his head, but I remain unmoved. Calyx's footsteps resound in my ears.

"I want to apologize, Castan, for offending you, for putting you in the worst possible situation imaginable." He inhales after that mouthful, and then my name is on his lips. "Corolla, all things considered, I don't think you should join the pelari on St. Helena right now."

"What are you saying?" Castan rises, and dust flies into my eyes as a result. I blink away the grit, tears springing to my waterline.

"I'm saying," Calyx answers at my back, "that it's time Corolla met our father. I'll send Maggie to meet you there, and she can take a look at your arm." His tone shifts, "Castan—"

"I'm not abandoning her right now." Where his voice has been jagged and unwelcoming, it is soft and pleading. I blink back tears, though there's no longer dirt in my eye.

"Of course." Calyx sounds as if he nodded. "Here are the coordinates for your geometer." There's an exchanging of paper. Calyx adds, "I wish I could go home with you, but I have to assemble the Valence and prepare. This won't be an easy war to win. I'll come for you two when I'm ready."

Castan makes a noncommittal noise and sinks down beside me once more. He tucks my shoulders under an arm, pulls my head to rest on his chest. In one ear, is the beat of his heart. In the other, is his low voice.

"Well, Tess, are you up for another family reunion?" Behind the shaky air of his comment, he masks more profound questions, ones I wouldn't know how to answer. I don't have to ask to know what he's thinking about. Death is on both our minds this evening.

"In a minute," I respond a little too late, though he makes no move to get up. "I don't want to leave just yet."

Unseen birds twitter over our heads. The sun descends until it is but a thin crescent in the horizon. I don't allow my mind to wander, to wonder about Kass, if she made it out, to wonder about Talan, Finis, Issak and the fates of every other loyalist at the Academy. If my mind begins to ask those questions, I focus my attention on the rhythm of Castan's heart. Consistent. Steady. But sometimes a little fast.

Castan traces a thumb along the curve of my jaw. "I'm sure James is alright. Aunt Laila probably got him out unscathed. They'll be waiting for us at St. Helena."

"Yes," I watch the heat waves rolling off the earth, "I'm sure they are."

It doesn't matter that strong arms encircle me. It doesn't matter how many times I count his heartbeats. It doesn't matter that the ground is right underneath me.

I am falling.

The sun has long ago set when we finally rise. Castan groans, helping me to my feet. The darkness of the night masks his expression. I imagine he's stiff from more than just sitting in place. *Kass. Talan.* I swallow and try not to think about it too hard.

"Marble Hill, Georgia," Castan muses, "I never knew where he lived. Only where he died." I glance at him. I only see the outline of his shape, but for some reason, I expected to see humor lining his face. But Castan has never been very good at jokes. He crumbles the paper in his fist and shoves it in his thigh pocket.

While he punches the coordinates, I press the tips of my shoulder blades to his back. Jumping used to make my pulse lurch to my throat. Now, I don't even consider the lavender bubble expanding around us. Like a pocket of puss, how much agony is contained within the shimmering veil because of our two bodies? My mind writhes, but my body remains still.

As the world begins to spin, Castan slips his hand into mine.

The dizzying sensation of twirling in repetitive circles is gone almost as quickly as it came. I never once blinked.

I tug my fingers from Castan's. If, somehow, my hand was a bridge to the pain in my heart, then I don't want him to know. I don't want him to suffer any more than what my brother has already put him through. If I'm not careful, Vels will be the death of him.

"Are you alright?" Castan plants firm hands on my shoulders, steadying me before I can answer his question. I can't look him in the eyes because then I'll see the real meaning behind his question. He's not asking about my arm, and I don't know how to respond about my heart.

"I'm fine. You?" I shift out from under his grip. He doesn't seem to notice. I pivot, following his narrowed gaze. My heavy lids absorb our surroundings with less enthusiasm. Tall pines and other trees I can't name line a sloping drive up a hillside. Birds twitter morning songs; the sun settles in the sky. It reminds me of the tunnel of trees leading into the Academy, but where those trees arched over the blacktop road like arthritic fingers, these trees stand straight. Not a drop of shade adorns the dirt drive. A wooden sign, near the iron-wrought mailbox, reads in intricately carved letters: Alba Creek Farm.

"I don't see a farm," Castan nudges my good shoulder. I manage a small turn of my lips. "I don't smell one either." I blink. Hard.

"Hey, Corolla." Castan places a finger under my chin. His eyebrows furrow, worry dripping from the pinched corners of his eyes. "Why—"

"We should go," I nod in the direction of the inclining drive. Without waiting for an answer, I place my feet on the soft grass banks and begin the trek up. After a moment, Castan follows me.

In silence, we walk. If I were listening, I'd hear the birdsong, the morning breeze ruffling the pines walling us in on both sides. If I were listening, I'd hear the world moving on when my brain cannot.

All I see is Castan, the pale morning sun reflecting off his chestnut hair like a halo. I study his face, the slope of his nose, and the way he tries to mask a wince whenever he steps on a rock. I want to touch him, to brush the stray hair from his lashes—I almost raise my arm, but I catch myself. I may want to touch him, but I can't. Because he walks on my left side, and I can't fit myself on his other side without being slapped by pines.

The dirt drive empties out into a blacktop clearing. On my left, stuffed between a copse of pine trees, is a two-car garage. The white doors are open, a cherry red Impala occupying one of the spots. On my right, chickens balk in a fenced-in pen. Chained to an apple tree, is a shaggy, gray goat. Before us, is my father's house.

Standing two stories tall, the house is enormous, the swell of the mountainside looming behind it. The siding is ivory, a literal white picket fence enclosing the front porch and disappearing on both sides of the house. Something tickles my brain. It's only when I cock my head that I realize what: The house resembles Allen Manor. My eyes dart to the curtained windows, expecting to see flickering candlelight there, a black-uniformed guard in the shadows.

Castan places a hand on my back, guiding me forward. All I can manage to say is, "This isn't where I thought he'd live."

In all my fantasies of my father, I never placed him as a farmer. I imagined him as a degraded man, living in some shack or cheap house like James and I did. Or a man surrounded, haunted by his own mistakes. A drunk. An addict. Grisly and unbearable, but lovely underneath the bloodshot eyes and stubbled jaw. I pictured him broken, and I portrayed myself as the only one who could fix him.

"I guess farm translates into chicken pen," Castan surmises. I welcome the warmth of the blacktop under my sore feet. When my soles slap on the cool concrete steps, my heart sinks a little more.

Castan rings the doorbell. It chimes a trill of notes, the sounds jarring to my ears. I fix my eyes on a hammock swaying in the wind on the porch. A litter of *People* magazines sprawls across the white net. A local newspaper displays flaming trees and fallen buildings. I avert my gaze.

Moments pass, and a woman answers the door. She's dressed in a black blazer, blonde hair clipped back at the nape of her neck.

I don't listen to the woman either. She makes startled noises, faces. A boy older than me pops up behind one of her shoulders. Mousy brown hair, blue eyes, he's too young to be my father. I wonder if we have the right coordinates. All the while, Castan speaks, his voice a low hum in my ears. I let him. Know how desperately he wants to be useful. He's just as lost as I am.

So while Castan explains, negotiates, while the woman nods her head as if understanding the impossibility of our situation, I see James. He's wearing his suit, blonde hair ruffled as if he just rolled out of bed. His hair never cooperates, but I don't care. I grab his hand. Squeeze it. I shoot him a look, and those pale blue eyes crinkle at the corners. *I know*, they say. *I missed you too, but I'm here now.*

I'm here now.

Castan's hand is pressing the small of my back again. With pleading eyes, I stare at James. His body dissipates, a thousand droplets of water in the sunlight. A mirage.

Castan and the woman sweep me up a set of stairs, into a room reeking of potpourri. I wrinkle my nose. Castan thanks the woman, who hangs awkwardly by the door. At some point, the boy left. Maybe he was never there either.

The woman nods her head, "I have another room down the hall for you, Castan." I don't like his name on her lips. The Southern accent twisting his syllables into something else. I want to pluck him from her mouth and send her on her way.

Castan fumbles, shooting me worried looks.

I glance over my shoulder at the quilted bed. I touch fingertips to his shoulder, so he'll believe me when I say, "I just want to be alone right now. Sleep, you know."

Castan meets my gaze for a short century. I blink. Turn away.

The woman's voice finds its way into my hearing, "I can get you some fresh clothes. A towel and washcloth for a shower."

"No," my own voice is dry compared to her hopeful tone, "I just want to sleep." I don't bother to see if they're gone. The door clicks shut, and the atmosphere plummets into stillness. The room is so small, it takes three steps to reach the only window. I push back the thin white curtains and peer outside. The chicken coop is below. The branches from the goat tree filter the view, but I see enough. The mountains sloping ever higher as my eyes travel the green land. Movement below catches my eye. I crane my neck and glimpse a red figure through the tree's leaves. Without seeing his face, I know it's the boy I saw earlier. I guess he does exist.

I tug the thin curtains back in place. Sit on the edge of the bed. My toes scrunch in the softness of the floor. After the unforgiving stone of the fortress, the hard-packed earth of Tilia's cavern, the carpet feels unreal. I don't want it.

I tuck my knees under my chin, wrap my arm around my shins. There's a high-pitched humming in my ear. A mosquito comes into focus, lands on my kneecap, and bites through the fabric of my nightgown. Instinctively, I raise my hand and smack it. Its body smears gray across my hand, blood across my knee. I stare at that brushstroke of crimson, tears lining my eyes.

I am rocking backward, body heaving with sobs. Agony rips through me, more painful than any lost limb. I bite my lip to keep from making too much noise. I know if I do, Castan will come running. Then I will have to explain what I cannot.

James, I weep, *James I never got to make you proud. I never*—I fold into myself, bury my face in the wrinkled quilt and sullied fabric of my nightgown.

"I can't do it," I hiss. "I can't." I don't know what I mean, only that there has always been James. And now there is a gaping hole within me where he is not.

I lay there, quivering with tears, for so long, a headache blooms behind my eyes. The tears stop flowing. I stuff a pillow under my head and try to sleep when I am restless. Where my old sleeplessness was the shut-eyed, inability to get comfortable type, this sleeplessness is the open-eyed, staring at a blank wall and the nothingness I cannot comprehend.

***

Morning dew wets my feet. The sun rises over my shoulder; a flock of indistinguishable birds soars overhead.

"James!" I skip towards the house where my uncle kneels over the flowerbeds surrounding its perimeter. Slick blades of grass slip through my toes until I feel like I'm running across water. For a long time, that was my favorite thing to do in the spring.

"James," I huff, hands on my hips, "what are you planting?" His back blocks my view of whatever plant his gloved hands grapple.

He turns, brushes the hair from his eyes. In the sun, his blonde locks are golden. By the youth in his face, the lack of worry underlying his

433

expression, I must be six or seven. When James had the job at the office. When James was happy, and I was a kid whose biggest sin was tattooing my name on the wall with Sharpie.

"Daisies," he exhales. "Want to help?"

"For Adian?" I cock my head, tiny chest heaving. I wear a lip-splitting smile. That's what James called my grin once. I always thought my lips would actually split. Sometimes, I tried to make them tear at the corners.

"Yes," he nods his head, sober. His own grin doesn't slip, though. A fist of apprehension loosens its hold over my heart. Asking about my mother was a risk, no matter how many years passed since her death. One Thanksgiving, I found James crying in his room. When I asked him what was wrong, he ducked his head, wiped the tears from his eyes. "Sometimes, Corolla, you just miss people." And even though Grandpa and Grandma had long since passed away, I knew James wept for his sister. For Adian.

I kneel beside James now, fingering the pale white petals. I poke one in the yellow center. I look from the pit he's dug for the daisies to the clump of gangly roots waiting to be buried.

"She'll love these." We used to talk about Adian as if she were still around; as if she hadn't been butchered in Tennessee.

"Yes," James sticks a cluster in a hole, "she will." He shows me how to cover the roots and pat the dirt to secure the plant. When we're finished, James disappears inside to make lunch. I race into the backyard, into the shadow of woods. I collect as many rocks as I can find and return to the daisies. Around each one, I make a stone perimeter. I did it for the rose bushes last week. The forget-me-nots, however, wouldn't follow the pattern.

My palms itch as if covered in poison ivy oil. I scratch sharp nails across my flesh, fighting the urge to shove my hands in the soil and undo all of the work James and I have just completed.

James returns with two plates of potato chips and ham and cheese sandwiches. I forget about my palms, the desire to destroy. We sit on the steps, tucking into our meal, and admire the beauty of the flowerbeds.

***

My eyelids flutter. Evening light floods my little room. For a moment, I can't remember where I am, why there's a sun-yellow quilt beneath me. I sit up, clutching my head. There's a piercing ache in my temples. I reach an arm to wipe the crust from my eyes, but a different pain cuts the movement short.

"Oh." That crust is dried tears. That ache is raw amputation.

James.

I raise my fist, facial muscles pinched. I unfurl my fingers, and there, nestled in the palm of my hand, is a white-petaled daisy.

Hadley
August 2020

"Your brother is dead." Numen's pen scratches across a sheet of paper, as my body goes rigid. *Which brother?* The question jumps to my tongue. I bite it back. Wait.

My gaze wanders around Numen's office. In the Complex, his mahogany desk was on the 23rd Level, near a sweltering fireplace. At the SA, his desk overlooks the fertile valley below. Sometimes, the clouds are so low, they blanket the sky and give off the illusion of a castle floating in the atmosphere. When those days happen, I find a high ledge in the Academy and perch there for as long as I can manage to be alone.

The day the Dentatas infiltrated Taxodium, the clouds were low-hanging blankets. But I couldn't lounge on a ledge like I usually do. Instead, I went through my father's desk with a fine-tooth comb. *Where's Mena?* Was all I could think, even as the raucous cheering from down below soared into the sky and through the office windows. Even as the clattering of chains, the whimpering of prisoners' cries, met my ears. I could only search for my mother's coordinates, coordinates I'm no longer sure exist. Mena may as well be dead.

A fountain splashes behind me, calling to attention the streams on either side of the walkway leading to my father's desk. I lower my head at the shimmering surface, the blue mosaic beneath the water. The streams vanish underneath the stone before they have the opportunity to swarm the platform that supports the desk.

Having grown up in crude concrete, I think the architecture is a little excessive. But it's better than being underground.

The harsh tone of my father anchors my gaze to him once more. Gray flecks the edges of his hairline. Wrinkles line his forehead, the hollows under his eyes. I never gave Numen the label of *old*, but he appears like so now.

"There's no way in hell I'm allowing Castan to be my heir. So," he sets his pen aside, "it's time that you married." Those black eyes focus on my hazel ones. I don't cower. He has that effect on many others, but he has never held that power over me.

"I suppose this means no more forcing weak-minded fools at me during dinners?" I whirl my wrist, feigning disinterest to mask my relief: Castan is alive. I haven't seen him in almost two years—Belarus doesn't count. I had to run from him when all I wanted was to embrace him. When that moment comes, I'll tell him all about how I told Maggie Delphi to place a tracker in his geometer. I'll tell him all about how I believed Mena to be somewhere in that bunker. I'll tell him all about my disappointment when I realized only a half-alive Alba was there instead.

But this also means Rosh is dead.

"No," Numen sighs, begrudgingly admits, "this means someone with *will*."

I don't dare say, "I could be your heir—I don't *have* to marry." I know better. Even with Renatus's forward thinking (women *can* be part of the Guard), my father would never hand the leadership over to a woman. He tends to depose strong-willed women. Manages to make them vanish.

I collapse onto an upholstered chair.

"So Rosh…" Emotion chokes my words. For a split second, I have to examine the lump in my throat. When acting is all I ever seem to do, it is difficult to know what's real. But this is. "Did they recover his body?"

Numen leans back into his chair, studies my reaction. "Yes, daughter. Baylor is taking care of the arrangements as we speak." Where there should be a drop of remorse, there is only stone. Even if Rosh was a cruel bastard, even if he was the most twisted soul in the world, I still loved him. He was still my brother. He was still a link. Now, staring into my father's pitch-black pupils, I am alone. Rosh had potential to change where Jon Xabier never could. Never can.

I prop elbows on my knees. Life and Death have only ever been reminders that the one cannot exist without the other. Everything is a moment, a flicker. I learned that when Numen took my mother away, when, six years later, Castan almost killed that boy in Carnage. Everything is fleeting.

But the Valence can make those moments last a little bit longer.

I *must* find Mena.

"Taxodium has fallen?"

Again, Numen nods.

"Good."

"Yes."

"Can I see his body?"

Numen looks up from his papers. "There's not much remaining."

I scoot closer, on the edge of my chair. "What do you mean?"

My father clears his throat. A low growl escapes past his lips, "Because Castan burned him alive."

I flinch. "Oh." Tuck the stray hair behind my ears. "Castan will suffer for this." My voice is hard, steeled over the way I learned from my father and his brother, Baylor. Numen doesn't pick up on the double meaning behind my words. Castan *will* suffer. Of that, I am sure. Guilt erodes people that way.

Numen glances back at the papers sprawled across his desk. The trickle of fountain water defeats the silence between us. He scratches something in ink, folds the paper in half, shoves it in a drawer. I track his movements, always aware. I put aside my fear of being caught long ago, but that doesn't mean I've lost my instincts. I have to be careful around Numen, the same way experienced marine biologists are careful around sharks. It doesn't matter how long you've been with the creature, it's still feral.

"Is Rosh going to be put in the Mausoleums?"

Numen's eyebrow raises a minute degree. "I suppose he will be put wherever Baylor chooses."

"You aren't—"

"Hadley!" His massive paw smacks the desktop. I do not flinch, but my pulse races laps in my ears. "I have more pressing matters to sort out than your brother's burial."

I cross my arms. Make a face. "More pressing matters than *your* son?"

My father's hands curl into fists. A muscle in his jaw twitches. When he meets my gaze, I don't bow my head under the weight of those black irises. His voice is the grating noise of bone rubbing bone, of inflicting pain. "Watch yourself, daughter. I am still Numen."

I almost smirk. *Rosh didn't think so*. There wasn't much Rosh disagreed with our father about, but Renatus's heavy involvement in Dentata affairs was one of them. I tend to side with my eldest brother: our father isn't as powerful as he believes. The Genocides flood this Academy, new faces every day. Though Gens and Dentatas alike have a common goal, they come for Renatus, not Jon Xabier.

My father folds his hands together. The action is more civil than he has ever claimed to be.

"Now go. I have things to prepare for Renatus's arrival."

I pause, elbows bent, butt hovering five inches above my chair. "Renatus's coming here? When?" Numen grins at the odd quality of my voice. It's not awe. It's not fear. It's something else altogether. Alarm, maybe.

"Yes. Now go, Hadley." He flicks his hand towards the exit. I stalk past the upholstered chair, my boots scuffing along the stone strip between the two steady arteries of flowing water. I make it to the brownstone pillars of the archway supporting the office doors, when

438

my father adds, "If you hurry, you may catch your uncle." I don't have to ask what he's referring to. In the shadows of the room, he can't see me, but I nod regardless.

Shuffling down the winding corridors of Collis Hall, I pass the black uniform of the Genocides who betrayed Taxodium. Some recognize me as Numen's daughter, acknowledge me with a curt nod of their head. Others don't give me a second glance. I shoulder through a crowd of young men, make sure they notice my fingers wrapped around the gun at my belt. Everyone is always looking at me, especially since I turned sixteen. Especially since Numen announced I am eligible to marry soon. Well, I guess *soon* is *now*.

Everyone here is so fucking primitive. I make a sharp right, shoulders relaxing. This corridor is empty, rectangles of sunlight striking the far wall. I glance outside the windows at the breathtaking view of the Cordillera. The South American Academy brags the highest altitude, the most isolation, and the best masonry. It doesn't surprise me at all that we moved here after Castan's departure compromised the Complex's location.

So far away from civilization, my mother would have hated it here.

Collis Hall used to house Major Tieko before she was deposed and executed. Her Commander was a Gen, plotted against her and facilitated the Dentata infiltration. Renatus, as always, was pulling strings from wherever it is that he operates.

I glance over my shoulder, see only the clear-cut brownstone of the corridor, and shoulder the main doors open. Cold mountain air greets my senses. I take in the cloud coverage, the structures of the Academy cut into the mountainside, and start down the steps. Baylor will be on the other side of the ridge, so I'll have to cut through the mountain using the pass. The Mausoleums scatter that side of the Academy. From the ground, the gray-brown stone structures blend in with the rocky mountainside.

I'll have to send Calyx a message about Renatus's coming. But Rosh comes first. My father may be callous, untouched by his son's death, but I will never be that calcified. My father has stopped appreciating death. That's the part of the Dentata disease nobody talks about. If you quit valuing death, then life will depreciate too. They go hand-in-hand.

Castan
August 2020

Some part of me always marveled with the knowledge that my brother was living and breathing, just outside of my reach. No matter how much I despised him, no matter how much I wished he would be captured or just drop dead, I was always conscious of his heart beating. He was a shadow, hovering over my head. I was used to him. And now he is gone. Gone. By my own hand.

I rake fingers through my damp hair and glance around the room again: a box of Legos on a desk in the corner, a sketch for some contraption taped to the back of the door. I don't have to recognize that handwriting to know this was Calyx's room. *Is* Calyx's room. My stomach twinges with nausea. The clothes Julli gave me to wear are probably his, too.

A head peeks through the crack in the door. Corolla slips inside and shuts the door behind her. I step towards her. She looks worse than those days she was bedridden in Tilia's cavern. Her hair is knotted and tangled, eyes rimmed red from crying. There are imprints of wrinkles on her cheek where she fell asleep. Her expression is one that could only translate as grief.

"What's wrong?" I brush back her disheveled hair. "You haven't been... you." It's a stupid thing to say, but I don't know how else to phrase it.

Her shoulders tremble. She bows her head into my sternum. It takes me a moment to realize she's laughing. She pulls away and holds up her cupped hand.

"Your paperwork lied." She doubles over with laughter, and I have to grab her hand to see what's resting in her palm.

"A daisy." I let go. "Did you pick this?"

"No," she gasps for breath. "No, I created it, Castan. My palms have been itching, and I assumed it was because of... something else. I—" she breaks off, face falling. Tears brim her swollen eyes. If I could decipher the thoughts flitting behind her eyes, I would.

I tug her to my chest, smooth back her hair. "My whole plan was wrong."

"I'm sorry." She's not laughing anymore. She's not crying either.

"You can't apologize for being everything you have been pretending to be. This isn't the *Importance of Being Earnest*."

She staggers backward. "I don't know that one."

"You're not volga, Corolla. And you're not pedes. You're pelari."

Her expression crumples again. Despair overwhelms her little figure. I want to reach out and grab her, but she backs away before I can extend an arm to touch her.

"What's wrong?"

Her eyes flit across my chest. "*Star Wars* doesn't look right on you."

"I'm serious."

"So am I."

"You're stalling. Corolla," I go to her, guide her to the edge of Calyx's bed. "What's going on?"

Just when I think she's resisting me, she exhales a single, whispered word, "James."

My body tenses. I reread her expression, and I know. My voice is dangerously quiet, sharp enough to cut glass, "Why didn't you tell me earlier?"

She takes my hand and sets the daisy in my palm. My attention remains glued to her eyes hiding behind thick lashes. "What's the point? Someone always has it worse, so what's the point in sharing and being sad together? There's someone else out there who has no arms, no uncles, no one to be her advocate. So," I wipe the tears trickling down her cheeks, and she raises her head, "what's the point? Here you are, after having to play George and put down Lenny, and you... you're just so strong, Castan. I can't be. I can't. But I must. Because someone's sadness will always one-up my own."

"Oh, Corolla," I grip her shoulder, "you're so backwards."

"Everything is backward, Castan. Look at where we are right now," she gestures to the room and winces. "Calyx is alive, and James is... and my father? Who the hell knows what's up with him. We shouldn't be here. We should be at St. Helena. Helping to end this war."

I don't say anything. She has a point.

"But you're wrong," I stroke the backside of her hand, trace the veins, "about sadness, I mean. You are entitled to feel anything you want, Corolla. I know I sound like Aunt Laila, but she told me this all the time when Calyx died—when I *thought* he died," I amend. "You just have to roll with it. Other people's circumstances aside, you have to allow yourself to feel your own emotions."

She leans her head on my shoulder but remains silent.

"I didn't know you knew *Of Mice and Men*."

She makes a noise.

"But you should know I'm not so strong. You know what I was thinking before you came in here? I was thinking about my brother. I wish the circumstances could have been different, but I am grieving for him nonetheless. As terrible as he was… It's the only way to get through… these types of things, Corolla. Is to feel."

"How can I feel when everything is so numb?"

I set the daisy beside Corolla on the mattress and sink to my knees. I cup her face between my hands.

"Look at me."

Her eyes swivel to meet my gaze. How could I have ever thought they were Calyx's eyes in her skull?

"I won't let you be alone, okay? We are bound together now, and I won't leave you behind."

Her mind registers my words, but I couldn't say if her heart does. She bows her head, still cradled in my grip.

"Okay," she exhales, "thank you."

I run thumbs across her cheekbones. Something inside me melts. She shouldn't be thanking me. I should be apologizing—without me, she would still have a home, an average life, an arm. She wouldn't have to kill to survive. And she would still have James.

But her Essence…

Her eyes flit to mine. She places her hand over my own. One by one, she removes my hands and puts them in her lap.

"It's not your fault, Castan."

I don't know how to tell her otherwise, so I change the subject.

"Julli left clothes and towels in the bathroom for you."

"Julli?"

"Tyto's wife."

"Oh."

I rise, tugging my hands from under hers. "She's downstairs now. Tyto'll be home from work around four." I comb fingers through my damp hair again. "If Calyx doesn't send Maggie soon, we're jumping out of here for St. Helena."

Too soon, there is a knock on the bedroom door. I jostle, Corolla tucked asleep at my side. Her wet hair has soaked through Luke Skywalker's face on my borrowed shirt, leaving my skin cool underneath.

The figure in the door crack clears his throat, pushes through. I nudge Corolla awake.

"What?" She blinks, groggy. "Is it time to go?"

The man in the doorway beats me to it. "Corolla Vel," he takes a step closer, "my own daughter."

Corolla jolts upright, blanket tossed aside. I try to see what she does: an estranged father. But it's just a man dressed in black slacks and a salmon polo. He resembles Calyx in complexion, though his skin is a shade darker, his eyes, a degree dimmer.

Behind her back, Corolla clenches her fist. She'll have a thousand questions, a thousand inquiries, but all she asks is, "Did you know about Luca?"

Tyto ducks his head. "Yes, Valeria keeps me updated."

"You didn't come see him."

"No." Tyto tosses his gaze out the window so he won't have to meet his daughter's reprimands. He claps hands on his thighs and faces Corolla once more. "But I'm glad you're here," his eyes skate over my hand on her waist, steadying Corolla's skewed balance. He glances away before he reaches the place where Corolla should be supporting herself but can't. "I heard about Taxodium. Another tragedy."

"Yes." How she keeps her voice so calm, I don't know. For reasons I don't understand, I want to shake this man until his eyes dislodge from his head. Maybe then he'll see her.

"But anyway," he rakes a hand through his salt and pepper hair, "dinner is ready downstairs."

Corolla nods. I add, "We'll be right down."

Tyto shoots me a look but doesn't say anything further. He returns Corolla's nod and slips through the doorway once more.

When he's gone, Corolla unfurls her fist. Crumbled daisies fall to the bedspread.

"So that's the infamous Tyto Alba."

I shrug. "He could have kicked us out."

Corolla hisses a breath of laughter. "I hoped he was unemployed. Something had to have kept him from finding me. I hoped it was drugs, drunkenness, financial inability, or maybe a severe concussion. But he's perfectly well off."

I slide off the bed and offer her my hand. "C'mon. Let's go eat."

Talan
August 2020

I wake to the sound of rattling chains. The noise grates my eardrums, along with hushed whimpers and bolder weeping. I don't have to crack my eyelids to know where I am. I'd see the brownstone masonry barricading us on three sides, the iron-wrought rods of the cell door.

I suck in a breath and wince. I didn't forget how I got here, but I did forget the bruises on my abdomen. I fell in battle. That's when they captured me, the foundation of the Academy crumbling all around me. But even when I was being kicked in the gut into unconsciousness, I could only wonder about Jura's resting place. Is it intact? Is she undisturbed? My finger feels naked without my ring of the Jura mountain ranges.

And Finis. He took off into the array for the Academy in Adelaide, and I haven't seen him since. I push away the hiss whispering that he's dead. I would know if he died. I would *know*. That's how love works, doesn't it? It binds you in ways science cannot explain.

Using my elbows, I ease myself into a sitting position. The chain around my ankle scrapes along solid ground. They bound our hands with Empara locks, devices designed to inhibit Essences, a biological lock. So far, they're working.

I glance around, groggy. Three others are cramped in the cell with me. I recognize one freshman from the Dining Hall. Slumped against the wall, he's in fitful slumber. The two girls, one blonde, the other raven-haired, I don't know. Judging by the fact that they speak Spanish, I'm assuming the Euro Academy fell too. Their deep voices slur together strings of words I can't comprehend. I wish I'd taken Spanish instead of Mandarin. I wish I knew what they were saying, eyes wide with fear. They might know something useful like *How long have the Genocides been camped out in the SA?* or *How long have the Gens been our* own *people?* I don't take the betrayal personally—I'm not the only one in chains because of the traitors. But a sense of battered pride surges throughout my being. We really were blind, weren't we?

I pull my leg, tugging the chain on the freshman's leg. He startles awake, black curls spilling into his eyes. He could be handsome, from certain angles.

"Over here," I wave, though we aren't *that* far apart. Our bare feet touch, the callus on his big toe rubbing against my soft underside. His hazel eyes settle on my profile, and the anxiety in his expression subsides beneath a layer of curiosity.

"You're closer to the door," I nod my head towards the bars, "what do you see out there?"

For a moment, he only stares at me, and I question whether he understands plain English. But then he cranes his neck towards the bars, pulse twitching in his throat. While he scans, I note the girls have stopped chattering and are studying the freshman as carefully as I am.

"I think we're in the Barracks. It looks like there are cells on this half of the wall only, though." I could have guessed that, based on our view of the stone wall.

The dark-haired girl shifts, yanking my leg in the other direction. She doesn't seem to notice. "Una salida?"

The freshman blinks twice. Shakes his head. "I'm sorry. I don't see one."

I startle. "You understand them?"

He replies slowly, "Yes."

I almost laugh. "I took Mandarin. I only catch fragments of their conversation."

The boy shrugs, "I've been listening to them for half an hour now. They've been here for a couple days longer than us."

"What's your name?"

"Thomas Azisio."

"Thomas, I'm Talan Taylor. I'd shake your hand if they weren't bound."

"Right," Thomas cracks a smile. In this cell reeking of human waste and drowning spirits, the act is a breath of fresh air. "That's Nena," he gestures to the blonde, "and Solenne, by the way."

"Are they from the Euro Academy?"

Thomas shrugs. "I'll ask." A ribbon of words spirals past his lips. He doesn't speak nearly as fast as Nena and Solenne, but quickly enough that I can't decipher a single word.

Solenne answers in her alto voice. Nena trembles, hugging closer to Solenne's side. Thomas's leg gets yanked, causing mine to drag towards him now. After a moment, Solenne's voice dies away. I don't like that eerie look in her eyes.

"What did she say?"

Thomas shakes his head to clear his eyes of his curls. "They're from Rome, yeah."

"But they don't speak English?"

"Well," Thomas doesn't meet my gaze, "they do, but they don't like to risk it after last time."

"Last time?"

"Apparently, our captors really only speak English, but," his voice dips into a whisper, "the two prisoners here before us were taken away because they talked too much, too loudly."

My shoulders sink. "And the girls never saw them again?"

"Correct. There's a group that flocks around the Barracks. They wear executioners' hoods. Black, Solenne said, so you can't see their faces. She thinks they're ashamed of being traitors."

Nena cuts in, a whirl of tearful words. I watch her lips, willing my brain to understand what's making her cry.

Thomas swallows, Adam's apple bobbing. "She said they call themselves the Vultures," Nena whimpers and Solenne sets her bound hands on the trembling girl's knee, "and that they aren't ashamed. Like pelari newborns, they laughed when they killed her friends."

"How does she know that? They weren't killed here, were they?" Though my tone is hushed to match Thomas's, horror rings clear in my voice.

He shakes his head. "No, they take their prey someplace else, but Nena swears she heard them laughing down the hall. You know," he gulps, and I remember how young he actually is, "over all the screaming and pleading."

"The Vultures?"

He glances at me, a bruise highlighting his left orbit, "Because vultures flock around the bodies of those they take away."

Corolla
August 2020

"It's kind of funny, isn't it?"

Maggie, glasses sliding down the bridge of her nose, inspects my arm. Grimaces. She asks in a voice that tells me she's not really listening, "What is?"

"Well," I glance at Castan's figure in the window, "that Tyto's estranged daughter shows up at his doorstep, post-battle, and he can't take time off work to get to know me." I shrug my other shoulder while Maggie touches gentle fingers to my flesh. I expect Castan to say something, but he's been very reclusive today. He met me in my room after Julli served breakfast, and though his place is more spacious, we've been lounging here ever since. Then Maggie appeared.

"Your fingers are cold."

"Your wound is inflamed," Maggie confirms. "I can take the swelling and infection away, but I can't grow you a new arm." She pushes up the sleeves of her shirt.

My voice is sharper than I intend, "I know."

"Of course you do," she radiates sympathy, "I'm too used to the hysteric. I'm sorry."

Maggie prepares herself, slow, methodical breaths, but I watch Castan the entire time. One leg is bent at the knee, the other draped across the window seat. Arms propped on his raised knee. If I had a photo of him the day we met side-by-side to his appearance today, I would see that his hair has grown long, little curls over his ears. The bags under his eyes are accented yellow with the fading bruises. But past that, past the physical, I would see more sadness. Against the morning sun, wearing Calyx's clothes, he is tragic.

I thought he was criminal, military, but he's never been that way. He's always been—

Maggie sucks in a gasp of air. My head snaps in her direction in time to see blisters bubbling around the circumference of her left arm. Just below the elbow. Exactly where I lost my forearm.

"Maggie—" I lurch forward to grab her, but she bats my hand away.

"I'm fine," she says through clenched teeth, "I just haven't done burns in a while. Don't break the connection." Her right hand grips my wound for a moment longer before slipping away. Her eyelids flutter with the agony I've grown accustomed to. Castan loops arms under her shoulders and guides her to the bed beside me.

Maggie shoves her glasses up the bridge of her nose, eyes filling with tears. I can only watch her suffering, so similar to my own. It's like watching someone adorn your own skin—I'm intrigued, amazed at how poorly she wears it.

It's a lot to bear, isn't it?

But she's a Healer, Castan likes to remind me, not a god. I doubt I could tolerate her suffering either.

Castan digs a hand into her satchel. "Here," he slips a bottle between her fingers. Maggie clutches the thick plastic container, brings it to her lips. I'm surprised at the ring of familiarity I perceive from her bottle. Back home, at school, guys would carry similar ones in the side pockets of their backpacks. Blender bottles, they dubbed them. For post-workouts. A wave of nausea rolls through my gut.

"Thank you." She takes a swig, but her body continues to tremble.

"Are you... alright?"

"Yes," she manages a grin, "the protein helps." She raises her bottle in a manner that makes me wonder if I should have a cup in my hand too, just so I can say, "Cheers!" How wrong such an action it would be, I can only begin to guess. I haven't been pedes in a long time.

Color comes back to Maggie's cheeks. Castan retreats to the window seat, his back to us. Calyx's shirts are too small for him, stretched taut across his frame like canvas pulled over an embroidery hoop. Yesterday it was the classic *Return of the Jedi*. Today, it's a ghastly blue and white striped polo.

The words slip past my tongue, "We should be at St. Helena. With you."

Maggie's gaze rests on my exposed arm. "It's like Ellis Island there. You guys are better off waiting until the chaos dies down." She touches fingers to my skin. They're still cold. "This is looking much better. Puckered, but clean."

"Who made it to the island?" Castan turns, and the concentration of sobriety is enough to make me want to throw up.

"Finis escaped the slaughter in Adelaide with a broken leg," Maggie doesn't even bat an eye, "and no one's seen Talan since the Sentries fired at the Barracks. Everyone else is fine. Kass jumped her entire family, one by one."

"She's alive?" I almost grasp Maggie's knee in disbelief. Would have, had she been perched on my other side.

"Yes," Maggie rises, "she has some choice words for Calyx when he finally arrives. I'm off to meet with the Valence now, actually."

Castan's lips part, as if he's about to say something, but I cut in before he can. "If Kass knows Calyx is alive, then shouldn't Tyto and Tate?"

Maggie shrugs. "I honestly couldn't say. Our plans to make Calyx disappear are null and void at this point." She stares in Castan's direction when she adds, "It was only ever to protect him from the Gens before we knew *who* that entailed." Castan makes two fists, and I hear the *pop* of knuckles cracking.

Maggie presses on, re-adjusting her shoulder strap, as if Castan isn't fighting back flames, no matter how weak they are. "But the African Academy was loyal. Mostly. It only fell because of some key leadership *impairments*." *Traitors*, she means, but neither Castan nor I ask. "The Gens, as it turns out, are mainly younger generation idealists. Inexperienced too. So even though Taxodium as a whole has collapsed, we still have a fighting chance at winning this war."

"Right," Castan half growls. I know what he's thinking: *We're part of the younger generation, and our only allies are a hospital full of patients on an isolated island.*

What was it he called them before? Cripples? I fight the urge to glance at my own handicap. Is that how he views me?

"Anyway," Maggie stretches her arms over her head, "I need to be going. I'm sure I'll see the both of you soon. Calyx will come for you when he's ready." She faces me, "Rest up and don't strain yourself. You still require recovery time." I nod, though all I really want is to make her disappear. Doctor voices have always had that effect on me. Maybe that's a good sign.

Castan walks her to the door, down the stairs, their footsteps fading. I strain my ears for the low hum of his disapproval—he won't want to wait for Calyx's say so to leave—but there's nothing. Only the click of the front door. Maggie will jump away, and Castan and I will be left with our thoughts.

I lie back on the bed, smoothing my palm across the pastel yellow quilt before pillowing my arm under my head. From this angle, the ceiling fan bulb really does look like a woman's breast. That's about all Castan managed to say to me before Maggie arrived.

I haven't laid eyes on my half-arm yet, and I don't plan on doing that now. The ache that usually accompanies movement of the appendage is gone now, though. It's... liberating. As liberating as a handicap can be, I guess. It doesn't change the fact that I have to ask Castan to help me clasp my bra.

"I *hate* this shirt." I glance up as Castan rips off the striped polo, wads it in a fist, and chucks it at the door. It closes completely, the brass handle glistening in the morning sun. My eyes wander his pale body, the healing bruises speckled across his abdomen like oversized sunspots. I follow the trail of dark hair diving down his stomach.

"I hate these shorts, too." He kicks off the too-tight khaki shorts, frayed along the seams. Despite the scowl twisting his features, he is the most beautiful man I have ever known. He catches me staring. Those emerald eyes flicker.

"Do you also hate those briefs?" I sit up to make room for his body, but he eases me back down. Cradles my frame in his strong arms. I feel the heat pulsating from his body in waves. It triggers a reaction in my own cells so that I gasp when his fingers slide under my shirt. He traces the hollow of my belly button, presses soft lips between the wings of my rib cage.

"You're warm," I mumble into the curve of his neck.

"Always." His hands fumble past the barrier of my bra—the bra Julli gave me. I've no idea where she got my clothes, and I don't care. All I feel is Castan's gentle fingers and the pulse between my thighs. Wanting. Needing.

"Is this you trying to drown your misery?"

"No," his voice is barely a whisper, "this is me loving you." Pleasure boils under my skin. Not because of his touch or his lips on my neck, but because of the words he uttered under his ragged breath. They *mean* something, something I have never truly felt for another person before.

I stretch for the buttons on my shorts, breaths coming in heavy bursts. I want him so badly, it's painful. My fingers are clumsy, but Castan catches on.

His husky voice is in my ear, "Let me." He chuckles, reaching for my waist, but I didn't want him to stop kissing me. I wanted to do this myself.

Like the blisters on Maggie's arm, frustration bubbles behind my eyes. Just as Castan unhooks the clasp, I shove his hands away. Open my eyes. The room is too bright, the colors too pale. Irritation bristles my flesh. It's a shoebox, too small to breathe, to scream, to be angry.

"What's wrong?" He drapes his elbows on my raised knees. I want to slap him, but I fumble to button my shorts instead.

"What's *wrong?*" I clap my legs together, pushing myself upright, and successfully knocking him off guard. He staggers sideways but catches himself on the edge of the mattress. "What's wrong is I can't undo my own buttons, and you've barely said a word to me before *this*." I gesture to his almost fully naked body, not trusting myself to actually look.

"Corolla—"

"No, Castan." All the emotions, the thoughts I didn't want, come crashing down upon me like a sword through my center. And the hilt is up to my sternum. "You can't just... do that." For reasons I can't comprehend, tears brim my eyes. "You can't just touch me when I can hardly manage to return the favor."

"*Corolla*—"

"Stop interrupting me," I shoot, even though a voice in my head reminds me I am the one interrupting him. "I can't..." The tears spill over, candle wax dripping down my cheeks. He raises an arm to wipe them, but I smack him away. "Stop *doing* that."

"Doing *what?* I don't understand." I wish he would shout, would grab my wrist and squeeze my bones until they cracked. I wish he would hurt me because that kind of pain, I could process. I wish Maggie hadn't taken mine away—it masked a deeper hurt, one I can't even begin to comprehend.

"She had no right," I splutter, shaking my head. "She had no right to take that from me."

"Who, Maggie?" Castan doesn't try to touch me, but he still tries to understand my misery when I cannot. "Corolla, you could have died from an infection. You *needed* a Healer."

Nausea overcomes me. My stomach is churning like a cotton candy machine on overload. Except instead of sugar floss, there's gray sludge. As if all my pain and fear and sadness have mixed together into some indestructible, slimy goo. As if emptying my stomach will empty my mind.

James would know. The thought strikes me with painful clarity. James would recognize my emotion. Even if I didn't, he would know what to do, just like how he knew to hug me when Averil left, to feed me chicken soup and popsicles when I was sick. He always knew things before I did, like when I came back from Belarus, and he spotted bruises on my legs that I wasn't even aware existed.

And I think, in some strange way, I was never like a daughter to him at all. I was like his kid sister, a chance for him to be a big brother again. All the things I'll never know, all the things he'll never know: that I'm so, so sorry about Averil, that I only took up the Cassena's offer to make him proud, that I love him. More than anything in the world, I love him.

The churning in the pit of my stomach spins faster and faster, rattling old hopes, old wishes.

If only if only if only.

Castan doesn't know. No matter how hard he tries to decipher me, he doesn't get it. And James isn't here to tell me what I'm feeling, to drop a hint that maybe—just maybe—all this anger I feel towards

451

Castan has nothing to do with him at all. Maybe it has nothing to do with anything.

Maybe that pain was the only thing left in the world that belonged to me.

Images flicker through my mind so quickly, I struggle to keep up. James weeding in the front yard. James coming home, a dirt-stained apron tied to his waist. James, blonde lashes fluttering, laughing at the stupid grin on my face when I first glimpsed red blood cells under the microscope he bought me.

All gone. All gone.

My breathing sounds wrong; my voice sounds wrong. Fingers tingling, I stagger off the bed, tug my shirt back down. Who is Corolla without James? Who is she?

I don't know.

"I can't do this right now." I bite my lip, another reminder of all that I've lost. My gum, I'm sobbing because I lost my gum. Castan doesn't move, doesn't stop me from flinging the door so hard, it smacks the wall and leaves a dent. I flinch, but I don't pause to inspect the damage, to say sorry. I'm done hesitating. Done apologizing. I've hesitated half my life and strove for forgiveness for the rest. James died on both accounts. And I never made him proud.

I'm done.

I don't pass anyone on my way out the front door, a fact I am grateful for. Swollen, teary-eyed, and half a left arm, I've probably never looked more repulsive. The sun beats down on the earth, blinding me. I've never hated the sun, but I wish I could pluck it from the sky and bury it six feet under.

Without thinking, I stalk across the lawn. Grass prickles my ankles, and I wish I could rip that out and bury it too. Wishing, hoping, praying—it all travels back to the same gaping hole of nothingness consuming my center.

Somewhere, a goat bleats.

I follow the sound, curving around the corner of the house where the picket fence porch meets the white siding. Trim flower beds snake around the house perimeter, flaring into nothing but a pile of rocks. My palm reacts to none of the flora.

"Delani!" My cousin's voice resounds in my ears. It's too nasally and too stuffy all at once. "Delani," I glimpse him kneeling under the pine tree, "you're very audacious today." Tate raises a fist, and the goat—Delani—jumps on her hind legs to reach it. Though Tate is years older than me, he giggles like a child at his pet's attempts. Around her neck, an iron chain links her collar to the tree's trunk. She bleats again, just as Tate bubbles a fountain of laughter.

On the border of sunny lawn and the tree's silhouette, I move to cross my arms. Think better of it. Scowl. "You're taunting her."

Tate, as I learned last night at dinner, is different than most twenty-one-year-olds. I don't mean that he still lives at home or that he wears socks up to his knees. I mean that he refused to eat his carrots when Tyto wouldn't call them *harvest discs*, that he wears neoprene gloves, like the kind nurses use to examine a patient, to eat his food; he prefers words that begin with A's and despises words that begin with C's. He won't even say my name.

Now, he lifts his chin and lowers his fist. Delani pushes her nose into his fingers, her tongue into his palm. With his other hand, he brushes his unremarkable brown hair from his eyes. If I hadn't dined with him last night, I would think he is the picture of teen angst. Through slitted eyelids, he watches me. I glare at him.

"I'm not taunting her. Taunting her means I'm rude. I'm not rude." His voice wavers, and with it, my reserve.

"No, of c—I mean, no, you're not. I apologize." He grins. Because I caught myself from saying *course* or because I said *apologize*, I don't know. What I do know is that his smile is the one thing I haven't wanted to destroy today.

I step under the tree, shade enveloping my body. Standing stock still between Tate and me, Delani seems to be bracing herself for an attack. Tate brushes his knuckles across her skull, ruffling her gray hair so it pokes out from her head in all directions. She steps back.

"Is it time to attend the doctor's?" He stands, so tall his head nearly brushes the lowest branches of the pine tree. The sappy clump atop his head indicates he's already bumped into them.

I shake my head. "No, I don't know anything about that."

He shrugs. "It's alright. Julli will alarm me when it's time to adieu."

"I—" A sigh replaces the words. "Okay. What are you doing out here?"

He pats Delani's head. "She abhors my absence as much as she abhors the metal links." He gestures to the chain dangling down her front.

"Then don't tie her up."

He bawks, slapping hands on his knees. "Delani would annihilate and devour Uncle Tyto's flowers and Julli's gardens. She ate through her rope last year. Metal links are the only thing that attaches her sufficiently."

"Oh." *Tyto's flowers.* I mutter under my breath, "Would that be so bad?"

453

"Don't mumble," Tate snaps, "Uncle Tyto doesn't appreciate that."

"Sorry."

"You're agitated."

I don't even try to fight it. "Yes."

"Why?" He cocks his head. Delani chews the already gnawed grass at his feet.

If I search through the branches and needles, I'd see my bedroom window, maybe even Castan. I focus on Delani's jaw, the muscles stretching to chomp and chew.

"I miss my uncle, James. I don't know who I am without him. It's always been the two of us, and I... I really wanted to make him proud of me," a lump catches in my throat, "and I... I've failed to do that. Because he's dead." Why I can say this to my cousin and not Castan, I don't know. Maybe because Castan's already shouldered so much of my burden. I couldn't ask him to carry more.

Tate's voice remains the same nasal tone, "You'll adjust."

I shake my head. "I don't think so, Tate. I really don't."

For a moment, his entire body vibrates like a just-hatched moth. Then, he is entirely still. "Accompany me to the barn?"

I glimpse over his shoulder, past the sap-dripping trunk, at the too-bright red barn. Scuffing my bare heels in the grass, I shrug, "Sure."

Tate is already pushing ahead towards the barn, which is nestled on the border of lawn and budding mountainside. Delani follows him at the calves, her sinewy legs kicking underneath her loafed body. When she can go no farther, she bleats. Tate either ignores her or doesn't notice: his long legs pursue his goal. I practically jog to keep up with him. I glance over my shoulder at Delani, standing in a patch of sunlight, jaw dropped. Abandonment fills her eyes. A shock of pity floods my veins. Though she's the ugliest creature I've ever laid eyes on, she reminds me of those ASPCA commercials with the big-eyed kittens and sad-eyed dogs.

I never thought I would sympathize with a goat.

Tate grunts, drawing my attention forward once more. With strength I didn't know he possessed, he slides the red and white doors open. Immediately, the scent of sawdust and paint chemicals splashes my senses. My vision smudges. James hated the smell of paint.

"This is our workshop," Tate beckons with one of his straw-thin arms.

"Our?" I step behind him, into the darkness of a shadow-cluttered barn, where he can't see the tears crowding my eyes. He flicks a panel of switches, white light drowning the space. The shadows flee, transform into shelves and tables of objects. The first thing I notice: the barn is divided by some invisible barrier. The left half is stuffed with wood carvings, metal tools, and chunks of wood. The right half is speckled with color: splotches of dull paints on the floorboards, the countertops; crumbles of paper towel and muggy jars of water litter the tables.

"Uncle Tyto and I are artists," Tate beams, fingers rapping on the nearest table top. He brushes away a tumbleweed of trash, and I can't tell if he's embarrassed or proud of his mess. Tyto's side appears to be in order.

The second thing I notice is the sculptures. Little clay figurines, no taller than six inches, clutter the shelves. Had they not been depicting various scenes, I would have thought they were all a part of one, long stretch of industry. Some are ballerinas; others, police officers and firefighters. A couple of the clusters are nudists, every detail captured. There's a fair share of goats too.

"This is *Home Improvement* meets Hobby Lobby." Tate laughs—I didn't know he perceived jokes—and I turn to face him. "These are remarkable. Do you sell them?"

"What?" He looks at me like I have three heads. "No, I throw them."

Now I give him a weird look. "*Throw* them? As in, you destroy your work?"

His expression falls. "I wouldn't annihilate another person's."

My eyes flicker from Tate's sculptures to Tyto's carvings on the opposite wall. Maybe it's my confirmation bias, but I like Tate's work better. My father's art consists mainly of signs (from *Alba Creek Farm* to *Made in America*). Some pieces depict figures or at least faces. One, I'm convinced is Tilia's profile etched into a polished plaque. Something tells me Tyto would never admit to that—he mentioned last night how he's "ceded from the pelari community."

I wanted to retort, "I wasn't aware that's something you could do," but Tate threw a fit about *ceded* and *community*. I didn't say much after that. Neither did Tyto. We just ate our meatloaf and harvest discs in a steady stream of silence. Occasionally, Julli would try to make conversation, but I wasn't inclined to speak for long; Castan wasn't inclined to eat for long. He retired early, said he was exhausted. I watched him slip around the corner towards the staircase and knew better. He was giving me a chance to talk to my father. But Tyto only shot me a grin, pushed his silver-rimmed glasses up his nose, and chewed each bite a little longer than necessary. The entire affair was so awkward, peeling my skin off would have been more comfortable.

"Does your mom sculpt too?"

Tate's voice changes completely, "My mother is dead."

I shoot him a look, confused. "I saw her."

Suspicion clouds his eyes. "Where?"

"In a memory," I begin, "Tilia showed me before she flickered away, and," I stop myself—Calyx mentioned Valeria was working at Intel. I note the futility in the conversation. "Never mind." I inhale the mingled scent of pine and paint fumes.

Mom, I add that to the list of things I can't talk about in front of Tate, right under microwaves and hospitals. He doesn't trust either.

Tate clears his throat, pushes off the counter he's leaning on. His countenance transforms again. "I'm awful with emotions," he says to the planked floor, "but Uncle Tyto and I sometimes get angry about Maurizio too." Since Tate won't say Calyx, he refers to my brother by his middle name instead. M's are still safe.

Before I can clarify that I'm not upset over Calyx, Tate snatches two goats—one speckled like a Dalmatian, the other, a tiny replica of Delani—and beckons me to the back of the barn. He places the Dalmatian goat in my hand and leads me down three rickety steps into a decent-sized cellar.

He flicks on another set of lights and announces, "Aim!" I don't have time to react—Tate swings his arm back and chucks his goat at the far wall. It strikes the concrete, shattering into a million gray and white pieces. They scatter to the floor, lost among previous ceramic ruins. Belated, I flinch, shoulders up to my ears.

"Why did you do that?" In my fist, his beautiful goat's hooves stab my palm, sharp enough to draw blood.

Tate exhales, grinning so hard, I'm afraid his lips with split at the corners. "It is animating. Your turn."

"I don't want to annihilate your work, though."

"Why not?" He places a hand on his hip, brow furrowing. "I gave you permission."

"It's too…" I struggle to find the word, "… absolute. No, alluring. Your sculptures, I mean."

"Oh," his shoulders sag with disappointment. He makes a face, irises skittering around the cellar. "Then here, take one of Uncle Tyto's mugs. He won't mind. He says the world accommodates too many mugs anyway." He retrieves a plain, off-white coffee mug from a little shelf beside the stairs. I pocket the goat, hesitating only when I think Tate is going to snatch the sculpture from my hand. He doesn't. Instead, he drops the mug in my palm.

"Go on." He nods his head in the wall's direction. I glance at the shards and carnage of fractured things, detached mug handles and identifiable figurine limbs. Somewhere in the clutter, I'm sure there is a little ceramic forearm.

These thoughts and perceptions race through my mind in seconds. Mimicking Tate's exaggerated movement, I swing my arm back and release.

The mug splinters into several pieces, clattering to the pile of shards like a fallen martyr. Tate cheers, clapping his hands. The curt sound reverberates off the concrete walls. I cast him a grin, my shoulders heaving with bubbles of laughter. I can't help it.

Breaking is much more amusing than being broken.

Calyx
August 2020

"Usurper, just like your father." Dull yellow candlelight flickers across the Russian's face, casting dark shadows in the hollows of her eyes. We agreed to meet in southern Tanzania, where the African Academy sticks out like a sore thumb. Metal fences, brick buildings to the sky... But the Genocides dismantled much of the Academy. The African Academy has long been the central training facility for the Guard—it was the best defended, the least damaged by the attacks. Maggie said I wouldn't want to see the North American Academy. After encountering Castan and Corolla, I'm sure she's right.

Maggie is late, but that's not unusual. Especially when I sent her to heal Corolla. Thinking about my sister's disfigurement, about Castan's anger, makes my heart hurt. It's too late for regrets, though. I tug on the metal chain around my neck, wondering why it feels so heavy. I never used to notice the tag's weight before.

I shift my attention back to the battle at hand. Against the brickwork of the African Barracks, the Valence gathers like a handful of convicts in what could be European catacombs.

Behind my back, I clench a fist. I meet Dinara's gaze. The Russian, arms crossed, doesn't flinch. Her haughty composure—loud fuchsia lipstick, ripped Official's uniform—grates on my nerves. Despite the grin on my face, my patience is spreading thin. Gasoline on water, this fire only seems to be spreading.

And the Valence is supposed to be infallibly united.

"Look," I fix my eyes on the recent cut above Dinara's eyebrow, "Tilia didn't leave instructions for her succession—"

"Precisely. A *boy* should not be our leader." Dinara's distinctly Russian accent—harsh and brutal—slices through the air. Nods of approval affirm her declaration. "You weren't at Hong Kong when the Asian Academy fell. You weren't at Adelaide, Peebles, Rome, or even here," she raises thick arms towards the brick and mortar surroundings. Sitting on a crate beside Dinara, the Okar twins scoff. Zoya and Kali were here when the African Academy fell. Their *armatus* glint in the candlelight, symbols of those who fell in combat.

"With all due respect," my voice is light, though I want to shout, "I was supposed to be dead. And Tilia herself was dying. I took care of her."

"That," Kali flicks a hand across the room to Umar and Nasreen, "was their job. Tilia didn't require a cabin boy." Her deep voice reverberates in the closed space. Her sister, Zoya, nods as if Kali just delivered a resonating religious sermon.

I want to raise my hands and say, "Fine, figure it out for yourselves, then." But I think of Tilia, fading so fast in those last minutes. She was too weak to speak, too weak to do much of anything. She lost so many, so quickly... The Valence was her design, and I can't allow it to fade into nothingness too.

"You're losing focus of our purpose here," Dinara opens her mouth to interrupt, but I raise my voice a degree, "Tilia chose us to root out Taxodium's corruption. Well, that corruption is gathering in the SA as we speak. Our inside operative, Hadley Dentata, has informed me that this mysterious Renatus is planning to make an appearance at the Academy. Genocides come every day, anticipating his arrival. The concentration of traitors will never be as high as it is when he comes. If we can organize an attack for that same day, we will employ the element of surprise, as well as—"

"You're not fucking Ethan Hunt," Dinara throws her arms in the air, "and this isn't fucking *Mission Impossible*, okay? This is the real world. The pedes' press is picking up on our counterparts' doings. It's only a matter of time before they realize pelari exist. The Rome Accords—"

"Oh, to hell with the Rome Accords," Henri, a French pilot, slurs. He reeks of alcohol, but if you ask him, he's been sober for a decade. He adjusts the old-fashioned leather cap and aviator goggles on his head. "The Rome Accords don't matter when there isn't a Taxodium anymore to unite, no? And so what if pedes find us out? We could use their... how do you say... *militaries* anyway."

Kali twists her body in Henri's direction, appalled. "You cannot be serious?"

Zoya completes her twin's thought, "We would lose our freedom if pedes became involved. Especially the Americans. They are always trying to control the things they fear."

A roar of noise follows, tongues accusing, arms flying in passionate speeches. People jump from their chairs and boxes, except for three. Unamused, Ramsey crosses his arms and regards his comrades. Umar drapes an arm across Nasreen's shoulders, her stomach bulging through her embroidered overshirt. Over the chaos, I meet Umar's steady gaze. He tucks his chin. I sigh.

"Okay!" When nothing happens, "Okay, *shut up*!" Slowly, heads turn. Smug, Dinara crosses her arms as if expecting my failure. Is this how my father felt when he was elected Major? I clear the thoughts from my mind.

"I appreciate your concern for the pedes problem, but that's not our priority right now. Your heads are in the wrong place, so focus. Please." I meet each of their eyes. When they cannot hold my gaze any longer, heads duck in submission. "We need to salvage what we can from the Academies—geometers, uniforms, weapons. The able-bodied survivors on St. Helena can assist us with that. Now, more than ever, they need our guidance and leadership. And beyond scavenging, we need a recon team to scout around the SA, blueprints of the Academy from any archives we have access to, and—"

"We need a bomb." Henri sucks his snot in the back of his throat through his nose. "Think about it, Cal. You said yourself the Gens will be most concentrated whenever that psychopath Renatus shows up. Well? Why not wipe them all out at once, Dentatas and Genocides?"

"Henri—"

"Is it *just* to bomb these people?" Nasreen speaks up, voice scratchy from disuse. "The Gens are only children. Confused."

Dinara scoffs, "Confused and *armed*. Henri's onto something. Extinction seems to be a better option than imprisonment. It is not like we can cart them all off to Adelaide anymore—we don't have cells to lock them in or enough guards to keep them there. We do not even have the Courts to try them. Death is punishment enough."

"We need to consider the ethics."

"No, boy," Dinara smirks, "we need to finish what Tilia started."

"But—"

"You want to be our collective representative?" Dinara raises a brow. "Then you need to realize that this is what we want."

"Fine, we can vote after some discussion."

"And," Kali adds, "we can vote you out of our missions. You are still an antidote to the Dentatas."

I struggle to be heard over the talking, "We need to be wary of that, sure, but—"

"But nothing," Zoya's interruption silences the room, "you may be our representative under one condition: you stay behind."

I maintain my composure as best I can, teeth nibbling the flesh of my cheek. I scan the faces before me. Nasreen ducks her head. Umar doesn't meet my flustered gaze. So then, they agree.

"And," Dinara announces, "your sister stays behind, too. We cannot risk either of your captures."

I am strong enough to admit when I've lost. I scrape the defeat from my expression and replace it with steel. "Very well." Something flickers across Dinara's stone-cut appearance. For a half second, she

460

almost looked soft. As if she's been holding her breath up until this moment. I have to remind myself that I'm young enough to be everyone's child in this room. If Maggie and Hadley were here, that wouldn't be the case. My eyes dart from Dinara to Henri to the Okar's *armatus*. Who have they loved and lost?

While I was speaking, people slumped back into their seats. Once again, I am towering over the Valence. No one pays me any attention now, absorbed in making plans and tweaking ideas. I almost feel a surge of pride—this is why Tilia chose us—but movement in the shadows catches my eye. A figure steps out from under the brick archway, silent in her scuffed Caeli boots.

Maggie's glasses reflect the candles so that I can't make out her eyes. She mouths a single word.

A name.

My body goes still, thoughts freezing in synapses.

Maggie nods her head to the door behind her, invisible in the darkness where candlelight cannot reach. Or refuses to.

All at once, breath rushes into my lungs, blood floods the chambers of my heart. Though I haven't spoken a single lie tonight, my ears flush red. Maggie makes me guilty. But I made myself a liar.

I glance around the room first. The Okar twins and Umar are sorting through who should lead what mission. Henri and Dinara are discussing differences between explosive materials.

I slip around the cluster of makeshift seats towards Maggie. Swallow. "How's Corolla doing? Castan?"

Maggie makes a noise, deep in her throat, almost like laughter. "If you're not back in thirty minutes, I'll send for help. She's just down the hall."

My eyes flit to the door's outline and back to Maggie's face. Exhaustion is a drape across her eyes, but she still manages to look amused. "How did she…?"

"She placed a tracker in my geometer, the clever thing. Maybe I never should have taught her how to do it in the first place."

"Hmm." My pulse is taking turns rocketing to my throat to plunging into my stomach. Without another word, I push through the door. In the hall, white light from battery-powered lanterns illuminate the brick walls and arched ceiling of the Barracks. Vaguely, my imagination connects the ambiance of the building to the image of a whale's esophagus. I dread what's behind the double doors at the end of the tunnel. I focus on my breathing, on my feet, padding against uneven ground. My thoughts jumble like alphabet soup. What am I going to say to her, the same thing I said to Castan?

There's no time to sort it out. I reach the double doors in record time—maybe I was jogging when I thought I was walking. I shoulder past the swinging doors, stepping quickly to avoid being hit from behind.

I don't notice the array of candles, like so many fallen stars scattered around the room. I don't notice the cupboards or the counter between us. I see her, and that's all my vision can consume. Slender as a willow, pale as a sheet of paper, she leans against a counter. Her hair is whipped into a long, flaming braid like it always was. She's wearing her black uniform, brown plates of armor like she always did. From all angles, she is the same. And then I see what she's doing.

A loaf of bread, a jar of Jif, and a dull knife in her hand, she lathers a piece of bread. The cathedral-style candles spread about the countertop cast an orange veil around her. In the dim lighting, the scene resembles some kind of summer camp initiation. But she's not trying to recruit me. She's trying to repel.

"Kassandra." Emotions, like a geyser, spurt from the cracks of my being. Awe, shock, or fear, I don't take the time to name them.

"I heard you came back to life. I had to see your resurrection for myself, I guess." Kass tends to swear when she's mad. The fact that she doesn't now means I've struck an unprecedented degree of fury. I have never feared her, but as she slaps a glob of peanut butter to a slice of whole grain bread, I do now.

"The Gens didn't care to ransack the kitchen cupboards. Lucky for me," she folds the slice in half and shoves it in her mouth, words thick with food in her mouth, "I love peanut butter."

"Oh." I can't think words—what do you even *say* to that? "That's cruel."

She raises an eyebrow, hiccups once, and washes the peanut butter bread down with a glass of water. "I can think of worse."

I can't bear the distance between us any longer—like a magnet, I go to her. I don't care about the jar of Jif opened on the counter, the butter knife in her hand, or the peanut butter in the corner of her lips. I have to kiss her. I have to erase the distance in her indigo eyes—

With a single hand, she interrupts my intentions. I only felt her acid once, and that was an accident. On the other end of her palm, knowing there's little that would stop her now, I dare not even swallow. Beneath the skin of her palm, her acid pulsates, like a low-growl in her being.

"Did you really think I'd let you kill yourself now?" Her peanut butter breath snakes around my face. She cocks her head, voice so low, my skin prickles, "No, it's not going to be that easy."

"Ka—"

"Don't," her grip on my throat squeezes my vocal cords. She discards the butter knife from her other hand. It clatters across the countertop and, though my back is to the counter, I know it slid clear across and crashed to the ground. "Was I really that untrustworthy? Was Castan?" She shoves my spine into the ledge. Palms on the counter, I brace myself against her attack. Heat radiates near my left hand, and I know I'm too close to one of the many candles. I'm too afraid to move. No, not afraid. Guilty. I am too guilty to fight back.

"Oh my god, Calyx, we grieved over you. We scattered your ashes, visited your mausoleum slot. My parents came to your Ceremony. They even gave me one of those stupid pamphlets about how to cope with losing someone you—" The momentum of her words comes to a halt. My entire *body* flushes with shame.

When Kass speaks next, her voice is that chilling low tone again. "Do you not realize how painful that was?" Though shadows cloak half her face, I distinguish tears pooling at her waterline. She blinks rapidly to clear them away.

I extend an arm, fingers curled to brush back the hair that's fallen out of her braid. She recoils, disgust lining her features. I gasp a breath, grateful for air, for her release. I smooth a hand around my throat as if feeling it myself will wipe away the imprint of her hatred.

"I am so sorry, Kassandra," I reach for her hand, hanging limply at her side. She maneuvers around the counter so that it separates us once more. "Tilia approached me. She needed me. *Taxodium* needed me."

Kass does the thing with her tongue where she drags it from one side of her cheek to the other. Hands on her hips, her gaze is fixed on the ceiling. "Unbelievable."

"Unbelievable." She said the same thing, eyes fixed on that poster of Brendon Urie in her room, where I taped my face over his in a jealousy-induced state. Laughter dribbled deep in her chest then, passed onto me when she pasted Selena Gomez on my ceiling with her face clipped clean over the singer's. Laughing was as natural as breathing back then. Loving Kass was easy. Easier.

Anger pricks my flesh. "It was hard for me to leave you behind too, you know." I scowl, "But it was only ever temporary while the Valence figured this shit out. Faking my death was the right thing to do."

A chuckle escapes past her lips. "I'm not saying faking your death was wrong—it was genius, sure. Especially the *cantus* 2.0. What's *wrong* is the fact that you left me out of the loop."

"It wasn't my choice." I move towards her. She takes four steps back. I don't know why her reaction would be any different this time.

All trace of humor, of understanding, vanishes from her tone. Her words are knives, cutting deep into my flesh, "I'm not your widow, your friend, or your colleague. If you want to live, then stay away from me. I don't want to see your fucking face ever again." Her eyes pierce my soul for extra measure before she slips through the doors. They swing violently, and through the crack, I glimpse a whip of orange hair. Then, nothing.

Without thinking, I drop my hands to the countertop—

"Ouch!" I retreat, whirling in the process. I glare at the candle, at the drip of hot wax on the back of my hand. I suck the burned flesh, scowling at my own carelessness. Kass's ghost fingers clamp my throat, and her venomous words ring in my ears. I'm lucky to have survived with only a little burn.

Castan
August 2020

The worst mistakes are the ones you know you're going to make before they happen, yet for some reason, you don't stop yourself from committing them. That wrongness pools in your veins like a poison, but your body still moves, your finger still pulls that trigger.

Even though my brother's blood stains my hands, I can't stop thinking about Hadley's ghost-white, horrified expression the night of Carnage. Most of that night is a blur, the stench of my own sweat and baking flesh, a flash of Ashley's pale hair. I almost killed my opponent, but I had the nerve to hold back. Because I knew, killing the bad guy doesn't make you the good guy. Things were black and white back then when they were only ever vast gray areas.

What will my little sister think now? Will she forgive me, scorn me, hate me?

I used to read books and the poetic deaths contained within their pages. But books never get it right—the smell, the emotion, the way it actually feels to be the killer, to be the killed. That rush of blinding adrenaline and then the terrible, frightening depression later, as if someone is holding you underwater and you can't breathe, but you can't die either. Or maybe there are no words to convey it. And besides, you can always flip back to the beginning of books, before everything spirals out of control. The first time I read *The Great Gatsby*, I did just that. Half of me refused to set the book down until Gatsby was alive again. Half of me resented Fitzgerald for having the literary genius to kill the man off.

Writing death is not the same as experiencing it. Reading death is not the same as knowing it.

I stopped reading when Calyx died because I would have understood when the protagonist talked about witnessing death. I would know what it means to see someone die. Now, I would know what it means to be the one *to* kill. And I don't want to remember how that feels. I don't want to remember my body, a combustion of flames, or my hands gripped around Rosh's throat; or his irises, so dark, they were solid black marbles in his skull. A bullet hole between his eyes.

I can dehumanize Rosh until he's a block of quartz, but he was still human. All of his quirks, his preferences and ideas have been snuffed out. I try not to reflect on our childhood together because if I do, I may just cry. And it's not that I'm too manly to cry, it's that Rosh would have snickered if I wept over him. So I won't.

Lounging in the living room, on a chair that's too comfortable to be real, I sip from a mug of black coffee. Julli made a pot before she and Tyto left for work, swearing she's been an avid drinker since age six. I used to love consuming this stuff, but lately, it's tasted bitter as sin.

I set my mug on one of the *Better Homes and Gardens* magazines littering the glass coffee table and lean back into the chair. Close my eyes. The sun streams through the windows, making my vision a film of red. Somewhere, I hear Corolla's voice. A door slams. Tate giggles.

I exhale.

Corolla hasn't spoken to me in a couple days, and I decided not to press her about it. She spends all her waking hours with Tate. They disappear into the big red barn on the edge of the property, doing Matrona knows what. Each time I see her at dinner, though, she looks happier. She doesn't even seem to mind that Tyto is increasingly late for his evening meal, claiming to have been working late at the office. He sits down around the same time Corolla and Tate get up to leave. I didn't think overtime was part of selling insurance, but then again, I wouldn't know.

Cracking my eyelids, I take in the flat screen suspended above the alabaster mantle and the matching white bookshelf across from it. I already skimmed its contents and found a lot of devotionals and every version of the Bible possible. Something tells me those texts belong to Julli, not Tyto. I don't think Tate likes reading, but I did find a handful of *Teen Titans* comics. *The Lego Ideas Book* was—is—probably Calyx's.

Is this what normal look like? I've been wondering about it. What if Corolla and I met in high school, rather than through break and entry. What if I took her out to see a movie or grab a coffee, rather than dragging her through pigeon shit in Florence and primeval forests in Belarus. Our biggest problems would be the SATs, college applications, and where to have sex without getting caught.

My heart stirs at the prospect. I almost laugh.

But who knows if our paths would have crossed otherwise? Where normal is difficult to visualize, imagining a life where I never met Corolla is like trying to think up a new color: impossible. I cannot comprehend never knowing her eyes, the way her nose wrinkles when she's deep in thought, or the chime of her voice.

The sudden urge to find her, to hold her, overwhelms me, so much so, I jolt when a hand obscures my vision of the rising sun.

"Guess who?" Her voice is light, immortal. Under her gentle pressure, my body relaxes.

"Tate?"

As her hand drops down to my shoulder, rays of sun beam my pupils. Corolla erupts into laughter, steadying herself on my shoulder. She saunters around the chair to face me, then plants herself on the coffee table, missing my mug by several inches. If her eyes weren't so clear, I would have thought she was high. Maybe Tate's Essence is joy, though from what Tyto was explaining, Tate didn't make any noise when he was born.

"Watch that," I gesture to the mug, but she throws her arms around my neck. Somehow, she's fit herself into my lap, legs curled to her chest.

"I don't think you'd want Tate to do this." She's so close, I count four eyes spread even across her face. Her breath touches the skin of my cheek, its own delicate current. She presses her lips to my cheek, thumb stroking the side of my neck.

"You're right. I'm pretty sure I saw him kissing Delani's mouth the other night," I frown, "but it *was* dark outside."

Corolla shrugs as if this is typical Tate behavior. It may be. She blinks, her lashes fluttering against my temple. She opens her mouth to say something, but at the last moment, I turn and catch her mouth with mine. Startled, she bites my lip on accident. I cup her face between my hands, and she settles against my body. My tongue pushes past her lips, exploring the ridges of her teeth, the warmth of her affections.

Finally, she breaks apart, breathless, lips swollen with passion. She grins so hard, a dimple I've never seen before spots one of her cheeks. I don't question her mood. All I know is that my heart's beating so fast in my chest, it may take off through the window any minute.

"You interrupted me," she chides, words breathy. "We have a surprise for you."

"We?" She places her hand on my chest, making to push free of my grip. I try to contain her in my arms, but light refuses to conform. She slips free, adjusting her shirt, which somehow became crooked in our entanglement. I notice her disfigurement isn't encapsulated in the knot of a long sleeve. The nub of her arm is fleshy and pink where Maggie healed it, stretched taut over bone and ligament. If she catches me staring, she doesn't react. I meet her gaze, where not an ounce of her joy has depleted. It's contagious.

"You're so lovely today. Always."

"Thanks," she says quickly, but I see the corner of her mouth twitch. "Now get up. Tate and I are anxious to see your reaction."

I stagger to my feet, standing a head taller than Corolla. "I think you drugged me. I feel drunk."

"Or maybe," she urges me up the step and towards the door, "my love potion has finally worked."

Crossing the barn's threshold, maybe Tate's Essence is artistic vision. My eyes flit from the distinct rustic half of the workspace to the scatter of paint jars and gallery of sculptures lining the planked wall. Tate's dressed in a white lab coat and plastic glasses. When he lays eyes on us, a smile breaks across his face. In that moment, a young Ramsey stares at me. I wonder if Tate knows who his father is. I wonder if Tyto does.

"Remember," Corolla squeezes my arm, "C words are okay, as long as you say them with a K. I konvinced him it was alright."

"We really should tell him about Calyx," my nose brushes her hair. She shakes her head, bowing with laughter to mask the horror absolving her expression.

"Kastan!" Tate grasps my hand before I can finish my thought. "We have the most appropriate art for you."

"Do you really?" I shoot Corolla a look. She releases her hold on my arm and jumps into step beside Tate. The pair—Tate dressed as a chemist, Corolla radiating something ethereal—beckons me through the weave of worktables, tin trash cans, and invisible paint fumes. In the back of the barn, I follow them down creaking steps. Staring down the cloud of musty darkness, I get the feeling of plunging into Dracula's lair. I keep that thought to myself.

"Watch your head," Corolla warns too late. I bump my forehead on something substantial, causing Tate to burst into squeaky laughter. He flicks the lights on, illuminating the dark pit and low-hanging ceiling I crashed into. I ease down the remaining steps, ducking my head until the roof is level with the ground.

I take one look at the shattered remains of pottery, glass, and raise a quizzical eyebrow. "Is this where you two disappear to every day?"

Rather than answer my question, Tate shoves glasses in my hand, identical to his own. At some point, Corolla slipped on a similar pair.

"We found it's better not to get kaught in the krossfire," she explains, "But anyway, hold out your hands."

I shoot her a suspicious look. "Do I have to close my eyes too?"

Corolla turns her back to me, and Tate exchanges something with her. She whirls, two objects hugged in the basket of her arms. Both are indistinguishable shapes. One is a large ebony lump, the other, smaller and construction-site-yellow. Corolla passes the ceramic objects into my hands.

"I wasn't allowed to say anything. Tate wanted it to be a surprise." When I don't reply straight away, she adds, "That yellow one is supposed to be Tilia. The other one is whatever you want it to be. I found I'm only good with basic shapes."

At her shoulder, Tate snickers. He slips a sculpted daisy into Corolla's hand. I notice a figure clenched in his other fist. Beyond the bronze arms and dark hair, I can't make out who it is.

"On the kount of three," Corolla grins, "throw one of those at the wall with as much force as you've got." The plastic goggles are too big for face, and she has to push them up her nose every couple of seconds.

Tate begins the countdown, Corolla joining him, "One, two, *three!*" Half a second late, I launch the giant ebony lump at the wall. It splits unevenly down the side, revealing a hollow inside. I don't know what I expected, but I understand what Corolla's trying to do. Without her giddy energy beside me, I probably wouldn't feel anything. However, I'm like a child again, when Hadley and I would take a basketball and chuck it down the hall to see how many doors we could strike.

Corolla bounces on the balls of her feet. Tate arms her with another palm-sized daisy.

She faces me then, stray hair caught in her lashes, "Today is a beginning." And as she teaches me how to throw—"I pitched an inning of softball in middle school. Make sure you *flick* your wrist."—as the yellow chunk of Tilia crashes into the cellar wall beside her daisy and Tate's figurine, I believe her.

Tate retires soon after for a nap, but Corolla is restless. With a look in her eye that could melt an iceberg into an ocean, she takes my hand and leads me up the mountainside. She follows a worn path through rock and tree. The higher we climb, the more the ropes anchoring me to the earth become irrelevant.

As we pass through pines and moss-covered rocks, I slip through some invisible barrier. I'm convinced we are the only two people on the planet. It's something you only experience once or twice in your lifetime, a moment where you see past the veil of your own mortality and into the world beyond. It all seems so fucking clear, you can't possibly be the same person you were five minutes ago; your soul can't possibly be bound to your body. There are no limits here, only us.

Corolla turns, laughter on her lips, locks of caramel hair tucked behind her ears. She's a head taller than me, fingers locked in my own, pulling, tugging, leading. She's been saying something, but I don't hear her. I memorize the waterfall of hair spilling over her shoulder, the way her eyes crinkle in the corners when she smiles.

I think back to all those weeks ago when I couldn't look at Corolla without seeing Calyx. I thought he was gone forever. Now, he's as distant as one of those stars suspended in the sky, so far away, he may as well be dead. But Corolla… How could I have ever compared the two? I was a moth: I confused a porch light for the sun.

All too soon, we're at the peak of the mountain, gray stone plating the ground beneath our feet. Through the spindles of pines, there is a view of the skyline. We gravitate towards the cliff, through needled branches, speechless. Down below, the highway cuts through the mountains, two winding ribbons. The zipping cars and semis threaten to break my enlightened trance, but Corolla's hand, brushing up against my arm, anchors me to this moment.

Everything outside of this bubble is a problem for tomorrow.

"Where do you think they're all going?" Her words are breathy from running up the mountainside. I realize I'm gasping for air too.

I shrug. "McDonald's. Maybe church. What day is it again?"

"They don't have real problems, do they?" She glances at me over her shoulder. I tuck fallen hair behind her ear, thumb smoothing across her cheekbone. She shudders under my touch. Maybe she feels the arrows shooting through my thumb into my core, too.

"That's what they say about us."

Corolla makes a throaty noise before crouching down and flinging her legs over the edge of the cliff. I do the same, my stomach flopping at the seducing height. A window of sunlight touches our bodies. Somewhere, a hawk cries.

"Look," my hand brushes her thigh, "I'm sorry about the other day. I didn't mean to be so… forceful."

"You weren't forceful."

Averil flits through my mind, like one of Kassandra's scouting posters. *Our brothers, our sisters, our society.* When I was searching the square for Corolla, I saw one of those advertisements. Splattered with red.

"Can I just say something?" Corolla shifts to meet my gaze. "Just one thing, and then we can stare into the distance like they do in the movies. You don't even have to say anything to me, I just need to get this off my chest."

The corners of my lips twitch. "Of course."

She sighs as if bracing herself. "I thought observing would help me find my feet in Taxodium. I thought to stand by the sidelines would be better than plunging into the unknown, but I just stood there, Castan. I just stood there and watched James… explode." This last word is barely a whisper. She leans her head on my shoulder. "Everything is different now. I'm not even sure people can be *just* good or *just* bad, you know? Everything is subjective, and everyone has their own intentions. It just depends on which way you're facing when the wind blows. You either go with it or against it. But you can change your direction at any time. Nothing is concrete. Does that make sense?"

"I think I know what you're saying. Nothing has ever been black or white, right or wrong. It's all just a gray... puddle."

"Yeah." She inhales deeply again. "It's weird, the things I took for granted. He had this one face that I absolutely hated. But if that were the only face he ever wore again, I would love it. As long as... As long as he just came back."

I wrap my arm around her shoulders. "I know what you mean."

"I used to write these things down, you know. All the things I did that hurt James. Averil, mostly. I just wanted to make James proud of me again, so I refused to let myself forget the bad stuff I did." Corolla ducks her head, "But I'm remembering the wrong things. That's the ironic part, I guess. I won't make that mistake again."

"He was proud of you." I watch the cars down below, so tiny and irrelevant. "He was proud of you, Corolla."

"Maybe." It's a speculative comment, and I imagine it will become concrete once she realizes what I already have. That James, even though he depended on Corolla, was in awe with her very existence. She was the daughter of his lost sister. Corolla never had anything to prove—she only had a life to live. That was enough for James.

But some things can't be spoken, and some things can't be explained. Like why I suddenly feel so at peace, despite the blood on my hands. Or why Corolla feels so *right* beside me, despite the trauma binding us together. All I know is that somewhere along the way, I stopped living on pain. I once admitted to Tilia that was the driving force of my existence. It's not anymore. I shoot Corolla a sideways glance and know for certain how that came to be.

We fall into a comfortable silence, a breeze sifting through fallen pine needles around us. Clouds take turns blocking out the sun. That hawk cries again, for what, I don't care to assess. Everything is... content.

The skeleton of a quote surfaces in my mind. I can't remember the exact words, but it was something about how someone who feels extreme sadness can then also feel extreme happiness. Alexandre Dumas knew what he was talking about. It's weird to think about these lessons people learned hundreds of years before me, yet I'm just now getting a taste of what those things mean. My head hurts with the philosophy of it all.

So for now, I draw Corolla closer and listen to the birdsong.

Hadley
August 2020

"You cut your hair."

I shrug. "Everyone is doing something to celebrate the coming of Renatus. They're really taking this *reborn* business to heart."

My father bristles, but he manages to keep his temper under control. I refrain from rolling my eyes—he's so pathetic, I almost pity his powerless position. Mena would have laughed, and with my hair cropped close to my head, I know Numen is thinking the same thing. *You cut your hair* really translates into *You look like that witch I was forced to marry.*

If only it translated into her location.

Sometimes, I think I imagined Mena. But the forced control on my father's face reminds me that she *was* real. She *was* my mother, and she *was* taken away from us, screaming. Her hair was cropped close to her skull, but that's how Jon dragged her from the room. By the hair.

"Did you need me for something?" I'm in his office so much recently, the dribbling fountain is just another accessory in the background. I hardly hear it anymore.

"I have something for you." Numen shoves a pile of folders into a drawer. He never used to deal with paperwork. I sometimes wonder if Renatus has made my father his personal secretary. "This way."

For all my father's age, he is still nimble as a boy—a boy whose biceps are as big around as my head. We tread down the walkway leading from his desk. I follow Numen through a veil of shadows into a corner of his office I've never seen before. He grabs what I think is a door handle (it's too dark to tell), and then there's a rectangle of white light. Enveloped within it, is Uncle Baylor; before him, a man is on his knees.

A prisoner.

"Hadley," Numen sweeps his arm, gesturing me inside. Baylor grins as if we are two relatives about to catch up over Thanksgiving dinner.

I glance from Numen to Baylor to the man cowering on the steel floor. If he weren't gagged, I imagine he would be begging. His ice blue irises are pleading, some of that ice melting in the corners of his eyes. "What is this?"

Numen growls, "A gift."

I laugh, clucking my tongue and crossing my arms. "Is this poor man going to be my fiancé, or are there vacant spots in Renatus's inner circle?"

"No," Numen thunders, "this has nothing to do with that bastard!" The acoustic panels lining the walls collect my father's fury and shoves it down my ear canals a second time. I flinch, bowing under the oppressive cacophony. Uncle Baylor is stone, hands gripping the prisoner's shoulders. The poor, whimpering man would blow over otherwise, like a leaf in a tornado.

Numen skims a palm over his bald head. "My men are calling you Siren," he says, quiet, "I want to witness what my progeny can do."

But I know better than that. Baylor and I may be the only two people left in this Academy who take orders from Jon Xabier. I see the desperation in my father's eyes—he's never appeared more human.

"Yes." My voice is flat, unwavering. Then I add, with a slight flare of eagerness, "Perhaps one day I can achieve a reputation like Rosh or Ashley."

Numen says nothing. Instead, he nods at Baylor. I watch the two of them pass through a second door into a soundproof chamber. A glass window reveals their eager eyes, grim expressions. They resemble one another so completely, one taller and slimmer than the other, that the image of a different pair of brothers flashes through my mind. When Baylor and I slid Rosh's remains into a Mausoleum slot, I couldn't help thinking, *Are you sure this is Rosh?* His body was almost a mirror image of one of those ancient Egyptian mummies, all warped and charred. But his face could have belonged to another.

These thoughts flit through my mind in a matter of seconds. Still, the eyes behind the window burrow into my body like flesh-eating worms.

My gaze drops to the prisoner. Despite his bound hands, he wriggles. Despite the gag pinching his skin, he mumbles. I pick out the syllables for *wife, daughter.*

I make the decision before I'm conscious of my hand unsheathing my knife. It happens so quickly, so suddenly—there is a spurting of hot, crimson liquid. The prisoner slumps sideways, and I exhale a quiet breath of relief.

"Enjoy the silence," I don't know who I'm talking to—the corpse at my feet or my father and uncle, slack-jawed, in the other room.

I pivot, remembering all at once that I chopped my hair to the bone, which is why I feel so *light*. Swiping the blade on my thigh, I fling the door open. Four eyes shoot arrows at my back, and I suppress a shudder. When I hear the door click shut behind me, I run. My legs know the way out better than my mind. In the corner of my vision, my shadow flees across flickering candelabras.

I wasn't going to use my Essence on a defenseless man, I tell myself. *I wasn't going to screech and make him suffer.*

Sprinting through those narrow corridors, blood sticky between my fingers, I understand why Castan was drunk with power at Carnage—such a tendency is in our veins. I never blamed him for almost scorching that boy to death. Two years later, when Numen threw me in the ring, I felt that current of fear my screech instilled in my opponents. I drank it up like nectar, felt those jolts of energy spike my blood. I burst eardrums. I made people bleed. All because my father willed it.

But his power is waning, and he knows it.

I dart up the steps cut into the mountainside, two at a time. The mountain air is thin, and even though my lungs have adapted, I'm gasping for breath. In the darkness, I lose my footing once, grazing my palm on the stone when I catch myself. In a whirl, I locate my room, slamming the door shut behind me. My back to the door, I flick the lights on.

I chose to occupy one of the dorms carved into the mountain. It's a single room, so small I could lie on my back and reach one wall with my feet pressed flat and the other, with my fingertips. I have a bed and a desk. If I were a boy, Numen would have insisted I stay in one of the Ward Suites, like Rosh did.

I undo my belt, shimmy out of my jeans, stained with that man's blood, and kick them against the far corner where the rest of my dirty laundry resides. I toss my knife, aiming for my desk—cluttered with dirty dishes and a set of throwing knives Rosh gave me for my sixteenth—but my hands are shaking. The weapon clatters to the floor, the blade streaked with rust-colored lines.

I exhale, forcing my body to be calm. It probably wasn't the best idea to disobey Numen. No buts. I will be punished for it tomorrow, I'm sure.

For now, though, exhaustion floods my bones. I sink to my bed, ready to slip into the soft folds of my bed. A tap, so subtle, I think I imagined it, breaks the rhythm of my breathing. Over my shoulder, I glance at my windowpane.

Laughter bubbles from deep in my throat. There, on my windowsill, is one of Calyx's hummingbirds. Engineered in vines, leaves, and one of Tilia's enchantments I cannot hope to understand, the tiny-bodied creature cocks its head at me.

Calyx can do amazing things with his Essence, but I've never been in the Antidote Boat. That's something my hysterical grandfather conjured, and for whatever reason, the idea didn't die with him. In desperation, people will believe in anything, I guess.

I cross the space in two strides and let the messenger in.

"Hello, little bloodhound." I pluck it from the stone sill and dig my fingers into its tiny breast. A tightly wound scroll tumbles out into the palm of my hand. The bird flies free from my grip, back to wherever Calyx is staked out. The hummingbirds are blood trackers, though they possess no other intellectual qualities—if they did, and if I had a sample of my mother's blood, I would find a way to send one after Mena. They only land to deliver their message but are hardwired to track for twenty-four hours. After that, they return to their master. Tilia and Calyx only made so many of them anyway.

Using my fingernails, I unravel the scroll and hold it under the single amber light dangling from the ceiling. It takes me a moment to decipher the tiny script. A grin spreads across my face; laughter shakes my body. I fall back onto my bed, holding the encrypted note to my chest like a schoolgirl clutching a love letter. My bloody prints smudge some of the ink.

It's finally happening.

I won Carnage, and I was lucky to escape for my *Humanitas* and join the Valence. Numen sent me out into the world like the Huntsman. And like him, I didn't come back with Snow White's heart either. I came back with the heart of an army my brother promised me all those years ago.

Corolla

August 2020

I'm missing and hating things I shouldn't.

Michigan winters always made *seasonal depression* a memoir, the blossoms of spring a promise of sunshine and open windows to come. I wanted summer in winter. I want winter in summer. I want knee-deep snow and a view of Lake Michigan's ice-capped shore. James and I would always make the drive to South Haven to see the lighthouse, a lonely red figure in the gray and white of the bleak weather. I never understood why we went, even when I was grown up enough to ask. Much to my irritation, James never gave a solid answer. It was as if he didn't trust the news anchors, had to see the lighthouse at the end of the pier himself to believe it had survived the previous winter.

Afterward, we would go downtown to Clementine's and fill up on onion rings and fried mushrooms, the hearty pub food sliding down our frozen throats like hot grease. Like the chime of a bell tower, the cold season never started until we made this venture.

Alone in my bedroom, the sheets a rumpled nest around my crossed legs, there's something hopeless about Georgia's sun. A persistent itch, it's always there, beaming through a window, through the curtains. It makes me realize how much I took blizzards, black ice, and slush for granted.

Downstairs, a frequency in the white noise shifts. Since Castan, Julli, and Tate all took off to pick up pizza for dinner, there's only one other person home. Unless Delani got in the house, but I just saw her chained to the pine.

Besides the fact that Julli is the only one who can drive a car, I am almost positive the three left for the very reason of forcing Tyto and me together. To *reconcile*, as a degreed professional would say. Funny how easily Tyto became white noise, how easily he inserted and let himself be inserted there.

But he can't run to a closed office on a Saturday. He can't avoid me anymore.

Instinctively, my ears strain to catch the difference in the background vibrations.

A woman.

476

An old pulse of curiosity charges my blood. When you spend enough time struggling in waves of change, it's refreshing to find yourself at a sandbar to catch your breath.

I move through the house, following the muffled voices, the *crack* and *fizz* of pop cans being opened. I've been here long enough to know Tyto and Woman are in the kitchen, perhaps lounging on the barstools. Grave tones and Tyto clearing his throat. Woman demands very clearly, "It's our responsibility. He's still our brother."

I tread on a floorboard at the bottom of the staircase, wincing when it creaks, low and obtrusive. I almost kick myself for forgetting about it, but it's too late to remain discrete.

"Corolla," Tyto calls, "come here. There's someone I want you to meet." And then, as if I haven't been living here a whole week, he adds, "We're in the kitchen."

As I cross the final distance, Tyto chuckles, "Remember when..." But I don't hear what he says. Aunt Val bursts into stifled giggles, "I know exactly what you're going to say! I can't believe we did that. We could have died from our own stupidity. Papa was *so* bereft."

"Well," Tyto shrugs, "it was his favorite bottle. And his last one, too."

Even before I lay eyes on Valeria, my thoughts collide with one another:

Tate's going to throw a fit—What's she doing here?

But then the poor woman is sitting before me, thick elbow propped on the counter. All at once, my mind pins the words *poor* and *tired* to her. She resembles little of her memory-self. Responsibility has sucked the youth from her figure, replacing it instead with skin so dehydrated, body so plump, she's a bruised pear instead. Though she's grinning, there's a weight to the corners of her lips, the corners of her eyes. Railroad tracks cross her forehead. Her short-cropped hairstyle, spunky on anyone else, is faded and ruffled brown on her. Her top lip is split, and I want to ask: Did you have to kill someone or did a structure fall on you too?

I guess I've endured both.

The subject of my scrutiny tucks her chin, a Diet Coke dripping condensation in her fist. "It's nice to finally meet you, Corolla."

My gaze slides across the counter to Tyto. Something about his immaculate reading glasses, genial smile, and white teeth. Something about his posture, the way he leans towards Valeria on two elbows. The words spark my tongue, an impulse.

"So you can sit here and do *remember when's*, but you can't say more than ten sentences to me?" I wish I could cross my arms, but they dangle, awkward, at my sides. I clench my fist instead, still not sure what will come out, despite Castan's training attempts earlier.

I know by Tyto's crestfallen expression that I've done the wrong thing. That I should have killed the impulse I knew was a mistake all along. That I should have just kept my mouth shut, but I don't think I would have believed myself until I saw his reaction. I fight the wave of shame flooding my cheeks.

But I'm not the absentee father.

"Seriously, you can erase my digital existence to keep me safe, but when I'm actually here, you act like I don't exist at *all*. You don't make sense."

"Hold on," Tyto raises a palm as if that will stop my voice. He turns to Valeria, eyes narrowed. "You got involved."

Her response is the quietest of the three voices, and somehow, the strongest too. "Of course I did. She's blood."

I glance between brother and sister, eyebrows furrowing. "What are you talking about?"

Tyto clenches his jaw, lenses flashing under the kitchen light. I can't see his eyes, and he won't look at me either.

Valeria shifts in the barstool. "I was the one who erased your existence." She shrugs one shoulder, "Well, I was going to put it all back once I knew you were safe. I've been deleting and reinstalling your life since you started preschool. And James... I've been changing the addresses for his bills so that I could pay for those myself. I didn't want you to worry about his debt, but I didn't want him to find out either. I almost had him out of the red..."

"Oh my god." I think I take a step back. I think my jaw actually drops because Valeria has been paying James's bills and I never needed to get involved with Taxodium and James and I would have been okay. Even though I know the answer, I have to hear Tyto say it. "You were never protecting me?"

His fingers curl into fists. "I—"

"She *died* for you," that photo of Adian with the flower in her ear, the chapel at her back, flashes through my rage, "Where were you?"

"I was *here*," Tyto tenses, "trying to explain to my two-year-old that he was not going to see his mother again."

I can't stop—something in my core urges me to press on, to squish Tyto under my scrutiny until he pops. It's like picking at a scab and not being satisfied, not even when crimson surfaces. Only when it drips, a bloody streak, are you content. Every argument I've ever had suddenly stems forward in time to this moment. My wrath was always meant for Tyto. This maelstrom was always his. I just never knew it until now.

"But what about me?" To make sure he heard me, I raise my voice, "Why weren't you there to raise me too?"

He tucks his face farther into the shadow hovering over his head. Heat flays my flesh, boils under my skin and spouts out from each of my pores. Does he honestly think he can just *ignore* me?

"Why—"

"Because I didn't want you!" His neck snaps, crazed eyes fixing themselves to mine. Chest heaving, he brushes hair from his forehead and asserts again, "I do not want you." Each word is a knife between my ribs, puncturing my lungs.

I should have known. And yet, deep down, I always did. *Why why why* always occupied my mind because I couldn't bear to think the truth. My father doesn't want me. He never did. And standing here, under Valeria's apologetic gaze and Tyto's fervent one, I don't want my father either. I don't want any of it.

I can't stay here any longer.

It was a nice idea, a voice croons. *But Mackenzie Clark was wrong about your father. He never killed Adian—he only ever murdered you.*

My voice is a swift dagger, "This should be James's life, but he was too busy raising me, providing for me, *your* daughter." The words tumble out before I can bite them back, "*You* should have died in the attacks. No wonder Calyx faked his death."

My satisfaction is borne in the cocktail of agony and shock shattering Tyto's temper. Valeria says my name, but I ignore her. I turn the corner—

And crash right into the bookcase. That translucent jug of dirt I always wondered about topples to the floor, spewing glass and earth so ancient, a cloud of dust fogs the air.

Choking on grit, I double over in pain. I bite my lip to keep from crying out, holding my left arm to my chest. I shrug off the hands patting my back. Shooting pain rips through my forearm. Instinctively, my hand grabs it, grabs for a section of arm that's no longer there. Irritation burns acid behind my eyelids. How can something that doesn't exist hurt?

Fucking ghost limb phenomenon.

Stomping up the stairs, hugging my arm to my heart, I clench my fist so hard, my fingernails make my hand go numb. I was wrong about new beginnings: they don't exist. But I don't have the heart to tell Castan life is just one long, downhill ride.

Especially when I want it to be untrue.

Talan
August 2020

"These cuffs are kryptonite. Even for you." Thomas grins, and I get a whiff of stale breath, a flash of cracked lips. I swallow a lump of frustration. It's not his fault I'm desperate for food and water. It's not his fault they shaved my head—they shaved all our heads, even the Spaniards.

Using my teeth, I clamp onto Nena's Empara lock. My breath isn't any better. I pry on the metal for all of ten seconds—Nena's wrist is the smallest—before giving up. Nena gasps, rubbing her hands close to her neck.

"Sorry," I push back against the wall and sigh in defeat. "If those lancets come too close to being dislodged, the cuff shocks the host." I apologize to Nena again. Solenne mutters to her, a prayer or encouraging words, I don't know.

"Lancets?" Thomas may as well be a child. Without his crown of curls, he resembles one. He's got an abnormally large forehead.

"The little needles embedded in our flesh."

"Oh." He relays the information to Solenne and Nena, though they understand English just fine. I think he just likes being able to speak Spanish, to show me he's useful for more than just being the lookout.

Since there are no windows, no regular food intervals, there's no way of us telling how long we've actually been locked in the Barracks cells. I gauge a week, Solenne thinks nine days. Thomas doesn't care for guessing games—he just wants to use a real bathroom. It's incredibly challenging to shift about in our chains, bound together by the ankles, so that one of us may use the bucket in the far corner. We try to stay away from that corner as much as possible. And, so it seems, as do the guards. The bucket hasn't been taken out in at least 48 hours, and it's starting to smell like it.

But I enjoy guessing games, and so does Nena when she's not whimpering like a kicked puppy (she realized crying only dehydrates her further). At a certain point, the guard patrol cuts in half. Nena and I (via Thomas) figure that's when the night shift begins. It's the safest time to talk, the most reliable time to plot and fascinate about our escape. To dream. Wakefully.

"So," Thomas exhales, "there's no way we can get out of the Empara locks?"

I shake my head. Close my eyes. Sleeping is a poor man's way out of his problems.

"But what if we—"

"Thomas," I snap without opening my eyes, "just drop it, okay? I don't know what else to try. Besides, I'm too tired to think right now." My stomach growls as if asserting my annoyance. Maybe Nena will become emaciated, and *then* we'll be able to slip her hands through the locks.

I sense Thomas shrink into himself. Solenne shifts, probably nestling with Nena, and tugs my leg, which tugs Thomas's.

The first few nights were hard, my mind configuring new ways to escape. But now I settle as easily as Solenne and Nena, my head used to the stone wall pillow, my spine forever crooked from leaning against it. Some mornings, I'll wake up on Thomas's thigh, or his head will be resting on my shoulder. I used to feel guilty, that if Finis showed up to rescue me, and saw Thomas and me that close, he would leave without unlocking the door. But now I don't care. Human flesh is better than solid rock.

Tonight, however, Thomas keeps his distance, even if it is only inches. I feel his body heat against my thigh, but my mind wanders elsewhere. I don't think about the Barracks, which I've come to accept as cylindrical, not rectangular. I don't think about Finis or Jura or whether or not Corolla managed to escape, that poor pedes caught in pelari crossfire. I think about nothing at all. And it is bliss.

I am on the verge of sleep, at that point of falling when every sound is suddenly amplified and warped—the rattling of chains in cells over, the muted song of a jailbird, and farther away, snoring—when a noise seems to scream in my ears.

"Wake up!" And though the voice is a hushed whisper, it is deafening, crashing against the stone walls like violent waves against a jagged shore.

My first thought: You're going to alert the guards! But then I see the figure on the other side of the iron bars. Barely distinguishable, the woman—at least it sounded like a woman—is hidden in the shadows of her own ebony cloak. No light pierces through that black cave masking her face.

Thomas has the sense to ask, "Who are you?"

The figure turns on him, perhaps drinking up his young, bedraggled form, before answering, "I'm with the Valence, a group established to fix things where Taxodium failed."

Solenne spits language at the strange woman. Beneath the curtain of fabric, I note the Caeli boots strapped to the woman's feet.

No wonder I didn't hear her approach.

"No, no," the woman raises her palms in response to Solenne, "this isn't a trap." She cranes her head left and right. I could tell her that the guard will be circling within the next ten minutes, but I keep my mouth shut. "And I can prove it." She crouches beside Thomas and reaches through the bars to grasp his bound hands.

"Don't struggle," she instructs. I watch with intense curiosity—and distrust—as she slides a key card over the left side of Thomas's Empara lock. The device falls limp into his lap like a beetle's shell hollow of flesh. Thomas massages his bruised wrists, stunned into silence. Nena makes an approving noise. Solenne holds her friend back.

The stranger snatches the Empara lock from Thomas's lap and shoves it in a satchel by her feet. "I'll have to put fake ones on you, but at least you'll have two arms and an Essence again. Who's next? I don't have a lot of time here."

Nena thrusts her hands towards the stranger, who takes them without question. One by one, we are freed from the constraints of the Empara locks. The stranger collects them all into her bag. In a hurry, she passes out the fake cuffs, explains that they twist together at the wrist to give the impression of being a single, metallic unit.

She rises, and a current of lost opportunity stabs my heart.

"Why don't you just free us?" It's the only thing I've said to her, not even a thank you for removing the Empara.

"Because," she slings the satchel under her cloak, "the Valence needs you all ready from the inside."

I don't need to ask why. Taxodium, the Valence, *whoever*, requires all the forces they can manage. "If you can sneak in here to replace our cuffs, then you can bring a little food and water, too."

The stranger tugs her hood farther over her head. Is that ink under her nails or blood? "This isn't *Orange is the New Black*, okay? I can't do what you're asking, and you're in no position to make such demands."

"Then you can't count on us to fight. We're weak as it is, and with the Vultures picking us off at random, your surprise army will diminish further."

The woman goes quiet for a moment. I pick out the distinct *clink, clink* of an approaching guard.

"Fine," the stranger hisses, "I'll see what I can do. But in the meantime, keep your Essence to yourself. It won't be long now."

And then she is gone, cloak billowing noiselessly behind her slight frame.

"What the hell was that?" But I don't answer Thomas. I go slack, slump against the wall, as the guard stalks closer still.

"Oh, Phaedra's Mother," he exclaims, just outside our cell, "that's some potent shit. Someone should really take that bucket out."

It won't be long now.

Castan
August 2020

"It's good to see you, Cassena," Commander Murphy claps a big-knuckled hand on my back. Around the slab of stone, heads turn to evaluate the reunion. Finis shoots me a small grin, stabilizing himself on crutches. A man and woman, who I can only guess are his older siblings, stand on either side of him, chattering about infiltration strategies. The luminant blonde hair and vivid blue eyes give them away.

"Dentata," I correct, gaze sliding back to the NA Commander. "My real name is Castan Dentata."

"I know," his grin doesn't falter, "word spreads like wildfire around here. Laila mentioned something about a deal with Tilia. We could use someone with inside knowledge of the Dentatas."

"Sure," I duck my head, "but I'm not sure how accurate my information is anymore. This Renatus figure seems to be messing up all the patterns." Commander Murphy nods, hazel eyes clouding in deep thought. A pair of arms wraps around my side, capturing my surprise.

"Castan," Aunt Laila—or just Laila—breathes. "I'm so glad you're alright. The customs officers said you and Corolla jumped here last night."

"Yeah," I puff my chest, prepared to explain everything to Laila, but the air pushes out my nostrils. "We're both alright." I already had to clarify everything from Rosh to Dani/Lola to Alba Creek Farm to the customs officers filtering through the survivors at the fortress gates. I don't have it in me to go through it all again. I don't have it in me to lie about Calyx again.

Laila whispers so only I can hear, "I passed her outside Luca's door. So, James really didn't escape?" I glance at Laila. I don't know what I expect to find, but it's not the careful self-control pinching her expression now. I nod once.

She exhales, shoulders relaxing. "Alright," her expression is hidden in curtains of black hair, "alright." The wispy syllable is enough; as if Laila is fighting nausea and saying the same thing out loud over and over again is the only thing that will settle her stomach. I don't know what occurred between James and her, but like many "adult things," James was only something she could love with her eyes. The pitiful sound of lost opportunities laces her voice—*I should have held him more, should have kissed him more.* If her hair weren't clouding her expression, Matrona *knows* what her face would reveal.

The air is suddenly more humid and saltier than before. With no AC or windows, the auditorium is more like a massive tomb. I expect to see clouds forming against the rough dome of the ceiling. Sweat pools in the hollow of my neck.

"Ladies and gents," a British man calls out. I recognize the Euro Commander, Robert Allen, by name only. His bones are padded with hard muscle, skin decorated in intricate, black ink. Like dripping oil, two ebony trails follow his carotids, disappearing beneath the collar of his shirt. Every so often, he smooths a palm over his bald head. At some point, Commander Murphy wove through the crowd and stands at Commander Allen's shoulder now. Murphy could bench press his own weight, but Allen could probably bench press Murphy. I guess he had a lot to live up to, though—it can't be easy being a descendant of Gentry and Dawson Allen.

It takes half a minute before silence falls over the conference room. Cluster by cluster, people sit around the elliptical slab. Laila crosses her legs at the knee, perhaps a little too focused. I pretend not to see the distance, like a vacant dirt road, in the shallows of her eyes.

Commander Allen grins, hard features over warm eyes. "Thank you, those of you who could make it again. And thank you, those of you joining us today for the first time. We'll start today where we left off yesterday, then. Scavengers in Rome have secured the latest project Intel was finishing up before the attacks. New uniforms, ones that can absorb high velocity hits and protect the wearer from internal damage. Those, as well as other supplies, will be dropped today by our only surviving aircraft."

I refrain from cracking my knuckles. I refrain from closing my eyes and taking a nap. The surviving Commanders—Euro, NA, African—debate amongst themselves, throwing questions and ideas at the assembly now and then. I soon realize how disorganized we are, how non-cooperative we are: everyone wants to do their own thing. Some are hunting for revenge, others, for a quiet surrender ("Why can't we just make do on St. Helena?").

"Where are the Majors?" I whisper under my breath.

Laila shoots me a glance from the corner of her eye, "They're all dead. Except Rex."

I lean back against the chair and chew on this for a moment.

"The Reserve," Commander Murphy explains to those who want to call for pedes military intervention, "are coming every day. It's just a matter of sending people to retrieve them, as our Communications are down as well."

"If we wait too long," the blonde woman beside Finis interjects, "then the Gens will have all the more time to reinforce themselves. They're just as scattered as we are right now."

"Yes," Laila speaks up, "but they're also barricaded in a mountain."

The blonde cranes her head to meet Laila's unspoken challenge. Her blue eyes flicker dangerously, "And when they organize themselves before we do, where are we sitting? On the edge of a cliff and half submerged in the ocean! We're making it too easy for them."

"That's enough, Mingo," the blonde man clasps a hand on his sister's shoulder. Finis is stone, caught between the two. His crutches lean against the backside of his chair, a glimpse of the reality outside this stone auditorium.

And to think, weeks ago, my biggest problem was nightmares.

Mingo shrugs the hand away. "We can't just *pretend*, Gideon. We're sitting ducks here, and yet, the Gens haven't tried anything. But it's only a matter of time."

"No," I mumble to myself, staring hard at the gray edge of the table, "they think they've already won." I didn't think I was talking loud enough, but some heads nod with assertion, brows furrowed and eyes grave.

"Maybe they're not wrong." I don't know who said it, but more heads bob to this comment, slow motion head-banging all around the table.

Commander Allen intervenes before voices can rise too high, "Taxodium has not fallen," his voice slices through the frustrated, sea-salt atmosphere, "its very foundation is right here, in this fortress. So long as its people live and breathe, we must defend our brothers, our sisters, our society!"

No soul dares contradict such straight-edge eyebrows, such conviction. No soul dares oppose a legacy. Sweat trickles down my spine.

"I believe," dozens of heads turn towards the double doors, tracking the sound of that confident voice, "that's where we come in." Calyx moves into the room, his presence filling even the smallest cracks in the walls. An entourage of people tail behind him—two African women, twins, an older woman with wild gray hair and purple lipstick, a lanky man with an antique pilot's cap snug to his head. Ramsey and Umar. I recognize the latter, burly black beard and quiet strides.

Betrayal stings my heart, alcohol to fresh cuts.

Calyx replaces the stunned Commanders at the head of the table. He tucks his chin in Murphy's direction but doesn't waste time with hello's or "I'm back from the dead!"

"Tilia herself created this group," Calyx gestures to the people surrounding him, "to root out Taxodium's corruption. Well," and here, the bastard has the audacity to grin, "it seems our work is cut out for us now." Umar hands him a scroll of paper I hadn't noticed he was clutching. Calyx smooths it across the table top.

"These are blueprints for the SA. My people and I have been... discussing... and we concluded that a bomb is our best bet. Shall we put it to a vote?"

"A bomb?" Laila grits her teeth. I wonder what she's thinking, Calyx living and breathing before a gathering of 60. "You want to wipe out everyone in the Academy? It's the only one we have a chance at taking back."

Mingo has to shout over the escalating discord, "But the Gens are all there *now*! I think it's our only option. If they decide to move someplace more populated by pedes, per se, then *more* innocents will die. This is a once and a lifetime—"

"Casualties true for any attack," an older man asserts in broken English. "But we kill everyone in SA, we are just as bad as Gens."

Calyx nods as if he's actually considering what the people are saying. I know he's not. He's already made his decision. "We have inside intel to reinforce this plan: Renatus is coming to the SA soon. If we plan our advancement accordingly, we may wipe out the roots of this pelari faction."

A fresh wave of chaos descends upon the room. Through flailing arms, soaring voices, I watch Calyx. Purple Lips whispers something in his ear, her tangled gray locks tickling his throat. He nods, face twisting as he chews his cheek, catches himself, and refrains from doing so again.

Is he a leader or a puppet?

"Ladies, gentlemen," Commander Allen raises his hands again, calling for silence. Gradually, the noise dips into scattered whispers and crossing arms.

And Calyx used to be so good at making friends.

As if hearing my mocking thoughts, his gaze latches onto mine. "Castan, what do you think?"

What do I think? He's asking for so much more than my opinion on the matter. "I think," I want to say, "that I was always meant to kill Rosh. Born the younger son, that was always the expectation. I can't blame you for that." I think Taxodium should have executed my ancestors. I guess this bomb is a chance to amend that crucial mistake. A *humane* way.

"Tax is running low on manpower." I fold my hands in my lap, palms sticky with sweat. "We should vote on it."

39 to 18. We're dropping the bomb, then. When Calyx announces the results, I absorb the information with careless regard. I voted with the 39. I can't say what Laila's slip said, yay or nay, but I have a feeling her vote canceled out mine.

My tee is damp with sweat, and when I lick my lips, I taste salt. I abandon the conference room in search of water, but St. Helena is a maze—winding stone corridors and artificial light. I don't dare take the elevator down past floor four, Housing, because my ears already feel the ocean and atmosphere pressing their weights down on me.

Instead, I climb sloping staircases, like DNA strands, higher and higher. Though St. Helena is partially underwater, it's not like the Complex, whose floors were flat, even concrete. Cold. St. Helena is a combination of underground caverns and architecture to connect everything natural and man-made. There are pockets of humidity in some places, refrigerators in others. Unlike the Complex, there is no pattern to this place.

I must have breached the upper floors, one or two, Hospital. I pass nurses, recognizable in their snow-white scrubs. The air resonates *antiseptic* as if the molecules themselves have been scrubbed with disinfectants and Biozide.

I hope to run into Corolla, Kass, Maggie, or even Júlia. But none of the haggard, sometimes red-eyed faces I pass are familiar. Eventually, I find a sort of common room. It's vacant of people, furnished in leather chairs and soft couches, a near-barren bookshelf coated in dust and outdated medical reference books. I gravitate towards the empty hearth. I snap my fingers, willing a spark to catch. When nothing happens, I throw myself back on one of the couches. My temples throb, limbs ache with weakness and exhaustion. I close my eyes, so comfortable, I could die here content.

I don't hear the door open, but suddenly, a shadow falls on my face. Without cracking an eyelid, I know exactly who's followed me in here. When we first began together at Tax, I always thought people would jab me for trailing him around like a dog. I gave him space, sure, but space is underrated when you've been hired to *be* someone's shadow.

"People spend all this time wishing their dead back to life, and when I finally do show up, nobody wants me." His voice rings bitterly. When he speaks again, I place him hovering in front of the cold hearth. "You've got to stop sending me mixed signals."

I drape an arm over my eyes. "Then maybe you should stop using people for your personal agenda."

"The thing is, Castan: you, Kass, my family were too important to know I was alive. Some secrets are too big to keep quiet, which, by the way, thanks for blowing my cover to my family before I was ready. That was a pleasant surprise to walk into this morning when I came to get you and Corolla."

I shrug, too tired to argue. "Tyto's an ass. He deserved whatever Corolla said to him."

"Are you feeling okay?" His voice is nearer, shadow thicker.

"Don't touch me."

I imagine him scowling. "I wasn't going to—"

"The thing that really pisses me off about you, Calyx, is that you never even considered who you were hurting. You just *did*, with no fucking warning."

Calyx folds his arms over his chest, his silhouette peeling itself from my skin. "And if I'd told you it was all a ruse, so I could go into hiding, what would you have done at Taxodium, huh? You wouldn't have mourned me, not really. You would have wanted to help the Valence eradicate the Gens, and I wasn't in a position to let you. Believe me, Castan, I was just following orders. I intended to bring about some good for the pelari community."

"Tilia lied for me first, Calyx. I don't understand why she never recruited me too."

"Who knows what her motives were? Maybe she needed you vengeful and depressed. Maybe she needed you to bring Corolla into this and show her who she really is. I don't know." Perhaps he shrugs. He certainly *sounds* dismissive.

"That's coincidental," I scoff.

"Tilia lived too long to believe in coincidences. Everything she did had a reason, even if she wasn't quite sure at the time what that reason was. Maybe she just wanted you to be free of obligation for a year or so until the Valence made itself known. She did care about you, Castan. More than anyone else who ever passed her threshold. You had the guts to leave the Complex and turn your back on the Dentatas. That's like breaking Amish and shit. It takes a lot of courage to leave behind everything you've ever known."

I crack an eye, and through my lashes, is Calyx. He's leaning over the hearth, one elbow propped on the brickwork. Rejection wrinkles his expression like soiled laundry. Something in my chest flows over, and I know I can't be mad at him anymore. He is, after all, my best friend.

I chuckle, the sound ripping through the somber silence, "I just wanted to read."

Calyx turns, surprise flickering across his eyes. He breaks into delayed laughter. "Well," he gestures in my direction, "there is that too."

Hadley
August 2020

"What the hell's going on?" I track bodies, racing through the streets, and have a flashback of the attacks launched on Taxodium: they came out of nowhere, too. Behind Collis Hall, fireworks—*when did we get fireworks?*—pitch into the sky, dull lights lost in the thick, white clouds. Eels of smoke curl through the atmosphere. Eyes foggy from sleep, heart beating in my chest as if it's the only organ I possess, I absorb all of this in the dead of night.

My grip tightens around whoever's arm I managed to snag when I staggered out of my dorm. Ropes of hard muscle but slim enough I can wrap my fingers around the circumference. It's only when my captive speaks that I let go. It's Colin, the boy Castan almost killed in Carnage. I catch his patchwork of facial skin in the eerie glow of auburn fireworks. Two years ago, he didn't even *have* facial skin.

"Renatus arrived—some of those Taxodium pigs brought out the kegs." His words are a tangle of excitement and vocal strain from the damage Castan caused. Even as he races down the steps carved into the mountainside, my brain configures what he's said. A loud roar of cheers and whistles erupts from farther down the mountain. Without thinking, I follow the noise, my heart willing Colin's words to be untrue.

But I have to see for myself. I have to see Renatus.

The air is bitter cold, cutting through the fabric of my jumpsuit—I stopped sleeping in pajamas when I joined the Valence, never knowing when I'd have to make a quick escape. By instinct, I snatched my knife—cleaned and sheathed now—from my desk. It hangs at my hip, slapping against my thigh with each step I fly down.

Even in navy blue darkness, it's impossible to get lost. Fireworks shoot into the night, crackling and sparking dull light over the Academy. I weave around those with lungs unaccustomed to the thin mountain air. My feet thud soundlessly as I jog towards the gathering crowd.

Of course, I almost roll my eyes when I see the building everyone is shuffling to get into. *Of course he chose to reveal himself in the Courthouse.*

I shoulder past jittering bodies, words a flutter of gibberish in my ears. The stench of alcohol smacks my senses in the doorway.

490

Colin wasn't lying about the kegs.

People stand on chairs, amber liquid sloshing in mismatched cups. Someone brought out glow sticks, vibrant, rainbow-colored manacles around wrists and throats. Beyond the ocean of bobbing heads, intoxicated bodies, stands Baylor, arms crossed over his heavy-set pouch. *Phaedra*, his expression reads, *I'm too old for this shit.*

"Where's my father?" I pull myself up onto the platform, the shadow of the Old Law flickering in the face of so much rebellion. Uncle Baylor nods towards the side room where the Judges would retreat for case discussion. Someone throws a glow stick at the stage, and the trend takes flight. I leave before Baylor loses his temper.

The chamber is strangely illuminated, blinding in its LED halo. I blink, eyes adjusting to the change. An unfamiliar voice reaches my ears.

"...think I wouldn't find out? You lost Luca Alba, and all that he contained, to Taxodium—"

"Hadley," my father is displeased, dare I say *pained*, "what are you doing here?"

But I can't answer. I blink, a dark suit taking form before me: Dark complexion, and, highlighted behind a trim suit, the lean body of a man who bikes twice daily. Wrinkled face, hair tediously dyed—there's no way it's *that* jet black—and hands pocketed in pressed trousers, he looks like he should be crunching numbers in a cubicle. There's nothing ominous about the man, and yet... There *is* something about him as if familiar eyes sit in an unfamiliar face. I can't put my finger on it.

So, I want to say, you're *Renatus, the man behind my father, behind all the attacks and killings.*

Okay. I can deal.

Or maybe, this is only a proxy Renatus. Maybe the real Brain just sent an advocate. Yet there's something about this man...

"Hadley," Numen grips my wrist, shoving me towards the door, "I want you to leave. Now."

"Why—"

"Don't you argue with me, too." My father pushes me towards the door, his hand gripped so hard around the handle, his partially-arthritic knuckles scream white.

"No," Renatus grins, and I get the impression of a snake eyeing a mouse, "let her stay. Perhaps she is the answer to our dilemma."

I don't do it for the Valence. I don't do it in spite of my father. I just can't *help* myself. I twist out of Numen's grip. "Dilemma?"

"You see, your father wants to share this newfound power." Renatus folds his hands over his stomach. A chill creeps into his voice, sending goosebumps along my arms, "And you've recently debuted, I've heard. Lovely."

Though Numen stands a head taller and inches thicker with muscles, he is powerless in Renatus's shadow. I admire my father for trying anyway. "No, you leave her alone." He moves to yank me back. Two things happen at once.

Renatus's hand flies from his pocket, a flash of black sleeve, and strikes my father across the cheek. My own hand unsheathes the knife at my hip, aiming the tip of my blade at the man's throat.

Renatus chuckles, Adam's apple bobbing against my knife's silver point. I have to force my lungs to calm, chest heaving with the power of adrenaline.

And all I can think is, *Numen must really despise this man if he doesn't want him to touch me.* It's not that my father whores me about like a prize, but he has been trying to marry me off since I turned sixteen. And didn't he say he wanted a strong-willed man for me? If Jon Xabier Dentata fears whoever Renatus really is, then how am *I* supposed to feel?

"That won't be necessary, little girl," Renatus flicks my knife away. A drop of blood trickles down his neck. "Look at your protector and think twice before you stand against me a second time."

I should cry—in joy, sadness, or relief—but I should cry. Instead, I regard my father's slit throat, crumpled body, and glassy eyes, with corneas so dry, I blink to replenish their moisture. Numen fell against the door, a clean slice through his left carotid. I thought Renatus struck his cheek. Despite his crimes, I thought I was defending my father. That's probably the last thing Jon saw, his only daughter drawing a blade in his wretched name. My father's only regret, I'm sure, is that he didn't die a traditional death—by the hand of his own child.

While these thoughts reel through my mind, Renatus's slick voice is at my shoulder, "Your father was foolish enough to share the reins with me before, and I am too selfish to return the favor." It's as if another person is speaking. Cool apathy on his tongue is a swift dagger to my ears. "I'm not the settling type, but I can already tell you're going to be a problem."

Head cocked, eyes tracing the slowing stream of crimson down my father's front, I let my guard down. A force knocks the knife from my hand, fingers stinging with the impact. Arms shove my spine into the masonry. His breath is toxic, I'm convinced, noxious vapors I shouldn't inhale. I hold my breath, his body pressed against mine. Between his legs, I feel his heartbeat. I swallow, take a quick breath and brace myself—

"I don't think so," a hand clamps over my mouth before the scream escapes. "I know all about you, Siren." My teeth clamp onto the flesh of his palm. He doesn't flinch, not even when I draw blood.

Some animal instinct coded within urges me to make him bleed, to make him die a pitiful death like my father. To make him human. Because that look in his dark eyes, that beam of lust and cruelty, causes a portion of my soul to shrink. Maybe he will rape me, but the zipper to my jumpsuit is smashed against the wall.

The crowd in the Courthouse grows impatient.

"Rena! Rena!" I pick out the slurred chant through the solid walls of the chamber. What will Baylor think, his birthright stolen from him by an outsider?

Renatus grins, white teeth in the shadow of his large beak. "Solitary confinement, I think, until I'm ready to deal with you."

The sour stench of spilled blood swirls in my nostrils. I wish I'd just stayed in bed.

Thank Pyrus I managed to deliver supplies to the prisoners earlier. But even this concession is small compared to the new reality stitching itself together in my head:

Renatus is early, and the Valence is not ready.

Corolla

August 2020

I never liked the ocean, but staring at it now, through thick glass at St. Helena, I can't help but admire it. Fear prickles my heartstrings, claws plucking a harp. I press my hand to the glass, absorb the depthless navy blue, and ignore the emotion shuffling through my neurons like a deck of cards. Or maybe I embrace it. Between the ache in my heart, the pain in my arm, the misery in my brain, I can't keep track of which I'm feeling anymore. It kind of blurs together like an amateur watercolor: messy, ugly, indistinguishable from *trash* or *art, physical* or *mental*.

James always said I should be a marine biologist, to "overcome my fear of the ocean." The ocean has never been a dormant, dying thing, has never been just a vast pool of hydrogens, oxygens, sodiums. It's always been a living, fluid beast, untamable. Uncontrollable.

My hand hovers over the glass now. Its reflection is a ghost of myself as if my body has been severed paper-thin a hundred times over. Each Corolla takes an emotion with her. But this one, the Corolla on the other side of the glass, she's warning me of... of what? Of loss, grief, love, and death? That's every human's birthright. It just took me until now to fully comprehend that.

But life isn't all that bad. I picture Castan's bare body hovering over mine, the symphony of muscle working beneath his pale skin, and my lips on his collarbone. Heat flushes my thighs, cheeks, and neck. I've got to stop turning myself on. Especially in a hospital.

Feeling more like a fish tapping my own bowl, I turn away from the oceanic view. Besides, I was just on my way from the Posted—a wall on the fifth floor dedicated to those lost in battle. I leave a fresh daisy-chain crown for James every morning. It's been three days since Castan and I arrived.

I hop onto an elevator, shiny and smooth as a bullet, relishing the quiet hum of gears turning, motors working. If Talan were here, he'd be going up to the hospital sector with me. But then again, if Talan were here, he would have found out Vera died from a second heart attack, not long after she was reestablished on the island.

I look for his name on the Posted each morning, too. As survivors arrive every day, so does the news of those who will never breathe again.

I practically leap out of the elevator and laugh at the noiseless impact of my Caeli boots. Calyx pulled some strings and got me an old uniform. It's a little loose on my legs, but I'm not about to complain. He's been helping me command my Essence, because he wants to or because he's trying to prove something to Castan, I don't know.

I tramp down the hall, passing under white lights and monotone *beeps*. Unlike the remaining four floors below, the hospital wing (floors one and two) are above ground. Which means they follow the rules: flat terrain, carefully constructed rooms. After three days of visiting Luca, the route is muscle memory. My thoughts wander to yesterday's session with Calyx.

"Vines are essentials. You can use them to choke, bind, pick locks, etc., etc."

I couldn't help the bitterness spiking my tone as I practiced. "It's poetic, isn't it, James's death triggering my... blossoming."

Calyx sucked in his cheeks, and I almost offered him a piece of gum (Castan got me a new pack). With more empathy than I expected, he said, "Strong emotional responses tend to trigger Essences. I'm sorry."

And to that, I clamped my jaw shut and worked on coercing a vine around my own neck, imagining it was Tyto's. ("Essences can never harm its host.")

I've been having erratic thoughts, but I think I don't care. *Roll with it*, Castan counseled. Okay, I will.

Luca is comatose, a spirit trapped in a chunk of barely-functioning flesh. Like a genie in a lamp. I fold my fingers around his hand, inhaling the clean air. I wish he would come out of his stupor. I wish I could talk to him. I don't know what I would say, but some chunk of me is pinning all my hope on his recovery. He is unlike Tyto, Valeria, and Calyx. He didn't *choose* to stay away from me all those years. Luca is a fresh start at family.

"You have so much love to give. That's why it hurts you to keep it to yourself."

Against a white pillow, folded under crisp linens, he is as thin as before. Skin and bones. Except for pink flushes his bronze cheeks; his chest rises and falls with content ease. Sometimes, his eyelids twitch, lashes fluttering like two, little black wings. Electrodes are stuck to his profile like suction cups.

The doctors say his brain activity is "unusual." The nurses say his vitals are "near perfect." I clutch his hand with ginger fingers and will his eyelids to complete what they've—no doubt—been trying to accomplish for weeks: to open.

I glance over my shoulder, see that the steel door is shut, and turn back to Luca. I heard somewhere that talking to people in comas is a good thing. I still feel strange doing it, though, like talking to myself in public.

"Laila has been pestering me about a séance," my voice doesn't rise above a whisper, "but I don't... I mean, if James communicates to me through Júlia, then where is he exactly? He was raised to believe in Heaven and Hell, but... I don't know. It hurts my heart to think of James, someplace drenched in shadows or covered in ash. He died in a world he didn't understand." I sigh, sweat collecting in my palm, "What is death like? I probably shouldn't know."

Like an expectant child, I look up. Luca's chest rises. His IV drips behind his head, bag half full. The monitor refreshes his heart rhythm, counting each beat the same mechanical way I count the days Luca's been like this.

Valeria's words tickle the back of my mind, *"It's our responsibility. He's still our brother."* It? What was she insinuating?

My hand goes slack. I tug my fingers free of Luca's.

"I'll be back tomorrow."

It's the little things. It always is.

I'm on the third floor, where the terrain becomes a little more angled and the pressure starts working its magic, when I witness a flustered nurse pushing a man in a wheelchair. I'm not near enough to make out the entire exchange, but the nurse parks the wheelchair at the end of the hall, says something about "not dealing with this today," and leaves the man to his own devices.

It's an overcrowded metropolis down here. People passing by either duck their heads to ignore the scene or talk louder to drown out their own guilty consciences.

They'll feel worse when they see what I'm about to do. I grin at the thought, but it's not about making other people feel worse. There's something about being crippled that encourages you to do things you know you shouldn't be able to. There's so much more to prove. To yourself. I don't even want to think about how much more horrifying it will be to put a tampon in now.

I go up behind the great gumdrop of a man, his flesh melting through the back of his wheelchair. His scalp is speckled gray, round as the underside of an egg. He grumbles to himself, confirming my suspicions. He's a permanent resident, was here long before Taxodium's survivors flooded the halls.

Without saying a word, I grip one handle and use my left shoulder to push. I shouldn't be able to move him, but I'm working against the odds now.

"Where are you going?" I almost steer into the back of some guy's feet. The man in the wheelchair grunts, the sound similar to laughter. He's a mean spirit—*that* I deduced the moment his nurse abandoned him. For some strange reason, it only makes me like him more.

"I don't like just anybody to push me, and the nurses know that." He crosses his arms over a stomach inflated with fat. I stop pushing and walk around the chair so he can see me.

"I don't think your regular nurse will be coming back." His eyes land on my arm, my eyes on his deflated basketball shorts. I almost laugh, one cripple to another.

He raises his eyes—pale blue of a cloudless sky—to my face. He licks his lips, "You from the NA, Euro or what?"

"NA."

"Hmm." I go back around and begin pushing him again. "I heard it was worse there. More panic than soldiers. Take a left up here. Lunch starts in six minutes."

The sight of a one-handed teen and a legless man earns us the entire elevator. People don't dare put themselves in such a small space with such a vast amount of tragedy.

"Why are we going down? The cafeteria is up."

I shake my head. "The one on floor five has better food."

"Floor five! How do expect to get me around down there?"

I shrug. "I was just going to push you down the steps and see how far you roll. I'm Corolla, by the way." I extend my good arm.

The man gives me a suspicious look before clasping his paw in mine. "Iatran."

Iatran insists on dining alone in the corner, so that's where I leave him. The cafeteria bustles, scents from the warm buffet creeping through the air. It's tantalizing, yet my gut roils. Nausea hooks the lining of my stomach. I sip from my water bottle, observing the interactions around me with cool demure.

"I thought I saw a redhead at the conference," Finis's older sister, Mingo, adjusts the sleeve of hair ties on her wrist, "Your dad?"

Kass nudges her younger brother, Lark. Besides his shock of red hair and pale skin, he's nothing like his sister. Shy. Collected. "Yeah," he responds. Lark digs into his heaping pile of macaroni and cheese once more. Before Mingo sat down, he was arguing with Kass about her *timing*—I guess she handed down a family heirloom, a *cantus*

497

blade, that's supposed to be useful for Hold transportation. Rendered *useless* now that the majority of Holds no longer exist.

Kass says something about her runs for the day—she's part of the team responsible for collecting members of the Reserve. She jumps around the globe all day, wearing herself thin, but the woman couldn't be more proud of herself.

Júlia angles towards me, clutching a pocket-sized agenda and pen. It's the most organized I've ever seen her. "Are you sure you don't want me to pencil you in for this evening? I have a slot available."

I swallow a mouthful of lukewarm water. "No thanks."

"You know," she tucks her pen behind her ear, "people find séances useful during recovery. Even if you're skeptical—"

"No *thanks*."

"Corolla." As I turn to face my brother, Kass recoils. His eyes flicker over her disgusted expression, and I witness his careful mask ripple with hurt. It happens in a split second. Then his eyes are fixed on mine, profile grave. "I need to speak with you. In private."

"Sure." As I follow him out into the hall, my heart hammers in my chest. Is Luca dead? Is somebody else? Castan spends most of the day in conference with the Commanders ("Once Allen starts talking, it's near impossible to get him to *shut up*.") and Valence reps, so I don't see him often. My heart almost stops—did something happen to *him*?

When we're in the hall, cool air sliding over our bodies like silk, I can't contain my panic. "Is something wrong? Is somebody hurt? Calyx, what *is* it?"

Calyx shakes his head. Chews his cheek. "No, my scavengers recovered this from Major Crivelli's office." From his back pocket, he withdraws a folded piece of paper. In my hand, it's thick, the kind of paper people use for wedding invitations or high-end parties. I unfold it, scan the fine print with hurried eyes. The muscles in my face tense.

"I don't understand. What is this?"

"A Mandate from the Board," Calyx rakes a hand through his coffee-ground locks, "Remember when I said Adian's death made no strategic sense? Well, now we know why. The Dentatas didn't kill her. Taxodium did."

Anger rises within me, not because Adian was murdered by her own people, but because Calyx seems to have a talent for resurrecting things that should just stay in the past. Like his own death. It *is* his fault heads turn every time he walks into a goddamned room. Whispers follow his every move.

He mutters so only I can hear, "The larger the signature, the more support that Major poured into the Mandate."

I shove the ridiculously thick paper in his hands. I don't have to look again to know whose signature dominates the article. I don't have to search to find the culprit either. I pivot, jaw clenched, and stalk through the cafeteria aisles. I don't know why I do it—a fierce sense of loyalty towards Adian, or a long overdue triumph over this cold-hearted woman I've never liked—but the impulse is there. Is *happening*, before I can think better of it.

"You had Adian assassinated." The accusation feels good on my tongue, like warm milk or a scrumptious dessert under candlelight.

"After she was killed, Major Rex commissioned a statue of Adian and placed it in the Garden." Guilt will make people do strange things.

Rex drops her napkin in her lap, thin-lipped smile fading into a straight line. "Take care what you say, Vel."

"Oh," I ignore the hundreds of thirsty eyes swallowing the scene, "I don't think you're in any position to make threats." I glance from the sling strapping her arm to her stomach to the bandage wrapped around her cranium.

Rex chuckles. "Fine, whatever. The Board Mandated your mother's death. After the attack on my Academy, we had no choice. The Dentatas would have festered and thrived had she lived. We had to protect pelari interests—"

"No," nausea rolls through my stomach again, "you had to protect your own interests. You hated my father for loving Adian. You hated him for having a *heart*."

I feel so sick—were Calyx and I to be Mandated to death too?—and tongue-tied, that I retreat back into the hall before I say something incoherent. Calyx is gone, back to his plotting and planning, but I hardly notice over the trembling of my own body. It's Life's ironies that the people least deserving of life should live.

Sweat collects under my nose, at my hairline. I clutch the wall for support, knees weak. My mind is a pool of shock. I can't escape it.

And then there are arms gripping my shoulders, helping me stand. I blink, recognizing those almond eyes immediately. His hair is longer, somehow, a testament to how time I've spent away. I throw my arms around Issak's neck. I think I love him, just for the sake of knowing he survived. One less name I have to search for at the Posted.

He pulls away, a pale-yellow hospital band around his wrist. He must have just been discharged. Though besides some minor abrasions on his cheeks and collarbone, he is fine. Maybe Maggie healed him too.

"Oh my god, Corolla." His hands tighten on my shoulders. For a terrifying moment, I think he's disgusted with my amputation. But his milk-white eyes are fixed on my alert ones.

"What?"

"Your…" his ears prick, "You don't know?"

Talan

August 2020

"It's been too long," Thomas hisses. "Maybe something bad happened to her."

I shake my head. Thomas knows better than to talk during the day. Especially since the Vultures have been more prominent in the corridors now. Thomas isn't wrong, though. The entire atmosphere has changed, gone from dormancy to excitation overnight. I thought I heard fireworks a couple night shifts ago, and I'm not the only one who thinks that either.

Something terrible has definitely happened. A pessimistic voice in the back of my mind says that Taxodium has failed, that their attack only resulted in mass casualties. That we are stuck here forever, with no hope of escaping.

Except that we do have a chance, albeit a slim one. Weak with hunger, and dry with thirst, each of us still carries the sliver of hope that, if all else fails, our proxy Empara locks will be our saving grace.

Nena and Solenne are taking the hunger harder, but they have been prisoners longer. They've gone mute, really, slouched against each other. They sleep most of the time. I somewhat miss their nonsense chatter, though I could never understand it.

I've succumbed to my thoughts, am deep in that place where you don't notice anything else around you except the hallucinations playing behind your eyes, when a ruckus echoes down the corridor. Screaming. Noises so animal, ripping through the quiet suffering of the Barracks, they're inhuman.

Solenne cracks an eye. Nena nuzzles closer to her friend's shoulder. Thomas sighs. Hunger appears to make him stupid.

"Another one."

I'm about to hush him when the disturbance escalates.

"No, no, no," a man wails. Women scream. And despite my deepest wish for a quiet evening, the cacophony travels down the corridor. Adrenaline shoots through my veins. Solenne perks upright. Even Nena, half-drunk with sickness, realizes something is wrong.

"The sound should be going away from us," Thomas states the obvious, poor kid. We established the Vultures use the east exit. So why are they parading towards the west? Towards *us?*

"Get ready," I shuffle in my chains, wincing, though the sound is lost in waves of others: human agony, cries and whimpering, the deep rumble of male laughter. I ignore Nena's surmounting, feminine squeaks of terror, and unclamp my Empara lock at the wrist. Using my Essence of brute strength, I swiftly detach the chains around our ankles.

I yank Thomas by the shoulder, "Keep up appearances until the last," I gesture towards the girls, "Tell them. Hearing it in their own language may give them comfort to keep quiet."

Thomas does as I ask, and not a moment too soon.

The party of guards comes around the edge of our cell door. There are at least six of them, each masked in black hoods, a prisoner clamped in four of their grips. The gathering is so overwhelming, there may be more Vultures in the fringes beyond. I don't dare ask Thomas to find out.

Why don't they fight? I glance from the men and women dangling on their knees, the whites of their eyes so profound, I feel haunted just staring, to their hooded captors.

They're afraid, I piece together. *They're weak and afraid.*

The Vulture nearest our door scans an ID card over the lock. Underneath the wailing, the praying, and the blood oozing from split lips, the lock *clicks*. It's the sound we have been dreaming of, the music of freedom. Pending.

"One from every cell," the Vulture has an unusually young voice as if he hasn't reached puberty yet. The lean muscle of his body suggests otherwise. He gestures delicate fingers towards Thomas, "Take him."

A different Vulture comes forward, arms outstretched to take Thomas away. To my cell-mates' credit, none of them make a noise.

"No," I hide my hands behind my back, "take me instead." I should have switched places with Thomas beforehand. I should have shoved them all in the back of the cell by the piss and shit bucket.

"Oh," the first Vulture crows, "it's Talan Taylor!" Without a face, I can't pin the voice to a name. "You fag. You two," he indicates Thomas and me, "have probably been getting each other off, like babies suckling a bottle—"

Thomas lurches upright, his hands replaced with clubs of steel. One clips the second Vulture in the knee; the other smacks into the jaw of the first. I hear bone crunching, the birth of our insurrection.

All at once, there is movement: Solenne and Nena plunging through the open door, Thomas and I clocking each Vulture. Once, I would have spared their lives. Now, the traitors are beetles under my shoe. I don't think twice.

My first mistake.

My second: believing.

Just as soon as we exploded into the corridor, freed the captives, shots ring through the air. Two-by-two, those we've just taken the time to liberate, clunk to the floor, a litter of bodies stacking bodies. Solenne and Nena fall simultaneously, fragile birds among the brutal muscle of the Vultures.

Beside me, I feel Thomas's gaze on my cheek. He crumples at my feet, hot blood pooling around my bare feet, between my toes.

A single figure stalks into view. Somewhere behind him, where the wall curves into shadows, guards shout to one another. I blink. I want to hang my head. So much for an army on the inside.

The man steps around one of his fallen men, stuffing his handguns in the waistband of his pants. He walks with catlike precision. I shudder.

"We'll have to start all over again now." He clucks his tongue, eyes grazing the collection of bodies clotting the corridor. His head snaps in my direction. Those dark eyes pierce my soul. "Taylor, huh? It really is a small world." He cocks his head with almost bored regard. "We'll start with you then."

Arms grasp me from behind. I squirm for a better angle, but something *cracks* on the back of my head. I fold, dropping to my knees. I think I land on Thomas's hand, knuckles popping under my careless weight.

Darkness swells in the corners of my vision. And like a sing-song tune stuck in my head, my mother's half-demented chant, *"Alba, Alba, Alba…"*

Castan
August 2020

I haven't slept in fifteen hours.

There are several reasons for this, but then Corolla walks into the room, and my memory is wiped clean. I cup my hands around my coffee, prepared to meet her at the butt of the breakfast line. Hotcakes and scrambled eggs with sausage today.

Across the linoleum and the artificial lights, she meets my gaze. I remember when I had to be sly if I wanted to look at her—peering through bodies, or when she wasn't paying attention. I grin. She frowns, soft concavity to her lips. My pace stutters.

Corolla turns. Issak Park steps out of line, drawn to Corolla by the same force gripping my heartstrings. He reaches her first. His lips move, and hers in response, but they conspire in low, indecipherable tones. Issak departs before I can ask, "What the hell was that about?"

I stir my coffee with my index finger. "The barista messed up my order," I relay in calm demure. "Do you want the whipped cream?"

And then I actually see her. The veil of jealousy lifts as I take in her baggy tee-shirt (mine), loose cotton shorts, and snarled hair. All three are signs of a rough morning. I don't think it's possible to be seasick underground, but that's how she appears: queasy and a pale shade of green.

I wipe whipped cream on my shirtfront. "Is it your arm again?"

She inhales. It worries me, her lack of direct eye contact. Months ago, I wouldn't have been able to read her this way, to know that something's up. With her thumb and index finger, she sweeps back the hair spilling into her eyes.

"I need to talk to you," she blows air through the O of her mouth, hand resting on her hip.

"Sure, yeah. Let's go up top, get some fresh air. You look about ready to keel over."

Though I'm on the verge of exhaustion, delirium, or just plain insanity, I toss my botched coffee order in the nearest trash and make the plight to the surface.

Island breeze whips through our hair, waves lapping the shore. St. Helena stronghold looms behind us, the only sign of civilization for miles. Sheer cliffs rise parallel to the shoreline, brownstone becoming green slopes. I glance out at the sunrise, pale purples becoming pale pinks becoming pale yellows. The ocean stretches for eternity, water and sky blurring in the horizon so that I can't tell one apart from the other.

Sand between my toes, I walk so that the waves lick my ankles. The water is a welcome relief, steaming when it strikes my skin. If Corolla notices this anomaly, she says nothing, just continues her pace, a foot away from the water's edge. If her expression weren't so concerned, I'd laugh at her irrational fear of the ocean and the way my shirt billows around her small frame like sails. Her jaw works on a piece of spearmint gum.

"So..." I drag a foot through shallow water, "what's on your mind?"

Rather than respond, she lifts her shirt and retrieves a Ziplock bag from her waistband. She hands it to me, and for a split second, I think she's given me a thermometer because she knows I'm radiating heat like a dying fire.

But then I flatten the plastic out and read the markings on that white plastic device. My brain works at a snail's pace. It's like one of those notes from the movies. Pregnant, Not Pregnant: please check a box and return to sender.

"I ran into Issak the other day. He heard a shift in my heart rhythm or something. I took a test just to be sure."

"Oh, Tess." We've stopped moving, bodies still as statues as the wind sways around us.

"If I'm Tess, does that make you Alec?" Two silver streams trickle down her cheeks.

"I didn't think you'd read that far."

Despite herself, she chuckles. "I'm a straight A student because of Spark Notes."

"But no," the plastic of the bag flutters in the breeze, "I suppose this would make me Angel."

"You said he's not good enough for Tess, though. When we first met. I remember."

"He's not."

She raises her head, strands of hair catching in her eyelashes. "Is that why you won't touch me?"

I shove the pregnancy test in my shorts pocket. Step back into the water. Steam swirls around my calves like smoke. "I won't touch you because I'm afraid to burn you."

"The disease?"

I nod. "I think this is the last of it. I can't summon even the smallest of sparks."

She doesn't budge from the shoreline. Just sits. Tucks her knees under her chin.

I peel my shirt off first, then shuck off my shorts. "If this is what menopause feels like…" I ease into the water, waves rushing to greet me like yapping dogs. I dig my fingers in the sand to stabilize myself against the flow. Salty droplets speckle my neck. I watch the steam rise from my surface area. Like any fire, I'm being extinguished. If Hadley were my witness, she'd laugh so hard she'd have to change her pants.

Hadley.

"Why don't you let me cure you? At least try?"

The muscles in my back twitch. "We've talked about this," I watch marine birds zip along the pink horizon, "you being the cure is probably just a myth. I don't know where my grandfather got the idea. And the procedure, I can only imagine, is a painful one. Regardless, I don't *want* this power. I never have."

When Corolla doesn't say anything, I try a different approach. "I wonder what our kid will be like then? Your Essence and my disease. They're both dominant genes."

She doesn't seem to hear me. "You didn't sleep last night. I didn't hear you snore."

I glance at Corolla over my shoulder. "I don't snore."

She massages the back of her neck, unimpressed and unconvinced. "Sure. Are you having those dreams again?"

Sand sifts through my fingers. "No."

"Then what?"

I retreat from the water, the sensation of its cool magic replaced with a lump of dread in the pit of my stomach. I settle down beside her, not caring where I'll have to rinse sand out of later.

"Calyx called me into confidence late last night. He hasn't heard from Hadley in four days. All of his birds return untouched."

For a moment, Corolla is quiet. The roar of the ocean fills the silence. I'm grateful her immediate answer isn't, "Well I'm sure she's alright. Your sister is a tough girl." Because we both know better by now. It doesn't matter if you're resourceful, if you're a straight A student, if you're innocent—bad things happen to everyone. No one is immune. It's the disease we all share, wound tightly into our DNA to remind of us of our own mortality.

"And," I exhale into the salty wind, "the scouts report fireworks. Celebrations."

She traces the sand around my left hand. "Renatus arrived early."

"Yes."

"So you're going to battle soon." It's not a question.

"At dawn. The Reserve is going in as the first wave. I'm in the second."

Her silence confirms what words don't need to: I'm breaking her heart.

I push off my palms and face her. "I don't want to be like the stereotypical dad from every pregnancy test commercial ever, but," my hand hovers over her abdomen, "oh my god. A baby."

"A baby."

"Hey," I cup my hand centimeters from her cheek, "I'm going to take care of you."

"Yeah?" Her eyes lock onto mine. A million questions float in the surface of her irises, like spirits of the underworld. Spearmint clouds my nostrils.

"Yeah."

And for now, that's enough.

She turns her gaze towards the way we came, a signal we should be getting back soon. On the beach, is her messy line of prints. Feet dragging, heart pumping emotion into her bloodstream. Fear and maternity. Where I walked beside her, however, the ocean's waves have washed away all traces of my footprints.

As if I never existed.

Corolla
August 2020

"You should sleep."

"You know I can't." Castan peels off his shirt and tosses it on the armchair in the corner. Our room, windowless and dim, is only big enough to sport a twin-size bed, an armchair, and a built-in closet. I flick the lights on, an orange glow flickering along our gray enclosure.

"Corolla." My back was to him, but I turn now. He's perched on the end of the bed, only inches from where I stand by the door. Though he could reach an arm out, he says, voice low, "Come here."

Teeth clamp my bottom lip, but I sink down beside him. The box springs squeak, a horrendous noise in the quiet.

Castan draws my hand into his lap, fingers tracing the lines of my palm. His heat occupies the room. I steal a glance at his pale abdomen, the trail of dark hair below his belly button.

A baby.

A baby.

I guess it's one way to avoid tampons for a while.

Castan opens his mouth, sucking in air, but I don't want to hear him say it—I don't want to listen to his goodbye, his ultimatum, or even a promise that he'll come back. That elephant's been tromping behind us all day. But it's not just us. The entirety of St. Helena is different, sometimes so loud you can't hear your own thoughts, and sometimes so quiet, you can hear the heartbeat across the room.

"I want to take you to Starbucks," I blurt. "When all of this is over, I want to show you all the pedes trends. You'd like Barnes and Noble. They have the most beautiful covers for the classics. I don't even like books that much, but they almost made me cry once."

His facial muscles relax. Whatever he was going to say dissipates in his realization: I don't want to talk about *it*. Those emerald eyes flicker over my face.

His half-grin fades. "You have to promise me you'll stay put." I guess he didn't pick up on my subtext. I exhale through my mouth. The Valence is making Calyx and me stay behind, "risky captures." Whatever. There are a couple *other* reasons why they won't let us join the barrage, but my apparent pregnancy is not one of them. No one but Issak and Castan knows. For now.

"I won't promise you anything, but yes, I'm staying behind."

Castan squeezes my hand between his sun-warm palms. He shoots me a wary look. "You have that look in your eyes."

"I'm not going anywhere," I laugh. "We both know I'm useless in battle." I shove my stub towards his face as proof.

"Yeah," Castan lowers my left arm, "that was *before* your Essence came through. I've seen you and Calyx training."

"He taught me how to pick locks with vines," I roll my eyes. "Don't mock me."

"I'm not!" Castan wraps his arms around my waist and tugs me backward so that our heads share the pillow. I tuck my cheek against his collarbone, inhaling the scent of him. Coffee grounds and sweat. He touches careful fingers to the blunt end of my bad arm.

"Does this hurt?"

I trace the hollow of his neck with my eyes. "No. Iatran says I'll probably have to get surgery, though."

"Well, he's not a doctor." Castan drags his lips across my bicep. I shudder and close my eyes against the dull light bulbs overhead. My body pulses with hormones.

"No, but he's... I don't know. Quit doing that. I can't think." I nuzzle into his neck, wrapping my good arm behind his head. My lips graze his jawline, the rough stubble there.

Castan slips a hand under the hem of my shirt. I sense his fingers hesitate over my stomach. *Yes, a* baby. There is nothing more sobering than the creation of life. But I don't want him to stop.

I pull away and sling a leg over his hips. He clutches my waist with renewed vigor. My hand on his heart, I bow down and plant my lips on his. He is an igniting flame, selfish, stealing the oxygen from my lungs. I can only keep him alive as long as my breath lives.

I break away, his hands working on the remainder of his clothes. I tug my shirt over my head and shimmy out of my shorts. And with every movement, the box springs creak and groan.

Castan catches me in his arms, but I scowl. "The bed will give us away."

His hot breath tickles my neck. "I don't care about the bed."

So for a moment—only a moment—I forget about him jumping onto a battlefield. I forget about that voice over the speakers, *"I am Renatus, the reborn."* And I forget my own, serpentine lies.

He doesn't want to be late, he says, rolling out from under the covers and leaving a pocket of cold air in his place. I feign a groggy, "Alright." Yawn. Because I really have to, not because I'm overselling it.

509

At some point, Castan got up to shut the lights off. He moves in the dark now, and for some reason, my flesh swells with fear. I told myself not to get sentimental, but I want to *see* him before he goes.

I swing my legs over the edge of the bed, wincing when the springs go off again. I flick the lights on, just as Castan finishes pulling on his new uniform. He leans into the closet, and I hear the *scritch, scritch* of pencil on paper.

He's probably writing down his coordinates. He's not good at remembering numbers. But for me, I memorized those digits six hours ago.

"Those pants are awfully tight." My eyes travel his lean frame, from the rounded toes of his Caeli boots to the gray tunic stretched taut over his broad chest. A yellow band travels the circumference of his right bicep, an indicator during battle to show who's loyal to Tax and who's not. My brows furrow. "No armor?"

Castan smirks, sliding the closet door shut. "This *is* the armor. New fabric that absorbs hits. I told you this."

"Right," I grin, "I just wanted to see if you'd repeat yourself."

He narrows his sleepless eyes. "Always testing the fire, aren't you?"

I cross the foot and a half separating us. Wipe my eyes so Castan won't see the restlessness there. So he won't know I've been lying, cuddled up beside him, awake.

"I never get up this early," I yawn again. "It's like Black Friday shopping with James all over again."

Castan cups the back of my head, pressing his lips to my forehead.

Don't say it. Don't say it. Don't say it.

"It's not so bad then, is it?"

I shrug, swallow the lump in my throat. "All things considered, no. It's not the worst thing." My throat constricts to the circumference of a pen. I tip my head back, Castan's arms smoothing my shoulders. I'm wearing his shirt. In his glistening, pea-green eyes, he's wearing my heart. Maybe that's why my insides feel like steel. Like someone scraped my organs out and replaced them with metal instead.

"Corolla, I love you."

I can only manage a whisper, "I love you, too."

"I'm going to take care of you. And our child."

This time, I can only manage silence. I nod. Bite my lip. I know we just have seconds—seconds before he will leave and seconds before I will run through my plan again—but time stretches between us in decades. We grow up, get married; we have a child, maybe two; we grow old; we die. It all seems so impossible and straightforward, I can't imagine how people do it. *But we live*, a voice in my head rattles, *we live.*

Castan cups my face between his hands and brings his lips to mine. The kiss is quiet, sweet. The ghost of his hands lingers longer than his kiss does. He steps around me, and with a backward glance, slips through the door.

I didn't know I was memorizing him until he's gone. I blink, conjuring the fresh image of his dark green eyes behind black lashes. The side of his face striped where the pillow impressed its wrinkles on his skin. The ends of his eyebrows stuck out in odd angles. I suppose I should have fixed them for him, but I found it endearing. Disheveled hair makes him real.

I drop to the edge of the bed. I don't cry—my nerves are too loud for that. Instead, my mind whirls with half-thoughts and broken sentences: Sixth floor won't be guarded. Approx. five minutes to get down there. Steal handgun. Snatch geometer. Enter blood. Enter coordinates. Jump. Find—*"I am Renatus, the reborn."*

Yes, find him. Whoever he is.

I couldn't sleep, drugged with so much adrenaline, I thought Castan would feel the *thump, thump* of my heart through my back. Thank God he didn't.

I squeeze my body into the old black and brown armor of Taxodium's glory days. I know my plan's not a good one, I just hope it's a *survivable* one. It's not about the war, Castan, or even me. It's about James. I couldn't live with myself if I didn't at least *try* to bring his murderer to justice.

I glance at my stomach, imagining the potion of a person bubbling in my gut like a cauldron. But no, I really couldn't live with myself. I have to try. For James. And besides, I almost shrug to myself, I can always find an isolated place and ditch. Jump back like a harried cat and forget I was ever demented enough to put myself and unborn child in danger.

But that's Plan B. My hand grips the cold doorknob. *I need to focus on Plan A.*

The hall is silent, and yet, my ears ring, faint echoes (or alarms) telling me to crawl back in bed, wait for Castan to come back. Wait. But my patience is worn thin.

I follow the dim light bulbs overhead towards the exit. I label the elevator *too obvious* and head for the stairs.

"Corolla Vel!"

I startle, my foot almost slipping on the first step. I whirl about, blinking, heart threatening to crawl out of my throat.

A figure stands in the block of vibrant light spilling out from the elevator. I recognize the white nurse's uniform but not the body underneath it. The man steps closer.

"You are Corolla Vel, right?" It's too dim to see, but I imagine his eyes dipping to my left arm. I square my shoulders, hiding my fist behind my back. Vines push through my clenched fingers. *Fight or flight*, they seem to hiss. I could race down the two stories, but would I have enough time to snag a gun, geometer, punch the coordinates and jump? I built my plan on the foundation of *undetected*.

"Yes," I nod. The vines are around my wrist now, prepared to spring.

The man's shoulders droop. "Oh, good." Did Castan send someone down to make sure I stayed put? "It's Luca Alba," the man says, "he's awake."

The vines shrivel to dust. "What?"

"Luca Alba," the nurse begins again, but I'm already racing past him, stabbing the elevator numbers, and am gone.

"Please, please, please," someone rasps. Someone I can only assume is Luca. Nurses crowd his door, alarm lighting their eyes.

"Get somebody from psych," a feminine voice pipes up over the noise. One of the nurses at the threshold responds, dashing down the hall like a wild rabbit caught then freed.

I shove through the thicket of bodies, elbows, to the heart of the commotion.

Luca squirms under the grip of two male doctors. The electrodes cling to his face like some kind of alien torture device. Sheets tangle his lower limbs where two other nurses hold his shins to keep him from flailing.

"Please, please, please," Luca repeats. There are tears in his eyes, panic in his weak voice. "Please get them out of there. Get them out."

I share a look with the doctor nearest me. I touch my hand to Luca's fist. "Luca, Luca," I croon, "you're alright. You're in St. Helena Hospital. I'm Corolla Vel, your niece."

Luca ceases struggling long enough for me to glimpse his eyes. Where his left one is chocolate brown, his right is a kaleidoscope, like stained glass. And then he is fighting again, pulling frail arms against grips stronger than his own.

"Get me a pen," he breathes, "get me a paper. Get them *out*. Before Jon comes back."

You don't have time for this. I crane my neck, "Give him a pen and paper. It may calm him down." Keyword: calm. Hands shuffle, and a ripped paper and black pen are supplied. Luca drops his head, staring at the items placed gently in his lap. He goes still.

"Corolla Vel," he rasps. "Corolla Marilena?"

"Yes," I nod. "That's my middle name."

Luca bites his lip, drawing blood. "Can I have my arms back please?" The doctors restraining him exchange a look. A concession passes between them. The one on the right releases his grip, but not the one pinning the left. Luca doesn't complain. He picks up the pen, raises its trembling tip to the blood on his lip. He touches the pen to paper, black ink slurring with crimson, and I think about that log we found in his hands. That ink was crimson, too.

I watch my name take shape.

Corolla Marilena Ve

"I'm sorry," his voice shakes. "I'm sorry. Just get them out." His pen scrawls the "L" in Vel. He looks up at me.

It happens quick as light. One moment, I'm at his bedside, hip pressing too hard into the hospital bed. The next, I'm alone, stranded on a dark plane. The edges of this world are tatters, suspended in space like ripped tissue paper. Pieces drift through the windless realm. The ground is like the sky: dusty brown. It's dim here as if someone put a towel over the sun, though I don't see one in the horizon. I spin, heart racing.

This is purgatory, I think. *Or this is death.*

That's when I see them.

My fingers begin to tingle, the tips of my toes go cold. Not four feet away, occupying an isolated patch of green grass, are two figures. My eyes stutter over the taller of the pair.

"Phaedra's mother," I stare at the woman, "I have to find Castan."

Hadley
August 2020

I never realized how cold it is up in the mountains until my woolen socks were taken away from me. And my Caeli boots. My knife too, though it never *kept* me warm. I always possessed a warm feeling carrying it around with me. Like taking a slug of whiskey.

I didn't know solitary consisted of me being forgotten in a vacated broom closet, but that's where Renatus stashed me what has to be *days* ago. I was searched by liberal hands, though not his. Empara locks bind me at the wrists, an awkward contortion. When someone does bother to bring me food and water, the Genocides seem to find it hilarious. How easily my father was deposed. His blood is still dried on my neck where speckles of it splashed during his fall. I feel it there, an itch. A reminder. I will kill Renatus myself.

The thought alone warms my blood in a way no knife ever has.

"I never liked cats." Somehow, the thought was funnier in my head.

I hug myself, sandwiching my chilled fingertips between my chest and thighs. There's not much I can do about my bare feet. The masonry doesn't help either.

If only my Essence had been fire.

Suddenly the ground vibrates. Had I been shuffling a moment later, I wouldn't have felt it. Unfurling from my cocoon, I strain my ears.

What—?

"Hey!" One of the guards outside my door shouts. "Hey, you're not supposed—" There's a thud against the utility door. A gunshot. I leap to my feet, positioning myself against the wall beside the door. I steady my breathing—Rosh taught me this—pushing the thought away. Crimson pools under the door. I catch my reflection in its ruby surface. I don't know what I plan to do, bound and unarmed, as I am. But sitting and letting shit happen, is not part of my coda.

The hinges groan as the door swings ajar. I brace myself, elbows poised.

A deep voice, "There's nothing in here, Din."

A thick Russian accent in response, "Well they can't have been guarding *air*."

I slip out from behind the door, not caring that I tromp right through the bloody puddle. It's body temperature *warm*.

"Dinara?" I only recognize the Valence operative by the fuchsia of her lipstick and the wild braids of her hair. Beside her, is one of the Okar twins—Kali or Zoya—I never really tried hard enough to learn the difference. Her jet-black hair is pulled taut atop her head, wrists cuffed in silver *armatus*. In her hand, a gun. Slung over Dinara's shoulder, a rifle.

The two bodies of my guards are crumpled in the doorway. I step over them, feet sticky with blood.

Dinara's thin lips quirk upright. "So this is where they've been keeping you." It's not the time for introductions. Otherwise, I'd thrust my hand out towards her. Dinara takes the butt of her rifle and smashes the Empara in the center. The cuffs fall away, my bones vibrating with the impact. She nods her head. "C'mon, girl. Let's get you some boots and enough menacing artillery to match that look in your eyes."

We move from the living quarters of the Barracks down to the garrison. Dinara fills me in as we go.

"Henri and some flyer called Mingo are working at setting up the bombs. We are rallying—or killing—to Collis Hall or the Dorms."

"Hold on," I pause over my bootstraps, "we're killing everyone here?"

Dinara nods. "Affirmative. This blight meets extinction today."

Kali or Zoya adds, "And we do not have enough forces to be merciful."

"The prisoners?" My eyes flit between the two. "Did they escape?"

The Okar twin grimaces. "They are all dead. Bodies stiff with rigor mortis. It appears they have been like that for a day or so."

I'm not sure what to make of that.

I arm myself with two daggers the length of my forearm. Dinara tries handing me an M16, but I refuse. I don't do guns. Something about a weapon more powerful than myself doesn't settle right with my bones. I've seen Rosh abuse that power too often.

Through the shuttered windows, a brew of muffled shouting and gunshots.

"So we're rounding them up like cattle then?" I've had to keep my emotions under wraps for so long, I don't bother now. "Since when do we kill everyone who opposes us?" I brace myself for Dinara's *The-Genocides-have-killed-thousands-of-pedes-Thousands-of-innocents-This-is-universal-justice* mentality.

"Ah, you poor Dentata girl," Dinara reaches out to touch my shoulder. I jerk back. She shrugs and tosses me a scrap of yellow fabric to tie around my bicep. "They voted on it."

I scowl. The Okar twin cocks her gun, and I don't wait for Dinara to include me on her manhunt.

515

High Rock. My gut is telling me that's where he'll be.

Outside, bodies litter the streets like some end scene in a movie. But these people won't be getting back up. Ashy smoke fumigates the wind, making my mouth dry. And because the campus is carved into the mountainside, a ruby river oozes south.

I do a double take—Chestnut hair, similar build, arm draped awkwardly behind his back, I think it's Castan lying in the puddle of mixed blood. But no, Castan would be wearing a yellow armband. I release a breath I didn't know I'd been holding.

I absorb all of this in seconds, body already propelling north towards Collis Hall. Through the plumes of smoke, I can almost see the peak of High Rock. Before the Gens moved into the SA, it used to be a summit for celebrations, bonfires. The Vultures have made it into something else.

I run up against a wall of crumbled rock. I bite my tongue to keep from screaming in frustration. The western passage is blocked with the rubble and ruin of the Courthouse. I'll have to cut through the main strip. My hackles raise at the thought—I can hear the sound of death from here. That's where it will be the bloodiest, the most frantic and dynamic.

I roll my shoulders and reroute.

Stone the color of deer hide lines either side of me, boxing me in. I have to keep looking up, apprehensive that one of the flyers zipping through the air will dive for me like a bird of prey.

Ahead, main street shudders with the battle. Through the passage borders, I glimpse arcs of yellow as arms swing. Cries for blood and calls for life. The metallic *zing* of blades clashing blades. An array of gunshots.

Your best bet, the voice in my head is Rosh's, *is to race through to the other side and hope everyone is too preoccupied to notice.* I guess this is what happens when you used to spend hours training with someone. You hear his voice inside your head instead of your own. I guess that's what happens when you *miss* someone.

I pick up my pace and clench the dagger hilts tighter until I get that strange sensation of not knowing where my fists end and my knives begin. Rosh called this nirvana. I call it adrenaline.

I decide it best not to hesitate: I plunge out of the passage and into the fray, aiming for the eastern pathway. It'll take me to Collis with as little intervention as possible. For all I know, Renatus has already made his escape. But something about the inhuman quality of his eyes tells me he wouldn't bother abandoning the SA. Like this battle is just an *inconvenience* to him.

I swerve around a man made of crystal, just as he pulls out a gun on a woman holding an injured arm to her chest. I wince, but I don't hear the shot. I don't hear anything over the drum of my own heart, like a hundred horse hooves clattering cobbled road.

Almosttherealmostthere. I leap over a fallen comrade—a big-boned woman—the clear-cut passage in sight.

My breath comes in foggy clouds. I can't tell if the white flakes falling from the sky are snow or ash. I get this flashback of Rosh, Castan and me on one of the rare occasions Jon let us visit the surface. We were playing in the snow banks, the moon our spotlight. Rosh puffed his cheeks and exhaled frigid clouds. "I'm a dragon." I remember—vividly—Castan scowling, crossing his arms over his chest and replying, "Dragons aren't real, so you can't *be* one." Snow in my boots, ankles stinging from the cold, all I wanted to do was go back inside by the fire.

I blink as if my eyes had been closed—*were they?*—and almost impale myself on a spear. I skid to a stop, blood thick on my boots. The Gen before me, lips a straight line, stands between the passage entrance and myself. She doesn't grin, doesn't say malicious words, only squares her shoulders for the blow. She has the most intriguing blue eyes I've ever seen. Piercing. But then she lunges.

I dodge the tip of the spear, whirling right, my own daggers raised for the woman's throat.

Don't hesitate. Again, the advice is Rosh's.

But when I center myself once more, ready to strike, someone else's dagger has already sunk into the soft flesh of her neck. Blood spurts on a hand. I follow it back to an arm, back to the body commanding it.

I expect him to say, "What, were you daydreaming or something?" I have to remind myself that he's not Rosh. That, even though they could have been twins, this is not Rosh. No.

So, *this* is Castan.

He comes to me in images. Shoulders hunched, breath a cloud of expiration from his cracked lips. His irises the color of avocado skin. Chestnut hair draped across his forehead. Too long. He needs a haircut.

Besides my grown breasts, the stubble spotting his jawline, it's as if those two years never separated us. As my hand grips my blade tighter, my heart swells.

I tuck my chin, a thank you, and continue onwards. For a split second, I experience crippling anxiety that Renatus won't be at High Rock. That, despite my evaluations, he's already gone. Untraceable.

A hand grips my wrist, yanking me back. I glance at the woman's bright blood smeared across his knuckles.

"It's not the time for a reunion," I want to tell my brother. I read the unspoken in his expression.

"High Rock," I gasp for oxygen, "that's where he tortures them. That's where he'll be."

No, his eyes aren't avocados. They're green lights.

That voice was my own.

Castan

August 2020

"**If** we weren't in the middle of something," I clip the Genocide in the throat with my fist, "I'd punch *you* for Belarus."

Hadley plunges her knife in the man's chest. A direct strike to the heart. He sinks to the street, and she withdraws her weapon. "I'm sorry about that, but not really." She frowns, head bowed over the body. But then she wipes the blade on her thigh and pushes on.

The first thing I noticed about Hadley was her hesitation in killing our cousins, distant relatives, and Phaedra knows who else. It doesn't matter. Because after a while, they all have the same generic expression, the same eyes, lips, and nose. But Hadley's not there yet. She still sees their individuality. For a couple different reasons, I respect her more because of it.

The path loops, taking us into a higher altitude. I suck in more air. I studied the maps of this place, but the streets are still a puzzle, worse than Iran. I'm the mouse. Thank Matrona for Hadley.

"You look like Mena."

She doesn't glance back, but the grin is in her voice. "Numen thought the same thing."

"I would've liked to see that." There are so many things I want to ask her, so many things I want to tell her—*I'm going to be a* father—but then the earth trembles beneath our feet. I think of Henri and Mingo planting bombs around the populated parts of campus.

We're outnumbered but not outwitted. I don't have to convince myself we're doing the right thing—the Gens have never played fairly, and we aren't about to either. *"Rally them up,"* Commander Allen instructed. *"Towards Collis Hall or the Dormitories. When Mingo Fletcher gives the signal, get out."* So that's what I'll do. End this thing. End the Dentatas and the Genocides in the same detonation.

Hadley stops abruptly. I almost topple her but manage to slow down just in time.

"What's wrong?" I notice her furrowed brow, the faint scar between her eyebrows from when Rosh tripped her and she cracked her head on a concrete corner.

"We'll have to go through Collis," her frown deepens.

I finish her thought, "But that's where we've been herding the enemy." I glance around the corner, craning my head to take in the size of Collis. The front of the structure reminds me of one of those English manors. It's carved in taupe stone. Two cylindrical towers frame the main entrance, glass windows and detailed finishing's in the stonework. But that's only the front of the building. The remainder shoots back into the mountainside. A delicate waterfall spills out the eastern side and into a manageable channel. The water flows down, past the courtyard before the Hall.

The trickling water isn't enough to mask the commotion echoing from inside. I picture people packed like cattle for slaughter, bumping weapons instead of heads.

If only they were mindless as cattle, too.

Hadley sucks in a breath and faces me. "Alright. How's your fire?"

"Oh," warmth floods my cheeks, "it's gone."

Hadley doesn't even blink. "Rosh's neutralization was early too."

"I didn't know that." This is the first time she's mentioned our brother. Does she know… Does she know the last of my flames devoured him? I don't have time to ask, a fact I'm grateful for.

Hadley sheathes her daggers, then unties her armband. "Hold the cloth to your ears when I say so. Tightly. Do you understand?"

I grasp her marker, thinking for the hundredth time how similar the color is to Tilia's yellow. I'm sure it's not accidental. Pelari grow up on symbolism. There's a reason why they still teach us Latin in school. Or did.

I wind the cloth around my palm. "You're too serious, you know that?"

She flashes me a half-grin. "Only when it counts." She doesn't waste any more time on words. We take the eastern entrance, droplets of water speckling my cheek as we pass near the waterfall. Inside, the stone-cut corridors echo with discord, a hundred voices working to be heard over one another. I trail close behind Hadley, knees bent into a crouch. I watch her shoulder blades work, remembering something Calyx said weeks ago.

"I think she wanted proof of her good-heartedness. Not for Tilia or me, but for herself."

Hadley presses her back to the wall. I copy her move, my head between two flaming sconces. Strange, I don't miss the fire in my veins. It's a relief—a relief to be… *pedes.*

Hadley drops to her hands and knees. We crawl around the corner where the stone balustrade overlooks the congregation below. An intricate chandelier hangs above the gathering, shards of glass glittering like so many flames. It's like we're children all over again, creeping around the Complex and hiding from Rosh. I almost expect to see him wandering down below, hands cupped to his mouth, calling, "Alright, you can come out now!" with that wicked grin on his face that means if we come out, it'll be a trap.

Through the tangle of voices and bodies, I locate Uncle Baylor's squat body, shouting to be heard. "Please! Calm yourselves! This is what they want!" And for once, he's right. But no one appears to be listening to the ramblings of an old, bow-legged man.

Without taking my eyes off the sea of black, I mutter to Hadley, "If this is where they're retreating, then where is Renatus to organize them for a counterattack?"

Out of the corner of my eye, Hadley's got that severe composure again, facial muscles taut. She's deciding. No, she's *decided*. She faces me, and I have to blink to wipe away the *Mena* impression.

"See that staircase over there?" She nods her head across the balustrade where I glimpse a doorway of stairs in the wall. "It'll take you to the roof. High Rock is directly west of that. I'm going to be your distraction. When I say so, hold that cloth over your ears and run. I'll catch up to you when I'm done." Her eyes flicker. I squeeze her bony shoulder.

"You're giving them mercy." I unwind the cloth from my hand. Sheathe my blade.

"Right." Her eyes flit back to the scene below. If I followed her gaze, I would see Uncle Baylor. "Ready?"

I cover my ears, and the world muffles around me as if I'm underwater. I nod.

I read her lips, "Go," just as she rises from the shadows of the balcony. I bolt around her, heart pounding in my ears. Do I imagine it, or does the air ripple with soundwaves? I leap into the doorway, feet landing on the clean-cut steps. Racing up the staircase, I'm at a disadvantage: I can't hear if they're people in the column with me. I don't dare take my hands away from my ears, though. I don't know how far her voice travels.

The air temperature plummets. I burst out onto the roof, wind whipping my cheeks and sending tails of snow flurries through the atmosphere. I drop my hand to my hip, grasping my dagger once more. I breathe in air so cold, it cuts my insides. Snow chills my feet through my boots.

If I glanced over my shoulder, I'd see the entire Academy sprawled at my feet. I don't dare tear my gaze from the summit. High Rock. Three stone pillars tripod around a pile of snow-capped wooden crates and firewood. Before the SA isolated themselves from Taxodium, High Rock was known for its parties. Of the three columns, two are occupied, each with a single body captured in chains. A slim figure stands near the first stone pillar.

Hadley comes up behind me, heaving white clouds of breath into the wind. "You pissed off a lot of people, Rena. Are you ready for the repercussions?" The figure, black against the porcelain snow, doesn't turn. His shoulders quake; I don't hear him laugh, but I imagine that's what he's doing.

Then I see who's chained to that first pillar. I should be terrified, furious. But my insides go warm. It's nothing like fire, nothing like the rage that used to consume me. It's like drinking hot coffee after hours spent in the bitter cold. My entire body grins.

The best mistakes are the ones you know you're going to make before they happen, yet for some reason, you don't hesitate to justify them. Because at that point, it's no longer a mistake. It's only *right*.

Corolla
August 2020

A wrinkled woman. A blonde boy.

As soon as my brain made this connection, Luca spat the three of us out, groaning like a woman in labor. The hospital staff about shit themselves. If it was chaotic and loud before, it's a maelstrom now.

"Who are these people?"

"How did this happen?"

"Watch his vitals, watch his vitals!"

I take one look at the woman's haunted eyes, the color of pistachios, and the boy's golden crown. At the foot of Luca's bed, he clutches Mena's frail hand, cheeks glowing pink.

"I'm Elliot," he answers the doctor's questions, animated. Mena cowers behind him, suspicion sparking her haggard expression. Her hair comes down past her shoulders, dark tangles.

Someone grasps my waist. I glance down at Luca, his skin a shade darker than mine.

"Thank you," he says. His eyelids flutter. I catch white-capped waves of the ocean in his right eye.

Anxiety rips through my core. I have to go. I have to tell Castan about his mother, about the child answering all the doctor's questions. Is he Mena's son? He certainly doesn't look like her, golden where she is obsidian.

I slip through the crowd, a part of me refusing to leave Luca's side. The thought of Renatus pulls me towards the door, down the hall, and into the elevator. On the sixth floor, there's not a soul around. Abandoned, the level is in disarray, gear scattered along benches, weapons missing from the wall.

I tuck a handgun in my belt. It's heavier than I imagined, and for the first time, I doubt whether I'll be able to use it, one-handed.

You'll think of something, a voice hisses. I punch the coordinates into the geometer. I mimic Castan's motions, pricking my finger and loading the strip in the butt of the device with a drop of my blood.

I don't hear him, but the air shifts, the way it does when a new organism enters the realm of here and now. I turn at the same time I punch JUMP.

Hands shoved in the pockets of his pants, Calyx cocks his head. His eyes flicker from the device in my hand to the gun at my waist. He raises his eyebrows.

"Please, Calyx," tears bloom in my eyes, "don't stop me. He killed James. He *killed* him. I have to at least try and do right. I can't let him die in vain."

The geometer *beeps* three times.

Calyx works the inside of his cheek. This time, I really do give him a piece of gum. He stares at the silver foil in my palm before accepting it. It must be tearing him up inside too—that Kass is out there fighting and he's here, bound by fragile contract as the leader of the Valence. He can't leave. If he did, what little foundation supporting this new coalition would topple.

"I'm sorry," he pinches the stick of gum between two fingers, "that our father was such a disappointment."

The lilac veil spills over me. Adrenaline spikes my blood. For a moment, I worry about breaking my bones, snapping my neck, dropping from the sky—I haven't had all the formal geometer training Castan has. What if there's something he does that I never noticed? What if jumping isn't healthy during pregnancy? I dismiss this last anxiety, an image of Nasreen popping out of a bubble surfacing in my mind.

I straighten my spine. Calyx rakes a hand through his dark locks. He really does resemble our father. But he has our mother's eyes.

And then he is gone, swept away in the whirlwind of fast travel. My body jolts. I clamp my eyes shut to keep from vomiting. Steady the gun at my hip, afraid it will dislodge and somehow fire during the jump.

I land on my back. Hard. I gasp for breath, rolling over in the snow. Cold. So *cold*. My wanting heart bursts, *We're in Michigan!* My rational brain concludes, *I mistyped the coordinates.*

My vision blurs, black dots in the edge of my view. Above, gray clouds are pregnant with snow. Pale flakes fall from the sky, melting on my cheeks.

A man appears, hovering over me, arms clasped behind his back. "The first time is always rough. Easier to lose your center of gravity. Especially over such a long distance." I must be dreaming—because the man has Orsino's face.

The world goes black.

I wake, numb with cold. It's only when I move to brush the hair from my eyes that I realize my arms are bound. In chains. The metal links dig into the fabric of my suit. I struggle against them, feeling so much like Delani, I could laugh. Vultures caw in my right ear, flocking in the corner of my vision like seagulls around French fries. I don't want to know what their presence means.

"You're as foolish as Adian."

I jerk my head at the figure standing three feet away. Dressed in a thick parka, snow boots, gloves, and a sock hat, he mocks my suffering. I drink in his face, his features. His nose is a dead giveaway. Like Maurizio's. Like Valeria's, Luca's, and Tyto's. And yet, his name is a question.

"Orsino?" I clench my fist. My fingers are fluid, telling me I haven't been out too long. My long sleeves have been cut up to my shoulders, the fabric hanging in tatters at my shoulders. "How...?"

Orsino shoves a hand in his coat pocket. He approaches with feline grace, feet kicking up powdery snow. My gun is in his other hand. His nose is inches from my own, breath sour.

"You deserve to know, I suppose. My own bastard children are tired of hearing the same old, same old. But then again," his eyes travel the length of my body, "none of them display an ounce of intrigue like you do."

I bite back repulsion, sick with nausea that has nothing to do with morning sickness. I'm stitching together my own version of Orsino's story, drowning in all the blood on his hands.

He makes a disgusted face. "Pelari are infinitely more superior than pedes. Had we reigned centuries ago, there wouldn't have been witch trials, world wars, economic depressions."

"You're delusional." I recall his voice over the speakers, *"She's not just your niece now, is she?"* I thought Renatus meant Luca. I never imagined he meant *himself.* I struggle against the chains again. "Reborn? That's subtle." Orsino shrugs as if I just gave him an F on a paper and he doesn't care.

"I put your father on top, hoping that could be my way in. He had old Rainier's ear, after all. But then Tyto became too powerful, and his only concern was dismantling the Attachment Laws. His mind was elsewhere, but it actually worked out for the better." Orsino opens the slit of my sleeve. He admires my damaged arm, bare fingers tracing the scars. I writhe, but my back is against a stone column: there is no place to go.

"By the beginning of 2004, I'd struck up a deal with the Dentata clan. The SA was already isolating themselves, so it was unsettlingly easy to convince them to turn their back on Taxodium for good too. We had a commonality: pelari domination. The Dentatas needed a way into Tax, and I needed brute force to topple it. The April Attack was the beginning of the Genocides, a preliminary trial of all that we hoped to accomplish."

"You *murdered* your own family," I spit.

His eyes flicker, then narrow. Like any old cat who loves you one minute and despises you the next. He raises, not fingers to my exposed bicep, but claws. Massive claws that not even the biggest of bears could boast.

"Yes, and my bloodlust has never been more satiated." He rakes the tip of a claw against my flesh, drawing blood. I bite my lip, focusing on that pain instead. "I plunged a blade in Marilena's chest. Maurizio was drunk on his own grief—slitting his throat was too easy. Giovanni didn't even hear me coming: he was singing to himself in the shower. Pas put up a fight, but he couldn't bring himself to pull the trigger on me. He hesitated, and I ripped his throat out."

Orsino pierces my flesh, a tally for each name. Marilena, Maurizio, Giovanni, Pasquale. Blood oozes down my bicep, scorching hot in the hostile cold.

"I kept Val and Tyto as leverage over Luca. See, Jon Dentata was having marital problems. Valeria and Tyto were Luca's reason to live and serve his purpose as jailer. And besides, Val had Tate and Tyto had Calyx. If I killed my siblings, it was only right that I killed their spawn. But ending children never brought me much satisfaction."

Reino. I weep for Reino. Orsino moves to my other arm. He carves my flesh, claws like a knife cutting butter. One, two, three.

"But Adian…" his lips curl, "she was alone when I found her."

I pull myself out of my own agony. I grit my teeth. Tears splash my cheeks, losing their warmth to the climate as soon as they fall. "What the hell did you do to my mother?"

His breath is hot on my cheek. "I stabbed her in the back. Symbolic, yes. Cliché, also yes. She deserved it for distracting my brother. But I also couldn't have the Dentatas getting what they wanted. I couldn't have them curing themselves and rising up against me. I promised them Calyx, but then Jon's son botched the capture. So I promised them you." He glances over his shoulder. I fix my eyes on the plumes of smoke, the flames licking the campus. My vision warps with pain and tears, smoke and fire. "I guess they won't be needing your DNA now, though."

I choke on a sob. Tears blur my vision, clouding Orsino's dark complexion like an elementary watercolor. A sick feeling swarms my stomach as if I've been socked in the gut.

"You took everyone from me." The admission is enough to make my body sag against my bindings. Tears drip with my blood.

Orsino crouches so that I am forced to look at him. "No, *Tito*, I didn't do this for you. I did it for me. I'm tired of tiptoeing around the earth, always holding back my true self so that pedes won't be shocked by the realization that they *share* this planet. Everyone has been a pawn in my game, right down to that 'spy' Tyto encountered in Allen Manor."

He gestures a clawed hand to the flaming Academy. "I haven't lost, you know. When this war is over, what will Taxodium tell the world? My actions have secured pelari rights across the planet. Pedes fear us now. They will be petrified once they discover who *we* actually are. Forget their mundane terrorists—we are of a different breed."

My tongue feels strange in my mouth. "Tilia showed me Adian's memory of meeting your family. She loved you."

Orsino squints at the vultures circling overhead. "Memories are fallible, Corolla." He pinches my chin between his hands, compelling me to stare into his smoldering eyes. "They don't last, and they don't matter."

This is where I tell him he's wrong. Where, in my defiance, I somehow break free. They do matter, I'd shout. They do. Because that's all I have left of Adian, of James. Memories. But none of that happens. Instead, my strength ebbs, melting into snow and blood, leaving me limp. I can't think.

My eyes slide over the smoking Academy, the flames so high in places, they touch clouds. Shots ring clear in the mountains, shouting and screaming fighting to be heard over the artillery. I don't know when the bombs will go off, but it can't be long now. My eyelids are heavy, the scent of my own blood swirling in my nostrils.

The world is ending.

"You pissed off a lot of people, Rena." I manage to raise my head. Across the snowy plane, are two figures. "Are you ready for the repercussions?" I don't recognize the stern voice or the young body it emanates from. But I do know the broad shoulders standing beside her.

Vitality returns to my bones at the same moment a familiar voice rasps behind me, "Castan."

Talan. How long has he been there, afraid to speak, to tell me I'm not alone up here? It doesn't matter. I need to get out the chains.

Orsino glances between Castan's poised body and my rattling chains. He reads the expression beneath my chapped cheeks and numb face.

"Oh," he clicks his tongue. "You licentious little girl. And with a Dentata, no less."

The girl beside Castan comes into focus. Square jaw, short-cropped hair so brown, it's almost black. *Hadley*, I name her, still struggling with my chains. Then it strikes me: Essence. Use your Essence. I calm, forcing my frozen hand to cooperate. I've all but forgotten my body's pain. None of that matters. Castan matters.

Castan and Hadley cut through the snow, dark warriors against the porcelain plane. The earth trembles, vibrating through the stone column and into my spine. Castan meets my eyes. The message is clear: we're running out of time before detonation.

My eyes flicker between Hadley's daggers and Castan's single blade. My heart sinks. They halt, the pair of them operating under some unspoken signal.

"He has a gun," I croak, face cold with wet tears. "And claws." It's not what I want to say: *Your mother is alive at St. Helena.*

Focus, Corolla. I feel the bud of a vine in my palm. I do as Calyx instructed me, sensing the chain with my abilities.

Orsino points the gun at Hadley's head. Though he is feet away from her, I don't doubt his aim. Castan tenses, eyes wide.

I've located the lock. The vine worms its way into the device. My heartbeat jostles my flora extension. I inhale through my mouth. Exhale. Focus on Castan's eyes. Focus on the green. The warmth.

"How pitiful," Orsino muses. "I could shoot her, but the scenario doesn't strike the right chords with me." He redirects the gun towards me.

The world moves all at once. Castan lunges for Orsino, grappling his wrist. He forces the gun toward the sky. The shot rings out, bullet zipping through the snow clouds. Hadley clips Orsino in the temple with her fist, but he flails his free arm, knocking her backward. I lose sight of her in a snowbank.

Almost got it. Almost—

My heart catches in my throat.

Orsino grips the gun between his two hands, a grin twisting his bronze face. I watch, horrified, as the gun's mouth wobbles between Castan's forehead and the empty space behind him. He turns pink with the struggle, arms shaking against Orsino's strength.

Everything explodes as if time and space have been suspended on a single peak up until this moment and they are plunging downhill now. Collis Hall goes up in flames, a mushroom of rubble and smoke. The earth trembles, ripples with the momentum of the detonation. In the process, the quake knocks Orsino and Castan off balance.

The gunshot erupts in my ears, more deafening than any detonation.

My lock clicks, and I shove free of the chains, legs propelling me towards Castan.

"This is *the armor. New fabric that absorbs hits."* But it doesn't repel lead.

By the time I reach him, he's fallen back into the snow. Crimson oozes from his chest, thicker than spilled coffee. In the ivory snow of the mountain, all I can feel is the heat of his blood. His eyes roll back into his head, but I slap his cheek.

"No," I can't hear myself over the high-pitched ringing in my ears, "No, you don't get to die." I press my hand into his breast, hot blood drooling between cold fingers. *Moss*, I try telling my Essence. *Moss to staunch the bleeding.* But nothing happens.

I bow my head towards his, faucets in my eyes. Some childish part of me believes that if I keep breathing against his cheek, his veins with catch flame and deliver blood to all his vital organs.

"Castan, Castan." I can't say his name fast enough. I feel so sick— *so* sick to my stomach—as if something inside me is gnawing on my organs. Maybe our embryo knows. Maybe it feels the grief, too. Bile threatens to surface, but I swallow it back. My body trembles with helplessness. "Castan. Your mother is alive. Mena is alive."

Sound returns as if someone pressed the unmute button.

He's saying my name, voice so weak, I probably wouldn't have heard him if my head wasn't so close to his. I pull away enough to glimpse his two beautiful, emerald irises. They latch onto me like hooks.

"Corolla," he struggles, throat bobbing, "you were right." He splutters, coughing up blood. I want to wipe the ruby spittle from the corner of his mouth, but I'm afraid to move my hand from his wound. His eyelids flutter, that wrinkle, like a familiar friend, resting between his eyebrows.

"You were right," he says again, "it is like watching a sunset."

I bow my head to his neck, not sure if the sound escaping my mouth is laughter or broken sobs. I press my lips to the heartbeat in his throat, hot tears slipping past my shuttered eyes. Maybe when I open them, he'll be alright—

"Corolla." His hand is in my hair. I glance up at him, those eyes watching me through tears of their own. His thumb traces my lips. "Corolla, I love you."

I nod my head, pressing my cheek against his hand. "I-I love you, too."

"It's—" he coughs again, spraying my face with crimson droplets, "—alright. Corolla, it's alright."

I shake my head, but I can't speak over the softball in my throat. I press my lips to his throat again, inhaling the scent of him. *Coffee*, my mind registers, *coffee and blood.*

His hand drops from my hair. The murmur of life fades from his body until even the hummingbird's pulse in his neck is absent.

"Come back," I whisper into his too-pale skin. "You are Tess."

Talan

August 2020

My locks fall to the ground, lost in the snow. I shiver, body trembling with bone-deep cold. I wring my wrists and find dried blood there. A figure steps around from behind the pillar. Though she's not wearing her cloak, I know her voice.

"We have to get out of here!" She has to shout over the raucous of crumbling buildings, of the earth's quaking. Blood pools at the base of her neck, hinting at some injury to her head hidden beneath her hair.

"Where's C-Castan? C-Corolla?" I woke up to her voice, her muffled cries. Orsino Alba had his claws in her, I could tell. But her sobbing reverberated a different kind of agony. Sobbing like when I found out Jura passed away.

"Ors-sino?"

"Gone. Can't find him." The stranger nods her head over her shoulder, eyes glossy. For the first time, I note the structure of her face, the uncanny resemblance to Castan in her features.

"Hey," a feminine voice shouts from above, "Allen's spotted mare—what are you still doing here?" Mingo Fletcher drops from the sky, swooping gracefully to land beside us. I have the ridiculous thought: *No, she's not the sister with six kids. She's the one who grooms pets for a living.* Her blonde hair is scraped into a ponytail behind her head, ash and sweat smeared across her fair skin.

She doesn't give us room to answer. "There's an avalanche coming from those peaks," she gestures someplace I don't care to follow, "we don't have time to examine the damage." She turns to the stranger, "I'll take Talan if you grab Vel…"

I don't *examine* anything—the SA is a swell of thermal radiation, dense clouds of smoke; charred bodies in places I can't see. The earth shakes again as if the planet is crying out in agony. I am convinced this is the extent of the world: smoke, flame, ash, and snow.

It's against the pale snow, the ashen clouds, that I spot Corolla. Her hair billows in a wave of heat—the remains of Collis Hall have just collapsed—lashes wet with tears. In her single hand, she cups Castan's cheek.

My teeth, which have been clattering in my head, cease moving.

"Alright people, let's go!" Mingo withdraws a geometer from her pack and shoves it in the stranger's hands. She holds an arm out to me. "C'mon, Talan. Finis has missed you."

Relief.

But then I look at Corolla again, and I'm not so sure.

Book Four
Spoken

"He who has felt the deepest grief
is best able to experience supreme happiness."
-Alexandre Dumas, *The Count of Monte Cristo*

Calyx
September 2020

"Kassandra," I nudge her shoulder. She whimpers in her sleep, eyes racing beneath pale eyelids. "Kass, you're dreaming."

She jerks awake, sweat budding at the base of her neck. Her indigo irises scan the room before resting on me. That animal look fades. She drapes an arm across her forehead and exhales. My gaze flits between her pale chest to the constellation of freckles across her nose.

"I saw the sleep demon again last night."

"Hmm." I trace her jawline with my index finger. "Where was it this time?"

She scrapes sleep from her eyes. "In the corner. On the ceiling. Sleep paralysis sucks."

"I'm sorry. Do you want to talk about it?"

"I just did." She swings her legs over the edge of the mattress, sheets like rumpled snakeskin on our bed. I've always found it striking, the black ink of the Mark between her porcelain shoulder blades. Kass is anything but fragile, and I don't have to remind myself of it.

"That abrasion on your hip is healing nicely," I remark. Kass makes a noncommittal noise and pulls her wardrobe from the closet. She slips on black leggings and a maroon V-neck. The light catches her orange hair, glinting amber.

"It's been a week."

I roll over in bed, flinging the sheets from around my legs. I don't need to ask what Kass is referring to: it's been a week since Castan's private Ceremony, since we placed his body in St. Helena's Mausoleums and cried *Bellator, vale!* in the pale morning light.

It's been a week since Corolla shut down and Hadley Wynter took off.

"It's like spotting a massive spider in your room, shutting the lights off, and then it's gone," Hadley grinned, but I saw the self-blame in her eyes. "I'm not coming back until Orsino is found. I can't face my mother like this."

"Hadley," I tried grabbing her shoulder but thought better of it, "He was probably buried in the avalanche. And even if he did live and escape, where would he go? That valley was in flames before it was covered in snow. He's dead. The scavengers just haven't uncovered his remains yet."

But she couldn't be convinced.

"I have that conference in New York today. Pedes press." I shove limbs into my good clothes as Kass twines her hair into a braid.

Neva Rex, the only surviving Major, stepped down several days ago, demolishing the ranks as she went. In her wake, a group of individuals banded together to represent pelari during this new era. It's a little nerve-racking to be a part of something historic: pelari are unveiling themselves to the public for the first time ever.

"Corolla's been writing for days, you know. I think you need to talk to your sister. She's quiet, but never this quiet."

I make a face. "I think she's experiencing psychosis."

"No, you idiot!" Kass turns, smacking my arm, "She's afraid of forgetting."

"Yes," I pause to admire her, "I know." Kass forgave me after she came back from the Battle of Cordillera and the war ended. She forgave me, and I can't imagine losing her again. I can't imagine losing her permanently. My voice is low, "I don't know what to say to Corolla. I mean, what am I *supposed* to say? I lost my best friend, but she lost—"

"Her best friend, too." Kass brushes her knuckles against my cheek. She has her tender moments, when that jaded heart of hers melts into flesh. "Just talk to her, Calyx. You know how important family is to her."

I flinch. *Family.* How can that still be important to her now, after everything that's happened?

"Okay," I nod, glancing at the clock hands *tick, ticking* away, "I'll see what I can do."

"Dad?" I come up short on my way to Corolla and Castan's room. "What are you doing here?"

Tyto jolts upright, pushing himself off the door. The sign is still flipped over to *Occupied*, reminding me all at once that, no, Corolla won't be in their old room. She's like a ghost—you see her floating around the levels, but never in the same spot. I was so distracted by my speech for the conference, I forgot this detail.

"Val gave me a geometer. They're hard on the knees, aren't they? I came to speak with Corolla," Tyto gestures towards her door, "but she's not in."

"No, this is probably the only place she's guaranteed *not* to be. Maybe try the hospital? She sits with the other amputees sometimes. Or Mena Dentata and that little boy."

Elliot. Kass and I speculate about him sometimes: where did he come from? Mena is no help, incoherent writing and mute, tongue cut out of her mouth like a peasant. But Elliot... He never stops talking, his eyes green as grass before spring strikes full bloom. And yet, he never once mentions his origins. Luca can't even remember where he came from, either drunk with drugs or repressing the memory.

There is one thing certain about Elliot, though: his aura is addicting, sweet as nectar but not so overbearing. He may very well be the Dentata cure Mena was known to have been working on.

"No wonder Jon wanted to keep him to himself," Kass scoffed. *"Elliot radiates something from deep in his soul. And it's* good.*"*

Tyto tucks his chin, shame flickering in his eyes. "I just wanted to apologize to her, you know? I didn't mean what I said." He raises his head, "What I meant to tell her is that everyone else was dead, so it was easier to pretend she was, too. Do you think she'll understand that?"

My gaze flickers from his expectant expression to the *Occupied* sign on Corolla's door. Tyto's always been like this, asking me for my advice. He asked for my blessing before he proposed to Julli. I was only nine. But saying *you're a terrible father to her* wouldn't matter now. Besides, I would be wasting breath telling him something he already knows.

"Yeah," I nod thoughtfully, "she may understand that."

Tyto buries his hands in his pockets. Silence stretches between us for a short eternity. I start to wonder if he knows how to get to the hospital levels. I'm about to ask if he's visited Uncle Luca when he says, "I keep getting college advertisements in the mail. It's almost like they don't know you're dead!" He laughs at his own joke. I force a chuckle. He took my "coming back to life" very well: he was more relieved than pissed. But still, it's hard to imagine he was ever good with words.

"So... how is everyone else? Aunt Val?"

Tyto swipes a thumb across a dark eyebrow. "You know, making the best of things, I guess. I can't believe the Rome Accords are spent. Attachment Laws, too."

"Yeah," I glance at the clock at the end of the hall, "which reminds me: I should be going, or I'll be late for the flight." Until the new Accords are negotiated and ratified, pelari representatives are suspended from geometers for the time being. Pedes don't want us *going anywhere* until they understand *why* their cities have been bombed, raided, and devastated this past year. I suppose it's a fair demand, all things considered.

Tyto makes a face, something mixed between nostalgia and resentment. "I remember those days. Alright. Well, safe travels."

"Yeah, and Dad?" Tyto raises his eyebrows, imploring. "She just lost someone important to her. I hope *you* can understand that."

Tyto dips his chin towards his chest. I wonder if he's thinking about my mother or if he's in such a sinkhole of denial that Adian doesn't even cross his mind.

I leave him behind and weave through the winding halls of St. Helena underground. Robert Allen, Alexander Murphy, Dinara, and the Okar twins were expecting me five minutes ago. Sweat prickles under my arms, much to my irritation. And for whatever reason, my brain connects this irritation to Castan.

I skip the elevator and jog up the steps as if exercise will pave over the cracks in my heart. It certainly won't help my pit stains.

It's like one of those dreams where someone you love dies, and you believe every, agonizing moment of it. Your heart breaks, your mind wobbles, and then you wake up, and none of that pain matters because it was never real. Except this isn't a dream. This is real, and the pain does matter.

Touché, Castan. Touché.

The cold blade of irony is too piercing to laugh about.

Kassandra
September 2020

I don't mean to find Corolla, but she's been missing for half the day and Talan is worried. While he searches the upper three levels, I scour the lower three.

I *am* searching, but not very hard—it's difficult to focus on things this week. My thoughts are bouncing between Calyx's stay in New York to my family's return home to the sleep demon. Maggie assured me it's a common occurrence during sleep paralysis, but sometimes, I'm not so sure. Like when I can't move at night, and that shadowy figure looms over me. Sometimes, I think it's the Devil himself, come to collect my soul for all those lives I ended in the war. But that's what being a soldier is: fighting, defending, killing. Honor. Nobody ever talks about the dreams, the sleeplessness, the demons. Alex Murphy said he would give me a medal since the ranking system is no longer applicable.

Since when do we keep medals in stock? We don't.

That's when I realize I'm on the sixth floor. And Corolla is perched on a bench, hugging a black backpack. Her upper arms are still bound in tight gauze where the doctors had to stitch her up. If I were a floater like Hadley Wynter, I would go out and hunt Orsino with her.

Found her.

Issak Park stands beside her, a similar bag slung over his shoulder. He doesn't glance up as I approach, but his ears twitch in my direction.

"Hey, Corolla," I wince at how demeaning I sound. I clear my throat. "Talan and I have been looking for you."

"Okay," she sniffles and has to set the bag down to wipe her eyes with a tissue smashed in her fist. I haven't really seen her since Castan's Ceremony. She was in black then, a pedes tradition I'll never understand. Her voice cracked on *Bellator*; silent tears streaked her cheeks. She glowed then, as she does now. I can't help but think, *She wears grief well.* Where others are gaunt, Corolla swells with something ethereal. Maybe she's the type to eat her misery away.

My gaze flickers between Issak's pearl-white eyes and her clouded ones. "Where did you jump to?"

Issak answers for her, "The NA. We had some things to pick up before the snow falls."

Corolla laughs—the sound is so unexpected, I startle. "The only crime he ever wanted to commit was a library heist—" She breaks off and tears at the tissue clamped between her knees and fingers. Little white flakes flutter to the floor.

I regard Corolla, eyes flitting from the tears at her waterline to the crumbling mess in her hand. And I know. I know what it feels like to lose someone you want to see every day, want to believe would be there every day. I understand that pain, but I can't offer any words to banish it. It could have been me. It could have been Calyx. It could have been anyone—and others *have* lost someone they love to this war—but Corolla is one of them.

Fierce protectiveness overcomes me, the kind only big sisters can experience. I snap my fingers at Issak. "Could I talk to you for a second?"

He follows my steps across the area, away from the lockers and benches where Corolla continues to shred her used tissue.

"What are you trying to do to her?" I struggle to keep my voice down. Issak's expression falters.

"She's looking for closure, just like everybody else on this island. I'm trying to help her."

"Don't you think your *help* is a little poorly timed? Castan—"

"She's *pregnant*, for Matrona's sake!" He goes red with anger or embarrassment, I don't know. The acid in my fists, on my tongue, abates.

"*What?*"

Issak rakes a hand through his glossy hair. His woolen scarf falls to the floor, but he doesn't pick it up. "I just don't want her falling through the cracks. We've all suffered so much already."

For a full minute, I can't say anything. Pregnant. With Castan's child. With a *fatherless* child.

"Right," I blink, licking my lips. "Well, I'm sure she appreciates that."

Over Issak's shoulder, Corolla's gone still. She's watching us with the cool demure of a caged lion. I shudder, the hair on the back of my neck standing on end. Caught in her gaze, I'm paralyzed. But this—this reality—is a different kind of demon altogether.

On my way to locate Talan, I pass the Posted on the fifth floor. I become distracted, lost in the flickering candles, names, pictures, and other paper clippings pasted to the wall. Pelari mourn all around, a river of bodies, a flood of grief. The air murmurs—*Bellator, Bellatrix, vale*—as if the walls themselves are breathing the phrase. We didn't used to do this—to mourn in public. We are a people who have experienced too many shocks in so little time. I think we're suffering an identity crisis.

In this, at least, we are united.

When the war ended nine days ago, new names crowded the Posted hourly. The overflow has come to a halt. Our dead have been accounted for, and those pelari hoping otherwise have been forced to accept that whoever it is they're waiting for is not coming back. I recognize some men and women, still as statues on the fringe of the crowd, from when I came days ago to light a candle for Júlia. Denial shines in their eyes, dimmer than the Posted's flames, but just as hot.

I recall something Júlia said after Calyx died. She laughed a little, lips red as roses, "The best souls go first, so what does that say about the rest of us?"

Rather than wear our *armatus*, people have set them on their ends, enclosing them around candles to protect the flame glowing within. There are so many candles, some cathedral-style, some small and disc-like, that this sector would be a fire hazard. Except the pyros are overseeing the flames, honorably.

It would be Castan's watch too. The last time I spoke to Castan was right before we deployed. He said he was shocked I outlived the attack at Cyprus. I said I was sorry I couldn't have stayed and killed them all. I know what he thought about me, but I'm not selfish. Not anymore. I see his name on the wall, a wreath of daisies surrounding it. Castan William Dentata in Corolla's shaky script.

Júlia Talhari, Laila Cassena, Umar Botros. My body flushes with a cocktail of emotions so strong, I suddenly wish for a weapon in my hand. The feeling fades just as quickly as it surfaced. I shudder. I don't want to touch destruction for the rest of the year, maybe longer.

Just when I'm about to leave for the flight of stairs, my attention latches onto two figures wading through the crowd towards the wall. Valeria grips her son's hand, something stoic in her gaze. In her other hand, a candle oozes wax down its stem and onto her skin.

Tate—I think that's what Calyx said his name was—stumbles behind his mother, wiping tears from his eyes.

"Why are they attending behind me?" He sniffles. "I won't allow it any longer." He turns and kicks at the ground. Something squeaks, and I crane my neck to glimpse a retinue of mice trailing behind Tate's heels.

Valeria turns a smile in her son's direction. "It's just who you are, Tate."

He grumbles, head craned at the little bodies crowding his feet. "What are we doing here anyway? I want to go home."

"We're lighting a candle for your father," Val replies with natural patience, "He died in the Battle of Cordillera."

Tate crosses his arms. "I don't have parents."

Valeria sighs but doesn't argue. She places her candle at the foot of the wall. I turn away, skin crawling with the idea of invading such a private moment.

"There is so much despair here."

I startle at the voice by my shoulder. I glance sideways at the blonde-haired boy standing beside me. He can't be much older than six or seven. He's dressed in denim overalls and a striped shirt underneath. In his front pocket, is a travel size packet of opened tissues as if he's been dispensing them.

"I feel it here," he touches a hand over his heart. "When they get too sad, it's enough to make my own heart stop."

"Are you supposed to be down here, Elliot?" This is the first time I've spoken to him, but I've heard a lot about him. Calyx and I discussed him a couple times, perplexed, just like everyone else.

"The nurses said I should have a break from Mena. I think they just wanted her alone."

I can't help myself. "Is Mena your mother?"

He shrugs, eyes following various people around the Posted, "I suppose she could be."

"What about the man, Jon Xabier Dentata? He visited you a lot, didn't he?"

Elliot nods, voice smooth as silk, "Yes, he liked to talk to me."

"About what?"

"Anything, really. He taught me about pedes and pelari," Elliot makes a face, nose wrinkling, "but I never understood. He said we are separated by our differences. I think differences make us stronger."

I lower my voice, crouching a little, so he can hear me better. "Was he your father?"

"Well," those wistful eyes latch onto mine. For a second, gold flashes in his irises. But then I blink, and his pale green ones are glued to me once more. "I wasn't *there*-there when I was born, but I suppose anything's possible."

My face feels strange. I touch fingers to my lips—

I'm *smiling*.

I glance at Elliot, his tissue dispenser and dimpled cheeks. What was the line Castan was fascinated with in Professor Hampton's class? The Jacoby Rainier one. The words surface as if they have been waiting to be recalled:

"When a great force of evil arises, nature also creates a great force of good to counteract the effects."

542

Talan
September 2020

A muscle in Fin's jaw twitches. I drop my gaze to his cast. Broken femur. He wobbles on his crutches and turns away from me. The island breeze chills my shaved head, and I lament for my long hair again. I shift against the railing on St. Helena's roof. Gauze clinches my limbs where Orsino Alba razed his claws through my body. I feel like a mummy. Wrapped outsides, vacuum dried insides.

"Things are changing, Talan." His hair is coming back from its buzz cut, just long enough for the wind to toy with.

Death of a Trainee.

"No shit. You're moping around because you couldn't fight at the Cordillera. Because Maggie couldn't perform a miracle on your leg."

Finis turns cold eyes on me. "Don't talk to me like that."

"Why, because you don't want to hear the truth?"

"Don't get me started," he scowls. "Your best friend was a traitor and a murderer," his voice cracks. My heart stings at the mention of Dani, but he doesn't need to bring Jura into this.

"You've been bitter to me ever since you found out," I counter. "You act like *I'm* the one who killed her. I didn't."

"You're right," his shoulders sag. I glimpse a fragment of his old self. "But this isn't about Jura. This is about us. I don't... we don't understand each other anymore."

He's not wrong. I remember how disgusted I felt with myself when he saw my bruises. If he knew there were fresh marks, beneath my gauze now, he still wouldn't understand—that sometimes, injuring yourself a little now saves you a lot of hurt later. And I will never understand why his soul is snow-capped, why he ever loved me when he's always loved my sister more.

But it's not about Jura. It's about the disconnect between us. It's always been there, we just chose to ignore it. Pretended it didn't exist.

"We're not made of the same stuff," I admit. "I think we should call it."

"Yeah," he bows his head into the wind, "I think we should, too." He's a stranger again, struggling to balance on crutches and eyes so blue they must be fake.

I leave him on the roof, descend the emergency stairs down into the hospital. Feet thudding on each step, relief spreads across my being, a warm blanket after a night of cold. Thomas's hazel eyes flash across my vision, remnants of a time that seems so far away, it must have been a decade since I was a prisoner, so weak and fatigued, Orsino Alba cackled when his guard brought an Empara lock to my wrists.

"No," he waved them away, "he doesn't require one of those."

Hospital air crushes my senses, antiseptic precautions and a sprinkle of stale urine. On the ground level, I search over geriatric heads, visitors, nurses, and card games in the lounge. Before Finis demanded to speak to me, I left her with Iatran by the potted plants and brochures for Essence retrograde and brain stimulation. It's not hard to find her now.

She's the only one sobbing.

I cut through a half circle of recliners, TVs turned up too loud, and nurses administering pills. Air conditioners pump cold air from the ceiling, making my arm hairs stand on end.

"—and sometimes the missing half still hurts. Sometimes it's so unbearable, I bite my lip until it bleeds because then I'll have a different pain to focus on." Corolla clutches a pencil in her hand, a notebook in her lap. She bows her head to rest on Iatran's shoulder.

Iatran strokes her head. "Physical pain makes sense." His voice is gruff, almost lumberjack quality.

"It makes sense," Corolla parrots, words breathy. Her body doesn't stop trembling, though. I picture that shrimp developing in her stomach and being jostled around like a marble in a soda bottle.

I raise my eyebrows, hoping to catch Iatran's attention. He continues to stroke Corolla's caramel hair, a faraway expression staining his wrinkled profile. His gray-white hair sticks out at odd angles, stiff as the spokes in his wheelchair.

"But you're bruised, not broken."

He understands. And for some reason, this thought alone causes me to yearn for my ring of the mountains. Jura and I were bound in the womb; the least I could do to feel *at home* is to wear her ring around my finger again.

Corolla
September 2020

I still expect him to waltz through the door, a mug of steaming coffee braced in one hand. I still want to tell him about how much I threw up this morning, or about how they're serving turkey sandwiches on the fifth floor, with tomato, mayo and everything, just like how he prefers it.

I want to say, "Damn you! Maybe if you wore the old uniform, this wouldn't have happened." Maybe if I'd stayed put, this wouldn't have happened.

People are nice. There's a bottle of water in my possession at all times. "Stay hydrated," they say, grinning like hired actors on commercials.

Okay. They don't know I lie on the lounge's couch at night, praying I'll wake up even though I'm wide awake. They don't know that I see his face at the end of that flaming tunnel, or that I shove my hands into the fire and try to climb to him. They don't know how afraid I am of waking up one day and forgetting the iridescence of his eyes, the smooth quality of his voice.

Paper and pen can only contain so much.

I don't even have a picture.

Pacing St. Helena makes me homesick. I have nowhere to go. Tyto offered me a room at his place, but I didn't respond. He can say whatever he wants—I'll just nod my head as if I care. I don't have it in me to be angry with him anymore. I don't have it in me to try to love him either.

I touch my hand to the glass, imaging the thrum of ocean life at my fingertips. I haven't seen any this afternoon, but that doesn't mean the creatures can't see me.

My reflection is the same, except for the white bandaging wrapped around my arms. I can still feel the stitches sometimes. Talan says we resemble walking mummies. I wanted to thank him for carrying Castan's body out of the snow, but the words stuck to the roof of my mouth like toffee.

"Corolla," I hear my name on my uncle's lips, watch his gaunt figure approaching in the reflection of the thick glass.

"You're out of bed?"

He comes up beside me, a faint current of wind sweeping the space around us. He smells like hand sanitizer. "Maggie told me the news."

"What news?" I observe his reflection, the way his chest heaves to catch his breath. He's wearing an eyepatch again, this one white as ivory.

"About your arm!" His reflection reaches out to grasp my own, then thinks better of it, shooting it into the air over his head as if that was the plan all along.

"Oh yeah," I touch the blunt root growing from my arm like a molar, "she said I may even sprout leaves and everything." I guess my Essence is good for more than just gardening and "defense." Clearly, the Dentatas were on to something.

"I can't even begin to tell you how good it feels to be out of that hospital bed and without captives in my head. I didn't want to become Taxodium's mobile prison. But look where I am now," he chuckles. The riant noise does something to my nerves. I turn away from the depthless aquamarine blue.

"How did Orsino escape your scrutiny? How did he keep his true intentions from you?" One eye may be a prison, but the other was a filter. A heart-reader.

"Sex. He was my brother—I wasn't going to delve into that!" His voice drops, "But maybe I should have."

I tap my fingers against the window and chew my lip until I taste blood.

"You know," Luca leans against the glass so that his back is to the ocean, "I told your mother once that Albas don't forsake Albas. I believe that—believe that still, in a way."

For a moment, his words settle. And then I comprehend their meaning. Their uselessness. The damage is already done.

"I want James," the tears bubble to the surface of my being, along with all the emotions I've been trying to categorize and understand, "I want Castan."

His tone shifts. "Sometimes the good guys die."

I glance at him then, wiping the tears from my eyes. The scar on his cheek is like a beacon, attracting my attention away from his expression. Orsino's claws have been embedded in everyone's lives for a long time.

They still haven't found his body.

"That's all Castan ever wanted." I wipe snot away with the back of my hand. "To do the right thing."

Luca nods, the corners of his lips concave. "You see how people are changed. Me. Val. Your father. It's up to you in the end though, how quickly you find your feet."

The door reads *Occupied*, though nobody's been inside for two weeks. Knowing that his clothes are still exactly where he left them makes my stomach turn with the sort of weight that could sink a boat. I grip my notebook tighter. My jaw aches from chewing gum so voraciously.

In the back of my head is James's voice, *"She's never come out of it."* That story haunts me, but I am tired of ghosts.

I inhale—

"Attention, Orsino Alba's body has been found." I crane my head at the speakers. "Orsino Alba's body has been found."

—and exhale.

I blink.

Occupied.

It's a start.

* * *

I inhale the earthy autumn air, leaves transitioning from green to gold. The array of pines doesn't bow to the seasons, everlasting through even the coldest of Michigan winters. Cornstalks taller than me shoot towards the sun, the faint scent of smoke in the breeze.

I clutch James's binder of blueprints and sketches under my arm. He drew up 22.5 designs, and I know precisely which chunks to piece together. That check we deposited all those months ago is still sitting in his bank account, along with the remnants of his inheritance. But I guess Aunt Val already paid for most of his debts. James just didn't know it yet.

In my hand, I squeeze the chestnut seed I plucked from a tree in the remains of the Twelfth Wall. Its leaves were the color of his eyes. I want our child to know that.

My gaze rests on the ashen bones of the house that once was. It burned to the ground and took every last possession with it. James's heirloom Bible, my microscope, that plaid couch in the living room. Without the house, the land is so much more vast. Full of *potential.*

I think back to the note Castan left in the closet. He was never writing the coordinates down—he was writing to me. It's a scrap of him, a clipping of who he was as a person. As a man. I want our child to know that, too.

The breeze catches in my hair, sweeping my testament away and planting it in the earth. A promise.

"What did I do this summer, indeed."

You didn't want to get into it. That's fine.

"I have felt her gravity since the day we met. And I'm still falling."
-Castan W. Dentata, This is NOT a Goodbye.

Also, if it's a boy, how about William?

Epilogue
October 17th, 2030

"The Pelari Wars—"

"Wars?" Daisy furrows her chocolate brows, "There was only *one* war."

William scowls at his sister, a faint wrinkle between his eyebrows. "If you let Mom finish, she would explain why." His face puckers with discontent as Daisy beams him with her emerald eyes. The twins keep telling me they're too old to be tucked in, but if I left them to their own devices, they would argue until exhaustion took the controls. They don't even share the same *room*, but Maggie and Hadley needed a bed to stay in. William offered his, no hesitation.

"Do you want to hear the reason why or not?" I manage to pull a reprimanding sort of look, but Daisy sees right through it. She's always challenging me, challenging everyone and everything. I don't know *where* she gets it from. By the smug grin on William's face, he *thinks* he already knows the answer, probably read it from one of the history books Calyx bought for him.

"Alright," she folds her arms over her chest, successfully choking the poor stuffed Labrador in her grip. "Shoot." This is a new phrase she learned from Kass. The other one being, "*Absolutely* not."

"Because," my gaze flits between them, tucked in their bunks, "all the people involved in the war were fighting with each other and themselves. It was an external and internal thing, making it *Wars*."

William bolts upright, "That's not what my book says!"

"Well, your book wasn't in the Wars. It was written by a historian, not a survivor."

Daisy rolls her eyes. "She's showing off, Will. Just because she and Issak wrote so many of their own books about pelari genetics." She clenches her black lab by the throat on purpose this time. Sometimes I wonder how she's my daughter and not Kassandra's—they both share aggressive tendencies. It's why William keeps Tate's little goat sculpture in his possession. Daisy would find a way to break it.

He settles back into bed, expression pinched. In his coffee-ground eyes, cogs are turning, trying to compartmentalize this new information. He's too black and white for his own good. I know where he got *that* from.

"Are Cat and Cal coming over again tomorrow?" Daisy speaks through a yawn, "They said they were."

"No," I shake my head, suppressing my own yawn, "Cataria and Calina went back to New York. Aunt Kass is going to have baby Kaden soon, and she wants to be home when that happens." I scan the floor to make sure my path is clear of Legos, books, and stuffed animals before I flick the lights off. "Goodnight, you two."

"Wait!" William surprises me with a cry.

"What?" I turn the lights back on, alarm raising the hair on the back of my neck.

"We didn't say happy birthday to Daddy yet."

My shoulders relax. I exhale. I didn't forget—I just hoped they had. It's already past 10:30, creeping towards 11:00. They're beasts in the morning if they don't get enough sleep the night before.

"You two need to get some rest—"

Daisy flings back her covers and jumps from the top bunk. I wince when she lands—that's how she broke three toes last year—but I know I can't stop her.

"I can't believe I almost forgot!" She punches William on the shoulder. "This is why I keep you around." She snatches the candle from her dresser drawer, while William races past me for his room. He comes back with a lighter.

"Where did you get *that?*" My mind is conjuring all the worst-case scenarios—house fires, flesh burns, and, knowing Daisy, accidental ingestion.

William rakes a hand through his dark hair. "Issak said I was responsible enough."

"It's not you I'm worried about," I glare at Daisy across the room.

"What?" She shrugs, "We can just have coffee in the morning. I can't sleep now anyway."

I sigh, seizing my children up: William bracing a lighter in one hand, and Daisy cupping their candle in the other. They saw it at Kohl's last December and wouldn't stop pestering me to buy it. It smells like brewed coffee.

"Alright," I hold my hands out, "let's go then." Daisy grips my right hand, and William clasps my left. He's gentle with it, even though I've told him a hundred times before that it's not fragile. Something about my Essence compelled roots to twine into the form of my missing appendage. And though I didn't sprout leaves or grow fruit, I do have full mobility back. It's a blessing I don't need to be reminded of.

As a unit, we descend the half-circle staircase down into the living room. Above, a glass chandelier twinkles, casting little rainbows on the wall. It was the biggest one I could find at Menard's, and I know James would be satisfied with it.

I glance left, at the kitchen counter and all the desserts that need to be packed away before I retire for bed. I love hosting the Accords party, Thanksgiving, and Christmas, but there's always the after party of cleaning. Aunt Val should have taken the brownies for Tate. Tyto and Julli's wine glasses lay empty by the sink. I could have sworn I took care of them already, but between Talan and his Berkeley husband, Adam, there's probably not any room in the dishwasher, anyway. Thank Phaedra Luca didn't mind jumping them home.

"Are you sleeping walking?" Hadley swings around in her chair. In the time that I've been up putting the twins to bed, she's moved from the end of the table to Maggie's lap. She swirls a cup of whiskey in one hand, ice clinking against glass. I don't know why they didn't just move to the couches in the living room instead. They're more comfortable.

Issak raises his eyebrows at me from across the dining room. I mouth with the faintest of breaths, "They pushed the right buttons."

"We're going to Daddy's tree," Daisy replies with the severity of a school teacher. William nods to confirm what his sister already said.

"Really?" Hadley pops up onto her feet, unsteady. Maggie grasps her wrist to support her. "I'll go with you."

We travel as a party under the October moon and porch lights. I let go of Daisy and William. They lead Hadley and Maggie to the chestnut gracing a large chunk of our property. Calyx and I planted it ten years ago, our Essences working together for a common purpose. My hand hasn't tingled with that itchy sensation since, and I can't help but think of two magnets, always attracting one another, no matter the distance. Even though questioning things is my job, sometimes questions hurt. I like to believe the absence of tingles has less to do with Castan's burial and more with the fact that I no longer have two hands of flesh.

The chestnut towers in adulthood now, trunk wide enough for William and Daisy to hug only if they link arms. The leaves rustle in the slight breeze, sending me back to the Twelfth Wall, the day I plucked the seed from its elder's branch. I wanted to steal away Adian's statue, too. In the end, though, I decided to leave her. It seemed right for her to watch over the land she loved so much, even if it was scorched beyond recognition at the time. But that's the thing about flora: we just keep growing.

I prop against one of the Greek columns framing the doorway on the stoop. Issak comes up beside me, a hand on my shoulder. I rest my hand on top of his, feeling his steady pulse in my fingertips.

"A decade of pedes and pelari equality. A decade of peaceful coexistence," Issak exhales in awed relief. His breath smells like something stronger than grape juice. "I don't know how Calyx managed it. I'm still convinced he got the New York Accords ratified on the 17th because of Castan."

"He would be twenty-eight today." William touches the flame to the wick. Daisy clasps Hadley's hand and together, they cheer like heathens. Though Hadley was neutralized years ago, she's still got lungs. The animal sound echoes in the night, quieting the crickets and cicadas. The moon observes with a maternal eye as serene as Maggie and William on the fringes. I wonder if Rainey and her sister, Isa, made it to St. Helena alright. I was hesitant to let them leave so late in the night, but Rainey also has tributes to pay. Umar doesn't lay too far from Castan.

"Thanks for getting him that, by the way. The last thing they need is a fire hazard."

Issak chuckles under his breath and tucks his chin in the crook of my neck. "That came to them by nature. You forget they didn't cry. They laughed. Who knows what the universe has in store for them."

I can't help but laugh—Issak and I have studied over two hundred samples of the Essence gene and published just as many papers and books on the subject. Daisy Laila and William James will be the first Dentatas cured. It's in their genes. We know *exactly* what the universe has in store for them. Well, almost. A microscope can only predict so much.

"I wish Calyx and Kassandra could have stayed another day to celebrate the Accords. But Calyx said Elliot can't govern the ship by himself. The Mundus Foundation wouldn't exist without him, though. He helps so many people every day just by being alive." Ever since Elliot was young, he's eased pedes and pelari into this new era. Calyx and Kass practically adopted him because Mena was never well enough to take care of him herself.

"I think Calyx just didn't want Elliot to be alone," Issak surmises, "It's only been two months since Mena passed. He counted her as his mother, even if he doesn't—didn't—know."

"He should have let us do a DNA test." The twins, Hadley, and Maggie are doing laps around the trunk now, pagan worshippers. William's laughing so hard at something (probably Daisy), he may asphyxiate himself. I grin.

"Some people don't want the magic spoiled. He's like that. He *is* that. Hell, every time he visits, I listen for a change in his being. I think, *Oh, he should be sixteen* this *year*, but I never hear a difference. He's a mystery science can't solve."

"Mom, Issak!" Daisy cups her hand over her mouth, shouting though we are only yards away. "Come down here and dance with us!"

Issak doesn't have to be told twice. He leaps from the stoop, making me wonder how much *he's* had to drink. He twirls around, offering me his hand.

"Mrs. Park?" When Issak grins, his entire body glows. It's infectious, like staring at the sun and trying not to squint. It's one of the things I love about him.

I place my hand in his as he guides me from the stoop and into the cool grass. Daisy does cartwheels around William. Maggie whispers something into Hadley's ear, moonlight reflecting off her dark hair.

Under the chestnut's canopy, in the halo of candlelight, I break free from Issak's grip for just a moment. Brewed coffee swirls in my nostrils, caressing my senses. Orange light flickers, casting shadows like prison bars in the ridged bark.

Sometimes it amazes me that beneath all this growth, there was devastation. That's how it is, I guess. I couldn't explain it to anyone— it's one of those things you have to experience yourself to know. But it's like this: Life is a flowing tide. It comes. It goes. And you never know what will wash up on your shore.

Coffee curls around me, and I imagine his fingertips grazing my cheek, his lips kissing the inside of my wrist. Those emeralds smolder through half-lidded eyes, saying everything he never could. All the cells he knew and touched are gone, replaced. Most days, the woman he loved is gone, too. The tattoo on my back and the scar on my leg are from another time, another life.

William slips his hand into mine, ever careful, always gentle. Daisy knocks into my side, jostling William and me like Newton's balls. She wraps her arm around my waist, perhaps the most vulnerable she's been all year. Maggie and Hadley teeter in the corner of my vision with Issak. We all feel it—the weight of the emotion hovering in the air— and we all participate in our own ways. But it's my children's voices that I hear, and the whispers sometimes present in the back of my head: *What would Castan think? Wherever spirits go, is he watching his children with wistful eyes now?*

Their voices are low, synchronized with the tradition of it, "Happy birthday, Daddy." Together, the three of us pucker our lips and blow. The flame flickers before it is snuffed out until next year. The wind carries the scent of smoke, but the candlelight stains my vision, a blot of red, for a moment longer.

Castan Dentata and Corolla Vel are gone.

But that doesn't mean I won't pretend some more.

Acknowledgments

I have been tinkering with the lives of these characters for six years. Along the way, I lost count of how many different versions I wrote, typed, or imagined. I can honestly say this is not how I thought it would end, but this was always the story I meant to tell.

This book would not be possible without the support and contribution of the many people in my life:

A huge thank you to my production team: my second, third, and fourth set of eyes, CJ and Rachel Hess, and Marianne MacRitchie. And to the Queen of Technology, Julli Bennett—without you, I would still be using pencil and paper.

Maggie MacRitchie and Kassidy Gregory for being the firsts to weed through my many, many drafts of *The Pretenders* before it was even titled that.

Many thanks are owed to those who lent me their names for this endeavor: Mackenzie Clark, Dani Cole, Jason Grubaugh, Colin MacRitchie, Júlia Talhari, Ashten Sienko, Kat Sides, and Orland Smith.

Special appreciation goes to Stephanie Hampton, my first real editor and advisor. You provided me with more insight on writing than any English class (at the time) could. I was thirteen then. Also thank you to Stephanie's friend, Ms. Steppes, for encouraging me (in the one brief encounter we had) "to write while you're still young!" It is all I have been doing since.

The bolster of English teachers from high school, specifically Jason Grubaugh and Alex J. Stacy. Thank you for finding my essays (at least somewhat) intriguing. Your praise and critique were fuel enough to motivate me to continue my work with *The Pretenders*. I told myself I wouldn't stop improving my skills until your names were in the acknowledgments of one of my books, and here we are.

I owe Dr. Kyle Lincoln of the Classics Department, here at Kalamazoo College, credit for all the Latin translations I threw his way. There are still many more to come.

Murphy Peters (1997-2016), whose memory still lives on in the sun, and Dave Howard, whose pocket quotes and persona kept me sane during a wretched season of ball.

Drake Babbitt—you'll find traces of yourself between my lines, however accidental they may be. I always knew you were stronger than you look.

Don Bailey, Abby Reimink, and the rest of the crew at Wayland Area EMS who believed this stack of paper could be more than a file on my computer. (Lindsey Hoffman, this is clearly *not* my diary, but it's just as dark.) It was Marilyn Hess who told me to "roll with it," and

I have been rolling uphill ever since. I love saving lives and kicking ass with you guys.

The MacRitchie family, who ~~bribed me with pizza~~ integrated me into your system. It was always about more than just pizza and road trips, though. Our Friday nights were the cure to breaking my writer's block every time.

Thank you, Papa, for your goat stories, and Orland from WAEMS for your true account about the Woman Who Never Came Out of It. She may rejoin society yet.

All five of my siblings—Forrest, Daisy, Zoey, Levi, Delani—your constant interruptions, irritations, memorable cat stories, coffee, and otherwise were (sometimes) welcome distractions between plot lines and editing sessions. I thoroughly enjoy being your big sister. For Gentry and Dawson Allen Bennett, who never saw the sun, but who are more than names carved in stone.

A shout out to my parents, Robert and Julli Bennett—*this* is what I was "doing in my room all the time." Thank you for being everything that you are, together and individually. I love you both very much.

And my readers: There is a lot I could say to you—Are you crying? Are you satisfied? Do you enjoy bittersweet endings just as much as I do?—But I want you to know this first: Thank you for reading until the end.

Made in the USA
Middletown, DE
13 March 2019